The Legend of Ahya
As Above, So Below

Matthew Colvath

This second book is dedicated to
My mother
For being that amazing inspiration in my life.

Books in the Legend of Ahya Series:
Target of Interest
As Above, So Below

TABLE OF CONTENTS

The Nation of **Zabökar**

Zabörian Sea

Tokishuo Ocean

trest
lezierz
maukoff
poanne
Bennes
xaracelles
Dhone Forest
ZABÖKAR
naumor
Lamen
hanigane
Curing Ranch
putmir
herron
yavignon
vitalis
fjordos
State of fjordos
Bavahuuy
Dirina
Girune Mountains
Grunesh Mountains
Galaria

FURMAP™

Trip Planner

A. Sunrise Savannah Cafe
Restaurant
133 Roaring St, Zabōkar City, Zabōkar

B. Zabōkar General Hospital
Hospital
85 Roaring St, Zabōkar City, Zabōkar

C. [Nina's Apartment]
Custom Location
23 Cygnus Ave, Zabōkar City, Zabōkar

D. The Fox Den
Bar and Nightclub
76 Ayjay Ave, Zabōkar City, Zabōkar

E. [The Marsh House]
Custom Location
64 Maximus St, Zabōkar City Zabōkar

F. [Jake's Apartment]
Custom Location
389 Luca Del Rio Ave, Zabōkar City, Zabōkar

G. [Fey's Apartment]
Custom Location
281 FettLocke Ln, Zabōkar City, Zabōkar

H. Church of Mereliah
Place of Worship
25 Main St, Zabōkar City, Zabōkar

I. St. Talia's Graveyard
Place of Interest
284 Rue de Olina St, Zabōkar City, Zabōkar

J. ZCN Tower
Corporate Office
30 Lagopus Ln, Zabōkar City, Zabōkar

K. The Real
Concert Hall
22 Roaring St, Zabōkar City, Zabōkar

L. Caelesti Spire
Corporate Office
1 Spire Circle, Zabōkar City, Zabōkar

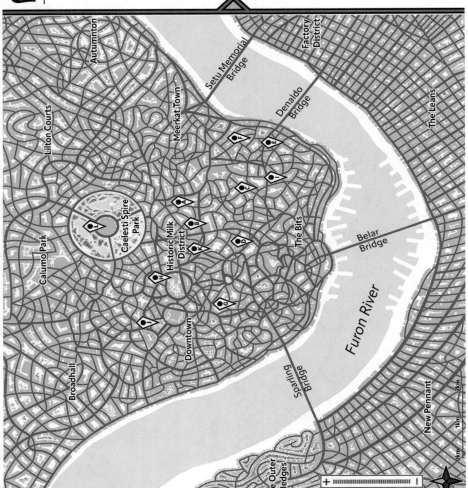

10

1.

SPONSORED

"What's the last thing you remember?" he asked.

Murana hadn't heard him, as she was staring out the window at the parking lot below. The multitude of police cruisers were lined up in symmetrical rows like beans on an abacus. Only a few were missing as it was Sunday, a slow day all things considered. The officers manning those vehicles were probably out on their lazy rounds throughout Zabökar, only to return late that night after a gruelingly boring shift. The remainder were downstairs, slaving away at their keyboards writing up end of day reports.

The planted row of trees flanking the perimeter of the lot was a nice façade for a peaceful, park-like ambience, but did little to cover up the hustle and bustle of city life. Several taxis and civilian cars honked loudly just meters beyond the glass as they nearly hovered into each other attempting to switch mag tracks. A taxi rose skyward to another line of hovering cars before angrily speeding away towards the skyscrapers beyond.

"Did you hear what I said?" he asked again, swiftly drawing the blinds shut with a clatter.

Murana's light brown ears flicked back with annoyance as she retrained her azure eyes onto the silver-striped kudu. His horns spiraled back into the moody darkness of the room, small bits of plastic at the ends to avoid scratching doorways or goring colleagues by accident. He was looking dapper in his brown suede suit, no doubt culled from organ donors now buried six feet under in the city's graveyards.

She smoothed down the blouse of her uniform, her paws drifting over her last name on the tag on her breast: "*Wolford*". She eyed him with some vexation. "Yes, I heard you. The last thing I remember was him gurgling on his own blood, talking about the new order the Arbiter would bring to the world now that we had 'betrayed' him – whatever that meant. I couldn't get much more out of him than that."

The kudu sighed, taking a long drag on his cigarette before placing it into the ashtray beside him on his desk. The smoke irritated Murana's nose, and she scrunched her muzzle at its acrid odor. "Let's take it from the top again, shall we?" He laboriously crossed his legs as he pressed the recording button on the tape, a small notepad and pencil in his hooves for any extraneous notes. "Can you take us back to the beginning of the raid? Do not leave out any detail regarding your interaction with the Arbiter's men."

Murana's shoulders drooped. It had been an exhausting day, and all she wanted to do was go home and sink down into a warm tub of bubbles. Maybe even enjoy a nice, intimate snuggle, like the one she shared the previous night with her husband, Anthony, who was no doubt out on one of those lazy patrols. Their superiors didn't exactly want them too close together on the force since they were married, and it could prove a conflict of interest in the heat of a critical moment.

So here she was, being grilled about her inner fortitude and emotional aptitude on being tasked with a new undercover mission.

Massaging her temple, she recounted, "As you are aware from the report, Kowolski and I went through the back while Buchanan and Lawrence went in the front. The suspects were in the middle bay of the warehouse at dock six, on the east end of town by the Furon River on The Leans. We had gotten wind of another group of kidnappings and had tracked them there, where they were being held for transfer to another undisclosed facility."

The kudu reviewed the report, flipping a page over as he browsed. "That was when Buchanan and Lawrence were discovered at the front."

Murana nodded. "Kowolski and I made a dash to intercept, but both were being held at gunpoint in the middle of the perps."

"Why did you not move in to save your fellow officers?" He took another drag on his cigarette, its flames lighting up his eyes.

"Because I saw who and how many they had taken. There were six of them and four of us. Although we could take them, they still had the advantage, and could incur more casualties if we went in without a plan," she explained.

"Yet Buchanan and Lawrence still died despite your cautions," he accused.

Murana winced. She knew the gravity of this statement. "I understand, but you see, there were women and children there. None of those kitnapped by the Arbiter have been seen again. Helpless innocents have been spared from whatever he was planning to do to them!"

The kudu exhaled softly, taking the glasses off the bridge of his nose and setting them aside. "Agreed, it was a good deed we did last night. However, it was at the cost of two of our troops, our colleagues, our friends," he stated for impact. "We do not trade lives for victory, Officer Wolford. Those innocents weren't going anywhere anytime soon. You were told to wait until backup arrived, were you not?"

Murana grimaced again. "Yes…I was."

The kudu leaned forward. "And yet you, as the ranking officer on scene, saw fit to put three other lives at risk to capture six armed lackeys of the Arbiter. Why would you do that?"

She looked away, wanting the blinds to be open again so she could escape into the city beyond. "I don't know. It seemed like we didn't have much time to waste. There were other trucks pulling off the freeway down the ramps to the docks." She turned back to him. "Not our trucks."

He set down the notepad and leaned over to reach into his briefcase. He carefully opened it, revealing a folder with a haphazard stack of papers bulging out, then sifted through the wealth of information inside. Several images of a time long ago flitted past Murana's gaze, paining her with their memories. Images of her suited up in garb that was a far cry from her current job and position, and certainly a far cry from any sort of legal notions of justice.

"It says here that you have a knack for finding people who do harm to such innocents, especially women and children." The kudu cocked a brow at her, daring her to refute his claim.

She waved a paw at him, but the terror of revisiting this time of her life was eating at her heart. "That was a long time ago. That isn't me anymore."

13

"Eight years ago, to be exact, and yet I cannot fathom any other reason why you would willfully disobey a direct order and make the nonsensical decision after years of training to go in without proper backup, except for this key piece of information of who was at stake inside that warehouse."

She met his stare accusingly. "Because we had no way of knowing if they would survive the night. They could have disappeared alongside the others we failed to save weeks prior. Unless you were privy to knowledge we didn't have out there, like the Script?"

"Deflect your decision all you want, but you and I both know that the Zabökar Police Department does not put stock in silly superstitions like the Script. If we did, we would have no reason to exist, as we'd be blindly trusting to the fates, ignoring the plights of the less fortunate. I, for one, am not a religious mammal. Regardless, your past unfortunately precedes you in this case." He readjusted the glasses back onto his muzzle before resuming. "You do know how tenuous your position is right now, Officer Wolford?"

A slight twinge of fear permeated her eyes as she looked at him. "Of course I do."

"We took a great risk secretly bringing you onboard the force, backed up by a multitude of recommendations to your character. You had skills that were useful and highly specialized that no one here could match." He waggled a damning photo at her. "You were saved from the consequences of your actions by joining us and putting in your time for the betterment of Zabökar. Free breaks like that don't just fall out of the sky."

Murana's resolve was breaking. The yawning abyss of her past was catching up to her insanely fast. The first time they punished her for her past was horrible, but it seemed this time was worse; she had a lot more to lose. "I know. I'm sorry. It was a lapse in judgment, and it won't happen again."

He leaned back, shutting the folder softly. "You're right. It won't." She looked at him curiously. "You were asked to come here to accept a new mission. A final mission, if you will. One that is more suited to your skills of old." He reached back and picked up a small binder filled with papers and handed it to her. "Inside you will find

14

contacts and materials needed to create a new identity for yourself. You will be infiltrating the Arbiter's syndicate as an undercover agent. You will do your best to find out why he wants these people, what he is doing with them, and if they're still alive, specific logistics on how to extract them."

Murana's jaw dropped as she saw the extent of her new role, flipping through the sheets to include a new ID card. "Sir, this could be a year-long endeavor or more. I may not make it back from this."

"I'm sure you will do just fine," he simpered. "Based on my knowledge of you, you were well-versed in the criminal underworld, and were quite adept at maneuvering your way around it. This should be just a return to form for you. Any and all tactics you employ that do not include murder will be authorized for this mission."

She looked up confused. "So, I am not being punished for Buchanan and Lawrence? Does Chief Bremingham know about this mission?"

The kudu scoffed. "The chief wants nothing to do with you. You've burned the last bit of good will you had with him with that stunt last night. If he had his way, he'd have you strung up in court with at least two counts of mammalslaughter, not to mention many other infractions."

This cowed her immensely. He must have noticed, as his demeanor softened. "Look, it was either this or jail for you. At least here, your unique set of skills will be put to one last good use, and will go a long way to atoning for that grand mistake you made."

Murana morosely gazed at the paperwork before her. The road ahead seemed vast and the path treacherous. This was a world she had been trying to escape from for years, yet she was now being forced back into it, or face the rest of her existence behind bars. She had tried so hard to turn her life around, to be free from the shackles of her past, only to have it crashing back down around her head.

To make things right, she had to go back to doing wrong to fulfill the greater good.

She looked up. "What happens after I accomplish this?"

He scratched his chin. "It is hard to say. The chief hasn't fully decided yet. Perhaps you could be pardoned, let off the force, and then monitored for the remainder of your days in early retirement. Or you could still be tried in court for your actions."

"None of that sounds encouraging to even try this in the first place." She closed the binder, not wanting to look at it anymore.

"I'm not without sympathy for your position, Officer Wolford, but you have little choice in this matter now. The legal wheels are turning, and this was the only solution that was offered in your favor." He re-crossed his legs with the other.

"Does Anthony know about this?" she asked.

He shook his head. "We will back-brief him when he returns tonight. He is to make no contact with you or he will blow your cover."

Her face wilted. "You mean I can't say goodbye to him or my boys?"

"No." His hoof tapped the armrest of his chair. "Unfortunately, you will be starting this mission tonight. Although your actions caused great loss in this department, it did serve to bring to light one thing: the Arbiter is moving ahead swiftly with his plans, and we can't afford to waste any more time. You need to be on the ground running with this."

"How will I communicate with you while I'm in the field?" She shifted uncomfortably, letting her tail flow out from behind her, dangling off the edge of the wooden chair.

"The Arbiter is too intelligent for wires and earbuds. He will be expecting it. So instead, we will discreetly meet at designated points and times pointed out in the paperwork you got there. There is a schedule to keep, and you will meet each one or we will count your mission as a loss. You will bring all information and evidence you have gathered to each meeting, and we will take it back to process." He put the folder of her past back into the briefcase. "This mission was tasked by the High Council themselves. We have been sitting on it for a few weeks now, waiting for the right opportunity and person to tackle it."

"And you believe you've found them?" Murana knew the answer before she asked it.

"Yes. Although, you made our choice simpler by your errant decision last night." He sliced a hoof through the air. "Make no mistake, this could very well be a suicide mission for you, Officer Wolford.

16

However, given the alternative, do you think you have much of a choice?"

Murana shook her head, looking down at her hind paws. "No, sir."

"Good. You have a few hours of free time to get yourself out of your uniform and prepare to execute this tasking. Do not talk to the chief. Do not talk to your fellow colleagues. Do not talk to your husband and kids. Go to your first rendezvous and meet with the point of contact there to begin assuming your new identity. You are dismissed." He waved her off.

Murana felt defeated as she got up from the seat, picking up the paperwork given her. She slid out the door, tail between her legs, and could hear the kudu get up out of his seat, turn off the tape recording, then shut down the camera perched on his desk filming the entire interaction.

Jake shivered. His eyes opened when he realized the covers were no longer on him, but rolled up around the larger bird beside him. The gangly stork was blissfully snoring away, seeds of Jake's aftermath all over the bed and underneath her. On the other side of him were two other birds just like her. At the foot of the bed were several passed out red pandas in various arrays of limbs, most likely hopped up on delirious sex dreams.

He groaned as he sat up; the ache in his loins from a night-long orgy of passion was draining on his physical fortitude. These girls were atrociously lustful for one of his kind. Not that he'd had much of a choice in the matter after he'd been commanded to be the main event at one of the bird's bachelorette party. The details didn't matter, it was all the same. One of them was getting married, and they wanted a night of passion before the ball and chain fell. So what better way to get their rocks off than with a rabbit?

Grimacing, he rubbed his paws through his fur, feeling the dry starchiness of their sinful deeds all over him. He would need to take a long shower when he got home from this. Gingerly scooting his bum down the length of the bed, taking great care not to wake his bedside companions, he slipped down the side of the mattress. He winced as his cottontail brushed past the face of one of the red pandas, causing her to stir.

"Oh… Humpings…is that you?" She groggily smiled, eyes half-lidded from the glare of the sun sweeping past the curtains, lightly blown to the side by the wind swirling in through the open window.

"My name is Thumpings," Jake reminded. He hated the nickname he would sometimes get from those who propositioned him for sex by the law, thinking themselves hilarious, as if they had thought of it first.

He had begun to rummage around to find his jeans when the red panda crawled to the floor and reached out a paw to encircle his ankle. "You were amazing last night," she slurred, her senses not fully present.

"I know," he said flatly.

It was always like this. For whatever reason, they would always tell him he was better than any lover they've ever had. The stamina of rabbit-kind was infamous, but he'd had the unfortunate pleasure of finding out himself just how much he had compared to others of his species. Looking back at the five ladies strewn across the bed and room, it was no wonder they loved him for keeping up with everything they demanded of him.

The panda giggled, whispering as if she was about to say something scandalous. "Hey, Jake… Did you want to have a little rendezvous before anyone else wakes up? Just you and me?"

"I'd rather not," he said truthfully, his tone cold. He had just found his shirt and was about to thrust his arms through it angrily.

Her expression soured. "Are you rejecting my demand for services?"

Jake stared straight ahead, ears dropping, his buck teeth grinding against all his others. He loathed it when someone reminded him of his civic duty and the law that governed it. "I am not," he replied, throwing his shirt down.

Without much emotion, he positioned himself above the eager red panda, who was getting more lucid by the second with the promise of what was to come next. He lost track of how long he was there straddling her, pounding away until he was forced to slap a paw over her mouth to prevent her unbridled screams from waking the others and the entire orgy, lest the night prior repeat itself. He simply didn't have time for this.

At long last, she lay there splayed out in ecstasy, eyes rolling back in her head as he came off of her. Not waiting for any compliments of his technique that were meaningless to him, he strode over back to his small pile of clothes and began putting them on. He was fully dressed and buckling his belt when she finally came around again, sane enough to talk.

"I could sponsor you, you know…" she said thoughtfully. Jake's nose twitched and he stood stock still. Unaware of his inner turmoil, she continued. "My family owns a big ranch south of here. I could sponsor you and you could live in freedom there. You wouldn't have to worry about making money anymore, where to live, or figure out how to put food on your table—"

"I know what sponsoring is," Jake interrupted. His breathing was rapid. He did not want this. This was a fate worse than death. If he got sponsored, all his hopes and dreams of being something better, as slim as they were now, would be completely annihilated. "What is your name?"

She cocked her head curiously. "Samantha. Samantha Curings."

Jake nodded without looking at her. "Give me some time to think it over, Samantha. It is a generous offer, but I need time to figure out what is best for me." He knew that by calling her formally by her name and giving her the promise of a hope that he would be hers, he would be let off the hook here.

"Of course, Jake. Anything for you." She shivered dreamily, still remembering their sex just moments before. "Do you have to go now?"

This time, he did look at her. "Yes. My job starts within the hour, and they'll wonder where I am if I am not there."

She waved a dismissive paw. "Of course, of course. I wouldn't want to be the reason you got in trouble." She knew the law as well as Jake did. A rabbit's appointed job was not to be messed with, and he was obligated to perform his paying job before accepting any offers from people like her for his services. She got up and sidled next to him, embracing him from behind as she stroked his stomach tenderly. "Just don't keep me waiting too long, ok?" she whispered into his ear.

Jake trembled, but not from any pleasurable sensations. Her touch was like fire to him, burning him at the implication of his potential future with her. He excused himself graciously, disentangling from her limbs and giving her one final farewell before silently slipping out the door and into the neon-lit hallway.

Trying to remain inconspicuous so he wouldn't attract any more attention, he scurried down the hallway. Some mammals could smell the scent of his musk after sex, and somehow that was more alluring to them. It was an unfortunate byproduct that he wished didn't happen, so haste was his utmost concern when getting home to shower. The sooner he had this smell off of him, the better.

While waiting his turn to exit out into the street, Jake bounded out of the way of an oblivious drunk horse who had barreled through the revolving door to the penthouse suites. The din of morning traffic was already in full roar. Multitudes of honking and revved engines overhead indicated the rush hour of people flying to their work in their souped-up cars, their bass speakers blaring out obnoxious tunes.

As expected, Jake was jostled to and fro working his way down the sidewalk. Unless people were insanely interested in early morning shenanigans right before work, nobody would typically pay him any mind. He used his rabbit anonymity to his advantage and slithered his way through the crowd.

He would normally have a vehicle to drive the surface streets here—the last remnants of an earlier time before the hover cars were introduced. Now only the poorest of citizens were regulated to such ground-based transportation, and he couldn't even afford that. It was a hard blow to take the day he had to sell his single-seater, having had it passed down to him from his father. Now all he had were his own two hindpaws to carry him everywhere.

His phone buzzed hard in his pocket. Jake tapped it open and answered without breaking stride. "This is Mr. Thumpings, official clerk services of Zabökar Police Department. How may I help you?"

"Hey, Jake, it's Tony!" A cheerful voice boomed on the other end of the receiver, causing Jake to cringe. "It's been a while since we talked! You will not believe what happened to me recently!"

"I'm on my way home to get ready for work, Tony. Make it quick." Jake sighed. He didn't really have time for another long-winded story from his sporadic friend right now.

"Of course, buddy!" Tony's voice was brimming with excitement. "I'm getting sponsored!" After a lengthy pause, he decided to expound for Jake. "You know that cheetah girl I've been seeing every Thorlag, right? Well, she's taken quite a liking to me and she said she's willing to sponsor me! This is it! I don't have to work anymore! I can be her personal servant and all my needs will be met!"

"That's great, Tony…really." Jake tried to sound happy, but his face was anything but.

"You're not all that thrilled, are you?" Tony could hear right through Jake's voice.

"Well, yeah…I am, but…" Jake dashed into a small alcove between buildings when another larger mammal almost stepped on him.

"Spit it out, buddy. What's wrong?" Tony's voice grew concerned. "You can tell your old pal."

Looking almost ashamed, Jake lowered his voice. "I might be getting sponsored too."

"That's great!" Tony returned to his normal volume. "We can be sponsor buddies!"

"I don't know… It doesn't seem like it's for me." Jake admitted.

"Alright, I know what you need. You need a pep talk from your old buddy, Tony!" Tony chuckled. "Tell you what, you got a bit of extra time before work today? Meet me at the Sunrise Savanna coffee shop on Roaring St. in about thirty minutes. Breakfast is on me! See you there!" He clicked off.

Jake glumly let the phone drop into his pocket before resuming his long trudge home.

Jake entered his apartment building, which resided in a less reputable section of town. The buildings for his kind were smaller and sandwiched amongst the larger ones meant for the bigger mammals. There were no birds nearby, since their abodes were nested further into downtown on the high rises with the rest of the elite. None would be caught dead living in the dregs with the commoners.

Shutting out the sounds of the outside world, he padded through the cracked tiling of the apartment foyer, its sleek surface marred by a plethora of pawprints that were never mopped away. At least the cargo elevator was open and inviting this morning. That was a lucky first. Getting in and shutting the extended grating to lock himself into the cabin, he pressed a button to begin his laborious ascent to his floor, the cables and wheels grinding all the way up.

After unintentionally swinging the grating hard enough that it rammed into the wall, Jake warily exited and walked down the hall to his room. The dismal lighting only seemed to accentuate his mood, flickering as he passed by. He shoved the key into the lock, turning it until he heard the click before pressing inward on the creaky door. It screeched all the way to its temporary resting place, only accepting sweet release upon closing.

Jake stared around his quaint two room apartment. It had a small den area complete with couch and television, the space shared with an equally small kitchenette. There was no room for a table to eat at properly. Just off the side was his bedroom with attached bathroom. It was sparsely furnished with minimal décor on the walls. He didn't make enough for much more than this.

He quickly discarded his clothes on the floor in a trail to his shower, which he turned on to full blast and let the steam rise up and permeate the room. The events of the night finally caught up to him and he pounded on the wall of the shower, tears flowing freely. He wept hard, his breath coming in ragged gasps as he tried in vain to get his misery under control. The scalding water did little to drown out his thoughts.

Shutting off the water unceremoniously, he didn't bother to dry himself off. Dripping into the bedroom, he went to his nightstand and pulled out the lone drawer just beneath his night lamp. He pulled the string to turn the bulb on and looked at the two articles that had shifted into view: a book that he had long since stopped reading about some silly dragon from his youth, and a gun, small enough to fit his paws with just enough bullets to fill the current chamber.

Checking the rounds loaded, he slouched onto the side of his bed, cradling the weapon in his lap. He stared at it for a long time. He placed the barrel into his mouth, angling it just right so as to cover the biggest mass of his brain. Quivering, he slid his finger into the trigger guard and held it there. Tears began to flow again as his entire body shook from the existential dread of the nothingness that was to come. There was no hope left for any future of his own design. All things would be decided upon by others over him. This was the last thing left he had control over.

His finger nearly slipped and depressed the firing lever when a buzz emanated from his discarded jeans across the bedroom on the floor. Trembling with the thought of how close he came to it, he set the gun down beside him. Sniffing, he went over and dug around in his pants until he found his phone. Swiping up on the screen, he saw a text from Tony.

"Hey buddy! I'm actually here early, come when you're ready! I'll be here." The obnoxious color of orange Tony chose for his text background was the only cheer to be found in Jake's dismal room.

Wiping the snot forming from his nose, Jake hastily tossed the gun back in the drawer and closed it. Committed to not killing himself that day, he picked a random shirt and pair of shorts, not even aware of putting them on as his body went by rote memory. He stuffed his phone into a pocket, then grabbed his keys and quietly went out and shut the front door.

The short flash that greeted him upon entering the business district was a stark reminder of how much his and everyone else's lives were slowly being controlled by those on top. Instantly, a lit-up screen built into the side of the storefront window began jabbering at him about the latest trend in rabbit fashion, using Jake's name and everything to advertise specifically to him. Another flash and the subsequent store began selling its wares to Jake.

He simply ignored them all as each scanner attempted to cash in on his presence. It was a relatively new system put into place in the last few decades, its usage only being within the inner city, but most folks didn't seem to mind. Not that it mattered. Those who would've objected didn't live in the inner city, but skirted the edges being poor like him. Only the elite enjoyed the entire world catering to them.

Still, that did little to deter the city from inputting every citizen's bio-profile into the system.

At length he rounded the bend to see the long line already out front of the Sunrise Savanna. Many mammals were already on their phones, tapping away messages to their colleagues about the coming day's events. Jake didn't really have anyone to talk to about his job; it was pretty much a vacuum—a lonely existence where he worked despite being among people.

Knowing Tony would already have a seat ready for him and his food ordered, he sidestepped the entire line and just entered in. He could already feel the stares at the back of his bunny ears from interested parties who were suddenly reminded that they might be hungry for something else this early in the morning. Praying he wouldn't get stopped as he searched for Tony, Jake made an effort to be nimble as he sifted through the larger crowd.

It was packed in the Sunrise Savanna. Multitudes of mammals were ordering their coffees or blended smoothies off the screens perched at their individual eye-levels. The workers behind the glass were a blur, rushing to make the drinks and linking them up to the proper tubing that would shuttle it to its intended recipient. Every now and then an irritated bray would resound when someone was delivered the wrong drink, but it was rare, given the efficiency of the system and its workers.

A cow cursed as she nearly backed into Jake after getting off her hover stool, which updated the occupancy counter outside above the door. She glared at the rabbit for being underfoot. Shrugging off her ire, Jake spotted Tony at last in the far booth in the corner. It was in the smaller mammal section of the cramped restaurant and he only managed to get a small two-seater, but it was enough.

Tony hadn't seen him yet, and was instead gazing out the beamed window that spanned the length of the section, his eyes darting back and forth amidst the rushing cars overhead. His cream-like fur color and species made him look much like Jake, but something about him, even right down to the square glasses perched on his nose, screamed happiness. Things had gone right for him in life, even if not much of consequence had happened. Unlike Jake, Tony was perfectly happy with the minimum. He never knew anything different or aspired to be anything more.

"Hey, Jake! Over here!" Tony had finally noticed him, waving him over.

Jake scooted into the tight spacing between cushion and table edge, doing his best to put on a bright face. "How you been these days, Tony? I haven't spoken to you in a few months." He graciously accepted his preordered coffee and began nursing it with his breath to cool it down.

Beaming at his great news, Tony leaned forward. "I'm doing great, actually. Sure I got dumped on by Sally, but she was a whore anyway." This caused Jake to raise a brow, but he did not interrupt. "So this cheetah chick, Sabrina, right? She comes into my bar and begins chatting me up. This was about six months ago. Well, every Thorlag night she checks in and always comes straight up to me and hits me up for a decent conversation."

"And she took a fancy to you." Jake couldn't hide his smirk. He enjoyed seeing Tony so happy.

Tony snapped his fingers. "Exactly! I didn't think much of it, but then she asks me two weeks ago out of nowhere if she could be my sponsor!"

"You done her yet?" It was an obvious question.

Usually these sorts of things didn't get to this point unless the benefactor sponsoring has tasted the goods, as it were. Most rabbits in job positions never really got beyond Jake's age when working since

25

most, if not all, were scooped up to become in-house servants. It was all reliant on the younger generation to shoulder the burden of doing the myriad of tasks set before them in Zabökar. In fact, Jake was actually on older side of the spectrum of still-available rabbits, being at the tender "old" age of twenty-five.

Tony winked at Jake. "Of course. She's just as fast in bed as she can be on the streets. She's pretty amazing. I'm so lucky to be chosen by someone like that."

"When do you see her next?"

Tony's brow furrowed. "Well, I don't know. It's actually been over a month…since she asked actually. Last thing she said was that she had a sudden trip she needed to fly off to.

Jake took a sip, still trying to be jovial. "I'm sure you'll see her again. Either way, I'm happy for you, Tony."

Tony frowned. He could see trouble underneath Jake's exterior. "All right. I could hear it in your voice and now I can see it in your face. What's got you down?"

Jake shrugged, looking out the window himself to avoid having to meet his friend's gaze. "I don't know… I feel like we should be doing more than what we are now. I tried to get into law enforcement and they just laughed me off. It's only after being persistent that I got a job at all in that sector. They threw me into their dungeon of storage cabinets to be sorted through, filing their case reports."

"Well that's a hard field to begin with, buddy," Tony tried to console. "Sometimes certain people are just better for certain things than others. I mean, look at us." He gestured to them both. "We're small rabbits. We are just naturally born to be perfect for specific jobs."

Jake snorted, looking down at his drink. "Yeah, like whoring."

Tony blinked. "Hey, not like that! That's just part of our civic duty. You know that. It's a way to bring the crime rate down."

"Like they keep telling us." Jake rolled his eyes, taking another sip. "And so we're not as big a whore as Sally is then?"

"Of course not!" Tony scoffed, waving a paw as if Jake was being ridiculous. "Sally has been breeding around other rabbits trying to get pregnant, which is against the law without proper permits."

"So you're going to rat her out?" Jake asked.

"Nah." Tony looked relaxed at the whole situation. "I don't give up my own. She may be a whore and it'll catch up to her one day, but it won't be because I sold her out. We rabbits got to watch after our own, you know? No one else is going to do it for us."

"Yeah...I know." Jake knew too well.

"Stepan believes we should step up to do more for our kind. As much as I'm excited to be with Sabrina, I do feel he has a point."

Jake tossed him a leery look. "I'd rather not discuss him right now."

"Why not?"

"I just don't like getting involved in radical behavior, especially with potentially dangerous types like that. I do work at the police department, remember? I don't want that on my record."

"Alright then." Tony lightly tapped the table. "That can't be all of it though. You were asked to be sponsored this morning too, yet I do not see you happy. This is the goal of every rabbit!"

"Not all rabbits," Jake reminded.

"Well, you were always an odd one. Right down to those pretty eyes of yours." Tony chuckled, indicating Jake's heterochromatic colors of aqua and emerald. "Many would love to have a rabbit with that rare trait. Still, you can't let what happened to your friend haunt your life, man."

Jake set down the cup on the platter a bit harder than intended, causing Tony to flop his ears back in annoyance. "Tony, I realize that. I know I shouldn't get so strung up on things I can't control like the murder of my friend, but I can't help it. He was the reason I wanted to become a cop in the first place."

"But you ended up being a bouncer instead," Tony prompted, oblivious to Jake's vexation.

Jake sighed and nodded. "It was all that was available and hiring without much discrimination. Did you know I was offered a job by a wolf to protect her daughter?"

Tony looked genuinely surprised. "I actually didn't. How did it happen?"

Jake stirred another cube of sugar into his coffee. "Like how any encounter with a predator happens: I was called upon for sex. How she came across my number to get me into her home, I've no idea. It was even on my private line. Still, her offer was legit, and I promised I'd keep an extra eye on her daughter as I could spare."

Tony inched forward. "Something tells me things didn't go well."

Jake shook his head. "Not in the slightest. Things were going good at first. The daughter was the backup singer and lead guitarist in that band, '*Bad Luck*'."

"I think I've heard of them." Tony scratched his chin. "Not my style of music though."

"Yeah, it was an easy gig mostly." A young wolf of what looked like red hair outside caught Jake's eye, almost as if he was seeing her again for the first time. "Most didn't really bother the performers, but being a rabbit, I was very useful for kicking rowdy revelers. However, I should have been more vigilant. I should have known someone as unique as her would have been attractive for people who could do bad things to her."

"I don't understand… What does this have anything to do with you being unhappy at being sponsored?"

Tony's question brought Jake's attention back from the outside. "I felt like I was actually making a difference in someone's life. Someone had tasked me specifically to watch over their daughter. Me! A rabbit! That's far more acknowledgement of my abilities than the police ever showed!"

"Not so loud, buddy." Tony looked around nervously. A few extra eyes were roving their way after hearing the loud outburst.

Jake calmed down, but he was disgusted. "See? You're just as afraid as I am of drawing attention to ourselves. Normally we rabbits go by unnoticed by most everyone, but we're afraid that if someone were to notice us that we might be accosted with an order to please someone in a back alley."

"It's not that…" Tony tried to backpedal.

"Then why are you so adamant and cheerful at being sponsored?" Jake pressed, arms folded. "You're happy that you'll have documented proof that you can show wherever you go that you're owned so that you no longer have to deal with any more strangers in bed, let alone be killed or eaten by those who are into that sort of sick shit."

Tony now looked uncomfortable, his true feelings about the matter evident. "Okay… Yeah, so what? I'm just happy I'll be off the streets and not fighting for scraps to make a meager living. My cheetah has a very opulent lifestyle, and I'll be enjoying it with her!"

"But not as her equal," Jake interjected.

"That's not the point. I didn't come here to talk about me, but to help you. You seemed a bit down in the dumps. So what happened to this wolf girl you were supposed to look after?"

Jake could see he was avoiding the issue, but it'd do no good to push his "friend" to divulge anything further; unlike him, Tony was a better psychiatrist than patient. Taking another drink from his now-sweetened coffee, he paused. His ears flicked towards the entryway instinctively. He thought he had heard some distant screams, but wasn't exactly sure if he was just hallucinating.

Sensing no immediate danger, Jake turned back to Tony. "She got kitnapped. I was told to give something special to her by her mother, and the very night I hand it over, she gets kitnapped."

"How do you know?" Tony's ears perked up as he scooted forward a bit.

"How else could you explain it? I was called off for my 'civic duty' shortly after seeing her last, and when I came back, she was gone. A mess and some blood left behind where she should have been waiting for me." He stared at his coffee, no longer feeling the need to drink. "I think about her still to this day… At how I failed her. At how I failed them both." His eyes rose to meet Tony's. "That's why I'm not happy. All my life I've been trying to be useful to something, somebody, anything, and I've achieved nothing but failure. If all I'm good for is my body, then what happiness can I find in being sponsored?"

"Aw man, that's rough… Maybe we should—" Tony's voice cut off as his ears turned to the commotion happening outside.

Jake wasn't alone now in thinking he had heard screams. They were getting closer, intermingled now with loud crashing and rending of metal. Many of the patrons of the Sunrise Savanna were already alarmed and getting out of their seats. Everyone was now looking outside the window at the throng of mammals running past, some glancing back in terror at an unseen malice.

Tony's nose was twitching uncontrollably, his flight-or-fight response kicking into high gear. "Maybe we should stay inside and get away from the windows," he suggested, scooting out of the booth and stepping away, eyes glued to the events unfolding outside.

Jake stood up tall in his own seat, determination on his face. "I'm going to head out to see what's going on."

Tony's eyes grew like saucers. "Are you nuts? There are mammals way bigger than us running away from something that's clearly dangerous and more than likely capable of killing us easily, Jake!"

Jake turned back to regard his friend. "If I die, I die. I was planning on doing so today anyway. Might as well have some excitement before the end."

Without waiting for Tony's reaction to his admission of suicide, Jake leapt off and made a mad dash to the front door. The rest of the customers already had it in their mind to begin a stampede towards the exit, so he was trying his best to make it there before full mob mentality took effect.

Jake skidded hard outside, hopping to the side to allow the panicked people a way out without trampling him. He could now see what was getting everyone spooked. Rising spires of magma were launching cars into the sky, heading towards them. Some of the vehicles were hurled so hard that they reached the first level of mag tracks above, knocking cars out of the air as they both plummeted to the ground, raining fire and hot oil debris.

A honking truck was propelled, back end first, up into the air by another rapidly cooling pillar of fire, its trajectory much higher than Jake had anticipated. Directly in its path of descending destruction was a small wallaby couple with their crying infant in a stroller. Without hesitation he bounded from car to car, all stopped and abandoned in the streets, towards the family. Without explaining why, he pushed them forward out of the way and jumped to the side as the truck slammed into the ground with a roar just inches from his hind paws.

"Is everyone okay?" He breathed heavily, looking for any cuts and bruises on the family. The stunned wallabies just shook their heads, eyes wide. "Good, go on. Get out of here!"

Without being told twice, they chittered hysterically and began to run opposite the looming danger. Sniffing the air, which was now reeking of sulfur and burnt fur, he saw a flash of red mixed with white flitting between the vehicles. Suddenly a bolt of electricity plowed through a string of cars, blasting into a nearby interior décor shop, shattering its windows into tiny pieces. All the lights inside went dark while more screams erupted.

"Jake! Oh my gods, are you alright?!" Tony had apparently had enough courage to follow his friend out into danger.

Jake's eyes were riveted on the blazing locks of red hair. Recognition smashed into him like a punch to his gut. He swiveled and reached out for his friend. "Get inside, now!"

It was too late. The young wolf with the red fur had covered that short distance in startlingly quick time. As if sensing a meal nearby, her unusual tail of crimson split open at its tip, revealing a jagged set of razor-sharp teeth and a dripping tongue of calculated malevolence. Scooping up Tony and coiling around his midriff as the wolf passed by him, it swallowed him up whole. Kicking and screaming, his tiny legs and arms disappeared inside.

"Oh, what the hell, Ahya?!" the girl shouted, now noticing the new weight in her tail.

"Did your tail just eat that rabbit?" the white swan next to her exclaimed.

The bird was holding the wolf's paw in her hand, as if being dragged along for the ride. She was sporting some dark leather pants complete with fishnet stockings. Her wings and bill were pierced with studs, and her chest was adorned by a shredded shirt with a metal band logo emblazoned on the front. The wolf and swan seemed like an oddly matched pair by their clothing alone.

Just beyond them was the source of the explosions and fire: an angry reptile of a mix Jake couldn't readily identify, or even guess. She seemed furious, slapping her spiny tail on the ground before another eruption of earth was sent careening towards their position. The wolf let

31

loose another bolt of electricity at the base of the incoming shockwave, causing it to explode out backwards towards the reptile. Rock and rubble spewed everywhere.

"Yeah… Yeah, she just did…" the wolf answered the swan, clapping a paw to her mouth like she was about to vomit. The writhing bulge in her tail was now gone. His friend, eaten. It was over so fast.

It was then she noticed Jake standing there staring at her with an unreadable expression. He didn't know what to do or what to think; the only thing that came to his mind was the name he remembered for her. "Taylor?"

Fighting back nausea at eating yet another person, she held a finger up to the swan beside her who was urging them to go now. Struggling with the fresh bloat in her stomach, she did her best to ask Jake, "Uh…hi. You just said my name. Who are you again?"

2.

KITNAPPING

The camera flickered on as the lines of static faded along the edges. The view was that of the Furon River on the west side. The Sparling Bridge gleamed in the dreary sunlight peeking through the clouds as the refracted rays reflected off the polished steel, spanning the water to the other side. Several warehouses perched along the pier opposite were dwarfed by the multitude of skyscrapers beyond, each with unique spirals and slanted roofing that seemed erratic in view, but served their purpose of keeping rain off the pedestrians below, walking alongside their tall structures.

The kudu adjusted his microphone to better protect it from the downpour, but his chosen spot for the rendezvous did not take into account for weather. He moved further towards the row of planted trees to better take shelter under their boughs. It brought little solace, but it was better than being out in the open with little protection.

He glanced at his watch again and gazed down the walkway. He was early, as he always was on these meetings. There were a few stragglers with umbrellas meandering down the riverside, but it was mostly vacant. His eyes scanned the environs and ensured there was nobody he could detect waiting there from the Arbiter. He needed to play his part in this, and ensure that everything was going according to plan.

His focus locked onto the figure running down the sidewalk just off the bridge in the distance. She was still tiny at this range, but there was no mistaking her running gait. Murana was a smart one. Identifying each of the rendezvous spots and the times she had to meet them, she had begun a routine of exercising in the early morning by jogging past each one. She'd sometimes switch it up and alter the order, but she'd always stop and rest to catch her breath at each spot. That way any malicious onlookers wouldn't think anything was amiss as she stopped today nearby to take a short break.

She was wearing a light grey tank top and shorts. She was completely soaked, but that didn't stop her from using her disc-pod ear plugs to listen to some tunes. Making eye contact with him, she began to slow and begin her cooldown as she appeared to all as catching her breath. She stopped several paces from him. With a nod, she acknowledged his presence before proceeding to lean up against the tree with an arm and pulling up one leg with the other for a deep stretch.

Without regarding him further, she spoke to the ground loud enough for him to hear. "I know the reason why they are hiring criminals to rob the banks." At a grunt from the kudu, she continued. "They are amassing a wide array of weapons and technical equipment in service to a bigger plan to change people, and he's using this stolen money to grease the hands of those who can get it for him, with traceable trade routes going as far out as Howlgrav."

Not looking at her either, he stared off across the Furon River. "Changing people? What do you mean?"

She shifted to the other leg, "It almost sounds like nonsense, but from the one time I met the Arbiter, he seemed passionate about this grand vision of his. He's aiming to mix something he called magic into people, into mammals of all types. Thought that sort of thing was reserved for fairytales and the Script. He's using the kids and teenagers that have been kitnapped as test subjects for this new invention of his."

"You already met the Arbiter? That is quite extraordinary," the kudu marveled.

Murana rolled her eyes, but continued the stretch. "You tasked me for this because of my skills. Why are you surprised that I'm delivering on them? Yes, I met the old tortoise. Not directly, mind you, but I was at least in the same room as his high-ranking lieutenants when he was going over his plans for expansion on his operations."

"Have there been any successful test subjects?" he probed, shifting his microphone to better pick up her response.

She dropped the leg and began a calf stretch against the tree. "Yes and no." She hesitated. "Those that succeed gain abilities I cannot explain. They are able to float, explode things, or even turn things to

35

solid ice. I don't even know how it is possible. He takes those that exhibit those powers and trains them for combat."

"And the no?" He shivered, the damp getting to him.

She continued to recall it in her mind's eye. "Each one of them screams in pain and agony for hours." Her nails dug into the tree, gouging it deeply to where sap dribbled onto her claws. "But they monitored those who didn't gain abilities for a bit until they showed positive for cellular cancer—the surefire sign that the process had failed with them."

"What do they do with the rejects?" His questioning was merciless.

Murana gritted her teeth. "The cancer would have killed them anyway in time, but they put them down right there. They called it a 'mercy'. Innocent children are being killed, all because their bodies did not meet the expectations of the experiment. An experiment they have no business being subjected to!" Snarling, she beat a fist against the tree, now looking at him for the first time. "Sir, we need to get in there now! Stop dawdling and let's send in strike teams to kill their operation! I already know where they are located and everything."

"Be still, Officer Wolford," the kudu clucked, his bray cutting her indignation short. "You mentioned these test subject gaining powers and that they were training them for combat." She could do nothing but nod her head. "How are these kids taking to this? I'd imagine they aren't happy being stolen from their homes and parents and forced to fight. Are there any rebellions within? If they are developing powerful abilities, as you claim, they should make little work of the Arbiter and his men."

She shook her head, swapping to the other leg to stretch. "That's the insidious part of it. He's making it out like they are going to be helping Zabökar and protecting their families and loved ones. He is using classic propaganda techniques on impressionable minds to bolster their courage and make them seem important to the future of their city. He is raving about a terrible reptile army from the south that will come raze Zabökar to the ground, and that each one of them needs to be ready to fight them off. Then he is giving them the tools to do so."

"That's scarily ingenious," he commented, turning away briefly to check if anyone new had appeared to potentially break up their meeting. "With this new information, we can't just barge in there against hundreds of trained child soldiers with abilities we can't possibly predict or account for." He eyed her more pointedly, ensuring he got his next thought across precisely. "We go in without more information with what we're dealing with, we may end up killing the very innocents we are trying to protect."

Murana growled. She knew he was right, and she hated it. "We can't just let them get away with this!"

"Wolford, I know you were once just a young wolf fresh off your stint as an assassin, for a group just as dark and seedy as the one the Arbiter is spearheading. You were a ruthless vigilante that gunned specifically for criminals who dared to harm young females and children. I understand your rage here." He sighed deeply. "However, there is too much at stake to go with your gut instinct to wipe them all out, especially when the very ones you are going in to save would be the ones to kill you if you tried."

"So what do you propose I do then, *sir*?" She nearly spat out the final word.

Ignoring her insolent tone, he took out a clear plastic bag with a thumb drive in it. He casually dropped it in the bush behind him, taking great care to confirm she noticed where it fell. "We need you to get access to whatever computer systems they are using to track, operate, and maintain these devices they are using to change these subjects. We need to understand the technology at work here, and maybe find a common thread to counter it when we go in to strike."

Her mouth dropped at the daunting task set before her. "I barely got into his inner circle by the skin of my teeth, and now you want me to gain access to his research division? A section I've barely heard mention of until this past week? As far as I can tell, his operatives within that section are highly secretive, and not even my contacts and those I associate with in his organization come within leagues of those operations."

He just smirked at her. "You got this far within a span of months, I'm sure you'll be fine." Noticing the irritation in her posture, he cleared his throat. "Unless you feel you can't hack it in this job? In which case, I can bring you in to be tried for your actions with Buchanan and Lawrence, alongside your entire history of crimes of ten years ago."

"You can't do that!" Murana was aghast. All pretense of stretching was gone.

"I'm sure I can," he sneered. "A well-known vigilante criminal resurfacing again deep in the heart of Zabökar police force, using us as cover for her clandestine operations for the Arbiter. Would make for quite the thrilling headline on tonight's news, wouldn't it?"

"This is entrapment! I'm already committing crimes on the Arbiter's behalf just so I can glean some precious information on his operations for you! Now you're using my own past against me for something the High Council ordered?" She jabbed a finger at him. "I'm going to be telling Chief Inspector Bremingham about this. I don't think he'd stand for it, even despite his opinion of me! I want out!"

"You will do no such thing. You *are* speaking to the chief inspector." The kudu stood tall, knowing he had won.

Murana's ears dropped as her tail sagged to the wet ground. "Wait... What happened?"

He shrugged. "Nothing happened, he just retired. Last week, actually. I was selected to take his place. I am overseeing this operation with you, and you answer only to me. You will continue to do as I ask, or I will see to it personally you are tried for every crime and murder you have committed in your life."

Murana took a few steps back. "You wouldn't."

"I would...if I must." The kudu noticed her bared claws. "Don't try it, Wolford. You may be a trained fighter, capable of bringing down the best of us cops, but this is your livelihood we are talking about. There is plenty of blood on your paws, and nothing you could do or say would hold much water in court. Your fiber of character would mean little in the sea of criminal acts you perpetuated in the pursuit of 'justice'."

At length, she backed down. "Fine. I will get the information you want. What specifics am I looking for?"

The kudu stuffed his hooves into his trench-coat pockets, inclining his head towards the bush where he dropped the drive. "All the things we require to know are included in a document on that drive. I hope you are reviewing these from me on a secured computer."

She snorted as she curled her snout. "Of course I am. I'm not stupid. I have a freshly imaged laptop not connected to the internet for this job."

He nodded approvingly. "Good. Check your schedule. We will meet again in two weeks' time. Hopefully you will have succeeded."

He turned to leave, but she called him back. "Chief?" She winced. She already seemed to hate calling him that. Regarding his curious gaze, she put a paw to her stomach. "I've been having morning sickness this past week."

His eyes enlarged, nostrils flaring. "You haven't been seeing your husband, have you?"

She glowered at him. "He's sterile, asshole."

"Check yourself, Wolford," he warned.

"Well, you knew he was to begin with!" She raised her paws in exasperation.

He pressed. "Fucking any of the Arbiter's men to get to where you are?"

She bared her teeth at this comment. "I'm more faithful than that!" She shook her head in disgust. "I haven't seen my husband or my two boys since that day I left your office. However, Anthony and I had sex the night prior my leaving. First time in a long while." She seemed almost reminiscent of that fact. "But that wasn't what got me pregnant. We had decided to make a trip to the local sperm bank the week prior and get myself inseminated."

He looked at her with shock. "And you didn't think to inform us that you were making this huge life change that would impact your career?"

She waved a paw in his direction, not wanting to look at him. "Not like it mattered, since you had already decided my fate before I stepped into your office. We were planning that I step down and separate while he continued his career. I was to stay at home to take care of the cubs."

Musing at this turn of events, he scratched his chin. "Convenient."

Suddenly, she turned back to him. "How are they? Are they okay?"

The kudu never liked Murana, but he wasn't heartless. His expression softened. "Of course they are. The news came as a bit of a blow to your family that you were on an undercover mission, but Anthony seemed to take it well. Them having no knowledge of your whereabouts and actions is probably the safest thing for them."

She nodded, almost reassuring herself of this reality. "Yeah…but I'm pregnant. I don't know how much longer I can remain undercover. After I do this last thing for you, can I get out?"

He studied her for what seemed a long time before answering. "I'll see what I can do, but for now just stay the course. I will see you in two weeks, and we will re-attack this discussion then. You are dismissed, Officer Wolford."

He gave her a tiny bow of the head before trudging off in the downpour towards the bridge where she had come from. He could hear her sifting through the leaves to snag the thumb drive which he had left, but was out of earshot shortly after.

Confirming he was far enough away from her, he took the camera off his coat and faced it towards him as he walked along the water. He spoke in a very clinical manner into the mic. "The subject's motivation is strong, but her willpower is lacking. She is a perfect candidate, but there is a new complication we had not foreseen. Will forward all data to the director for final analysis and determination of project viability. She would be a great asset if approached right."

Satisfied with his assessment, he switched the camera and microphone off. The screen went black.

"No! Wait! Please come back! She's not going to bite you!" Taylor yelled down the hall.

The poor wolf's screams echoed as he scampered further away. His pants were barely pulled up to his thighs, belt hanging loose, as he attempted to flee for his life. The constant thumping of the after-concert parties in her other bandmates' rooms drowned out any hope of him being heard, and thus garnering help for his supposed near death experience.

"Figures." She snorted, retreating back into her personal room with a slam of the door.

Taylor's backstage abode wasn't anything spectacular; one couldn't expect miracles in the slums of Zabökar. Unlike what she had heard of the high-rise venues downtown which sported carpeted flooring, plush furniture, state of the art entertainment systems, and more, her room and those of her bandmates was a bit more barebones. Hers consisted of a brick-and-mortar interior with a dash of illuminated images projected onto the walls as décor. There were also hanging lights above, along with a small vanity that had broken light bulbs and a small couch with ripped upholstery. It was scratchy, and revealed stains that she had long since stopped questioning.

Flopping onto the couch with disappointment, she glared at her tail. Ahya pretended to look innocent and attempted to nudge her arms in forgiveness. Taylor just pushed her away angrily, causing Ahya to wilt. She huffed and crossed her arms, staring off at herself in the mirror.

"I'm pretty, right?" She ran her fingers through her red hair which had been combed to one side. The other side had been shaved down to her base fur coat, all in service of that edgier punk look. Shaking her head in disgust, she turned back to Ahya. "I'm pissed at you. I told you to stay hidden and not reveal that you were real to him, and what did you have to go and do? Fucking lick his butt when he was over me! I could have had my first time tonight!"

Taylor was pretty wrathful. This was the first time she had gotten this intimate with anyone, and she was excited for it. She was finally old enough by social standards at the tender year of sixteen to enjoy herself, but having been on the run with her mom since her grade school years, she wasn't given many chances to truly learn about her sexuality until recently, since joining the band, *Bad Luck.*

One of her best friends and bass player on the band, Nina, seemed to be very supportive of her snagging one of their fanboys for the evening. She, alongside all of her other bandmates no doubt, were probably being shagged out of their minds by any number of rabid fans in the crowd. All she had was the one wolf who just left her room, screaming because of being spooked by a tail he had thought was just a stage prop.

Ahya sensed that she had messed up bad. The eye marks painted on her fur truly did make it seem like she was remorseful. She slowly edged back to bump Taylor's arm again for forgiveness. Taylor just sighed and opened wide to allow the tailmaw to slump its bulk onto her naked lap. Letting her head rest back on the dingy couch backing, she looked up at the cracked ceiling as she began to pet and work her fingers through the wrinkly skin beneath Ahya's thick, red fur.

"I really thought I had a chance tonight. That was the first time someone actually wanted to meet me after a concert." Taylor was talking more for herself than for Ahya, mainly as a way to get her thoughts in order. She was lonely, and many of her bandmates outside of Nina barely came to visit her if it wasn't a rehearsal.

Taylor continued to stroke her tail, its tongue slithering out to lick and coil around her fingers. "Who am I kidding? Like I'm going to find anyone who would see past you and love me for me. I just wanted some physical intimacy tonight that wasn't some hug from my mother!" She thumped her head back once on the couch.

The mention of her mother caused Taylor to stop petting her tail, something Ahya noticed, rising her head to "look" at Taylor. "I wonder how she is doing…" Taylor said.

She hadn't talked to her mother in almost two years—not since running away after their last fight. It was ugly. A huge wave of homesickness washed over her like a raging storm, and she felt sick to her stomach for having left. Even if she wanted to see her mother again, given how often they'd moved in those last few years, it was doubtful she would be at the last place they lived. Considering she didn't want to be found when Taylor was last with her, Taylor had little hope of reuniting with her mother again.

Wiping the fresh tears that had formed, she set Ahya off to the side. She reached over to her jeans that had been casually tossed aside in her earlier fervor to get laid, then shoved her legs through and buckled up both spiked belts. Seeing as there was little else to do now that her evening's activities were abruptly cancelled, she might as well occupy herself elsewhere until Nina was finished with whoever was banging her so they could walk home together.

With the bass blaring loudly down the dimly lit hall of doors, Taylor walked past her bandmates' private backstage rooms, since hers was at the end of the hall past theirs. She just shook her head upon hearing loud yowls and moans from behind their lead singer's door. What a whore. She never really liked him, nor did he care much for her either. Still, he reluctantly agreed that her tail was a big draw for their band now, and she knew he only tolerated her presence. One couldn't deny her raw talent on guitar or vocals.

"Hey, brother," Taylor whispered, passing by the framed picture of a brown raccoon smirking at the camera sitting behind a set of drums. Beneath the picture, on the frame, was a placard stating the name "*Max Thrash*".

Max was her idol, and also her older, adopted brother. A brilliant musician whom she had looked up to all her life. He was one of the major reasons she took an interest in music, and helped foster that love of song in her growing up. The day performing live on stage alongside her brother was something she'd never forget. Nowadays, it seemed he was just as distant as she was with their mother.

"Taylor." A small voice emerged from the shadows.

Jolted, but not unduly so, she turned to see a small figure step into the light. It was a rabbit with tan fur and dark freckles adorning his face. His white-tipped ears were drooped in deference to her as a predator, and because of his position as bouncer and bodyguard for the band. She was technically his boss, like the rest of the band, even if she wasn't actually the one who paid his paycheck.

She looked around, unsure of why he would be wanting to speak to her. He tended to hang out in the background, watching from afar as they got on and off stage, and usually helped propel unruly fans away from the band. They never really had a need to communicate beyond a cursory nod of acknowledgement that each existed.

Now that she thought about it, it was quite unusual to see a rabbit in this profession. It was usually lions or bears or even rhinos that were hired to keep the peace in these underground metal clubs. Still, the fact he was here at all and was given a legitimate payroll demanded respect all the more because he was a rabbit.

"Mr. Thumpings, was it?" She hoped she got his name right.

He nodded smiling. "Call me Jake."

"Was there something you needed to talk to me about? Why were you hiding there by those curtains?" She gestured off to the stairs leading up onto the stage just meters away, the venue hall now empty, with the exception of workers cleaning up the mess.

Jake looked back briefly to where she pointed. "I felt it was not my place to interrupt your quality time with your fans. I figured I'd wait until you were finished first."

Taylor clucked, rolling her eyes. "You probably saw as well as heard that idiot running out of here."

Unfazed by the appearance of Ahya peeking around and sticking her tongue out a bit at him in greeting, Jake folded his arms. "I take it he was not as used to seeing your tail as those who guard you?"

"Well, you're one of the only ones who guards us." Taylor had to admit that she only saw one other mammal besides Jake, and it was an older panda who seemed a bit too rotund and cumbersome to do his job properly. "Guess we are bottom of the barrel down here."

Jake bristled at this slant against his job, but kept his cool. "Look, I wanted to talk to you tonight because I was asked to give you something, and I made a promise to do so."

Taylor cocked her head confused. "You could have knocked earlier if you wanted just to do that. Was pretty clear I was going to be alone tonight." She sighed.

Jake shook his head. "Not while I'm on duty, Taylor. Maybe if you ask me after I'm off shift, I can follow less stringent job etiquette." This drew a curious look from Taylor, who didn't know exactly what he meant by that. "Regardless, here is what I wanted to give you."

44

Jake fished into his tawny slacks and pulled out a chained necklace with a single pendant. Rather it wasn't one at all, but an air freshener in the shape of a pine tree, much like the one her other older brother, Steven, used to wear around his own neck. She could already smell the fresh scent from where she was standing. It must have been recently bought and attached to the necklace. She took it off his paw and spread the chain opening wide with her fingers as she regarded it.

"It's from your mother," Jake said flatly.

Taylor's eyes bulged and locked onto his. "What? Where did you get this?"

"I told you. It's from your mother." He clasped his paws behind his back, maintaining his formalities. "She made me promise to deliver that to you. She said you would understand what it meant."

Wetness glistened at the edges of Taylor's eyes once more as she held it close to her breast. "Where did you last see her? Do you know where she is now?" Taylor had hoped that she could reunite with her mom and attempt to make amends for running off like she did.

Before Jake could answer, several giggling geese barreled out of her band leader's door. They were clearly drunk, and the scent of their lead singer was drenched all over them. Taylor wrinkled her nose at the two fowl as they stumbled down the corridor drunk and wasted from whatever hits they took while sexing it up with the hyena. They stopped short as they saw both Taylor and Jake together.

"Oh… Are you wanting him right now?" one of them slurred, pointing at Jake.

"We were just talking." Taylor responded, really wanting these two to just move on and go collapse in a gutter somewhere. Maybe even get run over.

"So you're not claiming him for tonight?" the other snickered, hiding her bill behind her feathered wing.

"Claiming what?" Taylor was confused. "No, he was just delivering a gift to me." She barely caught Jake's expression to stop answering a bit too late.

"Fantastic!" The first lurched forward, her breath reeking. "We need you to take us home safely, Mr. Rabbit, sir. Mr. Bouncer Rabbit, sir." She giggled, falling into Jake's arms as he had no choice but to prevent the goose from face-planting.

"You going to need any help?" Taylor offered tentatively, although she was in no hurry to deal with these two idiots.

Jake's shoulders sagged, but he shook his head. "I'll tend to these two first. I'm off duty in five minutes, but I'm still obligated to see that these two get home safely. It shouldn't be too long to take care of their needs. If you're okay with waiting, can you stick around here until I get back? It'll probably go quick, based on the condition of these two." His ears perked up, hopeful.

Taylor shrugged. "I'm still waiting on Nina to finish up with whoever she's got. Who knows how long that'll take?"

Jake nodded. If the geese were aware of their conversation, they did not show it. Their feathers were already fondling his body as he did his best to disentangle himself from their groping. He slowly led them outside, presumably towards their homes—or at the least a taxi. "Well, hopefully you'll still be here when I get back. I have another message from your mother that goes with your necklace."

"Okay…" She stood staring after them as the strong rabbit handled the two geese expertly down the hallway and around the bend.

She looked back down at the necklace in her paws. Just when she was thinking about her mother, Jake came along and delivered something directly from her. She never did quite believe in fate or anything like that, having seen what little good the Script did for her, but it seemed surreal to her that it had to happen tonight, and from a rabbit she barely had contact with. Just who was this Jake Thumpings, and how was he connected to her mother? She would need to discuss with him all of this when he got back.

Taylor slipped it over her head, adjusting the pine tree to align with the center of her chest before glancing back at Nina's door down the hall. Seeing no sign of her coming out anytime soon, she moseyed down past the communal break den. The depressed flooring gave way to a rounded, carpeted area with plush couches and a center table with a fruit bowl.

Grabbing an apple out of the bowl, she continued past to the one of the various back exits out into the alleys. It was better for her and anyone else in *Bad Luck* to not take any of the front doors, even if the majority of the crowd had cleared out by now. It was a less-controlled environment than their backstage quarters, where they were hidden behind the two lone bouncers of panda and rabbit. Being accosted alone by a rabid fan base was a dangerous prospect.

The side street she exited out on was a bit more active than most, but it was still off the main drag of the front entrance. Across the street was a noodle place, lit up by neon lights and an outdoor fish tank that one could see through to the patrons inside, the fish oblivious to their status of fancy ornamentation. The crisscrossing streamers of lightbulbs overhead, tied to rusted pipes and window bars, cast a pale yellow glow over the entire alley.

Taylor plopped down on the curb, stretching her hind paws out onto the pavement as she took a bite of her apple. Scratching the skin through the fur peeking out of the holes in her jeans, her attention was directed skyward as the hustle of late-night traffic was overshadowed by the looming hologram of a sexy vixen gyrating her hips in an advertisement to sell some lingerie. The fox was generated from projectors situated higher up on the surrounding skyscrapers, but was displayed in full view of the citizens below the upper-class echelons, their verandahs and catwalks overlooking them.

Taking another bite, she wondered what her mother was doing. She could scarcely remember their last home together, this past year having seemed like it stretched on for an eternity. Maybe it was some metal shipping container, or perhaps a large dumpster converted into a living space; she couldn't quite recall. She just remembered feeling trapped and wanting to be free. Now she had no idea how her mother was faring all by herself, and to suddenly get a present from her after all this time? Maybe there was hope she would see her again.

The azure-blue lightshow of the vixen splayed over, and directed Taylor's attention to an unmarked white van parked just a mere half block down her street. Her keen eyes detected a few bodies in the front seats, but it was turned off and it didn't seem they were interested in anything nefarious. Still, her inner instinct was alert now, and she figured she might as well hurry up this apple and head back on inside to see if Nina was finished. The reminder that she was a lone female wolf in the heart of downtown Zabökar was painfully evident, and the sooner she had a walking buddy home, the better.

Ahya was already caressing Taylor's paw. Taylor finishing up the last bite of apple, she held up the apple core. "Did you want this, Ahya?"

Ahya needed no coaxing to eat. She snatched it out of Taylor's paw with her tongue. Taylor watched it disappear into that maw, its saliva rushing to coat and dissolve the core within seconds. She could soon feel a small bead of fullness in her belly now that it had transferred to her body from within Ahya.

Getting up and dusting off her pants, it was time to head back in and knock on Nina's door, any partners of hers in the room be damned.

It seemed this act brought the attention of those in the truck onto herself. The lights blazed on, nearly blinding her. The engine roared, and it began squealing down the narrow street. Taylor, her heart beating out of her chest now in fright, dashed across the road and ripped open the back door with a loud bang against the siding. She moved past the threshold as she heard the sliding van door open and paws hitting the pavement.

She had no sooner gotten to the inner den with the fruit when she felt meaty fingers grab her by the tail with intent to yank her back. Ahya was upon them in an instant. A scream for help was silenced by sickening crunch, blood gushing across the floor. The maw had snapped him clean in half from the top down. The other assailants backed up at the sight of the rising menace before them, its mouth full of dripping blood and wiggling arms with nerves firing off their last hurrahs.

Taylor stumbled and gagged as Ahya dissolved her prey; whoever her tail just ate tasted awful, and the nauseous bloat threatened her ability to react. Seeing her prone on the floor, the remaining four kitnappers surged forward with cattle prods. Ahya swooped in on one, gripping him by the arm and flinging him skirling across the room, crashing into a couch, upending it. The others weaved beneath the enraged Ahya and jabbed their prods deeper into the folds of Taylor's clothes and skin.

"Help! Somebody help me!" Taylor howled, writhing in pain from the electricity coursing through her body. Even Ahya was having trouble focusing on protection. "Dear gods, no!" She cried again as one of them thrust a prod into Ahya's maw, making contact with the sensitive inner lining of her internal digestive sac.

Exhausted and panting from the onslaught of their weapons, she could barely crawl a few inches, trying in vain to croak out a cry for help. But the doors of her bandmates remained closed. The pulse-pounding music still beat a rhythm through the floor boards. Nobody was coming to help her. Nobody was going to see her being taken away.

She could feel herself behind dragged by the base of her tail across the floor. The yawning darkness of the van invited her into oblivion.

Panic settled in as she made one last ditch attempt to fight. She flailed out her limbs weakly and resisted when they tried to pick her up to dump her in the vehicle. One of the larger felines just yanked her head back by the hair and slammed their fist into her face.

Taylor woke up screaming. Her legs and arms were getting bundled up in knots inside the sleeping bag. Ahya was already alert and attempting to snap and devour anyone who came near. She could hear two voices shouting at each other, but she could barely focus on either. All she knew was that someone was laying hands on Ahya with a capable grip, curtailing her attempts at biting.

"Taylor, get yourself together. It is just us," a familiar voice rang out in her mind. Firm, scaly arms held her shoulders tight, forcing her to look at the source of the comfort.

Before her was the familiar visage of Ari, an odd face that many would consider downright unfriendly. She was a genetically altered mix of crocodile and tortoise, created by her father, the Arbiter, after losing his own wife to causes Taylor had yet to discover. Holding down her thrashing tail was Trevor, a larger wolf who sported a missing arm augmented by an iron mechanical replacement, alongside many other scars and indications of battle across his body and face.

Both of them were sent to capture her by the Arbiter and bring her back safely to him, albeit at different times and for two entirely different reasons. They were not the only people after Taylor, but she figured they were the lesser of the evils and would better align with her goals of getting back to Zabökar to reunite with her family, and more importantly, her mother.

"Ahya…it's okay. Calm down." Taylor relaxed, letting her entire body drop back into the sleeping bag.

Ahya's tension released and Trevor let go, catching his breath. "You've got one strong tail there. If it weren't for this arm of mine, I don't think I would have been able to contain her as well as I did." He was panting slightly.

"She's always been like that." Taylor yawned. The sleepiness was slowly ebbing back after the shock of waking from her nightmare. "She sometimes surprises even me with what she can do or manage."

"She's surprising in a lot of ways." Ari grinned, finally letting go and sitting on her rump beside Taylor. "You've managed to hold my interest."

"How comforting." Taylor shifted, not really sure how to take that comment.

"It should be." Ari grinned, showing off her row of jagged teeth. "I usually lose interest in my targets I've been tasked to go after and kill them too fast." At a look from Taylor, she added, "Although there was no talks of eliminating you, of course. You were merely meant to be brought in. All I'm saying is, you are a far cry more interesting than anyone I've had the honor of hunting down. Also the most fun too."

Taylor was flummoxed. "Most fun? How the heck am I fun?"

Ari pointed to Ahya. "You got a tail that eats people and can also heal and bring them back from the dead. You also got some mighty interesting powers of electrical impulses. You even have some imaginary friends you can conjure up that only you and I can see. I'd say that puts you pretty high on my list of wanting to know more of what you can do."

"Oh, right…" Taylor sagged. Being reminded that her two small companions of the past year were nothing but figments of her imagination did little to improve her mood.

50

"Certainly didn't help Gregor when he died," Trevor spat, still bitter about his friend who had been shot in the head by Finnley, an otter from an opposing faction's group of mercenaries, also sent to capture her.

Ari scowled at the wolf, but Taylor rose up to face him. "You're right, Ahya didn't help you when Gregor died. In fact, by extension, neither did I." She ignored his glower. "But if you recall, we were in a tense situation with your enemies ready to pounce on you should we turn our backs for even a moment. My sole purpose was to stop the fighting and prevent any further loss of life. Besides I wasn't exactly in a saving mood that night after you had torched two cities coming after me!"

"I understand that," he snapped. "But could it have hurt you to have at least tried to take Gregor into Ahya afterwards and do that magic like you did with Fey? Like bringing him back?"

"Fey was still alive and breathing," Ari reminded, edging closer to Taylor in case violence erupted. Taylor knew Ari's goal was for her safety back to the Arbiter, so she would prioritize that over any truce with Trevor. "Gregor was dead on impact from the bullet to his brain. There was no guarantee that Ahya could reverse something like that, and Taylor was in no condition to be exerting herself to try something of that magnitude. It nearly wore her out the previous time with Fey."

"So you were awake in that van coming into Cheribaum." Trevor waggled a finger at her.

"Somewhat." Ari shrugged.

Trevor huffed and looked back at Taylor. She still had bruises and missing patches of fur on various places of her body from previous injuries that Ahya had healed over. Even her right paw was bandaged up and braced so that her broken fingers could mend. It seemed not even Ahya could fix broken bones.

Taylor had been through a lot, and piling on yet another toil on her body by reviving Gregor could have tipped her health over the edge. There was no assuming the limits of what Ahya could do; they simply did not have enough information about how she worked, and Taylor was just as clueless as they were.

Trevor finally relented, looking away down the mountain path they had chosen to traverse. "So what's the plan when we get there, Ari? You still haven't revealed fully what's going to happen to me."

"All depends on my father." She rose up and started packing her own gear into the saddlebag on the back of her motorcycle. Equipment they graciously received from Mikhail's mother back in Cheribaum. "I know he'll want to test you, Taylor, to see what you can do. I won't lie to you that it might hurt, but it is all in the name of science. After all, this genetic manipulation is his area of expertise, and who better to examine you than the very person who created me and so many other mammals with abilities?"

Taylor shivered at the thought of being experimented on again. The dream that was slowly fading away was a stark reminder of when her life turned into more than just a horror movie. "I take it you won't stop them if they begin to hurt me?" Taylor looked up at Ari.

"Why would I?" Ari responded truthfully. "My task was to get you to my father. Whatever he decides to do with you after that is not my concern."

"Wonderful." Taylor dropped her chin onto her raised knees. "At least I know where I stand here."

"I probably would stop them," Trevor interjected, earning the attention of Ari as she fastened up the last strap on her gear. "I still have a promise to keep to your mother. Since Gregor is gone, it literally is the last thing I have left to live for before figuring out what I want to do with the remainder of my life."

Ari crossed her arms, her thick tail swishing. "If you cooperate in bringing her home to Zabökar with me and not interfere with my father's plans for her, I'll make sure you are well-compensated so that you don't have to worry about your future."

"I thought it depended on your father?" He mocked. "A promise made from the daughter of a convicted terrorist by the High Council, it'll be a miracle if I see any money at all out of this."

"Believe what you want," Ari hissed.

Taylor let her head sink further into her paws. These were the two people she had to be traveling with. She wished she was with Pine and Mitchell instead, but it had been a terrible realization that they weren't real at all. However, that didn't explain how Ari could see and hear them with her cybernetic left eye, and no one else could but Taylor. So there was at least something tangible to their existence, but Taylor was unsure of how she could bring them back again.

Pine and Mitchell were stand-ins, she realized, for her own two brothers. Being a skunk and raccoon, they mimicked so much of her family's mannerisms and personalities. It was no wonder that she felt so at home with them. If only she could figure out what they actually were, and if they weren't just some offshoot of another power of hers she wasn't aware of. Or maybe Fey, the leader of the other mercenary faction, was right: it was just a form of PTSD to cope with horrendous trauma.

"It's time we head out anyway." Trevor began to pack up his things as well.

"No breakfast?" Taylor was feeling hungry now that the terror had passed.

"Unfortunately not. Maybe we'll catch something along the way we can skin and cook," Trevor offered.

Ari licked her lips. "That sounds wonderful. I haven't had fresh meat in a long while."

Taylor looked at her curiously. She was part tortoise, which ate plants, but she was also crocodile which primarily thrived on meat…if her memory and education were correct. She wondered which side of Ari was the more dominant aspect of her personality, and if it influenced things like tastes in food. It'd have to be a question she'd need to ask later.

For the moment, Taylor was distracted by Ari suddenly walking off and placing a palm to her head as if listening intently. Her entire form grew rigid the longer she listened. Turning around suddenly, she zeroed in on Trevor. "We need to prepare ourselves to fight in case things go wrong."

"What?" He was bewildered. "What's happening now?"

She tapped her synthetic eye. "My father didn't get my messages in time before releasing his latest creation, Rakkis." Even Ari seemed nervous, which made Taylor immediately alert.

"Who is Rakkis?" Taylor asked.

Ari swiveled to her. "Much like you, but less stable. The message I got from my father was this: *'Your message arrived late. He is inbound. Do not try to resist, and let him bring Taylor to me. He should be aware not to harm you, but do not provoke him.'*"

Taylor was terrified. She recalled when Trevor spoke of the approaching threat of Ari with such anxiety, but now it was Ari who was worried in much the same manner. This did not bode well for the remainder of their trip to Zabökar.

3.

RAKKIS

The moment he walked into the restaurant for their impromptu meeting, he could tell something was amiss. Murana looked beyond agitated in her hastily-put-on black hoodie, her ears peeking through the holes in the fabric, and she had the bowstring drawn tighter than normal. She had chosen the furthest booth from the entrance, facing away from it, but within view of a mirror where she could survey the entire place. He couldn't hear it, but his keen prey senses detected the movement of her hind paw as it nervously tapped the carpet.

The restaurant was a little hole in the wall in a rough part of town—the type always seen in the movies with steam coming hot from the sewer covers and naked babes running amok in front of sandwiched apartment complexes, formed neatly all in a row down the streets. The establishment Murana chose even had a lovely fish tank as part of the wall, allowing views outside. The intricate red and gold interior décor was reminiscent of far western cultures like Livarnu, serving all sorts of dumplings and noodles that tantalized the taste buds with their cheap, exotic flavors.

He sifted through the busy throng of tables and made his way to the back. Sitting down across from her, she nearly jumped. Her claws were already out, but she immediately tucked them away into her pockets as she saw who it was.

"Chief Wendell." She nodded, her eyes flicking back to the mirror on the wall.

The kudu observed her for a few moments before clasping his hooves and leaning forward across the table. "This is highly irregular, Wolford. We were supposed to meet in three days, this Wanslag at the Setu Memorial Bridge overlook. I hope that phone you called me on was a one-off pay-per-minute cell. I took a big risk coming out to see you here."

Her irritation showed through for a moment, but was quickly covered up as she locked eyes with him. "I know, sir. However, if I didn't know any better, I would say you set me up."

Wendell grimaced. He didn't really like the tone she was setting for the conversation. "Mind your station, Officer Wolford. Do you mind explaining yourself, and why you would compromise your mission by bringing me here?"

"I think I may already be compromised." She took another look around. "The moment I tried to weasel my way into their research division, they seemed to be all over me. Questioning my background and what business I had in their operations. It was insane how much lying I had to do in a short amount of time and the forgery I had to conduct just to back up my lies when they checked. At best, I am now a liaison between them and some person named 'The Director', who is second to the Arbiter. That was the best I could do on short notice."

Wendell was genuinely impressed. "So I ask again, why bring me here?"

Murana scrounged around in her pocket before pulling out the thumb drive and sliding it across the table between their cups. "I managed to get what you asked me for. As far as I can tell, the Arbiter has created what he calls a 'DNA ray'. Basically he pulses his subjects with it and there is a fifty-fifty chance they'll either develop cancer and die, or they develop some sort of powers that can't be explained by current science."

"How does it work?" He nonchalantly put his hoof over the drive and slowly dragged it back to his end of the table.

"I browsed through the data, but it seems it actively rewrites a person's DNA structure on the spot. It removes part of their genetic code entirely and replaces it with something new. I have no idea where it comes from. I keep hearing that word 'magic' being thrown around, but it's hard to believe they'd just infuse something like that into the very DNA structure of a person."

Wendell tapped a hoof tip to the table. "But it would explain why some contract cancer instead. Perhaps it is the body's way of rejecting this forceful manipulation?" After a moment, he put the drive in his pocket and addressed her. "Was there any conclusive evidence as to why some take to the ray and others do not?"

Murana shook her head. "There seems to be no correlation between subjects. It appears to be completely random who lives or dies as a result of each experiment."

"That's unfortunate…for those that had to die," he added after seeing an odd look from her.

She put a paw on the table. "Can I please be pulled out now? I got what you asked. I want to see my family." She put her other paw on her belly. "I want to have my cubs in peace."

Wendell raised a hoof up to stave off her request. "A few more questions. As liaison to this 'Director', do you have access to or know the whereabouts of their successful specimens they keep? The ones that develop the powers."

She sighed, resignation filling her face. "Yes. It's actually in the sewers just below Meerkat Town, set in old bunkers that were built at the start of the city. They are bedding them down there, feeding them, training them, and filling their young minds with propaganda. This army of child super soldiers is ready to strike."

Wendell grit his teeth as he stared off towards the entrance to the restaurant. An elderly kangaroo couple had just hopped in to be seated for what was most likely their anniversary dinner. "And the High Council didn't take him seriously," he scoffed.

"What was that?" Murana's ears flicked forward.

He waved a hoof at her. "Nobody on the council took the Arbiter seriously when he made the proposal to formulate an army to defend Zabökar. Looks like he just went off and did it on his own."

"So what's the plan now, sir?" She was trying to be courteous here to him—not that she had much defense if she fought back against this with him. She wanted off the mission for good, after all.

"Well, it is certainly clear that whatever he is planning to do, it is imminent now." He flipped up his smart phone and began texting. "I will discuss with those on the High Council who entrusted me with this task to see what we should do next. In the meantime, I need you to fall back into your cover and continue as you were." This order caused

Murana to wilt. "I know that isn't what you wanted to hear, but it is safest for everyone—especially for you—that you do so."

"Shall we meet as expected at the bridge this weekend?" she said without emotion, her eyes vacant as she stared at her empty place setting. The place was so busy and understaffed, the lone waiter hadn't even bothered to come take her order yet.

"Of course." He nodded. He slipped a large bill across the table towards her. "Get yourself something nice to eat here. My treat." He got up and smoothed down his coat, taking care to have his horns not hit the hanging lamp just above their booth. "Hang in there just a bit more. I can't promise what will happen to you back out on the other side, but I can promise I've heard your request and I'll be actively looking for a way and time to bring you out. We just need to be smart about this. You're in pretty deep."

"I know…" she monotoned. She hadn't made a motion to even touch the money he laid out for her.

Seeing as he was going to get no more response from the glum wolf, he shrugged and wove his way back out to the front. He took great care to walk a fair distance away from the restaurant before turning off the camera and mic attached to the inner lapel of his undershirt.

"Eyes alive," Trevor called back, slowing his motorcycle to a crawl.

They were still a day's ride off from Zabökar, but the mountainous terrain had turned to rolling hills and sporadic clumps of forest dotting the landscape. Several rocky sarsens peppered the undulating landscape, giving it a wild and untamed feel. There were few other cars or hovercrafts on the paved road they took, the majority of the city traffic still closer to the metropolis itself.

Ahead of them in the opposite lane was a convoy of hovering trucks of military origin, all decked out in brown camo and oppressive headlamps. Three vehicles in total were gunning straight for their position, and it was no question that their occupants meant to intercept them. Diverging off the road and into the tall brush of the hills was no option, since their trucks could easily travel faster over such difficult terrain that their wheeled motorcycles couldn't. It wouldn't be much of a chase at all.

"Your father said not to resist, right?" Taylor recalled, pushing Ari's tail to the side and looking anxiously over her shoulder, having let Ari drive this leg of the trip.

Ari shut her engine off and kicked the stand out to park her bike. "I'd say so." Ari was tense, all her muscles were visibly taut. "He's in one of them. I can sense it," Ari muttered.

"Rakkis?" Trevor picked up her comment.

Ari nodded, nudging Taylor off the seat so she could stand and stretch her scrunched tail. "He's the first of his kind. My father has done gene splicing before, but not to this scale." She glanced back to Taylor. "He got inspiration from you... From the stories and data we stole from the High Council," she finished hesitantly.

"I'm not sure I understand."

"You'll see soon enough." Ari steeled herself, watching the trucks come closer.

"I don't like this." Trevor had to fight to keep his paw away from the gun on his hip. "I didn't like it when you showed up." His gaze met Ari's. "You threw off my entire plan of getting Taylor back to the Arbiter."

Ari snorted. "Seeing as how I first met Taylor in the hands of our competition, I'd say you were doing a fantastic job."

"Can you two please not fight? I'm getting pretty freaked out right about now." Taylor attempted to put on a brave face, but she was beyond terrified. Memories of being poked and prodded came back vividly, and the fact Ari and Trevor were taking her back to more of the same was not comforting. The Arbiter sending even more people after her filled her heart with dread. Just what was so important about her that they needed this many people to bring her in?

She needed to keep reminding herself about the reason she decided to tag along in the first place, about why she chose these two and not the other group. There was a lingering air of uncertainty if the other group's employers were even going to honor their deal with the job they tasked them with. It seemed even they didn't fully trust the High Council, and by extension, why should she? Going along with these two was just a means to an end to find out about who she was, how she was made to have a tailmaw, and above all, find her family again.

"I'm just saying there have been way too many complications for what was supposed to be a simple escort mission, that's all," Trevor grumbled, resuming his vigil on the trucks which had now come to a stop several meters from them.

The vehicles began to rev down and descend until they touched ground. All doors opened up to reveal multiple mammals of varying sizes in tactical armor and helmets. Each were carrying slung firearms, and several were already pointing mechanized pistols at all but Taylor. Curiously, she saw one door close all on its own without anyone there to shut it, but that detail got lost in the haze as the lead mammal spoke.

"Are you Taylor Renee Wolford?" the wildebeest huffed.

"I would advise your men to stand down and aim those guns elsewhere unless you want a very messy situation." Ari bared her crooked teeth. "I am the daughter of the Arbiter. You would do well not to cross me."

"We are well aware of who you are," the wildebeest responded. "We are just taking precaution to ensure that you both cooperate as we take you three back in to him."

"We were warned in advance not to react hostile. We will comply."

Trevor already had both paws in the air, seemingly aware that there was no winning this situation. His expression was very sour.

"Very good," an unsavory voice whispered close behind Taylor. "We were hoping for some delicious violence, but this'll have to do."

Taylor yelped and skittered away behind Ari, who immediately stepped one foot in front of her to defend. She could sense the presence of the intruder just moments before hearing his unsettling slither of voice tickle her ear. Before them materialized—as if from thin air—a chameleon of dark green complexion, with scintillating hues of blue that shown brightly in the sunlight at certain angles as he fidgeted this way and that, his two eyes bouncing randomly between the three of them.

61

What was the most shocking thing about this reptile was his tail. Swaying back and forth behind him with a devilish grin was a leathery maw of dripping drool and jagged fangs. Looking into that cavernous hole was like staring at something horrifying. Was this how people viewed her? Taylor could just imagine the terror people felt when Ahya frightened them, because now she was finally at the receiving end of such a shock.

Idly fiddling with the small fronds on his head, the chameleon quickly licked an itch from his left eye with a dart of his tongue. "Don't look so surprised at us. You seem to be the trendsetter, and now the rest of the world is catching up to your fashion!" He chuckled at his prose.

"There's another tail…" Trevor edged back. His paws did begin to move to his gun.

"That's quite naughty!" The chameleon slapped Trevor's paw with his tongue, its bulbous end sticking immediately to the fur and skin before jerking the entire meaty muscle skyward. Trevor, unbalanced from the sudden rise and twist of his arm, slipped on his hindpaws and fell to the ground in a tumble as the tongue released its hold on his skin.

"Ah… What the fuck!" He clutched his paw with his metal one. Some of the fur had been ripped away with the force of the sticky substance as the tongue retracted.

The chameleon put out a palm to stay the guns of his men. He was enjoying this reaction way too much. "We've orders from your father to spare you and Taylor, but we've not heard a thing about this lovely morsel." His tail began to grow and extend, much like Ahya could, its mouth getting wider in preparation to swallow the wolf whole. "We could use a midday snack. Shall we eat him?"

Taylor brushed Ari aside and stood her ground, her voice wavering being the only indication her inner self was in a panic. "Don't eat him! He's a friend to me!" This prompted an odd look from Trevor.

The inner tongue of his tailmaw had already slithered out and was dripping slimy, viscous drool on Trevor's head. The chameleon stopped and regarded her with roving eyes. "Interesting. That is not the impression we got from the reports we were given."

"You…you hurt him, then we're not going to comply," Taylor finished with some dignity, her eyes ever on the other tail.

"Bold words from someone so young. Very well…" His tail shrunk back down, retreating behind him, much to the relief of Taylor and Ari. "As hungry as we are, we've got a timetable to meet, and we've been promised a meatier meal than this scrawny pup."

"You're Rakkis." Taylor said it like a statement. It all seemed to click into place. The shock of seeing someone like her was fading, and what stood before them was a genetic experiment just like her. Just like Ari.

Rakkis bowed horribly. "Guilty as charged, my fair nibble." He licked his lips. "Do be so kind as to turn that cute little butt of yours to our car and hop in. We got a long distance to go." This caused Taylor to flush in a vexed way.

"What about the rest of us?" Ari moved over to help Trevor get back onto his feet. "I would like to ride in the car with Taylor."

Rakkis tapped a lanky finger to his chin. "Mmmm, we think not. Given the poor performance and why we had to be brought in to fix this mess, we think it is better to be alone with Taylor in our car."

He snapped his fingers and the entire contingent swooped in and began roughly handling the three of them. Each were shuttled off to individual trucks. Taylor was thrust inside the middle truck of the convoy while the other two were taken to others. The twin motorcycles were tossed in the trunks of two vehicles. Rakkis opened his door and slid in beside Taylor, his tail bumping heads with Ahya.

Ahya immediately snapped back at the unnatural invasion to her personal space, but was met with a small bite to the mouth from his. Ahya grew enraged and attempted to lunge at the offending maw, but was effortlessly dodged and bit back even harder, which caused Taylor to whine. All the while Rakkis was merely studying the sky outside, or some random spot inside the vehicle.

At length, he smirked. "We suggest you keep your tail in check, little lady, lest it get poked through with teeth marks. Trying to get the jump on us is fruitless. So stop trying."

Taylor fought hard to get Ahya under control, even to the point of grabbing her physically and placing Ahya on her lap, petting her to soothe the fraught nerves. "So does your tail have a name too?" Taylor asked angrily, upset this jerk was treating her this way.

Both his moving eyes turned to her now. His expression was odd, as if no one had ever asked him this question before. "It's Rakkis," he said finally.

"Rakkis? Then what are you called?" she probed.

"Rakkis," he responded again.

"Wait... You both have the same name?" Her anger was momentarily abated in light of this confusion.

"We are Rakkis." His interest now gone, his eyes began to rove about again. "Enough talk. We drive!" He signaled the driver up front to head out.

The entire truck hummed with energy as she felt it rise from the ground. In moments they were wheeling around to head back the way they came, effortlessly hovering and avoiding any potholes that were present in the road after being neglected for so long.

The sweeping hills rushed past in silence, the mountain range to the north slowly arcing its way back south in front of them, where it seemed they needed to pass through to get to Zabökar. Taylor didn't exactly remember traveling this far to get to Palaveve, the desert town she had been hiding out in for the past year. That whole trip seemed a blur in her memory.

Rakkis seemed busy with monitoring the inhabitants of the other two vehicles, ensuring that neither Ari nor Trevor made any drastic decisions. Taylor had to wonder why Ari didn't just immolate Rakkis and all them where they stood back there. She had more than enough power to do so. So what stayed Ari's hand and temper, for that matter? Taylor couldn't quite figure it out.

She took the opportunity to let Ahya lick the bite wounds that Rakkis's tail inflicted on her. The soothing saliva of her tailmaw soaked into the lacerations and began to slowly heal the flesh and mend the fibers, until the only indication she had been injured at all was the lack of fur in the spots where the teeth punctured through.

"Now that is very intriguing," Rakkis said with sincerity, his insufferable tone disappearing as he observed Taylor's tail mending her wounds.

Realizing what he was referring to, Taylor looked up from Ahya who was now licking her "lips". "Can your tail do this too?"

"We're afraid not, little bite." His smirk returned. "We just consume and devour. Nothing quite as special as yours. We might say we're a bit jealous, but then again we've got something a bit better up our scales."

"Like what?" Taylor was both curious and wondering if he'd actually spill his secrets.

One eye locked onto her, while the other monitored the side-view mirror. "Maybe one day you'll find out...if we choose to let you." A gurgle in his throat indicated laughter. Taylor found the sound rather revolting.

"Recon behemoth due south!" the driver of the front vehicle crackled out from the radios inside each truck.

All eyes turned to the indicated direction to see a large mechanical monster of reptilian design. Hunched over on all fours, steam erupted from the hinges of its joints as it lumbered each limb forward in its awkward gait. Each paw of this creature of metal pounded the ground, creating shockwaves that could be lightly felt through their trucks even from this distance. Its multi-eyed face was a new one to Taylor, who had seen several now, with each being a little different. It had thankfully not noticed them yet, considering its distance relative to them and their miniscule size overall.

These titanic marvels of engineering were a big mystery to Taylor and many others. There was much speculation about where they came from, but most agreed their appearance originated from the southwest, past the deserts and inhospitable rocky ranges. Only Ari seemed to have any idea of what they were, but she hadn't told Taylor anything of use. All Taylor knew was that they had enough firepower each to level an entire city in a single explosion.

Seeing as it was just her and Rakkis in the back seat, Taylor wondered if she could just slip Ahya over his head and bite it off completely at the neck. Would she have enough time for that? She could sense by the reactions of Ari and Trevor that the remainder of the militant contingent, although formidable, would be easier to manage with Rakkis gone. She would have to be quick, lest Ahya decide to dissolve the head after decapitation. That'd be the last thing she wanted to taste right now.

Before she could put her plan into action, Rakkis's maw surged up from beneath and snapped hard around Ahya's bulk. The teeth sunk in at specific points along Ahya's mouth, locking her jaw shut. Taylor cried out at the knifing pain digging holes into her tail and penetrating the fleshy membrane of the stomach sac within. Ahya began to thrash wildly, but was held firm by the other maw. Ahya's tongue was extended and slapping around in a futile attempt to get Rakkis off of her.

Rakkis whipped around, both his wandering eyes now holding still on her. "Don't even think about trying to get the drop on us, little girl."

Taylor's instinctual flight-or-fight response engaged and her fingertips began to crackle with electrical energy. Rakkis's tongue darted out, slapping its meaty end to the center of her palm. He jerked her forward as he released the mucus tendrils from her flesh and the tongue retreated back into his mouth, but not before gripping her cheeks hard with his palm and holding her face inches from his own.

"And don't try to shock us either." His tone was laced with deadly intent. Taylor tried to pull away, getting ready to raise her hindpaws up to kick him in the stomach, but he held onto her harder. "And don't try to hop out that car door, or we'll be forced to run you over with one of these trucks. The Arbiter didn't specify you had to be whole, just that you had to be alive. He'll find a use for you one way or another."

Taylor's eyes were wide with fear. It was as if he could read her very thoughts and motives. He knew exactly what she was going to do moments before she did it. Was he a mind reader? Was he reading her mind right now? Was he aware of how alarming it was to her that anything she did could be telegraphed to him by mere thought?

The driver and co-driver up front paid no mind to the altercation in the back; they seemed to understand very well Rakkis had everything under control. Taylor and Rakkis stared in silence for a time, but eventually Ahya calmed herself down and was no longer writhing, but Taylor could tell she was miserable, and could understand her pain for she felt it too through the piercing of his tail's teeth.

"We think we understand each other, Taylor," Rakkis cooed, releasing his hold on her face and giving her a small love-pat on the cheek. "Now be a good girl and just sit back and enjoy the ride. There is nothing you can do that we can't see. Remember that."

He released Ahya at last, who immediately retreated like a wounded pup into Taylor's arms, wrapping her tongue up around her arm for comfort.

Rakkis studied the interaction. "We're sure you two will be able to patch that bite up just fine."

Without waiting for her response, he turned away and relaxed a bit more into his seat. With seatbelt unbuckled and lifting one leg to put up on the back of the driver's seat, it was clear Rakkis was completely unconcerned with anything remotely dangerous in his vicinity. It was an air of haughty confidence about him that incensed Taylor. He had her beat; she was too scared to attempt anything else, and he knew it. All that was left was to pick up the pieces of her shattered pride.

Taylor could feel the rush of liquid pooling inside of her tail as the saliva built up to close the holes caused again by Rakkis's teeth. Pushing a lock of her hair back behind her ear, she moped. She needed to stop getting hurt all the time; it stung as the flesh regrew from Ahya's healing saliva. She regarded her tail as it lay prone on her lap, focusing on its interior stomach.

What a strange thing to be able to do with her tail. On one paw, her tail's saliva could heal even the gravest of wounds, but on the other, could turn into the most corrosive acid to dissolve anything for consumption. Even she didn't know the full extent of what Ahya could do. She had begun to test Ahya's limits in recent days, even reviving Fey completely from death after being riddled with bullet holes. What were Fey and the others doing now? Were Mikhail and Natalia okay?

Taylor's thoughts drifted to the other team of mercenaries who had been tasked by the High Council—in opposition to the Arbiter—to bring her in. Where Fey and his group questioned their employer's intentions, Ari and Rakkis were resolute in their objectives given them. Trevor was the only one of this bunch that seemed to be truly on her side now, and that was only because of a promise he had to her mother. This fact gave her little comfort.

With her tail now healed, she could do little else but watch the scenery go by. The behemoth pointed out earlier was still visible a ways off, but it had turned to the west and begun its journey in that direction. Ahead of them was a rising mountain range swooping in from the north that provided the last barrier between them and Zabökar. Extending all the way to the ocean to the southeast, it provided a natural barrier for the city, and was probably a good reason why none of those huge abominations had found it yet.

Taylor wasn't aware she had fallen asleep during the ride until the entire convoy came to an abrupt stop, lurching her forward in the seat. She quickly raised her paws to prevent her face from hitting the metal crosshatch grating between the back seat and the front. After a moment to regain her composure, she pushed her face up against the window to see what was amiss.

Ahead of them, blocking the pass out of the mountains, was a herd of what looked like six-legged bison—but they couldn't be that, since she remembered seeing a few back in the city when she was younger. These multi-horned beasts of burden were a bit less evolved and unsophisticated for speech or free thought. They were being tended to by a lamb who was serving as their shepherd. He had crossed his hooves at the vehicles, annoyed that they were disturbing his flock.

Rakkis sighed, wiping a palm down his face at this irritation. "Can't we just shoot one and scatter the rest?"

"I'm afraid not. Our motors can't even hover high enough to go over either." The dark furred jaguar in the front turned back, her eyes not giving Taylor the time of day. "The Arbiter said to not call undue attention to ourselves. These are local ranchers that provide valuable animal products and goods to Zabökar. Disrupting this economic system would certainly do just that. We'll have to wait it out until they all pass."

Rakkis clucked his tongue as he slouched back fuming. "Back in our country we never had such nonsense, and ranchers knew better than to let their cattle run free. You keep them in closed pens, well beyond the reach of roads where they'd just get run over."

"You're not from here?" It seemed an obvious answer to Taylor, but it was interesting to note that Rakkis was working abroad for the Arbiter quite possibly on his own free will.

He glared at her, squinting his tiny pupils. "Not by choice. Just keep your nosy little questions to yourself." Huffing, he folded his arms and watched the endless parade of livestock stroll past.

The convoy pulled off the underused road, hovering up a ramp onto a busy freeway filled with cars of varying types. Some were flying between designated mag tracks suspended in the air, their counterpart units keeping them there fastened to the pavement below. Nearer the ground were a mix of hover cars and those still with antiquated wheels. The huge variety of financial incomes of each vehicle occupant was evident by the both the condition of their cars and their paint job.

Honking a horn to be let into the fast-moving traffic, the three trucks barreled onto the highway. They were regulated to the slower left lane, then drove on for what seemed like hours. The rural huts and adobe-filled beam struts gave way to more modern aesthetic with slanted sidings and curved top awnings that was intended as shelter from rain. The congregation of housing grew thicker as well—from sporadic clumps of buildings to bigger metropolitan communities—but they still had not reached Zabökar yet. Did she really walk all this distance to Palaveve a year or so ago?

Then she saw it, just past a line of trees. The rising spires of Zabökar. She had grown up living within the city all her life, so she never quite appreciated its majestic beauty from the outside.

Before her, rising up from the center of the city, were several, spiraling towers of glass and steel three times taller than the next largest building on the skyline. Expanding out from these in eight cardinal directions were swooping beams, dipping down to levitating platforms with monolithic statues baring the faces of hardened predators. Each one looked out from the city, as if to ward off any dangers under their watchful eyes.

A slight jingle could be heard as the dangling rods of what seemed like light were swinging in the breeze off each beam. She could just barely recall hearing them daily growing up. When one was used to them, they had an innate sense to be tuned out, but being gone so long had reinvigorated her wonder at their beauty.

Taylor was entranced all over again about the city of her birth. Growing up in it, she never truly appreciated it for what it was. Being out in the harsh world and living in a desert city for over a year with nothing but scraps and dubious water to live off from made one reflect on the goods things in life.

Her countenance faded. The closer they got, the more sprawling the city became. How on earth was she going to find her mother in all of that? Let alone her two brothers, who could be anywhere, or not even in town at all. That and she had to meet this Arbiter first, and see if he would even allow her to find her family. There just seemed to be too many things restricting her. It was frustrating.

Rakkis seemed to be eyeing Taylor curiously as she continued to stare out the window. The rising buildings dwarfed her view until she could no longer see their tops. The flow of traffic began to slow to a crawl as they moved towards the inner city. Mammals of all shapes and sizes were walking the sidewalks in full business suits or casual wear. Many structures had elevated catwalks for the smaller mammals to traverse the city streets so they wouldn't be trampled on by the larger ones.

Taylor saw small lights flashing every now and then along the sides of the buildings, sometimes perched up in the corners of the windows looking into the stores and shops. Following these mystifying flashes, she could see holographic advertisements following several mammals for a few paces before vanishing into thin air. She couldn't hear what they were saying, but they were clearly advertising to the intended recipient. Most mammals glanced at it once and shrugged it off, continuing instead to go about their day.

"That's how they get you." Rakkis bapped Taylor's arm crudely, pointing at what she was looking at. "Those sensors flash your DNA profile, scanning you at a glance to identify you. You can thank the Arbiter for that. He introduced the technology, was denied, and then it later was stolen by the High Council for mass production." He cackled. "Good thing we're not even in the database at all. They won't be able to flash us!"

Ignoring Rakkis's laughter, Taylor turned back outside. Even Ahya was poking her head up above the level of the window alongside her to "look" out. Although she couldn't see anything, it was the thought that counted. Taylor shook her head at Ahya and continued to stare. Was she in any DNA database? Did Rakkis know she wasn't or was he just referring to him and his tail again? If she walked out onto that sidewalk, would she be flashed and then targeted by those advertisements? She didn't remember it being an issue back when she was singing in The Bits while in *Bad Luck*.

The convoy took a sudden right and descended below street level to the tunnels. A few more turns later and the traffic had all but died out. It wasn't until they turned one final time into a tunnel of darkness did Taylor realize that they had gone far off the beaten road. They were passing construction signs and road blockage warnings.

"We're here," Rakkis said.

The wall just ahead of them on the left began to indent into itself before sliding down into the ground, revealing a new route. The lead vehicle turned in, and they followed. Red lights were now visible at intervals as they continued their descent deeper into the underbelly of Zabökar. The tight corridor opened up finally to a larger, arched atrium of brick with an underground river flowing through it, algae in the water giving a nice glow to the entire area.

Parking just before the river at a girded bridge crossing it, Taylor was forcibly ushered outside. She saw Ari and Trevor being escorted out of their trucks too. Only Trevor was being handled roughly. Past the bridge she spied a bubble-like, metal container built into the wall with windows looking out, several mammals within monitoring their approach.

Rakkis snapped his fingers. "You two come with us." He indicated Ari and Taylor.

"Hey!" Taylor spoke up. "What about Trevor?"

71

Rakkis looked peeved. "What about him? He won't be harmed, if that's what you are asking. He is just being detained until we are told what to do with him."

"Don't worry, Taylor." Trevor jerked his metal arm out of the paws of one of the bears holding him. "I know my way around dangerous situations. I'm not about to make any stupid decisions." He winked and gave her a grin.

Uneasy, but unsure of what else she could do, she simply nodded. "Okay... But I'll be asking about him later."

"I would like to speak to Father first." Ari demanded, now stepping back up to be near Taylor.

Rakkis shrugged. "You didn't technically fail your mission, Ari. You just took a bit too long—well, longer than we'd like." He smirked, his tongue dabbing his eye. "So do as you please."

"I will." She shot daggers at him as she swept past, gently but firmly gripping Taylor's paw in her own and dragging her along.

Taylor turned back to see Rakkis eyeing them for a few moments as they began to cross the bridge to the bunker entrance, then suddenly he signaled his crews. They each disbanded and began to post-check their trucks for parking and storage. Once he could see they were doing their jobs, Rakkis followed close behind.

"This is not how I expected to come back home," Taylor whispered.

Ari kept walking but turned her head just slightly towards Taylor. "Well, how did you expect to be returning home?"

"Just with you and Trevor, on our bikes. Maybe we could have stopped at a few places downtown like somewhere to eat? I am starving." Taylor admitted.

Ari sighed. "Look, I'm just happy Rakkis is being agreeable right now. I wanted this job badly so that I could be depended on more often. The last thing I wanted was for him to one-up me."

"Why do you want that? Does your father not depend on you much?" Taylor asked.

Ari ignored her question, greeting the guards at the front. "I am Ariana, the Arbiter's daughter. Let us in."

"Of course, ma'am," the boar at the computer said. "Just procedure. We have to check everyone now. Security is ramping up lately, and we can't be too sure.

"It's me, idiot!" Ari slapped her palm on the table next to the computer he was looking at, causing him to squeal. "You've seen me a thousand times."

"Well, er..." He tried to loosen the top button on his shirt, now feeling it to be quite tight. "There could be a person with shapeshifting powers out there impersonating you. You do know he exists?"

"Of course I do! I killed him! Remember!?" Ari snapped, her hand heating up and beginning to melt the edge of the table, causing the boar's eyes to dilate in fear.

"It's her. Who else could pull that off?" Rakkis intervened, looking bored as he gestured to her overheating fingers. "You're just doing your stupid, little job in your stupid, little world. We get it. Just walk this one off and let us in." He grasped Ari's wrist and ripped it away from the table, nearly causing a violent reaction from her. He seemed unperturbed at the response.

The guard was sniveling in his chair as the three of them moved past into a more lit hallway. Ari took point as they navigated the maze of hallways and rooms, each one similar to the last. All sterile, cold and bland. The metal sidings and floor appeared to be purposefully crafted together to be impenetrable, either from the outside or inside. Taylor had the strange idea that it was like one big, metal cocoon sheltering this entire base of theirs.

"It's a bit complicated with my father." Ari returned back to Taylor's question. "Let's just say that things haven't always been this way." She glanced back meaningfully towards Rakkis, who seemed oblivious to this movement.

"This is where we leave you." Rakkis stopped.

"That's it?" Taylor was flummoxed. "You're not going to walk us in to the Arbiter?"

Rakkis turned to the side, looking back the way they had come. "Nah. We're bored. Her father knows who brought you in, Taylor. That's all that matters. Besides..." His tail rose up, tongue draping out of its toothy maw. "I'm feeling hungry right now, and I do believe that piggy back there might provide a good snack."

"Have fun." Ari was emotionless.

"You're just going to let Rakkis go off and eat him?" Taylor was horrified, watching his retreating form slink off down the hall and around the corner.

Ari shrugged. "Why should I care? It's not like I could do anything to stop him. He's as annoying as a cockroach and just as disgusting. Him eating that sap is a blessing in disguise in getting him out of our scales."

Taylor yanked her wrist out of Ari's grasp. "Just a minute. You are one of the most dangerous people I know. You single-handedly bested a full group of five trained mammals sent to fetch me, and you're not able to stop one single chameleon?" She paused a moment. "That is what he is, right? My knowledge of reptiles is a bit limited... I didn't actually finish school."

Ari exhaled. "Yes, that is what he is. What I meant was, there is nothing I can do that he won't see or counter. I've sparred with him many a time, and I always end up losing. The only reason I am not dead is because I'm the Arbiter's daughter."

Taylor looked back down the empty hallway. "He does seem just as determined to follow your father's orders as you are. When did he get to be so loyal? I mean, you I can understand. You are his daughter."

"That doesn't mean he automatically earned my loyalty." Ari swished her tail in impatience. "He saved Rakkis's life once, and he has been duty-bound to repay that debt ever since."

"Yet you seem very eager to prove yourself better than him to your father. Do you do it because you want him to love you?" Taylor pressed, genuinely interested in this dynamic between these three.

Ari thumped her tail on the ground. "I don't even know why I'm humoring you with these questions. He's expecting us."

Ensuring that Taylor was walking beside her, Ari led her deeper into the bunker. They passed by several bay windows where they could view barracks housed in cramped rooms. There were metal bars holding up to two beds in their frames, on which she could see a smattering of youthful mammals her age or younger sleeping, reading, or playing with each other. They seemed ignorant of their presence behind the glass.

Ari noted Taylor's interest. "This will all be explained soon when we meet my father. It has taken us nearly two decades to get back to what we once were, but we're now ready. All we need is someone like you to start."

"I don't understand. What is so special about me?" Taylor was not happy. Everyone had been after her for what she could do, but nobody could tell her exactly what they needed her for.

"He's behind this door." She stopped just outside a bulkhead door, with rotating wheel to depressurize the interior before opening.

Taylor looked around. "Not some big meeting room or throne hall?"

Ari scoffed. "Please, we're not that pretentious. This is where he sleeps. It is closed, so he is inside."

"Wait, his personal bedroom?" Taylor felt awkward walking in on this person while he could possibly still be in bed. It seemed odd that someone as supposedly important as the Arbiter would be so casual about meeting her like this.

"Go in." Ari wasn't fielding anymore questions.

Ari moved forward to spin the wheel, a loud hissing emerging, which caused Taylor's hairs to stand on end. Peeking into the gloom of red lights, Taylor could see a large shape facing away from them. Its large bulk sat on a sagging chair of steel. The entire body did not move a single muscle; in fact, it seemed like he had not even noticed them coming in.

"I've been looking forward to meeting you, Taylor," the deep voice before her rumbled.

4.

EXPERIMENT

The entire place was pandemonium. Young cubs and kits were screaming as the explosions rocked the structure, causing silt and debris to fall from overhead. A few of the more capable and level-headed of the youngsters were able to levitate some of the crushing stone and rock and fling it away from their friends.

Multitudes of police officers with chest-mounted flashlights and cameras were barreling through the newly opened entrance into the atrium of cots and bed stands. It was a sterile production factory of child soldiers. Their individual beds were lined in seemingly endless rows in an open bay of enclosed servitude. The dismal lighting in the indented sconces in the ceiling only accentuated that fact.

The cops fanned out as the lead officer took point. "Everyone be careful. They are well armed to defend themselves." He turned to address one of the frightened kits. "Do not be afraid, young one. We are to help get you out of here." The young ocelot had terror in his eyes and seemed ready to bolt.

"Armed? Anthony, they're just kids!" a colleague piped up from the side, getting a bit too close to a young fawn who was staring at him like she had been struck with headlights.

"I know that!" Anthony snapped. Changing tack, he went with another child: a young giraffe of stunted neck and amazingly violet eyes. She was clutching a small raccoon plushy tightly in her hooves, but she didn't seem as scared as the others. If he could convince her to relax, he might be able to reach out to the others. "It's okay. We're the good guys. We are here to help you." He reached out his paw. "Do you want to show me that cute doll of yours?"

"Marle, no!" another calf hissed, causing the uncertain giraffe to take a few steps back.

A strangled cry erupted from beside Anthony when all eyes turned to an officer being raised into the air before imploding in sickening cracks and squishing slurps. His entire body folded and caved into itself in a macabre display of horror. Blood seeped out of the condensed body as it continued to shrink. The lion was nothing more than a ball of bloody puss before he was dropped to the ground to splatter all over the defaced tile.

"Oh, fuck!" another officer cried out. "Which one of them did that?"

The jackal next to him began to skirl piercingly as blood poured out of every orifice in his body, causing him to collapse to his knees in abject misery.

"Doesn't matter! Shoot them all!" another yelled.

"No, gods damn it! Don't harm them!" Anthony roared, but it was too late. He turned to save and cover the small giraffe girl, but she had disappeared.

It was open season on the children as muzzle-flashes illuminated the bay. Several cubs in the immediate vicinity dropped like flies in the hail of bullets as several others went on the attack. One officer immediately burst into flames as another was flung into the concrete wall before sinking into it and being torn apart inside. All hope for control was lost as the modus operand turned to survival. No longer were these young children and casualties of war, but legitimate targets.

"You three, follow me!" Anthony jabbed his finger at his men, having a tiger and two additional wolves follow him as he sprinted through the mass of metal bed frames. "On your left!"

They all turned to fire with impunity on several gazelles and a zebra. The latter got off a round of concussive air directed squarely at one of the wolves. It hit him hard in the chest, flinging him up and over a frame, one of the jutting metal poles catching and shredding his entire leg off with the velocity of impact before the rest of his body slammed into the ceiling.

Anthony unloaded the remainder of his clip into the zebra before turning to watch his friend crunch to the floor below, bleeding and broken. "Damn it! We're losing too many mammals!" He jerked his head to have the tiger follow him directly. "Kowalski, you're on me.

Tannenbaum, see to it that you can staunch Henley's wound so he doesn't bleed the fuck out."

The other wolf nodded and turned to his fallen comrade. Anthony and Kowalski had already made a sprint to the far end of the room. The majority of the children had dispersed.

The sting was already a disaster. Their objective was to get in, secure the children, and maintain control for them to be extracted peacefully, but the Arbiter's guards made that hard, and forced them to stumble across their targets of interest in a less than peaceable way.

The calls over their radios had already been made to capture and contain as many of the kids as they could find with tranquilizer rounds, but the majority were already scattered to the four winds. Only the gods knew where they were now or where they would go. All that was left on their agenda was to secure the confidential informant that was said to be held still inside the compound, deep within the sewers of Meerkat Town.

Without that last data burst from inside the Arbiter's bunker from their informant, they would have never been able to find the entrance to his base of operations. Whoever it was gave them the access codes, and everything they needed to launch a surprise attack on the base. It was almost too perfect. Everything had been going smoothly up until their encounter with the guards.

"How the hell can they do those things?" Kowalski muttered, shaking his head. "Did you see that freakshow?" He was hot on Anthony's heels, keeping pace effortlessly.

Anthony slid up to a corner, pressing his back up against the wall as he peeked around the corner before looking down at his tracking device. "We were told to expect the worst, and that's exactly what we got. Now, if you'll keep it down, we're getting close to where their position is." His brow furrowed as he studied the schematics of the base on the device. "That's odd. Did we just pass them?"

Turning back around, he stalked past several doors before opening up the third on the left. Its entire metal frame screeched from the door sliding into place. The room was filled with hospital equipment and lab computers linked up to projector screens. There was a large apparatus that was dangling from the ceiling that looked almost like a gun, but the end tip was narrowed to a singular point, like it was meant for piercing. Below that was a rolling bed with a body on it.

Anthony's eyes enlarged as he recognized who it was on the operating bed. "Murana!" he shouted. He nearly dropped the tracking device as he rushed over to her. "Murana! Can you hear me?" He let the gun drop to his chest as he began to shake her and check for wounds.

"Oh shit, is that your wife?" Kowalski was stunned. His tail flicking restlessly, he kept his eyes glued to the door behind them.

Murana barely seemed able to register his existence as her eyes were rolled back into her skull. She was moaning and writhing like she was in pain. Anthony studied her and noticed several cords attached to her belly, hooked up to a device that was displaying a moving image. It was grainy and hard to make out, but it looked like a small body was moving around on the monitor.

"You're pregnant…" he mouthed. He looked up at the device above him and then back down to all the wires and devices meant to monitor her body and everything going on inside of it. "What were they doing to you? What were they doing to our cubs?" He slapped the arm of Kowalski as he indicated the device above. "I'm going to move Murana out from under this, but we got to destroy that thing."

Without asking questions, he readied his gun as Anthony rolled his wife, bed and all, a fair distance away from the kill zone. With a signal, Kowalski unleashed hell on the inanimate object. A few short moments later, it was hanging even further from the ceiling, half off its bolts and hinges.

Kowalski nodded with a grunt. "That thing isn't going to be working anytime soon!"

"Anthony?" Murana barely whispered, but he heard her clearly.

Ignoring all around them, he huddled close over her as he gripped her paw in his own. "I'm here, love. Are you okay?"

Murana cracked a small smile, wincing as more pain seemed to knife through her body. "You all got my message."

Anthony couldn't hold back the tears. "You were the confidential informant?" She nodded. He broke down completely as he wept over her. "Nobody knew what happened to you for months. You disappeared completely. We all thought you had gotten kitnapped or worse, killed! Steven and Max were distraught."

She raised a paw to caress his face. "I'm sorry to have worried you."

Another explosion shook the ground as Kowalski poked his head out down the corridor. "We need to move soon."

Anthony acknowledged the recommendation and looked back down at his wife. "Are you able enough to walk on your own, or shall I carry you?"

Murana coughed hard before slumping back into the bed. Whatever they had done had completely drained all energy from her. She shook her head. "Carrying sounds real nice right about now." She attempted to force a smile. She pointed a finger at the monitor. "Tell Steven and Max they're going to get new siblings." She had a dreamy smile on her face.

Anthony could tell he was losing her to unconsciousness again. He shouldered his gun so that it rested across his back as he snaked one arm and then the other underneath her after he had removed all her cables and medical cords. Lifting her up into his arms, he gave her a lick on the cheek.

"I got you, babe. Don't you worry about a thing. I'm bringing you home." His heart was brimming with joy at having found his wife again.

She was flitting in and out of lucidity, but she turned up to meet his eyes as she asked, "Did Chief Wendell give the order to extract me? Is that why you're all here? Am I free to go?"

"Chief Wendell?" Anthony looked confused.

"Who is that?" Kowalski added.

Taylor was panting heavily. The panic was settling in as her wrists and ankles writhed against the cold buckles of the clamps pinning her to the operating slab. The indifferent coyote administering the lab experiments was fiddling with some controls on the primary panel facing away from her position. Her entire body shook; even Ahya snapped her teeth in apprehension when the entire table began to move and slant. In a scant few seconds she was vertical, unable to move and vulnerable to whatever the "doctor" in front of her had planned.

Surrounding her was an unfeeling circular room of green brick and tile. The chamber rose high into the gloomy darkness above her. Hanging like a menacing spider was a device with a myriad of individual mechanical arms each ending in any number of unknown and unseemly attachments. Taylor couldn't fathom their uses just yet, and that disturbed her.

Why did she even agree to this at all? She had vowed never to be in this position again, yet agreed to submit to these experiments regardless. The Arbiter was very genuine and convincing with his arguments as to why he needed to do these things to her. She looked up towards the glass mirror looking down upon her, knowing he was up there observing and listening to anything the doctor would relay.

"I don't think I can do this..." Taylor's teeth were chattering, a deathly chill rattling her body.

"You agreed to this. You need to." Ari stood across the room beyond the doctor, leaning up against the wall with arms folded.

"I don't know why. I hated this the first time around." Taylor's breathing was getting faster; she was nearly hyperventilating.

"Calm yourself. I am here, and although I won't stop anything from happening to you, I'll try and make sure it's nothing horrible."

"Your bedside manner sucks." Taylor had to huff a laugh to keep from whining in terror.

Ari smirked. "Well, my father did say he wanted you alive through all this. My goal is to keep you that way. So don't worry."

"Will you two stop yammering? I'm trying to focus on these calibrations!" the coyote rumbled.

"Shut your hole," Ari snapped. The coyote glowered at her, but said nothing.

"Could you hold my paw?" Taylor asked.

Ari raised a brow. "Are you serious?"

"Please… I need… I need to feel like someone is with me through this." Taylor's eyes were darting this way and that. She imagined she looked pitiful.

Ari sighed and paced over. "Fine. This sort of pain is meaningless to me. I've endured much worse. Here I thought you were braver than this."

"From getting experimented on?" Taylor shook her head fervently. "No, not at all. I remember it being horrible, painful, and terrifying. The fact I can't move right now is freaking me out!"

Rolling her eyes, Ari offered her hand, which Taylor immediately grabbed and squeezed. "Ease up on the grip, girl. You will survive this."

"Like you survived your eye?" Taylor indicated Ari's cybernetic eye with her chin.

Ari chuckled. "I don't think we'll be doing anything like this with you today. As far as I'm aware, we're just getting vitals and overall body chemistry readings, as well as testing out what you can do."

"That's very comforting."

"First we need her blood." The coyote clicked a few buttons, lowering a metallic arm ending with a large needle that had an obnoxiously large vial attached. "Two pints should do it."

Taylor blanched at the looming device, it drawing ever closer to her arm. "Your father didn't happen to tell you what he needed all this for?"

Ari snorted. "Not really. It is not my place to question Father. He specifically asked me to not be present when he finally spoke with you. So in reality, I was hoping you would tell me what he intends to do with you. After having invested so much into bringing you back home, I'm genuinely curious."

"Your father is pretty scary, you know that?" Taylor began to grip Ari's hand tighter as the needle graced her skin, its cold tip like hot fire to her nerves.

"He never was one to show much emotion, even to me." Ari was thoughtful. "I can see how you could get that impression— Ah, ease up!"

Taylor yelped as the needle jammed in suddenly, causing Ahya to jolt and snap wildly. Crimson fluid began to flood the inner container of the vial. Taylor nearly passed out, having to be smacked awake by Ari.

"Now I'm starting to understand why you asked me to come join you." Ari grinned, showed her row of crooked teeth.

Taylor was fighting hard not to cry as the blood-drawing was finishing up, the needle pulling out with a sickening slurp. Another arm device was lowering to seal the wound with a skin adhesive, sewing up the skin effortlessly. "You were my only choice. I didn't want to be alone. I don't trust Rakkis, and you all won't let me see Trevor."

"The only choice? Was that the only reason then?" If Ari seemed hurt, she didn't show it.

"I figured you would understand better than most about being experimented on."

Ari drew back a bit, thinking on that. "I see."

She said nothing further, but continued to hold Taylor's hand as the coyote brought down a third arm that began to scan her irises, mapping them to a geometric model in the computer monitor alongside them. "It seems one eye has a deformity," the coyote noted.

Still reeling from the blood-drawing, Taylor was confused. "I don't understand. What do you mean deformity?" She tried to shy away from the bright lights that were now assaulting her blue iris, now having finished with her gold.

"Your right eye is not a natural color that is consistent with your species. It seems it is a mutation resulting from a catalyst event. Vision is still functional." He unhooked the filled vial of blood from the arm nearby and shook its contents a bit before placing it into a tube where it shuttled off to points unknown.

"I'm not even going to pretend to know what he means," Taylor stated bluntly.

"It means something happened during your gestation period in your mother's womb that caused you to have the golden color in your left eye," Ari explained.

"You can understand him?" Taylor's mouth dropped.

Ari shrugged. "I've been in this chamber too often to count. I've gotten used to his rambling."

"If you two ladies are done gossiping about me, let's proceed to the next test." The coyote seemed irritated.

A multi-fingered, claw-looking apparatus snaked its way down to the level of Ahya, poised expectantly at her tip. "If you wouldn't mind, could we have you stick out its tongue?"

Taylor complied with his request. The claw immediately pinched the end of Ahya's tongue and began pulling on it. Ahya did not like this sensation alongside Taylor, and continued to stretch herself to keep up with the rapidly retreating claw. Ahya got longer and longer until she was stretched taut, tugging gently at the base of Taylor's spine with the exertion of reaching out for the claw. Still the device continued to pull Ahya's tongue out further and further, until nearly her entire internal stomach sac was exposed.

Even Ari was impressed. "Now that is something."

"Stretching a full sixteen feet from tail base to tongue tip, the tail consists of an eight-foot internal stomach organ that can reach out to the same length of her tail." The doctor was hastily transcribing this into his computer. "It appears the tongue can be any part of the interior lining and stretch the length of it."

Taylor squirmed against her cuffs. "Can we release her now?" She was feeling like she was stretched too thin. She had never used Ahya to reach out this far before. Even to her, the full extent of how far Ahya could reach was surprising if not a bit frightening.

The coyote unceremoniously released the grip on Ahya's tongue, causing the tail to sag from gravity. Taylor had to keep her poor tail up as it coiled its tongue back into itself with some difficulty. It seemed Ahya was just as much done with this whole testing as Taylor was.

"So, did my father explain to you what he needed you for?" Ari asked nonchalantly, but Taylor could tell she was interested in the answer.

"Not entirely, no." Taylor tried to recall back to her conversation with the Arbiter. It was very much a nerve-wracking haze. She could barely get a read on the large, imposing tortoise with his non-emotive responses. "I remember him mentioning that I was a very important breakthrough in the realm of magic infusion, and that with the results of what they're doing to me now could help turn the tide of some war?"

Ari nodded. "Indeed. With you being the only one born with your powers, you are a unique specimen for study. The rest of us were given them artificially."

"That makes me feel all sorts of giddy," Taylor snarked. "So…magic is real, then?"

"As far as I can tell." Ari looked over to the doctor who was fumbling with a manual to figure out how to do the next test. "There is no scientific explanation for how we do the things we can do. My father has been able to isolate the very essence of it in the air, harness it through a machine, and inject it into subjects using a variety of methods—some more successful than others."

"Has it always been here around us? Why haven't more people been able to work with the magic that supposedly exists in our world?" Taylor didn't quite like the fact she had an aura of magic in her body. It reeked of being too similar to the Script and how it functioned off of magic, and she hated that with a passion. She did not like the idea of a mystical document dictating how everyone's life would play out without any room for freedom.

"I'm not sure." Ari ruminated over the question. "I recall my father saying that the common usages of it died out centuries ago with my people during the Hordos War, and now there are very few alive who remember how it used to be."

"Ari… What is he doing?" Taylor saw a huge slab of meat skewered on the end of an arm that was lowering itself to be at the level of Ahya's maw.

"We're feeding you," the doctor said without pity. "We need to see the extent of the digestion capability of your tail."

"No…no meat! Isn't there some vegetables you can feed her? Or fruit?" Taylor began to panic again.

"I'm afraid not. Open wide, because we got another slab for you after this one, where we are going to test out its regeneration powers, as reported by Ari."

Taylor's head swiveled to the side, her eyes rapt on Ari. Her cybernetic eye was studying her intently. "I needed to report everything that transpired, which included the miraculous resurrection of Fey Darner. My father is keenly interested in how this works with Ahya."

Taylor tried to forcibly keep Ahya's maw shut through sheer will alone. "I don't even know whose meat that is. Who did you all have to kill to get that?"

"Does it matter? Someone not worth mentioning." Ari began to squeeze back Taylor's paw.

"I don't want to taste it. I hate meat." Taylor began shaking her head in protest.

"You are the oddest wolf I've ever met. You disliking meat being the least of your curiosities." Ari couldn't contain her mirth.

"You just like to see me tortured. Ahh…what the fuck?!" Taylor shouted at the coyote as a cattle prod-looking arm shocked the end of her tail. Ahya was already grappling it between her teeth, trying to shake it hard to rip it off its hinges. "What the heck was that for?"

"Your tail's mouth. We need it open. Either open it now or we will shock it open." The coyote was merciless and unyielding. His demeanor never wavering from his task.

"Taylor, open Ahya's mouth." Ari urged.

After a few moments, the coyote did not wait further. The prod continued to shock her tail over and over until suddenly Taylor's will gave out and Ahya dangled with mouth ajar. The doctor expeditiously shoved the meat into the maw and using another clamp-looking arm, closed the jaws shut, disallowing any attempt to drop the meat.

"Now digest. We are monitoring all our instruments to see how this process works." The coyote flipped a button and several instruments hummed.

The intense fear of what was happening mixed with the adrenaline flowing through her veins and the awful taste inside her mouth, Taylor threw up. It splattered to the floor, much to the distaste of both doctor and Ari.

Taylor quivered, her lower lips shivering at the exhausting effort of hurling the new contents of her stomach. "Please…stop."

"You're going to have to clean that up." The coyote gestured to Ari.

"Like hell I am!" Ari snarled. "She's your patient, you deal with whatever crap she gives you."

"Thanks for the support," Taylor said weakly.

"Now we need you to half-dissolve this second piece and reconstitute it like you did with Fey." The coyote lowered down a larger slab of carcass before Ahya. Even her tail seemed unwilling to take it into her maw.

"I said stop..." Taylor could see the prod coming in for another round.

Coursing daggers of pain bolted through her tailbone and up her spine as the electricity crackled and penetrated through the flesh of Ahya's skin. Taylor grit her teeth and begin to whine as the doctor was relentless in his pursuit to shove another disgusting piece of meat up Ahya's maw. She didn't want to remember the rotten flavor of the meat another time. The first was bad enough. Who knew how long they had been keeping these hunks of flesh on retainer for just this moment?

"Taylor? You need to calm down right now." Ari had released her paw, having been shocked herself by the sparks now sizzling out of Taylor's fingers.

"*Make it stop,*" a voice rung out in Taylor's mind.

Taylor was done with the pain. She didn't care anymore about the consequences if she resisted. She was not going to get probed one more time by this stupid coyote. "Then tell him to lay off me! I don't want to get hurt again or poked with needles anymore! I don't even know why I agreed to this in the first place."

"Because you didn't really have a choice?" Ari offered.

"Or maybe it was because this was the only way I could see my mother and family again!" Taylor was in full rage. "I figured if I could just suffer... If I could just endure this, then I could negotiate a favor to go see my family. I don't even know if they're even alive. I just want to go home."

"*Let me kill them.*"

"Taylor, I don't think it's that..." Ari began.

88

The coyote prodded the tailmaw one last time too many. Taylor screamed as crackling bolts of pure electrical energy blew out through her paws, slamming into the floor with enough concussive force to crack the tiling with deep gouges extending all the way to the very edges of the room. The current hit the wiring for the device apparatus above that trailed along the floor and shot through them, sparking and popping fuses and blowing out dials along its destructive path. The blast shattered the mirror overlooking the room, displaying the Arbiter in full view above before all the lights went out.

The coyote shuffled in the dark to the backup PA system that ran on a different circuit than the rest of the room. "Unable to proceed further with subject due to cataclysmic power failure."

The low rumble of the Arbiter's voice echoed down into the room. "That will be enough for today. Daughter, go bring Taylor to her prepared quarters. We will begin again tomorrow."

"Yes, Father." Ari nodded, watching him lumber out of view above, his heavy footsteps audibly growing distant. "Taylor, you still with me?" Ari asked.

"I wish I wasn't," Taylor moaned, lazily lifting her head as if in a daze. Her whole body was limp, head hanging down onto her chest. Ahya dangled by her side. "My head gets very stuffy whenever I do that. I'm surprised I didn't pass out this time."

"That was not the worst I've seen you do." Ari began to undo the clamps. "I can still remember that time back in Howlgrav where you went to protect me from getting shot. You nearly brought down an entire city block."

"If this is magic, why is it so draining?" Taylor began to rub her wrists and massage her aching fingers that were still healing as Ari unhooked her.

Ari went to undo the leg clamps. "Because magic is part of you. Your body is using it like it would anything else. If you run a marathon, are you not tired? You are using parts of your body that need rest after the exertion. Likewise, when you use this aspect of your body, this electrical power, you feel exhausted too. I know when I use my powers to heat things up, I can feel the drain on my body, and I need rest after a time."

"Does it ever get better?" Taylor began to rotate her ankles to feel some satisfying pops.

Ari stood back up. "I've learned to train my body to withstand the fatigue, and over time I can use more of my power. It just takes practice, like with anything else."

"I wonder, what is so special about my magic that both your father and the High Council want me?" Taylor posed the question, hoping Ari might slip with some answers.

Ari shook her head before gripping her arm and showing Taylor the way out of the dark room with a finger. "That's what we're trying to do here. We're finding out together. You are unique in many ways even I haven't seen. Come on, let's get you to a bed to sleep."

Taylor was feeling awfully spent. Ignoring the mumbling curses of the coyote left behind to fix the mess she made of his equipment, the two of them entered the maze of sheet metal corridors. "So where exactly are we?" Taylor asked as she looked around at the red-hued halls they passed through.

"About a mile below the surface of Zabökar." Ari glanced over to Taylor walking beside her. "Don't think about attempting to escape. There are posted guards at every exit, and the labyrinthine tunnels out there would spin your head around. You'd be caught in no time."

"I wasn't even thinking of it," Taylor admitted. She knew Ari was just ensuring her cooperation, but it didn't take a genius to figure out that there was no realistic way of escape from the heart of their entrenched stronghold here under the surface of the city. "I'm just biding my time for a better opportunity to escape."

"I hope you're joking," Ari scoffed.

"Perhaps." Taylor smirked. The gesture was returned by Ari, but Taylor wasn't sure if the reptile felt the same way about it.

At length, they came to a stop right outside a sliding metal door. Ari flexed and pushed it aside, its automatic opening feature long since broken. She waved Taylor on inside. "These will be your quarters during your stay here."

It was pretty sparse, all things considered. There was a single mattress pad on top of a plate of iron bolted into the wall. Two pillows were the only saving grace on that pathetic-looking sleeping spot. A lone metal chair that Taylor could remember from her old grade school was the only other piece of furniture. Stacked on top of it were two dozen books.

"Figured I'd get bored with nothing to do and get into mischief, so you supplied these for me?" Taylor asked.

"Something like that." Ari was indifferent, getting ready to shut the door on her.

"Wait, aren't you going to stay and talk a bit?"

"No, why?" Ari looked confused. "I got a few errands to run for father. Someone will be by to serve you dinner. Just don't have Ahya eat them."

Without another word the door was closed, leaving Taylor to her thoughts. She was all alone in here. She had no friends to rely on. No family. There was no telling how long these experiments would go on for, and if the Arbiter would even deign to listen to her request to go find her family. Trevor was gone, and she had no idea what they did with him. Ari was aloof and distant at best. She didn't even have Pine and Mitchell to talk to, as imaginary as they supposedly were.

Shifting through the books, she spied a few she recalled from the Llydia series—a series about a dragon her mother used to read to her every night, filled with good morals and life lessons. Feeling nostalgic, she picked it up and flopped onto the bed with a creaking of the springs. She glumly stared about the dismal abode. She looked at her silent companion, bumping her paws for pets, then sighed. "I'm just lonely, is all…"

"I do not miss this place." Mikhail said, looking up at the congested mess of cars above them.

"You mean the city or the traffic?" Natalia chuckled.

"Both."

Mikhail, Natalia, Fey, Finnley, and Terrati had slowly worked their way back into Zabökar after being bested and given the slip by Ari and Trevor. Whisking away with their prize, Taylor, they had no choice but to retreat back to Cheribaum to lick their wounds. Finnley, the otter, now had both a back brace for his injured spine and a full arm cast with soothing gauze swatches to cool the lingering burn from Taylor's lightning that had struck his shoulder.

"You going to be okay back there?" Mikhail called back, looking in the rearview mirror of their wheeled vehicle at Fey and Finnley.

Fey, the elk, returned the gaze. "We're fine. We just need to get Finnley to a hospital. The sooner we can get him to a proper facility, the sooner we can help his injuries."

Finnley grit his teeth. "It still burns like hell. I swear to gods, I better not come across that stupid wolf and her freaky ass tail again."

"Then I guess it's a good thing you're not going after her like the rest of us are." The tiger beamed from the driver's seat.

"Hey, I still haven't said I was joining your crusade, Mikhail." Terrati, the gazelle, appeared put out.

"There's still time, even now." Mikhail looked over at the snow leopard. "How about you, Natalia. You still with me on this?"

"Of course," she replied in her thick accent. "I feel like she's a little sister to me now."

"Despite having eaten your real sister?" Finnley mocked.

"Shut it," Mikhail growled, honking his horn as a bongo swerved their car in front of theirs.

"Beside the point." Natalia was unperturbed. "I've come to accept what is and have forgiven her for that. For all intents and purposes, I view her as the sister I missed out on spending time with when I grew up. I would at least like to see her not used and exploited for what she is or can do."

"That's all very touching, but you're not the one with a burning hole in their shoulder as a reminder of why we should have never taken this job in the first place!" Finnley was frothing at the mouth.

"Honey, please relax. You're going to injure yourself again." Fey wrapped an arm around his small partner and brought him in closer. "If it also weren't for her, I wouldn't be alive now."

92

"Yeah, really reassuring." Finnley wasn't having it. "Only because the Script told you that we needed to take this job."

"You know as well as I do that no matter what I could have done, the Script would still have put me back in front of that hail of gunfire in Howlgrav." Fey rubbed the budding nubs of his antlers on his head, them having been sliced off during their escape from Howlgrav. "The Script has a way of fulfilling itself, regardless of what we do."

Finnley pouted and folded his arms. "Then that's one thing Taylor and I can agree on. That Script is no good and should be dealt away with."

"But can we really?" Natalia was thoughtful, looking back out at the shining store windows, the morning sun hitting them just right.

"I know Taylor can," Mikhail said gravely. "Like Fey, I was supposed to die back there. She saved us both, and according to Fey who checked our Scripts, we're no longer on it. We technically have no future, yet are still alive and kicking."

"I am still horrified and fascinated how she did that," Terrati said.

"She's got a very unique ability to heal people or even bring them back from near-death through her tail, Ahya." Mikhail was remembering being inside the squishy, tight confines of Ahya. The darkness constricting around his body as viscous saliva was flooding all around him, getting ready to dissolve him alive. Instead it soothed his burns, and he came out alive and unhurt. "Something we've only seen through the most groundbreaking modern medicine."

"And now she's in the hands of the Arbiter." Natalia slumped.

"Probably best for now, since we're still on the fence with the High Council," Terrati clucked.

"Well, technically we're disavowed," Fey corrected. "There's no point reporting back to them anyway. For all intents and purposes, we aren't welcome there, and we should expect to be treated as enemies of the state. So the sooner we can get our objectives done in town, the better."

"Speaking of which, your stop is here." Mikhail had to veer hard into the curb, ignoring the blaring of the cars behind as he parked it hastily.

Looking up through the moon roof of their car, they could see the rising spires of the Zabökar General, the most prominent hospital in the city—its multitude of catwalks joining each tower filled with occupants traveling to and fro to their appointments. There were several helipads perched at intervals along the upper reaches of each spire; some were meant for helicopters, while others were smaller and meant for avian patients that needed a direct route to medical assistance.

"You sure you don't want to find Taylor?" Natalia queried again, an imploring look on her face.

"As grateful as I am to her for my life, I think I've had enough of dangerous missions. With no Script to tell me what lies ahead, I don't want to risk my life any further than I already have." Fey looked down at his otter. "Besides, there is something else I'd like to research, and I can't do that chasing after a lost cause."

"See you when we see you." Finnley was eager to get out and get fixed, allowing Fey to pick him up and carry him into the building.

"You have our number in case you need anything that isn't tailmaw related." Fey winked at the three of them before shutting the door and entering the main foyer of the hospital, Finnley in his arms.

"So what do we do now?" Terrati asked after an awkwardly long silence after they'd watched the other two go.

"We should be asking you that." Mikhail turned around in the seat to get an eye on him. "You're the only one left in this car that hasn't really decided what they're going to do."

"We could always drop you off at your apartment," Natalia suggested. "Is your girlfriend still living there with you?"

Terrati flushed and averted his eyes from hers. "We're not really on speaking terms these days. That sort of happens when you're gone for nearly a year on a mission you can't explain anything to her about."

"Well, she understood going in that your job might need to call you away for long periods of time." Mikhail gave the gazelle a bewildered stare.

Mikhail's wife, when she was alive, was very understanding. She knew the job he held, and would always be waiting patiently for him to come home—worried for his safety, but always supportive and encouraging when he needed it most. He couldn't really fathom why anyone else would be anything less to the one they love.

"Ha… Try explaining that concept to a gal who wasn't raised in a military home like your wife." Terrati snorted, gazing out the window at the stop-and-go traffic just inches from their car. "I guess I'll stick with you two for a bit longer. Not like I have much to come home to now that I'm out of a job. I'd rather not move back in with Fey and Finnley."

"Fair enough," Mikhail grunted, flicking on the turn signal before weaving out back into traffic.

Their landlocked vehicle was the best they could find in the remote town of Cheribaum. It wasn't much, but it was cheap. Nothing like the fancy hover cars above them, which a majority of the wealthier citizens of Zabökar could afford. Still, it gave them some air of anonymity; nobody would go looking for them in a rundown piece of junk that their cramped car resembled. Even its green paint was flecking off, giving it the impression of being an old scrap piece.

"Do we have any leads on where Taylor would be held right now?" Natalia was observing the morning commuters taking the walkways and sideways along the street in vain, hoping that she might randomly see Taylor.

"Not really, but if previous reports of the Arbiter's operations are to be believed, then most likely underground." Mikhail turned off the main street and down one towards a quieter residential area.

"That could honestly be anywhere," Terrati groaned. "And with no High Council resources at our disposal, we'd be basically looking for a needle in a haystack. Do you even know how complex those subway tunnels and maintenance routes are underneath the city?"

"Pretty extensive, based on my prior experience in TALOS." Mikhail smiled.

"Not to mention his previous base of operations was abandoned during the major sting operation of twenty years ago," Terrati continued. "If anything, he probably dug even deeper and is more paranoid than ever. How else do you think he's evaded the High Council this long? He's taking his time and operating a bit less openly than he did before, now that he's been exposed once. If he's got Taylor by now, I don't think he'd let her out of his sight for any reason."

"Or maybe he might." Natalia's jaw dropped.

"What are you talking about?" Terrati seemed irritated at being corrected.

Natalia smacked Mikhail's arm and pointed out in front of them. "Slow down! Right there! Do you see her?"

Trying his best to not look conspicuous as he pulled over to park on the side in front of an apartment building, they all turned their eyes out the front windshield. They could see her clear as day, wearing casual clothes with a hoodie to cover her hair, but the red on her tail was unmistakable. If that wasn't enough to confirm it was her, alongside her was the half-shelled crocodile bodyguard, Ari.

"Who are they talking to?" Natalia leaned forward, as if that would get her a better view.

"I've no idea. Looks like a swan," Mikhail observed.

Terrati peeked over between their shoulders. "That's odd. Birds usually don't roost this far out from the inner city, or rather this low. They're mostly in the high rises and penthouse suites."

It appeared Taylor was having a lively conversation with the swan who was sporting dark leather pants with fishnet stockings. She had piercings galore, with spiked bands and a collar. Definitely a rebel—a far cry from the typical expectation for a bird of her stature. Ari did not look impressed at all, and seemed to be very displeased about their interaction.

"Do you think we should go see what's happening?" Natalia suggested.

Mikhail held out a paw to stop her from opening the door. "Not yet. We need to know what the situation is first. It seems Taylor is willingly out in public with Ari. Who knows what sort of deal she's involved in with the Arbiter to be allowing her topside. We might just be messing it all up if we intervene now. Let's just wait and see."

"Yeah, good idea." Terrati hunkered down in the back seat.

Ari looked just about done with the conversation and moved to grab Taylor's paw. Taylor jerked it out from her grip and began to argue with Ari. The swan seemed to step aside, unsure of what to do. The wolf and reptile seemed to be yelling now at each other when suddenly Taylor blew Ari right off her feet with an explosive bolt of lightning, causing the swan to flap away a short distance in shock.

"Oh crap, looks like things are getting ugly!" Natalia was unfastening her seatbelt.

"She's coming this way!" Terrati sounded terrified.

Taylor had already grabbed the swan by the wing and was barreling down the sidewalk with the scared bird in tow, Ahya's maw open and tongue flapping in the breeze as if happy. Ari was back on her feet in an instant and immediately uprooted a planted tree with a pillar of molten earth. It teetered and fell forward towards them, nearly crushing Taylor as it landed just inches behind her hindpaws.

Leaping over the front of their vehicle to get off the sidewalk and into the street, she bounced off the hood, dragging the poor swan along who was struggling to keep up. Mikhail made eye contact with Taylor for just a split second before she slid off the other side of the car and took off running. If she recognized him through the windshield, she gave no sign.

"Should we follow now?" Natalia was urgent, rebuckling her seatbelt.

"Oh crap!" Terrati yelled.

Ari had boosted their car from underneath with another pillar of earth, launching them off towards Taylor. They flipped inverted before crashing down just before another parked car on the other side of the street. The glass on all their windows shattered as the impact scrunched the headspace to nearly half, knocking the larger Mikhail out cold.

He woke up not even a minute later to see Ari running past them to chase after Taylor, the sound of carnage fading down the street as the screams grew louder.

He groaned as he ripped his seatbelt off and took stock of his surroundings. The other two were struggling to maneuver themselves upright in the overturned cabin of their demolished vehicle. Shards of glass pricked his paws as he tried to right himself and attempt escape through one of the now open windows.

"Is everyone okay?" he called out.

"I've been better." Natalia groaned.

"I'd say we found Taylor." Terrati laughed, panic evident in his voice.

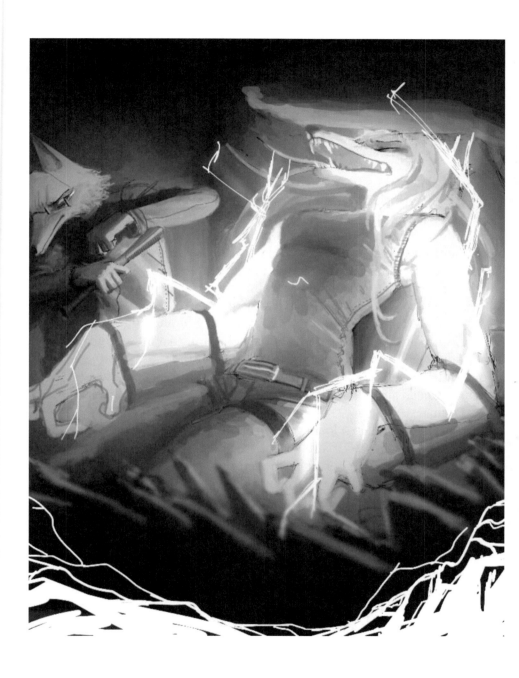

5.

MISSION

"Enter." His firm voice resounded in the tiny room.

The grizzled black bear wiped his brow as he huffed and let out a low bawl. The flimsy ceiling fan above, and the tiny one on his desk did little to dampen the immense heat in his office. It was the peak of summer in Zabökar, and the AC had picked the perfect time to crap out and leave the entire police station in utter heat lockdown. Many of his officers were taking frequent breaks in their cool, conditioned cars, and he hadn't the heart to stop them. It was miserable.

The door opened to the small form of Murana. She was a petite thing, smaller than most wolves her species, but that did not goad him into thinking she was helpless. She was one of the most capable and sometimes ruthless wolves he knew. Were it not for his knowledge of her past deeds and capabilities, he would have found the current sight of her comical.

She was given a loaner uniform meant for maternity cops, where the blouse was able to be stretched around the middle, only buttoned in place along the side of her ribs. Though she was well into her third trimester, the clothes lent were meant for a wolf of more common size; she was practically swimming in them.

Murana did little to hide her ineptitude of walking with the added baggage around her midsection. She waddled in, nodding her salute to her chief before heaving herself with some effort onto the offered chair before his desk. She took a few moments to adjust herself into a comfortable position, time that he graciously allowed her to have. She was just as hot as he was, if not more so given the extra warmth her accompanied passengers were giving off. She was panting up a storm.

"You wanted to see me, Chief?" She asked the obvious and most appropriate question.

He sighed, getting up with a grunt from his chair and walking around past her to shut the door she had left open. On his way back, he gestured to the tripod-mounted camera off to her left. "To set the record straight and to ensure we log everything legitimately so this does not come back to bite us in the ass, we are filming this conversation. Is that agreeable to you?"

She nodded and shrugged. "I'm no stranger to being videotaped, Chief."

He stopped briefly and gave her an odd look, but shook his head and dismissed it. He closed the slatted blinds on the two windows flanking his desk to ensure no more heat from the sun blazed in, making this already dicey conversation worse. Relaxing back into his plush chair, which screeched at his bulk, he scooted it up to the desk. A small ping came from behind him, probably a screw flying somewhere.

He pulled out her file and flipped to a part he had highlighted. "Officer Murana Delante Wolford, I have brought you in here to set a record straight, and to have it logged for archival and future legal purposes about the nature of your relationship to the Zabökar police, and what will ultimately be done with you in light of recent events involving the raid on the Arbiter's bunker deep in the sewers below Meerkat Town. Do you understand so far?"

"I do." Murana shifted restlessly.

"Against better judgment, we took you on into the police force under great secrecy as a confidential informant. Due to your previous experience as both a vigilante and former assassin for the notorious guild, The Claw, you were deemed a potential valuable asset to certain investigations and taskings that were to be executed under my strict supervision." He raised his glasses to his muzzle to better read the small print. "It is to my unfortunate regret that you gave us the leverage to negotiate a deal and your cooperation through your family, consisting of fellow officer, Anthony Wolford, and now your two sons, Steven 'Stinkman' and Max Thrash. Is that correct?"

Normally Murana was a feisty one when up against those in authority over her, but she knew that bringing up her family was no light-hearted matter. She simply nodded. "Yes, sir. I was afraid for my family, and that putting me behind bars for life would have a

101

detrimental impact on my boys' upbringing. It would also hamper the career of my husband, making him suddenly a single father. I had no choice but to cooperate."

The bear gave her a pointed look, but continued through his glasses. "It was agreed that instead of jail for the heinous crimes and acts incurred as both vigilante and assassin, you were to do service to your community in the form of assisting the Zabökar police in bringing various factions and agents to justice using the talents, skills, and connections only you had. The time spent fulfilling this duty was as of then undetermined, and still remains so to this day."

Murana went to speak, but he silenced her with a paw, instead resuming his rehearsed speech for the camera between them. "You performed exemplary in your duties, and helped clear the streets and underground black market of several dozen of Zabökar's most wanted. Within a scant five years, you applied to be a formal police officer and were inducted into training. You rose quickly up the ranks to corporal, and were reliable enough to lead raids and stake-outs. There was a lot of trust put in you that would not have been there, had your actions not shown your quality of character after we took you in."

He set the paper down and leaned forward clasping his paws with a sigh. "And this is why what I'm going to say next is so difficult, Murana." He could tell he had her undivided attention. "What we did ten years ago was unprecedented in the history of my department. Hell, this very city! We knowingly took in a criminal and mass murderer on good faith and recommendations alone from your family, friends, and various other citizens of high regard in Zabökar, and brokered a deal for your services."

"But sir, those vile men I killed were criminals themselves!" Murana interjected, knowing this would all sound damning against her on recorded video. "They were rapists, molesters, sadists…"

"I know!" he bellowed, cowing her immediately. "We've had this discussion before, Wolford, and although they deserved every bit of what was coming to them, it did not give you the right to mete out death and judgment on the law's behalf! Back to the point, we brought you into the force where only a select few knew of your existence. Even after your formal hiring as a police officer, still few knew of what you

102

were. This was to protect yourself, your family, and this department. The last thing we needed was headlines blasted across all of Zabökar that the police were harboring a known vigilante."

"I know that…" Murana used one hind paw to scratch the itch on the calf of the other, where the bear remembered she'd been wearing a tracked ankle cuff for years.

He slapped the reports on his desk abruptly. "And now this. A former criminal turned cop going rogue for some unknown reason, initiating complete radio silence for months, only to turn up suddenly giving an anonymous tip for the location and whereabouts of over five-hundred missing mammals that the Arbiter had kitnapped over the past decade. Now pregnant with one of my officer's children and prime candidate for research for what they've done to those kids."

"Well, actually the baby was…" Murana began.

The chief raised a paw and looked away, as if disgusted. "I don't care how you got pregnant, the news stations aren't going to care much either. Do you even know the position you've put me in?" He huffed some more, his rising temper exacerbating his heat levels. "Former assassin and criminal, now cop, potentially infiltrates the police force, marries a fellow officer, gets pregnant, goes rogue, and then suddenly delivers one of the biggest stings in Zabökar history?"

"That does sound a bit farfetched when you put it all together like that, sir."

He began to rub his temples. "Bringing you to light is only going to draw more questions, and the deeper they dig, the more they'll find regarding this matter. Not just I, but quite a few other good people will be relieved of duty—including your husband for his involvement with you."

"You want me to step down, don't you?"

He looked down at her from his higher position. "We will be reporting to the news that we had an insider tip as to the location of the raid, which is not untrue. We will keep your association with the whole thing under wraps, and simply give you the severance you are due for the services you have rendered. Your husband, Anthony, will continue to keep his job and current position as you get an early, yet small retirement package."

The chief sighed. It really was an exceptional offer. Second chances like she'd been given to even join the police force didn't come that often, if at all. Now she was being offered yet another deal which seemed to boggle the mind.

Murana cracked a grin. "Sir, this isn't like you. It is too generous."

He snorted and glowered at her. "I'm not doing it out of any fondness for you." He motioned off to the camera again. "I am doing my due diligence in accordance to the letter of the law, to properly compensate a paid employee of the city under extreme and unique circumstances. As stated, I am filming this to make sure that it goes to show on the record that we dealt fairly with you, and to recognize the full scope of what you did for this department and the city despite your past."

"Of course, how stupid of me. I should have known better." It came off as very flippant, but the faintest hint of a smile formed at the edge of his mouth. He was doing his best to hold it together, but she had grown to have a sort of rapport with him over the years. Recalling that, she suddenly sat up a bit straighter. "Excuse me, sir, but I just remembered something. This…Chief Wendell person. He said you were furious with me for what happened with Buchanan and Lawrence."

"I am furious at you for that, but that is not the point of this discussion." He eyed the filming camcorder. "We will address that issue at a later date."

"But do we know who he was at all?" she persisted. "I've only seen Wendell around the station once or twice before, wearing Major rank, and I just assumed he was someone I hadn't met yet, or a recent transfer from another unit."

It was not uncommon for some higher-up praised with accolades to be transferred to them in a management role to help "fix" whatever was currently wrong with their team. They usually didn't last long—most not beyond a year. He wasn't surprised she simply didn't question when someone of higher rank brought her in for an undercover mission. It wasn't like she had much interaction with those outside of her group of like-ranked colleagues. There were probably still people she had only seen or heard of, and not met face to face.

The chief tapped a claw on the wooden desk a few times, thinking. "That matter is being investigated by others right now. Whatever results come back from that will not be passed onto you, since at this moment going forward, you no longer have a need to know. Just be content that whatever actions you did under his direction are not being reflected on you in the final report. We have enough evidence now to at least support that fact."

Murana let out a sigh, relieved. "Thank you for that. After getting your call this morning, I was extremely worried this conversation was going to turn out very different."

"That makes two of us." His expression softened. "I had my doubts about you, Wolford, yet you held true to your promise, and you did not regress back to the ways of your past. I can at least respect what you have done for this department." He gazed at her for a few moments, his eyes suddenly alighting onto her swollen belly, as if noticing it for the first time. He motioned towards it. "How are you feeling? When they found you, you were in a state of delirium and were bedridden for several weeks."

She rubbed her belly, feeling the small sets of twin feet kicking her paw in response. Smiling, she looked back up at him. "Much better, actually. It wasn't very pleasant that first week, I can tell you that much. I'm not as lethargic or sick anymore, so I feel I'm on the mend."

The chief tapped his desk again. "You up for more rounds of testing at the hospital? The city is going to pay for all the bills. Each of the kids recovered had already developed powers or abilities as a result of whatever experiments the Arbiter was doing. You are the first we've encountered that hasn't yet. You just recently had been subjected to the ray he was building. City scientists would love to study and monitor your ongoing reaction to its aftereffects."

"I'd rather not." She grimaced.

He looked down at the missive on his desk. "They are offering a cash advance of half-a-million if you were to participate. It is completely up to you and optional, but if I were you, it would put both you and Anthony in a great position financially. Just my two cents. Take it as you will."

105

"I'll think on it," she said noncommittally. He couldn't necessarily blame her hesitance. It was a lot of money, but would probably be a lot of poking, prodding, and monitoring.

He nodded. "I have nothing further for you. Enjoy your early retirement, Officer Wolford. It goes without saying that you will still be carefully watched by the law no matter where you go."

"I know." She slipped down off the chair and saluted one last time before heading out of his office to go gather her things from her dusty desk and say goodbye to any friends she had left in the department.

The chief shut the door again behind her and turned towards the camera directly. "Case #2301 on the vigilante, the Dark Flame Wolf, is closed. Subject has cooperated with all protocols and regulations and is currently now a free mammal. The current decision is not to pursue additional charges against her."

He wanted to say more, but figured that was enough for the record. Rumbling his pleasure at how the meeting went, he strode up to the camera, blocking its viewport entirely before turning off the power.

Taylor had read the stacks of books they left for her a dozen times over; relearning all the morals and lessons Llydia had to teach her. Most of the books were for young adults or children. She recalled seeing a bunch of cubs and kits beyond the glass down one hallway when Ari first escorted her on the day she met the Arbiter. That was a week ago? Maybe more? Taylor wasn't sure in this perpetual gloom of red. Time seemed to stretch for an eternity, and this less-than-stimulating selection of novels did little to pass the time.

Looking at the book she had just finished, she recalled fondly the white dragon on its cover. She remembered snuggling up to her mother, Murana, reading these books to her as a young girl as she slowly drifted off to sleep imagining she was flying upon its wings. Very captivating for a budding mind, but not nearly as captivating now she was an adult.

Setting down the book and reaching over to the lone chair to pick up a small stack of papers, she flipped through the test results. Much to her discomfort, the Arbiter continued the experiments and stressed more aspects of her body and connection with Ahya. Both were utterly spent, and they were fed up with being poked and prodded. However, true to his word, they did not gratuitously harm either her or Ahya. There were no more accidents like they had that first day.

Strangely, Ari came by early each morning to hand Taylor a copy of the lab results. When asked about why her father was being so open about what they were testing her on, she just answered to build trust. Taylor's cooperation was to be rewarded with, at the very least, finished reports on what they had discovered about her unique body chemistry.

In her paws now was the results of her blood drawing. It had taken a long time for them to get back with her on it. Sifting through the pages, Ahya casually "looking" at them with her despite not being able to see herself, Taylor kept coming back to a single sheet. They had uncovered two strands of DNA inside Taylor's genetic makeup, though key individual chromosomes were vastly different. She couldn't quite figure it out, but the thought of having two sets of genes fascinated her.

Other, less important aspects to her were how her digestive system worked. She shivered at the memory. They had her drink a revolting solution that tasted like piss, but which helped them track movement within her body. They were still unsure how, but material dissolved within Ahya did not funnel through the base of her tail into her stomach, but rather seemed to magically transport directly into her belly. A curious oddity.

On the bright side through these feeding tests, they had acknowledged her complaint for better food and began supplying more fruits and vegetables to avoid the mess she provided them on the first day. However, be it that it was harder for them to gather such food down here underground or what, they did not give her much to eat each time. Taylor was in a constant state of hunger, but she was at least getting fed enough to maintain some semblance of health and sanity— an improvement over her food situation back in Palaveve, where she had to actually steal to survive.

She could feel his footsteps long before she could hear them. She bolted upright, sitting at the edge of her bed waiting for him to appear. This was unusual; the Arbiter did not pay her visits, and in fact was only visible when observing her testing. Something must have come up—or worse, maybe they were done with her now and he was coming to personally end her life? Her heart was beating fast as the booming thuds grew louder. Even Ahya was coiled around her shoulders, poised to reach out and attack if need be.

The sliding shriek of the door heralded the looming figure of the Arbiter. His wide shell was larger than the frame he was to fit through, but fit through he did. Taylor's toes curled as the scraping of his shell against the metal siding upon entering the now cramped room, filled with his presence, set off her nerves. She released her grip on the edge of her bed as she noticed Ari following in right behind him, her red eye ever fixed onto Taylor's position.

"Yes?" Taylor asked hesitantly.

"Testing is complete. We need to analyze the data now," Ari informed, her arms folded.

"What does that mean for me? Are you done with me? What's going to happen with the information you've gathered?" Taylor had a deep-seated dread for what they'd use it for.

The Arbiter regarded her silently, remaining as stoic as ever. At last, he spoke to break the alarming silence. "You are a far more unique specimen than any I've ever encountered, Taylor. You were one not of my design, yet were indirectly caused by it. A true success story far surpassing anything I could have hoped to achieve. Not even my false imitation of you, Rakkis, has come close."

"Um…thanks?" Taylor wasn't exactly sure how to respond to this odd praise.

"You are probably wondering why I am being forthright with you." He settled back onto his shell, using it almost like a seat. "A valid question. You see, your mother was a very interesting individual." He put his hand up to stay her burning questions. "I did not know her personally, but she was an unfortunate bystander to my Project Iapyx. A project designed to create super soldiers. We chose children as subjects

108

for the magic infusions rather than adults; adults are set in their ways, and are less malleable."

He faintly smiled at his allusion. "Did we go about unsavory ways to obtain them and subject them to our project? Yes, I will not deny that. I was a different person then, but my goal remains the same, and is why now, nearly twenty years later, I still persist in recruiting young talent to undergo testing to see if they are eligible to be infused with magic to develop powers."

"Why go through all this? What is the point?" Taylor didn't understand. She remembered hearing flashes of an impending war and that being the reason for all this, but she still didn't have the full story.

"You see, my daughter and I are not from around here." He gestured to them both. "You might expect me to be from the Vassal State of Hordos, where most of our kind in the northern countries reside, but I actually have traveled far from the southern empire of Talkar. There resides several hosts of nations filled with reptiles that have no love for mammals. Slighted from a wrong done to their people from an age past, they have been slowly building up over the centuries a formidable army to come raze the world of mammals to the ground."

"Centuries?" Taylor was incredulous. "Seems like an awfully long time to stage an attack when they could have just crossed the sea to get here." She vaguely recalled her geography from school to know that much.

"Us reptiles are deathly susceptible to the cold waters of the Goyanna. Previous ventures through those turbulent waters have been…costly." He shrugged, not seeming to care much for the loss of his brethren. "So, with the technology of true flight locked away by the avians and unattainable in the northern lands of Dirina, they instead constructed a more costly, yet far more efficient army to cover the stretch of land between us. You have already encountered such expensive creations: the behemoths."

Although Taylor was horrified at the prospect of a huge army like that, she couldn't help but ask, "Why do you care about us mammals so much then?"

The Arbiter sighed, looking over at his daughter. She chose not to return the gaze. "It was a promise made to my late wife. She was descended from a family of sympathizers to your plight, and wanted to ensure peace between our people. She wanted to stop the war from happening, or at least level the playing field so that neither side could win."

"And that's why you wanted to build up these empowered mammals." Taylor was putting the pieces of the puzzle together.

The Arbiter nodded. "I came to Zabökar with idealistic views and hopes, quickly dashed upon the High Council's hindpaws. I had no reason to believe they would betray me that first time. I was at a loss for what to do, but I discovered the common folk in your country had free access to the Script—something not quite accessible in Talkar. So I consulted my Script, which led me to my research. Through it, '*a being not of my own ambition would be born with the power of two*'."

"The power of two?" Taylor cocked her head to the side.

Ari stepped forward. "We are still unclear about what that means, but we believe the Script is referring to you. It could mean you having the ability to manifest more than one power, or it could mean the two strands of DNA inside you, or it could mean that you seem to be of two people in one body if we count Ahya, or it could mean any number of other things. What is clear is that you were born with your powers, not acquired directly from any one experiment through Project Iapyx."

"But wait…" Taylor's mind was getting confused. Even Ahya was furrowing her tail tip, as if thinking hard as well. "I don't have a Script. Sherriff Watters in Palaveve confirmed that for me. I'm a person without a Script. I was never born with one. How come you can find mentions of me in yours?"

"I no longer have a working Script," Ari explained. "Mine went off the rails the moment I developed powers. Mine ended the moment my father infused magic into me—or rather, it keeps predicting my death every damn day."

The Arbiter shifted, his shell seat seemingly not as comfortable anymore. "People with powers seem to be beyond the Script's influence and thus can sway it to varying degrees. You were born with the magic, not given it. Any mentions of you are only traces of your existence in others and their Scripts, at intersections where their lives cross with yours, and deviate from it through your actions."

110

"So what makes me so special then? Does the Script say anything about that?" Taylor pressed.

"Only that you will be the key to accomplishing my goals." He clapped his knee softly with a hand. "Which brings me to the reason I'm here in this room with you. You see, the High Council are a stubborn bunch, especially their elder, Barateon. They will no longer listen to reason, let alone coming from me. They declared my operations immoral and shut me down. They did not heed my warnings of the pending menace from my people."

"What makes you think they'll listen to me?" Taylor looked from the Arbiter to Ari. "I mean, that is what I'm figuring you want me for—to talk to them?"

"They won't listen to you. Not yet." He motioned to Ari. "You and my daughter will go up to Zabökar and research a growing problem that is happening right under the High Council's noses. There is a rising cult in recent years called 'power-eaters'. More and more people are disappearing, especially powered mammals. We're still tracking who escaped my labs twenty years ago. It is becoming quite the troublesome problem for the council."

"If we can discover and find out where these power-eaters operate out of, then we can strike them where it hurts." Ari flashed her crooked smile.

"But don't you have spies?" Taylor looked back and forth between the two. "You know, people who go out and find this information for you? Isn't anyone doing this research for you?"

"We are a science and development operation, not an intelligence one. We neither have the resources nor funds to split our objectives into two to manage both. I must forge ahead with what I must do to protect my interests. I'm merely doing this side mission of notifying the counsel as a courtesy to my late wife's dying wish." The Arbiter rose back up to his feet and indicated his daughter. "Ariana here has told me that you dislike unnecessary death. Doing this would most certainly prevent much future death."

"Which is why defeating the power-eaters at their heart would be so beneficial to our cause with the High Council." Ari's eyes were alight with passion.

The Arbiter nodded. "And using their defeat as leverage, you alone can prove the case that my operation is a success, and is necessary for the continued protection of Zabökar. The barrier they keep around the city will not be enough for the behemoths just beyond the mountains. They will raze Zabökar to the ground if we do not supply the means to fight back, or give the order now to evacuate the city. We need their funding, full support, and resources to have this entire project succeed. It has taken twenty long years to get back to where we were before all our previous research was lost," he finished, leaning back now that his plea to Taylor was finished.

"That is why time is of the essence." Ari uncrossed her arms and stood tall, pointing at Taylor. "You and I need to follow the trail of bodies that'll lead us straight to them. The sooner we get this done, the better. There is no telling when a behemoth will finally make it over the Grune Mountains."

"Do you understand what is at stake here and why we need you?" The Arbiter's eyes bore holes into Taylor's. He was not going to accept silence.

"I understand… I just don't think I'm up to the task," Taylor admitted.

"Do not concern yourself with success." The Arbiter let loose a rare grin. "Ariana here will be by your side to guide you and ensure you will not fail. I have trained her well. She knows how to navigate her way through difficult situations."

"I did bring you in with your cooperation and willingness, after all." Ari looked smug.

"After forcing Trevor to help destroy an entire city full of people," Taylor reminded, souring Ari's expression. "Yeah, don't think I have forgotten that 'small' detail. Just because I was willing, does not mean I was okay with it." As if getting a sudden thought, she turned to the Arbiter. "Where is Trevor anyway? He said he made a promise to my mother to bring me home to her. I should think he would want to be with us to make good on—"

He cut her off abruptly. "He has been given his due payment for services rendered and released topside into Zabökar. I will be taking over his promise to unite you and your mother together, but only after you resolve this power-eater problem for us."

Taylor was a bit miffed at having her goal tossed aside and delayed like that, but she knew she had no pull right now between these two. "And what makes you think us two can handle the power-eaters by ourselves? We're just two people, and it sounds like dozens of them."

"Hundreds," Ari corrected.

Taylor pointed at her. "My point exactly! And some even have powers like us? How the heck are we supposed to compete with that?"

"Inferior powers." The Arbiter snapped his fingers. "It is not a direct infusion like I have done, but rather an osmosis through the body by eating their victims. They are nowhere near as powerful as you two together. I am confident you will succeed."

"And what about Rakkis?" Taylor stood up when the Arbiter made a motion to get up and leave. "Wouldn't he be useful on this mission?"

Ari looked over at her father, clearly uncomfortable. The Arbiter did not return the look, instead staring at Taylor. "He has his own mission to accomplish. You have yours. It is best that you stay in your lane. Ariana here will see that all your needs are met, but do remember your place here and the job we have for you. This isn't just about you; this is about all the people in Zabökar. Now, you two ladies have a pleasant morning."

His task done here, he gave them both a brief nod before setting Taylor's hairs on end with his screeching out the doorframe. His lumbering gait could be heard all the way down the hallways for minutes. Shivering, she turned to Ari, who was staring at her with an odd look.

"So we're going to leave now?" Taylor broke the silence first.

"We need to shower first," Ari riposted.

"We?"

"Yes, you're all filthy from this week's worth of testing, and I can smell you from here." Ari gave a sniff to her armpits. "I probably need one as well, including a change of clothes. Come on, follow me. We managed to set up communal showers down here."

Taylor looked down at herself. She was still stuck with the clothes she had left Cheribaum with. She was high time due to be getting a new set. She waved a paw off towards the hallway. "Lead on then."

Ari glanced around the room. "Anything you wish to keep from here?"

It took Taylor a few moments to decide, but in the end, she grabbed her pine tree necklace and the small kitsune plush that she received from Mrs. Hircus in Palaveve. "Nothing else is really important to me."

Ari snorted as she looked at the articles Taylor picked. "Figures. Let's go then."

"You wouldn't understand." Taylor was upset that Ari would think so poorly of her belongings. She didn't have much, but it was all that was left of those she cared about. She didn't even have anything to remind herself of Pine and Mitchell, being as invisible as they were.

"Oh no, I get it." Ari swept out into the red hall of metal, knowing Taylor would follow. "People latch onto things that are sentimental to them. I grew up not having anything important enough to mean anything to me. It's so I can better leave everything behind and move on if need be. Sentimentality holds you back from your true potential."

"That's just sad." This remark got Ari's red eye to swivel back to glare at Taylor, but she didn't care. It wasn't like Ari was going to hurt her, given what her father just commanded her to do. "I'm starting to wonder what happened in your family to make you so loveless."

"Leave my family out of this." Ari grit her teeth.

"Then leave my 'foolish' sentimentalities alone." Taylor was being cheeky, she knew, but she didn't care for her feelings being dismissed like this. "I'm allowed to like and hold onto what I want, alright? You're not the one who has lost their entire family and been on the run without anyone to love them. At least you have your father still left to care for you!"

"Right, my father." Ari was being cryptic, but Taylor could tell she was struggling with the words she said. "He's an interesting teacher and father figure. He's never not been there for me."

"But he's never been there 'for' you," Taylor attempted to clarify.

"I never said that." Ari glanced back, irritated. "And stop twisting my words. Why do you care so much about what relationship I have with my family?"

Taylor shrugged, rounding a corner tightly along with Ari. "After seeing how insistent and sincere you were with fulfilling your father's order to bring me in, I figured there must be something special there between you two to have you willingly destroy an entire city and manipulate two sets of bounty hunters against each other just to get at me."

"So this is what it all comes down to, huh?" Ari stopped gruffly, turning to face her. "Like I gathered from Trevor when he got you out of Palaveve, I had little to no choice but to offer up Howlgrav as a sacrifice to use as a distraction to get that behemoth off our butts so we could escape with you safely. Howlgrav's finest wasn't going to give us any opportunity to get out of there alive. At the least, I saved Cheribaum from destruction, like you wanted. That has to count for something!"

"It did, up until the point I discovered Howlgrav going up in flames." Taylor stared back defiantly. "I know I'll never be able to avenge those people who died. I'm just one person, lost in the mix of everyone else who is after me. As long as I exist, someone will be after me. My mother tried to warn me about this when I was young and we were hiding, moving from place to place, but I didn't listen to her." Taylor broke eye contact and looked at the floor, ashamed to admit it. She wished she could have that time back when she was with her mom, but she made the choice to run away and escape, and now she had to deal with the consequences.

Ari's expression softened slightly as she mulled it over. "I won't pretend that I regret my actions. It was a means to an end, and failure to my father was not an option. However, what he is saying is correct. There is more at stake here than just you or me. If you're so upset about how many died to that behemoth, just know there are many more like them from Talkar, and they won't stop just because we want them to. So if you want to really solve the core issue here, which is the coming war, then you need to put what I did to get you here aside and focus on the task at hand."

"You're horrible when you make sense." Taylor puffed a lock of hair out of her eyes.

"Thank you." Ari smirked and resumed their walk.

It was only a few minutes, but they finally came upon a smaller corridor, almost like they stopped building it midway and just hastily put up a wall at the end of it. On the left and right sides were haphazardly placed portals leading into larger rooms. A small blue-green glow emanated from within, indicating a fresh change in scenery at least.

"The young cubs we've recruited get their own. Those are nicer." Ari ushered Taylor inside, batting Ayha away as she tried to bump into Ari purposefully. "We've rerouted the city water supply to come in through here on the way back from their destinations and greased some paws to turn the other cheek to it. It's a bit dirtier than freshly filtered water straight from the factories, but it is better than nothing, and it's not as stringently tracked."

"Smart, I guess." Taylor looked around.

It wasn't much. The sheet metal flooring was actually replaced with tile in here. As Ari had alluded to, it did look shoddy and hastily put together. Some sections didn't even have tile, and they just filled in extra grout to make up. The different colored lights were generated from hanging lamps with wires corded along the ceiling to some holes back out in the hallway. The walls were adorned with dismal showerheads aligned in a row down one side of the open bay showering area.

"So I'll take this one and you take the other?" Taylor looked over to the other portal opening leading into the second shower bay.

Ari shook her head. "Nope. That's the males. I'm going in with you."

"Wait…at the same time?" Taylor was a bit nervous now. She couldn't recall showering with anyone else for a long time. During the rare moments she had time to bathe, she was usually alone in the privacy of either a bathroom, or in the woods at a river when she was on the run.

"What, you've not showered with other girls before?" Ari mocked, pushing Taylor in before her towards one of the showerheads. "My father taught me that lesson early. Privacy is an illusion. One must always be ready to act on a moment's notice, even at your most vulnerable."

"Sounds like a pretty twisted upbringing." Taylor clutched her shirt, almost not wanting to undress now.

"It's a realistic one." Ari began to unbuckle her corduroy pants. "Let me guess, your mother was protective and denied you doing a lot of things because of Ahya?"

"She wasn't overly protective...not at first." Taylor flushed and looked away as Ari pulled her pants down and flicked them off to the side.

"Oh, please." Ari rolled her eyes, walking over to one of the water knobs and turning it on, the water splashing down in a torrential downpour that indicated a broken head. "We're both female here. Just get undressed and get clean. We got a job to do." After a moment, she probed to get Taylor to respond. "So, your mother?"

"Right." Ignoring the shelled reptile just feet away, Taylor began to undress, setting aside her belongings well out of water range. "She actually tried to give me a normal life growing up. In fact, the last time I recall showering together with other girls like this was back when I was in middle school. I was one of the cheerleaders of the school tramball team."

Ari's brow raised as she looked back over at the now-nude wolf, the stripe of red going down her spine on full display. "Seriously? You were a cheerleader? Why do I find that hard to believe?"

"Hey, it's true! I was. Ahhh!" Taylor jumped back as she turned the water knob and realized it was the blisteringly hot one. After mixing the two temperatures to something she liked, she got back into the water stream. "I couldn't exactly try out for sports directly, since Ahya would get too excited and competitive and try to reveal herself and eat the ball."

"Competitive? Ahya?" Ari chuckled. "Now that I can see."

Ahya "looked" at Ari, as if offended. She turned back towards the wall, acting like she didn't want to even look at Ari anymore. Taylor just petted her gently, bringing her into the water to let it run through her tail fur. "Strangely enough, she is. With cheerleading she didn't have much to do on the sidelines, and so my mother gave me some coping skills to keep her mouth hidden while I cheered on the team."

Ari turned and squirted the liquid soap bottle down the back of her shell, the suds rippling down her backside with the water. "And nobody noticed that you had a tailmaw at all this entire time?"

"Some of my cheerleader friends did. In fact, my best friend back then, Sarah, knew. She was one of the first ones to find out." Taylor began to get lost in thought, her paws rubbing the soap through her fur by rote memory. "They were all friendly to me for the most part, but they kept their distance. Sure, we all showered together and went to the games together to cheer, but I was always alone in the corner by myself showering. I was always the one at the back of the bus when everyone else was up front talking and having a good time. Sarah was really the only one who went out of her way to get to know me."

"What happened to Sarah?" Ari cleaned between her thighs.

"Ahya ate her."

Ari stopped and looked up at the wolf. Ahya seemed to be distant, as if not wanting to be part of this conversation. Taylor had stopped soaping herself down and was just standing facing the wall. "Are you alright?"

"I don't think I can do it." Taylor whispered. "I don't think I can face my mother again. Ever since then, our lives have been different. Mother was different." Taylor breathed in a ragged sigh. "I always felt like she judged me after that. All the hard times we experienced, hiding and running from place to place. I saw the toll it took on her body, and I couldn't bear the look in her eyes when she looked at me."

Ari finished up and turned off her water, turning around and looking directly at the still-bathing wolf, now unmoving. "Shitty things happen to everyone, Taylor. I never knew my mother, since she died before I was born. I never had friends like you growing up either. I've experienced my fair share of hardships and death. It never gets any easier, but that doesn't mean you need to stop living on the account of other people's deaths. It's just a natural part of life. Even people who believe in the Script understand that."

Taylor curled her lip. "Natalia said Sarah was to die that day. It was in her Script. I was the one that caused it. I hate the fact the Script said I'd be the reason my friend died."

"If not by you, then by someone or something else. The Script ultimately gets what it wants. However, you and I and every other person with powers can affect the Script."

That broke Taylor from her sad musings. Continuing to wash the soap out from her fur, she looked back. "Death by the Script or death by us, what is the difference? My influence certainly didn't help stop Sarah's death."

This brought a chilling leer to Ari's maw. "The difference is when. The Script could have them dying years from now, but you can push up the timeline a bit and kill them today. The Script will account for that and erase everything that would have happened afterwards. You were probably too young to realize the change you caused in Sarah's Script."

"Looked up someone's Script after they died, did you?" She caught on to Ari's explanation.

"I did." Ari looked proud of this fact. She pointed at Taylor. "However, you... You are much different. I'd be eager to see what has happened to Fey's Script after you brought him back from the dead. Nobody else has been able to do that."

"Or Mikhail's Script..." Taylor said softly to herself.

Would Sarah's Script still have ended that day by someone else if she hadn't been there to fulfill Sarah's death or was what Ari said true and that the Script accounted for her early death and Taylor had ended her life far earlier than it would have been? Is that why Natalia discovered Sarah's Script predicting her death, because Taylor pushed up the timeline?

Taylor finished up with her shower and turned off the water. She turned to see Ari putting on a new set of pants, now blue in color. She noticed a sizeable chunk of her right calf was nothing but a metal hunk separated into platelets that bended and folded as she moved her leg. It was shaped to look normal, but it was clearly artificial, and stretched from the inside of her knee to the bottom of her heel. It encompassed the entire backside and covered all the way up to just before the shinbone.

"And that?" Taylor pointed at it. "What happened there?"

Ari looked down with her good eye at the long forgotten injury. "That? That was failure."

6.

TERRIFIED

The camera view was all shaky, as if being held by paw. They were rushing down a hospital corridor, flush with sterile white light and fake plants hanging out of small indents in the walls, trying to help liven up a drab atmosphere. Murana and Anthony were paw in paw, sprinting down as they rushed up to the receptionist. The moose seemed flustered at the two wolves suddenly encroaching on her personal space through her tiny window.

"Excuse me, may I help you?" she asked in a slightly condescending tone.

Irritated, but not to be cast aside, Murana impressed upon the clerk the size of her belly. "I don't know what is going on, but I think I may be having a miscarriage or going into labor!" She winced, the cramping escalating to a fever pitch, requiring Anthony to hold her aloft lest she collapse to the floor right there.

"Can you please see if there's a doctor available to see her?" Anthony did his best to keep his anger in check, but it seemed the moose was not in any hurry to oblige their requests.

"One moment please." She picked up her phone and dialed a number, raising the receiver to her ear. "Yes, I have a male and female wolf here with a code 33. Requesting immediate attention and wheelchair for transport."

"Thank you very much." Anthony forced a smile as the moose just inclined her head and hung up the phone. He assisted Murana to the nearest waiting chair amongst all the onlookers in the room staring at them. "She wasn't exactly friendly, was she?" he muttered under his breath.

The camera-mammal filming this was getting abnormally close to her as she struggled to sit upright amidst the clenching pain stabbing her insides, making her gasp. "Can you please get him the hell away from me?" she roared, trying to swat away the buzzing muntjac who was capturing all this.

"Hey! I'm just trying to do my job!" he barked as he skittered back from the snarling growl of Anthony.

"Well, you could do it from a few paces back!" he warned the tawny deer.

"Geez, fine." He smoothed down his plaid button-up shirt before taking a seat opposite Murana, settling his camera phone to be facing the two so he could still record the whole event. He noticed a small Tamias chipmunk staring at him from beside his mother two seats down. He waved at the tiny duo. "Hello there." She just put her arm protectively around her son and drew him in closer.

"Ugh, why did we ever agree to this?" Murana moaned, gesturing dismissively at the muntjac menace.

Anthony regarded him as the deer was adjusting his plastic tip covers on both his horns. "Because the money offered was too good?"

She scrunched her face like she was attempting to will away a migraine. "Right. And if we refuse any more documentation and experimentation, we'd have to pay back the entire half-million. What was I thinking?"

Anthony massaged her shoulders and gave her tender licks on the neck to soothe her nerves. "It's for the future of our cubs, hun. We've already set up some great college funds for both our boys with it, and if anything, this research they're doing on you could help with any problems or complications that could arise from whatever the Arbiter did to you."

"You mean like what's happening now?" Murana whined, another pain knifing through her stomach.

"We don't know that yet. For all we know, it could just be some routine complication with the pregnancy," Anthony offered. He was no good in these sorts of situations, but he did his best to comfort her.

She shook her head violently. "No, any complication is not routine. This is something different. It feels…worse somehow."

The emergency room swinging doors slammed open as two nurses, one pushing a wheelchair, stormed in. They locked eyes on

Murana and whisked to her side. They helped lift her tiny bulk and straining belly onto the wheelchair before slapping the foot rests down for her to rest her weary hind paws.

They were heading back towards the double doors when the nurse pushing Murana noticed the muntjac following them with the smart phone. "Excuse me, sir. Who are you? You are not allowed to be filming anything in this hospital."

"Oh, right!" He beamed, flipping out an identification card and a letter of directive from the High Council. "I am on orders to document and catalogue all events regarding Murana Wolford by her acceptance and admission of this contract signed by the High Council."

The nurse brayed at him before clopping off with Murana in tow. The second nurse put a paw up. "I'm sorry, but only close family members are allowed beyond this point. You will just have to wait here."

"Mr. Wolford!" the muntjac cried out. "Can you at least take this phone and continue to record on my behalf?" Upon seeing Anthony's smirk that he wasn't going to oblige, he got serious. "It is either that or I tell the council you're willing to pay back everything."

That got him to comply. Anthony stomped over to the muntjac, ensuring his taller stature and predatory nature impressed all the potential fear he could muster upon the smaller deer. Surprisingly, the muntjac knew his rights and where he stood in terms of leverage, and stood firm against the imposing wolf. Grumbling, Anthony snatched the phone out of the deer's hoof and stalked after Murana who was already halfway down the hall with the nurse.

In short order, they had Murana propped up in a raised hospital bed with legs splayed in stirrups. The equine nurse was already wheeling around a clunky sounding device with monitor that they'd be using to conduct an ultrasound. She was prepping a small razor and trimmed some of the fur off Murana's belly, revealing the three faded, jagged scars beneath that were from a time long past.

The doctor, a small bobcat that was the on-call OBGYN for the night, stepped in. He was pulling tight some surgical gloves, snaking a hindpaw around a rolling chair before sitting comfortably close to the spread legs of Murana.

He smiled brightly to put her at ease. "Mrs. Wolford, I have already relayed a message to your current gynecologist, and he will want to follow up with you tomorrow after we are done here. All findings will be forwarded to him tonight so you two can discuss where to proceed, alright?"

Murana just nodded nervously. This was her first pregnancy; both of their sons were adopted. This was all new territory for her, and she did know what to expect. She had faced down hardened criminals and decimated underground crime rings, yet this daunting aspect of life terrified her.

The bobcat slipped two fingers into her, feeling out her cervix. After a few moments of fishing around, causing Murana to wince, he pulled out his paw and took off the gloves before tossing them casually into the nearby receptacle. "You aren't dilated at all, so you're not experiencing labor. So let's see what's going on with your cubs."

He motioned for the nurse to apply the gel and give him the sonar probe. Murana inhaled and squeezed Anthony's paw as the gel was applied to her belly, no doubt quite cold. The doctor wasted no time as he propped the probe onto her belly and began moving it in circular motions, his eyes ever on the screen beside them.

He pointed at the right edge. "That's the tail and one of the legs." Anthony struggled to maintained control of the camera, pointing it at the screen while simultaneously holding Murana's paw.

The bobcat's brow furrowed as he saw the limbs of the fetus fidgeting in a very erratic and distraught manner. He pushed the probe a bit more to the left, where his mouth dropped open. Then scan revealed another tail, but it wasn't attached to a full body. It too was shaking fitfully.

"Where is the other one?" Tears began to form at the edges of Murana's eyes.

"The other what?" he asked.

"There were two cubs in there. Where's the second?" Anthony was just as anxious as his wife.

The doctor was a bit unsure of how to respond. He pointed at the two separate objects. "Well, they're both right here, but I'm not entirely sure what I'm seeing with this second one."

125

Murana began to weep. "What is happening to my babies?"

Taylor simply stared at the device handed to her. She knew it was a cell phone, but it seemed so foreign to her that she at first didn't know what to do with it. She fumbled with the plain depression on the bottom of the screen and managed to turn it on. It had no password or lock to it yet, and brought her to a dizzying array of icons.

She must have been obvious staring at it, because Ari turned to her as they got out of the elevator and mocked her. "Please tell me you know how to work one of these things."

She shook her head. "No. My mother never really let me have stuff like this growing up. Guess you could say I was sheltered that way. I only had access to the internet during times I needed to do research for a project or paper for school."

Ari nearly facepalmed as she shuttled Taylor out of the elevator and into the maintenance tunnel beneath the city streets. "What about when you left her? When you were in the band?" she offered. "Surely you got into devices like this?"

Taylor shook her head again, finding it hard to walk straight alongside Ari and focus on the mesmerizing screen in her paws. "I never really had a need for a phone. My only friends...or rather friend, was in my band, and I usually saw her several times a week. Any other entertainment I needed was on the TV."

Ari looked irritated that she would need to play the role of teacher for this. "Fine. I'll show you how to operate it when we get to where we're going."

"What am I going to be using it for anyway?" Taylor finally figured out how to turn the screen off and plopped the phone into her pants pocket.

"In case of emergencies, or if we get separated and I need to find you or contact you. That's just for starters," Ari informed, firmly gripping Taylor's arm to redirect her to their new route towards the upper levels where the subways were.

The dank, featureless tunnels overgrown with a subterranean version of moss gave way to sleeker side plating that was a far cry from the concrete origins where they started their journey from the elevator. They could hear the wind and rumbling of the trains above them. It wasn't long before they reached a ladder leading up to a hatch that took them to an underused janitor closet, adjacent to one of the subway platforms.

Hauling herself up from the floor opening, Taylor looked around the cramped closet littered with cabinet shelves and cleaning equipment that hadn't seen action in years, if the spider webs could be trusted. Taylor kept Ahya close as they navigated a path through to the door leading out into the more public space of the railway station.

"This seems like an odd way to get down into the sewers." Taylor glanced back at the floor panel that Ari had replaced, its outline and the visible handle nestled into its groove the only indication there was anything underneath.

Ari popped the door open an inch to verify if it was clear to step out. She gazed back at Taylor, who seemed to be attempting to peek over her shell to check as well. "Zabökar wasn't always the city it was now. There have been several iterations built on top of each other over the centuries. My father and everyone else are residing in the earliest version of the city now—a place not even the High Council is aware exists anymore."

"Was it always that dingy and barebones?" Taylor wasn't really impressed with what she saw during her stay down there.

Ari shook her head and motioned for Taylor to follow her out. There were very few people on the platform this early in the morning. Several mammals were waiting patiently just before the yellow line, warning them not to get closer to the tracks. One was passed out on the bench nearest them—homeless, most likely—his sleep uninterrupted by the glaring neon marquee advertising above him.

Shutting the door behind them both, Ari surveyed up and down the platform before setting off towards the stairs leading upwards. "I'd imagine not," she responded, continuing the conversation. "If anything, they probably reinforced the support structures to handle the weight of the buildings on top. That tends to have the side effect of destroying

127

whatever charm the previous version of the city had. For example, the entire section beneath the Caelesti Spire in the center of Zabökar is completely closed off and probably full of supports for the towers above."

"It's like the only version of the city that exists is the now, and the past doesn't matter." Taylor looked around them as they rode the escalator up to the street.

Ari studied her curiously. "That's strangely poetic."

Taylor shrugged, continuing to soak in her surroundings. Maybe she just ignored it all growing up in Zabökar when she was younger, but now that she had returned after a few years abroad, it was like her eyes were opened. Around them, rising up on the escalator, were dozens of screens and holographic advertisements—some benign, while others shockingly graphic in the products or services they were trying to sell. There were even several flashes of light that stung the eyes as they moved, but nothing seemed to change about the nature of the images.

"You may want to pull up your hood." Ari gestured to Taylor's sweater.

Although Taylor did as she was told, tucking the bangs of her hair into her hoodie and drawing the strings taut, she regarded the brazen reptile with her head bare and her shell barely covered with an extra-large faux leather jacket. "And what about you? You seem awfully suspicious in a city full of mammals."

Ari snorted and stared down a couple of deer as they mewled and skittered off at the sight of her. "True, but I'm not the one with the criminal record and documented deaths to my name on social media right now. Besides, there are still a few reptiles around in the northern countries, as my father said."

Taylor's face soured at the reminder. After the events at Howlgrav, she was most likely all over the news in local regions. Who knew if those headlines made it all the way back here to Zabökar? Tucking her paws angrily into her front connected pocket on her sweater, she glumly stomped along after Ari.

The burgeoning morning commute seemed to be in full force the moment they hit topside. The noise of the bustling hover cars and busses around them roared over the soft jingling from the rays of light high above coming off what Taylor now learned was the Caelesti Spire. Hundreds of mammals were engrossed on their phones or tablets as they bustled down the sidewalks. The few that bumped into them gave them a brief, scared look before darting away, giving them both a wide berth.

Taylor noticed they were stopping just before what looked to be a large hospital. She gazed up to the dizzying heights of its spired peaks. "Why did we stop?"

Ari tapped her red iris. "Gathering some information for our mission from their databanks here. That's all."

Taylor stood waiting next to Ari while she gathered her "required" information. The honking of horns and the chittering of the plethora of species around them blurred together into a loud hum that made it hard for Taylor to filter or ignore. She saw Ari looking at her out of the corner of her eye as her ears twitched this way and that through the holes in her hoodie. Her annoyance at the continuous tumult was growing.

It appeared Ari noticed something troubling just a few meters away and lightly slapped her arm, gesturing her to follow. She took Taylor a few streets away from the main hub of traffic where they had started. The traffic was now a dull roar rather than an acute one. The sheltered boughs of the trees arching over the street seemed to provide a nice sound barrier from the traffic above.

Walking more slowly down the residential sidewalk, Ari smirked at Taylor's agony. "The sounds of the city getting to be too much for you?"

Taylor dragged Ahya back as she began to "investigate" a planted tree near them. "I just need to get used to it again, that's all."

Ari chuckled. "I understand. It's probably similar to my first experiences with this eye."

Taylor just looked away from her. "So, where are we going to first?"

Ari's cybernetic red iris contracted while it scanned for information. "We're actually a good distance away. A butcher from a local deli recently went missing. It's on the other side of downtown near the Furon River. We can start there since it is fresh, and look for clues on where the power-eaters might have dragged the body off to."

The mention of the deli got Taylor's stomach growling, and Ahya agitated. "That reminds me, I'm actually starving. Can we pick up a bite to eat before we get there?"

Ari shook her head, not deigning to look at Taylor as she continued to walk down the street. "We don't have time. This disappearance just happened yesterday. The sooner we act on the lead now, the better our chances of tracking down our targets."

"Can't you just do your internet research using your eye thingy and we just not walk all over the city?" Taylor pointed to Ari's cybernetic implant.

Ari rolled her eyes. "I could, but second-hand research does not replace being in person to catch clues that others may have missed."

"Fine, whatever." Taylor mumbled, defeated.

Taylor pouted some more. How easy would it be to just start running and get lost in this big city? Ari would give chase and use her powers to get her back, of that Taylor had no doubt. The reptile made no exceptions, and was not above destroying life and property to get what she wanted—that much was clear when they first met in Howlgrav.

That thought caused Taylor to remember something else. "Hey, what happened to Trevor? Is he getting tasked to do something else for your dad like everyone else?"

The snark in Taylor's voice caused Ari to curl her lip. "He's lucky he didn't disappear behind a locked door, never to be seen again, after his failures with you. The only reason he was let loose at all was because of the good word I put in for his part in helping me bring you in."

"So just like that. No longer useful, tossed aside when at the first opportunity," Taylor mused. "Just like what'll happen to me most likely when I convince this High Council of your dad's master plan. Just like you when you've outlived your usefulness."

This caused Ari to stop abruptly and spin around, stabbing a clawed finger in Taylor's face. "My father is not like that! He keeps his word, just like he taught me to keep mine."

Ahya looked unimpressed at this. Taylor folded her arms and coolly returned the glare. "And you did a fine job of that as far as I experienced back in Cheribaum, keeping one town safe that I wanted at the expense of another." Ari's eyes narrowed at this, but Taylor didn't care. "However, I found it quite interesting how quickly your dad dropped you the moment he discovered I had been handed to Howlgrav's finest. It couldn't have been a day or so without communication that he sent Rakkis after me. I call that being tossed aside. He could do so again."

"You wouldn't understand our relationship." Ari grinded her teeth. "He most likely sent out Rakkis to ensure my safety and to help bring you in."

"I understand now after the fact that my own mother gave up a lot for me." Taylor recalled her time with Murana, never appreciating the fact she was sheltering her from people who would want to use her for whatever abilities she had. "Did you know the night I was kitnapped from here, I had thought about returning home to my mom?"

"You were homesick."

"I was…a bit." Taylor shrugged. "But my time away has made me realize how good I had it. Maybe some time apart from your dad will make you see things differently than you do now."

"I don't think so," Ari retorted, turning to look ahead to their next destination, her red eye scanning for the most optimal path. "In all my years knowing him, my father has never once changed. He has always been stern, but fair with me. He would always allow me to prove myself if I asked, like going out to fetch you."

"Prove yourself?" Taylor scoffed. "I never once had to do that with my mom. That's not love, and that's not being fair either." Taylor pointed to Ari's metal replacement leg. "Or that." She shifted up to point at Ari's eye. "The one thing I learned from being hunted by all of you this past month is that I've been lying to myself about a lot of things." Taylor looked up briefly at some honking cars, just visible through the canopy. "Trying to hide the truth from myself to, what I had thought, better protect myself from the cruel nature of this world."

"And what truths are those?" Ari smirked, seemingly humoring Taylor with this line of talk.

"That I can't keep running away from my problems. That I can't fabricate emotional crutches like Pine and Mitchell to ignore the realities of my situation." Taylor looked down at the ground, feeling a bit shameful. "I know I'm a freak to the eyes of many. I know I have powers that make me a target. I know I'm truly alone in this world." She turned her eyes back up to Ari. "That's one of the reasons why I chose to come back to Zabökar with you: to find my family, or what's left of it. To find answers to the questions I've been running away from."

Ari snorted. "That makes two of us then. I'm a freak in a land of mammals. I've learned to deal with it. We'll find your family when we've completed our mission, not before. We're wasting time, so if you're done reminiscing about your past and poking into mine, we need to move."

Ari's last line triggered something with Taylor. "Wait, if you stand out among all the mammals and you're known as the Arbiter's daughter, wouldn't the High Council recognize—"

Taylor couldn't finish her sentence as she stepped out to be alongside Ari when a flustered swan bumped right into her, nearly toppling them both to the ground. The swan was awash with piercings, spiked bracelets, and collars. Her shredded band shirt and jeans, complete with fishnet stockings, were a sight all too familiar to Taylor.

"Ah, I'm so sorry!" the swan squawked, looking disheveled, her own feathers frayed on her head. "I didn't expect you to just step right out in front of me like that and... Wait, Taylor?"

Taylor looked up after dusting her pants off from any stray white feathers. She cocked her head curiously as she regarded the swan. She looked older than she remembered, like having hit puberty late and growing suddenly. There were more piercings down her bill and along the length of her arm bones along her wings, but it was the same person she could recall. There were even a few new burn designs, etching themselves through the feathers where none now grew, like modified tattoos, some matching the colors of the blue-dyed feathers on her head.

A final sniff confirmed it. Taylor's eyes shot open as she rushed in to hug her friend and former bandmate. "Nina! Oh my gods, it's been so long!"

"I know! Wow! What have you even been doing?!" Nina had to take a few moments to recover from the sudden hug to wrap her wings around Taylor. Ahya quickly coiled around their waists in loving gesture.

Taylor leaned back a bit to face her. "It's a long story. You might not even believe it if I told you. What brings you out here? It's pretty amazing that we even ran into each other!"

Nina looked a bit confused, flitting back and forth between Taylor and Ari. "Um... Well, I wasn't supposed to meet you today."

"I'm sorry, what?"

Nina broke the embrace and shook her head. "Don't misunderstand, I'm actually very happy to see you! It's just that my Script didn't have us meeting until tomorrow."

Taylor's mood soured slightly at this happy reunion. "I thought you never believed in the Script. You and I raged against it, even wrote a song about it, remember?"

"Oh, I remember!" Nina beamed, placing a winged hand on Taylor's arm again, rubbing it gently almost to convince herself that she was real and in front of her. "I still hate it. It's just that I can't ignore how much it governs our lives these days." She paused a moment to look down at Ahya. "Um... Hi to you too."

"Sorry about that." Taylor flushed, willing Ahya's licking tongue back into her maw and pulling the tail behind her. "She's just happy to see you. So why are you checking the Script then? What could have caused my co-writer of '*Script Hater*' to actually cave in?" Taylor chuckled at ribbing her old friend like this.

"Oh, um...yeah." Nina's response was hesitant, like she had spoken out of turn and needed to backpedal. She was not as joyful as Taylor was expecting, her bill turned down into a frown. "Things haven't been well these days, and it seems the future is more uncertain than ever. With what's going on, I don't have much choice but to check the Script to see what's ahead so I can better prepare for it." Taylor looked at her disbelievingly. That seemed like a load of bullshit coming from her.

"Excuse me." Ari coughed loudly. "Who the hell is this?"

Taylor turned to Ari, stepping slightly in front of the swan. "This is my friend, Nina. She and I were in a band together several years ago."

Ari's expression did not waver. "Right. That death metal band of yours."

"'*Bad Luck*' was what we went by!" Nina peeked out from behind Taylor, being helpful.

"Fascinating." Ari was not thrilled. "If you're done, exchange phone numbers and let's go. You got that phone now to do so. You can play catch up later!"

"Excuse me!" Taylor was angry now. She hadn't seen her friend in ages, and she wasn't just about to let Ari ruin this because of some mission that could wait a few more hours. "What if you had just met a childhood friend after so long, and you were told you couldn't visit with them? I mean, after all, you and your dad denied me seeing my family even after I did all that you asked of me, to include being experimented on! So what's an old friend to you?"

"This isn't about my friends or your friends. This is about our mission and how you're wasting my time!" Ari bared her crooked teeth.

"Oh, that's right! Because you don't have any friends!" Taylor snapped.

"Is...this a bad time?" Nina seemed to shrink and took a few steps back upon seeing Ahya rise up and enlarge in response to the growing animosity from Ari. "I mean, we could always hang out later, Taylor."

Taylor put a paw back to stay her friend's anxiety. "No, it's fine. Just pointing out the hypocrisy of someone who doesn't care about anyone because she never gave anyone a reason to care about her!"

"That's enough!" Ari snarled, gripping Taylor roughly by the arm, causing Ahya to expose herself, teeth flashing and tongue whipping out. "We have a job to do, and I'm going to see it done."

"Get your paws off of me!" Taylor was tired of being led around by the paw by people who didn't care for her. "In the end, you care for nothing but what your dad asks of you! You're no better than anyone else who wants something from me!"

Without thinking, Taylor jerked her arm away and pushed Nina a good distance. By instinct, she shot lightning from her fingertips straight at the feet of Ari, exploding the ground beneath, causing her to somersault back onto her stomach. The reptile did her best to retract her limbs into herself, but could only go so far due to her crocodile nature preventing the full protection of her semi-permeable shell.

Shocked at her own ability to surprise Ari, Taylor turned to Nina who had retreated a fair distance down the sidewalk. "We have to go, Nina!" she shouted, grabbing the rattled swan by the wing and barreling down the row of trees.

"What was that?!" Nina's bill had dropped open from shock. "How did you even do that?"

Taylor glanced over briefly, wanting to keep her eyes ahead of them. "It's a long story. I'll explain when we're somewhere safer."

Nina skirled as a tree beside them upended and broke free from its concrete planter confines, perilously teetering over their heads before tipping and crashing down behind them. They looked back to see Ari slapping her tail on the sidewalk and sending another tremor of flames along the ground towards the next tree in line in front of them.

They swerved left, then directly into a car. Taylor vaulted over the hood, though she misjudged the distance horribly and hit its front hard with her butt, causing her to wince. She thought she saw Mikhail from a quick peer through the windshield, but was unsure if it was just a hallucination. Sliding off the other side, her hind paws hit the ground running. Not looking around, Nina still squabbling in tow, her ears flicked back to the sounds of crushing metal and cracking glass.

"Who the hell is that?! Why can she do these things?! Why can you?!" Nina sounded like she was hyperventilating. "Why is nothing making sense anymore?!"

"Just focus on running!" Taylor jerked Nina hard to the side, the car crashing upside-down right where they were just seconds before.

"Do you know where you're going?" Nina attempted to flap her free wing to keep up, but it was quite the futile attempt.

"Not a clue!" Taylor had to laugh to keep from being terrified herself.

The last thing she wanted was to have one of her good friends hurt on account of her dumb decision just now to attack Ari. She didn't know exactly what Ari would do if she got ahold of her again, but she knew Nina would be receiving the worst of it. She couldn't take that chance now. So her best option was to just run and hope they came across an opening to lose Ari in the craziness that was the Zabökar morning commute.

She hadn't realized they were back downtown until she stopped short of a blaring horn from a rampaging bus that nearly ran her over, causing Nina to shriek. They needed to get lost in the crowd here, but they were quite visible from the street. Her keen hearing could hear the next tremor heading their way.

"Where's the nearest subway?" Taylor scanned quickly. She was not familiar with this part of downtown. It seemed to have changed drastically in the short span of years she was gone.

Nina was fidgeting hard, her feathers quivering with fear. Barely giving her direction a glance, her focus on the murderous reptile behind them, she waved her wing off to their left. "Across the street and three blocks down."

Taylor squinted. She could see the sign indicating the station entrance with stairs leading down. "Got it!"

"Why must you always make things difficult, Taylor?!" she could hear Ari shout.

Several swine beside them squealed, a dark shadow looming over them. Taylor looked back up and saw a flung vehicle hurtling toward them, getting ready to crush the hapless couple. She used Ahya to swat them to the side—unfortunately into the gridlock traffic of the road—saving their lives from the demolished car, the frame from which created an awful grating on her ears as it collapsed in on itself from the impact.

Without waiting for a thank you, she darted past the two whimpering pigs and ran out into traffic. The honking of the irate drivers did little to steady her nerves, but she knew she couldn't stop. Holding onto her friend's wing tighter, she ducked low and cried out as a bicycle railed past them, implanting itself firmly halfway into a vehicle opposite. She made eye contact with Ari who was already heaving at the exertion, but was not stopping, motioning with her arms as more cars launched themselves into the sky.

"She's bringing them down on top of us!" Nina fruitlessly covered her head with her wing.

"I know! Let's just make it to the subway!" Taylor barked.

It was a bloodbath. Taylor couldn't have miscalculated Ari's reaction any worse than if she had tried. The propelled vehicles were smashing into the hovering traffic above and raining hellfire and debris onto the bystanders below. Once people began to figure out what was happening, it was pandemonium. Hundreds of mammals were vacating their vehicles and shoving their way past Taylor and Nina, slowing them down.

She needed to stall Ari somehow, or they were not going to make it those three blocks to the train station. Flinging an arm back, she plowed lightning through two vans in a row, twirling them end over end through the air with sparks sizzling out in all directions. Ari dove to the side as both amazingly hit their mark where she once stood.

Satisfied that most innocent folk were gone from the immediate vicinity—other than the oblivious commuters above them—she kept running with Nina, turning back frequently to trade blows with Ari. She knocked down a lamppost with a concentrated blast of pure energy, it wobbling briefly before falling and creating a temporary barrier between them and Ari.

"This is horrifying!" Nina was wide-eyed at Taylor every time she launched a powered attack of her own.

Taylor leaned a bit on her swan buddy for support as a wave of light-headedness washed over her. "Yeah, well we need to get somewhere safe soon. I don't think I can keep this up for long."

Both were now out of breath. Nina was having to pant in-between words. "How is she even throwing cars at us?"

"She's actually melting the ground underneath each of them and pushing that up fast. That's how they're going airborne." Taylor fired back another bolt, not even aiming well. "Kind of like this one!" she yelped.

They ducked as a huge truck reared up ass-over-end. The liquid magma pushed its backend at an angle in hopes of blocking off their path. Taylor yanked hard on Nina and banked off to the opposing sidewalk, continuing to run down it. Ahead were a bunch of mammals fleeing a corner café, a singular rabbit alone in the midst of the chaos, seemingly unfazed by the din.

The truck smashed hard just meters in front of them, causing the rabbit to wince. "Jake! Oh my gods, are you alright?!"

Taylor didn't even know why Ahya did it. Maybe it was the rumbling in her stomach from having had no breakfast today mixed with the divine smells of the café next to them. She had intended to just run past the rabbit and keep going, but she felt the internal tug of both the will and the external jerk of Ahya reach back, enlarge, and swallow the rabbit whole.

"Oh, what the hell, Ahya?!" She could feel Ahya's tongue as it curled around the rabbit's midsection, locking him into her grasp, drawing him squealing into her maw and keeping him steady as the dissolving fluids began to rush into her sac.

"Did your tail just eat that rabbit?" Nina's eyes bulged, letting go of Taylor's paw for the first time since meeting.

"Yeah... Yeah, she just did..." Taylor did not have the mental acumen at this moment to contest the willpower of Ahya.

It was over within seconds. It was insanely scary how efficient her tailmaw was when it came to devouring someone. Her belly was obscenely full now, her hunger immediately gone. The taste of the rabbit hit her tongue like the bitter taste of grain plucked from a rotten field. She nearly hurled on the spot, her gagging reaction stymied by the calling of her name.

"Taylor?" another rabbit called out.

Blood was pounding in her ears. Fighting off the sickening bout of nausea, she did her best to turn to the rabbit. He was a cream-colored rabbit with freckled cheeks, his heterochromatic eyes standing out to her, screaming to recall who he was. She couldn't quite place him, but she knew he looked familiar.

"Um...hi. You just said my name. Who are you again?" she sputtered, licking her muzzle at the lingering taste.

"She's gaining!" Nina pressured, tapping Taylor's shoulder frantically.

"I'm so sorry...whoever you are! I need to get going." She felt terrible having to leave him there alone, with Ari most likely right behind, but the further she was away from him and everyone else, the safer they all would be.

Bolting off towards the subway sign, now just a block away from them, she realized her energy had come back. Like a shot to the heart, her legs were pounding like pistons on the pavement. The haze in her brain from firing too many bolts of electricity was like a distant memory. She was both sickened and awed at the effect eating someone had on her when she did not resist Ahya.

"Everyone, get out of the way!" she yelled as she shoved people, even using Ahya to move them. "Get back down the stairs!"

To accentuate her point, she blew a small hole into the side tiling above one of the escalators with a concentrated burst of electricity that was so powerful it pulsed a miniature shockwave, causing many ear-sensitive mammals to cringe. This got everyone to listen, and the screaming began to swell. People were trampling over each other, attempting to get away from her.

With most of the preventable casualties gone, she shooed Nina down the stairs to the base. Her ears flicked towards the huffing of Ari, who was most likely almost upon them. Taylor unleashed two blasts towards the cement overhanging the entry down into the subway, drawing two deep gashes that met in the middle above her. There were audible cracks and a cacophonous groan as the ceiling caved in on itself, blocking the entire route topside completely with rubble too heavy to lift.

"Will that hold her off?" Nina tried to peer through the minute cracks between the large cinder blocks and rocks.

Taylor motioned for Nina to follow her deeper into the station. "Not for long." She could already see the dull glow of red peeking through as Ari began to heat her way through it.

Nina screamed when a huge pillar of magma slammed up into the ceiling between them. Taylor knew Ari was grasping at straws and guesstimating where they were on the other side of the blockade. They needed to get out of her range.

As they entered the platform proper, the hood from her hoodie slipped off her head from a gust of wind created by a passing train. Dozens of people scrambled to squeeze into the limited-capacity cabins, their fight-or-flight instincts going full stop. Giggling with restrained terror, they both jostled their way into the train just as the doors were closing. Many noticed her crimson fur and attempted to keep a good distance, despite the cramped space.

They couldn't even breathe a sigh of relief as the train began to move when the entire vehicle lurched forward to a complete standstill, throwing everyone aboard to the ground at its violent nature. Struggling to rise up, using a seat to assist, Taylor spied Ari through the windows, her having skewered the train several cabins down. Taylor could hear the screams now through the connecting doors, a visible body oozing down the rapidly cooling pillar that had stopped them.

"How are we going to get away?! She's almost to us!" Nina nearly feinted.

"I never knew you to be this petrified," Taylor remarked.

Ari had not found them yet among the crowd, and Ahya was being nice and not revealing herself unnecessarily, so they had time to act. Looking down the tracks through the cabins, she spotted another train coming in to a stop on the other side of the platform for passengers going the opposite direction. It would reveal their position, but she would need to break through between the trains when they were stopped side by side.

The train beside stopped and its opposing doors opened. The commuters inside were clueless to what was happening just meters from them. Ari had already busted into a cabin one down from where they were. She wasn't killing anyone just yet, but she was getting the royal treatment of distance as many shied away from her, making it easier for her to search.

Blasting out the windows beside them, she gripped Nina hard with Ahya. "Don't think, just jump!"

The lights flickered between the two trains from the electric shock that plowed through them both. They leapt through the two adjacent windows, not quite making the second one as they both fell to the floor, paws in the air. Ahya opened wide and gripped a pole, pulling hard to avoid Taylor from smacking face first onto the dirty flooring. As expected, she could hear crashing metal and glass on the other train.

Terrified, but still not wanting to waste the opportunity, she rose up and held one paw towards Ari. Surging energy zigzagged out from her fingertips towards the reptile, just as her tail slapped the metal floor of her train. It hit Ari square in the chest, smashing her through the doors behind and clear across the platform and into the tiled wall, shattering the neon sign above her.

They watched shivering as the train they were on made an emergency start to leave the station early. Both their eyes remained on the form of Ari, rolling out of the big circular indent her shell made. She hit the ground on her hands and knees before she was out of sight past the wall and into the darkness of the tunnel.

Taylor collapsed onto the bench before her and began to shake. The last time she was in a fight for her life was right outside Cheribaum, with monstrous mechanical behemoths and savage reptile enforcers. She couldn't believe her impromptu plan worked, but she was thankful that it did. She gazed down the length of her train, to see a smattering of still brave mammals all staring at her and Nina. She didn't care. They could keep their distance. They escaped.

Nina slumped down next to her, absently putting her head on Taylor's shoulder. Ahya draped over both their laps as Taylor petted her fur. "I thought I was going to die," Nina stated plainly.

"I thought we both were." Taylor let loose a breath she didn't know she was holding in.

"So...is that rabbit dead?" Nina asked glumly.

Taylor grimaced at being reminded of her slightly bulging belly, just barely visible under her sweater. "I'm afraid so."

"That's sad." Silence between them. "Who was that reptile?"

Taylor looked down at Nina. She was still on her shoulder, just staring across at the empty seats across from them. "Her name is Ari. She's the daughter of...of a very dangerous person."

This cause Nina to look up. "Why were you even hanging out with her?"

Taylor looked away at the lights flitting past the windows, pushing a lock of her hair behind an ear. "It's complicated. Let's just

141

say it wasn't by choice. I'm back home in Zabökar for a variety of reasons."

"Why did you ever leave?" Nina looked sad. "I was so worried about you when you went missing."

"I was kitnapped." This caused Nina's eyes to grow in shock. "Ari and her father say it was the High Council who did it. They wanted to use me and experiment on me to figure out how to weaponize my powers."

"Your powers? Is that all you can do?" Nina hesitantly reached out and stroked her feathers against Taylor's fingers. The very ones that had unleashed so much destruction.

Taylor noticed a streak of red down the side of her friend's face. "Well, that's all I think I can do, but Ahya can do something else."

Nina jolted when Ahya's tongue placed itself on her face. There were some alarmed brays down the cabin as her tailmaw revealed itself. In short order, their entire section was cleared out except for them. Nina initially started to pull away, but was stilled when Taylor put a paw over her thigh.

"It's okay, just feel it." Taylor was confident this time. She had done this often enough in the past month that she could easily do this for Nina.

Ahya's tongue pressed more firmly onto Nina's wound and began to pulse. The saliva became heavy and thick around the location she was touching. Within a few minutes she pulled away from an astonished Nina. The bird reached up to her forehead and felt around. The feathers where the laceration was were gone, but the wound was healed and the blood soaked up by Ahya.

"You can heal?!"

Taylor pointed to Ahya. "She can. I've known she can do this for quite some time now."

Without waiting for permission, Nina surged forward and hugged Taylor tightly. Her wings connected together behind her back and she sunk into her friend's embrace. They sat their together for a time, lost in the bliss of each other's friendship. The jostles and bumps of the train as it levitated down the rails soothed their taut nerves.

"I've missed you so much," Nina said into Taylor's hoodie.

"I've missed you too." Taylor patted Nina's head.

"The rest of the gang is going to be so excited to hear you're back!" Nina rose up, now enthusiastic at the prospect of reuniting everyone together.

"You mean the band?" Taylor raised a brow. "I highly doubt all of them would be happy to see me."

Nina went back into the hug. "Well, two of them anyway. I'm happy to see you."

Ari groaned as she swayed back and forth on her hands and knees. That last blast from Taylor hurt; she was getting too adept at controlling her power. Maybe them experimenting on her and seeing what she could do wasn't a smart idea; she had learned from her tests.

While trying to catch her breath, she heard pounding footfalls headed towards her. Ari clucked her tongue. Thoroughly exhausted from doing all that she did in trying to get Taylor back, she was in no condition to fight. Taylor had won this round.

Good on her.

She rolled back onto her rump, letting her shell take some of the relief off of sitting upright. She beheld a tiger, snow leopard, and gazelle bear down on her. Turning her head to the side to spit a globule of blood, she sneered. "Good to know your friends didn't leave you for dead up on that mountain." She addressed Terrati.

Mikhail stopped just out of estimated range of Ari, his tail quivering with anger. They all seemed to be a bit worse for wear, with cuts and dried blood in their fur. "Just like it seems you were with Taylor just now."

"Where is she?" Natalia looked around at the now empty platform.

Ari waved off down the tunnel. "Gone. She gave me the slip."

Terrati seemed to be hot with anger at having to see her again. "So why don't we kill her now, and that's one less obstacle to getting Taylor back?"

"Because Ari knows why she's here and where she might be going." Mikhail bared his teeth but held his position.

Ari snapped her fingers and gave him a wink. "Right you are, big kitty." She tapped her cybernetic eye. "I can track her better than any of you can. We're not out in the wilderness anymore. I'm in my element here in the city."

Natalia's ears turned to the sound of rising sirens. "I hate to admit it, but she's right."

Mikhail pointed a finger at her. "You will be coming with us, and we'll discuss how we're going to find Taylor and what happens when we do. Do we understand each other?"

"Perfectly," Ari simpered, her eyes lidded.

"I don't like this." Terrati never stopped glaring at the smirking reptile.

7.

CLOSURE

"Murana? Please talk to me," Anthony repeated again.

She had been staring listlessly at some random corner for what seemed like hours. Sleeping in her arms was a resting cub, content and safe next to her breast. What was most striking about the child was its brilliantly gleaming red hair and tail tip that was just peeking out of the blanket it was swaddled in.

Toys were strewn about the playroom they had set up for the cub, using the corner room of the apartment suite in their high rise residence because it had two windows to better let natural light in during the day. It was a disaster, as was to be expected. What would be strange to visitors, however, was the sticky residue of saliva on all the toys that was quite unlike anything either wolf produced.

The crib beside her had gnaw marks up and down each of its wooden poles, with one almost eaten through completely. All these subtle signs added up to a scene of unusual curiosity. Of a cub that wasn't exactly what anyone had expected. Sleeping soundly in Murana's arms was a baby with part of her fur that was unlike anything else. No other wolf had red fur, especially not deep crimson that dazzled in the light.

"Murana, we need to talk about this. They need the documentation for the research," Anthony reminded. Her eyes limply drifted towards him, her focus coming back somewhat as she stared at him. "If we don't, we're going to be in a lot of debt. Not even my pay is going to cover what we'd owe if we terminate this with the city."

"I was supposed to have two…" she murmured softly.

"What was that?" Anthony sighed.

He hated these sessions. He felt like he was betraying their privacy filming these intimate moments with their family, but they both understood the implications of this long-term agreement when they signed the contract. He scooted up closer so she was more in frame, and better able to pick up her soft voice in the microphone.

"There were two cubs inside of me." She turned away again, not wanting to look at the babe nestled against her. "Now there is only one."

Anthony wiped his brow. He had no idea how to comfort his wife, and with this stupid requirement to document everything, anything he did next would make him seem cold and callous towards her. "These things happen. Nobody wants them to, but sometimes life doesn't give us what we want."

Her clarity returned with a vengeance as she grew hot with anger. She snarled at him. "These things don't just happen! I was pulsed by the Arbiter's men when I was caught! Someone gave me up in there! I had taken all the precautions, yet I still was captured! Someone wanted me to get pulsed knowing I was pregnant! I've half a mind to believe it was this stupid Wendell character that nobody seems to want to reveal who he is...if anyone even knows!" The babe had started to stir.

"Honey, you're going to wake her up." Anthony tried to calm her down.

"Who? This thing?" She lifted it up. It had now begun to cry, its red tipped tail slinking out and opening its tiny mouth as if in unison. "They ruined our cubs, Anthony! Whatever the fuck they did to me killed one of them and mutated the other, and now I don't even know if it is truly mine anymore! For all I know, it could be a complete abomination! That was a DNA ray I was exposed to! That rewrites your genetic structure! This isn't my daughter!"

The cub was full-on wailing now. Anthony knew this was not going to end well. He would have to stop the recording. He went to turn it off, but could see Murana was getting up from her rocking chair, intent to leave to do gods knew what with the child. He fumbled with it and dropped the small flip camera. It hit the floor perfectly angled up towards them as he rushed forward to stop her.

"Murana, just put the baby down." he warned, moving in with his paws to scoop the child from her.

"No! It's not ours! It's ruined!" She fought with him, jerking the cub away.

147

"Stop it! You're going to hurt her!" He shouldered Murana hard, shoving his hands around the bawling cub as he yanked it from her grasp.

She snapped. She was upon him with tooth and claw, biting at his face as she fought to get the child back. Anthony had the good sense to roll the baby across the play mat away from them as he prepared to defend himself from his own wife. He didn't want to hurt her, but she was completely distraught and in no condition to be reasoned with. She was a seasoned fighter just like him, if not more so. He gauged his odds as being pretty low he would survive this if he couldn't subdue her quickly.

He twisted their momentum to the left and they both rolled into the crib, knocking the rocking chair completely over onto its side, missing the now-flailing cub who had her arms free from the swaddling blanket. Murana bit hard into his neck, drawing blood. He dragged his claws down her back and sides, shredding her shirt, in an attempt to give her enough pain to loosen her grip. They crashed into the changing stand against the wall, upending all the stacks of neatly folded diapers, wipes, and bottles. All falling to the floor in a clatter.

"Mom? Dad? What's going on?" A small voice emerged from the doorway of the room.

Murana immediately released her husband and backed up into the corner, weeping uncontrollably. Anthony gasped for breath as he rubbed his neck before straining to rise up to a knee. He looked over to see his youngest son, an adopted raccoon with a delightful mix of tan and brown with black stripes alternating with them along his tail. He was rubbing his eyes, having just woken from a short nap.

"Max..." Anthony coughed. "Mother and I were just having a disagreement about something."

"Sounded like a pretty big disagreement." Max was starting to wake up a bit more fully now. His eyes rested on his now screaming little sister. "What happened to her?"

"Playtime got a little rough, that's all." Anthony was doing his best to hide his failure and shame at his inability to have stopped this turn of events.

He crawled over on all fours to pick up the little tyke. Her little paws immediately clung to him as she sought to get some solace from his mere presence. The tiny mouth that split open at the end of her tail had its tongue out, licking his elbow, as if reaffirming that it was him and was safe and could be trusted.

Max looked between Anthony and Murana, who was still huddled in the corner, head in her paws. "She still hasn't named her, has she?"

Anthony sighed, looking down at his unusual child, its eyes scrunched up in displeasure at the awful nature of the past few minutes. "No. No she hasn't." He regarded his wife with sadness. "Your mom... Your mom is just going through a hard time after pregnancy. She still needs some time to adjust to having a new kid in the house."

"Why are you recording your fight?" Max pointed out the red light still burning bright on the camera which was perfectly capturing the entire room.

"Aw shit!" Anthony was furious. Quickly setting the cub gently into the crib, he stomped over and kicked the camera hard into the wall, shattering it.

Jake pounded down another drink before placing it on the bar before him a bit harder than he intended, drawing the ire of the bartender down the way as he was serving another customer. Hiccupping an apology under his breath, he stared with glazed eyes at the five rabbit-sized glasses before him. This was about his limit, and he strongly considered going one more just to see where that would put him in the morning.

He couldn't get the events of the day out of his head. He vividly recalled that massive maw yawning wide, enveloping Tony into its darkness before visibly seeing his shape shrivel away to nothing inside that deplorable tail. What's worse, the person it was attached to, Taylor, didn't even recognize him at all. Such an acute dismissal of all the times he protected her while being the bodyguard for their band.

Jake tried to give chase when she ran off with Tony lost inside her tail, but had to promptly cut it short when a raging reptile with a shell barreled past him with the ground blazing behind her. The sight of that combined with what had happened to his friend was enough to send him into instinctual prey induced shivers. He had forgotten how long he had cowered up against that tipped car, eyes glued to the train station opening where he last saw several animals entering, perhaps in pursuit of the reptile. At this point, he cared not. Tony was gone.

A buzz from his phone caused him to jump. He fumbled in his pocket to pull it out and blinked his eyes to clear the blurriness of his vision to focus on the text in front of him. "Hey Jake... We heard what happened on the news." It was from one of his old coworkers back in the day before he branched off to take a law-enforcement route to his career. A rabbit, like him.

"News?" Jake texted back, having to delete and retype several times just a single word. Gods, he was beyond tipsy right now. He glanced up at the television angled down at the end of the bar. There didn't seem to be anything relating to the crazy events of the day yet.

"Yeah! They're playing it every fifteen minutes! It's all over the news!" Jake had barely read this when he noticed they were still typing more. "This is all the more reason why you should join us, Jake. We're worried about you. Ever since you left to go play hero, you've not been the same. You should come to one of our rallies with us. Stepan is planning a revolution against the predators! You above anyone else should be willing to agree with him after what happened to Tony. Don't throw your lot in with them."

Jake shakily set the phone face down on the bar. He didn't want to deal with this right now. He had just lost one of the only rabbit friends he could say he was remotely close to, and every other rabbit he knew was trying to rope him into an underground resistance faction spearheaded by this Stepan. It had started out innocently enough with casual get-togethers and meetings, but it had ballooned into this huge organization right under the noses of local law enforcement. The shared fate and communal experience of their existence under the service law was enough for every rabbit to keep this secret, even Jake; no rabbit ratted out their own.

He was about to order one more drink over his limit when the television caught his eye. They were running the report again. It looked to be shaky smartphone camera footage by a bystander across the street from where he was standing, having helped that family. The camera managed to capture the entire moment of Tony getting swallowed, forcing Jake to relive it yet again before the person holding the phone freaked out and the image became an indistinguishable blur.

"The current whereabouts of this 'wolf-in-red' are unknown, and has been deemed by the local authorities to be extremely dangerous. People are advised not to approach. Current guidance stands that if you are to see this unknown wolf to not interact, and instead contact your local police to deal with them." The small sparrow newscaster seemed to be shivering after having viewed the footage himself on live television, probably for the first time based on the fear evident in his eyes.

A snort down the row of barstools drew Jake's attention. "Not even two weeks after cutting me loose and they already lost her." The wolf shook his head in contempt. "And they thought I was the incompetent idiot who couldn't secure and bring her back." He chuckled as he gobbled down another hunk of burger, its grease splattering all over the plate and wooden counter.

Jake crinkled his nose at the repulsive way the wolf ate. Then again, what should he have expected coming to a dive like this place? It was primarily a predator frequented establishment. Deep down, Jake still felt that same sense of despair he had that morning and subconsciously chose this place in hopes he would end up like his friend Tony to the myriad of predators present in the bar. It would certainly end his current plight of having no future other than the ones in power gave him.

Still, the wolf did intrigue him for a variety of reasons. The fact it seemed he knew who Taylor was based on the newscast already piqued Jake's interest. He wanted to confront Taylor now and demand Tony back, if it was possible. This wolf might be just the ticket to finding her again. He noted the iron arm on the wolf as it reached over to grab his beer. Mercenary, by the looks of it. What sort of trouble had Taylor landed herself in?

Jake hopped down off the tall stool, nearly stumbling onto his face from landing from such a high up position. Regaining balance, he padded over to the wolf and did his best to look dignified as he leaped up onto the stool next to the gorging wolf. He barely even gave the rabbit a second glance and continued his meal, his attention now disinterested in the news above them.

"Excuse me," Jake said. He waited a few moments. The wolf didn't acknowledge him. "Excuse me," he repeated a bit louder.

Without looking at Jake, the wolf answered. "I'm not interested in your services, rabbit. Go find someone else to pawn your sordid body off on."

Jake bristled at this dismissal of his presence and the slam against his character. His ears flopped down. "Excuse me, Mr. shit-face wolf." This got his attention. He would have been trembling from the look he was given had it not been for his burning need to know the connection between this wolf and Taylor. "Yeah, no, I'm not here to pleasure you. That's the last thing on my mind." He pointed to the television monitor. "You said something about the 'wolf-in-red' that they were showing. Do you know that wolf?"

He smirked at Jake and swallowed his current bite, chuckling a bit. "What's it to you, little bunny?"

Maybe it was the alcohol talking, but Jake was feeling bold and he didn't like being talked down to by someone who could easily rip his face off in a back alley once he left the bar. "What's it to me?! That wolf just ate my friend this morning right in front of me, and I'd like to track her down. Then again, I guess a rabbit going missing in this city means little to you predators, doesn't it?" Jake jabbed a finger at the wolf.

The wolf roughly put his metal arm on Jake's shoulder and pushed him hard onto the stool to lower his profile. "Will you keep your volume down?" The wolf looked nervously at the wolverine bartender who seemed to have noticed the ruckus, and had the eye of being all too eager to stop it. "Okay, so she ate your friend. That sucks. Are you all hyped up on some sort of revenge quest? I can tell you right now that it isn't going to end well for you."

Jake had to stop himself from knee-jerk reacting to his question. It wasn't exactly revenge against Taylor. He wasn't sure what he'd do when and if he caught her. He was in no position even at the police department, filing paperwork, to do any sort of arrest. They simply did not give him authorization or jurisdiction for that. He was simply an office clerk at best, a far cry from where he wanted to be. So what exactly would he do if he finally caught up to her?

"I just want answers," Jake sighed finally, wilting in the firm grip of the wolf's iron paw. "I watched over that girl as she was growing up. Seeing her perform on stage and bouncing all the would-be creeps from getting at the band. I grew fond of them—almost like an extended family, since all of mine are either dead or sponsored out to people where I can't see them anymore. I thought she was different than other wolves on account of her tail, but it seems all of that was a farce. I just want to know why she did what she did."

"And if you don't like that answer?"

"I… I don't know. I hope it isn't as bad as I'm thinking." Jake was unsure.

His previous answer got the wolf's attention. "So…you watched over her? Do you even know what her name is? Also, what did you say your name was?"

"I didn't." Jake sniffed. "It's Jake, by the way, Jake Thumpings. And her name is Taylor."

"Trevor Novak." He smiled for once. "This is highly ironic that we'd be meeting here so soon after we delivered Taylor to… Well, to my former employer. I had just finished up with any lingering commitments here, and was actually on my way out of the city and to Livarnu when I overheard the trouble she caused. So I figured I'd stick around in the area and see the festivities." He chuckled. "When did you say you were bouncer for her band?"

The initial surge of adrenaline of confronting Trevor wearing off, Jake seemed to sink onto the stool. "It wasn't actually her band; she was just back-up singer and lead guitarist. Her tail sometimes played the drums."

"That's fascinating, but when?" Trevor pressed, his eyes tense.

"A bit over two years ago. She was sixteen then."

"So when did you get fired from your job there?"

"I was never fired." Jake tried to brush off the metal paw on his shoulder with little success, getting irritated now that his interrogation was backfiring on him. "She disappeared, and it was hard for the band to stay afloat after that. The wolf with the 'tail' was what drew in the crowds, even if she wasn't the band leader. They tried to limp on after that, but it wasn't the same. They fell apart and went their separate ways. So my job was gone the moment that happened."

Trevor looked like he was thinking it over and making connections in his mind. "That actually puts it near the time I was hired to go find her."

"I thought I was asking the questions here." Jake was miffed that he let the predator take over the conversation like that. He was better than this. He had fought off worse people back when he was bodyguard to the band. Maybe his depression of recent months had made him a bit soft and subservient.

"I didn't know I was being questioned like a common criminal." Trevor's mirth crawled under Jake's skin, causing the fur on his arms to quiver.

"So, you do know Taylor." Jake nodded, the answer confirmed by Trevor's responses. "You were tasked to hunt her down before, right? Even were paid to do it?"

Trevor coughed a laugh. "That's how I'm enjoying this wonderful meal right now."

"Then you can find her again for me."

Trevor slammed his normal paw on the bar counter laughing hard, releasing Jake finally from his iron grip. "Oh, that's hilarious. First off, you couldn't afford me, rabbit. I know how much your kind makes. Second, that is one mess I don't want to get involved in again. Trust me, you're better off forgetting her and going about your life."

"I've got nothing left but a dead-end job and no more real friends to speak of now that Taylor ate Tony." The reality of the situation hit Jake like a truck. He had been holding it in all day and he continued to be strong in the face of this wolf, doing his best to hold back the tears. "How can I forget her? She's taken the last thing that's

154

kept me from offing myself." Jake really didn't care anymore what Trevor thought of him now. It's not like this day could get any worse.

Trevor's face showed the first bit of concern that night. "Look, I don't know how I can help you. To be frank, I was lucky to be let off the hook like I was a couple weeks ago. The people who are interested in her are very powerful people. This isn't the sort of situation you stick your nose into if you're not prepared for it." He took another sip of his beer. "Besides, I lost someone too because of her. Not…directly, but lost all the same. His name was Gregor. He was a good friend, my best friend, and he fell in duty while bringing her in."

"So we both have a vested interest in finding her again." Jake's ears popped up again, hoping he could convince Trevor to help.

Trevor looked over from the corner of his eyes at Jake. "Oh no… Have you not been listening to anything I've said? You might have a vested interest since the pain is still fresh for you, but I've mulled it over and decided it best to leave that mess behind and live the rest of my life the way Gregor might have wanted me to, my promise to Taylor's mother be damned."

Jake cocked his head. "You made a promise to her mother too?"

Trevor snorted. "Gods, is there no person that wolf didn't enlist to look after her daughter?"

"I wasn't asked to look after her by her mother. I was already a bodyguard for *Bad Luck* when she contacted me." The conversation was remarkably sobering Jake up. "I was asked to continue watching over her and to deliver a necklace and message for her. I never got to deliver the message."

Trevor paused before taking another sip. "That would explain where she got that pine tree necklace. That was from you?" Jake nodded. "Do you think you'd deliver the message now after all that's happened?" Trevor looked genuinely curious, finally resuming his drink.

Jake looked off towards the television again, glancing away quickly when it happened to be replaying the moment Tony died. "I don't know. I don't even know if it's relevant anymore. I don't know how I feel about Taylor now. She was just a job to me. I was hired to protect her and her bandmates. Now I don't know if I should be furious at her or sad for her situation. Probably both."

"Honestly, it's all jacked up." Trevor finished the rest of his drink and stared at the repeating newscast as they showed the horror for the millionth time. "She was just a job to me too starting off. However, there is just something about her, like a sort of innocence despite what her tail can do, that I felt needed to be protected. It all got dashed though when Gregor died. Guess it would suck to be in her position right now. She's literally made herself to be enemy number one in Zabökar."

"What about that reptile that was ripping up the street chasing her?" Jake couldn't see any footage of the mysterious shelled character who rushed past him in pursuit of her.

"Ripped up the street?" Trevor huffed. "You probably mean Ari. She's the daughter of...my previous employer, and she's very deadly. If she was chasing after Taylor this morning, then something tells me Taylor got her own damn self into a mess." He shook his head again. "That girl will never learn. I thought she was done running away from her problems."

"Unless this Ari was the problem?" Jake suggested.

Trevor thought it over. "Possibly. I remember her willingly coming to Zabökar with Ari and I. So there must be some legitimate reason for her to break away from her now. Gods know that she's been with them enough time for things to go south for her."

"How long ago was that?"

Trevor turned back to Jake. "About two weeks ago. After they transferred my pay to my account, they dumped me off at the nearest ditch in downtown Zabökar and never looked back. I've no idea what they've been doing with her since."

"Probably starving her." Jake recalled something.

"Starving her? What makes you say that?" Trevor flagged down the wolverine to come over to check him out on his tab.

"I don't know for certain, but something I've observed about Taylor during my years watching over her in the band." Jake scratched his chin, trying to recall specific events. "Whenever Taylor was done eating or was full, her tail was never very aggressive and quite calm. I could always tell when Taylor was hungry because her tail was more…shall we say, 'touchy-feely' with everything and everyone. It was quite the hassle to rein in that thing until Taylor ate something."

It was starting to make sense now for Jake, at least his own theory. Taylor was never a chubby wolf. She was always very slender, but she still had some meat on her bones during her years as singer and guitarist with *Bad Luck*. However, he could vividly recall her gaunt features this morning—how much more emaciated she was than when he last saw her. It was a hunch that perhaps Tony was in the wrong place at the wrong time with Taylor. Didn't make the situation any less shitty, but it was at least some reason to not absolutely hate her for it.

"Well if you don't want to eat something you didn't put in your mouth yourself, I suggest you head outside with me." He slapped a few large bills on the bar. "That's for his tab too," he addressed the bartender.

"Why are you paying my tab?" Jake was confused, looking back at his abandoned glasses several stools down.

Trevor briefly gestured to the male cougar lounging with legs spread, staring at him with hungry eyes. "Given how crappy your day has been, I don't think being forced to service another right now is high on your list of things to do. Might as well make it look like you're with me instead at least until we're several blocks away from this place." He lowered his voice even lower. "For the record, I want to make it clear I'm not asking for any services, got it?"

"Oh, I get you." Jake truly did. He shivered a bit at the lustful gaze of that cougar. His interaction with Trevor was probably the only thing staving off that cat from coming over and demanding him by the law to do his duty. "Let me get my coat then and we'll be off."

"I'll be waiting at the front door." Trevor put on his own faux leather jacket, leaving it unzipped as he stepped over to the entrance.

Jake did his best not to meet the gaze of the cougar, his eyes lighting up with each puff on his cigarette. Still wobbly from his alcohol intake, he did his best to appear in full control of his faculties when he went to put on his coat and meet Trevor at the door. Giving a sidelong glance to the cougar, he noticed the disappointment in their face as he left with Trevor. Jake was usually pretty good at sensing danger around him, but maybe it was the combination of the drink and the conversation at hand that made him so razor focused on nothing but Taylor.

It all came back to Taylor, it seemed. Her tail was what rose her band to stardom in the underground circuits in Zabökar, and was also the cause of its demise when she went missing, thus losing Jake his job. Now that she had returned, she was the cause of his new pain and the loss of his buddy, Tony. Hearing about how more people wanted Taylor for one reason or another, it really struck Jake how odd it was that such a young teenage wolf could pull the interest of so many people. As upset as he was with her, he had more questions than anger right now.

The roaring din of the evening traffic had died down to just mild honking and squealing of levitation engines above them by this time of the night. The inner-city DNA flashers were pretty atrocious, but both Trevor and Jake had grown accustomed to ignoring their advertisements. The neon hologram of the gyrating vixen above them cast both their features in harsh relief as they walked down the sidewalk together.

"Thanks for that, by the way." Jake was definitely relieved to not have to do anything degrading tonight. He probably was in no shape to perform well anyhow, given how much alcohol he ingested.

Trevor waved his compliment off. "Don't mention it. I've never been much of a fan of your kind." He noticed the look and clarified. "I mean, in that way. I've never had a beef with rabbits. I just never found them very interesting."

"Still not helping your case." Jake raised a brow.

"What, you want me to use the law on you?"

Jake had to backpedal. "No, that's not what I meant! Just that…you're very different than most wolves I've met—Taylor excluded," he added her as an afterthought.

Trevor seemed to regard Jake a bit, prompting him to follow as they turned a corner down another street. "Gregor always did like your kind, given that guy's shortcomings with actual females of our kind. He was a terrible romantic and couldn't hold a date to save his life, so he turned to you all to satisfy."

"Sounds pretty typical." Jake felt this came out a bit too harshly given the look Trevor gave him. Jake cleared his throat and wisely shut up.

"He was unusually kind to your lot. Last time we were together, he must have paid the rabbit that serviced him six months in wages. Certainly made that guy's night." Trevor stared off, reminiscing.

Jake whistled. "That's pretty crazy. Why would he even do that?"

Trevor reached into his jacket to tighten his pauldron strap to keep his sliding iron arm firmly secured. "Gregor was many things, but above all, he was very kind to others. I'm going to miss him."

Jake noticed the motion. "What happened to your arm?"

"Blew off in the war of Del'varr. Gregor was the one that dragged my limp husk of a body all the way out of the warzone."

Jake knew that wolves were excellent trackers, and this one had already tracked down Taylor once. Perhaps he could convince him to do it again. The gears were already turning in Jake's head as to how best to approach him about it.

Nodding at Trevor's previous answer, as if taking it in seriously, he tossed out casually, "I can see how much Gregor meant to you now. Tony was like that with me; he technically saved my life this morning even if he didn't know it." He paused a moment to hopefully let it sink in. Trevor hadn't stopped walking or acknowledged his sentiment. "I don't want to find Taylor to get revenge or anything like that, but I would like some answers. Wouldn't you?"

"I'm sorry, Jake." This request did cause Trevor to stop and face him. "I told you already, I'm leaving that hot mess around her. You're on your own if you are so hell bent on finding her."

Jake's ears dropped. Just when he thought he had a lead on how to find Taylor, it just got dashed to pieces in front of him. "Didn't you want justice for Gregor when he died on account of Taylor? Even if indirectly, as you say? I want some sort of closure to the loss of Tony because of her, and knowing she's still out there and free after he's gone is not fair. You're the only one who has either seen or been remotely close to her and knows how to find her. How often do opportunities come across my path like that? Where's my closure?"

159

Trevor put both paws on his hips and sighed. He stared off down the road, noticing the cougar giving him a quick look before heading straight on across the street. "Tell you what, Jake, how about I help you find a good lead that'll take you straight to her? You handle the rest from there, cool?"

"Very cool!" Jake beamed. He couldn't believe that worked. He felt bad for manipulating this wolf's empathy factor, but he truly did want to face Taylor directly about what had happened this morning.

"Also, it might be best if you stick with me tonight. You can hang out at my flat for the evening." Trevor patted the rabbit on the back and ushered him back down the sidewalk.

"Why's that?" Jake looked around.

Trevor surveyed the road behind them a bit. "That cougar followed us out. I'm just making sure you're not being followed for bad reasons. It's what Gregor would have probably done for you."

"Thank you then, Trevor... And to Gregor too." Jake, for once, was not in a state of constant alertness when around a predator. Then again, it might also have been the alcohol.

There was a rustling in the trees as Fey's nostrils expanded and contracted to the sudden chill that blew through the city street. The cars barely moved from the wind, but the motion was perceptible enough to his trained prey eyes to know it wasn't some happenstance occurrence. The nearby streetlamp flickered a moment before remaining steady. In a moment, the tense sense of unease passed and it was a residential city street like any other.

However, Fey knew better. He hadn't intended to pull that young buck out of the way of a rampaging car roaring down the road at speeds far beyond what they should have been going. The words of thanks barely left the lips of the saved buck when the very air grew thick and oppressive. It seemed the buck sensed it too, and muttered a quick word of appreciation before clopping swiftly down the sidewalk and out of sight.

The only person who didn't seem to pick up on the strange occurrence was Finnley beside him, gently, but insistently tugging on his pants leg. "Can we please get home now so I can soak in a bath and cuddle up next to you? I'm so ready to be done with today." The otter normally didn't complain like this, but Fey couldn't blame him. It had been a torturous day at the hospital.

Surveying the road one last time to see if that strange feeling would come again, he finally looked back down at his small lover and smiled. "Of course. Let's go home."

"I mean, seriously, did everyone decide to choose today to get injured? So many freaking casualties rolling in after us like it was the apocalypse out here." Finnley shook his head, stomping his little paws down the sidewalk. "Here I am with a burning hole in my shoulder, and they see through fifteen other patients before me that came after!"

"Well, you yelling at the receptionist like that probably didn't earn you any favors, and probably just added to our waiting time." Fey had to smirk at Finnley's temper.

Ever since he had fallen for this little critter, things hadn't been the same. Fey finally felt happy for once in a job that made him lifeless. Having a special someone to share the toils of the day with was alleviating, and freed the burden on his chest of how much he had done in service to the High Council, an employer who had now since disavowed him and his entire team for completely failing their task in bringing Taylor in.

"I'll bet you it had something to do with Taylor," Finnley accused.

"Why do you say that?" Fey was amused at Finnley's blaming.

"Because anything horrible that happens these days is because of her." He looked back and held up two fingers. "By my last count, she's been essentially the cause of two cities being wiped off the face of the map. I wouldn't be surprised if Zabökar was next."

"I guess it's a good thing we're going to be getting out of here then." Fey continued to humor Finnley's rage and just let the little guy vent. There was a certain sort of endearing quality to these rants of his, and Fey did like working through them with him.

"First thing's first." The church across the street caught his eye. Sandwiched between two high rise apartment complexes, it looked almost laughable with its diminutive spires of importance. People weren't as concerned with the Script as folks were out in the rural and less industrialized areas, despite it still dictating their fate regardless of their knowledge of it. "Do you mind if we stop in there for a moment?"

Finnley scoffed. "Why? So you can kill another priest that says you shouldn't exist anymore? Fat chance!"

Fey shook his head. "No. I want to look up your Script right now. See if I have any more influence over your life now that I'm supposedly dead and not existing."

"What's that supposed to prove?" Finnley crinkled his nose.

"It'll help put my mind at ease about something. Can you just please do this for me?" Fey gave the otter a pleading look that he knew he couldn't refuse.

The disdain for the tactic was evident on Finnley's face. "I hate it when you do that to me. Ugh, fine. Let's go." He stormed off across the road to the still-illuminated windows of the church.

The chapel doors swung inward as the wooden frames audibly announced their age. This place was even smaller than the one in Cheribaum. There was a long aisle of pews leading down to the pulpit with the glorious stained glass etching of the written law of the Script, a document depicted with god rays emanating from its splendor.

There were two doorways leading off to either side of the primary vestibule. One looked to be the bathrooms, and the other the private space of the priest. This was going to be a bit harder than Fey thought; he would need to be both quick and subtle about this. The priest had already heard the bell jingle of the door and was coming out of his room to greet them.

The stoic alpaca bowed, his two hooves clasped together in the folds of his black sleeves. "My children. What brings you here at this hour, and how can I serve you today?"

Fey took the lead. "My friend here wants to know how his Script ends." Finnley shot him a death glare which was thankfully overlooked by the priest, but Fey could feel the heat of it on his cheek. "I was very much against this, but he was adamant about coming here."

The priest seemed to make note of Fey's shorn-off antler stubs, but turned to address Finnley. "I know the end may seem scary to some, my child, but knowing what is to come can bring a certain peace onto itself in your life. Do not be afraid of your fate. Let us embrace it together as I read your Script." He ushered both with a warm hoof into his quarters.

Fey ignored the wrathful looks of Finnley, knowing the otter would forgive him eventually for this. It's not like this embarrassing moment would matter much once they left Zabökar for good. Besides, Fey's mind was on the task ahead, which was to gather information he suspected would be on whatever computer the priest would have that linked this church up with the global Script Registry.

Sure enough, Fey breathed an inward sigh as he noticed a computer with the scroll delivery device next to it that would magically materialize Finnley's Script once it was recalled. It was an ingenious device that he hadn't the foggiest how it worked, only that it was hooked up to a network linked by individual computer terminals like the one present on the priest's desk.

He had worked with one of the Script Registry devices once before in Cheribaum, so he knew enough to know it could possibly be manipulated with standard hacking equipment.

Finnley's Script materialized in the receptacle with a hum. The priest pulled it out and began unfurling it by the glowing bangs on either side of the roll.

This was his chance. Fey surreptitiously pulled out his phone and undocked a side pin that had a special antenna built into it. He silently thanked the High Council for providing all this tech to them; he finally had a need to use this. As the priest was reading out Finnley's supposed final days, much to the otter's chagrin, Fey placed the small pin with its thin tip facing the computer directly behind the alpaca.

Getting up suddenly, he put a hoof to his abdomen as he sheepishly grinned. "Excuse me, Father, but may I use the restroom here?"

The priest seemed a bit lost at being interrupted, but quickly regained his composure. "Of course. Just head out of that door, hang right past the pulpit and the bathrooms are through the door on the other side."

Nodding appreciatively, Fey did what he was directed to do and immediately shut himself into a stall door and closed the toilet lid proper so he could sit comfortably. He tapped on his phone to access a few submenus, then found the app he wanted and immediately logged into it. Using the pin antenna he had left in the next room, he triangulated the nearest wifi signal in the area which just so happened to be the computer in that room. Once the signal was locked, he began to strip and log the packets as they filtered into his phone. Line after line filling in at insane speeds with data.

"Looks like I'm in." Fey grinned.

Switching over to another user interface, he was met with the primary desktop of the computer. No doubt Finnley would be able to see what he was doing on the priest's computer, but would most likely keep quiet about it. As long as the alpaca didn't turn around and notice, they would be fine.

He quickly opened up the menu options and scanned the various but minimal selection of programs. It was maddening, since he had no idea where to start to begin his search. However, one phrase did catch his eye: Authority Warnings. Clicking on it, it brought up a small roster of names, one of which was his: Fey Darner. It was a good thing he didn't ask for his Script to be read tonight.

So there was a list of miscreants like him that seemingly had no more Script. He recognized Mikhail's name and remembered Taylor sparing him from his Scripted fate several weeks ago. Nobody reported that one, yet here he was in condemnatory print.

Fey knew something was wrong the moment he saved that buck tonight. He was unbound by the Script, and could theoretically change others for good or for ill. He still hadn't the time yet to test his theories on what all he could do, let alone check against the Script to see if he was proven right. However, if this was indeed the case, the last name in that short list could very well be the person he saved earlier. He might have been Scripted to die tonight by that car, and Fey changed his fate.

Who was this Authority, and what happened when one no longer had a Script? These questions had plagued Fey ever since Cheribaum, and he needed closure. He was getting jumpier the longer they stayed in Zabökar. The more chance of interaction with people, the more he felt he was in danger. From what, he wasn't sure. He only knew that it terrified him, and he had no logical reason why he felt this way.

Seeing as he wasn't going to get any more information out of this terminal, he disconnected the link and stood up just as Finnley was banging the door into the restroom. "Fey, time to go!" The otter didn't seem happy.

Opening up the stall door, Fey nonchalantly took the proffered pin antenna from Finnley's paw, an unspoken secret between them. Finnley asked, "Did you find what you were looking for?"

He placed the antenna back into the slot alongside the phone's edge before stuffing it into his pocket. "Not entirely, no. Were you satisfied with your reading?"

"Oh, lay off of it!" he snapped. "This is such bullshit!"

Fey was perplexed. "Why? Not the ending you expected?"

Finnley waggled a finger at him. "First off, that's not nice to jump that on me so you can go off snooping around his computer! I never wanted to know how I was going to go out." He huffed, folding his arms. "Second, why in gods names would I ever die on Taylor's behalf?"

"Wait, what?" Now Fey wasn't enjoying this exchange anymore.

"*To the maw of red, you will make the ultimate sacrifice to ensure that the spirits of old tethered to the mortal domain are set free,*" he repeated from the priest. "What does that even mean?"

"The spirits of old? Tethered to the mortal domain?" Fey couldn't quite make sense of it. "I haven't the faintest."

"You're telling me." Finnley spat onto the floor. He didn't care. "Even the priest was confused about its meaning. He said he's going to consult with his peers about this in the morning."

"That...can't be a good thing." Fey was worried that course of action would lead everything back to him. "Let's get out of here." He made motions towards the door to leave the chapel.

"Agreed." Finnley was fuming again. "It just makes no sense. She's an abomination, and we already evened up our debts to each other for saving you. Why would I ever die for her?"

8.

EGGS

"So you are okay with everything now?" the muntjac questioned.

Murana looked at him with annoyance, eyeing his camcorder with intent to break it across his head. "No. It's always going to be a little weird that your own flesh and blood isn't exactly like you." She went back to watching the young toddler squeal and laugh as she played a silly game with her older brother, Steven. "My two sons seem to be taking to Taylor pretty well, but it's been hard on me to adjust."

"I can imagine. Several years with a wolf who has a mouth in her tail seems like it would come with its own share of problems." The muntjac had the undeniable talent for stating the obvious.

They continued to watch as Steven, her older adopted skunk son, was down on his stomach playing peek-a-boo with Taylor's tail. It was adorable as Taylor was moving it back and forth to either side to see if she could "find" Steven when he was hiding behind his paws. One time the tail even succeeded and nipped him playfully on the nose, much to his surprise.

The muntjac grew serious. "Your daughter represents a significant investment to the city and their continued research into what the Arbiter did to those poor children. Anything we can glean from her would be of use to the city as potential breakthroughs in how to cure these abnormalities, and perhaps even reverse them."

She turned to face him more directly. "Just what are you suggesting?" She made her stare as intense as she could.

He faltered for a few moments before getting back his voice. "The mayor has asked if it would be alright to deliver Taylor to special, qualified facilities where they can conduct testing to see what is going on with her... You know, at the cellular level."

Murana rolled her eyes in disgust. "It's bad enough that we go in for blood work. She hates needles. Besides, the High Council is what supposedly got me into this mess to begin with. Who is truly in charge here? The mayor or the High Council? I thought the council was just the advisory committee to the mayor?"

He checked himself as she grilled his intentions. "Well, technically they are both in charge. Just one of them is elected to be figurehead for the entire city."

"Sounds amazingly redundant. Why have a single leader at all when it is the committee that makes the decisions? Just cut out the middle man. This is why I hate politics." She snorted, turning back to Taylor and Steven. "Taylor, we're going to go out for ice cream. Get ready!"

"Oh... Ice cream!" Taylor clapped her paws while her tail licked its "lips".

"I think I'm going to head back to work, Mom." Steven pushed himself up onto his knees before standing. "The news isn't going to report itself."

"I know, baby." Murana strode over and bent down to give Steven a kiss on the head, ruffling the tuft of white fur between his ears. "I'm proud of you. I smile every time I see you on TV."

Steven blushed, but he pushed out his chest with pride. "Thanks, Mom. When I wink at the camera tonight, that'll be for you!"

She chuckled. "I'll be waiting for it!"

Steven smiled at his little sister one more time before flat-out ignoring the muntjac and plopping on his ballcap before heading out the front door. Hearing his tiny moped revving off down the street, she knelt and assisted Taylor in getting dressed to go outdoors. Her cute pink tank top was fine, but her pajamas bottoms were most certainly not. Swapping them for a pair of jeans, she lifted her onto her hind paws before grabbing the keys from the bowl on the counter adjacent to the kitchen.

"Mind if I tag along? I like ice cream." The muntjac beamed.

"Do I have a choice?" Murana walked past him without regard.

"I'm not the enemy, you know," he pleaded, shutting the front door behind them.

Letting Taylor go on ahead as she was playing hopscotch on invisible lines down the sidewalk, she initiated a slower pace so Taylor could not overhear them. "I'm sorry, what was your name again?"

"For the sixteenth time, it is Hank." The muntjac did a small bow of his head.

"I'm sorry, you can't expect me to remember someone who keeps dropping by unannounced and unwanted." She was not even trying to be nice.

Hank exhaled loudly. "Mrs. Wolford, need I remind you—"

"No, you don't." She cut him off, keeping her eye on Taylor ahead. "It seemed like a good deal at the time to sign that research contract. I figured, what could it hurt? It wasn't like I was expecting to have a special child out of it, or that those appointed to monitor us would be so irksome and annoying."

"You still haven't gotten over how she is?" Hank asked honestly.

Murana shrugged. "I've gotten over most of it. I've learned to make do in bad situations all my life. This is no different."

"So you're saying she's a bad situation?"

"Don't pull that word game shit on me, Hank." She nearly spat his name.

Hank grew quiet before looking back at Murana's quaint home, nestled at the end of a row of cookie-cutter homes with a line of perfectly spaced trees planted past the sidewalk, opposite the one they were on. Beyond them were wild, untamed fields of tall grass and wheat that seemed to stretch on for miles. Ahead of them, past the Outer Hedges, were the tall skyscrapers of Zabökar. They had a fair distance to go to reach the nearest ice cream parlor, being on the outskirts of the city.

"You seem to have a nice place here. What made you leave your penthouse back downtown?" He seemed genuinely curious.

"With Taylor being…as unique as she is, it was decided that we move further out and away from everyone. Take a right at this street, hun," she called out to Taylor as they came up on an intersection, the heights of the buildings not yet reaching three stories yet. "I realized one day as I was trying to get myself some coffee from Taurobucks,

170

Taylor on one hip, that she was going to be a much larger problem the older she got."

"How did you figure?" He panned the camera to have Taylor in view now. She had both arms out for balance as she was placing one paw before the other to tread along the edge of the sidewalk. Her tail's mouth was completely open, tongue flapping in the cool breeze.

"I had just purchased my drink and was waiting for the crowded line to shift for me so I could leave and exit when I noticed her tail nibbling on some of the mugs they had for sale on the wall shelf beside me." She shook her head at the memory. "Thankfully nobody saw what had happened, but I hurriedly got out of there. It was like she wasn't even aware of what her tail was doing. She was more concerned with wanting a sip of 'mommy's drink'."

"You still think people would freak out about it?" Hank kept the camera on Taylor. The tail was bumping her on the head to make her fall.

She glanced at him from the corner of her eye. "I'm surprised you haven't."

"I honestly think it's kind of cute." He smiled as the tail managed to finally succeed at knocking Taylor off balance, causing the little girl to get mad at it.

Murana stopped dead in her tracks, facing him. "You say that now. What happens when she gets older? She is still a predator and commands some measure of fear from others, even if she doesn't intend to. That mouth of hers on her tail is only going to grow and get bigger. Those teeth are going to get sharper. It is going to frighten others the larger it gets, and if my hunch is correct that she doesn't have full control over it, it is going to land her and me in a lot of trouble."

Hank scratched the tuft of fur under his chin. "I can see where you're coming from. I guess I didn't really think about that, seeing her as she is now."

"That's why we moved. That's why we have chosen to homeschool her while Anthony goes out every day as a cop to keep us afloat. The less exposure she has with others until she is grown enough to manage these hurdles and to gain control of her tail, the better." She punctuated her statement by resuming the walk, trailing after her daughter.

"You think having less socialization is going to be ultimately good for her?" Hank brought the camera back around to Murana.

Her ears flattened, tail swishing with agitation. "Says the guy who represents people who are only interested in Taylor for research purposes, and to possibly one-up whatever the Arbiter did to me and her."

"I won't say they aren't concerned for her in a capitalistic sort of way. They are worried that she may not be a productive and contributing member of society if she is cooped up for her entire life," he admitted.

"So it's all about the money and whether she will be a drain on their wallets, or if she'll add to them by becoming a normal member of society and finding a job and paying taxes." She glanced over to Taylor. "Dear, can you have your tail put its tongue back in? We're coming up on the stand!"

"Yes, Momma!" Taylor pipped back, doing as she was told.

Murana turned her head to look at him as they made a left down another street. "By her very nature, she is never going to be a normal member of society. There is nobody quite like her."

"Just like there is nobody quite like the five-hundred-plus kids with powers, many of whom are out there unknown and unseen at this point, in no small part thanks to you," Hank reminded.

Murana bared her teeth. "Don't even begin to get off on putting that blame on me. I'm happy they've successfully gone underground. After seeing the mayor and High Council's attitude about things, they'd be no better off with them than with the Arbiter. Tell me, Hank, do you have kids, specifically special needs ones?"

He shook his head. "I'm actually not married."

"Then don't tell me how to raise mine." She stopped abruptly. "We're here."

Taylor gleefully clapped and jumped up and down. Before them was a small shack parked up against a brick building series of apartments leading into the greater metropolitan section of town. They could even hear the distant hum of the hovering cars from this distance, their specks traveling through the air amidst the high rises. The trailer was not much to look at, being all slatted metal sheets, but the awning was colorful, providing shade as they ordered.

"Come to think of it, I'm actually not hungry anymore." Hank began to shut off his camcorder. "Don't forget to bring her in tomorrow for blood work." The screen and sound shut off.

"You hungry?" Nina's crooning voice broke through the inky haze of sleep.

"Give me a few moments and I'll have an answer," Taylor moaned into her pillow, rolling over to be facing away from the bright and cheerful swan, the bird's draping nightie hanging off her shoulder. Even Ahya flopped over and dug her "face" into the small of Taylor's back.

It had been ages since she slept in a nice, plush bed like the one Nina's apartment sported. Lacking room for much else, Nina offered her bed to sleep in and they shared it together that previous evening. It was both odd and comforting at the same time to be near someone during the night. Taylor couldn't recall any dreams, only that she felt well-rested, yet she did not want to leave the iron grip of those blankets and pillows this morning.

Nina looked beyond excited, her whole body quivering at something good. "I'm making breakfast for you! You'll never guess what it is!"

Taylor, her hair all frazzled, rose her head from the pillow to give her the sleepy eye. "Pancakes and hashbrowns?" She asked hopefully. She hadn't had something like that since Cheribaum, eating at Klera's home. She was really craving some sugary syrup.

Nina frowned. "Well…no. I was actually going to be making some scrambled eggs for you! A predator delicacy! My treat just for you!" Ahya perked up at this, now "looking" around, as if curious.

Taylor wrinkled her snout. She tried not to be rude. "That's very sweet of you, Nina, but I'm not a big fan of meat products or eggs. Do you have any fruits, like apples?"

It looked as though she had just shattered Nina's hopes and dreams. Looking away from Taylor, she said, "I just laid them this morning. I was going to bring them down to the market like I usually do to sell them off, but since you were here, I was planning on giving them to you."

Taylor's heart melted at her friend's sincerity. Meat or protein products for predators were highly restricted and controlled, not to mention expensive. It's why the birds were so established and affluent in Zabökar. This forced many to buy cheaper alternatives, and those weren't exactly ideal in quality or taste—not that it mattered much to Taylor, who swore off meat since Ahya's first kill.

The fact Nina was reserving her batch of eggs for her in lieu of the money she could receive from them was a huge gesture, since it could mean great financial loss. Who knew when the next time she would produce another batch?

"Planning on giving them to me? Did you just make that decision this morning when you laid them?" Taylor smiled.

"I did say my Script said I'd seen you again, right?" This reminder of how their chance meeting was anything but chance caused Taylor to grimace.

"Alright, alright, I'll have them." Taylor shifted onto her side facing Nina. "Hopefully they're not fertilized though?" She wasn't keen on eating anything growing inside those eggs.

Nina seemed to blush, folding her wings on her lap. "I'm not sexually active right now, and most certainly not with any cobs."

Taylor nodded, giving her a toothy grin. "I'd love some then."

"Great! I'll get to frying them up right away!" Nina gave a small pet to Ahya before bouncing off the bed and skipping into the next room.

Taylor could tolerate eggs, and was indeed forced to eat them on several occasions in the last month. She could grin and bear it for her friend. Like sleeping in the same bed, the thought of eating her friend's freshly laid eggs seemed odd to her. Nina and most other birds didn't seem to mind though. It was a profitable business; all they had to do was give up what they produced naturally.

All of this was unusual. They hadn't seen each other in several years, but it was like nothing had changed, even though a lot had changed. Nina seemed more sure of herself, and less prone to seeking validation from others. She was overly fond and touchy of Taylor last night, giving her many hugs or squeezes of the arm. Maybe it was because she hadn't seen her in so long, but Taylor had never known Nina to be this excited about her as a person.

Finally scooting out of bed, Taylor hit the carpeted floor and brushed down her pajamas. Nina remarkably wore her size clothing, cut large at the arm openings for the wings, and was gracious enough to loan her something to sleep in that night, even if it was a bit tight around the armpits; it was good thing Taylor was born a runt. For a punk bird like Nina, Taylor never guessed she would wear bright pink pajamas. Chuckling at this thought, Taylor quickly made the bed before heading out to the main living den.

Ahya was already curious, and attempted to be ahead of Taylor in hopes of snatching whatever food was being offered first. Taylor had to irritably push her out of the way and will her to stay behind while she avoided anything in Nina's apartment that Ahya could accidently knock over with her bulk.

It was a quaint living space. It only had four rooms to include the bathroom, but it was home for Nina. The incandescent tube of blue running up the length of the wall ended at a receptacle at the front door, still holding the mail from what seemed like several days. Nina seemed to have been purposefully forgetting it. Taylor's hoodie and Nina's jacket from the day before were still hanging on the hooks adjacent to it.

She sat down at the small round table that was pulled up from the floor where it was stored. Surface flaps locked up into position to provide eating space. Taylor could smell the delicious eggs being cooked. Looking over the day bar separating the living den from the small kitchenette, she could see her friend humming a few bars of a song they used to sing while she scrambled.

Normally Taylor wouldn't be looking forward to this sort of meal, but she guessed having had it once with Mikhail feeding it to her and again in Klera's home, it wasn't such a bad meal to have. It wasn't the flesh of a living person at least, so Taylor could learn to get over this disgust on eggs, especially if they weren't fertilized. That and it was from Nina, which somehow made it better for some reason she couldn't place.

"I really hope you like them… This is actually the first time I've ever had to make them for a friend." She looked embarrassed as she brought the sizzling pan over and scooped the eggs onto the plate already in place in front of Taylor.

Taylor's eyes widened. "Geez, Nina, did you save any of them for selling off later?"

Nina waddled over to lay the frying pan on the range before picking up a bowl of bread and seeds for her breakfast. "Of course I did. That's only five eggs there. I laid a total of nine this morning. I'll be alright with the money I get from what's left over."

"Five?" Taylor was shocked. That seemed like an awful lot. She was fighting and physically pushing Ahya down below the table from lapping them all off the plate in seconds. "Ahya, could you please not? I want to actually enjoy a fresh meal for once!"

"Well, they are definitely fresh." Nina looked proud of herself. She laughed at Ahya's antics. "She sure wants them for herself, doesn't she?"

"Yeah, and I lose out on the pleasure of actually eating them." Taylor was taking her fork and fighting off her tail, who was snapping at the makeshift weapon.

Nina covered her bill as she continued to giggle at the two of them. "Does what she eat not go to you?"

Taylor looked up briefly at her. "It does, but it isn't the same. Sometimes it just feels more satisfying eating it yourself, you know?"

"That I do," Nina mused, thinking about something. "I remember watching you back in the common room of our band house fighting over food, and it always used to make us laugh."

Taylor finally managed to get Ahya under control. Ahya proceeded to pout underneath the chair and bump up against it underneath incessantly, just to be annoying. "I'm glad to know that my fights with my tail amused you all," Taylor said with sarcasm.

"Don't take it wrong. We all liked you... Well, I did anyway."
Nina blushed.

With Ahya successfully subdued, Taylor finally settled into the chair proper and began to poke around the steamy eggs on her plate. "Could have fooled me. Usually after concerts, all of you went to your separate rooms, and I was typically left waiting on one of you to walk or bring me home. Nobody wanted to hang out with me."

Nina looked a bit guilty. "I'm sorry for that. Ramon was...very strict about things, and the rest of us weren't exactly wanting to cross him."

Taylor grimaced while she scooped her first bite onto the fork. "I almost forgot about Ramon. I always hated him."

Nina chuckled. "I think the feeling is mutual. His rich dad probably rubbed off on him in all the wrong ways."

"No kidding."

Ramon was the lead singer and leader of *Bad Luck*. He was a hyena with impressive vocal range and a temper to match it. If he wasn't of a different species to Finnley, Taylor would swear they might be related by personality alone. While every other band member tolerated Taylor with her freakish tailmaw more or less, Ramon was very vocal about his distaste for them both. He only relented when it was clear she was bringing in the crowds more than he, a fact he resented.

She raised the fork to her mouth, maw open wide before glancing up from her food to see Nina staring at her with anticipation. "I'm not going to lie. It's kind of creepy with you watching me eat something that came out of your butt."

Nina's feathers bristled and she looked affronted. "It wasn't totally out of my butt!"

Taylor smirked. "Close enough." She winked before taking the first bite, still feeling self-conscious about doing this in front of her.

"How is it?" She didn't even wait for Taylor to finish chewing. She hadn't touched her own bowl of food, so busy wringing her wings together for the worst.

Taylor swallowed, acutely aware of Nina's scrutiny. "They're...actually quite delicious. More so than any other eggs I've

177

had recently." She thought about it a moment. "Might also be because they were both made by Mikhail…"

"Who is that?"

Taylor waved a paw to ward off the question. "Nobody important to you. Don't worry about it." She scooped another helping.

Nina breathed a sigh of relief before turning to her food and spooning a mound of seeds. "Oh, thank goodness. I was so afraid you'd not like it. I've never actually had feedback on eggs I produce. I usually just sell them and never hear about it again."

Taylor was regarding the still large portion remaining on her plate. "Five eggs is an awful lot of food."

Nina pointed with a wing finger at her scrawny frame. "I noticed you might need it. Seriously, what have you been surviving on, leaves and dirt?"

"Just about." After another bite, pushing Ahya's sneaking tongue away from the plate, Taylor gestured to her. "How much do they usually net you? The eggs, I mean."

Nina motioned all around her. "I was able to finally get a place of my own separate from the band."

"You mean they're all together still?" Taylor had to quickly swallow before her laughter made her spew eggs across the table.

Nina shared the smile. "Living in Ramon's dad's rental apartment, yeah. None of them have really moved on from the band. Ever since you left, they're trying to rebuild it from the ground up and become 'even better' than we ever were, as Ramon puts it."

"I'm guessing not much success there, huh?" Taylor felt strangely satisfied that Ramon hadn't been able to recover from her absence. It was weird to hear after the fact that her kitnapping and disappearance was so detrimental to the band's fate.

"Not one bit. They no longer draw the crowds like we used to, and the songs Ramon writes suck!" Nina had to stop eating or she'd choke from laughter.

"What about Loray and Bailey? They still believe in the future of *Bad Luck*?"

Nina shook her head. "It's no longer called that. They're apparently the *Horny Toads*."

Even Ahya seemed to join in on the hilarity of the moment, her tongue lolled out and her mouth wide in a menacing expression. "And they actually thought that was a good name?" Taylor was rolling. She couldn't even get back to eating after that.

"It was Ramon's idea," Nina explained. "Now all their songs are about girls and sex. There's no real poetry to the music. No deeper meaning. That's why I loved it when you wrote our songs. They came from the heart and bared true pain."

Taylor pouted. "Yeah...because I'm the expert on it."

The mood changed drastically, and it seemed Nina could sense it. She reached a wing over to cover one of Taylor's paws. "I know you've not had an easy life because of Ahya, but I know a lot of what you wrote resonated with a bunch of fans."

"And here I thought they just came for my tail." Taylor tried to reclaim part of the earlier mood.

Nina cracked a grin in kind. "Well, that's one reason."

A flash of red from the muted television that was playing the news on the dry bar caught Taylor's attention. It was footage of Ahya swallowing a rabbit whole before the person who had taken the shot freaked out and it became a blur. Nina saw her countenance fall and turned to the source of her friend's sudden misery to see Taylor's face plastered all over the newscast with pictures of the dead rabbit in question as they identified him.

"I don't feel hungry anymore." Taylor let the fork drop onto the plate with a clatter, only a few portions left. Ahya took this opportunity to rise up and sweep them off the plate. "Damn it, Ahya!" She whapped her tail roughly as it slithered back down beneath the table contently, the remainder of the eggs digested and added to the growing feeling of fullness in Taylor's belly.

Nina frowned. "Yeah, you didn't exactly make the best return to Zabökar. I mean, it was only a rabbit and most people will probably forget about it within a week—less than maybe—but murder is murder."

"He was still a person, and Ahya ate him." She looked down at Ahya, who seemed to know she was being blamed and attempted to hide herself under the chair. She gazed back up to Nina. "Do you think less of me for what happened?"

"I've never been afraid of your tail." She leaned over to peek at Ahya, who was doing a terrible job at hiding. "For whatever reason, I always felt like she liked me and wouldn't harm me."

Taylor gripped both her elbows and brought her arms close, not wanting to meet Nina's eyes. "I wouldn't be so sure. I thought she would never harm Sarah, my best friend in grade school, yet she was the first one Ahya ate. I was so exhausted last night I didn't really give it a second thought when I fell asleep next to you, but maybe we should keep our distance while I sleep. I don't know if Ahya remains awake during the night."

"You kidding? If you hadn't come along yesterday, I'd still be going through the normal grind at my pizza delivery job with no friends to speak of." Nina seemed hot to defend Taylor against her own insecurities. "And for the record, Ahya sleeps. She didn't move an inch last night."

"That's good to know. Wait, did you watch us sleep last night?"

A slight pause and glance away. "No."

Taylor squinted, but dismissed the odd answer. "So, you don't still hang out with the rest of the band?" She asked just to change subjects.

Nina shrugged. "Not much these days, no. Loray and Bailey are still cool, but since they hang out with Ramon so much, I don't really like being around. I was feeling a bit lonely lately."

"Hold on, you said you'd be at your job now if it weren't for me…"

Nina reached over to the counter and flicked off the television with the remote before resituating back in her seat. "I called in sick this morning."

Now Taylor felt mortified. "You didn't have to do that on my account!"

Nina flapped a wing at Taylor, brushing part of her red hair aside. "Are you kidding? Why wouldn't I want to spend the rest of the day hanging out with one of my best friends?"

"Really? Best?" Taylor rose a brow. "I certainly didn't feel that way when we were still in *Bad Luck*."

"Come on, Taylor. We just went over this. I was the one that walked you home most nights. You can't deny that!" she pointed out.

Taylor smiled. "No, I can't. Thanks, Nina."

Nina pointed at the pine tree necklace around Taylor's neck. Apparently, Taylor had been fiddling with it without realizing. "Where did you get that? Is that new?"

Taylor brought the tree up to eye level, flipping it over in her fingers. "I guess so, since you last saw me."

"Where did you get it?"

Taylor studied it, thinking hard. "Now that I'm looking at it...I think it was from that rabbit we saw on the street yesterday."

"You mean the one you ate?!" Her bill dropped open.

Taylor shook her head tetchily. "No, no... The other one who knew my name. I think I remember him now. He gave this to me the night I was kitnapped. It was from my mother, he said."

"About your kitnapping. We all just thought you ran away from us."

"Oh, right..." She let the necklace drop. "None of you would have known. Yeah, to this day, I still don't know who it was that kitnapped me. I have suspicions it was the High Council here in Zabökar, but I don't know for sure. They did awful experiments on me."

"How did you escape?" Nina was riveted, her breakfast forgotten.

"I don't know. That's the part that's all foggy to me. I just remember being out in the desert running from someone or something I could not remember. It's like I became lucid in that very moment, and everything before it was a dream. I came to a town named Palaveve out in the middle of nowhere and stayed there for a time." Taylor lamented the fact that the town was no longer there.

"So why in the world would you even come back?" Nina seemed confused as she leaned back in her chair.

"Simple. These people who are after me, they are never going to go away. They'll always come after me wherever I go." She knew this wasn't making any sense to Nina yet. "Multiple bounty hunters were

181

sent after me and were fighting over me this past month. It seems different people want me for different things, and apparently one reason is for food."

"What?"

Taylor shifted part of her hair over to the side to showcase some patches of skin where the fur was just now growing back from lacerations that had been given to her. "Some person named Sabrina Fahpar drugged me or something and attempted to eat me. She bit me here and here. I overheard them talking about her after saving me."

"The very people who were hunting you down saved you?"

Taylor nodded. "Yeah. It's a long story. Apparently, she's something called a power-eater." Nina grew quiet and continued to listen. "But she's dead now. I came here with one of the people who were after me. That reptile you saw? Ari? She's one of them. I came to reunite with my family and find out answers as to why I was born with this tail and in return, I allowed them to…experiment on me." She shivered at the memory. Even Ahya shook at the mention of it.

"And you think they'll be able to track you down?" Nina looked nervously around. "To here?"

Taylor sat up straighter and leaned forward to assuage her fears. "No, I don't think so. We gave Ari the slip back in the subway, remember? She has no idea where we've gone. So long as we're careful going about Zabökar, we should be fine."

"So long as *you* are careful." She pointed back towards the television with her bill. "You're the one they have plastered all over the news, not me."

"Right, of course." Taylor was feeling pretty put out. She didn't mean to be a burden to Nina one day into their reunion. "Guess I should stay inside your apartment while you do what you need to do outside then."

Nina's expression melted as she smiled at Taylor. "I didn't say that. Just that we need to make some drastic changes to your look so you're not as noticeable anymore."

"Like what? Dye my fur?" Taylor scoffed.

Nina was thoughtful. "Well, now that you mention it… You were already doing that a bit when you fur-painted those eyes on Ahya

182

back when we were performing. We'd just be doing that to the rest of your red fur."

Taylor began to get self-conscious. "I guess... I sort of like my red fur, but I do see the point in covering it up. It would make getting around town a bit easier. Do you have anything like that here?"

"No. I used the last bit on my crown feathers." She spruced up her blue plumage atop her head made to look like hair. "We'd have to go find you something in a department store that'd work." She pointed at Ahya. "Until then, we'll have to dress you up pretty strictly and make sure she doesn't open up and scare people."

Taylor followed her gaze down to Ahya, who was trying to "look" innocent. "I can only do so much to control her. I just hope she understands the reason why." Ahya faced Taylor and was "staring" at her, as if trying to commune with the person she was connected to.

"I'm trying to understand the reason why you were with this...Ari, to begin with." Nina looked like she considered turning the television back on again. "Didn't you say in return for experimenting on you, they'd reunite you with family or something?"

Taylor's mood soured. She folded her arms. "Not quite. They sort of backed out on that one. I'm not exactly happy about it." The birdsong from the unevolved avians outside the apartment window attracted her attention. "I've no idea where my family is out there, or if they're even still in the city."

Nina thought about it a bit. "We could go visit the band. Was planning on doing that eventually soon anyways. I think Bailey still keeps in contact with your brother, Max."

Taylor brightened at this. "Max! Oh, I've missed him. I've not seen him in years, not since he left to go form his own career."

Max Thrash was Taylor's older adopted brother, the younger of two brothers that were not wolves in the Wolford family. He was a raccoon who was a bit more special than most, and seemed to excel when performing music. He was their drummer before Bailey took over that position when he left. Last she heard, he had started his own nightclub with nightly venues which drew in large crowds. She was very proud of her brother, but lacked the awareness back then to keep track of him and what he was up to.

"I liked him." Nina smiled. "Although he was a bit weird, there was no better drummer than Max. Don't tell Bailey I said that though!" She shared a knowing look with Taylor.

Taylor wiped her paws on the napkin hanging half off the table at this point. "So when do we leave to visit them?"

Nina put up both her wings. "Hold your horses there! I still got to put in all my piercings and look the part. I haven't seen the band for months now, and I'd rather not go back to them looking like this!" She gestured to her lack of temporary metal implants and make-up. "Besides, there is one last thing I'm curious about."

"What's that?" Taylor asked, handing Nina the empty plate as she put both dishes in the sink and let the auto-cleaning cycle flood the deep basin with soapy water and churn, the swan sliding the splatter shield lid over it.

"If they did experiments on you in return of reuniting you with your family…" she began.

"And finding out answers as to why I was born with a tailmaw," Taylor filled in.

Nina nodded. "And that. Why else were they letting you out with Ari then?"

"Certainly nothing gets past you these days." Taylor remarked. "I remember when you all used to get smoked up and drift nights away."

"I'm off that stuff." Nina looked like she was miffed about having to relive those old, bad decisions. "Ramon is probably still on the crap, but ever since then, my head feels a lot clearer. You still haven't answered my question."

Taylor grew silent for a moment. She wasn't sure how much she should tell Nina, or how much to involve her in problems she knew would come back to bite her in the ass. On one hand, there wasn't exactly anything damning about the information she had on the mission the Arbiter tasked her to do, but having Nina know about it might unnecessarily entangle her in something bigger that might get her hurt.

"Remember how I was telling you about power-eaters and the one that almost got me?" Nina gave a small squawk. "There are apparently a lot of them here in Zabökar, and the Arbiter said he wants me to track them down and figure out where their secret gatherings are so they can strike them where it hurts."

"What's that supposed to accomplish?" Nina looked a bit worried.

"It's supposed to give us the ears of the High Council. The Arbiter said he wants to warn them of a growing threat from his people and these huge mechanical behemoths from the south. They won't listen to him right now, because it needs to come from a product of his old research that was infused with magic and..." Taylor could see Nina's eyes glossing over. "Yeah, it's super complicated. Let's just say I was sent to do a job with Ari and you came along and it went sideways."

"Felt like I was falling over for a second there," Nina joked.

"Har har." Taylor rolled her eyes. "You're not the one involved in this whole mess."

"Unless I want to be."

The sentiment hung in the air between them before Taylor waved her off. "Go impale yourself with your metal rods, you crazy bird." Nina cackled at this and sauntered into her bedroom to get dressed.

"Speaking of metal rods," Nina called out from the other room while Taylor was staring out the window, enjoying the sun's rays trickling in. "I see you're missing all of yours."

Taylor reached up to feel her ears and the small indentations of all the piercing holes that had healed over. "Yeah, they went missing when I 'woke up' in the middle of the desert. Hadn't really gotten them back since."

"We got to fix that!" She came out with shredded jeans and a very revealing top with a faded bird skull printed on its front. Every hole and orifice was now glinting with brandished metal, the biggest being the big loop going through both her nostrils on her bill. "If I'm getting all dolled up to visit the gang, you will too!"

"Nina, seriously? We don't even have time for that."

Nina put her wings on her hips and glared. "You have all the time in the world as I see it! Your only goal was to find your family, and since you're no longer with this Ari person, you got no obligation to her either! Let's hang low, get you dressed up, get some metal in you and dye that fur! You'll be looking sexy hot in no time!" She let out a whoop.

Taylor couldn't help but laugh with her friend as she was ushered into Nina's bedroom to go change. The swan was immediately shuffling through her extensive wardrobe hanging on multiple racks in her closet, softly talking to herself as she judged one outfit over another. Finally she pulled out a pair of faded jeans with accompanying belt and looped chains, and tossed them over for Taylor to catch.

"I also think this shirt and coat can look good on you." Nina was eyeing a black leather jacket made from rare reptile skin cultivated from a foreign land. "They don't even make this sort of thing anymore in Zabökar."

"I like that shirt." Taylor pointed to a plain black tanktop with drooping arm openings for the wings, but that'd still work for her.

"Really? It's kind of dull." Nina looked at it strangely. "We should spice it up with this." Nina's eyes were aglow as she grabbed a spiked collar from her dresser and brought it over to fasten it to Taylor's neck. Taylor flushed, as she was unused to having someone fawn over how she looked. Not knowing what else to do in this situation, she let Nina undo the collar and clasp it around her neck. Nina stepped back to admire her handiwork. "It even fits!"

"You really are a beautiful wolf, Taylor." Nina didn't seem to be focusing on any one thing in particular, and was instead regarding Taylor's body as a whole. "And yes, you too, Ahya." She giggled as the tailmaw looked "offended" she was being left out.

"Thanks…" Taylor couldn't think of anything else to say to the unprompted compliment.

She never really thought of herself as beautiful. She was so used to people calling her a freak or a monster and wanting nothing to do with her. The Nina in front of her was not the same one whom she knew back when the band was together. This Nina wanted to be around Taylor, and didn't cow to Ramon and avoid her when forced to by his direction. Their only times they were truly together were the walks home after each concert. Times were certainly different then.

Nina could sense Taylor was a bit embarrassed. "Oh, right... You probably want some privacy to dress." She winked and waited out in the kitchen.

Taylor put on the jeans, having Ahya move around as she clasped the button over her tail so it could poke through. It was a bit shorter than what she was used to, having it end at the upper calves. She didn't truly notice a problem with the outfit Nina chose until she put on the jacket which had spacious sleeves. It was a short one that only went down to the middle of her stomach, and there was nothing that would cover the top of her head to hide the red hair. Not that it mattered too much when she had a blazing crimson tail as well. Nina's clothes on the whole were a bit on the small side.

"Nina! This is not going to work. I don't have anything to cover my hair."

The swan poked her head in. "Oh, yeah, that jacket actually has a rain hoodie to cover the head, but it's zipped up in a little pouch in the collar."

Taylor had to take it off to find the zipper. Sure enough, there was a lighter, but water-resistant fabric inside that she could pull up and over her head in case of rain. "That's clever."

"I know, right?" Nina chittered. "I actually didn't find out about that secret until after a year of having the jacket!"

"So where are we going first, oh Ms. Fashion Designer?" Taylor jokingly mocked, having now dressed herself properly. She was already starting to look like her old self, when she was lead guitarist.

"We need to do something about that fur." Nina looked up, rubbing the bottom of her bill as if in deep thought. "And that hair, it's utterly atrocious! It must go! Yes! Yes!" Her voice getting very pompous and playful.

"Shall we shave it all off?" Taylor shot back, smiling.

"Don't tempt my fashion sense!" They both laughed at this. "I've missed you, Taylor."

"I've missed you too." It was Taylor this time that initiated the embrace, sinking into those soft feathers of Nina's wings as they gripped each other tight.

187

188

9.

REUNION

Taylor grit her teeth and held back a whine as the piercer poked a hole through the outer side of her ear. He wasted no time in removing the needle and tossing it into a tin before grabbing another and slicing through the inner side opposite the first puncture. Tossing that needle alongside the first, he expertly slid a metal bar with a balled end through the two holes and secured it on the open end with another ball he screwed on to keep it in place in her ear.

"And it's over!" Nina honked happily, patting Taylor's paw which was crushing her other wing with a vice-like grip.

Taylor let loose a big exhale as she slumped into the chair. "I don't think I'll ever get used to that."

"I'm surprised, given how many piercings you used to have." Nina smiled.

Taylor nodded her thanks to the professional jaguar who had done her industrial piercing. "I didn't like doing them then either. I honestly just did them for the look, knowing it would enhance my street cred."

"Fake it until you make it, huh?" Nina ribbed.

"Yep!" Taylor wasn't even hiding it.

The jaguar pointed at the rod. "Now you must take care of this daily, young lady." His tone was not to be ignored. "Need to not fidget or play with it, and clean it daily with a sterile saline solution. Furthermore, try not to sleep on it for at least several weeks."

"Great, I have no way of knowing how bad I sleep." Taylor rolled her eyes.

"Don't worry. If you want, I can snuggle up beside you while you sleep on your side to make sure you don't roll around." Nina squeezed Taylor's shoulder with a wing.

The jaguar gave them both an odd look, but dismissed it. "Don't care how you two do it, just make sure you don't sleep on it." He waved them off towards the front of the cramped store for them to pay the fee.

"You're a weirdo," Taylor whispered as she got up out of the chair.

"I'm just making sure my best friend doesn't get herself injured on account of her tossing and turning all night long!" Nina whispered back.

"I could sleep on the floor." Taylor was thoughtful.

"That'd just make it worse!" Nina flapped her wings.

"That'll be eighty-five picuns" The jaguar dinged the register as the tray popped open.

Nina dutifully paid the entire bill regardless of Taylor's protests, and then guided her over to the mirror so they could have a look at her. They had already went to a barber earlier and dyed her fur a darker shade of grey than the rest of her body. Her red was so vibrant it required several applications for it to stick. Thankfully nobody either cared or were oblivious to the recent news, despite it being shown on the multiple monitors above the waiting area. It probably also helped that there were no customers at that time of day and the sound was muted.

Ahya thankfully remained silent and invisible for the duration of the dyeing, even though Taylor could feel that she wanted to expose herself when they were messing with her to apply the liquid into her fur because it felt so good. To complete the look, they asked the barber to shave one side of her head down to the base fur coat—the side with the wounds, since Nina said it'd look more badass—and then style the other half of her hair over it in a punk-like fashion.

Looking in the mirror at herself, she really did feel more confident. The chains, the spiked collar, the edgy hairstyle, the dark fur, and even the fake nose ring they put in her right nostril to compliment the very real rod piercing in her left ear all served to make her fit right back into her former band—not that she had any current plans of doing so. It felt nice to be able to express a bit of her individuality again. It only took Nina's insistence to do so, but she was grateful for it.

Nina beamed at Taylor's reflection. "That's the Taylor I remember." She paused a moment, looking at Taylor's swishing tail. "Well, except for the lack of red fur now. I loved that, but guess we'll have to get used to this for now, since you're a wanted wolf."

"I really wish I wasn't." Taylor sighed.

"Yeah, I know. Anyway, it's near noon now, and the gang should finally be waking up from their drugged stupors, no doubt." Nina chuckled, opening up the swinging door for Taylor to exit the store first.

"I never did understand why you all did that crap. The smell of it alone was enough to turn me off." Taylor grimaced just thinking about it.

They sidestepped a few antelope as they began their way down the street towards her former band's studio abode. They were still within the inner city, and the flashers were doing their rounds of advertising local sundries and goods to Nina. She didn't pay much mind to it until she looked over and saw nothing popping up for Taylor as they walked along.

"You don't get anything advertised to you?" She was flummoxed.

Taylor glanced over at the perky gopher who was tracking along in front of Nina, his holographic origins being displayed from an array of built in projectors perched along at intervals across the buildings in downtown—so well integrated that you had to actively look for them to spy their locations. There was nothing for her as she walked, despite being subjected to the same scans as her friend.

"I guess not." She shrugged.

"That's so weird." Nina waved off the gopher. "We had officers from the city come to our school to collect DNA profiles from every student. It was a citywide mandate. They didn't come to yours?"

Taylor shook her head. "Then again, I was taken out of school by my mother before I even hit high school. Ahya ate Sarah when I was only twelve."

Nina looked down at the ground in shame for forgetting. "Oh, right. You were very young then. They came to us when we were in high school. That makes sense."

"Yeah, I wouldn't be in the system."

191

"Probably better for it," Nina said with confidence. "They can be quite annoying, but it's not like I can do anything about it. So I just ignore them."

They turned the corner and walked past a noodle place with a window looking in, the view obscured by a fish tank filling its frame. Taylor stared at the place for a moment, shivering at a memory long since repressed. "Wait a minute." She turned around from it and looked up at the building opposite. "This was our old venue, The Fox Den. Don't tell me they're still living here?"

Nina laughed. "Sort of? They're actually one building down and eight floors up." She pointed down the alley to another side entrance, just as dingy as the one leading into the club hall proper. "We can take that to the stairwell leading to their place." They entered and proceeded up the floors.

"Isn't there an elevator to this place?" Taylor panted, already on their six flight of stairs since entry.

"Unless some miracle happened I don't know about, the elevator for this place has been broken for years," Nina explained, continually three stairs ahead of her. "The owner is too cheap and couldn't be bothered to fix it. Most tenants just take the stairs out of habit anyway."

Taylor paused momentarily, leaning up against the railing. At least they had a nice view of the grungy alleyway just outside via the full-length barred windows from the first floor to the top. "Not even bothering to check to see if he one day fixed it?"

Nina thought about it as if it had never occurred to her. "I guess we could have done that." Taylor moaned her displeasure. "We're almost there anyway, silly!" Nina assuaged.

They exited the concrete stairwell and into a more extravagant hallway with sconce lighting and blue, glowing bars of light that traveled along the ceiling, giving the entire corridor an unearthly hue. Nina strode forward with purpose until she got to the third door down on the left. The numbers on the apartment door had fallen off, and the stained outlines of them had all but faded away.

"I'm so glad I got out of this dump," Nina muttered to herself as she rapped on the door.

They could hear the thumping of the music beyond, drowning out her attempt at recognition. She rapped harder this time, yelling for Ramon's name. This caused the music to decrease significantly, but it was still audible through the wall. It was a good long minute before the door opened, smoke wafting out into the hallway, getting all up in Nina's face as she waved it away with her wing.

Nina coughed. "Gods, Ramon. Do you guys even care what the landlord thinks about what you do to his place? That stench will never come out of the carpet."

The taller yet hunched hyena stared at her with an indifferent look. He had the expected nose and ear rings to match Nina's. He was dressed down to a tank top and low-hanging jeans, its compliment of metal ringed belts doing little to hold up his dignity, revealing the stained underpants beneath. Taylor grimaced at his posture as he leaned up against the doorframe with a haughty look. His fur spots were a disgusting shade of black—no doubt tainted by the drugs he ingested into his body daily.

"The prodigal swan returns," he heckled, sniggering at his own humor. "What brings you groveling back to us? Want to get back into the glory of the band? Too late for that, missy. That ship has sailed. We're already looking to hire another bass guitarist, and I think we found him."

"I'm not here for you, idiot." She waved him to step aside. "We're here to see Loray and Bailey."

"They're indisposed." He wasn't budging an inch.

"Hell, are they doped up too?" Nina edged to peek past Ramon's bulky frame. He had clearly been working out since Taylor last saw him; she remembered him as a scrawny thing. "No wonder the '*Horny Toads*' are going to the shitter," Nina said with venom.

Ramon snarled. "Watch that tongue before I rip it out."

"You wouldn't even try." She did her best to stand up tall to him.

He sniffed dismissively, scratching his green-dyed mane. "Doesn't matter anyway. You only got lucky because you got old enough to crap out eggs and we couldn't. I bet if it wasn't for that, you'd be dead in some street gutter by now."

"Ramon, you're still an asshole." Taylor folded her arms.

He turned to Taylor as if realizing she was there for the first time. "Who's your stupid friend?"

"Her 'stupid' friend is Taylor." Ahya reared up and over Taylor's head, maw opened wide with tongue lashing out in an attempt to smack Ramon across the face. Taylor had to will Ahya hard to avoid actually doing that.

Ramon blinked twice before his mood turned even more sour. "So I got two gutter rats coming back to me. Did you all fail at life that you need a second chance at stardom and come limping back to the band? As I said to Nina here, applications are closed."

Taylor was about to snark back when a soft, elegant voice from within called out. "Who is that, Ramon? Is that Nina?"

Ramon wrinkled his snout, licking his muzzle in disgust. "Unfortunately."

"Oh! How is she? Let her in! I haven't seen her in months!" another drowsy voice sounded.

Nina gave Ramon a satisfied look, her eyes lidded with pleasure as Ramon reluctantly stepped aside. "Come on in. Why not?" His sarcasm was thick.

They walked in to what looked like a studio apartment. There was the main floor with a depressed den complete with L-shaped couches facing a wide screen television. Beyond that through the smoky haze was an open kitchen with even less amenities than Nina's, but with far more stacked dishes that were in dire need of cleaning. Spiral stairs on the left opposite the bay window on the right led up to the loft where haphazard bodies of mattresses, pillows, and sheets were strewn about. It wasn't exactly a positive impression of their cleanliness.

Lounging on the couches watching the music videos blasting on the big screen were a porcupine and an opossum that looked to be drowsing a bit. Both perked up as they entered. The porcupine spotted Taylor, recognizing her instantly despite her dyed fur. He ecstatically did his best to unpin himself from the blanketed cushion protector they had placed on the couch for him. The opossum merely stared blankly at the two of them, not entirely sure what he was looking at.

"Taylor! Wow… What happened to you?" The porcupine gawked at her new look before moving in for a hug.

"Whoa, hey! Nice to see you too, Loray!" Taylor backed off a bit, using Ahya as a deterrent with her teeth as she merely shook his paw instead. She wasn't about to get poked again. She had learned that lesson years ago with him. He meant well, at least.

"Is that really you, Taylor?" The opossum did his best to get up too, but it was like the weight of the world was on him and he slumped back down.

"Yeah, Bailey! Can you believe it?" Nina strode past the irritated Ramon, stepping down into the den area, leading Taylor by the paw. "I just ran into her yesterday out of the blue!"

"Eating someone, no doubt?" Ramon sneered, shutting the door loudly.

Nina whirled around. "Oh, come on! That was an accident and you know it!"

"Uh-huh, just like that poor kit groupie her first night out."

Taylor placed her forehead in her paw. "Don't remind me. Maybe coming here was a mistake."

Nina put a comforting wing on Taylor's arm and reminded softly, "Remember, we're here to ask about Max. It won't be for nothing." Taylor nodded her head at this. Ahya just looked embarrassed at this bad memory.

"Yeah, don't think I forgot about that," Ramon continued. "Her first night out during the afterparty, one of our groupies got a bit too close for comfort for Taylor and her tail swallowed him whole!"

"Ahya was scared! That was the first time we were among a bunch of fans who wanted to be close to us. She didn't know how to react!" Taylor snapped.

"Scared? She's a freaking tail!" He roared

"It's not her fault! She was just reacting in the only way she knew how to protect herself!"

195

"Ha! Tell that to the poor parents. Our band manager had to make up some bullshit story as to how he died to protect you!" He jabbed a finger at her. "I said it once then and I'll say it again, you are a danger to the group. A monster and a menace. I mean, why would he even cover for you?"

"Maybe because she had given us the popularity that you couldn't." Nina rebutted. "Face it, you couldn't hack it on your own as lead of *Bad Luck*. It took some random wolf with better singing abilities than you to do you one better!"

"Shut up!" Ramon backhanded her, causing her to honk before hitting the floor.

Ahya swooped in and jerked Ramon by the waist off the carpet with her big maw, her teeth digging in slightly into his sides. Taylor bared her teeth. "I have half a mind to let her bite you in half and toss your remains out that window! Don't ever hit my friend!"

"You…you wouldn't dare! If my father hears about this, he'll make your life a living hell!" Ramon whined, banging his fists onto Ahya to release him, which caused her to grip tighter forcing more sounds out of him.

"It already is." Taylor said coldly. "I was already marked for murder the moment I stepped foot in this city, and am probably already hunted by the police. What's one more dead body under my belt matter to me?"

"Everybody just calm the fuck down!" Bailey was fully awake now for once and had stood up between them, garnering the attention of all. "Nobody has to die today! What the hell has gotten into you two? Yeah, I know it was no pleasure fest the first time around, but it seems you two are out for each other's blood!"

Taylor looked down at the opossum a moment, before setting Ramon down roughly. "Sorry." She glanced away. "I can get carried away sometimes these days."

"That was an understatement," Loray commented from standing atop his couch space, having fled there once the argument grew heated.

Bailey smoked a huge inhale of the nearby bong to settle his nerves before flopping down on the cushion. "Why don't we all just chill and talk things out. We haven't seen Taylor in years, and the first thing you get her to do is want to kill you. Wasn't she our friend?"

"Calling me friend when you all specifically avoided me outside rehearsals and live concerts rings a bit hollow." Taylor cast a baleful look.

"We've gone over that." Nina sighed. "Even I admitted we may not have been the best of friends to you. For my part, it wasn't because of her tail that I didn't spend more time with her."

As if on instinct, all of them stared over at Ramon who was leaning over the mess of wrappers, condoms, food scraps, and more to find the remote. He looked up at the sudden silence. "What? If you're looking for an apology, you're not going to get it. Just because you could sing and play guitar didn't mean you were one of us."

"Good to know where I still stand then." Taylor grit her teeth. Ahya duplicated her reaction.

"I don't think that was ever true," Loray tried to mediate.

"Speaking of which," Ramon continued to look for the remote. "How are those new friends of yours, Nina?"

Nina scowled. "This isn't about me. We're talking about Taylor and how we did her wrong last time around."

"I think we just didn't know how to…relate to you, especially after that first incident," Loray attempted to explain.

"Ahya never did eat anyone else after that," Taylor pointed out.

Ramon slashed a paw through the air. "Doesn't matter. The fact it happened at all damned you in my eyes. You were only kept on because you were useful. Nothing more."

"You're a dick," Nina insulted.

"Thank you. One you enjoyed if I recall." He grinned maliciously.

Nina looked repulsed. "A mistake I regret to my very grave."

Taylor was shocked, pointing a finger at her. "Wait, you two…"

Nina put up a wing as Ramon cackled. "Please, I'd rather not get into it."

Bailey snorted, as if waking up from a snooze. "What if she was useful again? I mean, we have that gig at the Real two nights from now. Our music is hurting and we haven't been getting a lot of—"

"Shut it!" Ramon gave him a deadly look.

"I'm actually not here to rejoin the band." Taylor decided to finally sit down beside Bailey, who hastily scooted a half-cushion away. Taylor clucked. Guess some things wouldn't ever change. Taylor made sure Ahya did her best to be nice and keep her distance from the nervous opossum.

"Then why are you here?" Loray cocked his head curiously.

"I came back to find my mom and brothers." Taylor answered.

"Awww, you ran away from us and found no new friends, so you came back to the only people who could possibly love you? How adorably sweet," Ramon mocked, choosing to sit on the couch opposite Taylor, putting as much distance between himself and Ahya. He was still scratching the itching welts her teeth made in his skin.

"I didn't run away from you guys. I was kitnapped," Taylor retorted.

"You were what?" Loray was shocked.

Nina sat on the other side of Bailey, given him a gentle nudge to wake up from his sudden nap. "Oh, that's terrible! We didn't know!" He spoke with a start.

"I never did understand why Ramon hired him after Max left." Taylor was genuinely curious about the opossum's employment.

Bailey had a diagnosed case of extreme narcolepsy that struck constantly, even through live concerts. It was amazing that his custom-made drum set woke him up to continue playing when his head inevitably struck one of the perfectly placed cymbals. He had a talent to immediately grasp where they were in the song and pick up the beat without a break, which led to some off-timing quirks which lent itself to some charm with their songs.

"Because he was the only one good enough to replace him," Loray said, not getting the snark behind the question.

"Say, didn't you run away from your family? Isn't that why you were with us to begin with?" Ramon scoffed, leaning forward on a knee with one arm, his combed-over punk mane covering an auburn eye as he glared at her. "Why you wanting to go home to mommy after running away from that supposed 'hell-hole' that you were in?"

198

"It was not a hell-hole." Taylor was angry. She didn't like being reminded of her mistake to leave her mother. Yeah, it wasn't a picnic being dragged from place to place without any knowledge of the full why. "I was just frustrated with how I was being treated at the time."

"I'm sure. I bet you're treated a whole lot better now since you've had to come back to us." Ramon chuckled.

Taylor ignored that comment. "And for the record, I still have good relations with my older brothers."

"That's not what Steven tells me." He smirked.

"Ramon..." Nina warned.

Taylor looked back and forth between them confused. Ramon leaned forward further towards her. "Oh yeah, that skunk brother of yours came rampaging up in here a week after you disappeared, raving about how you were responsible for your mother's death!"

"Ramon!" Nina rose to go slap him as he backward somersaulted over the couch, backing off to hide from her wrath, giggling like a maniac the entire way.

"I...what?" Taylor sputtered.

Taylor's mind reeled from the revelation. Her mother was dead? Sure, her mother wasn't looking her best when Taylor left her, but enough to be dead from it? She always thought her mom as some indomitable force that nothing could control. She always noticed when her mom was angry, and it usually was never at her unless Ahya did something naughty. It was against others who had come to the house for some reason or another involving her. She seemed like such a strong person. The thought she could be dead now seemed unfathomable.

"That was a crappy move." Nina gave Ramon a death stare. He continued to cackle.

"You...knew?" Taylor continued to process this news. Even Ahya was slumped over Taylor's lap, feeling as depressed as Taylor. She absently petted her tail as she struggled to follow the conversation.

Nina's face wilted as she turned back to Taylor. "Yeah, I actually didn't want to break it to you until we met up with Max first. I wanted you to have a happy reunion instead of a sad one."

Although the intent to hide this from her was a bit misguided, Nina's heart was in the right place. Taylor sagged. "I didn't get to say goodbye."

"Maybe you should have thought about that before you ran away and disgraced us with your presence." Ramon stood up.

"I swear to the gods, I will shut you up myself if you don't can it!" Loray was already up and getting ready to turn around to shoot a few needles off in the hyena's direction. Ramon was already cringing and covering his face. Loray just huffed. He gave Taylor a more sympathetic look. "I'm sorry you had to find out like this. We all truly thought you ran off and ditched us, and thought that you had killed your own mother after what Steven had said."

"But…I didn't. I wouldn't!" Taylor shook her head. "She was sick when I left. I had no idea how bad it was until just now." Tears began to form as the reality sank in.

Nina rushed to put her wings around her friend. "I'm sorry, Taylor."

"On top of being kitnapped too…" Bailey was sounding remorseful.

Taylor's stomach was in knots. She held it tight and hunched over. "I don't feel so good."

Ramon sneered, staring right at Nina. "Maybe it was something you ate?"

"Will you just piss off, Ramon?" Nina glared.

"What will you do now?" Loray asked, plopping down looking just as defeated as Taylor.

Nina sat close to her and squeezed her shoulders tight as a reminder of their purpose. Taylor shook the haze that had enveloped her senses at the news of her mother's death. "Max… We came to ask where we could find Max now. Does he still own that nightclub down on Roaring St.?"

All eyes turned to Bailey. He was sound asleep again. Loray nudged him. "Hey, buddy. Wake up."

Baily rose with a snort. "No, actually, he just sold it last week. I was there at the auction."

"You managed to make it downtown on your own? Awake?" Ramon was incredulous.

Both Nina and Taylor cast him glares, but Bailey had missed the comment. "It was going under, and he called me to help him pack up his things and move him to his new apartment."

Taylor wilted. She had hoped at least one member of her family was having some good tidings, but Max probably had just as many problems as she did. Burdening him more with her presence and all the bad things that followed after her was probably not going to do Max any favors. She wondered if finding her family was such a good idea after all, especially now that she discovered her mother was dead. If Steven was furious at her and Max was going under financially, would her being around even be beneficial?

"Wait a minute!" Ramon broke the silence. "Did you say you're a murderer and the police are after you right now?" He miraculously found the remote right at that moment. He flipped the channel to their preset local news channel. "Is there a bounty for reporting you in?" He looked genuinely eager.

"Fuck you." Taylor was wrathful.

Sure enough, the newscast had horrendous timing. The image appeared of Ahya, far more crimson than she was now, swallowing a rabbit whole. The endless repeat of death bore into Taylor. First at Nina's place, then at the barber shop, and now here; it was like the macabre horror of what she was slapping her in the face with condemnation. She couldn't look at it anymore. The way Ahya expanded to inconceivable size, and suddenly the rabbit was gone, leaving nothing but a disgusting display of visible limbs protruding from within her monster of a tail.

Ramon snapped his fingers, leaping back to the couch and sitting. "I get it now. You dyed your fur to prevent yourself from being recognized now that you're back in town! After you murdered that rabbit!"

"Why would you do that?" Bailey seemed fully awake now, his eyes like saucers. He began to scoot away even further down the cushions.

Taylor looked down on the morose tailmaw in her lap, still seemingly caught in the grief of their mother's passing. "I have no idea. I didn't murder him. I never killed that rabbit directly. All I knew was that I was hungry and hadn't eaten in some time, and then I smelled freshly cooked food nearby and…it happened."

"It just happened?" Ramon was unconvinced. "I think it was premeditated."

"Will you please just lay off of it?" Nina squawked. She threw an unopened condom wrapper at him, smacking him squarely on the snout. Ramon just growled.

"That's probably another reason why we didn't hang out as much, Taylor." Loray expressed himself a lot with his paws, and he was doing his best to plead with Taylor to understand with them. "We all thought…" He looked at Ramon. "Well, most of us thought you were a wonderful girl, but that tail of yours is quite frightening. That video they're playing on the TV isn't really helping our impressions of the danger you pose."

"Yeah, I get it. I'm a menace. A freak. Tell me something I don't know." Taylor pushed Ahya off her lap away from Bailey. Ahya looked hurt at the gesture.

"Why don't you just tell us where Max is, Bailey? Then we can just be on our way." Nina tried to steer the conversation back to the reason they were here.

"He's actually a fair distance from here, on the other side of The Bits." Bailey was beginning to get drowsy again.

"Seriously, how did you manage to help?" Ramon squinted at the opossum.

"Did you need anyone to guide you?" Loray offered.

Nina shook her head. "We can manage on our own. Wouldn't want to take up any more of Ramon's precious time." She purposely ignored any expected looks from the hyena. Loray looked dejected, but Bailey seemed a bit happier Ahya wouldn't be nearby him any longer than she had to be.

"Specifically he's near Meerkat Town, on the north end of The Bits. He's on the basement level of the Marsh House. I even got a spare key to his apartment, but I'll never use it. You can have it." The opossum dozed a moment while shuffling his paw around his pockets. He barely was able to hand it over to Taylor before his arm dropped and he was snoring away.

"I'm surprised he's been able to survive this long," Taylor commented.

"The drugs make it worse." Nina seemed concerned. "But it's useless to try and talk them out of it."

Taylor looked at the three of them lounging on the couches. "Yeah, I see what you mean." What a worthless wretch of a band it had become since she had left. She almost ached at the sorry state it was in now under Ramon's complete command.

"Now that you've got what you wanted and reminisced with your 'buddies' a bit, will you just go now?" Ramon was already up and had the door open to the hallway.

"Yeah, we are." Nina rose, helping Taylor up with a wing. "Wasn't here on a pleasure visit anyway. Let's go, Taylor. We have a brother to find."

"It was nice seeing you two." Taylor smiled at Loray and Bailey. "And Ramon, I hope that stuff kills you one day, sooner than later." She swept past Ramon, saying it just loud enough for him to hear.

"Don't come back again or next time I will call the cops." He slammed the door behind them, bonking Ahya a bit with the force of it when she had barely crossed the threshold.

Taylor immediately swirled around and slapped her fist on the door. "You asshole! I wasn't even out the door yet!"

"Did you really have to be that mean to her?" they could hear Loray ask.

"You shut up!" Ramon shouted beyond the door.

"Now do you see why I left the group?" Nina sighed, looking at the key still gripped in Taylor's paw. "So did you want to go now or later?"

"Now." Taylor breathed a ragged sigh. "I want to get this over with. I came here to see my family… or what's left of it and that's what I intend to do."

"What if they don't accept you back? What will you do then?"

Taylor stared off down the hallway back to the stairwell they came up from. "I have no idea."

Jake shivered as he looked on the Sunrise Savanna coffee shop, now taped off and closed down due to being near ground zero of the disaster that struck with Taylor and his friend, Tony. He was not even several meters away from the spot where he last saw Tony leave this world. He could still envision that horrible moment happening again right before his eyes.

The rest of the street wasn't much better. Cars were pushed off to the side near the sidewalks and police tape was slathered all across the crime scene, stretching down several blocks. The cops had cordoned off nearly the entire street in their investigation. There weren't many there now; the horde of police had flowed through the area the day and night prior. What was left were those on clean-up duty, managing contractors to come out and help spruce up the area for business again.

"So why are we back here again?" Jake turned to Trevor, who was surveying the scene, looking for something specific.

Trevor still hadn't moved his chin off its perch on his paw. "You said you wanted to find Taylor and get some form of closure over all this, correct?" Jake nodded. "Then we need to first start at the scene of the crime, as they say, to pick up her scent and go from there. I did track her down once, I am confident I can do so again."

"Thanks for doing this."

Trevor waved him off without looking at him, the object of his quarry now located. He moved off in that direction with Jake in tow. "Don't mention it. I'll admit, I'm a bit curious as to how she's faring now since I last left her in the hands of the Arbiter."

"Where are we going now?" Jake couldn't see anything in the disaster before them that would attract Trevor's attention.

Trevor pointed to a nearby cop who was jotting something down on a personal notepad. "A way in. We can't possibly hope to have a chance to track her down from here, when we aren't allowed in to the crime scene. We need an insider."

The aging wolf officer looked up and raised a paw to halt them as they neared the tape. "You aren't allowed here. Official business only until we can get this— Holy shit! Is that really you, Trevor?"

"Vergin!" Trevor opened his arms wide.

"That's Officer Tannenbaum to you." The wolf narrowed his eyes, his familiarity disappearing into suspicion. "Why are you here?" He looked him up and down. "You look like crap."

Trevor chuckled, gazing down at his iron arm being scrutinized. "Yeah, I've seen better days. How you been?"

"Better than you, it seems." A hint of a grin began to surface again. "What brings you back to Zabökar? Haven't seen you since you quit the force!"

Trevor shrugged. "Here and there. Participated in a few wars." He tapped his metal appendage. "I'm actually here on a job for the High Council. I've been tracking down this murderer with a tail mouth for you." Jake looked up at him, but stood silent, he knew Trevor just lied out his teeth.

Vergin cocked a brow, obviously disbelieving. "This is highly irregular. Do you have any documentation or proof of this?"

Trevor shuffled in his coat pocket and pulled out a crumpled piece of paper and handed it over. "It's a bit old, but it is signed by the High Council about a year past. I'm still on the job, considering she's still at large."

Vergin snorted. "Doing a bad job of it I see considering it's been over a year." He studied the paper.

"So how is everyone at the precinct? How is old Harold?" Jake could tell Trevor was making idle conversation.

Vergin looked up at him. "Chief Bremingham is fine. He's actually due to retire in three months."

Trevor looked surprised. "Really? I thought he was going to stubbornly stay in that position until the day he died."

"Guess the job caught up to him finally, like it does to all of us. He's actually currently out of town on a business trip." Vergin shook his head, going back to studying the paper. "Kowolski resigned last year when it was found out he was cheating on his wife…with three other wives."

Trevor winced. "Good gods. That probably didn't end well."

Vergin laughed at last. "No, it didn't."

After a few more moments, Trevor leaned over a bit to read the paper he had handed over. "So you think we can take a couple minutes to investigate the scene and I can go about doing my job?"

Vergin folded up the sheet and handed it back. "I still will need to call this in. I just want to be sure. Procedure and all, you understand."

Trevor stuffed it back into his pocket. "Come on, Tannenbaum. For old time's sake. You won't even know we were even here. We're not going to touch or move anything, and it'll be as pristine a crime scene as when you last left it. All we need is five minutes." Trevor gave him his best sympathy look.

Vergin frowned and eyed Jake, who proceeded to step a bit further behind Trevor. "And who is this with you? He doesn't look like any cop."

"He's actually my associate on this contract." Trevor put a paw to grip Jake's shoulder jovially, something Jake wasn't exactly fond of. "He's had a firsthand encounter with this female wolf, and has proven invaluable in researching her places of frequent habitation."

Vergin studied the two of them. Jake did his best to put on a serious face and nod in confirmation at the lies Trevor was spouting. At length, Vergin lowered the radio from his mouth and clipped it back onto his belt. "You got five minutes, Trevor. Don't make me regret this." He stepped aside to busy himself in his cellphone for the duration.

"Much obliged. We'll be done in less!" Trevor did a two-finger casual salute and slipped under the tape. Jake just had to lower his ears to simply walk under.

Jake whispered to him when he felt they were out of earshot of Vergin. "I didn't know you were a former cop."

"You never asked, and it wasn't exactly important to our discussion yesterday." Trevor was already on a knee and sniffing around the area.

"You lied a lot back there. Was that contract you handed him even real either?"

Trevor glanced briefly at him, winking as he did so. "Well if by real you mean, did it have my name on it? No. I actually stole that off a group of mammals whose job was actually tasked to them by the High Council to track down and capture Taylor. I'm just glad Tannenbaum didn't inspect it closely enough or he'd see I was nowhere in the contract!"

Jake scowled. This sort of deception didn't exactly sit well with him. If Trevor was a former cop, his actions now definitely did not reflect the virtues he was supposed to wield. "I'm not entirely comfortable with this."

Trevor stopped sniffing and squinted at him. "You either want my help or not. If you don't like it, I can just stop now and leave. Otherwise, just shut up about it and let me do the job you asked me to do—which, mind you, I'm not getting paid for."

"Fair point," Jake admitted, defeated.

Jake was slightly peeved that he was working alongside an ex-cop in trying to find Taylor. It was a job he had long since dreamed of having, only to be forced aside to be a pencil-pusher for them instead. To have Trevor treat his formal profession with such callousness, it left a sour taste in Jake's mouth. Still, Trevor did make sense in that he was the one that asked for the wolf's assistance, something Trevor could have easily denied. There was no excuse for Jake to reject his help now.

Trevor was already nose to the ground on all fours at the very spot Tony was swallowed up. He rose to sniff the air and began to walk awkwardly hunched towards the sidewalk and a few steps down. "She was here." He looked off up the road towards the rising skyscrapers. "She came from that direction, where the scent is fading..." He turned 180 and gazed off away from downtown and towards a subway entrance. "And she fled that direction. I sense multiple scent trails here. She was traveling with someone."

"Yeah, a swan," Jake informed. "I remember her now. Her name was Nina. They were both together under my care when I was bodyguard for their band several years back."

"That's actually an insane lead." Trevor looked annoyed. "Why didn't you start with that? We could have avoided this step altogether!"

"You never asked." Jake smirked.

Trevor threw his paws up, ear flattening. "Ugh, let's just research where Nina lives now and just pay them a visit."

"So you're done here now?" Jake looked around. It didn't seem like they accomplished much of anything.

Trevor took another sniff. "Well, not quite. I think I smell a few familiar...faces. Follow me." He motioned for Jake to tagalong as he waved down Vergin. "Thanks, buddy! We're done here. See? As promised, not a single thing out of place!"

Vergin inspected the area. "Very well. Take care of yourself, Trevor!" He thought about something a moment before adding, "Did you want to hit me up later and go for a round or two?"

Trevor clicked his teeth and finger-gunned Vergin. "Sounds awesome, my man. Keep up the good work here!"

Both Jake and Trevor slipped back under the police tape and made their way down towards the subway stairs. Trevor was constantly following his nose until he rounded the bend and spied the caved in entryway, the rubble moved aside already to let pedestrian traffic pass. Cautiously, he held a paw out to have Jake follow him at a distance as he descended to the platform beneath.

"What are you tracking?" Jake's ears were up and alert.

"Remember that High Council contract I gave Tannenbaum up there?" Jake nodded. "Well, I smell three of those names on that paper here. It seems they gave chase as well, not just Ari."

"Do you think they captured her?" Jake looked around the deserted station. They had shut the area off due to a landlocked train being rooted to the spot by a pillar of earth that pierced it to the ceiling of the tunnel.

Trevor shook his head. "No, Taylor's scent and that of your Nina end here at the edge of the tracks. Ari and these three..." He pointed at a spot where dried blood was visible next to a massive indent in the wall the shape of a shell. "They caught up with each other here, and then went off further down the tunnel in the direction opposite the train Taylor probably took to escape."

Jake thumped a foot. He felt dumb. He probably needn't have involved Trevor at all. He wasn't thinking straight last night, booze-addled or otherwise. He should have recognized and remembered Nina yesterday, but things spiraled out of control insanely fast. The shock of seeing Tony die overpowered any other senses to recall Nina's presence until a few minutes ago out on the street. He could have just made a beeline straight for her residence and most likely found Taylor there.

"Since I can figure out where Nina lives now, I can take it from here." Jake attempted to sound confident in front of the occupied wolf.

"Yeah, that's a good idea. You go on ahead. I'll catch up." Trevor seemed distracted, his attention drawn to the dark tunnel.

"That's it? You're not going to stop me from going off and possibly hurting Taylor for what she did to my friend?" Jake didn't exactly have full intention to harm Taylor, but he was still angry at her for what she did. What he'd actually do once they met again, he still hadn't quite figured out.

Trevor broke his gaze and turned to Jake. He guffawed hard, drawing Jake's ire as he lowered his ears at the ridicule. "You? Hurt Taylor? Oh, you rabbits. I've full confidence that you'll do nothing of the sort to her. Not that she'd let you if you tried. I'm not worried at all. Go track down your wolf girl."

"What if she ends up hurting me?" Although Jake was slightly worried he might end up with the same fate as Tony, a part of him secretly did want some release from the pain that was his current life. This quest to find Taylor was the only thing that starved off his need to end it all.

"If you're that worried about it, go check your Script. Should be something in there about your death and if it comes at her paws." Jake couldn't tell if Trevor was being flippant or not.

Jake thumped some more. "So what will you do now?"

"I'm actually more interested why they chose to go with Ari. It's clear there was no altercation here once Taylor escaped. I want to know why they decided to leave together." Trevor faced Jake more fully. "This is where we part ways for now. Don't worry, if I need to find you, I can." He tapped his nose. "I sincerely do hope you find her and you resolve this matter with her. I don't think she meant what happened."

"I hope you're right." Jake's depression began to creep back into his voice.

Trevor stared at him for a few moments. "Tell you what, I'm going to send you a text and you can get my number off of that. Call me if you need me."

"Wait, how did you…" Jake was confused. He never even gave Trevor his phone number.

"Good luck, little guy!" Trevor hopped down onto the tracks and was already sprinting along them. Within seconds, he was lost to the darkness.

10.

LOSS

Hank sighed as he smoothed out his slacks, adjusting the new flip camera he had been issued just the year prior to bring to these meetings. Murana was sitting across from him in her reclining chair, looking a bit more pale than usual. Taylor was lounging in some black pajamas on the couch, watching cartoons on the television with a bowl of popcorn that both her and her tail was taking pawfuls of.

"She certainly has gotten bigger, hasn't she?" Hank noted. He had not been to their home in almost nine months, and it looked like the tail had been growing in size along with Taylor.

Murana didn't comment as she reprimanded the tail. "Ahya! Don't stuff it all in your face! Take only small mouthfuls! You're getting it all over the couch!" She pinched the bridge of her nose as the tail perked up confused, more kernels dripping from its maw and sinking between the cushions to be lost until the next vacuuming.

"Ahya?" Hank was confused.

She slumped into her chair further. "Yeah, that is its name. Taylor had her fifth birthday last week, and that's what she chose to call it."

"And it can actually hear you?" He tilted his head.

Murana nodded. "As far as I can tell. It seems sentient somehow. Like, Taylor can control it when she wants to, but it seems like it can also do what it wants without her input. It does respond when you talk to it."

"That's actually quite fascinating. I don't believe we've even logged that for the council." He set the camera on his thigh as he brought out a small notepad to jot a few things down. "The offer still stands to have her come in and get evaluated more thoroughly."

212

"And the answer is still no." She narrowed her eyes. "Not only was it not part of the original agreement, I wish for her to be free of that. Besides, that isn't what I asked you here for."

Putting the small pad away, he picked the camera back up. "So what did you bring me back here for? Without further examinations and research with Taylor, there isn't much more I can report on here. The High Council isn't really interested in the same dry statements over and over again with little to no change. That's why I haven't been coming lately. You're lucky they decided to just drop their investment and you don't have to pay it back now."

"I get that." Murana brought up a small cloth to wipe away some slight discharge from her nose. "I called you here to talk about me."

This perked his interest. "Why? Are you suddenly developing some sort of powers?"

She shook her head. "No. In fact, I think I may be one of the unlucky ones that rejects that DNA pulse. I would like to ask to be brought in for testing. I've been feeling lethargic and experiencing new aches and pains throughout my body. Simple wounds no longer heal as fast as they used to and—" She wiped her nose again. "I feel miserable all the time."

He stared at her for a time, the sound of Taylor's cartoons drowning out the silence between them. "Those symptoms could indicate any number of things. What makes you think it is the cancer described in your reports when you were investigating the Arbiter's operation?"

She eyed him suspiciously. "Well, if you had read the reports, I stated that roughly 50% of the subjects developed some sort of unnatural abilities, while the other 50% when exposed to the ray developed cancer."

"I do remember reading that, yes," Hank admitted. "However, their symptoms showed up much quicker than yours. It has been, what? Almost six years since then, and we're just now hearing of potential cancer symptoms?"

Groaning, she attempted to shift into a more comfortable position. "True, but they pulsed those poor kids several times if they did not develop the results wanted within the timeframe expected. I was only pulsed once. My dosage was less substantial than theirs. It would stand to reason I would develop cancer much later; it's the only thing that makes sense to explain what I'm going through." She wiped with the cloth again.

"And how long did you say this was going on?" He gestured to her nose.

"Maybe about two months now?" Her eyes wandered, seeming to lack the ability to focus.

A loud buzz jolted Hank from his chair, nearly knocking the camera off his lap and onto the floor. "What was that?"

Murana sniffed. "Just the doorbell." She took a tablet off the coffee table nearest her chair and swiped up to open an app to view the camera feed just out the front door. She called over to Taylor, "Honey, can you go get the door. It is Trevor from Dad's work."

"Okay, Mom!" Taylor seemed pained for having to miss part of her show.

Setting the popcorn down, she bounded off the couch and skipped over to the foyer. They could hear her excitedly opening up the door. "Hey, Trevor from Dad's work!"

Hank's ears flicked to the front entrance as the momentary silence grew. A solemn voice replied to Taylor, "Is your mother here?"

"Yeah, she's just in there!" She bounded back to the living room, running off to leap over the couch back into her comfy position to watch more cartoons, leaving Trevor to shut the front door behind him as he entered.

A large, scarred wolf appeared, his eyes serious as they locked on Murana's. "Mrs. Wolford?" His tone commanded attention from her as she sat up straighter in the chair.

Her eyes were wide and focused now. "What is it? Did something happen?"

"Ma'am, I think you're going to want to remain sitting." He grimaced and put a hand on his leg as he attempted to lean up against the couch. He took off his officer cap and set it down on the backing just above Taylor. "Your husband, Anthony, died tonight."

Murana dropped the tablet she was still holding. After a moment of silence she shakily asked, "How did it happen?"

"It was a routine traffic stop, ma'am." Trevor wrung his two good paws together. "A couple of punk kids were speeding, hyped up on drugs, and were pulled over. They had loaded weapons in the back and when Anthony went to ask for their license and registration, they simply pulled a gun on him and shot him. Point blank."

Hank sunk into his chair as Murana gripped the arms of her own, claws piercing the fabric with her intensity. "And where are they now? These punks? Please tell me you caught them." She was shaking with rage. Even Taylor had stopped watching her show as she could sense something was not quite right.

Trevor put a paw out to stay Murana's anger. "Mrs. Wolford, they are still at large, but they are being tracked down as we speak."

"They're not caught yet!?" Her teeth were grinding so hard they could hear it.

"The rest of the department has issued all units on your behalf in finding these kids," Trevor tried to assuage. "We all loved Anthony and appreciate the good work you've done for us when you were in. We all want to bring these perps to justice. So rest easy knowing everyone is on this case." He nodded with finality. "I have already identified your husband, but the question is open if you wish to see him at this time. You are free to say no."

Releasing the armrests, she began to nod in the affirmative. "Yes... Yes, I want to see my husband. I want to see what those rat bastards did to him." There was a burning fire inside of her, and all hints of the sickly wolf before Hank was gone.

"Maybe I should go." Hank suggested.

Looking at him as if he had just appeared from thin air, she agreed. "Yes, maybe you should." Her expression was determined. What grief she had was now buried deep within such fiery anger that one could barely tell she was affected by this news.

Not waiting for a further response, Hank got up and excused himself from the premises.

"So why aren't we tracking her down if you know where she is?" Natalia was a bit flustered with her own impatience.

Ari just swiveled her red eye to Natalia, her flesh and blood one still rapt on her phone app depicting a map with a beacon indicating where in Zabökar Taylor was located. "For the same reason why she left you all and came here with me: she's hot-headed and stubborn. Once she's made up her mind to do something, I've noticed, there is little anyone can do to change her mind."

"Sort of like you."Terrati pointed out, garnering a glare from Ari.

"Is that why you destroyed half of Zabökar above us in chasing her down?" Mikhail still seemed upset at the destruction of their car at the hands of Ari. The fresh cut above his eye was evidence of this displeasure.

Ari shrugged. "I'll admit I was a bit angry that she would defy me like that, but looking back on it I can completely understand. I overreacted. We denied her the very reason she chose to come with me in the first place: her family."

"So you're playing the waiting game and looking for an opening?" Natalia was pacing back and forth, her agitated tail swishing.

Ari's eye pivoted to her. "My father still has a mission set out for her. I will make sure she gets it done with me. However, I feel her discovering what has happened with her family would better benefit my cause, provided it doesn't take too long."

"I still feel it wrong of you to spy on her with that." Mikhail pointed to Ari's phone.

"Well, it's actually quite smart," Terrati surprisingly defended. "Why do the work yourself in tailing a target when you can let a machine do it for you?"

"Not surprising, coming from a trained spy," Mikhail grunted, folding his arms.

"I'm just glad she chose to take the cell with her this morning. After the conversation I overheard through her phone and the makeover this Nina is giving her, I half expected her to forget it in the bedroom," Ari admitted, still pressing the earbud up to her bald head where her ear cavity was.

216

They had taken up residence in a disused railway station that seemed forever in refurbishment. It was quite near the bird's apartment that Taylor was staying at, providing easy access to her should they have a need to go topside. Once it was established they could track Taylor's every movement through Ari's phone app, the tensions between them lessened, which suited Ari just fine. She'd rather have allies than foes at this juncture, with so many things going against plan. These three would do just as well as anyone else, provided they would go along with her objectives.

"Where are they headed now?" Natalia pressed.

"Stop your pacing. It annoys me." Ari returned Natalia's scowl. "They're heading to the Marsh House now. Something about visiting her brother, Max."

"Why does that name sound so familiar?" Mikhail seemed lost in thought.

"Are we going to follow them over there?" Terrati decided to plop down on the edge of the platform, his hind hooves hanging off over the rails.

"No." Ari turned the phone off, eliciting a cry of protest from Natalia. "We know where she'll be for the next hour and where she'll most likely be tonight." She pointed above them. "I'd rather not waste my time and effort in chasing after her all over the city."

"You don't seem to be in much of a hurry to fulfill your father's objective with Taylor if you're giving her this much leash." Mikhail was probing, Ari knew.

"If I know Taylor, she'll not wait for this to be delayed. She'll want to see what's left of her family as soon as she can. I'd expect a day or two at most for her to satisfy her longing to reconnect with them. Then I can remind her of her purpose and why she was brought back here at all."

"And what purpose is that?" Terrati turned his head to the side, one eye on her.

Ari thought on it a moment. It would probably be prudent to let these three in on at least a bit of their plan. It would only bolster their support and usefulness if she had them on her side, especially now that they were technically no longer with the High Council. Their goals wouldn't be opposing hers now.

"As you've seen from back in Howlgrav, the true threat here lies beyond the mountains to the southwest: those giant behemoths that can destroy cities in an instant. My father and I know this will inevitably happen to Zabökar. You know this. We know this." She looked at each in turn. "We have evidence to present to the High Council, but they are unwilling to listen to anything we have to say, since they banished my father from the council decades ago."

"And they won't listen to us either since we are disavowed," Mikhail continued her thought.

Ari clicked her tongue. "Exactly."

"But why would they listen to Taylor at all?" Natalia seemed confused. "She's a nobody compared to you, the daughter to the Arbiter, and us, former contracted mercenaries beneath the council."

"They'll at least grant her audience, which is all we need, because she is a unique specimen of mammal." She got up from sitting to stretch. "According to my father's records, she was born from the experiments that happened to her mother, which immediately made her attractive in the eyes of the High Council. They've been seeking her for years, first through diplomatic means, but after her flight from her mother, through more direct, illegal means."

"Why would she be attractive to them at all? I never did get that," Terrati asked.

"Why would any powered mammal be viewed as attractive to the High Council? She's got powers unlike anyone else. Powers they could use for their own ends. Seems as good a reason as any. They just duped you all into thinking it was some salvation mission for lost, wayward mammals with powers when they sent you out."

"So they grant her an audience, what then? What is the point? What could she possibly do or convince them of?" Natalia started to resume her pacing, but stopped when Ari glowered at her. "The High Council, in my experience, are not a group of mammals who will just capitulate to someone's demands."

"Interesting you phrased it that way," Ari noted. "I guess you could say we are using Taylor to ask something of the council, but it isn't as self-serving as you'd think of us. We're actually trying to convince the council to order a city-wide evacuation and relocation to somewhere safer in the sure event the behemoths reach Zabökar."

Natalia stood agape. "That could take days, weeks even to pull off!"

"All the more reason for their urgency." Mikhail nodded, finally understanding it.

"But why?" Terrati was suspicious.

"My father has his reasons," Ari answered. "I'm not about to divulge all of his plans to you though."

Mikhail sighed. "As much as I distrust you and your father, I will admit that the core reasoning is sound. I've yet to shed judgment on other aspects of your plan. Like how you could convince the High Council to even grant Taylor an audience that doesn't involve them overtaking her and throwing her in shackles for what she is and what she can do."

"Oh, that's the best part!" a seedy voice echoed from above them.

All eyes turned to the ceiling as Mikhail, Natalia, and Terrati trained their guns on the materializing chameleon above them. His green scales looked a muddy brown in the dim lighting of the subway. Terrati shrieked in fright as the chameleon's tail unfurled from a coiled position and opened wide in a slathering display of menace, its maw revealed for all to see. He dropped down to the tile below, causing Mikhail and Natalia to back away. Ari stood her ground at the smaller, yet imposing Rakkis.

"Gods, there's another tailmaw now?!" Terrati looked petrified.

"What the hell are you doing here, Rakkis?" Ari was adamant.

"Keeping track of you, of course. As we were ordered." His tongue darted out to lick one of his roving eyes. It seemed he kept one trained on her while the other bounced around at the other three.

"Why does it have a tailmaw too?" Natalia's grip on her gun quivered slightly.

Ari ignored the question and continued to address Rakkis. "By who? My father? Why in the hell would he send you to follow me? He entrusted this job to me, not you!"

His gurgle laugh caused her skin to crawl. "Maybe it is because we are insurance to finish the job in case you cannot."

Ari threw her hands up. "Ugh! He still treats me like a little girl! I'm unable to contact him for a few days after securing Taylor and he sends you to come meet me. I lose Taylor after day one here in Zabökar yet maintain vigilance on her location and doings, and he still prefers to have someone watch over me! When does it end?"

"Or maybe it is some misguided notion to protect you?" He stepped a few paces away before adding mischievously. "Or maybe because he doesn't believe you're up to the job, but gives you this independence so you can stay out of his way."

"Lies."

"Believe what you wish. We are only here to keep watch for now." He moved his tail to "look" at the three behind him, its bulk enlarging, causing Mikhail and Natalia to back up further, butting up against the drop off to the rails. "As for these three, you neglected to mention the method as to how you'll get High Council's attention! Might as well, seeing as you've revealed just about everything else to these nosy busybodies."

"What is he talking about?" Mikhail locked eyes with Ari.

Ari's shoulder slumped. "We were to investigate the disappearances linked to the power-eaters that now infest the lower tunnels of Zabökar. By researching and discovering their whereabouts, we could strike them at the heart of their operations and gain favor of the High Council."

"Then you'd send Taylor into that den of vipers with your proposed evacuation plan?" Natalia was aghast.

"I'll admit, that's leaving an awful lot to chance on the High Council's response." Mikhail's face darkened. "We may have worked for them and all, but even I have my reservations about their intentions regarding Taylor. They may have the best intentions for this city, true, but I can't say how far that extends to other things." He and Natalia shared a look.

"We think they're not sharing all that they know, Ari." Rakkis faced Mikhail directly, his tail slinking up closer to be face to face with the larger tiger. "Are you not afraid of us?"

Mikhail stared the tail down. "I've faced worse."

"Fascinating." Rakkis played with the fronds on his head absently.

"What things have you been keeping? What do you know about this High Council that I don't?" Ari stepped forward a bit, her posture now threatening.

Terrati answered first. "One of the power-eaters we encountered back in Cheribaum was a member of the High Council. She almost got to Taylor, and would have succeeded if we hadn't intervened."

"Terrati!" Natalia hissed. Terrati just gave a shrug.

This put a damper on Ari's enthusiasm for seeing this through. If there was one power-eater, she knew there would be more. "Are there any others we know of on the High Council?"

Mikhail was still firmly holding his weapon on Rakkis. "She was the only one we know of."

"My, my, this certainly has taken a turn." Rakkis looked pleased with himself, his tailmaw backing down from Mikhail. "And now with Taylor all over the news for murder, you're going to need to convince this High Council really hard to take her seriously—power-eater removal or not." He sniggered.

"One day you're going to have to tell me how you know things," Ari said.

"Mmm, yes, we believe we will." He got down on all fours and curled his tail up onto himself once more. In a flash, the light bended and he was invisible again, causing Natalia to gasp. "You understand we can be anywhere and listen in on many things. It truly is as corrupt above as it is below. You'd be surprised how much we know what goes on beneath the streets of Zabökar. Like the wolf who is headed your way right now." His voice trailed off along the ceiling down the platform.

"What wolf?" Terrati's ears were alert, his nostrils flaring as he sniffed the air wafting in from the darkness of the tunnel.

"Who was that?" Mikhail asked.

Ari stared off at the last place she heard Rakkis. "He's one of father's recent experiments, based on limited knowledge extracted from Taylor years ago."

"He can make more of her type?" Natalia looked worried.

Ari shook her head. "Not yet, but after last week's tests we did on Taylor, I wouldn't put it past him to perfect his methods."

"She's not some science experiment!" Mikhail grew angry.

Ari raised a clawed finger. "Her undergoing these tests in return for seeing her family again was the deal. She kept her end."

"You didn't keep yours," Mikhail reminded. "Which is why we're all here right now."

Ari waved off the accusation. "Beside the point. What matters now is to allow Taylor to get done what she needs. Only then should she be agreeable enough to do whatever else we require of her."

"Are you so sure about that?" Mikhail continued to grill.

"Guys, that Rakkis was right. I hear footsteps!" Terrati whispered harshly.

They all retreated from the edge of the platform and moved back to be behind several of the support pillars that trailed down at intervals across its length. They watched as a familiar cap strode in view, its shape visible from their position. They saw two paws reach up, one of iron, each lifting the wolf onto the platform. Natalia recognized him immediately.

"Trevor?" she asked.

"The one and only." He dusted himself off. "Speaking of broken deals... Yes, I heard a part of that conversation," he added, after seeing the death glare from Ari. "Decided I'm going to break mine and not stay away. It seems you might need my help with Taylor."

"Not exactly." Ari was not about ready to have her current plan be usurped by this wolf. It was bad enough that Rakkis was tailing her on her father's orders, but to now have this idiot back into her life?

"I think so. I might have an inside lead on Taylor, and getting her to do what you want," Trevor said confidently.

"Oh really? Do tell." Ari was seething.

"Let's just say I have a good feeling on a rabbit." He smiled.

Taylor could hear the arguing long before they reached the door. They arrived at the Marsh House in the late afternoon, the sun just dipping below the horizon of towering skyscrapers and spiraling hightops. The neon glow of the evening was just starting to buzz as the jingling off the ropes of light from the eight rods linked to the monoliths of the High Council began to fade into the din around them. She hadn't ever questioned their existence and just took them for granted, but now they were more intriguing than ever to her.

The Marsh House was a lot less impressive than they were led to believe. Even the surrounding area leading up to their destination were leagues apart from the slums littered around their former band's current abode.

In fact, it was even worse.

The Bits was a horrible place. Cracked pavement and flickering marquees were just the surface of a suburb gone wrong. Gaping holes in corner lots and broken or boarded up windows gave off a very unsafe impression, and prompted Taylor and Nina to bunch closer together.

Heading down the musty stairs to the basement, Taylor's heart fell. Things must be extremely rough for her brother, Max, if he'd had to sell off his lounge and move here to this dump. Even the corners of the hallways were squeaking with unevolved rats, huddled in their vile lairs, waiting for the next morsel to be dropped by a callous tenant.

Taylor had butterflies in her stomach as two familiar voices on the other side of a dusty door continued to argue, grease stains smeared along the edges of the frame. She couldn't make out the entire conversation, but it was clear enough for her to know they were talking about her. News of her abrupt entrance to Zabökar more than likely made it to them. The voice of Steven was pretty loud while the more reserved one belonged to Max. If what Ramon said was true, this would not exactly be a happy reunion with Steven. Hopefully Max would be more agreeable.

Nina squeezed Taylor's arm with a wing. "You sure you want to go through with this?"

Taylor nodded nervously. "It's the whole reason I came back here. I want to see my family again. If I can't see my mother, then I want to at least see my two brothers. Pine and Mitchell are no longer with me anymore, and I could do with some more family."

"Who?"

Taylor warded off her confused question. "Never mind. Just two boys you wouldn't know." She took a deep breath and rapped on the door softly. The talking stopped. It was dead silence on both sides of the door. She knocked again.

This time, she could hear Steven. "Were you expecting anyone?" His voice was a squeaky pitch. After a few moments, a thumping of feet stomping towards them heralded her eldest brother, Steven. He whipped the door open and took one glance up at her, his face immediately scowling. "How dare you... How dare you have the gall to come back after what you've done?"

"She didn't kill Mom," Max stated matter-of-factly, his form visible past Steven, relaxing in an easy chair, guitar perched upon his lap.

"I know that." Steven snapped, glancing back at him. "But she might as well have, given her broken heart! Leaving her in a state of need after all she had sacrificed for you to keep you safe!" His bulky glasses were quivering on his little nose.

Steven's skunk tail was standing straight up with trembling rage. His size and indignant posture would almost be comical if it weren't for the very real threat of the musk he could expel at any moment. His ball cap was frayed from years of use, his faded shirt emblazoned with the company logo of his news reporting job, "ZCN."

"Nice to see you again too, Steven." Taylor sighed, taking the initiative to sweep past Steven, ignoring his blatant protests. She waved at Max hoping for a better response. "Hey, bro."

He looked past her at the now empty hallway. "Hey, lil' sis."

Taylor looked beyond the tan, torch-key raccoon. There was not much room to move around. It was evident he had been forced to move from a much larger living space to a smaller one; there were heaps of unpacked boxes and piled up furniture that seemingly had no place in his household. There was barely a walking path from the front door to the cramped kitchen beyond the living den, and the hallway lead to what she guessed was a lone bedroom and bathroom. A single, wobbling ceiling fan was the only air climate mediator in the sparse room. A far cry from the fancy digs she recalled hanging out in several years back.

"I've half a mind to call the cops on you right now! What right do you have to come barging in here after the crap you pulled?" Steven shut the door harder than he intended, wincing as it slammed. Nina wisely stayed off to the side and remained quiet.

Taylor spun around on him. "The crap I pulled? What? Being kitnapped?"

"Kit...what? No!" Steven sputtered. "Eating that little girl..."

"Sarah."

"Whatever! Eating her and forcing mom to cut off all contact with me and Max and go missing for years on end." He jabbed a finger in her direction. "She lost everything because of you, to keep you safe! Then the next time we hear from her, you've run away to join some flunky band and leave her a former husk of what she was!" Steven was still breathing heavy. He reached into his pocket and brought out an inhaler, giving himself two good puffs to maintain his airflow.

"I was also in that band for a time," Max reminded coolly.

"Not the point!" Steven batted Ahya away as she attempted to nuzzle him in the side. "Get away, Ahya!" She looked sincerely hurt, drooping back around Taylor. "Then when it was found out you disappeared completely..."

"Kitnapped."

"Disappeared," he repeated without missing a beat. "We all thought you had run away and abandoned us. Mom died shortly thereafter of a broken heart. Her will to live and fight against the cancer was gone. We couldn't even say goodbye since she was laying low over hiding you after that murder you did. We only heard about her death from Uncle Sebastian. Because of you, she left us. Because of you, I lost the one thing that mattered most in my life."

"I'm still here," Max said without intonation, strumming a single chord on the guitar absently.

"You know what I meant," Steven said irritated.

"Mattered more to you than the rest of your family?" Nina asked.

225

Steven turned to her annoyed. "She saved my life when I was a young kit. Brought me out of a musk mill meant for black market trading of my musk. I could have died there, and she saved me. I will always love Murana for that, and now she's gone. And for what? Her only blood child? Like Max and I don't even matter?" He turned his back to Taylor. "Even since you were born, things were different. She spent more time with you than she ever did with Max and me—trying her best to give you a normal life, to ensure you got all the trappings of a successful future, and you just threw it all away!"

"Feel good to get it all out?" Max strummed another chord, a slight smile on his face.

"Not even close!" Steven seemed to be on a roll now, spinning around again to Taylor. The object of his ire now in front of him, he seemed ready to lay into her for all those years.

"I didn't throw it all away!" Taylor finally had enough. Steven might've been justified in his rage against her, but she didn't deserve to be treated like the trash of the family. "How would you feel if you were dragged from place to place, constantly on the run and never knowing when your next meal would come, let alone a place to sleep for the night would be?"

Taylor flung up her fingers. "Three full years of this I endured, and what answers did I get from Mother about all of this? Nothing! Zilch! She didn't deign to explain anything to me why we couldn't go back to being a normal family anymore. Why we couldn't ever see you two and Uncle Seb Seb anymore. I knew it was because Ahya had eaten Sarah, but looking back on it, I can't understand why she had to be so drastic in hiding me away."

"Because you murdered someone. Thought it'd be obvious," Max chipped in. She glared at him, but there appeared to be no malicious intent in his face. His emerald eyes were locked onto the curious poking of Ahya, her bulk wandering around the apartment, bumping into things.

"Yeah, fine… Well, I figured I'd just do my time for the crime and be done with it." Taylor was exasperated. These two diminutive brothers felt like a force of nature to overcome. "That didn't explain why what actually happened was so extreme."

Steven crossed his arms as he stared up at her. "That's easy: because she made it clear she loved you the most. A love she should have shared between the three of us, but because of your special tail, you got all the attention!"

"She actually wanted to kill Taylor at first," Max blurted out without inflection.

"What?" All three shouted. Even Nina was shocked.

Max shrugged, looking back down at his guitar as all eyes turned to him. "I was there when Mom and Dad fought over you. She was so certain you weren't her cub that she was willing to kill you. Dad stopped her."

"That's a lie." Taylor's mind broke. She couldn't really comprehend that her own mother wanted to kill her. It didn't seem real. After all she had been through with her mom, the very thought she wasn't wanted when she was born seemed crazy.

"I've never heard about this." Steven stepped around Ahya and walked up to Max directly. "What happened?"

Max looked up at Steven's ball cap. "Dad took Taylor away for a few months, visiting only a few times a week while Taylor was babysat somewhere else. He wanted Mom to get over the shock of Taylor's tail, and get to a point where she missed her as her baby. Then he returned with her. Things began to get better from there."

"I don't remember any of this." Steven was lost in thought.

"You wouldn't." Max adjusted his black-striped tail as he moved the guitar to a more comfortable position on his lap. "You had just landed that sweet gig at ZCN. You were busy and constantly running around working up your 'corporate ladder'. You never did get to see how bad it got."

Steven snorted. "Yeah...corporate ladder. What good it got me. The glass ceiling in that place favors predators more than it does us small fry."

"My point being, is that Mom loved all of us, but she had to learn to love Taylor. Which is why she ended up spending more time with her than either of us," Max said with finality.

"You seem wise well beyond your years," Nina commented in awe.

Taylor looked over at her; she had nearly forgot Nina had accompanied her here. "Max is...special. He was diagnosed at a young age. He doesn't think like you or I do. He also sees and notices things that we completely miss."

Steven nodded. "Mom had to explain that to me when we adopted him."

"And me when I was old enough to understand," Taylor added.

"You're okay with all of this then?" Nina broached the topic.

Max smiled, admiring her wings. "I'm not that dense to not know I was different from everyone else. Besides, I have medication these days to help with the worst of it."

Steven looked to be getting back his prior fervor. "Still, what makes you think you can just waltz up in here and expect to be welcomed back with open arms?"

"I didn't." Taylor had hoped this would have gone better. Now she had to salvage what she could of her family or this entire trip and all she had to endure to get to this point would have been a waste. "I was gone for so long and despite what you want to believe, suffered a lot of crap. After my kitnapping and managing to escape out on my own, I began to realize what was most important to me. It took two little friends to remind me of that." She smiled sadly at the remembrance of Pine and Mitchell. "I realized I needed to get home to you, to make it right by you two."

Steven huffed. "Well your chance to make it right died with our mom."

"That's rude," Nina honked.

Steven squinted at the taller swan. "Don't try to think you know better. I spent so much time with Taylor growing up. I invested all the spare time I could in playing with my younger siblings."

Max nodded. "I can attest to that. He would always stop by on the weekends before work to play with me and Taylor."

"I put my time in as older brother to her. Nobody loved her more, except possibly for Mom. Taylor was special to Mom, so she was special to me. That's all that mattered." Taylor could see that Steven was fighting back the tears. Taylor knelt down to hug her brother, but he shuffled away quickly. "I'm still angry at you for abandoning Mom

228

when she needed you the most. Angry that you took her away from us. Angry that you weren't there as the last breath left her lungs. Angry you weren't alongside us crying your eyes out at her funeral. All of this because your tail had to eat someone!"

"That's not fair to blame everything on my tail!" Taylor slapped her raised knee hard, frustrated at what she was being accused of. "How do you think I feel having a crazy monster of a tail that sometimes suddenly eats people without my consent? Having to be labeled a murderer and a criminal because of something I had no control being born with? To have my own family shun me because of the actions of our mother, which were completely out of my control? To cry in pain and agony at wanting to cut off your own tail because of all the shit it's brought you in life, but you're too damn scared to fucking do it? All I wanted was the love of my family, and not to be treated as some freak because of what I was born with!"

The stillness that followed was only broken by the evening traffic outside the raised window looking out at street level. Ahya was doing her best to hide behind a box, all this negative attention getting to her. Nina had a wing to her bill, unsure of what to do. Max merely stared at the space between Taylor and Steven, his expression unreadable.

"I never treated you like a freak," Steven said at last, his fury subsiding.

"You were an amazing talent on stage." Max grinned. "I was proud to play alongside you in the clubs. I love my lil' sis."

Taylor broke down crying. Steven didn't make a move, but Max set his guitar down against the side of his chair and got up. He moved over to Taylor and lightly patted her shoulder awkwardly. The cathartic release of getting all that out to her brothers spent her last reserves of energy. She just sagged under her brother's touch and just sobbed, leaning into the tiny body standing next to her. Ahya did her best to slyly snake around and coil about his legs. He ended up petting her too, an action causing much pleasure to Ahya as her tongue rolled out in joy.

Taylor gazed lovingly at her little, older brother, Max, as he pulled back from his momentary gesture of affection. "Still not used to it are you?" She laughed, wiping away her tears with her wrist.

Max moved over to the easy chair and flopped back into it, letting the cushion swallow him up as he sunk into it slightly. "Not really. I was never much one for hugs."

"A fact that Mom hated." Taylor continued to chuckle, feeling a bit better already.

"I miss Mom's hugs," Steven lamented, his tears now flowing.

"We all do," Taylor agreed.

It didn't exactly go as planned, but Taylor was happy that she was at least sharing a moment of shared grief with her brothers. They must have looked the unorthodox family back then. Two wolf parents with two adopted kits, a skunk and a raccoon, alongside a wolf cub that had a tailmaw. They were probably just as odd-looking now, despite their parents being gone. As different as they were in species, they were still family, and Taylor loved them dearly.

"I've missed you two so much," she said aloud at last.

"I'll admit I missed you too." Max finally looked at her directly. She knew he was making a conscious effort to do so, and she appreciated it.

All eyes turned to Steven as he stood off to the side, apparently wanting to get lost in the sea of boxes stacked up around and behind him. "It is good…to see you again," Steven said haltingly. "I don't think it can ever go back to how it was, but I don't hate you. I'm just…very upset with how things turned out."

"I think we all are." Taylor sniffed, opening up her arms to him.

It seemed like forever, but Steven finally relented and collapsed into her larger embrace. He wrapped his tiny arms around her ribs and wept bitterly into her chest. She licked his ears and nuzzled with a cheek his face and let him cry it out. Ahya looped around and did licking of her own as a show of comfort and love.

"I like the new look," Steven mumbled into her shirt.

Taylor patted him on the head, ruffling his head fluff. "I'm not too keen on it yet, but it is helping me get around town easier without being recognized."

"Smart," Max said, causing Nina to blush at the praise for her idea.

At length, Steven broke away and strived to calm himself down, taking another puff on his inhaler. "I miss Mom so much."

"I know. She was one of the major reasons I came back." Taylor could still recall the moment she decided to go with Ari to come back to Zabökar because of Murana. "I wanted to apologize for running away and make it right. Unfortunately I can't do that now."

"It is a pity," Max said, looking out his small, bar-mesh window. The sunlight was dwindling swiftly and it was getting dark. "How did you get back here?"

"That's a complicated story." Nina shook her head. "Even I'm not entirely sure on all of it even though she explained it to me. I'm a bit confused myself."

Seeing as Steven was doing better now, Taylor stood back up. "It's a bit worse than I would have wanted. I'm only here because of a debt I was forced into owing someone named the Arbiter."

"I've not heard of him." Max looked flummoxed.

Steven gasped. "I have! Are you serious?" At a blank look from Max, Steven continued. "It was all over the news several decades ago, long before I was born. I remember reading about him in the ZCN archives!"

"You nerd. You would." Taylor ribbed with a smile on her muzzle.

Steven looked insulted. "It's valuable history! For a reporter, you need to be knowledgeable about city history so you can apply it to the stories you report on today! It makes you look professional. Did you know that there was once a Project Draccos that was penned at the start of Zabökar as a mobile defense system for the city just after the Hordos War? It was deemed too costly, and all funds were funneled into the current system we have now surrounding Zabökar, linked to the spires of Caelesti as a sort of power source."

At the blank stares of all around, he just clucked his tongue at Taylor's dismissal of his craft. "Anyway, the Arbiter was once a formal High Council member who heralded from the southern country of Talkar. A place full of reptiles! Can you believe that?" He took a deep breath before plunging onward. "He was pure nuts, of course. He devised some crazy plan to alter Zabökar citizens into super soldiers, but needed council approval and funds for it. Of course they subsequently voted him off the council and banned all his research and funding. Last I read, he was last known to be behind the operations that resulted in many superpowered mammals escaping about nineteen to twenty years ago."

"Right around the time I was born." Taylor finished for him.

Steven's eyes dilated as realization kicked in for him. "Wait, what are you doing with him? Are you crazy? Wasn't he the one pulsing all those poor kits full of radiation to develop powers?"

Taylor bowed her head in assent. "And most likely Mom. I realize now that was probably what caused me to have the tail that I do."

"And Mom to develop cancer." Max looked as if he came upon the revelation himself just now.

Steven began to get upset again. "And you are working for him now?!"

Taylor raised both paws to placate her brother's wrath. "No! No, no, no. I was only using him as a means to an end. Too many people were chasing after me, and I had to choose someone to side with coming back here or I was going to get dragged back anyway, but maybe with someone I didn't want to be with. He was my best option at getting back to you, to my family."

"That's still pretty dangerous associating with him though." Steven looked unsure.

"And don't forget about that Ari girl," Nina reminded. "Wasn't she chasing after you because you ditched her for me, and you were on some sort of mission?"

"Ari who?" Steven was lost.

Taylor groaned. "Yeah, that'll probably bite me in the ass soon."

"And with the death of that rabbit all over the news, you've gotten yourself in a lot of trouble lately." Max was relentless with his truth.

"It would pay for you to be a bit more sensitive," Nina reprimanded.

Taylor waved her down. "It's fine. Max has always been like this, blunt to a fault. I honestly prefer him this way, rather than someone who lies or sugarcoats the truth."

"Well, now that you've reunited with us, what will you do now?" Steven asked the obvious question.

For once, Taylor didn't actually have a plan. Her entire purpose in coming here had been fulfilled. She was saddened she would never see her mother again, but she was overjoyed to have reconnected with her brothers. There was nothing else for her to look forward to. Nina was right, though. The Arbiter's due would come, and Ari would be the one to collect. What's worse, the mission tasked to her was in service to a greater need of a looming threat from Talkar that would blow over this city like a cataclysmic storm.

"I still need to help the Arbiter, I guess." She looked away from the damning expression Steven was giving her. "I know how it sounds, but I'm not doing it for him. I'm actually doing it for you two. I honestly think we should get out of Zabökar and go somewhere safe."

"Where would we go?" Max gestured to the littered box stacks around him. "This city is all we know. What could possibly be coming that's this important to leave our home?"

Flashes of Palaveve danced across Taylor's memory. "Something far worse than anything I've ever seen. I've seen entire towns get wiped out in an instant, and it's coming this way."

Steven began to visibly shiver. "There is such a thing that can do that? Which towns were they?"

"Multiple things, and they destroyed Palaveve and Howlgrav."

"Impossible!" Steven's mouth dropped. "We would have heard about it. Two country capitals wiped out? That surely should have made the news here!"

"Unless some people here didn't want us to know," Max mused.

"I don't like this," Nina said, scooting a little closer to Taylor for comfort. Ahya appeased her with a hug of her own.

"So how are you going to go about helping the Arbiter in supposedly saving Zabökar?" Max made direct eye contact again, his intensity boring holes into Taylor's own.

Taylor looked at each of them in turn, her paw rummaging around in her pocket, her fingers caressing the outline of the phone Ari gave her. "I'm not entirely sure."

How could she salvage this botched mission?

11.

JAKE

A dull roar echoed through the crowd. Murana was biting her nails as she waited for him to arrive. They would start the trial in just a few minutes, and she was still not inside the courtroom. She fastidiously adjusted the brooch on her blue suit lapel which doubled as a camera that would be recording the entire session. A technological relic of her bygone days as an undercover vigilante, it seemed well suited to bring it back out again here with no one the wiser.

"Mommy. There he is!" Taylor tugged on her blouse and pointed at the approaching wolf.

He had a charcoal shade of fur that encompassed his entire form outside of his white-furred forearms, paws, and front side. His braided tail swished behind him as he adjusted his scratchy green scrubs that he had yet to change out of. Stopping just a few feet from her position, he got to his knees and opened his arms wide for Taylor to jump into them.

"Uncle Seb Seb!" Taylor yipped, nuzzling her face into his fur. Ahya curled around his back as he hugged them both and kissed the top of her red hair.

"Sorry I'm late." He let go and stood up before ruffling the red tuft on Taylor's noggin. "There were a few critical patients in the ER this morning. I had a bit of a hard time getting away, but I managed it."

Murana breathed a sigh of relief. "I feel bad for calling you out of there like this, Sebastian. I know what our agreement stated, but I didn't know who else to turn to. This..." She gestured to the still open doors of the courtroom. "This is no place for Taylor. I felt it best she be with someone she knows and trusts while I'm in there."

Sebastian waved a paw at her. "No worries! I completely understand! Besides..." He nuzzled Taylor's cheek as she giggled, Ahya sneaking a small lick of her own against his face. "Why wouldn't

236

I want to spend time with Taylor? She's adorable." Ahya looked almost put out and offended. "And you too, Ahya. You're just as cute." He scratched the top layer of fur on the tailmaw.

A call from within directed her attention to the gathered throng inside. "I have to go." She said distractedly. "I'll call you when I'm done, ok?"

"We'll be fine, Murana. You be strong, alright?" He got back up to standing, regarding her seriously.

She nodded fretfully. "I'll be fine. Thank you, Sebastian."

A smile returned to his face as he looked down at Taylor. "We'll just go get some ice cream and be at the park." He encouraged Taylor to wave as they were leaving, forcing Murana to crack a smile and wave back.

Watching the two go, the zebra officer grunted loudly, indicating she was to enter quickly or remain outside. Acknowledging him, she swept past and entered the courtroom.

The social divide was thick inside that sweltering room. The families and constituents of the defendants were all stacked along one side of the room. A mix of fowl that had already begun to shed their feathers were causing an abhorrent mess for whoever had to clean up after this was over.

On the right side were Anthony's work family, the cops and fellow officers that he had served his time with over the last decade. The chief already had a seat picked out for her near the front. He stepped to the side and directed her to sit beside him. The eyes of the cranes, owls, storks, albatrosses, and more were tracking her down the aisle to her appointed seat. They were rich and powerful off the meat of their loins in their society, and they were not ashamed to flaunt it via the gaudy clothes that they wore.

Once everyone had settled down, they all rose for the judge as he entered. Murana muttered under her breath as she saw he was another bird, like the others—a heron. This already was not in their favor for a just resolution. The three kids were jostled into the courtroom by several burly warthogs. The kids squawked and threatened the officers with their jobs—that their parents would see to it that they lost them. Murana just sneered at the audacity of these rich punks. Just because their kind provided a beneficial service to all the predators in Zabökar didn't mean they were better than the rest.

"Order! Order!" The heron judge trilled, banging his gavel. Once the three defendants were locked and bolted to their chairs and table, he cleared his throat. "We are here presiding over case number 3489216. The Zabökar police versus the Hawkins family."

A small murmur skittered about the room. Many whispered and informed those who weren't in the know. The Hawkins family was an old one that had been instrumental in the development of Zabökar for centuries. These three swans who were indicted with Anthony's murder were the children of the venerable High Council member, Javier Hawkins. Murana inwardly grimaced at this turn of events. The rest of the police around her didn't look happy about it either.

The judge eyed both the defense and prosecutor. "You may give your opening statements when ready."

The ox rose up from his seat before the chief. "The prosecution will start, your honor." At a nod from the heron, he stepped out from behind the table. "I am representing all of the Zabökar police force for the brutal and malicious death of Anthony Wolford, husband to a wife and three children. At about 1842 on the night of Kristos's Victory by the calendar three months ago, Anthony was mercilessly killed by a shotgun blast to the face when doing a routine traffic stop."

He walked out to the middle between the two tables and pointed at the three stewing kids. "After speeding forty kilometers over the speed limit in a residential area, Anthony pulled them over to deliver them their much deserved ticket. I will today prove, beyond a shadow of a doubt, that he was murdered in cold blood by these three with premeditated intent to kill any and all cops they came across, as my further evidence will prove from the articles we secured from their vehicle at the crime scene." With a satisfied snort, he sat back down and smugly looked at the small marmot.

The tiny defense lawyer did not meet the larger ox in the eye, but instead hopped up onto the table in front of his three defendants and smoothed down his tiny white suit that shown brilliantly in the courtroom. "Your honor, I would actually like to give a closing statement combined with a singular piece of evidence that'll prove my victim's innocence in that premeditative accusation."

"This is a bit irregular, but proceed." The judge threw up a feather tip from his wing. "Just note that when you are done, you will not have another chance for further arguments."

"Understood, your honor." He sniffed confidently. Pacing back and forth across his table, he blared out firmly with his miniscule voice. "Did my defendants have guns in their car? Yes. Were they procured illegally? Yes. Should they be doing time for this crime? Yes. However, should they be blamed for outright murder? Absolutely not."

Murana snarled and grit her teeth. Another slew of whispers rushed through the room. A cautionary paw was placed on her arm. She looked up at the chief, his head silently shaking to indicate she should stand down and let the drama unfold. There might still be hope yet for a resolution that would do justice to Anthony's memory.

"You see, by law, for all traffic stops to not be labeled as entrapment, the cop must be prominently parked and in view at all times for oncoming traffic to see him. It is a gesture that reminds people of the law and to slow down of their own accord if they were accidently going too fast, correct?" There was a small flurry of voices.

The marmot indicated a small flat panel screen that was wheeled in prior to the trial stating: "Exhibit A." The screen flickered on with the press of a remote. On it was a camera view from a nearby gas station showing a car hidden behind a fence line flanked by bushes. "As you can clearly see, Anthony Wolford was completely out of eyesight from the direction my defendants were traveling. Their traffic stop was not only unjust, but illegal."

Murana's chief hissed near her ear. "That isn't even one of our designated stake out points!"

"Objection!" The ox bellowed, rising up.

"Overruled." The judge flapped a wing dismissively.

"To make matters worse, Anthony used excessive force in bringing them to heel, as seen here." The marmot pointed again at the monitor.

All eyes were rapt to the screen as the wolf that looked remarkably like Anthony was threatening the three swans to get out of the car. After several refusals, a gun was pulled out on the driver. Some more terse words were said and then it appeared Anthony opened fire. Two blasts later, his entire head got blown clear off his shoulders, making a macabre display of red paint on the sidewalk.

"What the hell is this?" The chief was angry. "I checked Wolford's gun that very night. There was not a single discharge on his weapon!"

Ignoring the fact the van with the swans drove off away from the decapitated corpse of Anthony, the marmot flipped the TV off. "So in a moment of terror, these poor kids did what they thought best to preserve their own lives under open fire from a person who had far more power then they. Given this indisputable evidence, I plead to reduce the sentence from murder to mammalslaughter, and for these three boys to be in one year incarceration provided good behavior."

"This is rigged!" the ox roared again, jabbing a hoof in their direction. "We have dashcam footage that refutes everything we just witnessed. This video is a vile mock-up of what really happened!"

The judge looked perplexed. "I don't know. Based on where the cop vehicle was parked, it does not look like any dashcam footage you may have would be of much use in determining how the events played out."

"Of course it would!" The chief now stood up and talked over the prosecutor. "Because Anthony never parked there! His car would be completely within the confines of the gas station parking!"

"Order!" the judge screeched. "You will sit down right now or I'll have you in contempt of court!" With a thumping slap back onto his chair, the chief glared at the judge before shifting his eyes to the three swans.

Content that he would not be interrupted again, the judge continued. "It appears to me to be a cut and dry case. Both sides were at fault, which led to the unfortunate death of one Anthony Wolford. A tragic loss by all accounts. However, the evidence shown does put the case in the favor of the defense where his death was instigated by aggravated assault unbecoming of an officer. So for that, I will sentence all three to a max of one year in jail with six months community service on good behavior. Dismissed." He banged the gavel.

The courtroom became lit with a rising din. The prosecution bolted up. "What about our evidence? Do we not get to present?!"

"This is a farce!" Murana's chief roared, standing as well.

Kowolski leapt from his chair pointing at the judge. "Who greased your feathers to do their dirty work and let these assholes off easy?"

"Order!" the judge was flustered now as more people began to rise.

"That's it? That's the justice my husband gets?" Murana's fangs were bared, her claws out. She was ready to kill and maim. "Just because their daddy's rich and powerful doesn't mean they can get away with murder!"

"My officers deserve better than this!" The chief was wholly in support of Murana and her righteous anger. "We risk our lives daily to bring peace and order to this city, and when one of us dies, it feels like nobody cares! You are just proving the point by letting these rich punks off easy, that their influence and power matters more to you than those that serve to defend you!"

"Order, I say!" the judge banged his gavel consistently, but it was drowned out.

"Such a shame," one of the storks simpered. "Maybe if you trained your boys better, they wouldn't be so trigger-happy and would follow the law themselves. What happened to Wolford was just punishment for his inadequate leadership. You all have only yourselves to blame."

That did it. Murana ripped open her blouse and tossed it to the floor, the camera's view going black as it hit the carpet. "I'll fucking kill you all!" she thundered.

What came next was an incomprehensible cacophony of growls, roars, squawks, screeches and cries as the entire courtroom erupted into a bloody melee. Several more thuds later from heavy hooves and the sound cut out too as someone stepped on her brooch, crushing the recording device.

Jake nearly lost his nerve when he saw Taylor walking down the street towards him with Nina next to her. She was no longer sporting her iconic red fur, opting to having it dyed a darker grey, but he still recognized her immediately. He had been going over and over in his mind what he would say to her as he waited the hours for Taylor's return, but now that she was mere minutes from his position, his entire mind froze. The tail's mouth was shut and looked like any other tail, but there was a deep-rooted fear in the pit of his stomach that it was still there, and could open up on him at any moment.

Taylor perked up and noticed him, alerting her friend to his presence. It was too late to back out now. On one paw, he longed for the death her tail might provide, having not much else to live for. But the memory of his buddy, Tony, demanding justice for his murder, kept Jake standing tall on his paws. The two of them slowed down when they got within several meters of him, both having recognized Jake.

"You..." Taylor's voice wavered, it seemed she was nervous as well. "You were the one in the street."

"I was the friend to that rabbit you killed." His voice came out far braver than he felt.

Taylor's face look like it sagged. "I'm so sorry! I didn't think that—"

"Think that, what? That'd you face the friend of the person you murdered? Well I'm here, Taylor! Deal with it! Deal with the damage you have done to my life!" The more words that came out, the better Jake was able to control his fear at confronting this larger wolf.

"That's not fair to blame her for what her tail did." Nina paused, looking at her friend. "How did you know her name anyway?"

Jake folded his arms and stood facing off to the side, like he was disgusted just looking at them. "I was once a bodyguard for your band. I'm surprised you don't recognize me either, Nina." He glared at her when he said her name. "Yeah, but I wouldn't expect young punk teens in your position to even pay attention to people like me. I'm just a rabbit, after all. Why would you care that I unknowingly saved your life multiple times behind the scenes when you weren't looking? Out of sight, out of mind, right?"

242

"You're… You're…" Nina was gesturing to him with a wing, fighting as if his name was on the tip of her tongue.

Taylor knelt down to his level. "Jake. Your name is Jake. Yes, I remember you now."

Jake groaned and waved her up off the pavement. "Get up. Don't even come down to my level. It's insulting." Taylor gracelessly did her best to stand up, looking hurt. "I may not have had many friends, but Tony was one of the few that I could reasonably call a friend. He did me a big service that day you killed him that I don't even think he was aware of when we last spoke. Now I can't even tell him thanks."

Taylor looked around to see if there was anyone else on the street overhearing their conversation, but thankfully it was just the late evening traffic and public transport rushing past over their heads, its railing bolted into the sides of the buildings. "I understand how you feel, Jake. I know the feeling of being unable to tell a loved one how grateful you are for them. I'm sorry Ahya robbed you of that. I know many people hate me for what I am and what Ahya can do, but I hope you have it in your heart to forgive me, and know that I never had any intention of harming Tony."

"And that you won't call the cops," Nina chipped in, drawing looks from both Jake and Taylor. "What? That'll just make things messy."

"Ahya is what you call your tail, right?" Jake wanted to confirm. He never interacted much with members of the band, and the few times he did with Taylor, her tail was barely in the conversation.

Taylor followed his gaze to Ahya, who was just now peeking out her tongue at him with a blep. "It's what I named her when I was a little girl. It's hard to get others to believe me, but she really does have a mind of her own. I can control her sometimes, but yesterday morning? She just flew out of control. There was nothing I could do fast enough."

"If she's truly responsible then she still needs to answer for her crime." Jake stared at the tail. It didn't exactly look repentant to his eyes.

"So you accept the fact she's her own person?" Taylor looked amazed.

"Unless you've been lying to us all these years and you plan to eat me too." Jake turned back up to her.

"No! Why would I do that?"

"You're not even that big of a morsel." Nina eyed him up and down.

Taylor whapped her across the shoulder. "Would you stop it?" It appeared she was trying hard not to laugh at Nina's dark humor.

"I don't think this is funny." Jake thumped a foot.

Taylor's expression changed. "I'm sorry. I know it isn't. This is just…all very awkward. To tell you the truth, this is not the first time I've had to deal with family or friends of the people Ahya has killed."

"And they were no doubt angry at you too." Jake felt some comfort in knowing that there might have been someone else who confronted Taylor about their loss.

"They actually forgave me." Taylor seemed lost in thought.

"What?" Jake's jaw dropped open. "Just like that?"

"Well, actually, no. They initially were contemplating killing me."

"This is quite fascinating, but it's getting a bit chill," Nina butted in. "Not trying to be rude, Mr. Jake, but unless you plan to do something right now about what happened, warranted or not, I would actually like to get back up to my apartment and get ready for a group meeting I have tonight."

Taylor was confused. "Group meeting? I didn't know you were a part of any group."

Nina laughed and dug into her shredded jeans for her house keys. "It's something I go to weekly. Let's just say it has been a lifesaver for me since leaving the band. The people there have helped me so much."

"Ah, sort of like a help group," Taylor reasoned.

Nina thought about it a moment. "Something like that, yes."

"Think I could go with you?" Taylor looked hopeful.

A shadow crossed over Nina's face, darkening her expression. "Mmm, I'm not sure that's a good idea at this time. They're really not accepting new members."

Jake cleared his throat to bring the attention back to him. "No, I don't think I can physically do anything to Taylor for what her tail, Ahya, has done. Nothing that I could easily defend in any court of law, especially considering I'm just a rabbit."

"Why should that matter?" Taylor clearly didn't understand his position.

"He's a servant-class mammal." Nina explained, extending her wing towards him. "The courts would first go through all the obligations he is required to do by law to see if he was in violation of neglect in his duties before they'd even get to the matter of whatever crime of revenge, self-defense or otherwise, he had done."

"And any findings that damn me in those would nullify any legitimate defense in my favor. So true, I could get you jailed for the crime of murdering Tony, but I'd also be landed in jail on any number of other possible counts. Not worth the risk," Jake finished for the bird.

"That's...horrible." Taylor looked mortified. "Why would any rabbit stand for this? I knew it was bad for rabbits by what Natalia told me about you guys, but I never expected it to be this awful. How do you even cope?"

"By sticking together." Jake shrugged.

"So, did you two want to talk this out upstairs or…" Nina prodded again.

Jake shook his head. He knew these two girls, but not enough to where he'd trust both of them in an unknown apartment alone. "For my safety, I would feel better if I stayed out here."

Nina turned her head to Taylor. "And you? You going to continue talking about this?"

Taylor turned upwards at the tall apartment complex that was Nina's home. "You know what, I think I will. I actually want to make this right with Jake. You go on ahead without me. I'll catch up."

Both Nina and Jake looked surprised. Nina spoke first. "Okay… Well, if you need in later, just remember where I showed you the spare key is." She regarded the rabbit next to them. "I remember you now, Jake. I always did find you cute. Did you want to come upstairs and—"

Taylor cut her off. "Nina! If you're going to ask of him what I think you are, you stop it right now! We only got the one bed and I'd rather not think about...that happening on it."

Nina honked a laugh. "What? I was more thinking we could share him!"

Jake flushed at this. "I am still here."

Taylor looked beside herself in embarrassment. "I'm so sorry for my friend's behavior! Sometimes I wonder how I even know her!"

Nina cackled further. "Well, I still need to get ready for later tonight. You got the place to yourself until midnight if you come home earlier. I won't keep you two love birds waiting. Let me know if you get bunny sore tonight, Taylor!" With that she ripped open the side door into her building and waddled in, still laughing.

The silence between Jake and Taylor was thick. The mere nature of what he was and what his purpose could be for Taylor if she just asked was hanging in the air. The law forbade him to refuse if he didn't want a quick trip in a squad car to the nearest lockup should he be reported. However, he wasn't feeling in the mood, especially considering the grave topic they were discussing regarding Tony. The last thing he wanted was to be having sex with Tony's own killer. Somehow, deep down, he hoped Taylor was feeling the same way about the whole situation.

"So..." Taylor was bumping her fist on her thigh repeatedly, probably unsure of what to do with herself. "How can I make it up to you? I can't bring him back...at least, not with how far gone he is now." She looked beyond uncomfortable talking about this, pushing back a lock of hair behind her ear.

"I don't think anyone can bring him back from that." Jake pointed at her tail, who seemed disinterested now and was wandering the sidewalk, looking for something.

"Yeah, I guess you're right," she said, but it felt like she was hiding something. "Did you want to go for a walk?"

Jake was a bit at a loss for what to do here. The conversation did not even go the way he thought it would. In fact, his righteous anger at Taylor had diminished some the moment he saw her coming down the street. The mere memory of the times he spent watching over her in *Bad*

Luck was enough to endear her to him, enough so that he couldn't be completely mad at her.

She never seemed like a murderer to him, and her actions now only complimented that impression. It still hurt that she was the cause of his friend's demise, but now he just wanted to understand her feelings and find out if she was truly remorseful. It would certainly go a long way to making him feel better about this whole mess.

"Yeah, that'll be fine," he agreed.

She slowly walked alongside him at his pace. Neither one of them had a plan of where they were going, so they just went straight down the sidewalk. "I am a bit ashamed of my friend back there." She spoke at last after a few minutes of silence. "I'm still shocked she'd even think about asking that of you."

He tilted his head slightly up at her. "About what? Servicing her in bed?" He snorted, looking ahead. "It's what we're here for. I know my place. Maybe one day I'll be sponsored and I won't have to deal with anymore strangers like that." He scoffed, his mind on that red panda, Samantha, and her offer of sponsorship.

"Sponsored? What's that?" Taylor had to pull Ahya back behind her, as she was about ready to bump into a lamp along the street.

"You seriously don't know?" He gazed up at her.

"I wasn't in school when they taught anything about rabbits." She looked lost in the conversation.

"Are you pulling my chain?" After a few moments, it did look like she was sincere. Jake sighed. "It's when someone of sufficient wealth basically buys me up. They would then own me and my life. I go move in with them and service them to the end of my days, but hey, at least I get to live in opulence!" He laughed bitterly.

Taylor shook her head. "That is so wrong. I wouldn't stand for it if it happened to me."

"Well, you're not a rabbit."

"Even still, haven't you all fought back against this law?" She remembered the time Natalia first explained it to her. "I think it's all so stupid."

"We have." Jake stuffed his paws into his pockets, edging away slightly and speeding his walk up as Ahya got a bit too close behind him. "The cases never go anywhere, and are summarily dropped every time."

"I'm surprised you all haven't revolted by now."

"Funny you should say that." Jake motioned for her to follow him down a brighter lit street. They were walking headlong into a darker, seedier side of Zabokar. Probably best to at least be heading in the general direction of his apartment, which wasn't far from here. "There is this rabbit, I think his name is Stepan. He's been organizing rallies in the sewers for just us rabbits. My other…'friends' have been wanting me to join for months now."

Taylor mulled on this for a bit. "This Stepan, is he a dangerous rabbit? Do you think they would have any success in overturning this law by force?"

"I don't think so. Stepan just seems to be some rabblerouser. I don't think he'd actually incite a riot, but then again, I've not met the guy." Jake stopped suddenly and turned to her. "What's it to you anyway? Why are you so interested in what happens to us?"

She scrunched her face up, like she was overthinking it. "I remember when I first heard about this law. It was maybe a month ago?"

Jake raised his brow in disbelief. "Really? First the lack of schooling, which I find hard to believe, and now this. Why didn't you learn about us in school? Everyone else and their cousin Fred knows about us."

"Cousin Fred?"

"Because no rabbit names their son Fred?" Jake waved a paw irritably. "Nevermind. Figure of speech. Forget it."

Taylor shook her head. "No, I was taken out long before then I think. But when I first heard about rabbits, I thought it was such an awful thing to be subjected to. I'd feel pretty miserable if I was forced to do such things."

"You've no idea." Jake looked away, not wanting to meet her eyes. "Still, it's a bit weird to have you sympathize with us."

Taylor shrugged. "Why not? I've been in much the same position." Jake gave her a disbelieving look. "Well, not the same, but I know what it's like to be crapped on by those above you and have little

248

control over your own life. Ahya has not done me many favors, and my life is just a series of miserable events because of her." Ahya rose up and moved in front of Taylor, "looking" directly at her face. "Well, it is!" She tried to excuse. Ahya just wilted.

"How much does she truly understand?" Jake was a bit fascinated at the level of intelligence the tail was supposedly showing. It seemed almost cognizant of their conversation. He recalled being in awe over how dexterous Taylor was with her tail on stage when she used it to play drums. It having a mind of its own would seek to explain some of that behavior.

Taylor studied Ahya. "I'm not entirely sure. Sometimes she seems in perfect sync with me, and I have a feeling she gets everything. Other times, well, I feel like she's completely clueless or just ignoring me on purpose. I don't know exactly how she understands things. I wish I did. It would have made so many things a lot easier."

"You know that sounds like a load of crap, but I guess that makes sense." Jake began to walk again. Taylor followed along looking aggrieved. "Still, I don't think you have any idea what we rabbits go through on a daily basis." He gestured to her. "You're still free to hang out with your friend at night, without worry about your sexual and personal wellbeing."

"That's not entirely true."

"More true if you're a rabbit." He countered.

"Do you think I'm a monster or a menace then, Jake?" she asked suddenly.

"I don't believe so, but it's hard to say right now. Your tail can be scary, I'll admit. It can do horrible things, like devouring Tony." he responded bluntly.

"I said I was sorry about that, but it's not all my fault." She was exasperated. "Ahya sometimes does things I can't explain. What is it with people blaming me for what my tail does?"

Jake creased his nose. "You know what? I don't even know why I bothered to get a sincere apology or closure from you. It's clear you won't take responsibility for what your tail did, and it shows a clear lack of respect for me and the one you killed. If I didn't know you, Taylor, I would have simply called the cops on you, risks be damned. As it is,

249

your mother's promise stayed my paw. I'm done, Taylor. Don't follow me."

Taylor called out to him, but he just kept walking, speeding up his gait. He noticed a strange scent on the wind, his ears shooting up as he noticed a dark figure leaning up against a building, his eyes like slits, watching him. Jake recognized him from the day prior. It was the cougar Trevor protected him from earlier. How in blazes had he been tagging him for this long?

The cougar had noticed Jake break off from Taylor and moved in with predatory menace. He intercepted Jake brusquely, stepping directly in front of him, close enough Jake had to stop suddenly and back up a few paces or he'd would run right into the cougar.

"Can I help you?" Jake was infuriated. He just wanted to go home.

"Yes." The deep voice of the cougar sent chills. "I was wondering if you were finished with that wolf for tonight?"

"Excuse me?"

"That wolf." The cougar repeated. "If you were done servicing her, I would like you for your services tonight. I have a nice place we can go back to. Promise I'll treat you right. All nice-like."

Jake jerked when he suddenly felt Taylor's fingers grip his arm firmly. "I'm not finished with him, thank you very much!" Her eyes were hot with anger.

The cougar looked up to address her. "Not done yet? That's fair. If you want, we can share him now and I get him after you're completely done?"

"What sort of sick crap is this?!" Taylor reared Ahya up over her head. Ahya's tooth-filled maw grinned wide, her tongue lashing out and smacking the shocked cougar upside the head. "He's my rabbit for tonight and I'll be claiming his services! He is not yours until I'm done with him! Now get lost!"

Ahya snapped her jaws with a clatter inches from his face, causing the cougar to stumble back onto his ass. He scrambled backwards on all fours desperately, caterwauling bloody murder at the terror of seeing Ahya. The last they saw of him was his flapping tail, scurrying around the nearest corner.

"What are you doing?" Jake was depressed as her words felt like they stabbed him in the heart. Was she just getting back at him for not accepting her apology? Was she now going to force him to have sex to mock Tony's memory?

"Making sure he didn't have you!" Taylor puffed out her chest, petting Ahya for a job well done. "That guy seemed like a sleazeball to me anyway."

A sudden wind blew through street, rustling the planted trees and parked cars. One alarm went off. Jake noticed several lights flickering up and down the streetlamps, and a few in the windows of the stacked buildings across the street. The air became thick with dread, and his heart was racing for no apparent reason. His eyes darted here and there as he thought he saw a shadow flit across above them.

"Taylor?" He anxiously tapped the paw gripping his arm. "Do you sense that?" His thoughts about what she'd invoked were gone from his mind.

She was scanning the area too. Even Ahya seemed alert. "Yeah. Where did you say you lived?"

"Not far." He began walking faster.

It took several minutes to get to his part of town, where the buildings were smaller and more sandwiched together between the larger ones. The feeling of panic continued to rise within him the longer they were outside. Taylor could sense it too. She had already grabbed his paw and was nearly dragging him along behind her, guided only by his directions. He looked behind once and could see lights going dark one by one, as if trailing after them. His keen ears could detect some sense of low gasping, like from the depths of some nightmare that he couldn't wake from.

They barreled through the double doors of his complex and skittered forward through the cracked tiled foyer, Taylor nearly toppling over onto him. Just like that, the feeling was gone. They both were panting hard, paws on knees as they recovered from the unknown threat. As if in unison, they turned to look back outside through the glass and could see the lights flickering back on down the row of buildings. Whatever it was had passed over.

"What was that?" Taylor gasped.

Jake's eyes were still wide. "I have no idea. I've never experienced anything like that."

Taylor attempted to catch her breath. "Well, we're here. I walked you home." She chuckled, but Jake could tell she was trying to laugh to prevent herself from screaming. Whatever just happened scared the hell out of them both and he couldn't explain why. "Which floor is yours?"

With his heart rate decreasing, the reality of what was to come next set in. "Three floors up." He motioned to the cargo elevator in front of them. She had to hunch over a bit to fit inside the elevator, but she dutifully waited beside him as they ascended.

Taylor appeared content about something as they walked down the hallway to his apartment, humming a familiar tune. He wanted to ask, but wasn't sure if he should. Was she happy she was going to be serviced by a rabbit? He was disappointed in her for it. After that entire talk they had just prior to the cougar, if she truly meant what she said, why then did she fight that cougar off for his services? Maybe his gut instinct was wrong, and she was just like everyone else. He began to regret watching over her on behest of her mother.

"Taylor, did you mean what you said to that cougar?" he asked softly.

"Of course!" Her mirth hadn't changed. "He didn't deserve you!"

He numbly stared at the lock to his door, the keys limp in his paw. Even after all that, he was still just a rabbit. She just buttered him up so she could get serviced. Maybe even to eat him like she did Tony. Did their prior history together mean nothing? He'd watched her grow up from when she was a young teen, for gods sake. Now she seemed happy about being fucked by him, probably to get back at him for their falling out minutes prior. He wanted to continue to grill what her intentions were and if she was serious about what she said back there, but he was afraid of being seen as defiant of the law.

"What else did you want to do? I'm home now," he probed, hoping his wild thoughts weren't true.

She looked at him flummoxed, as if not realizing his intent. "Oh, if it isn't too much trouble, I was hoping I could come inside. I've always been curious what a rabbit hole looks like. We can continue what we started in there."

His heart sank. "As you wish, although it isn't exactly a hole."

He opened the door and let her walk in ahead. It wasn't much, just the den area and the bedroom alongside it. It didn't seem to matter to Taylor though. She was looking around with wonder at the miniature furniture, having to duck down to avoid some of the light fixtures as she explored the mini-kitchen. At length, she giggled when she tried to situate herself on the tiny couch which seemed to fit her entire frame, where for Jake, it could have been a seat for two.

"This is comfy. I actually like this spot." Taylor smiled at him. Ahya was irritated she couldn't fit in comfortably alongside her.

"Just...stay right there. I'll be back."

He turned and shut the bedroom door behind him. He was trembling all over. He wasn't sure if he could go through this with her. He remembered that promise he made to her mother and that he'd watch over her, but he never thought it'd be like this. However, she did invoke the law quite blatantly on him, and he needed to comply. He took several deep breaths, calming his nerves. There were worse bed partners out there. That tail might be a problem—he had no idea how he was going to deal with that—but if this was what Taylor wanted, he had no choice in the matter.

The fates were laughing at him. Tony's killer, sliding back into his life under the guise of a caring and empathetic wolf he thought he knew better, only to spite him by forcing him to service her. It all seemed like one big joke. He tried to fight back the tears as he heard her out there.

"Jake? Are you going to come out here with me?"

"Just one moment!" He controlled his voice. He had been languishing over himself for a bit too long.

Sniffling to present himself better, he still prided himself on maintaining some sense of dignity about this. He unbuckled his belt, dropped his drawers, and tossed his shirt. His mind was in many directions at once, but he needed to focus on the here and now. He calmed himself and began to think about pleasing this wolf in the next room. He needed to forget everything else except that, otherwise his will to go through with it would falter.

After a minute, he was sufficiently hard and he felt zoned off enough that he could mentally separate himself from the task at paw. He opened the door and attempted to strut in confidently. "So, Taylor, did you want to be on top or bottom tonight?"

Taylor saw the naked form of Jake saunter in from his bedroom, his member upright and bold. She practically yelped and lurched backwards over the side of the couch, trying in vain to cover her eyes from the sudden lewdness of her friend, or who she thought was her friend.

"What the gods are you doing, Jake?" she shouted, trying her best not to look at him.

He stuttered and fell back to the bedroom, hastily pulling up his pants to cover his loins. "I...I thought this was what you wanted? Did you not tell that cougar you wanted me tonight for my services?"

"Freaking hell, Jake! No!" She was heaving. She was shaken that he had approached her like that. The shape of him lightly throbbing was seared into her mind's eye, like a vision she couldn't get out of her head. "I only said that so he wouldn't abuse you or hurt you! What is it with you rabbits and misunderstanding me and what I want from you?!"

Jake was confused. "You mean...you didn't want this?"

"No, I mean, yes! I mean... I relieve you of your service! I relieve you of your service!" she repeated frantically, remembering how she got Francis to stop. "Can you please just put your clothes back on?"

There was a frantic shuffling noise coming from the bedroom, and Jake partially emerged moments later, fully-clothed. "I am so sorry about that, Taylor!" He seemed to be doing his best to keep his distance. "I just thought... Well, it seemed like you were just like all the others when you told that guy what you needed of me."

"You thought I wanted your services?" Taylor was incredulous, finally peeking over the small sofa. "After all we just talked about? How big of a hypocrite do you think I am? I've been trying to convince you this whole time that I'm not fully in control of Ahya and that I feel horrible and awful about what she did to your friend. Why would I then lie and say I understand your situation, just to abuse your trust the next moment? How could I get you to trust me about Ahya then?"

Jake looked guilty. "I'm sorry about the misunderstanding. It's just that...I'm so used to assuming that's what others want or expect out of me. I didn't mean to imply you were a liar."

"And I hate liars." Taylor meant it. "You know what... Um, I should just go."

"You just got here..." Jake fumbled over his words. He looked like he really messed up.

"Yeah, I know, but it just got a bit weird. Maybe we can talk some other time?" She grimaced. She hadn't actually meant to leave the future open for a subsequent visit. It was embarrassing enough right now as it was.

"That sounds good..." he muttered. She was getting up off the floor and heading to the door when it seemed he remember something. "I still do have one last thing to relay to you. It's from your mother. A message. After that, you'll never have to see me again."

Taylor stopped in mid-stride to the door. She looked back at him, her tone serious. "I will come back to discuss that with you. I promise. I just...can't right now. Will you forgive me for what happened with Ahya?"

He looked between her and Ahya. "I'm trying to forgive you, Taylor. Ahya... I think she'll need to work more for it."

That seemed fair. She nodded. "I get that."

"Don't think ill of me for what just happened. I didn't mean to make you uncomfortable." He was wringing his paws, his ears were drooped. The sight of him almost made her heart break.

Her expression softened. "Of course not, Jake. I'm sorry I even implied I wanted that from you. I just didn't care for that cougar having you; I had a bad feeling about him. Catch up with me at Nina's tomorrow morning? We can continue our talk then, and you can give me mother's message. I'd truly like that."

"Then it's settled. I'll see you bright and early tomorrow, Taylor." A glimmer of a smile began to creep back into his face.

"Good night, Jake." She bowed her head and shut the door.

Taylor was out of the building in a flash. Her ears were burning and her heart racing. The entire scene continued to play out in her mind over and over. She hadn't had these sorts of thoughts for years now. Last time she was this excited about such pleasures was that one wolf back in the band that Ahya had scared off. She could recall how close she was to getting her cherry popped. With what happened up in Jake's apartment, all those feelings came flooding back.

She barely realized she was up the steps of Nina's complex and knocking on her door. Taylor's mind slammed into the present as Nina opened the door with a smug grin. "Wow, back already? How was he? So good you forgot the spare key to get in?"

Taylor threw up her paws as she pushed Nina aside. "Ugh, we didn't do anything, Nina! I'm not like that!"

Nina gawked at her. "You mean you didn't hit that cute piece of bun ass? They've got great stamina, you know! I remember I was sore for days afterward. I'm shocked you came back so soon!"

"I'm not talking about this!" Taylor dropped herself roughly into a dining chair, pouting and not wanting to look at her insensitive friend. "The whole situation is just disgusting! I'd not do that to him."

Nina slinked up beside Taylor, flitting around Ahya before sitting adjacent. "You're not kidding? You two did nothing? No bunny soreness for Taylor?" She tried to smirk and bring back the humor between them.

Taylor's arms fell to the table with a thud, demonstrating her vexation at Nina. "He was our bodyguard back in the band. Someone who worked for us! That just seems so wrong!"

"He doesn't work for the band anymore and we're no longer in it. What's stopping you?"

"He's older than me."

"Not much older. Not an excuse." Nina was relentless.

"He's too small." Taylor was grasping at straws.

Nina shook her head. "Also not an excuse. Rabbits are skilled lovers." She slapped her own wings on the table. "My gods, Taylor! You seriously don't even know?" She reached over the table and dragged her laptop in front of her, flipping it open. "They got love videos filmed of them in action over at Pawtube!"

Taylor shunned off the laptop with a paw, facing away. "I don't even want to see it! I can't believe you're even condoning this with rabbits. Don't you see it's forced service?"

Nina didn't seem to fathom Taylor's reasoning. "It's just how things are, Taylor. I don't see what the big deal is. So Jake fucks you. So what? He's a rabbit. He'll get over it. You'll enjoy it and get over it too. They do this all the time. They like it. Why else would they agree to sponsorship? Because they all secretly want to belong to someone forever."

"Don't you have a group meeting to get to?" Taylor refused to look at Nina now.

The swan slumped back in the chair studying her friend. "Fine. Be obstinate. I guarantee the moment you see what they can do, you'll wish you took advantage of the opportunity. They're amazing."

Seeing as she was going to get nothing further out of Taylor, Nina just squawked with irritation and stormed out the door. Taylor could still hear her friend grumbling to herself down the hall and into the stairwell before the rest of the nighttime sounds around them drowned her out. Taylor was left alone in the room with the open laptop. She had half a mind to believe Nina purposefully left it unlocked with browser open to taunt or even tempt her.

Taylor crossed her arms and stared off towards the bedroom. This attitude of everyone when it came to rabbits was ridiculous. It's like everyone else was treated like a real person, but rabbits were somehow beneath them. The worst part about it was that she could empathize with Jake's position. She knew what it was like when the only reason people were interested in you was for what you could do for them. Sex for Jake, Ahya and her powers for Taylor. They were almost two sides of the same coin of being used and abused.

Despite her best efforts, her thoughts continued to linger back to the sight of Jake coming out of that bedroom and Nina's words echoing in her mind. Ahya could sense a change in Taylor's body chemistry and swayed a bit as she "stared" at her, as if she knew Taylor's body was betraying her.

Taylor stuck her tongue out at Ahya. "Stop it. So what if I'm a bit turned on? It's not like I'm going to do anything about it! It's wrong to think of him like that and you know it!" Ahya was silent and continued to "judge" Taylor for her thoughts. Taylor wasn't sure how long she had sat there facing off against her tail, but at last she just groaned. Curiosity got the better of her. "Fine, we'll just take one peek!"

Taylor had some experience with computers, primarily after she had run away from her mother. She was a bit peeved about her sheltered upbringing, but she knew now her mom only did it to protect her. She stared at the blank search bar, unsure of what to type in. Remembering what Nina said, she typed in "Pawtube" and "Rabbit." What came back was a dizzying array of video thumbnails, some in scandalous positions and views. She clicked on the top one.

Taylor's eyes were opened that night as the moans and pounding slaps were heard in that tiny apartment. She barely realized she was covering her mouth in stunned silence as she ingested minutes and minutes of video. This was foreign territory for her. Her mind was blown that people would even think to record themselves like this, let alone make it public for everyone to see. It was like a train wreck that she wanted to look away from, but couldn't force herself too.

She could sense a type of yearning deep between her legs forming—a yearning she had not felt in a long time. Her gaze back over to the bed was one of longing now. Ahya seemed to have a similar idea, because she was moving away from the table, tugging gently on Taylor's tailbone as if prompting her to do something about this new feeling.

Taylor trembled slightly as she relaxed herself against the headboard, her pants off and legs spread. Ahya was coiled up and around like a critic over the proceedings. Taylor knew enough about what was supposed to happen if a boy was with her, but never if she was by herself.

She began her first tentative steps in massaging and prodding. Some of it was pleasing, but most of it was just weird and awkward. Much to her initial resistance, she began to think of Jake and those Pawtube videos again to help things along. It helped some, but in the end she let her hands drop. Her still-healing fingers, broken at Cheribaum, were aching and hindered her success. She began to cry. It just wasn't coming for her.

Nobody ever taught her what to do to please herself. It was just never on her radar growing up. She wished she had been taught about these things, but she was ripped from her life too young. She was denied the ability to grow and mature as a young teen should.

All she was left with was fear. Fear that someone would come and snatch her away from her mother. That fear drowned out all other things, to include her sexuality. When she tried to capitalize on it when she was singing with the band, Ahya ruined it all.

So she simply gave up. Resigned to the fact she may never get to experience this.

Her tears began to subside as Taylor noticed Ahya swaying in a very odd way, her tongue dangling out in a display of utter tranquility. She sneered. "Well, I'm glad at least one of us is enjoying this."

She stopped. She stared at that long tongue just hanging down in front of her. She had no idea why she thought about it, but the tongue was something like what a guy has, right? Might be a bit more wet and slimy than the real thing probably. Would that work just as well? Unsure of herself, she hesitantly reached out to her tail and held Ahya steady. It was like Ahya knew something was up, something new and unexpected. Something neither of them had done before. Taylor softly bit her bottom lip as she committed.

. . .

Oh gods… Oh gods… It was everything…and more.

12.

SCRIPT

"I'll be there in a minute," Murana called out as the banging on the front door grew more intense.

The call was unexpected, but the chief wanted to sit down with her while Taylor was away at school to talk over some serious matters. It didn't sound good at all, and she knew to document everything in case it could be used against her later. Adjusting her final miniature recording device in the form of a small sparrow pin on her blouse, she checked herself in the mirror.

She lightly tapped the metal pin. "Better not let you get crushed this time."

Her days of being vigilante were long since done. Her weapons and technical supplier was pinched in a sting unbeknownst to her until much later, and all access to gear she had so abundantly was suddenly severed. Everything she had now were just remnants of a time where she was far more deadly and lethal. She had to preserve what she could and make it last; she was not going to get anymore replacements.

"You never were patient!" she snarked loud enough so that he could hear on the other side of the door as he pounded yet again.

Jerking the door open, she saw the imposing black bear completely framed within the small opening of her front door. He was glowering at her, but she paid him no mind. Stepping aside to let him in, he squeezed through as best he could with a few grunts. Once inside, he took off his brown hat and began looking around for a place to hang it.

"You're looking pretty casual today," Murana remarked as she offered to take his hat and put it on the rack behind the door. She stepped back and took a look at his *Metal Birds* t-shirt and cut-up jeans. "I'd almost say you're trying too hard to blend in."

"What?" He scowled. "I happen to like their music. Don't judge me."

"Like you judged me when we first met?" she bantered, showing him the way into the living area where they could sit down.

"Touché," he admitted, accepting the offered seat on the sofa with the glass trimmed coffee table between them. The sofa creaked under his weight. "I think you know why I'm here."

Smoothing down her blue slacks upon sitting in her chair, Murana relaxed into the cushions. "To state my punishment for what happened in the courtroom last year?"

The chief scratched his neck a bit before coming out with it. "That was about six months ago, but yes, that is part of it, although the lot of us got off extremely lucky."

"So then what is it, Chief?" she said stoically.

"I'm not your chief, Mrs. Wolford." He sighed, looking a bit defeated. "I haven't been for years. You know that. Just call me Harold."

She shrugged. "Sorry, force of habit."

Eyeing her suspiciously, he continued. "I'm here to let you know you are under house arrest and surveillance." This caused Murana to raise her brow, but he barreled on before she could interject. "With the murders of the Hawkins boys fresh on the media, we felt it was in everyone's best interest to not just keep watch over you, but to protect this home from retaliation."

"Protect me from what?" She was a bit flummoxed.

"Are we being recorded? Is there anything on that could capture this conversation?" The chief was suddenly acting very unusual. He looked around the living room trying to ascertain if any object looked out of place to be a camera.

"No, of course not. It's just me and Taylor living here. We have no need to record anything," she lied. "I've long since given away the baby monitor I had years ago."

Wary, but satisfied with the answer, he leaned forward. Keeping his voice to a hush anyway, he pointed a finger at her. "Look, we all know it was you who killed those three swans. Those Hawkins boys."

Murana attempted to look offended. "Now why would I do such a thing? I know better than to stick my neck out any more than it already is and ruin my life and Taylor's by doing that."

Harold scoffed. "Please, I know you better than that. I spent nearly a decade tracking you down before we finally caught you and made you work for the city. I've spent every waking moment studying your kills, your movements, and your methods. I would almost like to say I'm the expert at the Dark Flame Wolf."

She leaned back into her chair, folding her arms. "You did get annoying, I will give you that."

He guffawed, causing her to jolt. "I'm glad I was! If I wasn't, I was not doing my job well! I even earned my promotion thanks to you. Got Chief right after my predecessor retired."

"Congratulations," she said dryly. "Is there a point to this?"

His face darkened. "Point being, I know the work of the Dark Flame Wolf when I see it. Not many would have the resources and skills to get into a fortified jail facility and murder those kids in broad daylight. Sure, they were not burned alive as is your calling card, but every other piece of evidence matches up."

She squinted. "So is that it? You're going to bring me in and answer for their deaths?"

It was Harold's turn to lean back and relax. "As a matter of fact, no." This brought a look of surprise to Murana. "We at the precinct all loved Anthony. He devoted nearly twenty years of his life to the job. Most of us were just starting off when he did. His death and farce of a trial over his killers hit all of us pretty hard."

He tapped the backside of the couch a few times, thinking. "We all believe they deserved what you gave them. That is why those who knew about you and who you were said nothing, and will continue to do nothing against you. We cannot publicly state we approve of the murders and the investigation is 'ongoing', but it'll most likely end up in a cold case with no leads."

"That's pretty convenient." She smirked.

He clasped his paws and leaned forward again. "Which leads me to the next point. Due to the highly sensitive nature of what you were and how you assisted the Zabökar police, it would do us no good to

263

reveal that we knew who you were and that you were working with us publicly. The fact you killed those boys would cause a huge uproar and most likely incite retaliation to both us and yourself. To that end…" He reached into his jeans pocket and pulled out what looked like a brand new ankle bracelet. "We are putting you again on house arrest and you will be tracked wherever you go."

Murana groaned, putting her face into her paws. "I thought we were past this."

"We were." He dangled the bracelet over the table for her to grab. "However, I cannot have you going off and killing folks anymore, even if they do deserve it. Those three boys were your last victims. The one, small bit of solace I can bring to Anthony's memory is to let that slide, but I cannot ignore what you've done. So it's either this or jail for the remainder of your life, and Taylor will be put into the foster home care system."

Murana's eyes bulged. "But…she wouldn't fit in well there. You know how she is… What she has…"

He nodded solemnly. "I am aware of the special traits of your child. However, there would be no other choice if you were to be taken away from her. I'm giving you this option for three reasons alone: In honor of Anthony Wolford, who I consider to be a dear friend and outstanding police officer. In honor of you, for what you've done for the city and this department, and how you turned your life around against all odds. And finally, so that the child of Anthony does not go parentless."

He jiggled the bracelet again, directing her attention to it. Murana looked like she was going to cry. It took her years to finally get it off the first time after they captured her and forced her into the deal of becoming a confidential informant. It was like a cage where her freedoms were greatly reduced or removed altogether. The yawning abyss of darkness emanating from memories of that time was threatening her calm as she stared at it.

"Please, Mrs. Wolford. Do this for Anthony and for Taylor." Harold was sincere.

Stifling a sob, she took it from him and lifted up the leg of her pants. With grim resolve, she wrapped it around her right ankle and snapped it shut. A small hum emitted from the device as it turned on, and the yellow LED began blinking a few times before turning green. She stared glumly at the light, her entire day ruined. Possibly even the year.

"Thank you, Mrs. Wolford." Harold seemed to visibly relax. It was clear he was expecting more resistance than that. He looked happy she listened to reason. "You will have weekly police check-ups and free access to our psychiatric services should you need to vent and talk about anything regarding this situation. It is going to be tough, of that I have no doubt, but you knew there would be consequences from your actions. Things could have turned out a lot worse for you."

"I know." Her eyes turned back to him finally. "I know what I deserve."

His voice softened. "Yes, you did a lot of bad things, but I read your case file. A lot of bad things had happened to you in your life prior. The pattern of abuse lives on if left unchecked. I'm actually glad for Anthony's sake that we got to you before you reached the point of no return."

"Oh, why's that?" She wiped a tear from her eye.

"He, too, had a troubled past as I'm sure you know." He smiled. "Probably not as checkered as yours, but I've known him since we were teenagers. He never really did find true happiness until I saw him with you and your boys. And with Taylor, he was beaming with pride about her birth. Everyone in the station could see it. None of that would have happened for my friend if not for you. You gave each other what each of you deserved."

"You don't have to save my feelings." Murana shifted, still uncomfortable with the new weight around her ankle.

"I'm not." Harold groused. He rose up, towering over Murana's small form huddled in her chair. "Just stay out of trouble from here on out, ok? No more killing. No more vigilante work. Nothing. You've got a good thing going here, and I'd be loath to see it come crashing down around you."

Murana tried to crack a smile. "I'll be good, Chief."

He gave her a stink eye, wagging a finger at her flippant calling of his title after he had told her to disregard it. "Gods help me, if you do anything more to bring further flak onto my department and the jobs of me and my crew, I will do what I should have done when I first caught you and put you behind bars for good."

"Is that a promise?" She maintained the grin, but her will was dwindling. She could feel her cancer slinking back into her bones. She had been having a good day.

"Always." Harold winked at her. "Ma'am." He bowed his head before grabbing his hat from the rack and opening the door to leave. "Say hello to Taylor for me, will you?"

"Of course." She dropped the smile as he shut the door.

She stayed sitting there, watching the unwavering green light on her ankle until the sunlight entering the room had turned a rich shade of red. Rousing herself from her stupor, she fidgeted with her sparrow pin. The video and sound went dark.

Something was nagging Fey, but he couldn't quite put his hoof on what. They had stopped running Taylor's killing of that rabbit on the news late last night, but he had the video link saved on his computer. He kept watching it on repeat over and over again, but he was no long paying any attention to it. If anything, it was just background noise for his thoughts.

Finnley slowly crept into the room, his small squeaks indicating to Fey that he had just woken up from his sleep and his lower back was aching. It was still dark outside, but it wouldn't be long until the sun would crest over the lowest of buildings and slink into their apartment with its warmth. He could feel the tiny, clawed paws of his otter grasp his striped pajama leggings and clamber up onto his lap, curling around in a small ball as he snuggled into the elk.

"Morning, Finn." Fey leaned down to give Finnley a kiss on the head. "How's your shoulder?"

"The ointment is helping." Finnley drowsily looked at the news report Fey was viewing and grumbled. "Will you lay off that? We're done with that thing and her monster tail. What's so gods damn important that it keeps you up this early in the morning?"

Fey reached over to grasp his coffee mug to bring it over for a sip before explaining his concerns. "There's something I'm missing from all this. I am off the Script, and because of that I can, in theory, affect other people's Scripts that was never written for them."

"Yeah? So what's your point?" Finnley seemed more awake and already done with the conversation.

"When I saved that buck the other night, I felt something horrifying."

Finnley looked up at Fey with concern. "I didn't feel anything. I maybe felt a strong gust of wind, but that was it."

"I felt that too, but I also felt terror. The kind you get when a predator or killer is hunting you. I can't explain why, but I think the reason I felt it is because I'm off the Script and you're not. You were not in any danger from the Authority. So it makes sense why you didn't feel that sense of panic like I did."

Finnley unfurled and put a paw on Fey's arm. "I worry about you. You've been on this crazy Script kick ever since we got home. All I want to do is pack our things, resolve our bank accounts, and get out of dodge. Why are you so hyped up on this Authority thing, or whatever it is?"

Fey took a bigger sip. "Because I think that's what is after me now. For whatever reason, I feel like it's getting closer—like it was further away before and the more things that change, the closer it gets."

"But there's nothing?" Finnley seemed confused and fretful over him. It was endearing to Fey that Finnley cared so much about him.

"I think there is. Take a look at this." Fey stopped the video clip of Taylor and swapped over to another window. There was a news report about a horrific death that happened in the early hours of the morning. He reset the video clip and turned up the volume.

"The body identified at two o'clock this morning down on Forrester Lane," the feline reporter began, "was a bank teller named Terry Fitzgerald. He was last seen earlier last night heroically stopping an armed robbery at his bank. He was lauded a hero as he delayed the two robbers long enough for police to arrive to contain the situation."

An image popped up with what he looked like. Finnley sat up a bit straighter on Fey's lap. "Isn't that...the buck you saved?"

"Yeah, just a few blocks from here." Fey nodded. "Keep watching."

"Fitzgerald was found this morning lying face down in a pool of blood by a homeless mammal who immediately reported it to the police. The footage I'm about to show you is graphic, so viewers are warned. Fitzgerald was victim to a vicious attack that coroners are calling unprecedented in all of Zabökar's history." She continued.

The aircam footage from a drone showed clearly the spotlighted location of where Fitzgerald lay next to a dumpster. It was pixelated to prevent it being too graphic, but it was clear that all his skin, organs and muscle had been striped clean. All that was left was his bones, which were remarkably intact. The massive sea of red around him, they assumed, was the rest of his body liquefied.

Fey turned down the volume as he paused the clip and pointed at the blurry body. "I'm no coroner, but I've have had my fair share of investigating deaths and causes of it. Terry was running from something. Gauging by the way his legs are splayed, one slightly bent and his arms tucked under his body, he literally toppled over onto his belly from some force and died in that position. He never got away from whatever stripped his bones clean."

Finnley turned back to look at Fey. "You think... You think it was this Authority?"

"Almost positive. I saved him that night from a hit and run that would have surely killed him. Since I proved I was off the Script, there should have been no one to save him that night. So if my theory is correct, he was off the Script up until this morning when he died."

"But how can you prove it was this Authority that did it? It could have been anyone and anything that killed him."

Fey shook his head vehemently. "No. Look at the manner of his death. What animal or weapon do you know of that could do that? Think back to your training. Nothing, right? At least, no weapon or animal I know of. This is a wholly unique method of killing. It has to be the Authority."

"I think you're grasping at angel strings here, Fey. Making connections when there are none." Finnley was putting on a brave face, but Fey could see his macabre musings were getting to him.

"Don't believe me? Think about what the last thing he did was: saving his bank and most likely several other people's lives from death by this robbery. More lives than the one life I saved. That's a lot of Script-changing. Shortly thereafter, he dies a horrible death at the hands of...nothing? Does that seem right to you?"

"That doesn't mean anything. I mean, you've been alive this long since Taylor saved you. Shouldn't the Authority have caught up with you now as well?"

"That's the thing. I've been thinking about that a lot." Fey was going over all the events in his mind since his miraculous resurrection inside Ahya's maw. "The only thing I did of any consequence since I was given a second chance at life was kill that priest in Cheribaum. It was then that I noticed in his Script that the Authority was notified. We went to then save Taylor and that cheetah, Sabrina, got killed. I barely had a hand in that and it was Taylor who ultimately killed her; the rest of us merely distracted Sabrina for Ahya to deliver the killing bite."

"I don't see where you're headed with this."

"Just wait." He set down his mug, his thoughts now going into high gear. "What else did I honestly change about the Script since then? Nothing. Sure I went with Terrati up on the mountain to help snipe Howlgrav's finest, but Ari was intending to be Terrati's spotter anyway. It wouldn't have ultimately mattered if I was there or not. It was an inconsequential contribution on my part. The Script was fulfilled one way or another, through myself or Ari. I ultimately had no say in how that entire plan went when we lost Taylor to Ari."

"So what changed from then to now?"

Fey looked out the full-length window spanning from wall to wall of their luxury suite, paid for by lucrative funds of successful missions past. "Answer me a question before I finish. Would you have killed Gregor and attempted to take Taylor back from Ari if Taylor had not revived me from the dead?"

"I would have done it out of spite, actually," Finnley said after some thought. "I would have liked Taylor a lot less and might have even smacked her around a bit more often, but I would have tried to bring her back to the High Council because it was your mission to. Our mission. I would see it through to the end just for you."

Fey nodded. That confirmed it. "Then Gregor's death was destined to happen anyway, not because I was alive by Taylor's doing. No wonder the Authority didn't find me then."

"You mean to say that since saving that buck was your first major change in the Script, the Authority found you again?" Finnley seemed confused and was trying to follow Fey's thought process.

"That's exactly what I'm saying. It found Terry quickly because of the mass of people he probably saved from Scripted death in that bank. The more I interact with others and change things, the sooner I think I'll be meeting this Authority."

Finnley shivered. "Well, hell! All the more reason to get out of Zabökar and go somewhere secluded where no one can find us! Live out our lives in peace!"

Fey's shoulders slumped as he petted Finnley. "You know that's not how it ends. You read your Script. Your fate is intertwined with Taylor's."

"Well, fuck Taylor!" Finnley fumed as he hopped off Fey's lap and began pacing around on the table. "Nothing good has ever come out of being involved with her. The further away from her we are, the better."

Fey tried to remain calm and patient. Finnley would come to see things like he did. "It's not that simple. The mere act of removing ourselves from everything on my account, to keep me safe, effectively changes the Script. Your Script. Don't you see that? You are changing your Script because of my influence. If we leave Zabökar now, you'll just attract the attention of the Authority back onto me. We need to stay here, follow your Script, and figure out if there is a solution to this mess, and I think Taylor is the key."

Finnley threw his paws up. "This is crazy. You know that?" He balled his fists and pouted. "None of this makes sense. It feels like some crazy conspiracy theory you want to believe is real! Like, how can we even be sure?"

"Why was the High Council so interested in Taylor then?" Fey said softly.

Finnley blinked. "Well, they wanted to bring her in to safeguard her from the Arbiter."

"You and I both know that is a lie. Their motives were never altruistic in all the years we've known them. They'll do seemingly selfless things if it benefits them in the end. They were supremely interested in Taylor for a reason. That contract they put out on her that we accepted was not like the others put out on the other powered mammals. They made a specific stipulation of her being alive. Didn't that strike you as odd? Why bother keeping her alive and accept the dead bodies of the others if her being alive wasn't a special requirement for something?"

"It wasn't our job to question the orders," Finnley tiredly said. "We do the mission, get paid, and go home. That's it."

"Except now it could be my own life at stake if we don't question it." Fey clicked open a few more windows on the computer and showed Finnley what he was researching. Showing him what had kept him up all night. "Power-eaters, as we know, eat the corpses of the powered mammals to gain their powers in some limited form. It has been proven by Ari and others that these powers, when used, can shorten people's Scripts. Taylor is the first person to ever be able to extend a person's life beyond their Script, effectively ripping them off of it completely."

Finnley brought a paw to his cheek and tapped. "Okay, I get it. Taylor is more special than most."

Fey stared at him. "Don't you see? A Script can be shortened, because it can account for that. It can write that person's new end and finalize their Script. That doesn't attract any attention, otherwise Ari would have been killed by this Authority long before now. If you keep living past your final end, there's no more parchment roll, as it were, to keep writing your future. You now have no more Script!"

"I think I see what you're getting at, but why would the High Council want Taylor for this? It's not like any of them are going to die soon, right?"

Fey shrugged. "Perhaps, perhaps not. However, I did more digging, and I discovered these power-eaters actually go by another name: Children of the Unwritten Script. Or at least, their founding members were originally a part of that cult. Their sole goal is to get society and effectively the world at large off the Script. That's their entire focus. Why else would they be so interested in eating the slain mammals with powers? To gain the ability to change the Script!"

Finnley nodded in understanding. "Yet none of those mammals have the power to truly change the Script, only to modify it to still fit within its parameters."

Fey snapped his hoof fingers. "Precisely! Dingleberry tarts! You're getting it!" Finnley's ears flattened at the jovial mocking. "Oh, don't give me that look. Taylor is the only one to completely change it, and every person she affects this way can as well! Who else do we know on the High Council that targeted Taylor is a power-eater?"

"Sabrina Fahpar. And we still don't know if she was working alone or if other members of the High Council were in on her plan." Finnley began pacing again.

"Which is why I need to break in and investigate her residence and see if I can find more clues as to her involvement, and by extension, the High Council's," Fey finished with satisfaction.

Finnley smirked. "Now I know you're nuts. That's in downtown, Caelesti Spire, dead central High Council tower. How are we going to sneak in there—after we've been disavowed, mind you—to go snoop around a dead council member's abode when they've no doubt figured out her death by now? And what would we be even looking for anyway or trying to prove?"

"I can't answer the first one yet," Fey admitted. He hadn't thought that far ahead. "But what I'm there to prove? If these power-eaters have definitely infiltrated the High Council, then the Arbiter was right all along and Taylor would be safer in his hands."

Finnley snorted. "Please don't go sympathizing with him now."

"I'm not."

"Good." He stared at Fey a bit longer, seeming to make sure he got his point across.

"I'm also going alone," Fey added.

"What? No!" Finnley spun on him, fists on his hips. "I just got you back from certain death. Your second death might be around the corner because of this stupid Authority thing. There's no way I'm going to let you wander into High Council central by yourself and get caught!"

"Your Script does not have you going to the High Council, does it?" Fey asked calmly.

"I don't know!" He threw his paws up. "I don't like hearing my Script."

"So who is to say the Authority won't find me if I make you go there because of me?"

Finnley was attempting to keep his rage bottled up, with limited success. He glowered at Fey as intensely as he could. "That's a risk I'm willing to take! I'm not going to leave you, Fey."

Fey sagged in the chair. "I'm not going to talk you out of this, am I?"

"Not a chance!" Finnley said confidently, crossing his arms like a job well done. After a few moments, he continued. "So the High Council gets their hands on Taylor, then what?"

Fey wasn't exactly sure. He hadn't even thought of the ramifications of what could happen, but the more he ruminated on it, the worse his heart felt. "Then a lot more people are going to die. If they use Taylor to accomplish getting themselves off the Script, then they could cause a cascading effect throughout the entire city, and whatever this Authority is will be having a field day of a graveyard digging."

"Yeah, I agree. That's bad." Finnley sighed. "As much as I hate to say it, you're right. Taylor is stupid important and I despise that. I'm willing to bet the Arbiter doesn't even realize what he has yet, or he wouldn't have gone and let Taylor roam around the streets of Zabökar like that." He gestured to the news clip of the rabbit getting eaten, buried under other windows now.

Fey squinted as the first rays of the sun hit his eyes. He was reminded of a text he needed to send to Mikhail about all this, given he was off the Script as well. He spoke with fear as he tapped in the letters on his phone to send the information off to the tiger, "And Taylor is more vulnerable than ever."

273

The incessant tapping woke Taylor up. She glanced around and noticed she was alone on Nina's bed, bottomless and covered only by Ahya's thick fluff. She must have fallen asleep right after she finished. She flushed hard as she could smell and detect the presence of Nina in the other room. She hoped that Nina didn't find her like this when she got home last night. She panicked a bit when she remembered she also didn't close the windows with Pawtube up—on full, damning display for Nina to see.

She quietly slipped off the bed and tucked her legs into her jeans, hoping Nina wouldn't notice her movements too much in the bedroom. The tapping continued on. Trying to act casual, she stepped out into the living den. The sun was already shining brightly into the room, illuminating the shape of Nina sitting in front of her laptop. Taylor flinched inwardly as it seemed Nina was looking directly at the screen.

"Hey, Nina." Taylor tried to sound chipper, even if she was feeling anything but.

Nina glanced up from her thoughts. The tapping of her wing on the table stopped. "Oh, hey, Taylor. I see you enjoyed yourself." Although it sounded like playful ribbing, there was a certain unease about the swan this morning.

Taylor shied away and didn't meet Nina's eyes. She sat down at the furthest seat from her, feeling some distance might help matters. It was probably fruitless anyway. "I really don't know what came over me last night. I'm sorry about—"

"It's okay." Nina cut her off, terse but not completely upset. "I was the one who prompted you to do it, teasing you and all."

"I'll go clean and make the bed if you want," Taylor offered. She felt weird discussing this with Nina. This was a situation she had never been in before.

"I'll do it. Besides, I got the key to the laundry room downstairs anyway." The tapping resumed. "Just a shame I wasn't here to see it."

Taylor looked at her oddly. That was quite an unexpected thing to say. "Are you alright, Nina? You look pretty tense."

Nina looked down at her knee as she followed Taylor's gaze. Her leg was bouncing in tune to her tapping. She stopped both. "No, I'm fine. What makes you say that?"

"I don't know. You seem…different. Distant, somehow. Did everything go alright with the group last night?" Taylor offered her paw to grab as she extended her arm across the table.

Nina looked at it a moment before draping her wing over Taylor's paw. "It went fine. Everything was great. They're all pretty friendly there." Nina cracked a smile, but it still felt she was holding something back.

"So what's eating at you then?"

Nina chuckled nervously. "Well, my father called this morning and wants to see me at church. He demands I show."

Taylor cocked her head slightly. She was almost positive her father shunned his daughter's very existence when she decided to rebel and go full metal with the band. "When was the last time you spoke to your dad?"

"Since before you first joined us." She looked distraught. Taylor could feel her trembling over her paw.

Taylor whistled low. "That's a long time. Did he even say what he wanted from you?"

Nina shook her head. "Only that mother was worried about me. She's…never been worried about me. Like ever."

Taylor gasped. Her thoughts went to the television still sitting on the kitchen day bar. "Do you think they saw you yesterday on the news with me?"

"Well, they never really had any issues forgetting about me during the entire time I was with you and the band back when we were together." Nina seemed like she was going numb emotionally, her countenance drooping.

"Maybe so, but that was before I was labeled a murderer on live TV."

"Damn it." Nina shut her eyes, clamping her bill shut in frustration. "Why did it have to be now? My last day off before work tomorrow and they want me to spend it with them! Ugh, I'd rather spend it with you."

Taylor placed her other paw on top of Nina's wing and squeezed gently. "You still can. I'll go with you."

Nina's eyes shot open. "Are you whacko? They never approved of anything I did nor anyone I have made friends with. They definitely won't like you showing up, especially if they caught wind of Ahya's recent killing."

Taylor was resolute. She steeled her gaze and looked Nina directly in the eyes. "I don't care. You're my friend and I want to do this with you."

"What if they call the cops the moment they see you?" She was fidgeting.

Taylor sighed calmly. "Then we'll run and figure things out then. Besides, they won't recognize me initially. What was the point of dyeing my fur and changing up my look if not to blend in better? Besides, you've done so much for me since I arrived here. I could be dead or out wandering the streets by now if not for you. You gave me a temporary place to sleep and stay. So of course I want to do this for you. Let me be your crutch; lean on me like I did on you yesterday."

"They're going to have the Script there, reading it off to people," Nina reminded, her humor returning to her.

"So? We don't have to pay attention to it. We're only there to hear out your mother and father, not to get indoctrinated into the church when we wrote a song directly hating on the Script." Taylor smiled.

"Can we go somewhere fun and nice afterwards?" Nina looked hopeful.

"Only if I can call up and invite my two brothers!" Taylor was getting excited now.

She knew Ari would come around eventually and reality would slam her against the wall, but for now, Taylor needed an escape from the pressures of what was looming on the horizon. If it meant dealing with this nonsense with Nina's parents and then enjoying the rest of the day off, it was worth it. Zabökar's fate could wait one more day; Taylor needed this. Besides, she hadn't quite figured out how to approach Ari again after all she had done to her. With the recent trail of the power-eaters now cold by two days, there was no plan to follow either. Might as well procrastinate.

"I'd like that, actually." Nina got up and walked around the table to hug Taylor.

Taylor rose and embraced the swan, wrapping her arms tight under the wings. It was always awkward to hug Nina because of those wings, but the warmth of their plumage was so wonderful. Taylor could just sink into those feathers and just be at peace. Nina seemed to sense this feeling and tightened her grip further.

"Thank you for being a good friend," Taylor whispered.

Nina broke off the hug, but continued to keep her wings around Taylor. Ahya had curled around Nina's back and was idly licking her pants. "Thanks, Taylor. Between all the members of the band, I'd say you were the one I disliked the least."

Taylor rolled her eyes. "Oh geez, thanks for that backhanded compliment!"

Nina made a kissing sound with her bill and winked. "You know I love you, Taylor." She cackled. "You were the only sane one among us. Even I'll admit I was a bit lost to the drugs and sex of that time, and didn't really appreciate you much then. I'm sorry."

"I know." Taylor stuck her tongue out. "You made me wait to walk home with you while your groupie horn-dog friends banged the shit out of you! I was beginning to question your taste when I found out about Ramon yesterday!"

Nina put a wing up in defense and feigned innocence. "Don't remind me. We all make mistakes. Granted, at least I learned from mine!"

Taylor's face fell. "Yeah, unlike Loray and Bailey."

Nina dropped her wings and began to move away, softly pushing Ahya out of the way so she wouldn't trip. "Yeah, it is a shame those two are still hanging out with Ramon. I feel like they could be doing so much more with their lives, but instead they are just wasting away with him. Still, we need to look out for ourselves first, right?"

Taylor nodded. "Right!" She gazed around the empty, yet clean kitchen counters. "Did you want to eat some breakfast before we go?"

Nina waved a wing at her. "No, I'm actually quite stuffed. I've already eaten. Don't worry about me. Get yourself something and we can head out. Oh, and Taylor?"

"Yes?" She was already pouring herself a bowl of cereal.

"Thanks again."

"Anytime." She watched as her friend returned the smile before heading into the bedroom to get dressed for church.

"You really should have fucked that rabbit!" Nina called out.

"Shut your mouth!" Taylor roared. She stuffed her arms through a new shirt, hurriedly getting dressed to head out with Nina. Despite her being reminded of her missed opportunity with Jake, Taylor had a nagging feeling she was forgetting something this morning.

The Arbiter was sitting silent and still on a reinforced stool that seemed way too small for his bulk. His eyes were roving over the plethora of screens in front of him. News reports of a liquefied deer. Local crime lords being busted during a sting. Old recordings of Taylor's rabbit killing. And that was just the public channels.

Some of his surveillance feeds were giving him different views of Zabökar. The High Council was in session, discussing something mundane and most likely not worth his time watching. What was most pertinent to him now was the screen depicting the lower subway tunnels and a small gang of mammals walking alongside his daughter, Ari.

He had finally tracked her down the night prior after she had gone missing on day one. It wasn't until Rakkis reported back her location that he was able to move the tiny drone cameras to better expand coverage in the tunnels and locate them. He was thankful Rakkis was around as a backup to his daughter. As much as he trusted her resolve, she was still a young teen and prone to error. Taylor's escape and disappearance proved that, even if he did plan that.

Still, it looked like she was on the job and actively tracking Taylor through her own means. It was interesting to him that she chose to ally herself with both the lone bounty hunter they casted off, and a good portion of the ex-mercenaries from the High Council. Obviously a shared interest, or she wouldn't be so chummy with them; he knew his daughter that much. She had a bit of a temper and would have turned violent long before now if they were a threat.

The timetable to accomplish their task was shrinking further with each passing day. There were already reports of behemoths navigating the western mountain range. They were not built for such terrain, so it would take them some time to make it across the peaks, but it would not be long now.

His eyes drifted back over to the High Council meeting. What were they playing at? They surely would be aware by now of Taylor's presence because of her abrupt destruction of Roaring St. and her face plastered all over the news. So why hadn't they made a move?

They revealed their hand and Taylor was visible earlier than they wanted her to be, but it still was odd they were content to ignore her existence. Did they not want her to begin with? He was beginning to think his plan wasn't as sound as he expected it to be. The fact various factories of the Harutan brand in the old subsections of the city beneath Caelesti Spire were shut down and cleared out a week ago was alarming enough on its own.

A small intercom buzz alerted him to an incoming call from the weapons lab. He pressed it firmly. "Arbiter here. Please tell me you have good news."

There was an audible exhale of breath on the other end. This did not bode well. "Sir, I tried to replicate the tissue growth on damaged bodies like you asked me to based on all the samples we extracted from Taylor's tailmaw."

"And the results?"

"It seems we're missing some key enzyme that activates the regenerative capabilities of the saliva. The only thing I've been able to manage is to get it caustic to where it can melt through just about any substance." The technician sounded defeated.

The Arbiter wasn't too disappointed. "That could have other applications. That is a worthy discovery. Keep one section of your lab working on that aspect of her tail's saliva and see if we can weaponize it."

"And the other sections?"

"Have them keep focusing on getting this healing ability working. We need to see if we can replicate how she managed to bring an entire person back from death. I'd rather we be consistent with those results than a fluke streak of luck like we had with Rakkis." He was keenly interested in Ari's report that Fey Darner, the leader of the mercenaries hired by the High Council, managed to be revived from within Taylor's tail after certain death from a hail of bullets.

The technician's voice was weary. "Yes, sir. If we could just get Taylor to come back and provide more samples for—"

"Negative," he said firmly. "Too many pieces are in motion right now with our packing and moving of our subjects, and kitnapping her back now would draw too much attention to ourselves. You need to work with what you've been given."

"Yes, sir. I'll report if I have anything new." He clicked off.

The Arbiter leaned back and continued to watch the screens. The fate of this Fey was intriguing to him. He had sent Rakkis to keep an eye on them as well. With eyes and ears in nearly every corner of Zabökar, he felt confident he could control the evolving situation and coming events. Taylor was playing nicely off of Ari, but then again, Taylor's mother was obstinate too, he recalled.

13.

FALLOUT

"Hey, honey, I'm home!" a male voice called out from the entryway, followed by the sound of a door closing and coat being hung on the rack behind it.

The psychiatrist looked up from her current round of notes at the sound and curiously looked over at Murana. "I wasn't aware you got remarried."

Murana was trying hard to suppress a grin. "I didn't. That's just Sebastian. After many years being the impromptu nanny sometimes to Taylor, I hired him on a semi-permanent basis to be my in-home caregiver." She coughed a few times, wiping the red spittle with a cloth from her mouth.

A dark, charcoal-furred wolf strolled into the room with deep sepia scrubs. He was looking matted and hot, his tongue out and panting. "It was a rough day today, but I managed to get off a bit early." He smiled, leaning over to give an affectionate lick to Murana's cheek which she leaned into longingly.

"I'm just glad you're home." She gripped his paw when he placed it in hers. "Would you mind making dinner tonight? I'm not really feeling well again."

He petted her head and scratched her ear gently. "Of course. Anything in particular you'd like?" She just shrugged. "Then tomato soup and grilled cheesed sandwiches it is!"

"That sounds lovely." She squeezed his paw in appreciation.

He leaned over to whisper into her ear, his eyes darting over to the gazelle sitting patiently in the chair opposite Murana. "Maybe even a bath later? Just you and me?"

Murana flushed, looking a bit embarrassed for the gazelle, but lightly bapped Sebastian on the arm. "Not in front of Kiera...but maybe if I'm feeling up to it. Today hasn't been a good day for me."

He nodded, giving her one last kiss before heading towards the kitchen. "Then I'll make sure these are the best sandwiches I've made yet!" he chortled, wagging his braided tail happily all the way to the stove.

The gazelle smiled after him. She pointed with her pen. "Does he know about...what you were back then?"

Murana shook her head. "No. He knows nothing about my days as a vigilante; he only knows about my career as a cop. I prefer to keep it that way. Wanting a fresh start, you know?"

"I can understand that." Kiera lingered on Sebastian a few moments more. "He seems sweet. How did you two meet?" She raised a hoof at the raised brow from Murana. "If you want to tell me, that is." She pointed at the notepad on her lap. "It would be good to round out your profile with all details so I can give a favorable report back to the precinct."

"Indeed," Murana mused.

She had been seeing this psychiatrist for well on five years now, ever since her services were offered by Harold. In the beginning, these sessions were sorely needed and it helped alleviate a lot of what was on her chest. It was insane how much this gazelle now knew about her life, from its horrid beginnings to the strained present. She could almost say Kiera was like family, if only in a professional sense. At least the bills for her therapy services were all paid for as promised by their chief.

Shaking off her thoughts, she put on a happy face for Kiera. "Anthony and I actually met Sebastian before Taylor was born. Since then, he's been a very good friend of the family all throughout her life. He's like an uncle to her."

"Soon to be dad?" Kiera couldn't help but rib Murana playfully.

Murana flushed again. "He already is." She gazed off to the kitchen to see his cute butt swaying with some insufferable tune he no doubt had in his head while he was cooking. "After Anthony died, he was a great help in getting us settled afterwards. He had his own life and job to tend to and I had mine. It wasn't until recently with my health deteriorating further that I decided to hire him on officially as a part-time care giver to me. His relationship to Taylor was already great, and with his skills and knowledge in the health industry, it seemed a perfect fit since we trusted him already with so much."

"And it turned to love?" Kiera pressed, leaning forward as if hungering for the juicy gossip.

Murana couldn't help but smile at this casual conversation about her love life. It was strangely welcome. "I guess you could say that. Nothing official though, but we've definitely moved past professionalism, if that's what you want to know."

Now this brought a blush to Kiera's cheeks. "Well then..." She fake coughed. "I'm going to leave that specific detail out of my notes."

"Appreciated." Murana chuckled.

"He seems a bit young for you." Kiera winked.

"Only by ten years or so, but I've still got it!" Murana clicked her tongue knowingly. They both laughed at this.

Attempting to regain her train of thought, Kiera scanned her notes. "How is Taylor these days? Is she adjusting to her new school?"

This question caused Murana to sag. She wiped her brow with her paw. "Not entirely. We've had to resort to the old methods of coping with Ahya when we first put her into public school because we had no other choice. Anthony was gone and I wasn't equipped to homeschool like I thought I was. But even those methods aren't working now."

It seemed Kiera's heart went out to Murana. "It is just simply dreadful what happened to you. I read it all in the report before taking you on as my patient. You were set to have twins and then only gave birth to one cub, but with such abnormal qualities as a result of what you were subjected to. I can't imagine what you've had to deal with raising her."

Murana grimaced, wiping the dribbling snot from her nose with the cloth. "She's not abnormal. She is just Taylor. She's a little girl like all the others, but she needs a bit more assistance than most. That's all."

"And her brothers have been helping you with her?" Kiera was jotting things furiously.

"Not recently, no." Murana looked sad. "I can't expect them to take huge swaths of time out of their day like Sebastian to come care for me and Taylor. They got their own lives too, and they are adults now. As much as I miss them, I realize that my time with them under my roof is over. All I have now is Taylor." Murana shifted in her chair after another fit of coughing, revealing her ankle bracelet, still attached after all these years.

Kiera noticed the movement and gestured to the device. "I know the chief did not specify an end date to that tracking bracelet, but if you want, I could put in a good recommendation for you to have that removed finally. After so many years of good behavior and stable lifestyle, I can say with the backing of my degree and opinion that you are fit enough to be free of this restriction."

Wiping more blood from her mouth, Murana tried to laugh. "Gee, thanks, right as I'm going to die soon from this cancer anyway."

"Better late than never, right?" Kiera tried to keep the mood light.

"Of course." Murana did laugh this time. "I was thinking that we…" Her ears suddenly sprung up, hearing the heavy patter of pawpads on the sidewalk outside. Combined with sobbing and panting, she was immediately alert. "Taylor?"

Taylor used her keys to bust into the home, slamming the front door against the adjacent wall, causing Sebastian's coat to drop to the floor. "Mom!" she wailed. "Mom!" She rushed into the living room crying and flopped onto Murana's chair heaving.

"What is going on? What happened?" All thoughts and feelings of her sickness were gone. The adrenaline rushing through her body alleviated any aches and pains and all she had eyes for was Taylor.

"I ate someone!" she yowled, looking at her with tears streaming down her face, snot rivulets flowing out her nose and ruining the upper blouse of her drenched school uniform—the rain still pouring outside.

"Ate who? How?" Murana was getting panicky.

"Ahya!" Taylor pointed at her tailmaw who was looking guilty and trying to roll up and hide under Taylor's skirt. "She ate Sarah! One minute she is next to me talking, the next, she's inside Ahya being eaten alive!" Taylor began to dry-retch. "Ugh, I still taste her on my tongue. I feel like I'm going to be sick."

Without a further thought, she pitched over the armrest of Murana's chair and vomited onto her lap. Taylor was shivering and crying as she howled louder at having ruined her mother's clothes. Murana didn't care about that, she cared more for what was going to happen next. Her eyes met and locked onto Kiera's. The gazelle's nostrils were flaring and her pupils wide like her fight-or-flight response had been activated.

"Kiera?" Murana warily called out, trying to gauge her response.

"What's all the fuss?" Sebastian rushed into the room, seeing the mess Taylor had made on Murana.

Murana turned to him with fear in her eyes. "Her tail ate someone."

"Oh gods…" he breathed.

"Taylor… Taylor!" Murana gripped her hard and forced Taylor to look at her. "Go with Sebastian to clean up and we'll figure this out together. Maybe there's a way we can get Sarah back."

Taylor began moaning again, shaking her head vigorously. "There's no way! She's gone! She's gone! She's not in my tail anymore! I feel her now here!" She put a paw to her stomach.

"Taylor, honey, just come with me," Sebastian tried to soothe. He picked up the distraught Taylor and carried her upstairs, dripping all the way, to clean up and get redressed. They could hear her cries all the way up and into the bathroom.

"Kiera?" Murana probed again.

This caused the gazelle to shrug off the lapse in coherency. "We have to report this. I have to report this."

Murana rose up from her chair. "No, you don't. Let's just stop for a moment and think about what we can do next. We are talking about Taylor here. She's only twelve years old."

"Yes. A twelve year old who just killed another girl." Kiera reminded, quickly flipping her notepad shut and stuffing it into her briefcase. "There's going to be a police report on this. We need to address the grieving family. They're going to want to know what we're going to do about the killer, your daughter."

"But it's not her fault! I've already told you several times that her tail sometimes has a mind of its own. She can't always control it! She's not a killer." Murana's tone grew firm.

"Yet a girl has died regardless. There must be some accountability for that lost life. I need to report this to the chief." Kiera reiterated with more force.

Murana took a few threatening steps towards her. "And what do you think they're going to do to her? They're going to take her away from me, possibly for months, years until they can get this legal mess sorted out because of her tail. If they convict her, I know exactly who is going to have her: the High Council. They've been wanting to experiment on her for years, and I've denied them. This would be the perfect opportunity for them to do it. The perfect excuse to take her away from me. She's a danger to society, so might as well lock her away and figure out how she works!"

"What crazy, delusional theory is that?" Kiera was aghast. "The High Council is not like that at all, and you are spouting nonsense. You don't know that is what will happen!"

"In my years working for the city and my dealings with the High Council, I think I know more than you here, Kiera." Murana stabbed a finger at her. "They are not the stalwart defenders of our city like they've convinced the majority to believe. You go and report my daughter to your chief, I will lose Taylor. Do you want that on your head?"

"But I must. A death has occurred, Murana. You know as well as I do that there are procedures to be followed." Kiera began to make for the front door.

"Don't do it. Stop, Kiera." Murana warned, baring her teeth.

The forgotten camera Kiera had brought to document the session was perched at the edge of the coffee table, capturing everything. The gazelle's wide eyes were shifting erratically between door and wolf, unsure whether she should take the chance to make a dash for the opening or find some way to talk Murana down so she could leave safely.

With a flick of her ears, she decided to make a run for it. Murana roared and was upon her in a heartbeat. She barreled Kiera to the ground and began digging her claws into her soft flesh as she attempted to hold the gazelle in place. Kiera immediately bucked, narrowly missing Murana's entire head with her horns.

"Don't make me do this!" Murana grunted, fighting the bleating gazelle. They continued rolling across the floor until Murana was back on top.

Kiera tried skewering Murana's face again with her horns, causing the wolf to grab one of them and yank her head off to the side. Murana underestimated her own strength, and she heard an audible snap as Kiera's entire body went lifeless beneath her. The gazelle's eyes stared up past her towards the ceiling, the neck twisted at an awkward angle.

"Oh gods..." Murana gasped, instantly dropping her hold on Kiera as if she were poison. "Oh, no, no, no..." She fell onto her rump and scooted backwards until she bumped up against her chair. Placing a paw to her mouth, she began to weep. "Why, Kiera? Why?"

Sebastian thundered down the stairs, halting abruptly at the entryway to the living den. His eyes alit on Kiera's corpse. He stared stunned at the scene, his gaze slowly traveling over to Murana who was a miserable wreck, rocking back and forth against her chair on the carpet. Taylor was still distressed, but she was curious now what had happened, tears and wailing only coming back again upon seeing what had happened.

"What did you do?" Sebastian couldn't think of anything else to ask.

"They're going to come for her now." Murana sniffed, looking around the room as if it was no longer her home. "They're going to take her away."

"What are you saying? Stop. Let's slow down." Sebastian looked to be struggling with how fast things were moving.

Murana focused on him, as if just seeing him for the first time. "I killed her. She said she was going to report Sarah's death and I killed her."

"What was she doing? How did it happen?"

"Don't look at me like that." Murana could see the pity and sadness in his eyes. "I said don't look at me!" With decision made, she struggled to get up using the chair for leverage and strode directly towards her daughter. "Taylor, you and mommy are going to be leaving now. We're going to have to find a new home."

"Wait! Stop!" Sebastian grabbed Murana's arm hard, trying to keep her from walking out. "Can we just talk about this peaceably? Maybe I can help you figure out a way we can get us through this?"

Murana wrenched her arm violently from his grip. "I know them. This is exactly the opening they wanted. They're going to take Taylor away and I can't let that happen."

"Who is? What are you talking about?" Sebastian was completely lost.

"You wouldn't understand." Murana was already grabbing the coat that had fallen to the floor, slipping her arms through it. "I know things that you couldn't even fathom."

He stared at her looking disheveled and a mess. "Let's at least get you cleaned up. You still got barf all over your pants."

"No need." She brushed him aside.

"What about your ankle bracelet? They'll track you down wherever you go." Sebastian was getting more upset by the second.

"I know ways of removing it. It's a non-issue," she said impassively.

"I'm sorry, Mom…" Taylor hiccupped, clinging hard to Murana's coat.

She bent over to kiss Taylor on the forehead, smoothing back her red hair. "Nothing to be sorry about, dear. We'll figure this out together." She rose up and turned back to grabbing a jacket for Taylor as well. "I can't involve you, Sebastian. You're too good a person. You have a good life going. I don't want that ruined on my account. Please, just forget that you knew me."

This got him angry now. "No! You know why I can't do that!" He indicated Taylor. "You signed the contract and you made it open. I have just as much right to see Taylor as you!"

"Like that'll matter at all when they come to carry her away." Murana looked at him with sadness.

"Then I'll stop them from taking her!" He beat his chest with a paw.

"No, you won't. Live your life, Sebastian." She quickly thrusted her paw towards his jugular, hitting key pressure points all along his neck. In a flash, he collapsed to the floor twitching, unable to move or speak. "Consider this my blessing to you in this madness. You are innocent of all this."

"Mom! What did you do to him?!" Taylor shrieked. Ahya was poking herself out to see what was going on and why Taylor was upset.

Murana patted her on the head. "It's fine, baby. He's not dead, just incapacitated. He'll be able to move in a few hours." She scanned the living den one last time, noticing the camera still filming everything. She frowned. "Taylor, we have a long way to go tonight. Go into the kitchen and grab any sandwiches you see that Sebastian made. That'll be our dinner."

Taylor sniffled, still unsure about what was going on. Her mind still probably reeling from eating her first person. "Okay, Mom..." She shuffled crying into the kitchen. She didn't want to leave her home.

Satisfied that Taylor was being a good girl and obeying, Murana made a beeline for the camera and grabbed it. She was going to take it with her. She now had a plan and a new purpose. This video would be the first step. She quickly turned it off and pocketed it into her messy sweatpants.

"Did you see that? There he is again!" Taylor slapped Nina's wing arm with the back of her paw.

"What? Where?" Nina looked over by the tree planter in the middle of the brick-tiled resting area outside the church, just two sets of rock stairs below them.

The cloaked figure in black was gone. Taylor had just seen him moments before perched halfway behind its trunk, like he was spying on them. The devilish grin of that bleached wolf skull adorning his face, hiding his true identity, bore holes into Taylor's mind. She scanned around the other planted trees that beautified a mostly mammal-made structure leading up to the church entrance.

"He was right there!" She pointed again. "Behind that tree! He was wearing black robes, and a skull mask with antlers coming out of his hood!"

Nina looked baffled. "I don't see anyone, Taylor. Are you sure you saw what you saw?"

Taylor looked again and sniffed. There was a different scent in the air that was unique from all the others in the local area. A scent that wasn't there five minutes ago. "I know what I saw and what I smell now."

Nina shook her head. "I'm sorry, Taylor. I've no idea what you're talking about. You sound like Ramon when he's far off his rocker on drugs. I know you're not taking anything right now, but maybe you worked yourself too hard last night and you're seeing things now?"

Taylor fumed and rolled her eyes. "Har, har. Will you lay off that? I'm being serious! Why would I lie about this?"

It was frustrating that Nina didn't believe her. That was the second time she saw that robed figure this morning. The first was right as they exited the apartment building. They'd stepped out on the street, and across the road from them in broad daylight was that thing, staring straight at her. There was no movement. Just staring. She turned to ask Nina if she knew what was going on with the stranger, but when she turned back, he was gone. And now here he was again at the church. Taylor began to feel that pit of terror in her stomach return, like it did years ago when she was being chased.

"I don't think you'd be lying. I think you're just tired. It has been an exhausting few days." Nina sighed and looked up the final set of steps to the double oak doors into the chapel.

It was situated on a hill between two taller skyscrapers in the richer part of downtown, where several sets of crisscrossing stairs of rocks with resting side areas leading up to the modest, yet impressive structure. Above the entrance were multiple stained-glass windows indented into the meticulously stone-crafted structure. The centerpiece window depicted a roll of parchment with words on it, descending from the heavens. Taylor thought it a ridiculous notion about where the Script came from.

"Fine. Whatever." Taylor didn't like the fact she might be seeing hallucinations. Maybe she was going crazy. It was just as bad as her hearing that other voice in her mind recently. She still hadn't figured that one out.

"Come on, we're already late. They've started the service." Nina tugged on Taylor's arm.

Taylor let Nina lead her into the church. The stork usher clapped to attention as he pressed one of the large wooden doors inward with a wing. He bowed low in reverence as they passed by.

Inside, the foyer opened up into a wide atrium a few meters ahead where hundreds of pews were lined up in four rows, two on each side of the main thoroughfare. Many of the land-based mammals were seating in their pews, none looking back at the entrance since the sermon was already underway.

Looking up above them, Taylor could see racks of hanging bars in much the same orientation as the pews below. Hundreds of fowl and flying folk balanced themselves on these precarious fixtures, each one rapt on the priest at the front. There were statues adorning the stained-glass alcoves on either side, each one representing a former High Council member in some form of holy, angelic pose. Each one holding a book that was intended to be a Script of their own.

Taylor just grimaced at the fake opulence of the place. There was no reason for all of this; it was just a roll of parchment with words on it. Words that ultimately meant nothing since people could damn well choose what to do for themselves. Yet people fawned over it like it was some gift sent from the gods. What had the gods ever done for anyone? She may not have been in school long enough to have learned much about that part of world history, but she certainly didn't recall learning about any of the gods intervening in their affairs for centuries.

The heron up at the pulpit droned on as they shuffled and excused themselves between peoples' legs and hindpaws as they made their way to one of the far ends of the back row of pews. Several of the churchgoers were giving Nina some odd looks, probably wondering why she just wasn't flying up above to be with the rest of her brethren. Not many gave Taylor much notice since for all intents and purposes, she just looked like some edgy punk teenager that they wanted no part of.

Finally securing a seat together at the very edge, Taylor wrapped Ahya across her legs and petted her. She could tell Ahya seemed tense in this place and was doing her very best to be good. She had held remarkable restraint the entire morning, not revealing herself at all.

She made sure she had three bowls of cereal to combat her hunger pains so that there would be no accidents in the dense population of the church. Last thing she needed was Ahya snarfing up an innocent Script-believer. If that wouldn't brand her as a heretic in the eyes of the congregation, nothing would. She chuckled at the thought. A female badger in front of her turned around to glare at her impertinence for laughing during the reading.

Taylor couldn't focus much. Nina was just tapping away on her phone, texting someone. Taylor tried to be attentive. The priest had received a second Script. "By Mereliah's blessing, we have been honored to read today's Script for a..." He paused momentarily as he was handed by a deacon in sage robes a Script roll. He unfurled the sturdy parchment by the slightly glowing handles and read the name. "Javier Hawkins."

Both Nina and Taylor sat up at attention. Nina glanced over at Taylor and mouthed silently, "That's my dad."

Taylor was more alert now. She had to keep Ahya under control by pressing her down on her lap, as she was curious why Taylor was so agitated. Taylor began looking around above at the various roosts the birds were occupying. Nina indicated the one at the far right up near the front. She could see a pair of older swans dressed up in elegant clothes and jewelry. Her mother had white plumage like her daughter, but her father was jet-black.

Taylor may not have been much of a believer in the Script, having had it govern none of her life, but she at least understood its importance to others. She, still felt it was bogus, that people could still choose to not follow the Script and they'd be just fine, but it could serve as a nice guideline as an option on how to go about their day. Taylor never believed that people were slaves to it, or that they couldn't escape the fate written for them.

However, the fact it involved the father of her friend, she began to pay extreme attention to what was being recounted.

"As it is written for Hawkins: *Your sole cherished heir will return to you by force. Wrapped in the arms of a vile demon of red, they shall be pursued to the edges of your home. The abomination of the Script will be forthwith bound in chains to the city's loyal blue. Trials will be met as you shower your heir with the responsibilities that are due, for a greater boon is coming to the one that is faithful.*"

"I don't like this," Taylor hissed, leaning in to Nina. "We shouldn't have come here."

"No shit!" she snapped back. "I had thought things would be different."

The priest rolled up the Script before handing it back to the deacon. A small murmur flowed throughout the crowd. Another was handed to him and he proceeded to read that one as well. Taylor was no longer listening anymore. She knew exactly who the demon of red was. The sole heir must be Nina, since she knew of no other siblings for the Hawkins family. What worried her most was being bound in chains and being pursued. That was supposed to happen today?

Taylor's focus was now scanning the entire church's attendees. She began to notice quite a few more people who were in full police uniform, which was most definitely odd to come dressed to church in. She began to squirm in her seat. Did Nina's father call her here knowing what today's Script would be? Did they know Taylor would be here with Nina, and so deliver them into a trap? Her mind was racing with conspiracies.

They attempted to see if they could leave the service early, but already noticed all entrances being blocked by armed police officers. When the heck did they get there? They certainly weren't there when they first entered. They had no choice but to sit out the Script readings and hopefully exit out with the rest of the crowd when it came time to dismiss.

After just one additional reading, they were free to leave. Taylor and Nina immediately stood up with the congregation and began to flow along with them to the front doors. They kept their heads down, and Taylor kept Ahya close. It was a lot of jostling and pushing, but they were almost to the twin oak doors leading out when they heard a firm voice from above them accompanied by a flapping of wings.

"Nina!" Nina's dark-feathered father flew down within feet of their position. "There you are, darling! We have been so worried about you!" The officers nearby took the hint and began to subtly close in. They were being cornered.

"We almost didn't think you'd come!" The nurturing voice of her mother flapped down beside the husband, the pearls around her long neck clinking.

"I really shouldn't have." Nina began to edge back into Taylor, who put arms out to hold her wings gently. "Since when did you ever care about me? The moment I left, you all dropped contact with me and never once attended any of our concerts, even when I sent you invites!" She looked around as more cops closed in.

Javier spoke first, giving Taylor the stink eye. "Your mother and I never approved of the things your three brothers got into. They were to be our heirs to our estate, and one was to rise to my position as High Council member when I retired. With their deaths in jail for that stupid murder they were unjustly accused of, you became our sole heir."

"Dear, we worried for you day and night when it looked like you were going down the same path they were." Her mother waved around her wing as she talked. "When you ran off to be in that vile band, we were just hoping it was a phase. That you'd come to miss what you had with us."

"You flat out ignored me!" Nina raged, finally gaining the strength to stand up to them. "When I lost my brothers, what I needed was my parents! What did I get? Nobody! You were so focused on the deaths of your 'favored' children that you neglected the one who needed you the most!" Her father attempted to butt in, but she shut him down. "No, it's my turn to talk, *Dad!* You two were so intent on keeping up appearances and attending all the memorials and wakes and gatherings that lasted weeks, that you completely missed the fact that you profited off your children's deaths!"

"How dare you talk to your father that way!" Her mother's tone changed instantly.

"I can, and I will!" Nina puffed up her chest. "Don't think I didn't notice the slipped checks between feathers as gifts of sympathy for your loss, or the fundraising you did in their honor to help the communities and schools they were a part of, which you skimmed off the top from. I sat around waiting and hoping you'd finally get over whatever you called mourning and come comfort me. And what did you do? Go back to your jobs and daily routine! You left me alone!"

"Gulia— I mean, your mother and I figured it was best not to pressure you into moving on so soon." Javier exchanged a quick, worried glance at his wife. "We know you were close with your brothers, but each person mourns in their own way and in their own time. We were just giving you space."

"How? By never interacting with me at all?" Tears began to form at the edges of Nina's eyes. "You used to love me once. You used to play with me when I was younger. I remember it all. Then things changed. When my brothers got older and began getting into gangs and drugs, you stopped caring about me and focused on getting them back on track." She waggled her wings in mockery. "Woe be to our family and reputation if your boys get out of line and slander our good name! They were threatening your job position with their antics, and so they became your priority. Because they were to be the future of our family, clearly. Not me. I was just the last born."

Javier sighed. "I know we haven't been there for you in the past. We both realize that. This is why we both felt we should reach out to you now and bring you back home."

"Why now? Why ignore me all these years and suddenly take an interest now?" She wiped some the snot from her nose holes on her bill with a sleeve. Nina was beyond distraught. Taylor attempted to comfort more, but it seemed Nina didn't want to be touched.

Gulia put a cautionary wing on Javier's shoulder to ease him back as she spoke for him. "Singing about hating the Script and other heresy? We thought we had lost you forever with that horrid band, but when we heard you weren't with them anymore and no longer under that negative influence? We were overjoyed. Then we heard you were getting back in with bad company, so we felt now would be the best time to reach out to you. Now that you might have realized how hard it is to live on your own, you might remember more fondly the luxuries you had at home waiting for you. They can be yours again, darling. Just come home."

"As hard as it is, I have been living fine on my own, Mom." Nina was looking drained by just mere minutes of arguing with her parents. She went rigid. "Wait a minute… How did you know about me leaving the band? That was a long while back, and I never told you anything."

"I told them." A sniggering cackle emerged from behind two of the encircling officers. They stepped to the side to reveal Ramon, dressed unusually nice in a pair of slacks and buttoned-up shirt with tie. He looked abnormal in it, and it did not suit his multitude of piercings. "Told them just who their 'darling' daughter had been bunking it up with these past few days."

"You asshole!" Taylor spat. It took every ounce of her willpower to keep Ahya from revealing herself right there and blowing the entire situation straight to hell.

"Participating in occult rituals and practicing deviant sex with this wolf?" Javier shook her head, disappointment in his face. "I'll admit we were appalled when we first heard it from Ramon, but we knew we needed to bring you in now rather than later. Gods know where you'd end up next week! Probably dead in a ditch somewhere, violated and mutilated."

"Occult rituals? Deviant sex?" Nina sputtered.

Taylor knew they were both lies. "And you believe this hyena over your own daughter?" Taylor jabber a finger at Ramon, now stepping in-between Nina and her family, drawing tense looks from all the cops around. "If you recall, Ramon is still lead singer of that 'vile' band you hated your daughter being in. What gives him the authority of trust over your own daughter?"

"Yeah, Dad, Ramon is still with that 'horrid' band! Why believe him? Why not chastise him?" Nina was furious.

Javier was stern. "Ramon is not our flesh and blood. You are. What he chooses to do is between him and his family. We're talking about you. Don't change the subject." He flapped his wings at her.

"For your information," Gulia huffed, "Ramon's father is an influential banker in this city, and he is heir to a vast fortune. He is well-respected and sought after for his financial advice. There is no group, sect, assembly, or party that hasn't heard of him. Unlike our daughter here, Ramon has not once been in trouble with the law, despite his substandard taste in music and style."

If Ramon took offense to that statement, he didn't show it. He just winked. "I know better than to embarrass my family and screw up a good thing. That's why I felt compelled to tell her parents what was truly happening with their daughter. What was happening to her weighed heavy on my heart."

"You're so full of shit!" Nina moved to punch him. The cops all moved in to break them up as Ramon giggled away behind the biggest one. "I swear to gods, Ramon, when I get my wings on you, you're dead!"

"That's enough fuss now, Nina. It's time to come home and your friend to answer for her crimes of kitnapping you, among…other things." Javier clicked his bill and signaled the officers to take her and apprehend Taylor.

"You're all forgetting one important thing!" Taylor shouted, causing all to stop and stare at her. "Did not your Script say you would chase me to the bounds of your home? Might as well make it fucking come true!"

Taylor went to a knee before slamming her fist into the floor, sending electricity in a wide circular arc around her position while at the same time looping Ahya around Nina's waist to lift her off the ground as the tiles beneath them erupted into a million fractured pieces. The concussion of the blast threw every person around them off their feet and into the air several meters. They all landed in various positions of tangled or twisted limbs.

Ignoring their groans, Taylor set Nina down on the now decimated floor. "You all right?"

Nina was shook, but nodded quickly. "That hurt like hell, but I'll live. Feel sorry for these suckers." She looked around in satisfaction.

"They're onto us now. Let's run!" Taylor grabbed her by the wing and bolted towards the oak doors, plowing one open with a bang.

"Just like old times." Nina laughed hysterically.

"Yeah, as of two days ago." They were bounding down the staircases two to three steps at a time.

"That's what I meant!" Nina giggled when they reached the bottom. "Did you see the look on their faces when they went soaring into the air?"

"Yeah, real goofy." Taylor wasn't paying attention much, her focus more on the scene ahead of them.

Sirens were already audible up and down the street. It seemed in their time inside the church, they had cordoned off the entire road in three blocks in all directions. They meant business. Taylor looked around and stopped. She thought she saw that cloaked figure again standing beside a cop looking at her, but after a blink, he was gone.

"Where to now? They got all avenues blocked!" Taylor was beginning to panic.

Nina looked up. "To the skies."

"We have you surrounded. Let go of the swan and step away with your hands up." An officer with a megaphone stood on top of a police cruiser hood.

"That car there." Nina pointed at a taxi cab in one of the lower maglev freeways above their heads. It had two rail bars, one on each side, that they could grip onto.

"Got it!"

Taylor and Nina ran headlong toward the gaggle of officers ahead of them, but their goal was the last planted tree at the base of the hill leading up to the church. Taylor unleashed Ahya and vaulted her length upwards to the nearest branch, her maw's teeth clamping tight onto its thick girth. Leaping up on the trunk, using her tail as leverage, she assisted Nina onto the next branch higher.

In no time at all, they were already in the higher foliage and in prime position to jump to the hovering taxi cab. Flouting the cries to desist below, they both jumped onto the nearest rail bar, causing the entire vehicle to yaw hard to the right. Dozens of horns sounded around them as the taxi veered across several lanes of traffic. Many cars tried swerving around them while others tried going over and under the errant vehicle as best they could within the maglev field of their lane.

They scrambled up the slick siding to the roof, all while the occupants inside cursed loudly. They both didn't care; they were already ducked low, on the lookout for the next vehicle to hop to. Two helicopters zoomed in feet above their heads. They curved around, doing their best to avoid the flow of traffic as they angled themselves towards Taylor and Nina.

"You know you can just fly. I can take care of myself." Taylor readied Ahya to grasp the next oncoming car.

"I know, but I'm not leaving you!" This brought a smile to Taylor's face as they shared a quick look of appreciation.

Ahya stretched up to grab the next car. Taylor wasn't ready for it as she was dragged by her tail down off the taxi, her weight forcing the smaller vehicle to descend. "Nina? Help!"

"You're going to drop out of the maglev field and fall like a rock!" Nina flapped her wings and dove down to grab Taylor's paws with her hind talons. "Crap, you're heavy!" She struggled to maintain aloft, her wings beating the air hard.

"Be glad I'm freaking thin, then!" Taylor shouted back.

When she was finally pulled up high enough to get her footing onto the side of the moving car, she swapped Ahya to the top and slammed her teeth into the metal roofing as an anchor. She walked up the side and dropped Nina down alongside her. They were already heaving with the exertion.

"This car is going to fall." Nina pointed at the maglev units on either side. They were sinking down below the level of them.

"That train there." Taylor pointed at a moving multi-cabin transporter traveling along the bolted rails across the side of multiple buildings. "We can leap down to that."

"Only if I slow our fall. That would hurt, otherwise!" Nina looked worried.

Committing to the action, she jerked Ahya up out of the roofing, eliciting a cry inside, before bounding over to the train. Nina did her best to soften their landing onto the swift-moving cabin, though its sleek, orange surface still bounced them horribly as they hit hard. Nina squawked as both of them tumbled and rolled down the length of it. Taylor screamed as she grasped one last handhold, her broken fingers still not healing. She used Ahya to grab Nina by the leg before she soared off the edge.

This is freaking crazy. Why were they having to do this? With every ounce of strength she had, she pulled Ahya close to where Nina could lay down beside her, gripping the maintenance ladder rungs on the top of the train. It was slowing down and going to be making a stop at a tall building with an exterior elevator of some sort. Taylor pointed at it in hopes she could get Nina on board with the plan. Nina just stayed there, shivering with her head down and her cheek pressed against the cold metal.

"Come on, don't bail on me now." She reached over to rub Nina's back to soothe frayed nerves. "Let's go."

The carrier stopped. Everyone inside was shuffling out quickly, none wanting to be below them long. Taylor used her lightning to shatter the glass panel just beneath them. Dragging Nina in with her, they landed on the floor deftly. They ran into the tram station, Taylor disregarding the slivers of glass puncturing her pawpads. The station was small, but it was visible from the outside, with all its walls just reinforced glass with metal beams giving it structure. The helicopters outside were still keeping tabs on their every move.

"Up the elevator!" She jostled and pushed people aside, Nina flailing behind. "Move! Out of the way!" Taylor yelled.

Everyone vacated the cabin for them. Taylor pushed the button for the top floor and tapped her foot anxiously as the doors laboriously closed. She stared down the twin helicopters, filled with a squad of cops each as they rose floor by floor. She saw one of them open up their side compartment door and an odd object rotate out of it. It was black and cylindrical.

"That's a minigun…" Nina quailed.

"Are you kidding me?" Taylor put a paw to Nina's back and slammed both of them onto their stomachs. More glass exploded and sprinkled above them like deadly rain.

Nina cried out as a wayward bullet splattered blood across Taylor's cheek as it sliced through the swan's shoulder. Taylor cursed before putting Ahya's tongue through the wound, wriggling it into the bullethole and pulsating. Nina stared with horror as liquid began to ooze, and then gush out of her body where the tongue was penetrating. At length, Ahya removed herself and it had cauterized. It was already starting to heal, but it would be a while yet before it fully closed up.

"What... What did you do?" Nina was in shock, staring at Taylor.

"Saving our asses." Taylor gritted her teeth. "Ah, screw this!"

Taylor rose up onto her thighs and took aim at the helicopter firing on them. She let loose another bolt of lightning. It tore through the entire thing, causing red mist to spray out the sides and back. It began to wobble and tilt, its front pointing downward. She had killed the pilot. Her momentary joy at her victory turned to dismay as the helicopter was making a sinking beeline straight for their elevator.

"We got to jump! Let's go!" Taylor yanked Nina back onto her feet and dove out of the broken glass walls of the elevator right as the helicopter crashed into the building where they once were, sending rippling shockwaves across the shiny exterior. Windows shattered.

They hit the first car hard, but they managed to stay steady on top of it. It dipped slightly, but was sturdy enough to maintain their weight within the tracks. Taylor got a bit woozy looking down. They had at least five layers of traffic between them and the ground. It would not be a pleasant stop after that fall.

They began hopping from car to car across the lanes. Nina cried out behind her. "Do you know where you're going?"

Taylor briefly glanced around. "Not a clue. That building over there looks nice!"

More bullets whistled over their head. Taylor ducked and launched another salvo of electricity. It clipped the rotary wings above, causing the entire engine to whine as the pilot struggled to maintain control. She had misjudged the force of the blast. It pushed Taylor and Nina off opposite edges of the small truck they were on. They both began freefalling down the levels of traffic.

"I got you, Taylor!" Nina swooped under the truck and plunged towards Taylor.

Taylor reached out with Ahya, having somersaulted upside down, narrowly missing an oncoming car. Nina almost had her hind talons on Ahya when another car rushed past her, slamming against her wing and causing her to falter. She twirled away as Taylor called out for her, another near miss by the third row of traffic. She had two more to go before the sudden stop. She had lost sight of the helicopter, but heard another resounding explosion somewhere off to her left. Another near miss and then impact. She smashed through the roof of another taxicab, her fall halted by a loud screech and a soft pillow.

It must have been seconds for the daze to clear. The taxi she was in was still driving erratically, horn honking and pitching hard left and right. She moaned miserably. Her entire back and tailbone ached as she stared up at the wolf-sized hole in the canopy. Senses still muddled from the fall, she looked around and noticed she had landed on top of what looked to be a very dead rabbit. The roofing panel she ripped through had squished the poor thing.

It wasn't until she heard a frightened mewl that she looked over at the passenger seat. In the farthest corner of the seating away from her was another rabbit, his legs and arms splayed against the frame of the taxi in an attempt to keep away from her and steady himself against the crazy driving she had caused. His tawny complexion and freckled face almost reminded her of…

"Jake?" She squinted, rubbing her eyes, doing her best to get up to a sitting position.

The rabbit shook his head. No, it wasn't him. He didn't have Jake's heterochromatic eye colors; this rabbit's were just a simple blue for both.

The taxi finally slowed down enough to have pulled into an alley, enough maglev units to provide this necessary pitstop for uncanny situations such as these. The anteater swirled around in his driver's seat and began berating Taylor in a language she couldn't understand.

She grimaced as she attempted to get off the poor rabbit beneath her, hearing more squishing sounds with every movement. "I'm so sorry about this. I didn't mean to…" She pointed upwards. "I was just…" She dropped her paw and gave up. "Never mind. It's a crazy story anyway. Just tell the driver to drop me off at the nearest alley that isn't this one please. As far away from the city center as possible."

The rabbit nervously did what he was told; it seemed like he could understand multiple languages. He was finely dressed with a proper suit and overcoat, his tie a deep magenta hue. Definitely a businessman sort of rabbit. Did they have those in this city? She clumsily moved over to sit beside him, being mindful of the space between. He was probably scared out of his wits after what he just witnessed.

"I'm truly sorry." She gestured to the dead rabbit. "I know I can't really make it up to you, just know it was never meant to happen." She sat in silence as the taxi pulled out back into traffic, the driver grumbling nonsense.

"I've seen you," the rabbit finally spoke. "On TV."

She shuddered inwardly. "Yeah… I'm Taylor, by the way. Just a wolf, not a monster." She spot-checked Ahya to make sure she was being hidden.

"I'm Stepan," he replied back nervously.

14.

TRAJECTORY

"Well, that was a disaster!" Terrati looked on as they saw Taylor smash into the roof of the taxi cab.

Ari had gotten wind earlier of some police radio chatter being broadcasted into her cybernetic eye. There was a hunt for Taylor, and they had a lead on where she would be this morning. The five of them went topside and pinpointed her exact location, but were unfortunately too late. The police had blocked off the entire downtown section of Zabökar surrounding the church she was in.

They arrived on the scene just in time for the fireworks to start. Ari had relayed to them the entire event as she zoomed in with her eye on Taylor, tracking her every movement. It all culminated in the clash with the second helicopter, it spiraling out of control before colliding with the church on the hill. The cops dragged their avian charges down its slopes before the explosion demolished the front entrance to the structure.

"Can you tell who owns that cab and where it's going?" Natalia was still keeping an eye on the swerving taxi.

Ari zeroed in on the license plate and ran it through the internet database. "Yeah, it belongs to Harutan Technologies."

Mikhail keyed into that name. "The same contracting company the High Council uses. I wasn't aware they made cars, let alone a cab service."

"You'd be surprised about a lot of things the High Council dips their paws into." Ari was already moving along the perimeter of the cordoned section of the city. Her real eye navigated the mass of irate drivers in their gridlocked cars, police standing guard looking dumbly

306

up at the sky, while her cybernetic one fidgeted around like it was having a seizure.

Trevor was casually strolling up alongside Ari, keeping remarkable pace with her as he licked the plastic spoon on his morning egg noodles, tossing the box in a nearby trashcan as they reached the sidewalk. "So I assume you're tracking them. Can you see where they are going?"

"How can you be so relaxed about this?" Natalia indicated the food he had spent time ordering while they were rushing to intercept Taylor before the cops could. "Her life is at stake and you don't seem to care!"

Trevor looked at her coolly and belched. "Look, I'm helping you guys out because I made a promise to a rabbit to get them together." Even Mikhail gave him a look. "Hey, it was his idea, not mine. He's got his reasons. Point being, I'm basically done with trying to go after Taylor or save Taylor. I'm doing it for this rabbit, because hey, why not? It amuses me. Besides, we got Ari here who has that super wifi eye of hers to track Taylor down, right?"

"What was the rabbit wanting to do?" Mikhail was immediately suspicious.

"Well, he wasn't interested in pounding her brains out if that's what you mean." Trevor whooped hard at this, drawing an irate stare and flattened ears from Natalia. "I swear, you two treat her like a little sister or daughter of yours. She's not your family; she's her own person and can make her own decisions!"

"Apparently not that very well," Terrati muttered, waving a hoof at all the madness around them on Taylor's account.

"Ari?" Natalia noticed the reptile had stopped. Both Ari's eyes were tracking something—her real eye was going far slower than her mechanical one—both moving the same direction. By the time Natalia was able to follow her flow of direction, they were all staring off down the congested street at nothing but gridlocked vehicles. "What were you looking at?"

"Did none of you see him?" Ari turned to each of them. They all shook their heads. "That person in the black cloak with a wolf skull over his face? Nobody? He literally walked right past us."

307

"Where is he now?" Terrati was looking nervous, his head darting to and fro.

Ari looked back again. "Gone now," she grumbled. "Whatever, the taxi is heading towards the Outer Hedges on the west side of town."

"Well, let me know where they stop." Trevor pulled out his phone and was tapping through it.

"What's it matter to you? What are you planning?" Mikhail was already up on Trevor's backside, breathing down his neck.

Trevor shivered and jerked away. "Could you lay off your parental instincts for one gods damn minute, you crazy cat?! I know it's hard to break away from those tendencies, but you need to let me do my thing."

"What thing? You already said you weren't in it for Taylor," Mikhail continued to grill, but maintained his distance now. "If I had known you had other reasons for coming back, I wouldn't have let you come with us to begin with."

"I said I'd help you with Taylor, but only to find her for this rabbit." He continued to scroll through his phone. "There he is! Jake's his name. He wants closure from Taylor for the friend she ate on live TV. Surely you've all seen it?" He looked up smirking.

"Trevor!" Natalia looked stunned. "And you want them to meet? After what Taylor did? How do you think that's going to end?"

"I don't. That's the fun part. I'm curious to see how a rabbit and a person like Taylor would do meeting up after something like that. Maybe they already have and worked it out?" He gave Mikhail a smug look. "Or banged it out..."

"Now I know you're certifiably insane." Mikhail glowered and looked off, disgusted, focusing instead on Ari ahead of them leading the way. "Is Taylor's life some sick joke to you? She isn't some person you can just cast aside."

"Uh-huh, and Gregor was?" Trevor grew serious. "My best friend was killed on account of your little otter buddy claiming your mission was far more important than my friend. We had already won. All you five needed to have done was just step down and walk away. Live to fight another day, as they say. But no, that little shit shot Gregor

308

in the head, and I was left to pick up the pieces on the way home and wonder why he was worth the sacrifice for someone like her."

"Well, she has healing powers the likes no one has—" Natalia began to explain.

Trevor cut her off with a snarl. "I don't want to hear it! So yeah, I'm just in it for the curiosity now over what'll happen next. I got my money. I could go retire somewhere, but what good is it with nobody to retire with? Might as well stick around and enjoy the show. Oh, don't worry, I'm not going to harm Taylor or snatch her away. It really isn't even in my interest anymore."

"I can't speak for Finnley, but I know I was no longer going to stop you when we last saw you out there near Howlgrav," Natalia tried to console.

"Yeah, Finnley." Trevor sniffed around. "Where is that little bastard anyway?"

"Not with us." Mikhail gruffly answered. "Like you, him and Fey didn't want anything to do with Taylor. So they left to do their own thing. Only us three decided to go after Taylor to prevent her from falling into the High Council's paws."

"Well, technically, I'm only here because I got wrapped up in the insanity of Ari chasing after Taylor," Terrati reminded them all.

"If you've all completely aired out your so-called grievances against each other, we got a bigger issue that we— Freaking hell! What is that?!" Ari immediate dove to the ground, her red iris fixated on the sky above.

All four of them sunk to the ground and looked skyward along with Ari, but were confused as they gazed about. All they could hear was the rustling of the leaves on the planted trees, and the feel of the wind brushing across their faces. Even the hovering cars above seemed to wobble a bit if one looked close enough. It was momentary, but it passed.

"What did you see?" Natalia's tail was twitching fast, her ears flipping back and forth to capture every curious noise.

Ari looked frightened. Trevor knew Ari. He had never seen her this terrified before. She was still rooted to the ground while the rest of them had recovered from whatever imaginary thing she was talking about. "Ari? You okay?" Trevor leaned forward. He had to admit, this reaction from her was unnerving him a bit.

Mikhail seemed to have picked up on the unusual nature of Ari's behavior. He knelt down beside her, putting a paw on her scaly shoulder, shaking it a bit. "Ari. What's going on? What happened?"

"No... Nobody saw that?"

"Another invisible cloaked figure?" Terrati offered.

She shook her head violently, her breathing still tense and rapid. "I can't even describe it. It was...horrifying. A twisted form of something I can barely imagine. Did none of you feel a heaviness in your heart like all your happiness was gone?"

Mikhail frowned. "I did feel a bit of that just now, but it was fleeting. I didn't see anything like you did however."

"Did either of you feel something?" Trevor asked Terrati and Natalia. They shook their heads no. "So just you and Mikhail. Interesting." He snapped his fingers, back to his normal self. "Anyway, Ari, can you get any sort of feed into that taxi cab? Maybe some camera or audio link we can snoop in on?"

Ari nodded her head tentatively, still reeling from whatever she had just witnessed. "If they're not too far outside my reception range, I can try to get a look."

She sat down in the middle of the sidewalk, drawing curious glances from the foot traffic around them. She closed her good eye and let the other reach out to the waves in the air. It was only a few seconds, but her brow consternated, as if she was straining against something.

"I have a live feed view from the camera in the cab. It's facing back to the passengers. There's two rabbits and Taylor. She's just... She's just removed a rabbit from Ahya's mouth. It looks disoriented."

Natalia shared a look with Mikhail. "Do you think she revived another person from near-death?"

"It's possible," Mikhail mused. "She did hit that taxi hard, and possibly crushed anyone underneath her."

"Can you identify the rabbits in the car with her at least? Is one Jake?" Trevor asked excitedly.

"Yes… No…" Ari was struggling. "Crap! They're out of range." She grit her teeth. "I only was able to get the bare minimum information on one rabbit, but I can research more on him now."

"Well, who's the one rabbit?" Trevor pushed.

"Stepan Longare." She paused a moment as if she was scanning something. "Fascinating. He's actually the leader of an underground resistance movement involving the rabbits. I'm pulling up recorded videos of his rally speeches. He's promoting civil unrest and violence to the people in this city who have oppressed them."

"And she happened to land in his cab?" Terrati was aghast.

Mikhail seemed thoughtful. "How the Script turns. This is indeed an interesting development."

"And he's just casually riding a taxi like that? Why haven't they been arrested yet after all those rallies?" Natalia looked concerned.

"I didn't say these videos were on public channels," Ari said. "More like in places where you got to dig a bit deeper to find."

"That's great!" Trevor sent off a text. "I just let Jake know who she's with and most likely what area of town they're going to be in."

"You what?!" Natalia shouted. "Not only is Taylor with one of the most dangerous rabbits in Zabökar, you want to send Jake to meet her and let Stepan know she killed a rabbit? How is that going to help her case at all?"

"It would cause enough commotion to get the High Council's attention, wouldn't it? You can thank me now." Trevor grinned. He patted Ari's knobbed shell as she was getting up, much to her chagrin. "And you were wanting Taylor to get an audience with them to begin with, right?"

"Yes, but with me there!" Ari shook his paw off. "The last thing we need is Taylor to fall into the High Council's paws alone!"

"Not really my concern, as I've said." Trevor shrugged. "I'm just following a little white rabbit. So with that, I think I'm going to break off here. You can continue your chase after Taylor. I'll just keep in touch with Jake here and enjoy a nice dinner tonight." He shook his cell phone at them tauntingly.

"Mind if I go with you?"

Both Natalia and Mikhail swerved to look at Terrati in surprise. "You're leaving?"

Terrati looked embarrassed. "Yeah. I told you that I wasn't sure if I was wanting to go on some crusade after Taylor. I was only following you guys until I figured out what I was going to do. And I've figured out that I don't want anything to do with Taylor either. All this talk of reviving more dead people and horrifying things we can't see… It's too much for me. We're already disavowed and no longer welcome here by the High Council. It's best I got out of dodge too."

Trevor clapped him on the back. "My comrade! Come! You're more than welcome to be with me and get sloshed tonight! My treat!" Terrati looked uncomfortable.

"So you going with him?" Mikhail asked, his face unreadable.

"Well, technically no, but definitely away from here." Terrati responded sheepishly.

Natalia moved in to hug Terrati. "I understand. This isn't your fight. Not your mission. Don't be a stranger, and when this is all over, I'd love to see you again. You have our numbers."

"Likewise." He melted into the embrace.

Mikhail shook a paw with Terrati after Natalia parted. "It's been an honor."

"Taylor is getting further away, and it won't be much longer that the police will pick up on her scent again," Ari warned.

"Right, we best be off then." Terrati waved as he continued to give lingering glances back at his friends.

Trevor wrapped an arm around his shoulders and leaned in all conspiratorial-like. "Don't worry about them. They'll be fine. What matters most is that we're away from all that when it finally goes down, and it will. Mark my words."

"What will you do when it does?"

"Raise a toast to Gregor."

"Extraordinary!" Stepan appeared dumbfounded.

He was nibbling and doting on his now-very-much-alive wife, whom he had pointed out to Taylor as being dead just minutes before. Taylor felt such a surge of emotion and regret that she had basically killed this poor rabbit's spouse that she begged him understanding for what she was to do next. Lacking resistance from the frightened rabbit, she took his wife's body into Ahya's mouth and let Ahya do the work of flushing her saliva through the rabbit's entire being.

Taylor just slumped exhausted. It was quicker this time around, as the injuries weren't as grave as Fey's. There wasn't as much to patch up. The wife came out safe and sound, albeit very messy and sputtering incoherently as Ahya assisted her out of her mouth with her tongue. Stepan was in amazement at seeing his wife living and breathing again. He kept looking back and forth between the grisly maw of Ahya and Taylor's tired face smiling at the two of them.

"Who are you?" he finally asked, after having inspected his wife thoroughly.

Taylor felt weak after having performed yet another miraculous recovery. Between her labors of using all that lightning against the helicopters and then following it up with bringing someone back from the dead, she was thoroughly spent. She was glad she was with some harmless rabbits and not some other people she could mention. If anything, because of their status in this city, she felt safe around them. She already felt safe around Jake in the limited time she was with him, if she was being truthful with herself, him exposing himself be damned.

She waved a paw in the air to let him know she heard him, taking the time to gather her thoughts. "I told you already. My name is Taylor Renee. I'm not a monster, just a wolf who is more weird than most. Yeah, I know I got a mouth in my tail. Yeah, it just healed your wife. Yeah, I'm being chased by cops, High Council, and gods know who else right now because of what I am. Does that answer it for you?"

He nodded hurriedly. "This is certainly quite the meeting. Why did you bother helping me? Helping us? We're just rabbits." He squeezed his wife tight and helped her sit beside him. She seemed tired too, laying her head against his chest, ears flopped over his shoulder.

"Because you're like me." She grinned faintly. This brought an odd look from both rabbits. "You're looked down on and ignored. Chased only when people want you for something, and never given a normal life free to live on your own."

"You're certainly an intriguing wolf." Stepan looked ahead. The cab driver was doing his best to weave in and out of traffic to bring them to Taylor's requested destination in the Outer Hedges.

"So people keep telling me." She sighed. "All I've ever wanted to be was normal. For the longest time growing up, I felt I was." She brought Ahya up into her lap, her devilish maw smiling. "Then she usually makes things more difficult."

"What is she?" It was a logical question.

"She's my tail. I was born with her. Beyond that, I'm not entire sure."

The cab driver said something unintelligible at them. Stepan's wife arose from her stupor. "We're almost there? Where are we going? Are we not heading back to the Marsh House?"

"No, dear, we need to drop off this nice wolf who saved you." His eyes were only for her as he caressed her face. Taylor's heart melted at the affection shown, that she wished she could get right now.

Her ears perked up at remembrance. "Wait. Did you say...the Marsh House?"

Stepan looked over. "Yes. I did. Is something wrong?"

"No! Actually, that's great!" Taylor rose up in her seat, feeling a bit more invigorated now. "My brother lives there. I actually want you to drop me off there instead!"

"For saving my wife? Anything." He yelled up to the driver new directions.

The driver was beginning his long tirade of cursing when the entire cab shuddered out of the sky. Stepan's wife was screaming bloody murder as the driver wrangled with the uncooperative wheel. They fell through one layer of mag tracks, clipping a car, causing that one to careen into another above them as they continued to plummet. The driver engaged the manual hover thrusters, bringing them out of the freefall. He had reversed polarity and was now being drawn towards the nearest lane of hovering magnets.

"What the heck was that?" Taylor was already on the floor of the cab on her knees, looking out the window to see what hit them. Ahya was alongside her, pretending to do the same.

Nothing was outside. All she saw were streams of vehicles navigating along their paths in the air through the inner-city skyscrapers, multitudes descending and ascending to new lanes before pushing forward to their eventual destinations. She looked up and saw nothing but the towering buildings glinting in the morning sun, the dangling chains of light from the central High Council towers flittering in and out of view as they were blocked partially by structures around them.

Stepan leaned forward and shouted for the driver to keep going. "The Marsh House isn't far from here. We stopped heading in the opposite direction just in time!"

Taylor eased herself back into her side of the cab, being mindful of the rabbits and the space she felt they needed. She was a predator after all, and even though she'd saved one of them, old ingrained habits were hard to kick. "So why are you going to the Marsh House? Do you two live there?"

"As a matter of fact, we do. So it's no trouble at all to take you there with us." His cheeks bunched up in a cute way as it seemed his entire face smiled when he closed his eyes.

Taylor looked up at the hole in the roof. "What about that? I can neither pay for my fare nor for the damage I've caused."

Stepan dismissed her concerns with a paw. "Pish posh! I'll cover it all. After what you did for my Eleanor, I'd give you all my riches if I could."

"Pay for it all?" Taylor was doubting with the size of that hole. "That's a lot of riches. Where'd you even get all that?" She winced the moment she realized the question she uttered and the look on their faces. "Oh, are you two sponsored?"

Eleanor shook her head while Stepan spoke. "No, otherwise why would we live where we do? We've had to resort to other, more degrading work to make ends meet. Profitable work, yet very soul-draining."

Taylor's ears wilted. "I'm sorry. I feel it's just horrible how everyone treats you guys. This one rabbit, Jake, he assumed I wanted something from him and embarrassed both of us when he realized I was just trying to help him out. I wasn't asking for anything in return."

Stepan didn't miss a beat. "You mean his services?"

She regarded him, wondering if he was as squeamish as she was to talk about this, but he seemed very straight-faced. "Yeah, but I relieved him of that immediately. I was just helping him out from another prick who I didn't want to see him with. He had a bad smell about him."

"That's very admirable of you. Not many I say that about." He thought about something a moment, looking out the taxi window. "What did you say his name was again?"

"Jake Thumpings." Taylor was hopeful. "What? Do you know who he is?"

He looked back and shook his head. "No, but we rabbits tend to stick together, so if I query around, I'm sure some of us may have heard of him. What were you wanting with him?"

"I just wanted to apologize for the misunderstanding last night. I did leave abruptly after it." She glanced away awkwardly, suddenly recalling what she forgot: she'd promised to meet him at Nina's apartment this morning.

"No need to be ashamed, honey," Eleanor finally spoke up, tenderly reaching out to put a reassuring paw on Taylor's leg. "We're not strangers to the needs of other mammals. This is just a normal day for us rabbits. You can talk freely about such things with us. We understand."

Taylor had never encountered such sexually adjusted people as these rabbits. Growing up with not much recourse to learn or explore such topics and recreation, Taylor had a skewed vision on what was normal. She knew enough by the relationship her mother had with her dad—and later with Uncle Sebastian—that sex was a positive thing between two people that loved each other. But with rabbits? With how everyone treated them? It seemed very wrong, and discussing it with them so casually seemed like it would be offensive, especially in her position.

"Growing up, I never knew anything about rabbits. I knew you all existed, but I never reached the grade where I was supposedly going to learn about what you do for us—for society, I guess. If I had, this entire conversation might have gone different, but I don't know. When I was first told about what your purpose was and what opportunities you all had in life, I was shocked. I felt disgusted. This waiter named Francis, I was humiliated on his behalf that I had unknowingly asked him for his services."

"No one blames you for that." Eleanor patted. "It's what is expected. We take it in stride and then go about our day. The fact you thought so much about Francis's feelings is warming to my heart."

"Agreed." Stepan nodded. "Tell you what, are you going to stay at the Marsh House for any length of time once we get there?"

"Well, since I don't know where my friend Nina is, and most likely she's either caught or being watched right now, my brother is the best and safest place for me."

"I won't presume to know all the trouble you've got yourself into, Taylor, but for what you did for me and my family, I'd hide you myself." He chuckled, causing Taylor to finally share his mirth. "To think, I assumed I was going to die by your paws a few minutes ago, and here I am pledging my life to keep you hidden from the police."

Taylor's face dropped again. "Yeah, you saw Ahya eat that rabbit. Please believe me when I tell you that it was an accident."

He gestured to her tail. "That begs the question, why were you able to bring back Eleanor, but not that other rabbit?"

Taylor put a hand on Ahya, the maw slipping open just enough to let her tongue out to lick Taylor's paw softly. "It's very hard to describe. I have to really concentrate and tell her what I want her to do, but I found out I had this ability to heal wounds with her several years ago. Then I discovered I could bring someone back from the dead not even a month ago."

"That's unbelievable."

"I didn't think she could do it the first time. It takes a lot out of me. The rabbit she ate, she was hungry. Well, I was hungry. She goes off my needs, I've noticed. I didn't mean for it to happen. I lost focus for just a second and it was over."

317

"I think I understand." He was eyeing Ahya with a fearful interest. "You talk like she's her own person, that she can think for herself."

She returned his stare. "How would you describe it then? The way she acts?"

"Good point." His attention was distracted by the slowly descending ride down to the surface. "We're actually here. You go on out first and I'll settle the tab with the driver. Don't feel bad about any of this. I can personally say I feel elated to have met a wolf as unique as you!"

"Thanks." She didn't feel that special.

After some gruff interactions with the driver and a fat wad of cash mysteriously disappearing into the anteater's hands, Stepan waved off the taxi as it rose into the air and mingled back in with the traffic. He motioned for Taylor to walk alongside him and Eleanor. It must have looked quite the sight, a wolf accompanying two rabbits.

They had just entered the front lobby of the Marsh House when he turned and looked up at her. "Do you know the way to your brother's suite, or did you need an escort?"

Taylor waved him off with a smile. "No, I can manage on my own. And suite? I didn't know they had those in this building. Could have fooled me given the living conditions Max is in on the basement level."

Stepan clucked his tongue against his two buck teeth. "Suite, apartment... It's all relative to our station, Taylor. What a suite is to us is a hovel to the birds that live above."

"No kidding." She chuckled. "Thank you very much, Stepan."

The rabbit was about to turn away before waggling a finger in the air. "I just thought of something. I do these...group meetings, you could say. Seeing as you sympathize with our plight, I think they would be of great interest to you. Perhaps you could join us one evening? We have a rally going on tonight." He pulled out a small business card from inside his coat pocket and handed it to her. It was small, meant for bunny paws, but she was able to still read it. "If you're up for it, it would be an honor to have you come join us. Regardless, I shall be singing your praises there whether you come or not!"

318

"You really don't have to."

"Don't mind him, dear." Eleanor stepped in. "When my husband gets passionate about something, he won't stop at anything until he sees it through. For what you did for us—well, for me especially—I am eternally grateful."

It took several more minutes and much bowing from both rabbits before Taylor was able to disentangle herself from their friendly clutches. Despite the odd nature with which they met, connected, and then parted, Taylor was feeling very good about herself. She did a good deed today, despite all the crap that had happened. To top it off, she felt more passionately than ever about helping rabbits in Zabökar get the justice and treatment they deserved. If Nina could have her secret help group to go to, Taylor could have hers.

Bouncing off her high of helping those two rabbits—despite it being initially her fault—she was excited to see Max again. The morning didn't start off extremely well, and she had absolutely no idea what she'd do or where she could go to sleep tonight, but she was determined to make the rest of the day better.

She rapped on Max's door lightly. There was no response. She couldn't even detect any movement on the other side of the door. Her ears were rapt, listening for it. She pounded a little harder. Still nothing. Hopefully he wasn't gone. Then again, she wasn't sure what his work hours were or where he even went to for a job. She began slapping her fist on the wood, causing the hinges to rattle.

This brought the attention of an ornery zebra with baseball bat brandished down the hall berating her for her rudeness. "Sorry!" she called out, watching as the zebra shook their head and shut their door roughly.

At last she could hear Max shuffling past boxes and his footfalls getting closer. He opened the door, looking up at her with sleep-filled eyes. "Taylor… You do know that it is just past noon, right? What do you need at this hour?"

"Crap!" Taylor was suddenly reminded that Max was nocturnal. Ever since he left when she was just eight, she no longer had to adhere to his schedule just to find time to play with him, so the thought never

319

crossed her mind here that he'd be sleeping at this hour. "Look, can you let me in, bro? I'm in need of a place to stay."

Max yawned before stepping aside and allowing her in. "Of course. What trouble did you get into this time?"

Taylor scoffed. "You really think that badly of me that I'm automatically in some trouble?"

He shut the door and stared at Ahya numbly. "Well, aren't you? You aren't exactly the most inconspicuous person in the world."

"Not including Ahya in that one, are you?"

"You get her into trouble, she gets you into trouble." He shrugged. "It's all the same."

"You always did know how to cheer me up," she snarked, taking a seat on the floor since there was a distinct lack of chairs beyond the lazy one Max claimed for himself.

Flopping into his appointed, cushy spot, Max kicked up his feet over the armrest and stared out over some boxes nearby Taylor's head. "I heard some remote sirens off in the distance. Am I to guess that was you?"

Taylor sighed and nodded. "Unfortunately, but we were set up. Nina and I were meeting her parents who asked her to come to the church uptown. We were then surrounded by cops and we had to escape."

"And it caused all that ruckus outside?"

"We couldn't take the ground route; they had all that blocked off. We took to the cars above and might have destroyed a few. I'm not entirely sure. It all went by pretty fast."

Max chuckled, muttering to himself. "Mother could probably have broken through the line without getting detected."

"What about Mom?"

"Nothing." He waved a paw. "Carry on, sis."

Taylor gave him a dubious look. "Hmmm… Well I hitched a taxi ride with some rabbits who live here, but now I don't know where Nina is, and I think going back to her place might be a bad idea since it may be watched. Ramon sold us out."

Max scrunched his short muzzle. "I never did like that guy."

"I don't think anyone does."

"So what will you do now?" Max looked around his cramped apartment. It didn't seem like he bothered to open up and unpack a single box since last time. "I don't think I can host you for more than a couple nights. Do you know where you're going?"

"That's it? No brotherly love and assistance to help me get away from Zabökar so your darling sister doesn't die, get captured, or worse?" She said it playfully, but deep down, she was a bit worried about his response.

"Not that I don't love you, Taylor, but you're not actually my priority these days." He flopped down off the lazy chair and moved into the kitchen. He hopped up onto a stepping stool and began pouring some grinds into a coffee maker. "If you hadn't noticed, I'm a bit down on my luck. The club scene isn't exactly working out, and now I need to find a new way of living if I'm going to keep this place longer than a month." He finished pouring the water and pushed the "on" button to start the brew.

"You could always come with me, Max. Just you and me."

He turned around on the stool to gaze over the kitchen counter. "And what about Steven? I'm sure he matters to you as much I as do." It was a probing question, Taylor knew. He was probably curious as to her feelings on her older brother.

"He seems well established here, and doesn't seem to want to leave." She paused. "That, and I don't think he's still gotten over this issue with Mom and me."

He hopped back down and walked up to her. "I think you've not gotten over it. Steven isn't the one to hold grudges long when he knows a sincere apology is made. I know my brother that much." He went to pat her leg, but thought better of it and moved back to the chair, climbing up the side. "You have a hard time letting go of things, Taylor. You tend to take all the guilt for what you've done upon yourself, and let it fester. You did it all the time when we were younger. Eventually you'll need to face yourself in the mirror and accept the things you've done and move on. Otherwise you'll just be wallowing in your own misery."

"Do you ever look at yourself in the mirror?"

Max looked disgusted. "Ugh, no, of course not. I hate looking at myself. You know that!"

Taylor rolled her eyes. "Thanks for your brutal honesty. I knew I came here for a reason."

"A service only I can provide, I know." He squirmed a bit to be more comfortable. "So let's say Steven doesn't come with us, what then? Didn't you say there are some things out there that are headed this way that can burn Zabökar to the ground? Shouldn't we get our brother out too? I wouldn't think you'd be that heartless to let him die."

"I wasn't meaning to leave him to die. I just don't know how to convince him."

Max pondered for a minute. "How sure are you of these…monsters beyond our borders? Is it a sure thing they'll come here?"

Taylor turned inward. "I saw two of them wipe out entire cities already. I know there are more out there than just two by what Ari and her father are telling me. From what I've seen, I don't have any cause to doubt them on this point."

"Can they be destroyed?"

She shook her head. "Not that I could see. We didn't really have anything that could pierce their hides. They're just too big."

"I believe you." He tented his fingers, and sat like that as the coffee finished brewing. It was starting to get awkward when he finally spoke again. "I'll see if I can convince Steven to join us."

Taylor's heart fluttered in her chest. "You'll come with me?" She couldn't believe it. She would adore it if her remaining family could join her on the road.

"Yes, but need I remind you that I hate change." He got back off the chair to go pour himself a cup. "I'll probably be cranky the entire way."

"That's a price I'm willing to pay." She laughed. He graciously poured two cups and offered one to her, which she gratefully took. She relished the feeling of warmth between her paws as she blew on it. "Do we know anything about where Uncle Seb Seb is?" she asked hopefully.

He shook his head. "Headed out of town shortly after Mom died." He didn't seem willing to say more on the matter. "I recall you had other problems out there as well." He poured an insane amount of creamer into his cup. "This Ari person and her father, that Arbiter guy. I'm imagining some big, secret conglomerate organization with unlimited resources are after you. Got any plans about them?"

"They're not exactly that, but they do have a lot of people working for him." Her ears flicked back as she heard several sets of paws enter the primary building, sounding as if they had come in running. "I think that part of my visit here to Zabökar is about to rear its ugly head, Max." She put her cup down.

He paused, looked her directly in the eyes, then flitted them over to the door. He caught the sounds too; they were making their way down the hallway. "I'm going to need at least one sip in me first before this goes down." He practically gulped half the mug before setting it on the counter with a loud clink.

Taylor stepped in front of him, Ahya at the ready and maw open. "It's okay, bro. I got this. You don't need to fight."

"I don't need my little sis protecting me." He stepped alongside her.

"Wouldn't that be big sis?" She looked down at him with a smirk.

"Never. Not on my watch." His eyes stared straight ahead.

There was a loud hissing at the doorknob. They could see it turn bright red in between the door and the frame, getting superheated and beginning to melt. Then a loud crash and it was kicked open, banging against a stack of boxes behind it, causing one to tilt and fall to the floor. Ari led the charge with Mikhail and Natalia close behind. Taylor was going to blast Ari in the face with a bolt of electricity until she saw the other two. Her paw faltered and lowered.

"You've had enough playtime, Taylor!" Ari snapped, her fingertips glowing white hot. "You will be coming back with me and doing what my father ordered!"

"Mikhail? Natalia?" Her mouth dropped, ignoring Ari's threat. "What are you doing with her?"

The tiger gave Ari a glance, reaching out a paw to hold her back. She seemed raring to go and subdue every single person in that apartment. "A joint venture is the best way I can describe it."

Natalia stepped forward. "The only reason we are here is to ensure you are safe. Both Mikhail and I agreed that we would look after you. With no job to speak of and enough money in our accounts to at least get by for a while, we wanted to make sure nobody exploited you for what you are."

"That's very thoughtful and all, but I feel like it's just exchanging one method of control for another." Taylor was very suspicious. She already knew Ari's loyalties. She didn't quite know Mikhail and Natalia's yet. They were the nicest of the bunch from the mercenaries working for the High Council, but she had no valid reason to trust them completely.

"We're not going to be asking anything of you or asking you to go anywhere," Mikhail tried to assuage her. "We just want to be nearby because we find that we care for you, as surprising as that sounds."

"That's very generous of you." Max pointed back the way they came. "But unless we're still going to fight, can one of you close my door? You're letting in a draft."

Ari snarled. "You deliberately defied me and embarrassed me in front of my father. You made him use Rakkis to check on me to see if I was doing a good job! I left you alone for a while, figuring you needed to get whatever sentimental crap out of your system, and then I would come collect you when you were done." She gestured out the window to the street. "Then you get yourself in harm's way and then bring more attention to yourself? This is where I draw the line. You need to be brought back underground and focus on what we set out to do."

"And what exactly is that?" The sizzling crackle of energy was still dancing across her fingertips.

"You know damn well what! To get the High Council's funding and cooperation in either defending or evacuating this city before those behemoths come."

"Given my run-in with one of the council members this morning, I highly doubt that plan is going to work anymore." Taylor laughed maniacally, like it was the funniest thing in the world. "It's all a big joke. They won't listen to me, or you or your father. At this point we'd be lucky we just get our friends and loved ones out."

"So you don't care anymore about precious lives lost?" There was scorn in Ari's voice. "What about that tirade you made at Howlgrav? What about Palaveve?"

"Says the person willing to let Howlgrav burn! Ha! Of course I care!" The arcing intensity of her energy was humming louder. Both Mikhail and Natalia were edging away from Ari and attempting to flank Taylor, but she just moved her paw in their direction to indicate they should stop. Ahya kept her "gaze" on Ari. "But with a city this big? With people in power who don't care about it? With the behemoths this close just over those mountains? What hope do we have to do anything worthwhile? There's nothing we can do on the grand scale of what your father is asking. It's stupid!"

"That's not for us to decide! You're coming with me, now." Ari slapped her tail on the ground.

That was her cue she was on the attack. Taylor dove to the side and released her bolt at the reptile. Ari shoved up a column of flooring to block the blast, sending the rapidly cooling shard of cement and carpet off in all directions. Max was up on top of the boxes in a flash, leaping from one to the next until he was upon Ari. A blade appeared in his hand as he coiled around her neck, its edge digging into her throat.

She attempted to glare angrily at him. "I could roast you right now, little bug."

"Perhaps." He breathed next to her ear hole. "But I'm confident I have pretty good reflexes to drive this straight through your jugular and let you bleed out. You wouldn't be good to anyone dead."

"You're bluffing."

Max shook his head slowly. "Just ask my sister. I don't bluff." Ari looked over for confirmation. Taylor just nodded vigorously, Ahya keeping Mikhail and Natalia at bay. Max continued his warning, "Picked up quite a lot of skills moonlighting with my mother. She taught me a lot. I'm dying for someone like you to test me. If not, then let's rewind this conversation and start over, shall we?"

Taylor's jaw hung.

15.

MOURNING

The video flickered on, the view covered by Murana's blocking paw. She was setting up the camera to be in a pristine position to capture her fully before she backed up to sit on the haphazard bed in the center of the small, metal room. The entire place was a mess with clothes strewn about decrepit pieces of furniture and bed sheets half off the mattress. There were even several dozen half-empty to crumb-ridden paper plates scattered across the floor.

Murana rubbed her eyes a few times, willing her tears to go away, but they would not acquiesce. Sniffling and resigning herself to a miserable recording, she looked directly into the camera. "Taylor? Baby? Please come home."

She broke down again as her voice cracked on the last word. The entire day had been an unequivocal disaster. Smearing some snot on her shirt as she attempted to recompose herself for another try, she looked up again. "Taylor, I know we've not had the best three years. I know I've not always been there for you, but everything I have done was to protect you. To protect us. You may not understand that now, but hopefully in time, now that you're on your own, you will."

The words spilling from her mouth now gave her the strength to carry on with more determination. "I knew the moment you had eaten Sarah that our lives were changed…forever. There are forces at work now that are beyond my control. They are seeking to find you and claim you for their own. Sebastian wouldn't believe me, and I've lost all my friends and livelihood trying to track down information to support my theory that I know to be true. That unfortunately left you in the horrible position of being left alone, stuck in whatever temporary hovel or shack I could find, praying nobody stumbled across you. I'm sorry I left you alone for so long and so often."

327

Murana took a deep, ragged breath. "I know it must have been hard on you, Taylor. You were frustrated you couldn't go out anymore, that you couldn't go back to see your friends or go to school. I tried to get you to understand why I was afraid for your future, about why people are interested in you because of Ahya. You were so strong for so long. I was proud of you, but I never truly realized how much I was harming you with my over-protectiveness until…you ran away."

The tears threatened to return, but Murana shook her head vehemently. "I tried to reach out to you several times, but now I realize it is futile. You don't want to hear from me, your old overbearing dictator of a mother. You want to experience your own life and make your own mistakes and live freely. I get that. The problem is they are still out there, the ones seeking you for their own gain. You may not believe me, but I pray they do not find you.

"To that end, I've made the resolution to watch you from afar, and to employ others as best I can to watch over you in my stead." She paused a few moments, contemplating a harrowing thought. "I am dying, Taylor. I cannot take care of myself much longer, let alone keep you safe."

Shedding another tear, Murana coughed hard, ignoring the blood dripping from her mouth as she did so. She leaned over to pull a stack of folders and paper into view, then regarded them. "In the meantime, I will continue to do my best to pull every last connection and resource I have to research these vile people and expose them for who they are. I just hope that you will remain safe until I have completed my mission."

She set the evidence down on the bed beside her. "Once I have the information I need and broadcast it to the public, hopefully our names can be absolved and we can walk freely without fear of being arrested, captured, or worse. I don't know how much longer I have left to live with this cancer, but I hope to see you again one last time before it all ends."

The crying began anew at this. "Mommy misses you so much. You were the star of my life. I hope one day you will see this and come to forgive me for what we both had to endure."

A loud banging shook the entire room, rattling the metal façade in which they had lived in. A familiar voice called from outside, "Murana? Are you in there? Unlock this door please."

Murana wiped her face one last time. "Sebastian is here. I called him finally to come pick me up. He has agreed to take care of me in secret since I can't anymore. Be safe out there, Taylor. Wherever you are…"

She wobbled a few moments trying to stand up before leaning forward to turn the camera back off.

Taylor could hear the pitter patter of rain as it began to flow down in earnest just outside the bathroom as she finished up cleaning her bloody paws. She had tried to go to the bathroom, but with her stomach all tied up in knots and feeling queasy, she instead let her mind wander to Eleanor and how she saved her life. She certainly had broken bones from the impact of her squashing, yet Ahya healed them fully. Could they have been healed because there were openings for Ahya's saliva to seep into?

With that thought in her mind, she found some small scissors in the medicine cabinet mirror and with a hand towel in her mouth to dull her whines, she made a deep slice into the skin of the broken fingers. Shivering from the pain she inflicted upon herself, she had Ahya flow her healing salve into the lacerations and let it encase her finger bones.

Within moments, she could feel it working as she could bend those bones better and the cut skin was beginning to heal. She marveled at her new revelation. Ahya could mend broken bones or internal injuries. Like Fey before Eleanor, the saliva just needed to get inside to where it could do the most good.

Seeing as she was going to get nowhere in the bathroom with her upset stomach, she stepped out into the living den where Mikhail and Natalia had helped Max move a few box stacks to the sides of the room to better accommodate them all in the center. Max was pacing back and forth between the three of them as he absorbed all they were telling him.

Max was quite the effective mediator, and his no-nonsense way of speaking got everyone on board with the idea that they needed to work together to accomplish all the goals they each had. He glanced up briefly to see Taylor and indicated his lazy chair, that she could have it. Taylor smiled at him and took her now-warm mug of coffee over to the chair and slowly sank into it, much to the irritation of Ari. She certainly did not seem happy about this turn of events, but she was being nice on account of Taylor promising to be extremely difficult to manage if Ari wasn't.

"So let me get this straight." Max pointed at Mikhail and Natalia while still staring at his carpet. "You two literally have nothing else to do right now but to protect Taylor from harm?"

"We've been disavowed from our jobs with the High Council." Mikhail's shoulders drooped. "It's highly unlikely we'll find any job in Zabökar or surrounding areas that'll hire us right now. So until such time we get a sufficient distance away, we wanted to spend our current energies and investment into at least keeping Taylor safe."

"Besides." Natalia beamed at the relaxing wolf, sipping her coffee. "Everyone keeps accusing us of this, but I personally would be lying if I didn't see a bit of my little sister in Taylor." This brought a flushed smile to Taylor's muzzle. "So of course, lacking any family currently alive outside of my friend and colleague, Mikhail, Taylor is the closest thing I got."

"Welcome to the family then," Max said without inflection, turning around to Ari without bothering to observe the response his words had on Natalia. "Those two aren't a threat, but you..." He tapped his chin in thought, still staring at the ground. "You're the violent one."

"Excuse me?"

"Point proven." Max continued to pace once more. "Your entire objective is to get Taylor before the High Council so they listen to your father's plan to either defend or evacuate the city. Well, clearly defense is not an option, since I've yet to notice anything regarding them fortifying this place. Either they don't know, or they don't care, as

Taylor has stated. Yet if you don't accomplish this, you'll be a failure in your father's eyes. Do I have that right?"

Ari stared directly at Taylor lounging with her coffee. "And you remember what happens to failures in my family?"

"You get a nice, shiny new upgrade?" Taylor smirked at her own humor. Ari was seething. "Sorry," Taylor mumbled into her drink, quickly looking away.

"Why am I bound in these cuffs? You know I could escape very easily, kill you all, and just take Taylor." She was calm, but her words carried deadly intent.

"It's the principle of the matter," Max stated matter-of-factly, stopping once more in front of her. "I never really expected them to hold you at all. They're merely there as a reminder that you're not the one in charge here. Technically, no one here is except I'd wager Taylor, since you all so desperately need her for one reason or another."

"Ha!" Mikhail busted up laughing, causing Natalia to regard him as loopy. "He used the same tactic Ari used on us! Brilliant!" He shook his head, wiping the tears from his eyes. "Oh, that was a good one, Max."

"What is he talking about?" Max was directly staring at Mikhail.

Taylor shrugged knowingly, taking another drink. "I've no idea. Go on, brother."

"So to me, it's clear we need to satisfy Taylor's wants of getting her family and loved ones out of Zabökar before those behemoth things come, since we agreed it's a bit pointless to stop them now," Max concluded.

"If everyone had just listened to my father years before, none of us would be in this mess to begin with, and Taylor may not have been so involved in the first place!" Ari fumed.

"Well nobody did, and here we are." Max was pitiless. "Since going to the High Council is a moot point now, I'd say the Arbiter's goal and Taylor's are basically the same: get people out of Zabökar. The difference is in the scale of it. As we are now, there is no way we can reach a broad range of people without exposing Taylor to the High Council. So unless that problem is solved, we are only limited to getting out those we care about."

"And who are those to you, Taylor?" Natalia leaned up on Mikhail's shoulder, looking tired.

Taylor held her mug in both paws as she thought about it. She barely noticed when Ahya was dipping her tongue into the cup to lap up some of the liquid for herself. "Both my brothers, of course. Maybe Loray and Bailey from the band if they're willing. Definitely Nina if we can find her again. I think that's about it."

"That's not a bad list." Mikhail nodded approvingly. "Seeing as the rest of our team has dispersed and got their own plans for leaving Zabökar, the most we can do is shoot them a text regarding the condensed timeline and what we plan to do. Hopefully they'll figure it out on their own, and we'll check in with them after."

"I agree," Natalia chimed in. "Spreading ourselves too thin to go beyond the bounds of what Taylor wants would increase our chances of failure."

"And Jake!" Taylor said suddenly. "I'd actually like Jake to come along. And Stepan, Eleanor and as many bunnies as we can get."

"Now you're just making things more difficult!" Natalia rebutted.

"Well, at least Jake then." She brought the mug back up to her mouth, talking into it now. "I owe him that much."

"My father is not going to be as understanding of this plan." Ari was calmer now. It seemed her mind was working, and she was no doubt planning three steps ahead like she usually did.

"Which leads me to my next point." Max plopped down, propping his cheek on his fist as he rested his elbow on a leg. "Since I know barely anything about this Arbiter, I don't know how we're going to convince him to change his mind." He turned to look at Ari's shelled chest, covered partially by the leather jacket she was wearing. "Do we even know why your father is so adamant about saving this entire city? What does he even gain from it? It seems like a fool's errand to affect something as big as Zabökar."

Ari looked away, her sight obstructed by a stack of boxes nearest her. "All I could ever get out of my father was that it was a promise made to my mother before I was born. He normally doesn't ever talk about the past, and I don't pressure him to. I've found that it's better this way."

Taylor frowned. For someone who was so intent on pleasing their dad, Ari was definitely not making any attempts to go beyond simple recognition. Taylor only had her mother and how she was raised under her as a frame of reference, so she had nothing to compare the type of upbringing Ari had under the Arbiter only, without her mother's influence too. Taylor was lucky to have two dads during her childhood, if Uncle Sebastian was to be counted.

"So, how'd you get to be so savvy, Max?" Mikhail leaned forward with interest. "That brief moment of you in action was quite impressive. I haven't seen such skill since I left my old special forces unit, TALOS."

Max gazed over and noticed Taylor's coffee, prompting him to get up to pour himself another. He didn't ask anyone else if they wanted any. It appeared he ignored the question entirely until he pointed at Taylor as he came back to the group. "Our mother was what you'd call a crime-fighter before she was a cop. I used to go out with her when I was younger, almost like a sidekick. We busted so much butt." He chuckled before realizing he forgot his creamer, frowning he went back to pour some.

Taylor eyed him as he walked past. "I never knew any of this. Where did she even get the training for that?"

Max brushed past with his newly minted beverage. "Like Ari here, I didn't really pry much into her past dealings. I just know she was a lot more brutal and malicious before I was adopted and joined her. I guess having a family changed her perspective on things. Regardless, she raised Steven and me alone before marrying our dad, Anthony, and having Taylor shortly after that. Somewhere along the way—before Taylor but after Anthony—she got caught and was forced to either work for the city using her unique talents, or be jailed for the rest of her life."

Natalia was engrossed. "I guess we can assume which of the two she chose."

"She chose to help. To protect me, she didn't say a word about my involvement in her crime-fighting and instead left me to pursue what one would call a normal kit's life. I never did help her again out in the field, but I never forgot what she taught me." He sighed deeply, remembering. "I honestly missed trying to make this city a better place. Now look where I'm at."

"You still have me and Steven!" Taylor tried to be cheerful about it.

"Not exactly comforting, but you did your best." He slurped some of his coffee.

A soft tapping at the door got everyone's attention. All eyes turned to Max. "Were you expecting someone?" Mikhail asked, rising up with a paw going down to his holster.

"I was not." Max seemed unconcerned, and continued to enjoy his drink.

Mikhail stayed Ari's hand with a paw as he moved towards the door. "Last thing we need is to wreck up more of Max's apartment. I should think a simple gun can handle this."

Seeing as Ari was going to be cooperative, he ripped open the door and pulled his gun on a very shocked rabbit. Taylor called out as she recognized those dual-colored eyes, doing her best to get up from the lazy chair that was seeking to suck her back in. Ahya perked up with interest upon hearing the rabbit's name.

"Jake!" she cried out, handing her coffee to Max so she could use both paws to get out. She had sunk too deep. "How did you find me?"

He waggled his cell phone visibly. "Got a text to reach out to Stepan, who said you'd be here. Gave me the address and everything. You missed our meeting this morning."

"Yeah... I'm sorry about that." She did her best to look innocent.

Jake scoped out the room and saw everyone present. "Did I come at a bad time, Taylor?"

Taylor tried to push Mikhail away from the entryway of the door, but he wasn't budging, causing her to glare up at him. "No, of course not. Did he, Mikhail?"

Mikhail's eyes darted down briefly to meet Taylor's before continuing to scrutinize the rabbit. "You going to harm Taylor for what she did to your friend?"

It looked like Jake got caught off guard by the question. "Actually, no. We already settled that account last night. I'm just here to relay a message from her mother and then I'll be on my way. I'd actually prefer..." He scanned around the group. "That it was a bit more private."

"Not a chance." Mikhail was unyielding.

"Would you give it a rest?" Taylor sparked Mikhail's arm, causing him to grunt in surprise, but at least it brought his gun down. "If Jake wanted to kill me over it, he would have last night when we were alone together." She caught both his and Natalia's eyes. "Don't start. I remember what happened back in Cheribaum. All went well, and hey... I'm old enough now, what's it matter to you?!"

"You're straying off topic." Max said, still staring straight ahead, relishing his coffee. "He's here to give Taylor a message."

"Can't it wait?" Natalia looked unsure. "I mean, we're still trying to figure out something important here."

"And this last message from my mother is important." Taylor put a paw on her hip as she squinted at Natalia. "Honestly, it's the last thing I'd like to do or hear before we proceed with whatever plan we go with. Besides, I did say Jake was one of the ones I'd like to bring with us, and here he is!"

"I'm sorry, what?" Jake looked confused. "Oh...okay, then." He was now flustered as Taylor reached out, grabbed him by the paw, and brought him in so they could shut the door. He was now standing uneasily in the middle of them all, getting stared at.

Taylor could sense his apprehension and probably what was on his mind. Remembering not to kneel down to talk to him, she simply put a reassuring paw on his shoulder. "Don't worry, Jake. There will be no services rendered today if I can help it." She turned her head to Max. "Is there a private room Jake and I can go talk?"

"Actually..." Jake sounded hesitant. "We need to walk somewhere. It's a requirement from your mother that I take you someplace first before delivering the message."

"Out of the question." Ari sat up straighter, her focus intense on Jake. "With what's going on right now and the amount of people

335

looking for Taylor, it is no longer safe for her to be wandering around Zabökar."

"I don't care. I want the last thing my mother left for me. If it's just a message, then I'll take it." Taylor was not going to back down.

"Maybe we could tag along, you know, at a distance, to make sure nothing happens to her?" Natalia offered.

"Sounds reasonable," Max agreed. "Unless someone recorded Taylor recently, they're probably still looking for a red-headed wolf. So she's disguised enough for a brief walk outside."

"Thanks, bro." She smiled as he just inclined his head slightly without looking at her.

Mikhail groused his displeasure. "Fine, but maybe we should ask Jake first if he wants to go with us before assuming he'll agree."

"That's fine. I'll fill him in along the way." Taylor was cheerful for once.

She had her brother at her back and a new friend in Jake. With them and two pseudo-trustworthy people proclaiming themselves her bodyguards, she at least had a small group with which to feel safe around. That was definitely a first. Even during the time of being chased from Palaveve to Cheribaum, she never could quite fully trust anyone.

Except maybe Mikhail's mom, Klera. She was nice.

"And what about me? Do I get a say in the matter?" Ari appeared sincere enough in the question, despite what her facial expression showed.

Max simply pointed at Taylor, not even turning around to look at her. "She's the boss right now. Since all our vested interest is to help her, then we should let her decide instead of by committee, unless that decision is stupid and we overrule."

"Just whose side are you on anyway, Max?" Taylor scowled.

"Yours, of course."

Taylor sighed, looking at the shaggy carpet. After a moment, she looked up at Ari. "You are welcome to come. After what we've been through, I can't say I trust you more than the rest of them. However, as long as you're going to be nice, don't destroy any more cities and agree to tag along for protection, then you can come."

"How gracious." Ari rolled her eyes. "Can I at least get these cuffs off?"

"Of course, I'll tend to that." Mikhail stepped forward. "Natalia, you go on ahead with Taylor and Jake. I've got a few matters to discuss with Ari first. It's about what Fey texted me." He and Natalia shared a knowing look.

"What about you, Max? You coming?" Taylor leaned over her brother. Ahya mimicked the movement beside her.

The raccoon finally got up and stretched. "I actually need to go see Steven if we want him to be with us. I think it would be easier coming from me than you. I've been with him longer, and I know what makes him tick. I'll make sure he listens to reason."

"Steven can be a bit stubborn, but thank you, Max." Regardless of how Max felt about it, she rushed in for a hug, picking her brother up and nuzzling his cheek with her own. Even Ahya looped around and pressed into his back as her way of showing affection.

His legs and arms were squirming. "Taylor! Taylor! You know I hate this."

"And I know I love you." She poked him on the nose with her own. "But fine, I just wanted to hold my brother a bit before we leave." She set him down lightly, causing him to shake out his tail and brush his clothes down.

"Touching, but would prefer you already be out of the apartment before I un-cuff Ari here," Mikhail reminded.

"Do you have an umbrella, Max?" Jake asked, showing his small one. "The one I brought with me is a bit inadequate for two."

Max considered the mass of boxes. "Somewhere in all that."

"You know what? Never mind." He handed the rabbit-sized umbrella to Taylor. "I may be just a rabbit, but I won't let anyone say I'm not a gentlemammal."

"I like him already." Natalia grinned.

Taylor began undoing the strap and fluffing the umbrella in preparation to open it once they got outside. "After you, Jake. I have no idea where we're going."

"Of course." He walked a bit ahead of her, but made sure he was keeping pace with her strides so it didn't look too odd. He looked up at her as they made their way down the hall, Natalia having shut Max's broken door behind them. "If anyone accosts me for services, I would like it if you say I'm currently servicing you all. I know you won't mean it this time, and there won't be another misunderstanding."

Taylor blushed and looked away. It's a good thing rabbits couldn't read thoughts; that comment made the naked image of him last night appear vividly in her mind. "That makes sense. I'd rather not be interrupted when you've been trying to give me this message for years."

His eyes rose in amazement. "You remember?"

"I do now. It came to me recently. The night of my kitnapping. You were there to hand me my necklace, and told me you had a message to give me."

Jake's ears dropped. "I was disheartened when I came back to find you gone. I noticed signs of a scuffle, but honestly didn't think anything of it. I remember looking back with those two ladies and seeing you go outside, so I didn't put two and two together until much later that you went back in and got kitnapped."

"It all happened pretty fast." Taylor's mind was going to dark places with the memories.

They stopped at the front doors, the rain ahead looking quite the downpour. He pointed up towards her neck. "What happened to that necklace?"

Taylor's eyes bulged as she patted down her breast a few times. Her face sagged at the realization. "It's still back at Nina's apartment! I forgot it."

Jake frowned. "As long as we can get it back, we should be fine. We'll worry about that later. Let's walk. What I want to show you isn't far."

They both turned back to see Natalia a few meters back. She gave them both a nod, ensuring she would be following at a distance. "Don't worry about me. A little weather isn't going to bother this cat." She winked, bundling up her dreadlocks in a tight bun.

They pushed through the doors and stepped out into the rain. Taylor propped open the umbrella and held it aloft. Jake wasn't kidding when he said it was meant for his size; it was just barely large enough to cover her head and shoulders, but not wide enough to prevent rain from pelting her from the waist down. At least her top half would be dry. She did her best to angle it over so he could get some of its protection, but he seemed content to bask in it, letting it drench his clothes.

"Several months without rain and the first day we get it, it's a lovely storm." He laughed. As if on cue, a flash and thunderclap was heard on the far reaches of the city.

Taylor observed the sky, the bright chains of light above the buildings being the main thing that stood out against the darkened sky. "Shouldn't we actually take cover if there is lightning?"

"Probably, but ever since Tony stopped me from doing something terrible and then meeting you afterwards? I've been feeling pretty free."

Taylor felt sad for Jake. He seemed so blasé about his personal crisis. "Terrible? Were you thinking of suicide?"

His bouncing ears faltered a bit as his pace slowed. "I was."

"Well, feeling free out in a thunderstorm just seems to be trading one form of suicide for another."

"Perhaps." He turned his face to the rain and closed his eyes. "But I can appreciate things a lot better now."

"So how did it happen?"

"I guess you could say I was at the end of my rope. I had been approached to be sponsored the morning of our encounter on the street. I'm ashamed to admit it, but I was the main attraction at a bachelorette party. Being tossed around from girl to girl multiple times until they couldn't walk anymore, I felt like my life had lost meaning and direction."

"Do you not have a good job?"

"Not the one I had been wanting all my life." He glanced sidelong at her, following the length of Ahya until it ended just above him. She was warding off some of the rain from his head. "Thanks for that, Ahya." They kept walking as he sighed. "My job as bouncer and bodyguard to your band was supposed to be a stepping stone. It was to be my big entry on my resume to getting a more noteworthy job, like being a police officer."

"And they denied you." Taylor's ears fell with Jake's mood.

"Worse than that. They put me in record storage and had me do paperwork for them. While everyone else was out here on the streets proving their worth, I was stuck behind a desk doing all the critical things to keep that department afloat, but never being recognized for it. And before you ask, appealing to a court of law about this injustice is a waste of time. Despite what it may say on the black and white letter of the law, many judges would refer instead to the higher law that governs us rabbits. That gives me little leeway to make my case."

"It's that law that's the problem." Taylor pouted. Jake looked up curiously. "Still, I'm sorry Ahya ate your friend, Tony. He sounds like a great rabbit, given that he saved you from doing something awful."

A smile peeked at the edges of his mouth. "He was. But if I'm being honest with myself, he wasn't exactly a 'best' friend of mine. I actually don't have anyone I could call that. He was just the only rabbit I talked to on a semi-frequent basis with. We rarely got together outside of the few times we had early morning chats over breakfast. Still, I was sad to see him die."

"And I'm sorry Ahya caused that. That sounds like a good friend to me. They don't have to visit you every day, or even every week to be a best friend. I wish I had someone like that."

Jake could probably see her downcast expression. He reached up gingerly and patted Ahya to get Taylor's attention. It worked, but not before Ahya patted him back on the head with her full bulk. "Oh geez, not so rough!"

"That wasn't me."

"I know, but still…" He stared up at the grinning maw. She was apparently having a field day with herself. Rubbing his head, he continued, "I guess when you put it that way, I guess he was a good friend. So, what about you? Nobody in that apartment your friend? What about Nina?"

"Nina and I just got back together again only a couple days ago. It's not exactly like old times, but it feels nice, you know?" The thunder was receding, but the rain hadn't lessened in intensity. She did her best to arrange the tiny umbrella over herself. "She's much friendlier than when we were still in *Bad Luck*, and she has her quirks. That, and her father is on the High Council. I'm not sure our friendship is going to last long because of him. She also kind of rubbed me the wrong way with how she talked about you."

"About using my services?" Jake shrugged. "I actually didn't really notice. It happens so often that you could almost tune it out. I had forgotten all about it when I went to bed that night. I was more interested in confronting you at the time than whatever she wanted." Taylor wasn't so sure. "And what about your brothers? I know you and Max were close on stage before Bailey replaced him."

Taylor's heart felt heavy at his question. "By the time I was of an age where I could play more with my two older brothers, they had both grown up and moved out. I was basically an only child from six onwards. They'd come visit from time to time, but I usually only had Ahya to play with. I only reconnected with Max during our music jam sessions. Outside of it we didn't interact too much, although he still remains my idol to this day for his talent."

"The three of you aren't close?"

"Yes and no. Up until yesterday when Steven yelled at me for leaving Mom, I had no idea anything was wrong between us. Hopefully that's patched up now, and Max is willing to help. I still love them both as brothers, because they were also kind and nice to me whenever they came to visit. Steven played with me the most, and I always enjoyed our time together."

Taylor's body shuddered with a sigh. "I came back primarily for my mom. I wanted to apologize to her for what I had done and hope she would accept me back. Realizing she's gone now, all I have left of my family is my two brothers. I don't even know if Uncle Sebastian is alive or even where he is."

"Speaking of which, we're here." Jake stopped suddenly, pointing across the street.

Ahya shook the droplets from her fur, causing Jake to sputter underneath her as they gazed across the road. Taylor hadn't realized how far they had walked, but it was definitely beyond a half dozen blocks. Entrenched between a cluster of buildings was one of the city's graveyards. One of the last hallowed grounds left untouched by the advancement of technology around it.

It was kept by the church, so it made sense why they wanted to keep it pristine. Nobody questioned the Script, and all people had their appointed place, even in death. The spike-topped metal rod fence surrounded the grassy enclosure on the edges not flanked by a towering construct of forward progress. There were nice, orderly rows of walkways, and leveled hills with varying tombstones reflecting class and the wealth behind each that seemed to stretch for several city blocks.

Taylor glanced back to see Mikhail and Ari catching up to Natalia. They were keeping their promise and maintained some distance. "So why did you bring me here?"

"When we get there, it'll all become clear." Jake didn't look exactly happy with what he was going to show her.

She followed him across the street, being mindful of the ground car traffic. They walked past a tall wolf with an odd snout in a dark grey trench-coat, a black beanie over his head being the only protection from the elements. Their eyes met briefly, but Taylor thought she saw recognition there. His gaze followed her all the way up the steps to the graveyard entrance.

Jake opened the small gate that reached up past his head. They flowed onto the gravel pathways and meandered up and down the sloped hills of the expansive graveyard. Taylor never realized how expansive Zabökar truly was until now. She had heard of the city having a couple dozen graveyards, but never expected each one to be like this. She honestly hadn't a need to go explore one until now.

"Do you know that wolf?" Jake asked quietly, having noticed the exchange.

She turned back briefly. "No, I don't think so, but I can't shake the feeling I've seen him somewhere before."

"Alright. We're almost there." Jake said.

Jake abruptly turned to two unassuming gravestones side by side. They were not much to look at, being almost featureless. On them she read:

Murana Delante Wolford
Jase 20, 2182

Alahon 19, 2229

Anthony Wolford
Alahon 22, 2192
Sempah 13, 2218

A smaller stone placard between the two of them read: *In life they hid their true selves from each other, but in death they are as one.*

Taylor was shaking all over. "Why would you show me this?" Ahya had dropped all pretense of sheltering Jake from the rain and just dropped away from him.

Flinching at the sudden rush of rain now peppering his head, Jake knelt down next to Taylor as she fell to her knees before her mother's tombstone. "I guess I should start at the beginning. I was already watching over you in the band when Murana called my phone specifically asking to come over for services. I felt it odd that she could find my private number, and even more so that she was aware of how close in vicinity I was to you. Over the course of our visits, she filled me in on all that had happened with you."

"So you know about Sarah." Taylor's paws were fists.

Jake nodded. "I know enough. It's why I faltered at being completely mad at you over Tony. Yes, it hurt. Yes, I felt you owed me some closure over that, but upon seeing you again and talking with you, I feel that you may need it more than I. Tony was a good guy, but he's just one of many in a sea of friendly acquaintances that never go past the professional stage. I've never been one to really make close relationships with others."

"Did you sleep with my mom?" She now looked at him, his face level with hers now. Tears were streaming down her face. "Did she use your services?"

Jake was immediately flustered. "Oh gods, no! She was like you. She relieved me of my services the moment I visited every time. She didn't want me in trouble with the law, so she made sure our arrangement was business only regarding you. She was very proper."

Taylor just nodded before turning back to her mother's grave. That eased her mind somewhat. She was happy that her mother also didn't treat rabbits like pleasurable fodder. She wouldn't know what to think if she had. "So what was her final message to me?"

"There's the problem. It involves that pine tree necklace I gave you years ago." He peered off to where they entered the graveyard, and she followed his gaze. The other three were hanging back, but within the confines of the fence. "She embedded a data chip inside of it so only you could find it, and tasked me to give it to you for safe keeping since she said keeping that information on her person was foolish. They could take it away and destroy the evidence she worked so hard for."

"Who is they? What evidence?" Taylor's mind was a jumble of thoughts. She couldn't even think straight. As calm as Jake was talking, this was all coming at her too fast.

"Murana wouldn't elaborate. However, she knew getting this information away from her was the safest thing for it, and better its chances of being leaked to the public where it could do the most good and the most damage. Unfortunately she didn't have a single person she could trust to hold onto this information until it was released, except you. While it would have been suspicious in her paws, it'd look like only a sentimental memento for you."

"And that's where you came in."

"Yes. Me. An innocent rabbit that no one cares about or gives a second thought to, hand-delivering supposed damning information about an organization that she said she had tried to protect you from for years." Jake exhaled, his shoulders untensing for the first time since the conversation had started.

"So that's why she did it…" Jake cocked his head over at her inquisitively. "All those years running from place to place, sleeping in old, rusty shipping containers, scrounging for scraps from trash cans or stealing food. It was all to protect me. To protect this information she was gathering on my behalf. All that time spent alone while she ran off to gods knew where. She was doing it all for me. And now… Now the damn necklace was left in a place most likely swarming with police!"

Taylor broke down weeping. Ahya seemed to be mourning as well, her slightly open mouth bobbing up and down on the slick grass covering her mother's grave. Everything seemed to make sense now.

All the questions burning in her mind about what had happened back then started to fade away as she put together the fragments of her past.

"So why show me her grave? You could have easily told me all this without bringing me here." She tried to wipe the tears off her face, but it didn't matter given how wet they both were, the umbrella on the ground beside her, forgotten.

"That was the one other thing she told me." Jake looked miserable he had to recount this. "Murana knew she would never see you again before she died from her cancer, but she wanted you to know that it was those that are after you, those that did this to her and gave her that cancer, they are the ones that put her in this ground. They were responsible for her death."

Taylor's vision began to tunnel as only the words on the tombstones stood out to her. Then it was the Arbiter who did this. He said her mom was an unfortunate bystander to his project. Does that mean he was responsible for her cancer? Was he responsible for the way Taylor was born? What exactly happened twenty years ago? Did Ari know? If not, what would she do if she found out? Would she still side with her father?

"Taylor?" A fearful note was in Jake's voice, but her mind couldn't quite pick up on it until he was forcibly shaking her out of her concentration. "Taylor! What is Ahya doing?!"

Her eyes snapped back to reality and she saw Ahya digging a deep gash into the dirt, clods of grass flinging into the air. "Ahya! Stop! That's Mom's grave!"

She began pulling back on Ahya by the base of the tail, but she was incredibly strong. She continued to bite and hurl more and more dirt, creating a hole already several meters deep. Her maw was covered in filth. Mikhail and the others already sensed something was up and were running over. The strange wolf beyond the fence was staring through intensely, his paws on the metal.

"Is she digging up that grave?" Natalia was appalled.

"Stop her, Taylor!" Mikhail roared. "This is a holy place protected by the temple and its Script-keepers."

"I'm trying!" Taylor sobbed, now clawing at her tail and trying to jerk it back. "I don't know what she's trying to do!"

"Do you think she intends to eat the body to heal her?" Ari suggested, looking intrigued.

"Not the time!" Mikhail shot her a death glare.

Ari just studied from a distance. "It's an honest question. I'm curious to see what she'll do."

"Well I'm not!" Mikhail reached forward and gripped Ahya hard with his claws just as she hit the coffin beneath. Ahya writhed and jerked backwards and up to shake off his grip, enlarging as she did so, and lunged forward. She enveloped Mikhail down to the waist and lifted him clear off the ground.

"Ahya! No! Don't eat him!" Taylor was a wreck.

Ahya spit him clear across several plots of tombstones, his body hitting one to where it tilted slightly from the impact. He lay still before it. Natalia rushed to his side. Ahya made an attempt to bite Jake as he squeaked a cry at the sudden violence, but he bounded out of the way just seconds before her jaws snapped shut. Ari jammed a thin, but potent pillar of super-heated dirt up into the underside of Ahya, knocking her maw back hard causing Taylor to fall back on her rump as her tail hit the grass with a thump.

"Can you control your tail?" Ari asked firmly. There didn't seem to be any malice in the question, but there was a hint of a threat behind the words.

"I... I..." Taylor began to crawl back on all fours, her butt dragging across the ground. "I don't know. The longer I stay, the more chances Ahya could go out of control like this. Maybe they were all right. I am just a monster and a menace. I'm nothing but a danger to you all. I'm a danger to everyone. I can't ever get any peace." Taylor looked over at Jake, his nose twitching as he stared at her with fear in his eyes. "I'm sorry, Jake. I'm a monster to you too."

"That's... That's not..." he began, fumbling with his words.

"Stop her." Natalia cried out as she looked up from inspecting Mikhail to see Taylor getting up and running.

"No! Leave me alone! I'm a dangerous freak!" She screamed and shot enough lightning directly into the ground between them to cause huge plumes of earth soaring dozens of feet into the air, extending outward from her position, uprooting walkway and tombstone.

346

Ari and Jake bobbed and weaved to avoid all the falling debris as thick slabs of stone pounded into the ground at dangerous ranges, sinking in to rest in their new homes. Taylor was already running to the opposite end of the graveyard towards the other exit, her balance shaken and her head woozy. That one exertion nearly spent everything she had, but it was enough to buy her time to get away from Ari, her biggest threat.

Slamming the metal gate open, she ran down the steps to street level and bolted down a random avenue sidewalk. Ahya appeared comatose, her entire maw being dragged along behind Taylor. She did her best to lift up her tail so it wouldn't hit or catch every bump on the sidewalk, but Ahya had grown to a large degree and her mouth was open, tongue out as it left a nasty, thick trail for others to easily follow.

Sensing the gawking eyes of pedestrians around her, Taylor realized she wasn't safe running around aimlessly with a dragging abomination behind her. She quickly picked up Ahya and held her to her chest as she continued running down the streets, pushing and jostling through those who didn't move out of her way fast enough. The bodies and faces of the people around her were a blur as her breathing thundered in her ears.

At long last, she felt she was far enough away that she dipped into a narrow alley, complete with ankle-deep puddles and refuse dumped from the condos above. She walked into the alley far enough to be beneath crisscrossing clotheslines, then slumped down against the metal brick siding and dropped Ahya to the cement. She bunched her knees to her chest and wrapped her arms around as she wept into her legs, hoping the rain would drown her.

Ahya began to rouse and was attempting to nudge Taylor's arm to get her attention. She pushed Ahya away. "What the hell is wrong with you?! Is that all we are?! Just some freak? Some monster? How can I have a normal life if you can't be controlled? You killed Sarah. You eat people without reason. You make me a danger to everyone, so that I'm always left alone. It's true then what they say, that I am a monster and I'm better behind bars where I cannot hurt anyone ever again."

347

Ahya attempted another show of affection, but Taylor shoved her this time. "No! Don't even try to apologize to me! You were digging up Mom's grave, and for what? She's dead! Dead... Dead! You hurt Mikhail and almost ate Jake! Are you nothing but a demon stuck to my tail? What are you? What do you want? To torment me? Is it funny to you that my life is so fucking miserable that you have to ruin every gods damn good thing to ever happen to me?! What is it? Answer me!"

Taylor began to slap and punch her tail. It hurt every time she did so, but she didn't care. Ahya did not fight back. It was trying to avoid her fists, but since she was unable to see or escape being Taylor's tail, it could only do so much. Taylor landed some hits, but most glanced off, though still stung as Ahya made futile attempts to escape.

"Now you're being all remorseful? Where's those teeth and that anger you showed, huh?" Taylor slapped her tail again. "Why don't you turn them on me and just fucking end it all?! End this miserable, sorry excuse for a life! You fucking tail! I hate you! I hate you!" She kept hitting, but her urgency was dying with each declaration of hate.

"Please stop, Taylor. You don't understand."

"What the hell?" Taylor backed up and slapped herself against the wall. "Who said that?" Nothing answered in return. Ahya rose up weakly and "looked" at her. The sound of rain filled the silence between them. "What's the use?" Taylor gave up and sunk down. "Now I'm going crazy too..."

She was ignoring Ahya and observing her bloody knuckles, incurred from hitting her tail, which now had a dull throb throughout its tip. Out of the corner of her eye, she saw the top of a white card peeking from her pants pocket. Sniffling, she took it out and stared numbly at it. It was Stepan's calling card. She snorted. How silly.

She was an outcast. She had no home. She had no friends. If she was going to be an enemy of the system, she might as well act like one. If these rabbits want to rebel against those that oppressed them, then maybe she should join them and help them succeed in any way she could. After all, what else good could she do with her life? She couldn't get her life straight to save it, so she might as well fix others in the most law-breaking way.

"Taylor?"

She nearly yelped at the sudden proximity of the voice. She had barely sensed him coming. "Who are you?" She looked up at the large wolf she had seen at the gates to the graveyard. "Do I know you?"

"I should hope so." His light brown eyes were filled with kindness as he got to a knee alongside her. His dark grey fur on his head was covered by the dark beanie. The weirdest thing about him was the small, interlocking black platelets that went from his nose, up his snout, and underneath the beanie. "I was the one who drove you out of Zabökar. Do you not remember me?"

Taylor shook her head. Ahya just laid on the ground, awash in her own misery. She didn't seem to care about this conversation at all. Taylor pointed at his muzzle. "You're…not a normal wolf, are you?"

He smiled. "You said the same thing last time." He held a large paw out to her. "Come on, let's get you out of the rain. I saw everything. If you wish, I can take you out of Zabökar once more."

"I don't understand." She felt like a lost, confused girl all over again. She had no idea why this wolf would make her feel this way.

"I'll explain when we've got some time."

She drew back. "No. Wait. Can you come with me here tonight?" She showed him Stepan's card. "This rabbit is hosting a rally tonight. I would like to go. I'm going to call him and ask if I can come."

His smile faded, his face unreadable. At length, he responded. "Yes, I know of Stepan. I'm aware he holds these rallies. If that is where you wish to go, Taylor, then I shall accompany you."

"Thank you." She took his paw, her own swallowed up in its size. "What's your name?"

"Liam." His smile returned before lifting her back onto her feet.

349

16.

STALLING

A younger Jake stopped in mid-undress. His nose twitched and his ears stood on end as the red light glowed on the camera Murana had set up to record them. Shyly maneuvering his bare ass away from the camera and pulling his pants back up, he gestured to it. "Um, what is that for, ma'am?"

Murana was reclining in a comfy lounge chair. Her limbs looked thin and frail, as if she had lost a hundred pounds dramatically. Sebastian was nowhere to be found, but her living circumstances had improved. She was now in a proper home, complete with some carpeted flooring and loving pictures of herself, Taylor, and Sebastian adorning the walls around them. She gazed over to the recorder perched on the tripod she had set up for this meeting, having turned it on via remote.

"That's to ensure I have physical evidence of the promise and the deal I'd like to make with you tonight," she said cryptically. "Why? Does having that on unnerve you? You ever been filmed before?"

Jake was wary and continued to buckle his belt, all thoughts of servicing this elderly wolf apparently gone from his mind. "I have…" He haltingly began. "Just not with a large predator before."

"Is there something wrong?" Murana asked.

He nodded slightly. "One of my friends died on camera for the sick pleasure of those predators who drafted him to be their partner for the night. I was unfortunate enough to see that snuff film when it was leaked online. So excuse me if I don't seem altogether eager to continue further, Mrs. Wolford."

"But if I asked, would you?" Murana's face was inscrutable, her intent unclear.

Jake's nostrils flared, his inborn fight-or-flight response kicking into high gear. "By the law, I must say yes, I would continue." She

351

could tell he was leaving more off, but she didn't want to press him further.

Murana casually waved a paw to assuage his fear. "Don't worry. I'm not going to eat you, or have you service my 'needs'."

"Then what did you call me here for?" Jake kept his distance now from the wolf. The uncertainty of this entire transaction was clearly unnerving him.

"I have a proposition for you that I will pay you for," she began.

Jake put a paw up and shook his head. "Ma'am, I already have a job, and any services required of a rabbit does not need to be paid for per the law. What we do to sexually please you is free of charge, as is our lot." He seemed very matter-of-fact, as if he had memorized the entire regulation of the law.

Murana chuckled a bit, wrapping her shawl around her gangly body to keep out the coolness of the room. "I understand that. It is just incentive for you to do what I ask."

"This is very irregular. I do not think the law requires me to be exploited to do underhanded deals under the pretense of doing what is required of me." Jake's demeanor was getting a bit flippant.

This refusal got Murana to scowl. "Who do you think they are going to believe? A wolf, or a rabbit who refused to do the services asked of him?" she lied.

She knew she had no power here, especially given the entire situation with Taylor and her current relationship with the law for having absconded with her. However, Jake was unaware of any of this, and probably had little clue as to who she really was. This worked more in her favor than in his. She hated threatening him like this, but she needed a trustworthy person on the inside that would do as she asked. Holding a rabbit hostage by the law, although contemptable, was one of her last options left.

Jake thumped his foot on the ground, his own glower matching hers. Folding his arms, trying to keep the irritated tapping of his foot in check, he spoke with an icy tone. "What is it you require of me?"

Unfazed by his defiant attitude, she carried on with her proposal like nothing was wrong. "I have been doing some digging, and I've come to find out you are quite the adept bodyguard at the local rave club, The Fox Den."

He shrugged, still maintaining his stance. "So? What of it? It's just a job."

Tightening her shawl further, she pressed. "I also know you tried out for the police academy, wanting to better yourself and apply for a job well beyond the station of a rabbit."

"Yeah?" His nose wiggled. "There is nothing in the law stating we can't go after any career we choose."

"But most don't," Murana pointed out, waggling a finger at him. "So why did you go beyond what most others wouldn't? Why try for the near-impossible for one of your species, and then fall back to something simpler like being bouncer at The Fox Den? It is clear you had aspirations for something greater."

Jake shifted uncomfortably, looking up at the wolf in the chair. "As I stated before, I lost a dear friend to this law you're using against me now. No justice was done for him. I wanted to be able to better defend myself should the same thing happen to me."

Murana clicked her fingers. "And that is why you are perfect for the job." At a look of confusion, she clarified for him, "You understand what it is like to be living in fear for what you are and what you can provide to others. You have a protective instinct for your own preservation—and I'd wager for those of your fellow kin when you tried for the academy."

He flicked an ear in impatience. "So what are you getting at?"

"Do you know of a young singer who recently joined the band, *Bad Luck?* They sometimes plays at the venue that you work at." Murana tried to not appear too eager to hear news of her daughter.

Jake looked at her curiously. "The one with the tail that has the mouth that everyone thinks is a fake? Yeah, I know of her. They're actually performing tonight, and I'm slated to work rear door duty."

Murana paused a moment, considering if she should reveal everything. "Well, she is my daughter." Realization crept into his face. "She and I did not leave on good terms, and I know she has no interest in me right now. However, in the future when I am ready, I would like to request that you deliver something to her on my behalf that I wish for

353

her to have, but until that time, could you just keep a close eye over her and make sure she is safe?"

His light thumping on the ground stopped as he considered this sincere proposal. "Well, it wouldn't require me to do anything above and beyond what I'm already doing at The Fox Den," he reasoned, which prompted a nod from Murana. "I can't promise anything, but I'll do my best to keep a closer eye on your daughter. How long do you think before you'll need me again to deliver whatever it is you want me to?"

Murana sunk into her chair, the conversation having already exhausted her. "I don't know. Could be weeks, could be months…if I live that long." As if on cue, she began another coughing fit, bringing a faded rag to her mouth out of courtesy for her guest. She shivered uncontrollably after the spasm passed.

Jake's countenance melted at the sickly wolf before him who was nothing more than a concerned mother. "Is everything alright with you?"

She shook her head weakly. "I'm afflicted with an incurable cancer. Nothing contagious, mind you. Just very much lethal."

The rabbit's look turned to one of pity. After a few seconds it looked like he wanted to say something else, but instead he just gazed around the room, considering something.

Unbuckling his belt to get her attention, he offered, "Would you still mind if I eased some of your cares if only for a few hours? It would actually be my pleasure this time. I'll promise to go gentle."

Murana flushed as she began to cough again at the seizure of laughter that devolved into more bloody heaving. She warded him off with a paw. "No, that'll not be necessary. I'd be a terrible bed partner at this stage anyhow. All I ask is that you watch over my daughter, and come when I call so I can give you my final gift to her. Please watch over her."

Fastening his belt again, he strode over to her and gripped both her large paws into his tiny ones, staring up directly into her tired eyes. "I can promise that." This brought a warm smile to her face, which he returned. He rose up, patting her paw gently before giving her a nod and leaving.

The front door shut quietly. The remote for the camera had slipped during the conversation down into the small space between the armrest and the seat cushion. She was too weak to go grab it herself. Cursing that she was unable to turn off the camera, she just let it run out, falling asleep in the chair as she did so.

The rally was a lot larger than she had anticipated. Taylor didn't know what to expect, but she wasn't thinking hundreds of thousands of rabbits jam-packed into a large, abandoned, underground power plant. The old steel and copper pipes and generators were still left intact from the moment the entire factory was shut down in favor of new technologies and energies to help power Zabökar. The time spent neglected, but not demolished, was evident in its exteriors smeared with rust and grime.

It was literal wall-to-wall rabbits standing so tight together that Taylor could not see any gaps. There were some hidden behind cylinders of unknown purpose and other structural obstacles; they would most likely not be getting the full viewing experience of this rally. However, it did not matter, since all Stepan had to his name to conduct them was a megaphone and several drapes of his face and slogan hung along the concrete wall behind him. Portable floodlight stands were brought in to illuminate the vast atrium, leeching off the power from the grid above.

She had drawn many a curious glance from hundreds of rabbits, but she was not the only non-rabbit attendee there. She had seen other mammals, primarily prey. She was one of the few predators present. Taylor wagered they just assumed she was a rabbit sympathizer and left her alone. Many did not want to interact, however, despite Stepan assuring she was a wonderful person. The mistrust ran deep.

It pained her to think they assumed she would enact the law on them at any moment and treat them horribly. If Stepan hadn't vouched for her, she doubted she and Liam would be allowed in. None had recognized her for being Tony's murderer, at least; that was a small respite. For now they were up front, sitting in chairs behind Stepan up on the stage.

Liam was stalwartly at her side the entire time. She had given Stepan a call on her cell phone and asked where the next rally was being held. Since she had no clue where the location mentioned was, Liam was kind enough to show her the way. He asked her no questions, and kept respectful distance from her. She was still recovering from her rage at Ahya for doing what she had done. Her mother's grave was now forever desecrated, which was lingering on her mind.

"We didn't get a chance to really talk yet, what with you being so intent on getting here. How's she doing?" Liam leaned over to whisper into her ear, indicating Ahya with a tilt of his head.

Taylor only looked long enough to ensure Ahya wasn't getting into trouble. "I think she's either pouting or depressed. I can't tell which." Ahya did indeed look like that. She was just lying on the floor limply. The only time she moved was when Taylor moved her herself. Like Ahya had simply given Taylor all control and was not caring anymore.

"I did witness the end of what you had done to your tail." His tone was soft. "I can't imagine what you've been through since we last saw each other."

Taylor took her eyes off Stepan and his speech; she wasn't paying much attention anyway. It was mainly recounting the atrocities committed upon the rabbits and getting unanimous approval of his views—stuff Taylor already knew and agreed with.

She turned to look at Liam, his eyes welcoming. "Seriously, where do I know you from? I remember your eyes now, and that nose of yours."

"I'd be almost hurt, but I can understand." He smiled, showing his teeth. "I found you over a year ago, half-naked running through the streets of Zabökar. No, really! I did." He saw her look of disbelief. "I had no idea what happened to you, but I knew you were in trouble. Since I was on my way out of the city anyway, I offered you a ride in my truck. You didn't even hesitate. You flopped in and passed out."

"I did that?" Taylor racked her brain to remember.

The time of her kitnapping all the way up to the point where she was a few miles out from Palaveve was a fever dream of fog. Whatever experiments they had done to her back then nearly made her lose her mind if she couldn't remember that section of her life. What other things happened that she could not remember?

Liam nodded, the smile ever-present. "You were talking nonsense for quite a while. I just took it in stride and made sure you were fed and kept safe when you were sleeping."

Taylor paused as the crowd roared another assent of agreement towards Stepan's speech. "Why would you do that for me? Surely you saw Ahya and how she is."

"I did." He looked over at the inert tailmaw. "I just wish someone had done that for me when I was your age. Sometimes all of us could use a bit of a helping hand, and I'm just glad I was able to do that for you—twice now if you'll let me."

"But what do I owe you?" Taylor found it hard to believe Liam would just cover expenses for her well-being yet again. "We don't even know each other. I haven't earned this sort of charity."

"Owe? Nothing. Let's just say I'm not the type of wolf who likes to see unfortunate things happen to good people." He mulled it over a moment. "You could call it a fault of mine."

"Thank you for the offer, but it might be best if you left me behind." She turned back to the crowd, her face downcast. "I'd just be more trouble for you."

"Why, because of Ahya? I'd actually welcome the challenge." He chuckled.

She turned her head to give him a disapproving look. "It's not funny. Ahya is dangerous, and I honestly don't know how I've been able to control her for this long. There's no telling when she'll go off and try to eat someone else."

"We'll cross that bridge when we come to it."

"So, you said you were on the way out of Zabökar last time. What brought you back this time?"

Liam gazed off across the sea of rabbit ears. "I had unfinished business in the city." He left it at that before motioning towards Stepan, who seemed to be coming to the climax of his speech. "What do you think of all of this?"

She breathed deeply, taking the sight of the crowd in. "I never knew there were this many rabbits in Zabökar."

"This is certainly not all of them."

"I get that, but where were they all hiding? I knew this law was a problem, but I never knew how much of a boiling pot it had become." Her eyes scanned the sea of ears, her attention stopping only on the one odd figure in black. She recognized the antlers from his head and wolf skull on his face. He was just at the far back of the rally mob, lingering at the edges of the entrance back to the tunnels. It looked like he had a phone to his ear. "Do you see that person? Black robes, antlers, far back where everyone came in?"

Liam's ears were alert and he focused hard on where she described. He narrowed his eyes and shook his head. "I don't see anyone." He sniffed. "Hard to tell with all these rabbits either."

The cloaked figure was gone now. Taylor trembled. She wondered who he was and why he was following her. How did he know to find her here? "I've seen him already a few times, but he never talks or moves. He just stands and stares. It's freaking creepy."

"When did you first notice him?"

"Actually this morning. He didn't start showing up until..." Her voice trailed off.

A sudden, outlandish thought came into her head. That was two times now Ramon had accused Nina of something, and both times he was quickly silenced on the matter. She shook her head passionately. No, she needed to keep the faith and trust things would be alright. Might be just paranoia getting to her after these past few days.

"Never mind. It's nothing."

Liam didn't look convinced. "I think you should stick close to me for now."

"What are you? My dad?" Taylor snorted, trying to laugh at her humor.

He frowned. "No, and I don't claim to be. I'd hope I'm a bit too young for that. However, I'm not about to let you get snatched up and potentially murdered on my watch if you're sincerely concerned over this robed figure."

"I'm still surprised you'd stick your neck out for someone you barely know, especially some 'punk teen' with a monster for a tail." She slouched in the chair, puffing up the hair that had fallen over her eyes.

"You can believe what you want, Taylor. I know what I'm choosing to do." He rose back up, satisfied he made his point, and continued to stand stoically beside her, observing the gathering.

Taylor hadn't been fully attentive since it seemed more a speech of dissent than a rallying cry for action, but that changed as her ears perked up at Stepan's latest proclamation. "And that is why we, as rabbits, must rise up and raze the city to the ground if need be! They have given us no quarter all these years, where we can't even remember a time before all this despair and grief! We should give no quarter to them! Destroy their homes, their businesses, and their livelihoods! Make them suffer and watch like we've watched our brothers and sisters get torn apart in sick, perverted films for their twisted pleasure! Tomorrow night, we strike!"

"Whoa, whoa!" Taylor was already up on her hindpaws. Liam tensed behind her. She strode right up to Stepan, placing a paw on his shoulder. "Hold on right there. I agreed to come aid your cause in fighting for a better treatment for rabbits. I didn't sign up for looting and killing!" A murmur went through the crowd.

"What would you suggest?" Stepan looked at her smugly. "Talking hasn't worked. Appealing in courts of law hasn't worked. Even minor peaceful protests hasn't worked. Nothing changes when there is nothing sacrificed. All my kind are in agreement that a more forceful paw is needed to change our living circumstances."

Taylor's mind was reeling. The entire situation had escalated insanely fast, and she had no idea what to do to stall the inevitable. Yes, she wanted to help them get better living circumstances and rights, but the last thing she wanted was Steven, Max, Jake, Nina and anyone else that she might remotely consider friendly to be swept up in the massacre that Stepan was proposing. Stepan really was dangerous.

"Can you give me until the night after tomorrow to give you an answer about that?"

359

To her amazement and to some in the crowd closest to the stage, Stepan's eyes glazed over a bit and he mumbled, "Of course, Taylor. I'm sure we can wait just another day more."

Taking this crazy opportunity, she asked, "Do you think you can help me spread the word about what I want to do to everyone here when I'm ready?"

Stepan nodded lethargically. "It would be my pleasure."

"She's practicing witchcraft on him!" A rabbit in the crowd cried, pointing at her.

Taylor backed up from Stepan, letting go of his shoulder. He shook his head a bit before addressing the accusation. "She is not! She did a great service to me today, saving my dear Eleanor. I would be remiss if I did not grant her this request of one additional day. Their time of reckoning above will come one day or another. What's another night?"

Taylor looked down on her fingers in amazement. What just happened?

There were some grumblings and jeers from within the herd. They were not happy to be silenced after the riling up he had done to them just minutes prior. They were eager for blood. Stepan went to calm down the crowd and promised them justice, but to wait patiently one more day while Taylor and other mammals who sympathized with their plight paved the way for their uprising. He framed it in such a way that Taylor would make it easier for them, when that was not what she promised.

She stepped back near towards Liam as he regarded her impassively. "What are you doing? Do you even have a plan?" He motioned out to the growing din of the crowd. "You just promised in front of thousands of rabbits of a better solution in only a day's time!"

She waved him off, irritated. "I know!" She swept past him, pacing back and forth in a small circle. "I think I have an idea of what to do, I just need to hope I can get what I need to pull it off."

Taylor knew she had nothing to provide for these rabbits. Coming here was a mistake. She had no plan; she was only stalling for time at this point. Time enough to get her brothers out of the city, as well as track down Nina and hopefully get back that pine tree necklace from her apartment. Her mother's last message to her was on it, and she needed it now more than ever. If the impending riot overran Zabökar before she could get to it, the last remnants of her mother would be lost to her forever. She couldn't afford that.

She was gazing at her paws, her mind tuning out Liam's annoyingly calm reprimand of her impulsive behavior with Stepan, when she noticed a red panda coming straight towards her from across the stage. She stopped just a few paces away and smiled with a small bow. "So, you're Taylor. That was a brave thing you did. I'm very happy you are standing up for these rabbits. They deserve better treatment than they've been getting."

"Who are you?" Taylor tilted her head.

"Oh, how rude of me!" She giggled, putting a paw to her chest. "My name is Samantha. Guess you could say I'm a sympathizer of sorts, like yourself."

Taylor clucked her tongue. "Yeah, but I'm not much of one."

Liam cleared his throat, getting both their attention. He addressed only Taylor, giving her a small business card. "Since it is clear you are not listening to me or not caring, here is my number. I am concerned about your well-being, Taylor, but I will not be party to this foolishness you are getting yourself into with these rabbits. Yes, they deserve justice and a better shake at life, but getting involved with this crowd will only bring ruin. Trust me, I know. I've seen enough of these things to predict how they'll go."

He sighed, putting a paw on his hip. "When you've finally come to realize that, call me. I'd be more than happy to take you away from Zabökar once again to safer pastures. Until then, I will not be risking my life with someone who so callously risks their own. It is one thing to help someone who is struggling with what they cannot control, but it is quite another when they walk right into that trouble themselves. I had hoped you were smarter than this, Taylor."

Liam didn't even wait for a response and simply left, taking the path of least resistance down off the elevated stage and through the crowd of rabbits alongside one end of the room. All gave him a wide berth.

Taylor stared off after him. She felt conflicted for what she was doing, but she didn't know of any other path to take. She knew she needed to get her family out of here before a behemoth came to destroy Zabökar off the map. She knew she needed her mother's last message to her. And though she would love to have Jake and Nina come along— maybe even Loray and Bailey— the real question was, would anyone allow her back after the disaster at the church and graveyard? Or would Ahya ruin it all once more and she remain forever a dangerous monster?

Samantha leaned into her view and beamed. "Wow, that guy was a bit gruff, wasn't he?"

Taylor shifted her eyes back to her. "I think he means well. I just wish I could remember more about him. For some reason...I feel safe around him, and I don't know why."

"Well, no matter." Samantha got closer as the rally adjourned and the rabbits began to filter out. "You said you needed a day to get together a better solution? Did you have any idea of what that might be?"

Taylor nodded her head. Last thing she wanted was to let loose that she hadn't a plan. "I think I have a few ideas, but I need to get back something that belongs to me first."

"That's fair." Samantha hooked an arm through Taylor's, barely garnering a reaction from Ahya who still lay listless on the ground. "Mind if I accompany you? It's rare I get to see another female around these parts, when it comes to rabbits."

Taylor glanced back at Ahya. She seemed to be docile enough to have company after what happened earlier. "Sure, but could you keep some distance from me?"

"Oh... I'm sorry." She released Taylor's arm and stepped back. "I didn't mean to get chummy. We just met and all."

Taylor shook her head. "It's fine. I just...have a thing about physical touch right now."

"Me too." Samantha smiled. "But probably not in the way you do." She giggled. "It's all cool with me. We can walk abreast."

"Where will you two ladies be going? Did you need a ride anywhere?" Stepan offered, having finished up any last-minute administrative decisions regarding the end of the rally. His volunteer workers rushed off to their appointed tasks.

Taylor bowed her head. "If it isn't too much trouble, I have a place in mind I'd like to be dropped off at. It's not too far from the inner city Milk District."

"And you?" Stepan turned to Samantha.

"I'll be tagging along with her for now."

Stepan grinned. "Splendid. I have a taxi waiting for us above."

"I don't like it." Finnley stated the obvious.

"I don't either, but we've got no choice." Fey set Finnley down beside him, leaning up against a car across the road observing the high glass towers in the center of Zabökar. At its peak were the penthouse suites and board rooms of the High Council.

They gazed up at the dizzying heights of the tall structures. In Fey's hooves was a small, homemade bomb he had made earlier that day. It wasn't anything fancy and its purpose was not any sort of wide-scale destruction. They only needed it to provide a distraction so they could walk right in through the front doors of the building and work their way up to Sabrina's quarters. They still had her cell phone, complete with her DNA print on it. They only hoped it was still valid for their entry. They were going to find out either way.

Finnley had been here many times before, and was well acquainted with the shift schedules of the guards of the Caelesti Spire, its eight chains of light at its combined peak diverging off to their respective monoliths. It was nearing the night shift, and they could more easily move under cover of dark to set up the bomb. The panic of the evening crowd who would be leaving work at this time would be their cover.

Using his small stature to his advantage, Finnley took the miniature bomb and scampered across the street and up alongside the council garden. He sifted through the bushes and shrubs, making it to a corner of the building where he glued the small device onto a nook of the architecture where it wouldn't be easily spotted. Then he made his way back to Fey, scoping out for guards on the way.

He hopped up onto the car hood and stood beside the elk, gazing on the path between the separate gardens that led to the primary entrance to the tower, draped in windows and spiral horned pillars. "I'm here for you, but we get only the information we need, get out, and pass it off to whoever we need to. I do not want anything further to change on the Script and this…Authority to find you."

"I understand. Thank you for supporting me on this." Fey squeezed Finnley's shoulders warmly as he looked over at the otter. "We need to know if any other members were in on Sabrina's dealings with Mendezarosa in Howlgrav, and if more of them could be power-eaters, and if everything we've been doing for them has been furthering their ends at ending the Script."

Finnley low whistled. "Seems like a tall order, but hopefully we can find something here that can help protect you from this Authority." Finnley gave a big, ragged sigh. He did not want to lose Fey. As much as he hated this entire mission and the fact Taylor was tied to it all, he couldn't deny Fey's fate was at stake here. He only hoped it was worth it. He handed the detonator to Fey. "You ready?"

Fey took it and, hoof finger hovering over the button, he unclipped and drew out a small pistol. "I have what we need to avoid detection."

"From the guns too?" Fey was nervous.

"I hope so."

"Let's do it then." Finnley was resolute.

Fey clicked the button and the entire front right corner of the Caelesti Spire exploded outwards with a deafening roar. Perhaps Fey had crafted the bomb a bit too well. Huge chunks of metal, rock, and glass splintered across the walkway and rained upon the gardens surrounding. Alarms began to sound and voices were shouting as the civilians nearby and within the building began to panic.

They slapped on their hats, pulling them low just enough to cover their eyes as they surged forward into the gaggle of runners who were exiting both the building and gardens. Using the commotion, Fey took aim at the two cameras flanking the entrance and shot a small electrode module that attached itself swiftly to each. Within seconds, the devices were shorted out and useless.

Sliding to the side as more guards poured out past them, they slipped inside, and Fey took down four more cameras aimed perfectly down their planned path. Their skills at subterfuge served them well. The receptionist at the information desk barely gave them a second glace as they continued to walk with purpose through the diminishing crowd. If they were lucky, the High Council members many floors up would be evacuated too, giving them more freedom and time to play with.

They entered an elevator and gazed up to fire on and dismantle the small camera watching them. Fey opened the cylinder of the pistol and checked his bullets. "Only got 3 more shots left."

"Better make them count then." Finnley continued to stare straight ahead, not wanting to watch the floors count upwards as they rose. "I know we'll be long gone from here before they dispatch a strike team to eliminate us, but it's best we don't have to worry about them identifying us at all." They rode in silence for a moment. "Guess we made it past the guns."

"Guess we did." Fey chuckled uneasily. "Surprised our DNA profiles are still valid." Finnley nodded, continuing to stare forward. "I'm scared, Finnley." Fey said at last, his breath exhaling at having kept it in too long. "Scared of what we might find."

Finnley broke his internal concentration and looked up at his love. He put a reassuring paw on the elk's leg. "So what if the power-eaters have infiltrated the High Council? We're not going to be acting on this information. It's not our fight anymore. At best we pass it off to more crusade-driven people like Mikhail and let them handle it."

"It's not just that. I know I'm doing this partially to discover the link between the High Council, Taylor, and these power-eaters, but I'm also stalling for time on affecting your Script. You are to remain here in Zabökar. The moment we head away from where your Script places you and we start interacting with more people, the sooner I think I'll be found. I mean, you're not even supposed to be in Caelesti Spire with me right now."

365

Finnley gripped Fey's pants tighter. "We won't let that happen. I won't let that happen."

The door opened just shy of three floors from the top. They were deadly close to some of the tightest security in the tower. They did their best to hug the wall as they walked out into the carpeted hallways, accentuated by domed archways with pristine fountains, statues, and paintings. It was alarmingly open; they had forgotten just how little cover there truly was in the upper levels. It was all spectacle and awe, meant to cow those beneath the council before meeting them for business or political purposes.

"Do we know where Fahpar's quarters are?" Finnley looked around to see if he could spy obvious locations of cameras. He unfortunately couldn't find any.

Fey nodded. "I researched the council's information on their public website. It amazingly has some pretty extensive information released from their PR department." He laughed. "Since Fahpar was a relatively new addition to the council, they would most likely have her near the north side of the building in the smaller suites. That would be the first place I'd check."

Other than quickly ducking behind a statue of a former council member when a troop of guards came running past—probably to contain the breach downstairs—they had a relatively uneventful trip through the wide corridors. It didn't take them long to find Sabrina's place of residence. It was already taped up and left to be neglected until the council decided a successor to take her living quarters.

"They made it easy for us." Finnley cackled, handing the phone to Fey.

Fey turned it on and entered the app menu, Finnley having cracked it wide open earlier. He used the hacking app Finnley installed onto it to snag Sabrina's fingerprint she had put in to unlock her phone so it would display prominently on the screen. Flipping it around, he put it on the print panel and waited for it to scan. The internal mechanism clicked, and the door light turned green.

"And now they know someone who isn't Sabrina is here." Fey took a deep breath, bending low so his nubs of a rack wouldn't catch on the police tape.

"If we're quick and that diversion below is enough, we won't have to worry about anyone." Finnley tried to reassure Fey, but he was feeling the pressure too.

Shutting the door behind them, they quickly scoured the suite. For a smaller abode than the more venerable council members, it was quite sprawling. Full bar-paneled glass windows adorned the exterior of each room, looking out across their grand city. Containing no less than eight rooms to include three bedrooms and an expansive bathroom with Jacuzzi, it was the epitome of decadence. A far cry from what the common folk enjoyed in just about everywhere else in Zabökar.

"Here's her office." Fey pointed to a minor alcove off the main den with a fake fireplace.

Popping in a small drive into a port, they opened up her laptop and began to run the cracking program to unlock her desktop. After a few tense minutes of waiting, it opened up to a bunch of applications scattered across the screen. Sabrina's organization was atrocious, and did not bode well for what they wished to research. Where would they even begin in all this mess?

"There!" Finnley pointed at a folder mixed in with all the rest named "Howlgrav".

Clicking on it, they spotted several different documents and letters saved complete with itinerary to Howlgrav. One linked to a program which opened up the email in question.

"Chief Mendezarosa, it has come to my attention that you have secured a high-value target that is of interest to me and the council. I will be taking a bird to fly out to you tonight within the hour. Expect me soon. Interrogate who you have to until I get there. Our previous deal remains solid, but do not let anyone go until I get there and I say so. Sincerely, Council Member Fahpar."

Finnley's brow furrowed. "That still doesn't confirm one way or another that the rest of the council members were in on it or not."

Fey's eyes shifted to Finnley. "Nor her connection to the power-eaters. Let's keep looking."

Finnley grew frustrated and hopped off the desk, letting Fey pilfer through that mess of data. They were wasting too much time already, and had little to show for it. He began inspecting the bedrooms and other furnishings. He was about to give up when he noticed a drawer slightly ajar on the nightstand in the third bedroom down. Opening it, he found yet another cell phone.

He excitedly ran back to Fey who seemed to be even more frustrated than before. "I think I might have found something!" Finnley swiped it open and was surprised to see it wasn't locked like her other phone. Fey stopped his search and leaned over to look. Finnley scrolled through the names. "There's far less contacts in this one. Most of the High Council is in here except for a couple. Then there's this one... COTUS."

"What's that?" Fey asked.

"I don't know." Finnley tapped to open up more information on the contact, but it was all blank. Empty. "There's nothing else listed. Just the acronym."

"Children of the Unwritten Script, you think?" Fey was probably grasping at straws.

It wouldn't be that obvious would it? Then again, who else knew about the power-eaters and their original name to begin with? Not many, Finnley wagered. He tapped the number and put the phone up to his ear with bated breath. It rang several times before it clicked over as someone picked up.

A soft, yet stern voice came through the speaker, despite a lot of background noise and voices. "Ah, Sabrina Fahpar. How nice of you to finally return home after your little unexcused vacation in Howlgrav. Pretty astonishing, I dare say, since you seem to be dead."

Finnley immediately hung up. "Fuck."

"That was High Council Elder, Barateon." Fey had recognized the voice. "They know where we are now." He shut the laptop and was proceeding to take it for investigation later when Finnley slapped his hoof.

"We have no time for anything now. This was a horrible idea from the start!" Finnley dropped the new phone into his pocket and began to make a dash for the entrance. "Come on, we need to go!"

Fey's ears flicked forward. "It's too late. I can hear footsteps out in the hall now. They were probably alerted to us the moment we used Fahpar's phone on the door."

"Gods dammit!" Finnley immediately drew out his dual knives, sliding behind a cushy chair adjacent to the front entrance.

"No, we do not kill anyone!" Fey rushed over to put a hoof on Finnley's quivering paws.

"Why not? They're going to kill us if they discover us in here!" Finnley grit his teeth.

"Because of me. You're not supposed to be here. You're only here because of me. If we kill anyone, that'll be me changing the Script through you. We need to get out of here without killing anyone."

Finnley's heart broke as he looked upon his lover with grief. It was either go out in flames together, or do something that might attract something neither of them had any concept of. Nothing but an indescribable fear. Reluctantly, he sheathed his blades and gripped Fey strongly.

"Fine, but that won't stop me from scratching them up will it?" Fey shook his head at him. "Good."

No sooner had they parted when the door slammed open, the guards kicking it in hard and swarming in. They were armed to the teeth with electrified batons and handguns. Finnley got behind the nearest potted plant stationed just at the corner of the entry hallway and used both hindpaws to shove it at the legs of the first guard, pushing him off balance. Landing sideways towards Finnley, he got knocked out cold as the otter punched him in the face the moment his head hit the floor.

Fey used Fahpar's laptop as a projectile and winded the next guard when it nailed him in the stomach, causing him to keel over. Running up fast, he kicked him hard in the face, drawing blood with the edge of his hooves. He fell to the floor alongside the first. Both Fey and Finnley dove to the floor behind various furnishings as gunfire erupted into the den. Upholstery and filler were flying through the air at the multitude of holes penetrating the expensive pieces.

Fey turned up a dial on his pistol and aimed at the nearest guard just as he came in view. The electrode module hit his neck and began to expel electrical shocks throughout his whole body. He quivered uncontrollably and spastically fell to the floor. Fey succeeded in quick order to down two more with the remaining rounds he had left. This caused enough of a distraction for Finnley to move from cover to hop onto the second to last guard and twist around his neck, clawing and biting.

Ignoring the skirls of the frenetic guard under siege, Fey charged the final one with head down and gutted him in the stomach with his antler nubs. It didn't penetrate far, but it was enough to knock the wind out of him. Fey slammed the guard against the wall then withdrew his head, cerise on his budding rack, and punched the guard hard, breaking his nose causing blood to dribble down as he slumped to the floor unconscious.

Finnley was breathing hard as he finally put a good stranglehold on his victim until he passed out. He released the guard as he dropped, then alighted softly on the carpet next to Fey. Admiring their handiwork, he clapped his paws. "They certainly don't train them like they used to."

"Or how we were trained." Fey smiled.

Finnley's eyes went wide as one of the previously comatose guards groggily rose his head and took aim with a gun at Fey. "Look out!" He cried as he instinctively grabbed an inert body and lifted it high to block the shot. The aim was low, but it was true. The guard fired and it pierced straight through the chest of his comrade.

"Shit!" Fey slammed his hind hoof into the firing guard's head, knocking him out again, then raced over to see the damage done to the shot one. He inspected the wound. "It hit his lung. If he doesn't get medical help immediately, it'll collapse and he'll die."

"Fuck!" Finnley knew the implication of this. "We don't have time to fix him up."

Fey looked at him knowingly. "No, we do not."

"Let's just go. We have her new phone. We can figure this all out later."

They raced down the hallway and entered the elevator. A feeling of dread was enveloping them both. The guard was now dead. Their breathing became heavy, and it was an effort to get out each one. The lights within the cabin as they descended seemed dimmer than normal. A loud rattling seemed to shake the tower as a gasping wheeze was heard on the wind in a space where there should be none. Fey seemed to be panicking, rocking back and forth on the carpet. Finnley was terrified for him, having never seen him like this before.

"It's coming… It's coming. I can feel it," Fey kept repeating.

"Just stay with me, hun." Finnley was patting and rubbing Fey's back as he held his elk tight. "We just need to get out of this elevator and—"

The entire cabin jolted and stopped. The lights nearly gave out as the gloom permeated the small space. Fey began to freak out and rammed his head against the metal basing of the interior wall. Again and again he slammed his head, jamming his budding antlers deeper into his skull, causing it to bleed. The fur began to flake off, then the skin as more and more of his head began to strip away at the brutal beating he was giving himself.

"Fey, get a hold of yourself! There's no one here! It's just me, Finnley! Your honey!" He began to cry as the larger elk was more powerful and relentless than he was. He hadn't the strength to stop his love from goring his entire head into the wall.

The low, guttural gasp returned with a single phrase. "Entity detected. Executing."

Fey unleashed a blood curdling scream as he raked his eyes out with his hooves, his entire body going rigid. Finnley cowered in the corner as a pall of death seeped into his heart. There was a presence in the room that was beyond terrifying, yet he could not perceive it fully. Fey continued to shriek as his clothes turned dark red. Blood was pouring out of every orifice and drenching the floor. Skin began to melt, and Fey's entire body shrunk to nothing but a mangled husk of bones.

As swiftly as it came, the presence was gone, and the lights flickered back to full brightness. The elevator began to move again after a few seconds. However, Finnley was rooted to the corner, his eyes mesmerized in terror at the macabre display of clothes and bleached bones that was once his lover, surrounded by a sea of crimson. The Authority had come for Fey, and it had found him.

"Fey…" Finnley began to weep, crawling over to tenderly hug the bones of his loved one, not caring how filthy he got in his blood.

Taylor had caused this. Taylor had removed Fey from the Script. Finnley couldn't say which death was worse, being riddled with bullets or being reducing to nothing. All Finnley knew was that more of this was to come if Taylor was left free.

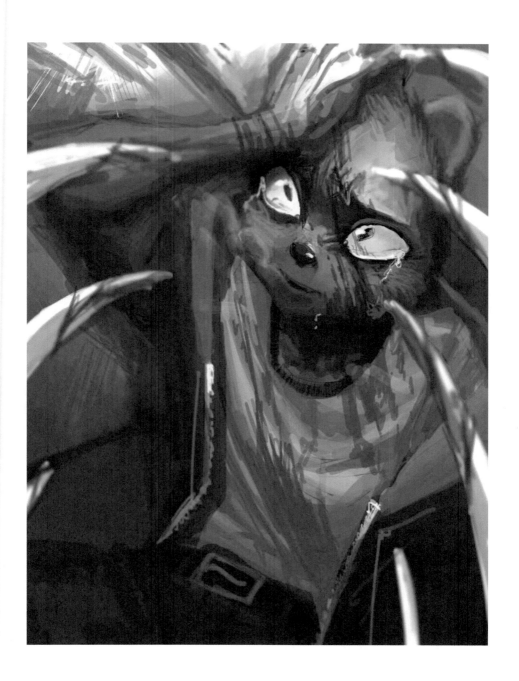

17.

REVELATIONS

Stepan had directed the taxi to drop them off after the surprisingly lengthy drive from the rally. "You two ladies have a pleasant evening. Oh, and Taylor…" He leaned out of the cab side door. "If there is anything at all you need, just let me know. You have one full day to find a better solution than what I proposed tonight. I wish you luck, because we certainly haven't found anything better." He smiled at her in an unsettling way before shutting the door quietly and directing the driver to rise up and hover off into the night.

"So how did you get to join the rabbits and their cause?" Samantha asked, not wasting any time diving right into the conversation now that the only rabbit between them had left.

"I wouldn't say I 'joined their cause', at least not in the violent way they want, but I did want to do something about it." She looked around the city streets as they walked, scoffing at how different it looked to her eyes now compared to a few days prior. "Now I'm not so sure I want to join them directly, not that I have the power to do much of anything at this point."

"I don't think that's true. We're all powerful in some fashion or another." Samantha sounded cheerful. "Maybe your part in all this hasn't been revealed yet. The Script could help, you know, to find your way. Sure, it may not detail every aspect of your every waking moment, but the biggest future moments are at least recorded. Maybe you don't know what to do, simply because you haven't consulted your own Script about it?"

"I don't think that'll be necessary." Taylor wrinkled her nose as she did her best not to glare at the red panda. "So, what about you? What brought you to Stepan's rally?"

"Me?" Samantha seemed to look inward as she thought about an answer. "I guess you could say I had sex with enough rabbits to begin to question how they felt. It was probably several years ago that I sponsored my first rabbit."

"Are you rich?" It was an obvious question to Taylor. She had heard of this sponsoring just yesterday, and how it was only reserved for the elite.

"Me? No, but I saved up enough money with my parents to register a rabbit to myself, and then I set him up with a home far to the south of here that my family owns where he can live out his life in peace." She beamed proudly, like she had done a good deed.

"Living there doing what?"

"Oh, you know, helping out on the ranch and growing crops. I'd say it is a far better life there than in the city where anyone can take them to their bed and abuse them."

Taylor's brow furrowed. "You said your family owns it?" Samantha nodded. "Sounds like you just traded him from one service to another. Seems like they still have no freedom regardless."

Samantha bristled. "I'll have you know that I've saved two rabbits so far from this awful place, and I'm about to save a third! I check up on them twice a year, and they're always happy to see me and are in good spirits!"

"So they tell you. Rabbits stick together." Taylor repeated something Jake had said to her.

"Look, we're both trying to do a good thing! Let's not get mired in the semantics of how we accomplish that." Samantha seemed a bit put off with Taylor's attitude. "Where are we headed anyway?"

"We're actually here." Taylor stopped and looked up at The Fox Den, its top visible by the neon lights around. One block down the side alley was the entrance to the stairwell leading up to her former band's flat. "I'm going to meet up with some of my friends in hopes one of them might be able to sneak past the cops guarding my friend's apartment and get some of my stuff back. They might have a better chance than me, since they're neither Nina nor myself. Let's just hope Ramon isn't back yet or things might get ugly."

"Oh geez, what sort of crap are you wrapped up in, Taylor?" Samantha was looking very nervous.

"Far more than I bargained for. That's for sure." Taylor sighed. She glanced over at her. "Still want to tag along?"

Samantha was hesitant. "Um, for now, I guess?"

"Why did you tag along then?" Taylor was slightly amused.

"Because you were the only other female I saw with a similar interest in rabbits."

"That's all? Somehow I highly doubt my interest matches yours." Taylor did her best to hide her mirth. "Follow me if you want, but thanks for keeping me company this far."

They had entered the stairwell and were going up the first flight when Samantha asked, "Have you ever thought about sponsoring a rabbit? I mean, not for just sexual needs and such, but to give them a good life?"

Taylor felt uncomfortable with the topic. "It still feels like owning them, even if you are doing it for a good cause. Even if you supposedly put them out on the ranch, I still feel that there is some part of them that feels like they owe you and would influence how they act around you. You'd never truly get to know them for who they are."

Samantha was thoughtful. "I never really looked at it that way."

"Besides, how do you know they would do better in that new job and role you suddenly gave them? This is still dictating the type of life you wish to have for them rather than them choosing for themselves. What if they wanted something else for their future?"

The red panda seemed awed at this line of thinking. "How do you figure that? You ever sat down with a rabbit and asked him how he feels?"

Taylor had to stifle a laugh. "As a matter of fact, I have. He seemed unhappy with how things turned out in his life, and was quite bitter about the topic of sponsorship. I can sympathize with him because much of the freedoms he never got was kind of like me, and how I had my freedoms ripped away from me."

"Oh, I hope my Jake doesn't feel like that when I finally sponsor him. It would be awful if I found out he hated it." Samantha looked despondent.

Taylor stopped briefly on the third landing, looking back at her. "Jake? That's…a nice name. How did you two meet?" Taylor's heart began to pound in her chest, her mind swirling with thoughts of Jake and this red panda.

"Oh, you know…how most rabbits come around. He struck my eye and I asked for his services." She giggled, unaware of Taylor's inner turmoil. "We here? Or are we still climbing?"

"We got a few more floors," Taylor said numbly.

"Well, it wasn't until my girlfriends asked for him to be the entertainment for their bachelorette party that I made the choice to free him from this life. He's an amazing rabbit, and handsome too! I would hate to see him wallow away in obscurity here."

"Sounds real generous. Did he accept?"

She frowned. "Well, not quite, but he did say he needed time to think about it."

Taylor let out a small breath in relief. She didn't know why, but she was getting extremely possessive all of a sudden over Jake. She shouldn't feel like that, especially after denouncing the insanity that was this rabbit law. Fighting over Jake would simply render him less a person, something he would most likely be hurt by if she ever did it to him. Was all this recent exposure to rabbits and how other people viewed them already coloring her view? She hoped not.

"We're here," Taylor said, entering the blue lit hallway leading to her band's apartment.

Her ears flicked forward as she heard several voices in heated exchange beyond the door. She went to knock when it flew open to reveal Nina before her, disheveled but intact. She stood staring at Taylor for a few seconds before sweeping into her arms and hugging her tight. Even Ahya reacted slightly to this sudden influx of physical touch, but she maintained her cover and did not open.

"Taylor! Oh my gods, I thought you had died when you fell from that truck! I tried flying back up to find you, but had no idea where you went!" She was breathing rapidly, trying to expel her entire experience. "I was searching everywhere up and down the street, praying I didn't find your body splattered on the ground."

Taylor patted her on the back. "It's okay. I'm alive." She drew back to look at her, still enveloped in her wings. "Why are you here? I thought you and Ramon were at odds?"

"We are," she sneered, "but this was the only place I could think of to lay low and hide out. I went back to my apartment after we were ambushed at the church this morning and police were everywhere. I barely had enough time to get a few of my things and get out by the window. It's a good thing most of them can't fly, since such work is beneath most birds." She laughed sardonically at the irony.

"Crap. That's what I was afraid of." Taylor sagged. "I was hoping to get my pine tree necklace from your place before they ransacked it."

Nina brightened up. "Oh! I did get that for you. That and some…doll. I knew you were carrying that around with you and it seemed important to you, so I figured I'd pick both up."

Taylor began to cry and hugged Nina again. "You have no idea how much that means to me! Thank you!"

It was Nina's turn to pat. "Is everything okay?"

Taylor sniffled and nodded. "I'll tell you inside."

"Who is this?" Nina finally turned to the red panda.

"Um…this?" Taylor didn't really know how best to introduce her. Some random person she just met at a rabbit rally designed to incite violence on everyone in the city?

The red panda extended her paw towards Nina. "Samantha Curings. Taylor and I actually just met, but she's been super friendly."

Nina shook her paw with a wing, letting go of Taylor. "That's great, but I meant, why is she here?"

"I'm still trying to figure that out myself," Taylor admitted, walking in with her following Nina. The cloud of smoke was still in the air, but not as heavy as when they were here last. She waved at Loray who bowed at the two of them, and Bailey who seemed content to lay where he was. "Hey, you two." She looked around as Nina shut the door. "Where is Ramon, anyway?"

"He left in a rush this morning. According to Nina here, he met you two at the church downtown," Loray explained.

Bailey woke himself up with a snort. "He hasn't been back since, and we have a concert to perform tomorrow night!"

"Concert?" Taylor looked perplexed. "Just the three of you?"

Loray looked peeved. "It's all we've got since you disappeared— I mean, were kitnapped, and Nina dropped out. Things just haven't been the same." He put his fists on his chubby hips. "However, if he doesn't get back by tonight, we'll barely have time to rehearse before tomorrow. If we don't nail this gig, this'll probably be the end of the *Horny Toads*. Our current manager won't be willing to front the money for another event."

"That sucks, but I fail to see how that's our problem." Nina sighed, pinching her bill between her wing feathers. "You see, Taylor? I came here to lay low, and these two have been pressuring me to join them tomorrow to help out when I made it clear I don't want back in the band."

"You mean you haven't told them what Ramon did to us yet?" Taylor glared at her.

"I just... I didn't want to make waves. I was hoping to have been gone before he even showed back up." Nina looked guilty.

"Huh, well, Ramon sold us out to the police and to Nina's parents today. We barely escaped," Taylor informed the band matter-of-factly.

Loray gasped. "I am so sorry! If we had known..."

Baily struggled to stay awake. "We didn't know he would turn on you like that. We wouldn't have bothered Nina so much on rejoining."

"It's fine. I was about to leave just before Taylor got here. Even if I wanted to rejoin, I wouldn't do it under the *Horny Toads*." Nina cringed.

Taylor bobbed her head in agreement. "'*Bad Luck*' was the better name. I'm just glad you two weren't in on his plan to rat on us." This brought smiles to Loray and Bailey's faces.

"Oh, snap!" Samantha blurted out, causing them all to jump. She was pointing at Taylor specifically. "You are 'that' Taylor? Taylor Renee with the awesome mouth for a tail? I almost didn't recognize you with your new fur color! Is it for real?! Was it some technical prop?! I must know! Show me!" She looked like an excited fangirl.

Taylor was a bit unnerved at the shower of adoration she suddenly received, something she never truly got personally during the band's heyday. "I never pegged you for a metal fan, Samantha."

"I have a wide variety of musical tastes, but I remember you now!" She clapped her paws together as she attempted to inspect Taylor's tail, causing Taylor to turn around to keep herself between Samantha and Ahya. "So are you going to show me?"

"I'd actually rather not. Ahya and I are having...a bit of an off time right now. I don't fully trust her to do what I ask." As if in response to this, Ahya seemed to lay even lower to the ground, resting lethargically. Samantha looked supremely disappointed.

"Never mind that." Nina flapped a wing. "What brings you here? After what Ramon did, I figured you wouldn't come back here."

"It's complicated, but I actually came back for my necklace. Where is it?"

"One moment!" Nina smiled as she walked over to the bag dropped unceremoniously on top of the coffee table and all of its mass of trash. Rummaging through the contents, she pulled out both the kitsune doll and the necklace. "I'm actually glad I went back to get these."

"Me too." Taylor grabbed the two articles from her wings and then went rigid when Nina attempted to go in for another hug, her bill touching her cheek. "Ah, you okay, Nina?"

Nina flushed, backing off slightly. "Yeah, sorry. I'm just happy to see you again. I seriously thought you were dead."

"I'm glad I'm not." She returned the grin.

"Mind if I sit down?" Samantha asked awkwardly, clearly being the fifth wheel to all this. She just seemed jazzed to be in the presence of one of her favorite bands, even if they had broken up.

"Go right ahead." Loray beamed, offering the cushion next to him, which she promptly took.

"So why did you need the necklace?" Nina sat down next to Bailey, who woke up once more when her weight pressed down beside him.

Taylor's face dropped. "It has some sort of microchip embedded in it with data regarding my mother's last message to me. I was told by…" She looked over at Samantha. "…someone that I could access it somehow."

This information perked up Bailey's torpor. He finally stood up on the couch for once and regarded Taylor more clearly, the haze of the drugs lifting from his eyes. "A microchip you say? With hidden messages? That sounds very interesting!"

Loray laughed. "Ah yes, our resident hacker. If he stays awake enough to assist, he 'might' be able to get you what you need off that pine tree."

"I'm not that inept!" Bailey was affronted. Taylor's jaw dropped alongside Nina's as the opossum slipped off the couch and raised his tiny paw towards Taylor. "If you don't mind parting with it for a bit, I'll see if I can't crack it wide open and have whatever's on it viewable for you."

Taylor glanced over at Loray for direction. Loray just shrugged. "That's the first I've seen him be this invested in anything in a long time. I say let him have at it."

"Alright, I still want the necklace back intact after you're done." She gingerly let it drop into his outstretched paw, strap and all.

"Don't worry about a thing, Taylor! I'll be sure I give it back in even better condition than when you gave it to me!" Bailey was brimming with pride, having been tasked with something important for once. He marched off to the other room where she could see him climb up onto a hyena-sized chair, and began booting up the computer on the desk.

"Wow," Nina marveled. "That's the most lucid I've ever seen him be."

"It comes and goes." Loray sat back down and looked up to Samantha with a grin. "So how did you first hear about us?"

Taylor walked over to sit next to Nina, wrapping the inactive Ahya across her lap, as Samantha answered, "Well, actually I only heard about *Bad Luck* because of her." She pointed at Taylor. "Her monster tail was the talk of the town, and that's how I heard about you all from my colleagues."

Loray snapped his fingers. "I knew you were the money-maker! Ramon wouldn't believe me!"

"Yeah... Because of my 'monster' tail." Taylor sighed, looking down at her dark-grey-dyed tail.

Nina observed Taylor for a moment before placing a wing on her leg, taking care not to touch Ahya. "What happened to you after we got separated?"

"I landed in a cab with this rabbit named Stepan. He invited me to his rally this evening, which I went to, and that's where I met Samantha." She looked up at the red panda.

"Rabbit? Rally? What are you on about?" Nina looked confused.

"Oh dear." Loray clucked. "I don't know who this Stepan is, but I've heard of these rabbit gatherings. Don't you remember, Nina? Just last week there was a small break-in at several Pali Marts in the Milk District. Many goods were stolen and several stores set on fire. By the time the police came, they had very few rabbits to arrest since most scattered."

"Really?" Nina was shocked. "I didn't know it was because of rabbits."

They heard a small thud as Bailey quickly called out from the other room, "It's okay! I'm alright. The keyboard is fine!" They summarily ignored him.

"What happened to the rabbits that got caught?" Taylor was concerned.

Samantha stared at the ground sadly as Loray revealed the ugly truth. "They were tried and convicted that same day and euthanized. Was a pretty cut and dry case without much fuss."

"He was right..." Taylor muttered to herself, thinking back to what Jake said.

The rabbits were never given a fair shake, and were literally doomed to failure the moment they stepped into any courtroom. No wonder Stepan was promoting such violence against the rest of the mammals in Zabökar. They had no other option, since the entire system was rigged against them from the start. Yet she abhorred the idea that more people would be killed or injured for a law that they were never taught was wrong. She felt incapable to change what was going to happen tomorrow.

Nina's head swiveled back to Taylor. "And you are going along with these rabbits?"

Taylor gripped Ahya tightly. "No, not exactly."

"Well, you did say in front of everyone that you'd find a better solution than simply rioting," Samantha reminded, much to Taylor's chagrin. "I thought it was very brave!"

"You promised what?!" Nina's feathers were fraying. "Was Jake there? What did he think about all this?"

"Well, that's the thing. He wasn't. I actually left him when… It's really difficult to explain what all happened." Taylor wasn't even sure how much was even relevant to tell.

"Wait, Jake? You mean Jake Thumpings?" Samantha clued in on his name. She leaned forward. "When did you two meet? Where is he now?" Her tone got suddenly hostile.

They were all interrupted when Bailey reentered the room. "I got it out from the tree and it's in a reading device. You just need to access it like you would any other folder and file system." He looked really proud of himself as he crawled back up onto the couch and collapsed back to sleep beside Nina.

Taylor got up suddenly, looking around at all of them. "Would you mind…if I viewed my mother's last message to me alone?"

Samantha looked like she was about to refuse, but Nina stood up to deflect the red panda's hot jealousy. "Of course, Taylor. I wish I had the sort of relationship you had with your mom. Well…not at the end, of course, but before then." She was wringing her wings in front of herself.

Taylor nodded. "Thank you."

Without waiting for further permission, she swept past the couches and into the small office beneath the loft bedroom. Shutting the door quietly behind her, she could hear Samantha grilling Nina on what she knew of Jake. That would be an issue she'd have to sort out with her when she got back out of this room. For now, she turned to the computer and took a deep breath before sitting in the seat and reaching for the mouse.

"So I says to him, why don't you find your own booth, buddy? This one is for me and my harem!" Trevor slapped the table, guffawing at his joke. Terrati cackled right alongside him, putting a hoof on his shoulder to prevent himself from tipping over.

They had both gotten thoroughly sloshed that evening. Trevor meant what he said when he would get Terrati completely wasted. From the sounds of the stories coming from the gazelle's mouth, this night of stress-relief was something he sorely needed. They stayed there throughout the afternoon and into the late evening, drinking beers and ordering round after round of finger foods, and cheering the sports games on the television as Trevor put his hard-earned cash from the Arbiter to good use.

"Aw, I never thought of it like that!" Terrati attempted to wipe the tears from his eyes as he tried to control his laughter, only succeeding in rubbing his forehead instead.

"Whoa, maybe we should just call it a night for you." Trevor chuckled as the gazelle nearly swooned into his lap. "I may like to be close to my bros, but not that close!" He helped Terrati back up to sitting straight beside him.

He waved off Trevor with a limp hoof. "I'll be fine. Just need a break," he slurred.

"Uh-huh, and I'm a High Council elder. I think I'm calling it for you, young buck." He made a signal over to the bartender that his tab was to close. "Besides, we should probably start thinking about figuring out how we're going to get home. You think you can make it back to your place on your own, or are you going to crash at my place?"

This question got Terrati serious. He stared into his near empty glass of Tallup. "I actually don't have a place to stay here. My girlfriend kicked me out before I even got back. Before she came along, I just always bunked down with Fey and Finnley. Fey had always looked out for me, and when I was floundering under my own bills, he just up and helped me sell my meek apartment and move in with him."

"Why then did you split from them and hang with Mikhail and Natalia?" Trevor set his drink down. He wanted to know how this group of mercenaries ticked. It seemed there was a clear divide between the five, with Terrati in the middle.

Terrati hiccupped. "I guess I'm just indecisive. Part of me wanted nothing more to do with Taylor and just to leave with Fey and Finnley when we first got back into Zabökar. The other part was curious to see what happened to her. She is quite the extraordinary specimen."

"Specimen, huh?" Trevor snorted. "Is that how you view her these days?"

Terrati frowned. "I wasn't meaning that. I know she's a person. I just know how many would view her. People like the council. She can heal people, even from death! That's something modern medicine has a hard time doing! She could be very valuable."

"Then you realized how much trouble she actually was." Trevor rubbed his chin.

"A lot of trouble." He nodded, downing the rest of his Tallup before setting the glass on the table, nearly causing it to tip over.

"Think calling Fey might be a good idea tonight? I can stay with you until they come to pick you up," Trevor offered. Although they were on opposites sides once, Terrati wasn't a bad guy. He had an amazing wealth of experiences that most people could only dream of, and that was just looking past his initial timid exterior.

Terrati stared glumly at the table. "Yeah. I think that would be good." He fumbled around his slacks pocket and pulled out his phone. He called Fey first. He grimaced at the disconnected tone. "That's odd." He tried Finnley next. Same thing. He hung up and dropped the phone to the table. "Both lines are disconnected. I wasn't aware they cancelled their phone lines."

"And there's no other way of contacting them?"

He shook his head. "No. Not unless they check their email constantly, but they said they're heading out of town soon anyway, so…"

385

Trevor regarded the gazelle a few moments. He did look quite pitiful just sitting there all flaccid. With his primary residence currently unattainable and Mikhail and Natalia off to gods knew where, Trevor was stuck with him. Guess Terrati could crash at his place for a bit, but he was planning to head out of Zabökar shortly too, and never come back. Terrati would need to reconnect with Fey before then, because he certainly wasn't taking on extra weight upon leaving.

His eyes and ears focused on the sudden trill of the emergency alert as all the televisions in the tavern turned rainbow colors for a few moments. The din of the patrons died down as the broadcast aired. The screen changed to one of a helicopter flying through the night sky near the Grunnesh Mountains southwest of here. Other choppers were flitting in and out of view of the cameraman. It appeared to be a whole contingent of reporting aircraft hovering together.

"What we're seeing is a behemoth crossing over the barrier ridge near the town of Herron. It was spotted and reported by the local populace earlier this evening at around 1930 local time. There is no indication of its intended course of travel, but be advised that contact with Zabökar could be imminent within a day or two. Residents are strongly encouraged to begin making plans on—" The signal cut off and the rainbow emergency screen popped on, followed almost immediately by the previous programming.

Both Trevor and Terrati sobered up pretty quick. "How many people do you think saw that broadcast?" Terrati asked.

"I don't know. May not have been many. It's pretty late at night, and most people are either asleep or drunk or in places that may not have TV or radio. Judging by how quickly that got silenced, something tells me the higher-ups do not want the people of Zabökar to know."

"To prevent a panic?" Terrati looked around as the patrons began to get restless and started forming a line to pay their bills before hastily leaving. Some simply snuck out, they noticed, without even doing that.

Trevor nodded. "Possibly. Question is, why? Not wanting to have a panicked evacuation of the entire city is preferable, but the fact nothing has been done about it even now is concerning. If they're this close, something should have been done long before now. They're controlling the information for a reason, and I bet you not for a good one." He looked at the watch he had bought earlier that day as a gift for himself from Gregor's share. He would have wanted Trevor to have it. "Looks like my timetable has been moved up a fair bit."

"There's no way they can evacuate a city this big. They should have started days, even weeks ago!" Terrati nearly wailed, his senses addled enough by the alcohol to be oblivious to his own volume.

Trevor's phone buzzed in his pocket. Pulling it out, he spied Jake's number. Furrowing his brow, he picked up the call. "Hey, Jake! Bun buddy! What's up? Did you get your darling wolf all sorted out? Did you get the closure you needed?"

"I…did." Jake's voice seemed shaky, which caused Trevor's senses to trigger. "She's gone, Trevor. Her tail tried to eat…um…this tiger, Mikhail, and then tried to snap at me after I had talked with her. It's a long story. But now this reptile, I think Ari is her name, ran off after her and now we don't know where she is either."

"Shit." Trevor knew this was not going to be good for anyone. Two crazy, powered mammals loose in a city was a recipe for disaster. Sure it was like that not even a day ago, but at least they were roughly on the same side, but now with Taylor having run away again, they were most definitely not together. "Where are you now, Jake?"

"I'm with Mikhail. With Ari gone, we've lost our primary ability to track Taylor, so we need someone who can catch her scent so we can find her before Ari does."

"Jake, I'm glad you found Taylor and all, but what does what happens to her matter to you anymore? You got your closure like you wanted for your friend, isn't that enough? Something big is coming this way, and I'd rather you get out of dodge before it hits."

"I know about it. This behemoth. They were telling me about it. That's why I want to find Taylor, so she isn't around when it gets here."

Trevor put his iron paw to his head in exasperation. "Why though? What's so important about her? It's not like she's family! Get out of town!"

Jake's voice was now firm. "Because I promised her family that I'd watch over her. I've nothing left in this city worth a damn, Trevor. My last real friend died a few days ago and I'm stuck in a dead-end job with no future for me except sponsorship—something I don't want. Doing the one, last damned thing asked of me by a wolf I respected is all I have left to give my life meaning. Do you have any idea what that means to me? A rabbit?"

Trevor sighed and slumped in his chair. "Yeah...I think I do. Just text me your location and I'll come find you. See you soon, buddy." He hung up with a scowl.

"Are we getting pulled back in?" Terrati seemed miserable, talking louder than normal.

"I'm afraid so." Trevor attempted to shush his volume.

"But why?" Terrati looked so confused. "We both agreed Taylor was nothing but trouble and we were done with her."

"That we did." Trevor massaged his forehead roughly. "The only reason I'm doing this is for Jake. That silly rabbit who has the balls to white knight for this wolf and her tailmaw. If it weren't for Gregor, I probably wouldn't even be considering this."

Terrati tilted his head. "What's Gregor have to do with this?"

"He always had a soft spot for rabbits. True, he used them like everyone else does, but he treated them nicer, like actual people. It could have been any rabbit in Zabökar, but I'm choosing this one to save. For Gregor." He looked up at the ceiling. "Don't say I never did anything for the less fortunate, buddy." He sighed, struggling to stand up. "Let's pay the tab and get going."

"I don't think I'm that stable." Terrati nearly stumbled.

"Doesn't matter." Trevor belched, holding Terrati by an arm. "We got a rabbit to save, and by extension a young wolf. Let's get our shit together and go do this so we can hightail it from here before it all hits the fan." At a sudden thought, he took a still filled shot glass before raising in the air in a toast. "To you, Gregor."

The scene blurred into view. Murana seemed smaller than before, sitting cradled in Sebastian's lap in a large, plush chair. Beyond them was a cozy bedroom with strung-up lights on wires crisscrossing the room over a large, king-sized bed. The amber glow from the bulbs gave off a warm feeling that was no doubt the intention of Sebastian to give Murana the best environment possible for her final days.

Sebastian squeezed Murana's shoulders, giving her encouragement as he held her up against his chest. It was clear the cancer was destroying her body, and it had accelerated to a pace she was unable to keep up with. Barely able to do much but lift her head and stare at the camera, she appreciated the nuzzle from him as he did his best to keep her aloft. Her limbs were shrunken and bone structure was now present both under her fur and on her face. It wouldn't be long now.

She gathered her strength and stared directly into the lens. She spoke, wincing in pain as she did so. "Taylor, honey... I love you so much. I'm so very sorry for all the times I was harsh on you, but I want you to know that I only ever wanted what was best for you. If you haven't already, you'll soon find out that there are people who want you for what you are, and they are not nice people."

Murana hacked hard, causing her entire body to convulse, blood spattering off-screen as Sebastian looked pained at how miserable the love of his life was. He covered for her as she struggled to put a cloth to her mouth. "Murana has spent the last three years gathering information, videos, voice recordings, and more from the police, her High Council-appointed counselor, and more...most likely breaking a few laws to acquire these bits of evidence." His expression indicated he didn't approve of her methods, but he was supportive all the same of the end result.

Images and videos began to display as Murana pushed a few buttons off screen to route to the stream she was recording on the computer she was building this all on. Sebastian continued to speak for her. "We are arranging and saving all this data that you see before you now on a small chip that can be accessed and viewed at your leisure. Everything you see here will prove beyond a doubt the corruption that lies within Zabökar at the highest level."

The images flashing past the screen showed damning evidence of the High Council members collaborating with masked individuals, and even participating in the kidnapping of several young cubs and kits.

Videos of them practicing unholy rituals on young children and sacrifices were shown in all their visible, gory display.

Tears were beginning to form around Murana's eyes. She gestured to the screen. "My younger brother was abused, tortured, molested, and sacrificed by being burned alive before my eyes when I was a child by these very same people. They set my life on a path of despair and vengeance that it has taken decades to even recover from. To this day, I am still in their shadow. Now these same vile monsters have infiltrated the High Council and every facet of our government." There was quivering rage rattling in her voice.

Sebastian patted her on the shoulder to rest so he could speak next. "They are called Children of the Unwritten Script, although you may now have heard of them as power-eaters. They are one and the same cult. Their goal has been, and always has been, the eradication of the Script. To that end, they have delved deep into occult practices to rid themselves of the Script's influence, even at the harm of young children and other unfortunate victims to their rituals."

Sebastian looked just as angry as Murana. "Seeking more power and resources to combat the Script, they have weaseled and connived their way into positions of lofty power unbeknownst to the greater public or their peers in the field. These power-eaters are the same ones who allowed the Arbiter to make his DNA ray in secret and to experiment on other mammals. Once they saw the promise that these mammals had on influencing the Script, they launched a campaign to end his operations so they could benefit."

Holding up a paw to Sebastian, indicating she was ready to speak again, she raised her eyes back to the camera. "So a Manchas Wendell snuck into the Zabökar police department and tasked me to go undercover to report on all that the Arbiter had been doing. I gave them everything. I blew the whistle on his entire operation and provided the police the means to find all the affected children. This was so to not have anything link back to the council."

"Then something went wrong. Several people within the Arbiter's ranks and in the police force were power-eaters themselves, and they botched the entire thing prior to the sting. Hundreds if not thousands of the afflicted mammals were let loose into the underbelly of

Zabökar, and I was caught and pulsed as a result. Some were captured immediately by the power-eaters and consumed to gain their powers, but a majority were able to escape and find homes and refuges to hide. All this time, the Arbiter was unaware he was being manipulated into providing fodder for the power-eaters to rewrite Script." Murana shivered visibly, as if a cold wind had chilled her to the bone.

Sebastian wrapped the pink wool blanket tighter around her as he gave her cheek a comforting lick. Settling her back down against his chest, he pressed on for her. "Murana was rescued, but Wendell was nowhere to be found. We cannot prove it yet, but we both suspect he was working for the power-eaters within the High Council, and allowed Murana to be captured to see what would happen if she was exposed to the DNA ray while pregnant."

Sebastian bared his teeth. "It was all some sick experiment to see if the unborn child would produce extraordinary results. Unfortunately for you, Taylor, you did. They immediately offered a lucrative deal of surveyed monitoring as you grew, in exchange for money. They were curious about you and what extent you were capable of influencing the Script. Your mom here though—" He gave her shoulders a squeeze. "—stonewalled them every chance she got. She knew something was not right, and forbade them from ever being alone with you."

Murana's voice sounded raspy now, tired from the strain of speaking so much, but she needed to get this all out. "They lost interest in you when it was clear you weren't providing the results they expected. Ahya was uninteresting to them, and did not indicate anything remotely useful for their plans, so they stopped monitoring us. It wasn't until Ahya ate Sarah that opportunity arose for them. If they had stripped you from me and tried you for murder, it was an easy way for them to take you from me to experiment on or worse, eat you for whatever powers they felt you had."

"That's when she left me," Sebastian interjected. "I was distraught, not knowing what I had done wrong. I had no idea where you two had gone for years until she called me one day crying, saying that you had run away."

Murana placed a loving, apologetic paw on his. "We've since made up, but ever since that day, I was on the run with you. True to my prediction, they were hunting us. They were hunting you. That is why we never stayed in one place for more than a few months. That is why you never went back to school anymore, or made any more friends. That is why we always had to eat scraps and steal for basic necessities like clothes and food. That is why I always left you alone in our safe-houses while I did my research and gathered evidence to indict them of all their crimes."

She shakily wiped her lip as she felt another drop of blood trickle. "I'm so sorry for the life I had you live these past few years, Taylor. Your mother was never much of a good person. Because of them, these Children of the Unwritten Script, my life was turned upside down and I was pushed to revenge. I was a terrible person for years, hunting them down and killing them. I had become that which I hated for decades. It tore at my soul, and made me a worse person for it."

Sebastian shifted his focus from Murana to the camera. "Which is why she will be unable to blow their cover on her own. She has too many dirty stains on her history to be taken remotely seriously, no matter how damning the evidence. They would shut her testimony down. She tried to turn her life around when forced to work for the police, and then later becoming a fully recognized officer, but it won't be enough to clear her entire record...especially after she ran off with you after killing Sarah."

Murana was sickly, but she stared determined at the screen. "This is why I am entrusting all this data over to you, Taylor. I wish it had never come to this, that I could have no one else to trust. Sebastian is already implicated by sheltering me, so he can't do this either. I'm going to die soon, and I'd rather he live the rest of his life away from the fear of being followed every day. I couldn't bear to leave him with that, and I couldn't lay this on your brothers since they are still free and clear of this mess."

She pointed at Sebastian to get something for her. Placing the chain across her finger, she lifted up a pine-tree necklace. "We will be uploading all this to you on a hidden chip within this necklace tab. I have entrusted a rabbit named Jake Thumpings with the knowledge of this chip and how to access it. He is someone you can rely on. He has been watching you for weeks now, and is letting me know you are safe. He can be trusted. I will give him this to give to you once we've finished. I pray that you'll keep it."

She brought it to her nose and sniffed it. "It still has the scent of the forest, much like the same kind your brother, Steven, got for me with earrings just like these. I figured it would be a good reminder of my love for you, and that you still have older brothers you can rely on for support if necessary. Please don't shun them too. They do not deserve that."

Taking back the necklace from Murana and setting it down, Sebastian leaned forward to hold her tight. "She and I will respect the distance you wish to have right now, Taylor, but know that we both love you very much. We do not expect you to blow this corruption wide open yourself. That would put you in far too much danger. However, if you can find someone you trust to broadcast this to the entire city, you will go a long way in destroying their plans and hopefully getting a bunch of them behind bars where they belong."

Murana began crying again. "I'm so sorry to have to dump all of this onto you, Taylor. It should never have been your responsibility to bear, but mine. However, I am too weak and frail to go on anymore. Cursed by the decisions and lies made by those above me, put in the path of the Arbiter and his fucking DNA ray. You lost a sister to that awful thing. I was to have twins…two girls. I just hope that wherever your sister is, that she is at peace. I never got to meet her, but I am glad to have met you…for as long as I loved you."

She kissed her fingers and pressed it against the lens, smudging its view. "You are my little girl. I love you more than life itself. I'm sorry I wasn't the best mother to you, but I did my best to give you a good life. Please forgive your mother, she never meant to push you away. I just want to see you succeed. Please come back to me…"

"Please come back to both of us," Sebastian agreed, resting his head on Murana's. She leaned up into his neck, taking comfort in his warmth. "Your mother is in good hands. I hope this gets to you. We look forward to being a family again. Please be safe, and let's hope we can kick these bastards where it hurts."

"Bye, baby…" Murana waved feebly, her hand dropping to her lap, her eyes ever-lingering on the camera, as if looking directly at Taylor before Sebastian leaned over to turn it off.

Taylor was bunched up on the chair, knees to her chest, crying when the final video ended. There was more files and incriminatory documents about the High Council on the chip, but she didn't care about that right now. The one thing she knew for certain was how much her mom loved her.

The true scope of her teenage years slammed into view. She had explanations for everything that happened to her. It was all right here.

She turned her head to regard her tail. It had slowly risen off the floor the more she watched their mother's last message. By the end, Ahya was just as engrossed as Taylor was. Now they were looking at each other in silence. Taylor put out a paw and pressed softly into the fur, feeling the wrinkled skin beneath. Ahya leaned into the touch and seemed to relish the affection.

Taylor couldn't stop crying. "Are we… Are we sisters?" She raised her other paw to grip the other side of Ahya, facing her directly. "Is that why you keep giving me a hard time in life?" She attempted to laugh through the tears. She sniffled hard, shaking her head. "Doesn't matter if you are or not. I'm going to consider you one. Mother said she was to have twins… Maybe that's exactly what she had? Maybe that's why the Arbiter said I have two strands of DNA in me?"

She moved forward to embrace her tail, wrapping her arms tightly around the tip. Ahya's maw opened as her tongue slithered out to curl around Taylor's neck, petting her shoulders gently. They held on to each other for what felt like minutes. Two sisters finally discovering each other after so long thinking they were not.

Taylor whispered into the tail fur. "I'm so sorry I hurt you, Ahya. I just… I just hate some of the things you do. I wish you could talk so that I could understand." She exhaled a ragged breath. "I always wished for a sister, I just never thought it would be like this." She chuckled again through the tears, hiccupping as she did so.

Her eyes shot open as she remembered what they had done together on Nina's bed the previous night. "Oh gods…" She released her tail suddenly and straightened herself in the chair, facing the computer head on. "Yeah, we're not going to do that again," she mumbled to herself, leaving a very "confused" Ahya hanging in the air.

She perused the remaining documents, and the more she scoured them, the angrier she got. A plan began to form in her mind, getting more solid with every article she read and video she watched. With a growl, she shot up out of the chair and barreled back into the main den. All eyes turned to her. The four of them were watching some music videos. Ramon had not dared to show his face yet.

Nina was the first to rise. "Well? Was it what you expected or wanted?"

Taylor's face was set in grim determination. "It was…and more." She locked eyes with Loray and Bailey. "We're doing that concert tomorrow night. Nina and I will be there."

"Wait… I am?" Nina sputtered.

"I knew it!" Loray whooped, a few quills shooting into the couch protector from excitement. "We're going to sell so many tickets with you! We should headline you!"

Bailey roused enough to comment, "But isn't she being hunted by the police? Won't they arrest her at the concert?"

Taylor had an evil glint in her eye. "Not if what Loray is saying is true. The crowd is going to want to come see me. Might as well give them what they want. The mob would not dare let the cops touch me during the concert."

"But what's the point?!" Nina was so flustered a few feathers were molting from her wings. "You're chancing your own safety by doing all this!"

"Do you recall the lyrics to one of our songs, *Bring the Fall?*" Nina nodded nervously. Taylor snapped her fingers. "We're going to do that, but on the scale of the whole city!"

Samantha clapped her paws. "Oh, this sounds exciting! Can I have an exclusive backstage pass at the concert?!"

395

Taylor grinned at her. "Sure, why not? You can help too!"

Samantha's smile faded. "But what about Jake?"

Taylor winked. "I hope he comes too. We're going to ring out the end of Zabökar with a bang! I have a plan!" Ahya's mouth was wide open, teeth menacingly bared and tongue whipping around with wild, gleeful abandon. Samantha squealed in delight that the tail was actually real.

18.

CELLPHONE

The sun's rays were just starting to turn a reddish tinge, heralding the coming of the evening. They had gotten a lot done that following day, and she was surprised it all went so smooth. She was petting Ahya, who was now the vibrant red that she always was. Taylor was just putting on the finishing touches to her fur paint job on her tail, drawing angry eye lines to simulate that Ahya had a face. She was going to give what fans wanted once again.

Ahya seemed to enjoy the attention, and looked proud of her new look. She was baring her teeth at the glass as they both occupied the bay window perch. Taylor was looking out at the city above and below her vantage point. She was getting butterflies. What was going to happen tonight would change her entire life, she just knew it.

Feeling anxious, she brought out the phone Ari had given her. There weren't many contacts in the device, but she did have Liam's card in her jeans pocket. She had no idea why she decided to call him now, of all times, but he seemed the best person to be objective about her position currently. She dialed his number and held the phone to her ear. It rang and rang until the voicemail picked up.

She frowned, but decided she might as well leave a message. "Hey Liam, it's me, Taylor. I know it's a bit weird calling you like this out of the blue, but you did say I should call you if I needed a ticket out of Zabökar. I mean, there is still one last thing I need to do before I leave tonight. We're performing this concert down at the Real at nine o'clock. I've asked Stepan to get the word out to all the rabbits."

She nervously cleared her throat. "I know you said this deal with the rabbits was a stupid idea, but I got another plan in mind for them. I think once they see what I have to show them at the concert, their

398

destructive riot should be channeled to a more focused location. Less widespread death, I hope."

Taylor scratched a spot under Ahya's maw, drawing a pleased response. "How can I explain… My mother left a message for me that revealed the corruption of the High Council, and that the people making the laws and enforcing them are not duly elected leaders at all, but fanatic cultists who eat people in secret. Yeah, I know that sounds really crazy. I couldn't believe it myself, but it's true!"

Taylor was miffed as the voicemail cut off her message, its length too long. She dialed again, waiting for it to pick up before she resumed. "All I ask is that you attend the concert and then take me and some of my friends away from here. It would mean a lot if you could come. Why? I'm not sure myself, but you were really nice to me, and I'd like to sing for you." She pulled the phone away from her ear briefly. That was probably a bit too weird.

Bringing it back to her ear, she continued. "You know what, never mind that. Just come, ok? Loray and I got with my brother Steven to advertise the concert on social networks, and Bailey drafted up a poster and got with Stepan to spread the word about it. You can't miss them. I even got my picture taken for the poster with my original red-furred look. Loray said it was the best idea since people would want to see me front and center in the band."

Taylor paused a moment. "Liam, I'm sorry if I disappointed you. I'm not just some little, teenage girl running around making stupid decisions. I really am trying to do the right thing. I owe it to my mother to get this last message of hers out to the people of Zabökar. After that, I can go, but this is just something I need to do. Something I owe it to my family to see through. It may not make sense to you, but it's everything to me right now. I hope to see you there. Bye, Liam."

Nina popped into her view as she put the cellphone back into her pocket. "I didn't know you had a cellphone plan already. You just got here a few days ago." Nina chuckled, holding a plate of scrambled eggs with sliced avocado and tomatoes.

"The phone isn't actually mine. Ari gave it to me when we first went topside here." She pointed at the plate. "Is that for me? Whose eggs are those?" She regarded it suspiciously.

Nina looked disapprovingly at the phone bulge in Taylor's pocket after her explanation, but dismissed it. "Mine, actually. Remember I had a bit leftover from my previous batch? Figured they'd do no good wasting away at my apartment getting stolen by whichever cop fancied some eggs. Better bring them here and save them for my best friend!"

"Again…you didn't have to." Taylor graciously took the plate and recalling how amazing her eggs tasted last time, began scooping them politely into her mouth.

"For you, I'd lay a hundred!" Nina chuckled, wringing her wings as she watched Taylor consume the late lunch. "Are they okay? I always feel so weird asking that, but since I did produce them, I feel like I have a personal stake in how they taste. I know it's silly."

Taylor licked her muzzle. She finished that faster than she anticipated. Guess she was hungrier than she thought. "They were delicious. Probably even better than last time!" She handed the empty plate back to Nina who took it with excitement.

"I'm so happy!" She blushed before turning an evil eye to Loray and Bailey, back in their usual positions. "Those boys didn't make it easy. I had to clean up that entire damn kitchen of theirs before I could even see the countertop space I had available to work with to cook this!"

It was Taylor's turn to blush. "You did all that…for me?"

"Well, of course! I am certainly not going to do it for those two knuckleheads on the couch over there. My exquisite product would be wasted on them anyway." She flapped a wing at them. "Neither one is a true predator, so they have no need to curb any such cravings."

"Mmm, I think Ahya helps me curb those cravings just fine, Nina." Taylor patted her tail, who was in much better spirits than the previous night.

"Still… I wouldn't mind being the one to curb your cravings." Nina blushed hard as Taylor looked away embarrassed. "So, when do you think you'll be telling me what was on your mother's necklace— besides the fact your tail is your sister—or am I going to find out alongside everyone else tonight?" Nina smirked, changing subject.

"I figured it would be a surprise to everyone. Don't worry, it'll be a good one. I know you and I both hate being told what to do by those in authority over us, and this information is really going to fuck them over." They each shared an evil smile.

"I should hope so! If it's about my dad, I really hope it embarrasses the hell out of him!"

Taylor didn't say anything. She was unsure if the truth of Nina's father was known or not to Nina, or how she would react if it wasn't. Taylor still didn't know if the entire council was compromised, or just part of it. Murana was resolute about trusting no one with this information, which was why it pained Taylor that she had to keep it a secret still from even Nina. That and the fact her own mother was responsible for Nina's brother's deaths also wouldn't sit well, Taylor wagered. Best to keep that to herself.

"We'll see. You seem much more receptive to performing on stage with us now. What changed?" Taylor wrapped her arms around her knees, waiting for the answer.

Nina frowned, unsure of how to respond. "I honestly didn't want to, but since it seems like you are hellbent on leaving Zabökar after tonight, I consider this one last hurrah for all of us."

"Except for Ramon."

Nina chuckled. "Yes, except for Ramon. Fuck him. He doesn't deserve to be on stage with us." They both laughed at this.

"Are you coming with me when I leave, Nina?" Taylor's eyes beseeched Nina. Despite her oddities and secrets Taylor knew she kept, she felt comfortable around her, and truly did want her to come run away with her. She could use a friend in her corner, not just her brothers.

"Well, you know I would love to…" she began, but was interrupted by a phone call. She took the buzzing cell out and checked the number. She had an unreadable look, but she was staring at the number for what seemed like a full minute. On the last ring, she picked it up. "I'm sorry, Taylor. I need to take this."

Taylor was confused, and looked after Nina as she walked off miserable, phone to her head listening. Samantha saw her opportunity and got up from the couch, promptly plopping herself down on the bay window seat opposite Taylor, forcing Ahya to be hastily moved out of the way before she was sat on. They each stared at each other for an awkwardly long time without saying anything.

"Can I help you, Samantha?" Taylor squirmed a bit back against the wall.

"I know Nina told me what happened, but you and Jake really didn't have sex?" Samantha's face looked pitiful, like her heart would break if Taylor said yes.

Taylor rolled her eyes. "For the last time, no! Nothing happened. It ultimately was one big misunderstanding. 'Your' Jake is still an eligible bachelor to sponsor." As friendly as Samantha was, she still had this annoying fixation on rabbits, and on Jake in particular.

The red panda breathed a sigh of relief. "That good! He really is a sweetie. I'm actually so happy he finally managed to get your mother's last message to you. He held onto that for such a long time! It goes to show how caring and dedicated he is! That's one of the reasons I love him."

"I'm sure." Taylor thought about it a bit, looking the small panda up and down. "Hey, Samantha, is it possible you could do me a favor?"

"Of course, anything!" She seemed a bit too bubbly for Taylor's tastes.

"You have Jake's number, right?" Samantha nodded enthusiastically. "Okay, good. If something happens tonight…and I'm not able to meet up with you, Jake, or anyone else, can you reach out to him and take him out of Zabökar tonight? Maybe to that ranch that you own."

"Yes! I was planning to do that anyway!" She giggled. "I am going to sponsor him, after all!"

Taylor raised a single finger. "If that's what he wants. I only said to take him to the ranch and away from here. Anything else beyond that is up to him, as it should be." She looked at Samantha dead in the eyes to ensure she got her point across.

The red panda looked suddenly put out from the realization of what Taylor was asking. "Right. I need to consider his feelings too. I think I understand, Taylor."

Taylor smiled finally at her. "I'm trying to account for everyone here. I know that I may not be able to round everyone up in one nice, big group and all leave together—not with what is going to be probably happening tonight."

Samantha looked out of the bay window. "Yeah, I don't think what you're doing tonight is going to be stopping Stepan and the rabbits from rioting. I do understand your reasoning though for wanting to delay them. I don't want to see my home get torn up either."

"But it can at least distract and redirect them to a more worthwhile target. Hopefully my songs and the message my mom left will be enough to guide them to where I want their righteous rage to go."

"You're very brave," Samantha said suddenly. "My entire life I've just been flying under the radar, just doing what was expected of me. But you... You have raged against the system, ran from the cops, and forged a new life for yourself here it seems. You're taking risks and promoting this concert using your face as the draw knowing full well the police are looking for you, and many people have seen you murder someone on live TV. You're fearless. Something I won't ever be."

"That's not really something to aspire to..." Taylor was caught off guard by the response.

Taylor was seeing a new side to Samantha. She was stuck in the ways trained and ingrained into her during her formative years in Zabökar—something Taylor never received since her mother kept strict control over the household and what Taylor was ingesting from society. There were a lot of annoying traits Samantha picked up, like the attitudes towards rabbits, but Taylor attributed that mainly to her schooling rather than any of Samantha's personal held beliefs.

"That's also not entirely true," Taylor assured. "You were at that rally last night. You were there hoping to make a difference. That's a big step."

Samantha shook her head. "More like pretending I was. Look, I just love rabbits. I want to be serviced by as many rabbits as I can, but that doesn't mean I want to abuse them or take advantage of them!" She saw the look Taylor was giving her. "Hey, I just like them a lot! More so than my own kind! Now you got me overthinking about what I'm doing with Jake and the two I've already sponsored and…ugh." She put both paws to her head, covering her face. "I'm a mess."

Taylor reached out to put a paw on Samantha's knee. "It's okay. I'm a mess too. I'm just happy you're starting to see things the way I do about rabbits. To tell you the truth, I'm pretty scared right now. I'm wondering if all I'm doing is the right decision. I've been wrong in the past before, and others have paid the consequences. I sometimes feel like I'm just a small pup again in a world full of adults, just trying to stumble through life and hoping each choice I make isn't something that'll screw me over."

"You sure don't seem like it. You seem very confident." Samantha looked up at Taylor, their size difference evident as they sat across from each other on the ledge.

"Only because I don't know how else to act. To me, this is just being normal. To others, they call it confidence." They both chuckled. "I just hope what we're doing tonight goes as planned. Nothing I've ever done goes to plan, so I'm hoping this one just might."

"It was really smart to advertise your tail. It looks like fans remember you." Samantha pointed down through the glass at the alley below.

"Oh wow." Taylor pressed up against the glass as she got a better view. There was already a crowded line on the sidewalk for the Real just five blocks down the street. What concerned her more, however, was the police presence beside them. "You aren't kidding."

"I think your little selfie stunt I suggested worked." Samantha smirked. "Your post went viral."

Taylor did not want to look at the red panda, feeling her cheeks flush. The last thing she wanted to be reminded about was how exposed she felt "advertising" that Ahya was in fact real, and not a stage prop, to countless unknown viewers on Nina's social media account. "Don't remind me," Taylor muttered.

"So, can I see her fully?"

This ratcheted Taylor's attention back to Samantha. "What? You mean Ahya?"

She nodded vigorously. "I was never able to attend your concerts when *Bad Luck* was still in the club circuit. By the time I had heard of your music, you were long gone and the band was dissolved. I never did get to see Ahya up on stage banging out those drums or snapping at the crowd to their cheers. All I had was some shaky phone footage to go by to experience it."

Taylor felt self-conscious. This was the second person in recent months to want to see her tail in all its glory and know more about it. "Alright." She hesitantly gave Ahya control.

The tail rose up and expanded over the small red panda, whose eyes were entranced at the gaping maw growing larger over her head. Its teeth were sharp and menacing, tongue dripping saliva onto her pants—a fact she was either unaware of while in the moment or didn't care. The size of that maw was large enough to swallow Samantha whole, should Ahya get the urge to chomp down on the hapless girl. Taylor was tense as she readied herself to take immediate control in case it went south.

"Wow, how did you get one of these?" Samantha's eyes were rapt on the cavernous darkness inside the tail.

Taylor put a paw on Ahya to steady her and hopefully remind not to do anything rash. "I was born with her."

She finally looked back at Taylor's eyes. "And you said she's your sister?"

Taylor regarded her tail thoughtfully. "I believe so. That's what I want to think going forward. There will always be that question if she is or isn't, but I'd like to believe she is."

"But she tried to eat others before. Harmed some of your friends, I recall you mentioning. Why do you think she did those things?" Samantha now just began to brush off the spit on her pants.

There was a pained expression on Taylor's muzzle as she remembered the look on Jake's face in the graveyard after Ahya attempted to hurt him. "I don't know. If she could talk, I would want to know the same." This triggered Ahya to close her mouth, retract back to a smaller size, and turn to Taylor in curiosity. "I really wish we could communicate, Ahya. So you could explain to me why I had to go through the crap I did because of your actions."

"You think she purposefully meant to do those things?" Samantha's paw hung in the air as if in an unspoken attempt to ask to touch Ahya.

"I hope not. I have a hard time trusting her at all these days. It would be awful if I found out I couldn't trust her period. Especially after I found out she's my sister."

"Such an odd thing to have—a sister for a tail."

"Lucky me."

Probably realizing that the request would be too forward, Samantha brought her paw down and looked away towards Loray and Bailey, then Nina pacing in the kitchen on the phone. "What are we going to do now?"

Taylor relaxed back up against the window frame, enjoying the last few rays of sunlight. "Nothing. We've done all we could. I needed Steven to let me into the ZCN tower with Bailey so we could hijack the city's fiber signal for tonight. Bailey couldn't get in himself to do the job and Steven didn't know how to hack the signal, so Nina suggested I could sneak Bailey under my shirt since the DNA scanners downtown and in the building can't pick me up while Steven let us in."

"That's really clever! And Steven was okay with you two messing with his job's fiber infrastructure?"

Taylor smiled in a mischievous way. "I wouldn't say he was happy about it, but thankfully my other brother, Max, got to him first, and had already convinced him to leave Zabökar before I showed up. I don't know how he did it, but he got Steven to turn in his two week notice and agree to leave the city tonight. Allowing us into restricted areas of his job site wasn't as big a deal to him anymore."

"So they won't be at the concert then?"

Taylor's expression dropped. "No. I would have loved to have them there, especially Max who could whack those drums like nobody's business!" She gazed out down the alley again to spy a homeless person delving around a trashcan. "They're probably on the highway out of Zabökar by now."

"That's a shame."

"I'm trying my best to get those I love out of here before…" Her voice trailed off.

406

Samantha tilted her head. "Before what?"

"Nothing... Just promise me if you see Jake before I do, concert or no concert, just take him far away from here."

"I promise I will." Samantha was serious about it.

"Thank you." As much as she disliked the idea of Jake being with Samantha, she couldn't get mired in the thoughts of being possessive over him. He was a rabbit and his own person. He could choose whom he wanted. Samantha was still the best chance for him to get away from Zabökar before a behemoth blew it to smithereens.

Taylor was stressed. There were too many variables to consider, and that still wasn't accounting for Mikhail and Natalia. If they meant what they said and only wanted to protect her, shouldn't she help get them out too? Taylor still needed to stay, at least through the concert, because it would be her last chance to get her mother's last wish accomplished. There wouldn't be another time where so many elements aligned this perfectly to broadcast her last message.

Samantha bundled up excited on the ledge. "So, are you all ready for tonight?"

Taylor shrugged, looking over at Nina who had just hung up the phone. She appeared to be very troubled. "I hope so. We rehearsed a bit this morning. We're going to fall back onto a bunch of our old standbys, none of this *Horny Toads* crap. I even wrote up some lyrics for a new song we can just sing over an existing tune tonight. I'm rather proud of it." Her eyes continued to follow Nina as she made a beeline for the two of them at the bay window.

"Taylor, where did you say your phone was from?" Nina asked sternly, wings on her hips.

"From Ari. I told you this. What's going on? Hey!" Taylor struggled as Nina jammed a wing into her pocket and yanked out the cellphone. Ahya was already open, teeth bared, bewildered as to what was going on.

"Last night, you told us she found you again without ever knowing you were at the Marsh House." She held it up for all to see. Even Loray and Bailey were looking up over the backing of the couch at her. "Ari is tracking you with this! She probably already knows where you are right now!"

407

"What are you doing?!" Taylor made a grab for it, but it was too late. Nina had opened the side window of the bay and threw the phone out to where it smashed onto the concrete alley below. "What the hell, Nina?"

"Like you had an attachment to it, Taylor." She scoffed. "It wasn't even your phone anyway!"

"Yeah, but it had numbers of people I would like to keep in contact with! Like my brothers, Jake, and Liam!"

"Who is even Liam?" Nina threw her wings up.

"Doesn't matter now! Who were you talking to?" Taylor made a grab for Nina's pants pocket, but she just fluttered away to the other side of the couch. "You were on a long call with someone and then you come roaring over here chastising me over my phone usage. Who were you talking to?!" She repeated again with ire.

Before Nina could answer, the apartment door exploded inward, superheated hinges zinging off the glass coffee table, shattering it as the trash on top fell through. Slipping in through the door was the visage of Ari, her crooked smile and bulky shell taking up the entirety of the frame. She locked eyes on Taylor and began moving in her direction.

"You've been a very busy little bee, Taylor!" Ari cackled. "Promoting concerts and riling up the rabbit populace. I dare say you're doing a far better job of getting the High Council's attention than my father ever did, but can you gain their trust? Trust in the legitimacy of your words and my father's goal of defending Zabökar from my people?"

Taylor was immediately off the window seat, pushing Samantha behind her and towards the kitchenette. "The High Council are not the people you think they are. They would not listen to me anyway. Just give it up, Ari. Your dad sent us on a fool's errand. You were doomed to fail anyway from the start."

"I was not!" Ari raged.

Ari slapped the floor with her tail, shooting a streak of steaming carpet towards Taylor, the trail sinking a long hole to the floor below— its tenants visible as they stared up in horror at their ceiling melting before their eyes. Taylor squeezed through the window Nina had opened earlier just as the blistering conflagration reached the sill, exploding it upwards and shattering all the panes of glass outward.

"Everyone run!" Taylor shouted back inside before leaping from the metal catwalk balcony across to the fire escape on the building opposite. She nearly missed, Ahya reaching forward and catching the rungs on the floor above as Taylor slammed into the railing below. Grunting from the impact, she clambered over and sprawled out on the open metal floor beneath her.

"To think I was beginning to like you, Taylor," Ari spat, smashing the support beams of the primary panels of the bay window so she could step out as well. "Now you're really starting to piss me off." She looked down from the height with trepidation. "Damn it."

Ari lowered her fingers to the metal bars and trailed the heat along its length until it separated from the wall. Forcing it to propel one side of itself across the alley, it merged and fused with the catwalk railing opposite creating a haphazard bridge across. Taylor was already leaping up the flights of stairs two steps at a time. Her goal: the rooftops.

Ari calmly liquefied the metal around her and continued to manipulate it beneath her feet, pushing her up higher through fire escape. Each subsequent set of stairs was just more fodder for her rising, twisted elevator of molten metal. In no time at all, she was beside Taylor. She stopped short at the top of the next staircase, the roof still dozens of floors higher. Ari had blocked off her route.

"Don't make this harder than it has to be. You're a smart girl. I know this. Remember when you decided me over them?" Ari sneered.

"And I'm starting to question that decision." Taylor was beginning to develop sparks along her fingertips. This did not go unnoticed by Ari.

"So you feel being with the High Council now, the very one you say we can't trust, would have been the better alternative?"

"No." Taylor was looking all around for another way out. "I think neither one of you was a good choice. I was never given anything good to choose from."

She sighed. "Taylor, we could keep fighting all night long, but what would it accomplish? If I wanted you dead, I would have killed you already. We both know I have the power to do so."

"So you'll take me back, then what?" The ball of lightning was increasing in intensity above Taylor's palm. Ahya was looking vicious. The line of people waiting below were already pointing up at them and filming on their smart devices. "We both know there is little we can do against those behemoths coming this way. This city is a lost cause, and I think your father knew it!"

"That's for him to decide, not us!"

"Think for yourself for once, Ari!" Taylor yelled. "Why are you blindly following your father when it's clear he doesn't truly care about you?" She pointed at Ari's leg and eye. "No father who loves his daughter would put them through that shit!"

"You don't know a damn thing about our relationship!"

"You're right, I don't! But I do know what a loving one looks like! If what you and your father have is love, then I guess my childhood was damn right abusive!"

"Shut up!" Ari slapped her tail on the metal grating and blasted a pole directly at her. Taylor had only enough time to let loose the electricity from her fingers, causing a mini-shockwave as it slammed the heated metal tip deep into the brick siding of the building next to them.

"Don't harm my friend!" Nina swooped in from the sky behind Ari and kicked her, feet first, off her metal perch. Ari hit and crashed into several metal railings on the way down. The reptile gave a scream of fright, but did her best to retreat into her semi-effective shell to alleviate the worst of the impacts.

Nina alighted next to Taylor and offered her a wing. "Hold onto me tight. We're scaling this thing, mainly because you're too heavy for me to carry otherwise."

With the awkward grace of a swan with a wolf on her back, she climbed up the side of the fire escape, using her wings to gain the extra momentum that allowed them both to travel triple the speed than what Taylor was originally making on the stairs. They weren't far now from the roof when they heard a vengeful cry from below.

410

Taylor dared a glance down. Ari was now literally ripping the very ground and buildings around her apart, boosting her up the side of the building with their swiftly cooling debris. Taylor didn't know how much energy Ari had left in her, but if she knew Ari, she wouldn't stop until she had recaptured Taylor or exhausted herself completely doing so.

"We need to go!" Taylor squeezed around Nina's midsection.

"I'm going as fast as I can, but I'm tired now, Taylor!" She was breathing heavy.

A shocked cry from below caused both to stop and look. Another reptile had joined the fray and was fighting Ari up alongside the building. She was melting and pushing out patches of wall for step holds as she blasted flaming bricks at the darting and jumping chameleon. He was crawling on all fours along the walls, shifting colors to camouflage before leaping out to strike Ari again.

"What is that?"

"That's Rakkis," Taylor responded. She had hoped never to see that chameleon again. If he was fighting Ari now, then the Arbiter probably had a good reason to stop her from chasing them. "Let's just get to the rooftop first!"

They finally reached the top and collapsed together side by side. Spread eagle and looking up at the stars that were just barely visible through the haze of the city, they began to laugh at their fortunes of escaping Ari with their lives. The sounds of the fight had died off, and neither Rakkis nor Ari had shown their face above the edge of the rooftop. It seemed they were in the clear, yet neither wanted to look down to find out.

"Are Loray, Bailey, and Samantha all safe?" Taylor asked at last, her breath finally returning to normal.

Nina nodded. "They escaped with me shortly after Ari went out the window after you."

"That's good. She has a thing of not hurting my friends as some perverse way of gaining my trust. You could say I've wised up to that now." Taylor shifted onto her side, stuffing her pine tree necklace back into her shirt. She'd never let go of this thing as long as she lived.

"Oh?" She noticed that her small kitsune plush had slipped out as they were laying there. She picked it up.

"What is even the story behind that anyway?" Nina asked.

Taylor studied the multi-colored button eyes, its colors changing with the angle of light hitting it. "A reminder of the old magic of this world. A gift from…a person I guess you could say was a surrogate mother figure to me back when I was on the run."

"Do you believe in the old magic?" Nina got up and dusted herself off.

"I don't really know for sure, but it would certainly explain the weird things I can do as well as what Ari can do." She stuffed it back deep into her torn jeans. "Just another sentimental memento I like to keep around."

"I'm sorry about earlier." Nina looked remorseful. She was gazing out at the police lights dancing across the building walls below them, having been attracted by the altercation. "I didn't mean to get that rough with you about the phone, but you see what I was talking about. Ari followed you yet again because of it."

"You're right, Nina. Thank you," Taylor admitted. "But you will need to tell me who you were talking with on the phone just prior to that."

Nina turned back to Taylor. "I will. I promise. Just…not now, okay? We got a concert to get to. We don't have much time before it starts. The place was booked for the *Horny Toads* weeks ago, but it'll do no good if we're late. Loray and Bailey should already be on their way there."

Taylor nodded. "Fine. I trust you, Nina. Lead the way. Maybe we can slip in unnoticed, even this late!" They both scampered off across the rooftops, looking for an easier way down to street level for Taylor.

Jake was shivering uncontrollably. That had to be one of the worst moments of his life. The feeling of fear and despair was something he never wanted to experience again. Beside him was Mikhail, his larger bulk sitting alongside him on the curb as the rustling wind in the planted trees began to fade away. Lights flickered back on in a street that was just shrouded in darkness. Whatever it was that had sought them had lost track, and they had no explanation why.

"Can anyone explain to me what the hell that was?" Trevor was regarding the two with anxious sniffing, trying to pinpoint what was on the air.

They had stopped running and were in a residential part of the city, a far cry from the more commercial district they had found themselves in when Jake was attacked. The terrifying feeling of darkness and demonic gasping felt like it was on their heels nearly the entire way. Now the street seemed like any other, brightly lit at intervals by streetlamps and the reflected light from the neon holograms from within inner downtown.

Jake shook his head again, elbows resting on knees, head in his paws. "I've only ever felt that once before, two nights ago."

Natalia knelt down beside the two, putting a paw on Jake. "What happened?"

Jake gazed across the street as Terrati and Trevor listened in. "I was with Taylor. We were doing nothing special, just talking. I had left her, but then a cougar came up asking me for my services and she defended me. She chased him off. It was then that both she and I felt this same feeling. This same...dread."

Mikhail looked over at Natalia. "I think he's off the Script too."

"How do you figure?" Terrati's nostrils were flaring. "I didn't feel anything, not in the way they did. All I was aware of was the gusty winds from nowhere and the lights going out."

"I felt it once before, but only fleeting when we were with Ari." Mikhail stood up and shook himself out.

"She did seem pretty crazed for a few moments." Trevor scratched his chin as he remembered. "It was quite unlike her to be absolutely terrified of something none of us could see."

"I think it is this Authority that Fey and Finnley were talking about," Mikhail said with grim resolve.

Jake looked up at the tall tiger. "Who is that?"

"We don't know." Natalia glanced over at Terrati who shared her fear. "Taylor saved Fey from certain death after being shot up by dozens of bullets. He should not have lived. As a result, he no longer has a Script, and can supposedly alter other people's Scripts now, just like Taylor can."

"Fey killed a priest well before his time and changed his Script. He mentioned that at the end, some 'Authority' was contacted. He said to me he was going to do research into this while he was in Zabökar." Mikhail finished for her.

"Can you get in touch with Fey? Do you guys have their numbers?" Trevor was now beginning to pace. "Terrati here tried calling and he couldn't get through."

Both Mikhail and Natalia tried on their phones, calling each number in turn. She just shook her head. "The lines are disconnected."

"So we must assume that whatever this…thing is, it got to them." Mikhail clenched his fist, something Jake noticed and began to quiver again.

"I've dealt with drunk predators twice my size when bouncing for bands. I've dealt with unruly mobs and crazed fans like it was a lazy Soonlag. But I've never dealt with anything quite like this, and I don't think I want to." Jake's heart was still pounding from the experience.

"You were supposed to die that night, most likely by that cougar I'd wager." Mikhail was reasoning it out. "Just like I was supposed to die weeks ago to her tail after I had given her the lesson I had wanted to pass on to her. That's the reason why I think only he and I felt the full extent of what this Authority is just now."

"What caused it this time?" Trevor stopped pacing and faced Mikhail.

"I think me killing that rabbit." Mikhail looked at his paws, the fresh crimson barely dried in his fur as he had to rend that rabbit's head off. "I should have known better. Fey texted me yesterday to not change anyone's Script, and here I go by instinct and save Jake's life by killing

414

another who shouldn't have died. It nearly cost me my own." He shivered from an unknown terror.

"What else were you going to do? Let Jake die just now?" Natalia was still upset it had happened at all.

"Of course not," he snapped. "But I shouldn't have been here to stop it."

"And neither should Jake have been there to have started it," Terrati reasoned.

"Why did that rabbit assault you, Jake?" Trevor walked right up to Jake, looking down on him still sitting on the curb. "And why did he claim your death was in Stepan's honor?"

"I don't know!" Jake truly didn't. "We rabbits usually stick together! Rabbit on rabbit crime is non-existent in Zabökar. We got a shitty enough life as it is, there's no reason any of us need to make it harder on each other. I was even offered to come join their underground rallies in hopes of rising up and bettering our lot."

"Did you go to any of these rallies?" Trevor continued to grill.

"No, of course not. I was hoping to be a cop one day, remember? Before that all got dashed by the system. I would have put a stop to these things if I was one." Jake felt more miserable than ever.

"That might be one reason to target you, but feels very flimsy of a reason. That rabbit knew your name before charging to kill you." Trevor folded his arms. "What rabbit would have enough power to hire others like this?"

Natalia snapped her fingers. "Wait, how did you find us at the Marsh House yesterday? You said someone texted you the location. Wasn't that a rabbit?"

Jake's eyes shot open. "Yeah, that was Stepan...the leader and organizer of these rallies."

"But why would he want to kill Jake? That makes no sense. Even if he was against the rallies and didn't attend, that's no reason to off him." Terrati was flummoxed.

"Because of Taylor?" Mikhail offered.

"He did say where she was, so that means they must have met before." Jake finally stood up and turned to the tiger.

415

"This is all getting too confusing. We need to find Taylor and get out of here. We've spent too much time today trailing along after Trevor on her scent trail. It's like she's hopping all around the city." Terrati pressed. "The behemoth is already over the mountains and is lingering on the outskirts of Zabökar."

"Do we know why it isn't attacking yet? It's clearly got enough firepower to do so." Natalia asked.

"It's waiting for something, and I don't want to be here when that comes." Trevor repositioned his shoulder pauldron, flexing his iron fingers with whining gears.

"Here's what we're going to do." Mikhail pointed at each of them in turn. "Natalia and I will go pick up Taylor and get her out of the city. Terrati and Trevor, you take Jake and secure us a form of transport to get out of here. Steal it if you have to. I don't care. It won't matter anyway once that behemoth gets here."

"I'm coming with you after Taylor." Jake was adamant.

"No, it is too dangerous," Mikhail growled.

"I don't care! I got no job of note, no future in Zabökar and no more friends. All I've got left is this promise to Taylor's mother to watch over her, and that's what I'm going to do! I'm going with you whether you like it to or not." He crossed his arms to match Mikhail, glaring up at him as he thumped a foot. "We're both off the Script, so we're both in the same sort of danger. I can handle danger."

"Just not the 'Authority' kind." Trevor tried to insert some dark humor into the situation.

"Really?" Natalia just shook her head. Trevor just shrugged.

Mikhail scowled at him for a few seconds. "Fine, but stay close and try not to kill anyone—or save anyone's life, for that matter. This is going to turn into a real shitfest."

"Where will you find Taylor?" Terrati asked, preparing himself to leave with Trevor.

"Huh, I actually don't think it'll be that hard." Trevor pointed at several posters he just noticed plastered onto a rotting fence between two buildings.

"Oh, good heavens!" Natalia was shocked.

"Still making those bad decisions, I see." Terrati clucked.

416

Taylor was displayed naked in all her punk glory with tongue out, a wink and twinkle in her eye, Ahya open and slathering, Taylor's fingers in the universal metal salute. "We know where she'll be tonight." Trevor whistled admiringly. "She's not half bad."

Natalia whacked his arm. "You keep your paws off!"

"Yeah, where she'll be drawing the attention of every single person who wants her. Just what the hell is she thinking?" Mikhail was not happy.

"Best get going and find out; Terrati and I won't wait forever." Trevor clicked his tongue, surreptitiously stashing a poster in a pocket as they all turned to leave. "Behemoth is coming whether we want it to or not!"

Rakkis nearly threw Ari down to the steel floor. She managed to stumble back upright onto her feet before even hitting it. She glowered at the chameleon, his tailmaw split wide in a visage of silent laughter. She hated the fact he could sense her every move against him, and when she did strike him, it was healed over within a matter of minutes. Her father created an utter monster with Rakkis.

"Daughter, come here." The Arbiter's voice was deep, with a hint of sadness which caught her attention.

It was then Ari noticed how sparse the command room was. Most of the equipment and telemetry had already been packed up and moved out. Her father was staring at a lone screen which depicted live coverage of the concert Taylor was a part of. It was to start within the hour. Looking around, there was no one else but him and Rakkis in the room.

"Father, what's going on? Where is everyone?"

"We're leaving. By tomorrow this place will be nothing but dust, and I want us far away from here." He wasn't looking at her, his eyes still watchful on the screen. "We have several vans already on their way out of the city as we speak. We will load up on one of the last ones and go ourselves. Most of our test subjects have been secured at a more fortified location."

"What about Taylor? Why did you have Rakkis bring me in? We weren't even done with the mission you tasked us with!" Ari was furious. What was the point of sending her out only to give up only a few days later? Sure, it hadn't all gone to plan like she wanted, but it could have still been salvaged. "What changed?"

"What changed? Nothing. But you should take a look at those." He pointed over to the lone folding table next to him. There was a stack of photographs taken from surveillance sources. She thumbed through them to reveal the behemoth crossing the Grunnesh Mountains. "It arrived far sooner than we had anticipated. Something is happening to bolster their timeline, and I have a suspicion it is Taylor. She was there at the death of Palaveve and Howlgrav. Through her actions, she is causing these to seek out targets well in advance of our predictions and against the Script."

"I don't understand. Are we to leave her here? What was the point of even capturing her at all and bringing her here?" Ari was confused. She spent so much time and effort in bringing her home so her father could be proud, and the most she got was another task that was doomed to failure from the start, just like Taylor had said.

"Why?" He finally looked at her. "To finish the experiments we began years ago on her. I did not have all the data I needed to create something as unique and complex as her." His eyes traveled back to the shadow that was Rakkis at the doorway. "Now that I do, she is of no more use to me, other than as bait for the behemoth so that it destroys Zabökar and her along with it."

"So, this entire mission to convince the High Council was a ruse?" Ari was stunned.

He nodded, turning back to the screen. "Indeed. My only goal was to get her captured by the High Council. I had no more need for her. Whether you succeeded or failed was irrelevant. The goal was to get their attention and for them to go after Taylor. What they did to her after that mattered little, since her involvement would most likely bring the behemoths down upon them, which is exactly what's happening."

Ari's red iris was scanning the various data signals rampant around them. "Why isn't it attacking yet, Father? It's still dozens of miles away not approaching."

"It's waiting for something." He continued to mull something over. "Waiting on something from Taylor. I think more research back home is needed."

Ari's eye grew wide. "We're going back home? Don't they hate you there?"

The Arbiter rumbled a laugh. "Perhaps in certain circles, but no matter. I have need of knowledge that can only be found in the archives of Al-Talkar. So we must return to the land of my birth."

"You'll leave Taylor to her death, then? What was the point of sending me with her at all if you were just going to throw her at the council in the first place?" Ari was angry. Why put her own life on the line for a lost cause?

He smiled. "Because if I just released her to her own devices, she would have most likely went underground, and not made waves like she's doing now. She needed motivation to cause trouble, and you going with her tasked with a mission by me was the perfect way to force her to show herself to the world."

The Arbiter chuckled as he regarded his daughter. "Why else did you think I refused to acknowledge her request to go see her family? Why else would I task you with a mission I knew you would uphold over all else and force her to leave you? You played off each other so well, drawing the council's attention off of us and onto her; they aren't even aware we've got what we came here for and are now gone! We're finished with the mammals."

"Finished? What about mother's promise? What about the saving the mammals from eradication like you proclaimed to me for years now? What about building super soldiers to assist them in combating our people's armies? You're just going to let them destroy the biggest city of mammals in the northern countries?" Ari was struggling to find the logic in all this.

"You still have a lot to learn, my daughter." The aged tortoise eased up off the stool, its form creaking under the movement. "I gave up that quest decades ago, when my operation was destroyed by the High

Council. There was no true recovery from that, and no salvation I could give to this place. By letting Zabökar die, the biggest city in the northern countries, it'll send a message to all the mammals that they will need to unify under one banner or be annihilated." He chuckled some more. "A unified banner I'm sure the High Council themselves would not mind being the head of."

"But why not unite the northern countries sooner? Why not when Palaveve was struck? Or Howlgrav? Why wait until they strike Zabökar, their biggest city and manufacturer of wartime technology?"

The Arbiter scratched his chin. "That indeed is a puzzle. They've blanketed knowledge of those cities' destructions from the local populace for a reason I can't fathom. I had noticed years ago of concentrated work around Caelesti Spire—Harutan Technologies being one of the major contractors—but earlier this year they all were disbanded and the entire substructure locked down. They have something planned, but I am not privy to it. Not that it matters much, since we got what we came for."

"And the promise to mother?" Ari persisted.

He stared at her. "It'll be fulfilled, but not this way. I did my best once for them, but the mammals can't be trusted to their own salvation, so we must look ahead to our own people to give it to them. Let this city fall. We have more important things to do, more critical research to conduct. What we've learned through Taylor will be extremely important in destroying the Script for good and bringing peace to our nations, no matter the cost."

"But you made a promise!" Ari was angry. "You always taught me to keep my word, just like you claimed to have kept yours! Was the word you promised mother just a lie then?"

"We leave now, sir," Rakkis intoned from behind them.

"Things change. We have to change with them. You did your part well, Ariana. Do not fret." He reached out to put a hand on her shoulder. She trembled at his touch. She hadn't felt him touch her lovingly like that in years, except now it felt like icy cold daggers. "I'm taking what I wish to save with me, and that includes you. Forget what's left here and let's go home."

"Yes, Father," she said uncertainly.

His point made, he turned to lumber out with Rakkis, fully expecting her to follow. Ari turned around to view the television covering Taylor's concert. After all this time spent chasing after her, and with what her father intended to accomplish with her once she was here, she was still shocked that he so casually tossed Taylor aside now that all the experiments he wished to have done were completed. Just what did they learn from her that was so useful? What made Taylor so special that he waited years for her here when he could have up and left long before now?

This all seemed wrong somehow.

19.

CONCERT

Taylor and Nina were splayed out across the thin carpet on the floor of their dressing room as the opening act was revving up the crowd. They both rolled in when Loray and Bailey were arguing with the venue director. There was some misunderstanding about who was performing in their stead, and they had to smooth things over that "technically" the *Horny Toads* were still performing tonight, just that Taylor and Nina were covering for Ramon.

With the initial legalese settled and their gig still valid for the evening, they retreated to their backstage abode and began to practice. Loray and Bailey were already well-versed in their former standbys when *Bad Luck* was their life. Taylor and Nina were jamming out to an old cassette of their songs, earbuds shared between them. They were memorizing the words and relearning the songs they were going to be performing within a few dozen minutes.

"I've missed this," Nina spoke suddenly, her eyes still closed as she internally thrashed to the metal.

"I have too," Taylor said with closed eyes, her head bobbing on the carpet to the tune. "I remember when we used to spend entire afternoons away with nothing but a bunch of tapes and CDs of our favorite bands."

Nina tilted her head to look at Taylor, her body laying opposite the other way. "Thanks for letting me dye your fur back to red. You look better this way."

Taylor chuckled. "Well I certainly wasn't going to let either of the guys do it for me!" She glanced over at Loray and Bailey, but they were busy with their practice instruments set up in the room. "Besides, I couldn't reach all parts of my back and tail without someone to help."

Nina flushed. "It was nice. I enjoyed spending that time with you."

"Me too."

"Do you really have to leave tonight? Are you certain that…behemoth thing is coming to Zabökar?" Nina's voice was hushed.

Taylor popped the bud out of her ear and turned her head more directly towards Nina. "Pretty positive. Even if it wasn't, I don't think I'd want to stay any longer here. I thought coming home to family would solve many problems, but in the end, they just showed me new ones. I would really love it for you and the others to come with me."

"I'd love to, Taylor, you know that. It's just that—"

An elderly doe stage attendant knocked on the door and opened it. "You guys are on in ten! Hustle your butts!"

"That's our cue." Bailey nearly slipped off his chair, held up only when Loray stopped his head from hitting the floor.

"Alright, the sooner we can get you to that drum set, the better off you'll be." Loray laughed, winking at the two girls. "I'll get Mr. Sleepy here to the stage. We'll see you there."

Taylor began packing up their musical tapes and players when Nina put a wing on her arm. She looked up at her. "What's up?"

Nina looked apprehensive. "It's been a long time. I don't know if I can do this. I'm nervous."

Taylor could relate. Her stomach was doing somersaults right now, knowing they were to be in front of thousands of people. "You're nervous? How do you think I feel? I'm about to be in front of everyone after they've seen my body all over Zabökar!" She had to force out a laugh. "Come on, we did it before. How did we manage to entertain hundreds of fans the last time? We just got out there and played. I guarantee the moment we start, it'll come back to us. I already have rememorized the lyrics to our songs. It was like riding a bike; I only needed to rehear them once."

Nina nodded nervously. "Yeah, I know. It's just that lingering fear that somehow I'm past my prime and it won't come to me up there."

"Remember what you said? Fake it until you make it?" She gripped the bird's shoulders tight. "That's all we're doing here. We'll both make it."

Nina nodded with more determination. "All right. You're the star of the show here; even I can see that." She chuckled. "They're all waiting for your appearance on stage with Ahya. We'll build up your intro, just be ready to roar in on cue, ok?"

"You know it!" Taylor's smile broke as Nina rushed in for a hug. Ahya wrapped around as Taylor melted into it. She could feel Nina rubbing the side of her face into her neck as she held on tight. At length she broke away, staring at Taylor with an odd expression of regret. "You going to be all right, Nina?"

She nodded hurriedly. "Yeah. Let's bring the house down." Gripping her paws one last time with her wings, she turned and jogged down the hall to be with the others in setting up her instruments on stage during the intermission.

Nina was acting oddly clingy of late. Something wasn't adding up, but maybe it was both nerves and the fact both their lives would be changed after tonight. To be honest, Taylor would feel nervous and clingy too with people she loved and cared about. The only reason she wasn't was the path ahead of her. She knew exactly what she was going to do tonight; it was so clear in her mind. The song list was all picked out in order to build up to the grand reveal her mother wanted. She clued in everyone on the order before they rehearsed.

Holding the edges of the lone vanity in the room, she gazed into the light-adorned mirror at herself. She really did look like a rock star. Her hair was combed over the shaved part of her head, complete with piercings up her ears that meshed well with the torn clothing, ribbed arm bands, and spike collar. The fur-painted eyes on Ahya were just icing on the punk cake with how menacing she looked beside her. It was like nothing changed from a few years ago—except maybe a few years older, but maybe not wiser.

"You can do this," Taylor told herself in the mirror, steeling her eyes back onto herself.

Confident she wouldn't balk, she swiftly walked out of the room. She hadn't gotten three feet beyond the door when she was

425

slammed up against the hallway wall, a clawed paw around her neck. She hacked something fierce as a waft of alcohol and an earthy scent mixed with fire and ash assaulted her sensitive nose. Before her was Ramon, his leering gaze lopsided as he looked completely smashed.

"Oh gods, Ramon. What the hell are you on?" She was fighting both Ramon's grip and Ahya's inclination to eat Ramon whole for his violation of her personal space. The last thing she needed right now was a bad trip from consuming the hyena.

He hiccupped, his yellow-stained teeth glinting in the mood lighting of the hall. "You little bitch. You thought you could come back up in here and take my spot as leader of my band?" He waved his paw in an erratic fashion, attempting to indicate something neither of them could see. "Don't think I didn't see your posters all over town with your ugly face on it! How dare you take this away from me! I built this band from the ground up!"

Taylor continued to struggle against his superior grip. He had an abnormally strong stranglehold on her windpipe and she was struggling to breathe. "You were never a player in your band, Ramon. Just face it, we only ever became popular because of me." She gagged as he tightened his claws. "Even now, my fans have proven it by showing up to our show without you even there." She attempted to laugh, but he strangled the sound out.

"I never did like you, with your snarky attitude and pompous self-importance." He gazed off down the hall, as if remembering the moment. "If it weren't for Max and his recommendation, I wouldn't have even allow someone like you to join us—what with your freakish tail!"

Taylor did not want to hurt him too badly; she did not need a dead body to be found in the backrooms during the show by concert staff. She kneed him in the groin, causing him to release her as she dropped to the floor. He keeled over in pain as he gripped his loins tight. She had to suppress a laugh, knowing it would only worsen the situation.

"If it weren't for you telling the others to ignore me, maybe Max wouldn't have left due to my bad treatment, and then maybe Bailey wouldn't have been hired! We all know you don't like him, but you have literally no one else willing to join your sorry-ass group now!" She pointed a finger at him, still on his knees before her.

"Shut up!" he snarled. "I had known Loray and Nina long before you. You took their trust from me within weeks of joining! Why else did I have them avoid you? You were stealing my band from under me! You eating that stupid wretch that first concert was the perfect excuse I needed to isolate you from the rest of us—to present you like the danger you are. I had hoped you would leave shortly after that, but no... Like a cockroach, you kept coming back time and time again!"

"Because the fans loved me and Ahya! Not you! Just admit it, you're nothing but a hack! A no-good bastard child riding on the coattails of his father's fortune, failing at being a musician and afraid to be forgotten as he pretended to be good at something he's not!"

"You stupid whore!"

He swung his leg out and tripped her. She flopped onto her back, squishing the bones connecting Ahya into her spine from the impact. She cried out in pain as Ramon leapt on top of her, spreading her legs apart and restricting her paws by the wrists. Ahya was enraged and did her best to stretch out beneath Taylor to arc around to bite the sniggering hyena.

"How can I be? I've never had sex, you asshole!" she spat in his face.

He cackled, his noxious breath causing her to retch. "Maybe it's time we changed that! You did look kinda nice in those posters!" He began to fondle her roughly as all his sense of decency and common sense went out the window with his drug-addled brain.

"Get off of me!" Taylor shouted, trying to shift her paws out his grip, touching his fingers with her own.

The din of the crowd mere meters away drowned out their altercation, but her cry of protest was enough for Ramon to stop and stare down at her with a glazed look in his eyes—like he was devoid of soul. Taking the opportunity, she loosed her wrists away from him, charged her fingertips and popped him in the chest with her claws, sending a focused explosion directly through his body. He went soaring up, busting a hole into several of the foam tiles above in the grid ceiling.

427

Taylor rolled out of the way as Ramon crashed down where she once lay. He seemed disoriented and looked around, groaning in pain. "What...what happened?"

"Ahya, no!" Taylor surged forward to make a grab for her tail.

Ahya wasted no time. She loomed over the prone hyena, maw wide and dripping. She plunged down onto his form and snapped his legs at the femur. The amputated hindpaws twitched once and lay still as blood poured out of them, staining the carpet. The remaining hyena's mass writhed and screamed inside Ahya as she began to flush the insides with dissolving fluid.

"Stop, no! Let him go! He's harmless now! Ahya!" Taylor began to claw at her tail.

Her sister wouldn't listen. They fought against each other with their wills, but Ahya had the stronger. The jerking motion of limbs grew weaker until there was nothing but a bulging stillness inside her tail, now a red bump on the carpet. Taylor couldn't move or get to stage with this weight in her tail. As much as she fought and screamed at Ahya to release, it was an agonizing few minutes as her tail gorged on what was left of Ramon.

Suddenly there was a sharp taste of smoked pine on her tongue alongside the after-scent of burnt flesh going up her nostrils. Her eyes dilated as the entire hallway swooned in her vision. She lurched forward to clutch the wall with all her might as the light intensified within her vision. The disgusting fullness in her belly paled in comparison to the hyperreal thumping of the ground caused by the crowd and the blinding coronas of the twinkles from the bulbs lighting her path towards the stage.

If she could vomit, she would, but her senses were skewed completely out of whack. She didn't know what to do. She had avoided all these drugs, so no one taught her how to handle them. Fumbling down the hall, her paws ever on the wall, she swung her head loosely as she looked for someone to help. She needed something, anything that could dowse the full impact of whatever she just ingested from Ramon.

She staggered over into the main area with Ahya dragging behind her, tripping over something and falling face first into the carpet. The rug burn when her face slid across its surface seemed super

428

magnified and she began to cry at its lingering scald. Doing her best to roll back over and slump up against the nearby wall, thumping her head against it, she felt hopelessly adrift.

"Fuck," was all she said as she stared over at the steps leading to her crowd.

"*Did you know that this feels awesome? We should do this more often!*" a voice screeched into her head, causing Taylor to wince.

"Shut up. Just shut up." She moaned, her head lolling to the side.

"Oh, freaking hell! Did you just get drugged up right before going out there?" The stage director had come backstage to figure out what was taking Taylor so long. He stood over her as she ogled him from below. He used his burly bear strength to lift the tiny Taylor back onto her paws. He studied her pupils for a moment. "Yeah, you did yourself good. Let's get you back up and out there." He rolled his eyes and led her to the concessions table for the performers. It seemed he had dealt with this sort of situation before.

"No…" She tried to limply point back to where Ramon's hindpaws were still resting. "There was a guy… He attacked."

"Yeah, yeah." He clearly didn't believe her. Probably assumed it was something she saw while on whatever drugs she took since she was little worse for wear. "Well, if I don't get your ass out on stage, we're going to lose a lot of money on this lot." He lightly smacked her cheeks a bit, barely eliciting a response from Ahya, but it did get Taylor to zero in on his face. "Look, I'm going to be giving you something to eat. I need you to eat it all, can you do that for me?"

She nodded, her focus on his nose. What a silly, little thing it was. So cute and black. It almost didn't seem to fit his face with it being as bulky as he was. She had the urge to just boop it with her finger, but something was in the way. His eyes demanded her attention and she gazed down at something thick and white. It felt like bread when she bit into it.

"Eat all of it. I'm going to need you to fill your belly with some simple carbs to get you back on your paws." He held her firmly, but was not slowing down on getting her to eat the remainder of that interminably long loaf of bread. She attempted to shy away from him, but he continued to grasp her neck by the scruff and keep her steady as he fed her. "There you go. Now drink all of this." He offered her an energy drink. He was very patient in her struggle to drink it all down.

"One last thing before we get you on out there. I swear to gods, teenagers…" He mumbled that last part under his breath as he let her go to grab something.

She could hear the masses chanting her name over and over. She fixated on the large paw in front of her nose as she bent over with paws on her knees. "What's this?" She examined the rolled-up joint.

"Something I learned back when I was your age. Take one good drag off this." He smiled at her, placing a caring paw on her back. "It seems counterintuitive, but this will help mellow out whatever you hit yourself up with. It'll give you some focus."

Taylor did what she was instructed and put her mouth on the end of the proffered joint. She breathed in deep, feeling the smoke hit her lungs. The reaction was near instantaneous. She began hacking up hard with big wheezing gasps. The stage director continued to pat her back as he massaged it out.

"There, there. Amateur. Now get yourself up. You have a set to perform!" His hearty laugh jolted Taylor from her reverie at contemplating how grossly nauseous she was. "No seriously, get out there." He gripped her face and smacked her a few more times. He pointed at the stairs. "Up there. Sing. Perform. Go."

The world seemed to fade away as her head grew lighter. She barely remembered walking up the steps and onto the stage, stepping out behind the curtain to roaring cheers caused her to pause as the spotlights dazzled her senses. Everyone was trained on her. She forced Ahya to rise up off the floor, her bulk dragging behind her as she had ascended the stairs. She turned and made Ahya open her maw wide, tongue drooping out. The crowd went wild.

Nina and Loray could immediately see something was not right. Nina went straight to her side and helped her get to her position front and center. Picking up the guitar placed there for her, Taylor unsteadily pulled the strap over her head and let the instrument dangle off her shoulder. Taking one end with a paw and a pick in the other, she took several steady breaths.

"How is Zabökar tonight?!" she yelled out into the ground, not even aware she had said it. "Did you miss me?!" The roar was unanimous. Ahya whipped her tongue in a frenzy to their cries. There was one odd shriek from a random corner in that sea of heads.

A bit stunned from the reception, she turned to Nina and nodded. It was like her fingers were acting of their own accord. They strummed the strings and pressed the chords. launching into their first song, *Outcast*. Everyone went savage as fans recognized the tune. Taylor was beginning to enjoy being out on stage. Stepping up to the microphone ahead of her, counting the beats, she inhaled deeply and let loose an insanely deep death-growl to the delight of all.

"Dammit." Natalia was biting her nails. "I was hoping she wouldn't show."

Mikhail, Natalia, and Jake, perched on Mikhail's shoulders, were watching with hearts sinking as Taylor walked out onto that stage. She looked a bit startled at first, but with Nina's help, she took position before the crowd. The band struck up their first bit and the entire underground amphitheater got pumping. Lights were flashing and oscillating back and forth, creating a frenetic atmosphere.

The Real was an interesting venue in that although the foyer and entry concessions were at ground level, the real stage was underground. Once going down the primary stairs, it opened up into a vast, metal-beamed room with a low flooring that dipped in the middle. Seats were perched all up the sides with walkways in-between them. The stage was set at the far end, jutting out a bit into the center where performers could get up close and personal with their fans.

The long growl emanating from Taylor caught all three of them off guard. "Good heavens, she can really bring it!" Natalia's mouth dropped open.

"I had heard her sing before, but not like this." Mikhail was just as amazed. That girl could scream-sing with the best of them. She was raging against the machine as the lyrics hit hard and fast.

"We got trouble though!" Jake pointed out several positions of cops along the edges of the amphitheater. They were situated at all the exits with a few spares that were using the tumult of the crowd to slip between the dancing bodies as they made their way slowly to the stage.

"What are they doing? Are they going to try and arrest her live on stage?" Natalia asked.

"Not now, no." Mikhail confirmed grimly. "They'll get close enough to make it easy, but wait for an intermission between songs as she goes behind a curtain for a break or drink of water and then nab her then."

"We need to stop that from happening!" Jake thumped Mikhail's chest with his heels.

Mikhail directed Natalia with a finger motion. "You take the right side of the stage, I take the left. We'll need to remove those going after her first before we get rid of those around one of the exits."

With their plan in motion, they split off. Jake watched Natalia blend into the crowd as they hopped, jumped, and head-banged to the music. Mikhail was jostled roughly here and there, but he kept his focus as his bulkier frame pushed the smaller revelers out of the way. Jake had to hold on tight since the thought of his little body being in the middle of a sudden mosh pit did not sound appealing.

"How about that? You all like that?" Taylor was laughing. "We're all outcasts in some shape and form, aren't we? A little bit of rebel in us, yeah? Fighting against the system and what brings us down, am I right? Maybe we should just...*Bring the Fall*!" She announced her next song to cheers and howls.

"She can command that stage." Mikhail whistled.

Jake nodded, holding onto Mikhail's cheeks, as he shouted down to the tiger. "I've watched her do this countless times. It's why Ramon hated her so much. She just had a feel for the crowd and she owned it. It's what I admired about her when I watched her perform from behind the curtain those few years."

The chorus was deafening as nearly every head bowed in unison to each pound of the song. Taylor's growl was joined by Nina's lighter pitch and they belted out the words with reckless abandon. However, their eyes were on the two intimidating rhinos in uniform who had already made it to the left side of the stage just where the center strut was extending out into the raved concert goers.

Take advantage of one of the louder portions of the song, Mikhail slammed his fits into the kidney of one of the rhinos as Jake hopped off and roundhouse kicked the other rhino's snout in midair. Mikhail tripped the first as his buddy tumbled over him. The mammals around them saw the two fall and screeched out in joy, "Mosh pit!"

Mikhail had to snag Jake out of the air as he fell from the kick, clutching him close to his chest as he backed off from the impending mess before them. People were bouncing and ramming into each other with the hapless rhinos beneath their thrashing paws and hooves. Jake smiled as they worked their way back through the crowd to one of the exits. Neither one of those two cops would be able to subdue Taylor after that beating.

It was hard going back towards the edges with the mosh pit behind them expanding in scope. Taylor had already finished her final howl when she began panting loudly. "You guys are awesome!" She chuckled maniacally, almost falling backwards before catching herself. "You probably all saw me do some bad things before tonight, didn't you?" Her smirk seemed a bit off kilter. "Maybe killed a couple people, who knows? I've been a bad girl!" She turned to her tail and began kissing and sucking on Ahya's tongue, something it seemed they both enjoyed. A large contingent of males and females in the crowd trilled at the top of their lungs at this wicked display.

Mikhail exchanged glances with Jake. "Is she okay?" Even Nina and Loray on stage looked nervous. Bailey was snoozing in his drummer chair.

Jake shook his head, squinting at her, nose twitching. "No, she's never done something like this before! She must be hyped up on something bad. She doesn't look well. Can't you smell it?"

Mikhail shook his head. "My sense of smell was destroyed a while back—torture and all that."

Jake winced. "I'm sorry."

He shrugged. "It's in the past. We need to get Taylor off that stage now. If she's drugged up, she is in no condition to fight or escape without our assistance."

Despite her confession of murder, which seemed to be taken as stage presence bravado, it only seemed to excite the crowd further. Licking her lips from the sloppy kiss, she chuckled and walked back up to the mic. "Or maybe he was just slated to die and there was nothing I could do to stop it? Maybe it is the Script that's the problem! Maybe I'm just a *Script Hater!*" she roared, joining back with everyone in attendance.

The band took their cues and began blasting out the hard intro to the next bit. Jake looked over to where he saw Natalia last and noticed both her targets were gone too. She made eye contact briefly across the large space and gave a single bow of her head.

"Natalia hit her marks," he said as the people cheered when Ahya got in on banging the drums with a stick.

"Good, we need to get through one of these doors and make our way backstage so we can grab her before it gets anymore out of paw." Mikhail made a beeline for the closest exit nearest the stage.

It appeared the two police guarding that exit were alerted to their determined gait towards them. It wouldn't be an easy fight. One was a large horse while the other was a lion. Jake was inwardly stewing. No wonder they rejected him out of hand; they only wanted the biggest and brawniest mammals to become cops to intimidate, even if they weren't as skilled as he could be.

Without waiting for them to get closer to intercept, Jake leaped off Mikhail's shoulder and wrapped himself around the horse's neck. Mikhail bellowed at the lion and pitched forward, pummeling the big cat straight through the double doors and out into the stark hallway beyond. Jake was yanked by the ear with a hoof and jerked off the neck. Landing in the arms of the horse, he kicked hard upwards several times into the cop's jaw, snapping his head back and staggering him.

Taking the opportunity to escape the horse's clutches, Jake bounded up off one of his forearms, and as the cop looked up to see where Jake was going, he got his snout caved in with the force of Jake's feet smashing down one and the other onto his nose. Jake hopped off his head and onto the now ajar exit door, then used the momentum to rebound back into the horse's throat feet-first. Gurgling on spit and a bit of blood, the larger cop stared at him dumbfounded as he collapsed to the ground clutching his windpipe.

Jake hit the floor lightly and stood up, dusting his paws off. "I always knew I could do the job better," he huffed with satisfaction.

He turned to see Mikhail scratched up and bleeding but with the upper hand, his beefy arm straining with the force of strangling the air out of the lion. The big cat beneath Mikhail was slowly losing the fight as his limbs and tail began to thrash less and less with each successive spasm. At length, his head dropped and Mikhail let go.

"Is he dead?"

Mikhail stood back up, panting. "No, is yours?" He turned to the bleeding, immobile horse.

"Eh...possibly? I don't think so. Probably won't be able to speak normally again at least." Jake actually wasn't sure.

Taylor had just finished her song and was addressing the crowd again. "That's right. We must forge our own destinies! But they can be destroyed by those in power over us! Those that we have elected to lead us and guide us!" She took a few moments to steady herself before continuing, her grip on the mic tight. "What about our leaders? Our very own High Council? Who holds them accountable for their *Betrayal*?"

She made a motion back to Loray, who then appeared to be making a quick text message to someone on his phone. Within moments, the dual screens above the stage changed to images and video footage of some atrocious things happening. "You may know the song, but here's a new version of the words!" Taylor strummed her guitar and launched into her next song.

The effect was not one anyone could have predicted. Although the band on stage was thrashing out with all their heart, the words Taylor was screaming were hitting home too deeply. The new lyrics over a familiar tune seemed to reach out and the crowd began to grow silent as they watched little cubs and loved ones get murdered before their eyes. Recognizable people from the High Council current and past were caught on damning camera eating young kits and rabbits, and performing unholy rituals.

Natalia had finally made it over to them, but she was just as shocked as they were. "This…this is awful."

"She wanted to rout them," Mikhail spoke with admiration. "One last 'fuck you' to the High Council."

"Murana's final message." Jake nodded. He had an idea of what it entailed, but he had no idea it was this horrific.

True to Stepan's word, there were many rabbits in the crowd who had attended the concert. They were incensed at the treatment their brothers had received at the paws of the High Council—to these cultists claiming to be their honorable leaders. If they were this deceptive, what's to say the rabbit law itself was just as much bullshit as their accountability? They began to rage as the chittering of their brethren grew to a fever pitch. The remaining cops left their stations and attempted to quell the rising violence.

Jake turned when he thought he heard a familiar voice, and saw a red panda standing beside the comatose lion, looking uncertainly at him. Taylor and the band faltered and stopped playing as pandemonium erupted in the amphitheater.

Taylor was crowing with glee as she struggled to keep up with Nina dragging her along. They had exited off the stage and left the Real through a back entrance. Loray and Bailey must have left via other means. She didn't know what happened to them.

Taylor pointed out as they passed by windows of taverns or restaurants that her broadcast was reaching more than just the people inside the concert hall. Nina didn't seem to acknowledge this much, focusing instead on keeping Taylor moving.

The late-night ground traffic seemed denser than normal as the public transport had halted all operations. The flying cars in the mag tracks above were thinned out. All these elements Taylor focused on, but could barely remember even moments later.

There seemed a different feel to the city in the air. Something was happening, and it was not quite apparent on the surface. Taylor just enjoyed the pretty lights of the advertisements that were still harassing Nina as they swiftly strode down the street the few blocks back to her place.

The cops had abandoned their posts around Nina's complex in favor of putting all their forces at the concert. This worked to their advantage as they took the stairwell up to Nina's apartment. Using the spare key, she ushered Taylor inside and locked the door behind them. It was a bit worse for wear, having the entire place look upended like a hurricane went through. The police did their best to search the place top to bottom for whatever they could find.

"We really stuck it to them, didn't we?" Taylor collapsed hard into one of the chairs at the dining table. "Those High Council pricks won't know what hit them when those rabbits come storming through their front doors! Did you see what they've done?" Taylor was feeling really happy with herself. She finally felt like she had made a difference.

"Yeah...Taylor. I did." Nina had her wings folded and was regarding her strangely. "I really wish you had told me what was on that chip. I didn't really like finding out about my dad and his other council members like that."

Taylor snorted, giving Nina a bemused look. "I thought you hated your dad. You said he never did anything for you and neglected you all those years! I thought you would be happy!"

"Well, I'm not... Not like this." Nina began to squeeze her elbows with her wings, looking away at the front door. "Is this what you had planned from the start?"

She nodded languidly, the drugs still flying through her body. Ahya was having a grand time feeling up the table leg with her tongue. "Because of those fuckers, my mother died. Because of them, I was born with a sister attached to my butt!" She snickered, finding the idea incredibly funny. "Look at it this way, Nina. You can now say you hold the moral high ground over your own dad!"

Nina still didn't look joyful. Her gaze now fell onto her bedroom. "Taylor, were you serious about leaving with me?"

Taylor had begun to slouch in the chair—something that surprised even herself. "Well...yeah." It seemed obvious to her. "You're my best friend. I'd do anything for you." She giggled when Ahya snuggled up underneath her shirt, lapping at her neck with her tongue.

Nina looked wracked with some unknown guilt, which confused Taylor greatly. Having made a decision, Nina let her wings drop. "Okay, then I need to pack."

"I think I'll help." That was not the best decision when Taylor stood up. She fell forward right into Nina's arms.

"Oof, maybe tonight is not such a good night to leave. You do not seem well enough to travel." Nina looked concerned, putting a wing to Taylor's forehead. "What the heck did you smoke? You were like a wild wolf out there. I had never seen you like this before."

Without evening thinking, Taylor blurted out, "Ahya ate Ramon. Yep. That she did. He's right here, in my tummy." She leaned on Nina as she dreamily patted her belly, which was bulging slightly. Ahya seemed super proud of herself.

"Oh gods... You are completely smashed." Nina heaved as she attempted to lug the dead weight that was Taylor into the bedroom. Both fell hard onto the mattress as she disentangled herself from Taylor. "As much as I'd like to say I'm glad Ramon's gone...I don't think he should have gone out like that. You also shouldn't have eaten him. Look at you."

"I tried to stop her. She wouldn't listen." Taylor lazily waved off in the general direction of where she thought Ahya was. She was actually up alongside her head, completely zoned out with Taylor.

"Guess it'll be good to sleep one off then," Nina crooned. "I think we'll talk more when you're a bit more coherent."

"You got a cute bill." Taylor poked her friend's nose before dropped her head to the sheets.

Taylor's eyes fluttered open. Nina was still beside her, legs wrapped over hers and her wing across her chest. She was staring intently at her face. Taylor was feeling lightheaded, but she could think a bit better now. "What happened? Where are we?"

"Back at my place. I already packed my bag." Nina looked up and over at the nightstand where her suitcase was.

Taylor's ears perked up as she heard gunfire and screaming outside at multiple distances. "What's going on?"

"Riots are happening, but it isn't just rabbits." After a pause, she continued. "Because of what you revealed tonight, the entire city is up in flames. You've only been out for over an hour, maybe two, but it seems to have gotten worse. We won't be safe out there for much longer if we don't leave soon."

"We really did it, didn't we?" Taylor marveled.

She didn't like that people were most likely dying in this upheaval, but she had completely foiled whatever the High Council was plotting for her and this city. Maybe even outed them as leaders, no longer free to harm and destroy other people's lives, like her mother's. Would Mom be proud?

"Yeah, you did." Nina was still giving her an odd stare. "Did you really mean it when you said you liked me?"

"Well, yeah. Why wouldn't I?" Taylor seemed confused.

Nina lay there holding onto Taylor for what seemed like minutes. Without warning, she gently moved her head forward and placed her bill on Taylor's mouth. It was a sweet, tender press of her head, but Taylor could feel the emotional weight behind it. Somehow the lingering ingested drugs Ramon passed onto her caused her to hyper focus on every minute application of pressure and movement of Nina's lips across her own.

Nina rose up, her breathing starting to increase as a certain scent began to diffuse into the air. She looked uncertain at Taylor, as if awaiting rejection. "I really like you too, Taylor. Always have. I hope you're okay with this?"

Taylor's senses were pinging off her skull right now. She could only focus on Nina's eyes, seeing how they contracted and expanded. Even Ahya knew something was up and was already investigating the tail feathers of Nina, seemingly eager for something more. What was happening right now? Taylor wasn't fully aware of the full implication of what Nina was asking. Had she always felt like this around her, and she was too blind to see it?

Sensing no resistance, Nina moved forward again, this time slipping some tongue between Taylor's sharp front teeth. Positioning herself to be more on top of the wolf, Nina's movements became more urgent as her wings began searching for bare fur to touch underneath Taylor's clothes, finding purchase as she cupped a breast. Ahya was getting more excited too, and dipped her tongue between the plumages of Nina's tail, prompting moans that traveled through her kisses into Taylor's mouth.

Reality slammed into Taylor's mind as she did her best to put her paws on Nina's chest to push her gently, but firmly off of her. "Nina... What? Whoa... What are you doing?" She willed Ahya to stop licking Nina and hold off at the edge of the bed.

The haze of lust was still evident in her friend's eyes. It was clear she wanted to quickly get back to what they were doing. "I thought you liked me. I thought you wanted to be with me."

Taylor pushed up harder as Nina made a move to descend back onto her. "I do like you...just not like this. I see you as just a friend, Nina. A good one. One of the very best, but I just don't see you as...this."

The haze evaporated and what was left was stark realization of what she had done. The silence between them was deafening. Nina made no moves to get off of Taylor, nor did she attempt to push the matter. It seemed she was about to cry, a little sniffle snort coming out of her pierced nose on her bill.

"Do you think we'll ever?" She followed Taylor's head shake with her eyes. She pleaded again. "Never?"

Taylor's heart was broken. She loved Nina beyond all measure, but she couldn't see her friend romantically like this. She just wasn't into girls like that. She wished she didn't have to trample her friend's hopes like this, but she needed to get her to understand that despite this mishap, she was more than willing to maintain the friendship if Nina wanted to.

"I'm sorry, Nina. I love you, but as a friend—a sister of sorts."

The dam broke. Nina began weeping horribly. Taylor couldn't think of anything else to do but wrap her arms around her friend and smooth down her back with a paw. She had felt emotional anguish before, and she knew the toll it could take on your heart. As awkward as it was, she would be here for her friend as she trudged through this quagmire of pain.

"I still want you to come with—" Taylor's eyes moved over to the doorway where the cloaked figure in black was standing, his head tilted to the side and antlers just scraping the top of the doorframe. "Nina, get back!"

Taylor rolled to the side to toss Nina to the other end of the bed as she lashed out a bolt of lightning towards the robed figure. In a single blink of the eye, he was in the corner of the room next to the closet. The bolt smashed some cutlery in the kitchen beyond. Confused, but no less determined, Taylor sat up now and loosed another arcing blast. It splintered the closet door into a million fragments, but now he was across the room behind them by the window.

"What the hell?!" Taylor fumbled with her dexterity and coordination as she attempted to get out of bed. She simply slid off the side and landed roughly onto the carpet.

Grasping the sheets tight, Taylor pulled herself up halfway onto the bed, her senses still muddled. She took aim again but was struck with a knifing pain in her gut. It was like a thousand little daggers had stabbed her insides and were doing somersaults up and down her stomach. The sparks on her fingers fizzled and disappeared as she bunched up into a fetal position and began to cry.

The skull opened its mouth and a soft, yet stern voice slithered out. "Child, did you feed her your eggs?"

Nina was still recovering from the ordeal of Taylor's denial. She nodded glumly. "Yes. She ate all of them."

"Good. Make sure she does not resist."

With a clenched wing, Nina extended it towards Taylor. Taylor howled in agony as the daggers turned to jagged scythes that ripped around her insides like a maelstrom. It felt like she was being torn apart. Her guts were on fire, and every movement of Nina's feathers was like a spear through her heart. Nina had powers too, and whatever she had ingested from Nina was its conduit. All those times attempting to go relieve herself in the bathroom were stopped by this bloated clot of eggs festering inside her belly.

"I really wanted to run away with you, Taylor." Nina continued to sob. "I had hoped we could live together free from this place and..." She glared at the masked one. "These people."

"Why..." Taylor gasped in-between bouts of unbearable pain. Ahya was writhing on the floor alongside her, unable to do anything, feeling everything Taylor was.

"I just wanted one person to love me. One gods damned person to not neglect and treat me like trash. I had hoped it would have been you, Taylor." The cloaked figure seemed to be enjoying this, allowing her to bare her heart to Taylor. "Then you had to go eat Ramon and ruin our chances of leaving earlier...before he came. Then you had to out the very people I had sworn my loyalty to days ago live in front of the whole city. You had to ruin everything."

The dark figure gurgled a laugh. "Our dear Nina here was honored two nights ago with her first kill. We had saved a mammal quite like yourself from the Arbiter." He leaned over to rub his hoof against her cheek in mock sincerity, but she just jerked her head away from his touch. "Yes, I know you are aware of him and what he's done, Taylor. Yet she enjoyed every bite and morsel of her prey and now has his powers. Call Nina our little insurance in securing you when all else failed at the concert. We had her handpicked months ago when her own Script had her crossing your path, promising her that she could make a difference. We were almost certain she'd blow her cover due to her feelings for you, but as you can see..."

"Why, Nina? I thought you loved me?" Taylor could look at no one else but her friend, or whom she thought was her friend.

"I do, but you'll never love me." She cast her eyes down to the bed where they once laid together just moments before. "No one ever will."

Several more robed figures in various mammal skulls filtered into the bedroom. The primary figure beside Nina snapped his fingers. "Pick up that wolf and bind her paws and tail." He regarded Nina a moment. "Bind hers too and take her with us."

"Wait, what?" The swan looked up at him.

Nina's power over Taylor instantly evaporated, but it was too late. Dozens of paws were already upon them both, and the last thing Taylor could recall seeing was the grinning skulls of the slain as a black hood was pulled over her head.

20.

RITUAL

The drugs from Ramon were still persisting in Taylor's system, but her senses were far more alert than before. Through the black hood tied around her neck, she could still hear them rustling past screams and gunfire. Several explosions could be heard from what sounded like a few blocks away. She could see flashes of light accompanied by loud bangs. The acrid odor of smoke penetrated the fabric.

She was bound with her paws behind her back, but it felt like Ahya was restricted in an entirely different way than she had expected. She felt like Ahya was floating behind her without gravity or weight, but she was unable to move her. There was some sort of force keeping Ahya immobile, and her strength to control her own body was powerless against it.

One tiny voice could be heard through the din. It sounded like they had jumped onto a car hood. "Bunny uprising! To me, brothers and sisters!"

Several times their group was attacked by unidentified assailants. The robed figures around her made movements she could detect with her ears. Then suddenly an unknown sound or strident roar grated her hearing, but was almost always followed up by screams of pain, then the disgusting squishing or gurgling of blood from the poor saps who dared to attack. Every single kitnapper around her had powers like she did. This would not be an easy situation to escape out of.

The clamor of the riot started to subside as the air began to take a more musty scent. They were underground. The buzzing of the fluorescent bulbs above and their light illuminating through her hood at intervals signaled to her that they were in the subways. A low rumble and mechanical sounds heralded a descent into darkness. She supposed

445

some secret entrance off the platform led somewhere deeper into the underbelly of the city.

It was faint at first, but she could just barely hear the low rumblings of chanting. It was in a language she could not decipher, but it sent chills through her body. It was incessant, and seemed to be repeating. It felt like the space opened up as the sound echoed out in a much larger chamber. Through the black fabric, she could see many specks of twinkling light. The aroma of incense was thick here, and it stung her nose. It had a harsh smell of sulfur that reminded her of burning flesh.

She was dropped unceremoniously onto what felt like a stone slab. The hood was ripped off and she saw dozens of similarly robed figures, each and every one with a skull for a mask. Some were predator in nature, others were prey; she even noticed a few rabbits in the crowd near the front. Their shrouded forms looked eerie in the wavering light of the torrent of candles surrounding the natural stone chamber.

She tilted her head back and up. A large effigy of rock had been intricately chiseled to depict a horrific, multi-limbed god with claws the size of both her forearms put together. There were real mammal skulls perched like studded ornaments down the length of each claw and on the spikes protruding from its armor. Its face was split into thirds at the chin like a giant maw with several rows of meticulously crafted teeth encircling a void of darkness. It was sculpted in the very act of tearing a small foal apart.

Taylor's head ratcheted over to a second slab beside hers, almost within touching distance. Nina was tossed onto it, her hood ripped off. She was also looking around, frightened. The terror in her eyes indicated to Taylor that she had never been to this part of Zabökar. Whatever cultish sins she committed with these people, it was not here. This was a place of sacrifice, not initiation.

Their eyes locked on to each other. Nina cried. "I'm so sorry, Taylor! I didn't—"

The antlered figured swiftly strode over and smacked her across the cheek, drawing blood with his hoof, its red bleeding into her white feathers. It looked like she tried to raise her wing to rub her cheek, but she was just as pinned down by an unknown force like Taylor was. Her gaze wandered out over the vast sea of skulls. If every single one of them had powers, then it was hopeless to even try to fight back. The two of them would be massacred.

The chanting had risen to a fever pitch, their incense shakers jangling with the motion of their wrists. Then all was quiet as the leader between Taylor and Nina raised his arms for silence. The soft, but commanding voice from earlier captivated the congregation. "We are gathered here tonight, on the eve of Zabökar's destruction, to garner proof that we can change our Script!"

"All hail, Barateon! All hail our unwritten Script!" they replied back in unison.

"Too long have we been biding our time, waiting for a solution to rid ourselves and our destinies from the curse that is the Script. Chained upon us by birth from a time and a war nobody can remember. We are slaves to its words." He swiped his arm through the air to emphasis his point. "No more! Through much observation and studying, I believe this wolf holds the key to what we've always wanted: a future without fate!"

"All hail, Barateon! All hail our unwritten Script!" they repeated.

"Our dear wayward sister, Fahpar, was a lost cause, but she did demonstrate one key piece of evidence in her failed excursion: this wolf can bring people back from the dead after their Scripted end!" There were murmurs of joy and elation from the grinning skulls. "Without the Script to govern what we do and where we die, we can reshape this world into what we want. We can take back what is ours and annihilate the reptiles that dare march upon our borders!"

The leader flashed out a knife and, pointing at the crowd with it, walked back and forth between the two girls. "Which one of you has the courage to step forward and die for the cause? Which one of you will enter that gaping maw of death and be reborn without Script?"

It was a violation of her entire being, but she felt Ahya's mouth open of its own accord, like it was a compulsory action. A figure next to Ahya manipulated out her tongue with some sort of power and bared her tail's fangs for all to see. It was a frightening sight for those in the front rows. Taylor tried to struggle and bring Ahya close to her, but this insidious pull within her was denying all attempts at re-commandeering her own body.

"Nobody?" The wolf skull chuckled. "Yee of little faith." He stepped over to Nina, grabbing a hoof-full of feathers off her head, jerking her up to the crowd. She yelled in shock at the rough handling. "It is good then that we have brought a willing sacrifice."

"You let her go! You let her go right now, you fucking assholes!" Taylor seethed.

"Silence, little girl." He motioned over to another figure with a coyote skull.

The coyote figure waved a hoof towards her. Taylor's screams were muffled as her jaw fused together and closed off her entire mouth. There was nothing left but bare skin grown over where her maw used to be. Taylor was beyond petrified now. She couldn't move. She couldn't talk. She had absolutely no control over her own body.

"For a sacrifice to be, it must first die to the cause." With the knife, he pointed out several members from the gathering. Five stepped forward. "Take off your masks," he commanded them.

The skulls removed, Taylor saw that they were a mix. There was a zebra, a beetal, a tiger, a ciconia stork, and a wolf. Reverently placing their skulls at the feet of Taylor, they moved over to surround Nina, who was whimpering and attempting to shrivel up into a tiny ball. She began to honk and flap as they took each of her limbs and spread them apart. The leader remained quiet and let the swan squawk and squirm without restraint.

"My brothers and sisters. You may dine," he said without inflection.

Nina's blood curdling screams rebounded off the rock walls as the five bit into her flesh. Rending and tearing with their teeth, they took bloody hunks off her body and chewed, swallowing fully before going back for more. Taylor shouted into her closed mouth until her throat was hoarse, her tears flowing at the brutal slaughtering of her friend. She could feel Ahya thrashing within that powerful grip of magical force, but it was useless. She was bound tight.

They had already made it to Nina's bones. They were now working on her belly, chest, and face. Nina squealed out. "Taylor! Help me! Help!" Her cries turned into nothing but strangled bubbling as blood was frothing out her mouth. Her body went into spasms at the shock of being eaten alive.

A few excruciating minutes more, the leader intoned, "Enough! She is dead."

The five followed the command and set the swan down. Nina's head rested on the cold stone, staring at Taylor with that vacant look. There was nothing recognizable about her body except for that. Taylor wept for her friend and vowed she would kill them all if she ever got free.

She didn't get that chance, as she quickly felt herself lifting off her platform and floating over the mutilated corpse of Nina. She tried her best not to look, but they wouldn't allow it.

The five mammals, their faces covered in red, stepped back into the crowd and reapplied their masks. The leader nodded to each before addressing Taylor. "Now we have your tail eat what's left of your friend." Taylor shook her head vehemently, but he just chuckled. "That was not a request."

Again Taylor felt the violating pull deep within her body move Ahya over Nina and begin to open wide. She screamed some more inside her mouth as she saw Ahya reach out to wrap her tongue around the body of Nina and pull it deep into her maw. Ahya's jaws snapped shut, then Taylor was set down on the bloodied slab where Nina was killed. She tried to fight with all her might, but mere sparks fizzled out of her paws. Their powers were just too much for her.

"Now heal." His order offered no refusal.

Taylor could feel Ahya's saliva gush into her inner cavity, soaking the corpse of her friend through. She shivered in revulsion as she could sense every bitten, chewed orifice and laceration of Nina within her tail as the fluid touched every inch. The entire bulk of Ahya began to pulse as she went to work at rebuilding the tissue within. Taylor no longer cared about the feeling of her friend's blood beneath her, seeping into her clothes and soaking her fur.

Raising his hooves high, the leader bellowed out, "Through death we are released. Through death we are free! Reborn in the tail we

449

can change the future. By the divine grace of Alacoth, we will rend this world asunder with our freedom!"

"All hail, Barateon! All hail our unwritten Script!" they cried out with fervor.

The chanting began anew as the incense began to flow with the clatter of their burners. The wolf-masked figure walked up to Taylor and knelt down. She could see his blue eyes dimly through the holes in the skull. He was regarding her strangely. He flicked the knife up and jabbed it into her artery in the crux of her arm with expert precision. Blood began pumping out. Taylor raged behind her sealed mouth. He quickly brought a deep bowl and began to position it to collect her essence.

Bringing the coyote skull over to staunch the flow with his powers, Barateon lifted high the earthen bowl, filled to the brim with her life blood. "For those rare few tonight who will receive this honor of rebirth, we will drink of the blood of the Script killer."

Holding the bowl steady with a hoof, he removed his mask and revealed himself to be a stag—his antlers tall and proud and not part of the wolf skull he was wearing. His eyes never leaving Taylor's, he tipped the bowl and drank deeply from it. He then passed it around to each of the five who had eaten Nina. They too drank deeply. It was all gone by the time the fifth had finished.

Carefully setting it aside on the stone altar Taylor was first on, he turned back to the assembly. "We chosen six will bear the pain of death so that we may alter the course of the future. It is the will of Alacoth that we do this! With the blood of the wolf that will heal us in our bodies, we will be immune to the Script's reach. Now come, each of you. Surround her with your presence."

He pulled out an arm from each willing participant, rolling back the sleeve of each. Using his knife, he made two rough incisions down the length, ensuring a clean cut into the arteries of each mammal. "Hold out your arm over her and let her be drenched in the poison that is your blood, tainted by the Script! She will take onto her all the wretchedness of that unholy magic and bring forth a renewed purity for each of you."

Taylor did her best to thrash to avoid the blood spilling over her, but she was held in place. She could do nothing as the warm liquid washed over her and stained her clothes, making her look like a mass murderer with all the red upon her fur. She wanted to die. She didn't want to be here anymore. This was worse than death—to be at the mercy of vile cultists, the very same ones that ruined her mother's life. She would be yet another casualty to their wicked cause.

Then she felt it. There was a small, muffled cry within her tail. Movement was heard as Nina thumped her body against the stone through Ahya. The leader motioned for the five cut to step aside, but to keep letting their blood flow over Taylor. He moved down and around to her tail, watching the bulges within writhe.

"She has done it! She has cheated death!" The cheer resounded throughout the cavern. He waggled his hoof to a nearby robed figure to bring him something. It was a faintly glowing Script roll. "This is the Script for Nina Hawkins! We will bear witness to a miracle!"

He unfurled her Script by its blooming handles, ignoring the rising urgency of the swan within Ahya. He belted out a laugh as he folded the parchment to just the part where she died. "There was nothing further in her Script. She was slated to die anyway tonight. Like all powered mammals and us gathered here tonight, this wolf has the capability of ending people's Scripts earlier than expected. However, although Nina's Script now has her death for tonight, she is alive and well inside the tail!"

He casted off the Script into the crowd for hungry onlookers to grab and paw through it to verify for themselves. He turned around and, with a tight grip between Ahya's mouth, flipped it open wide to reveal Nina inside sputtering and messy, but very much alive. There was an awed hush that had descended among the people. A new worded chant began to rise from the first as they began to fall to their knees.

The five above Taylor grinned, knowing they would be next to experience this divine rite of passage. All smiles faded when one of the mammals reading the Script called out. "Barateon, who is this Authority?"

"What?" It seemed that was the first time he was caught completely off guard.

He stormed down the plinth steps and jerked the Script from the quivering ocelot. He scanned the bottom of Nina's Script. A cold chill began to envelop the congregation. The flickering candles began to waver and then blow out. First one, then another, then more as it traveled across the chamber. Several mammals held their paws aloft to generate balls of light so that those without night vision could see in the gloom.

Taylor recognized this feeling. She had felt it once before with Jake. Her ears flicked this way and that as a low, wheezing gasp could be heard. It was like a lode stone had been pressed upon her heart and was weighing her down deeper and deeper into the stone dais she was on. She trembled at the terror that was filling her core.

There was a shriek that set everyone on edge. Nina began to toss her head back and forth, her wings gripping her temples tightly. Without warning, she slammed her head down onto a tooth of Ahya, puncturing her skull. She did it again. The stag was in shock as he stared at the self-mutilating swan still encased within the open maw of Ahya. Nobody said a word as everyone's flight-or-fight instincts were kicking into high gear.

"Get her inside me now!" Taylor heard a voice screaming in her head.

The coyote skull had released his hold on her, and blood began to pour once more from her arm. She could feel her mouth break free as it was reopened back to fresh air. Gasping to fill her lungs, she realized she could control Ahya again. Not questioning what she believed to be Ahya's voice, she used her tail's tongue to grip Nina tight and bring her deeper into that maw, away from the teeth. Slamming the jaws tight, she kept Nina restrained as best she could with Ahya's tongue, fighting against the thrashing bird who seemed intent on killing herself.

It was here. This Authority was here. It was like a darkness that nobody could perceive, but was among them. It reached out with feelers that could be felt but not seen. People dropped unconscious as it searched the room for its target. The conjured balls of light disappeared one after another. Taylor was shaking hard as she felt this "thing" pass over her. She couldn't even describe what she saw, only that it was terrifying.

The longer it searched, the more they all could feel its growing malice. At last, it spoke. "Entity lost. Searching."

Nobody dared move a muscle until the presence was gone. Taylor was too panicked to begin calming down right now. Ahya took the opportunity to heal whatever damage Nina had done to herself. Finally, the swan settled inside the tailmaw. Taylor looked up at the five who had poured their blood over her, but they were now on the ground, having bled themselves to death.

"Well, that was certainly interesting," a steady voice emanated from the far corner of the cavern. The blazing balls of light re-illuminated as all eyes turned to its source. Standing casually with his arm resting against the cool, rock wall was Liam. He idly scratched the platelets down the length of his snout as he regarded the group with contempt. "I do believe you have there a friend of mine. She called me to come take her away from Zabökar, and that's just exactly what I'm going to do."

Barateon chortled. "Oh, really? All by yourself? Do you even realize who we are? What we can do?" Every skull in the gathering turned to Liam.

He continued to inspect his claws, unperturbed. "I honestly couldn't give a damn. The real question is, do you know who I am and what I can do?"

"Ridiculous." Barateon swooped a hoof at him. "Kill him."

"However!" Liam shouted to retain their attention. "I think I should warn you about my new friend here that I just tossed up onto the ceiling not too long ago."

All eyes turned skyward as they saw what looked like a tortoise superheating a huge, roughly circular patch of ceiling in the rock. Satisfied that her work was done, she dislodged it with a jerk of her arm, its entire bulk plummeting down to the crowd below. Catching a ride with the falling ceiling of death, Ari bundled herself up as best she could into her shell as it splattered dozens of cultists beneath it.

"Kill them both!" Barateon roared, backing up towards the dais where Taylor lay.

Liam snarled as his clothes began to rip and tear. He grew and enlarged, his muscles bulging out and his body extending tall. His tail elongated to an insane degree. Scale platelets began to form and trail from his shoulders down his back to the tip of his tail. Horns burst

453

through his beanie as he thundered like an almighty dragon, his form nearly triple the size of what he once was.

Several cultists took a few steps back. Taking advantage of their shock, he gripped the underside of the huge slab Ari had dropped, now that she had hopped off of it, and began to lift. His whole body strained at the weight of its mass, his own hindpaws creating cracked indentations in the rock beneath him. He finally got the leverage he needed and flung it head over end towards the altar, squishing dozens more cultists.

Anarchy broke out as bolts of fire, ice, and other powers blasted across the room. Pillars of swiftly cooling magma lit up the darkness as robed mammals were impaled, their bodies melting from the inside out upon each. Liam trampled into the fray, claws out and fangs bared. He was rending them apart, splitting them in half with his strength and tossing others dozens of meters across the cavern.

"Nina, get out now!" Taylor was literally pushing Nina out of Ahya with the tongue. She slipped off the dais and grabbed Nina by the wing before she stumbled forward down the steps.

Spinning her around, Nina was distraught. "Oh, Taylor..." She collapsed into her arms, hugging her tight. She sobbed into Taylor's chest. "I never meant for any of this to happen. They told me they only wanted you to destroy the Script. That you had the power to do so with your tailmaw. I never..." She gazed around at the carnage happening before them, all the cultists' attention focused on Liam and Ari. "I never expected any of this to happen. I just wanted to make a difference for once in my miserable life."

Taylor drew her close once more, her voice weak. "They lied to you. You fell in with the wrong crowd. I feel hurt that you did what you did, but I forgive you."

Nina pulled back. "You... You do?" She stuttered. "But I hurt you so bad. When you rejected me, I felt angry. I was devastated. I got you captured and now you're injured!" She looked down at the weakly pumping artery in Taylor's arm. "You're bleeding!"

"Just one moment." Taylor smiled faintly. She took Ahya's tongue and wrapped it around her elbow, covering the wound in the fold of the arm. The tongue pulsed and Taylor felt sweet relief enter her body as the saliva traveled through her bloodstream and began to heal what had been lost. "It'll take her a few minutes."

They both scooted more firmly behind the dais, hopefully out of view, when a body went flying over their heads to get impaled on the statue behind them. Nina gazed at herself. "I... I was dead." Taylor nodded. "But you brought me back. Healed me completely." Taylor nodded again. "You're amazing!" She rushed in for another hug. "I'm sorry for ever doubting your love for me."

Taylor pulled away, partially because Nina had squished Ahya and interfered with the healing. "Back when we were in the band, I always felt like you were another sister to me or a best friend, like Sarah was—at least during the brief times we hung out. I can't love you, Nina, not in the way you want me to."

Nina wiped away a tear with a wing. "I understand. I don't know how I'm going to, but I'll just have to learn to live with this. That is…if we live through this." She glanced out into the chaos nervously.

They went to embrace once more, carefully now with Ahya between them, but Barateon had turned to see them active and well. He pointed at the coyote skulled figure beside him, his focus on defending Barateon against errant rocks or flailing bodies thrown at them. "Manchas, get the bird. Leave the wolf."

Taylor's entire body twisted to the coyote skull. "Manchas?" She recognized that name. She knew exactly who was behind that mask now—exactly who had forced her to do those vile things and sewn her mouth shut. She had watched her mother's final video several times to have that name imprinted on her brain. "Manchas Wendell? You're the one who killed my mom! Got her captured, pulsed and rotting with cancer! I'll kill you!" All thoughts of healing were gone.

Taylor had pushed Nina behind her with Ahya and was running full tilt at the kudu masked in black robes. Wendell had already lifted her off the ground, jerking her limbs out wide, but not before she let loose an arc of lightning at his chest. The sudden movement of being levitated and controlled threw off her aim and it blistered through his kneecap, causing him to falter. She fell to the ground in a heap as his powers released her, but was up in an instant.

Ahya had unfurled her tongue from Taylor's arm and gaped her maw wide, swinging in from the left, Taylor surged in from the right to pincer the kudu between them. "You bastard!" she raged, fully intent to maul and maim.

Wendell shot his hoof up and halted Ahya in mid-bite, her quivering teeth just inches from his face. The sudden jolt of her tail pulling her back caused Taylor to lose balance, but she forced herself to fall forward into the kudu, knocking them both to the ground. Placing a paw fully onto the coyote skull, she unleashed the full force of her power. The concussive shockwave reverberated throughout the chamber as it knocked everyone near her to the floor, to include Barateon. Taylor nearly passed out, with only Ahya folding under her chest to catch her from falling atop the kudu.

Wendell screeched and thrashed beneath her as he tore off his mask, his face burning and flaking off at the magical fire that was consuming it. With the hold on Ahya gone, she was getting ready to eat his head off when a whistle from behind distracted her intentions. Glaring angrily back, her wrath dissipated when she saw Nina in the clutches of Barateon, the mask off and his eyes glinting at her.

"Lay off him or you will not see Nina alive again. There will be no coming back for her." He leaned his muzzle down to her cheek and gave her one long lick from jaw to head, causing Nina to cringe within his grip.

"Fuck you!" She cast an arm backwards, aiming at his head.

The bolt did not hit. Instead it split apart the effigy beyond at the base of one of its arms. The limb began to dip and then fall to the ground, destroying more of itself along the way, slicing the body impaled on it in half. Before Taylor realized what had happened, Barateon was right atop of her gazing down at her straddling Wendell. He did a vicious kick to the face, propelling her off of the kudu.

She flipped over quickly onto her back, wiping the blood from her lips, and unleashed another strike. It hit the ceiling above, causing rocks to crash to the stone floor below, crushing one cultist on his way out as he fled. Barateon avoided that too. It was like he was teleporting, and she couldn't get a good bead on him.

456

He appeared by her head next. She willed Ahya to snap at him, fully intent to rip him in half. He materialized behind Ahya, kicking Taylor in the ribs. "Look again!" he cackled gleefully. A scream emerged from where Ahya snapped shut. Nina had taken Barateon's place. She was crushed between the powerful jaws of her tail, blood pouring anew from the fresh wounds Ahya was creating.

"No!" Taylor immediately had Ahya release Nina, but the swan was already past the demonic effigy, on the stone ramp leading up and out. Barateon was beside her.

"Farewell, cursed wolf. May this city be your tomb." In an instant, they both were gone.

Taylor scrambled to get back onto her hindpaws, but was barreled over by Wendell. With one hoof raised to keep Ahya at bay, he had the other around her neck, choking her windpipe. His muscle and bones beneath his fur were visible, Taylor's lightning still burning him to pieces.

"You filthy wretch!" Wendell frothed, gory spittle getting on her face. "I knew I should have stolen you from your mother the first chance I had! Now look at you! All grown up and worthless to us! Putting such thoughts in your head of rebellion. You could have been so much more compliant if we just took you as a babe and raised you ourselves! Should have put a bullet in that bitch of a mother the day she birthed you."

"I'm going to kill you!" Taylor tried to slam her claws into his chest to release every last ounce of her powers into him. She wanted him deader than dead. But his powers to restrain her were too powerful. He had sewn her maw shut once more.

"You really should watch that filthy mouth of yours, Taylor. It's unbecoming of a young lady!" He head-butted her twice, causing her to see stars. "What a glorious power this is! It was a real find, let me tell you. If only I had this when your mother was alive, I would have seen to it personally she suffered for days. Guess I'll just have to settle for watching you die quickly!"

His laugh swiftly choked in his throat as a blazing pillar of molten magma pierced him up the ass and along his spine. A calm voice from behind him called to her. "We need to stop meeting like this, Taylor. Move away from him."

Taylor scooted back from underneath the dying kudu. She looked up at Ari and could see she was going to intensify the heat and liquefy him where he was. Taylor growled and flung Ahya forward, decapitating him at the neck. Spitting the shocked head to the side, Taylor watched with grim satisfaction as the rest of his body went limp on the smoldering rock before oozing to a puddle beneath it. Her mouth had reopened again.

"He's dead, Mom." Taylor closed her eyes and exhaled loudly.

A fresh peace came upon her heart for just a brief moment. She wanted to relish in this before reality snapped her back. She dropped to her knees and panted heavily. Her head swooned. She knew her body needed a rest to recharge after expending all that energy, but life was not so kind.

Ari reached down to grasp her arm and pulled Taylor back up to standing. She looked around and saw that the majority of the cultists had either died or escaped. Liam was lumbering up beside Ari, shrinking as he came closer. He was head or two taller than Ari when he finally stood next to her. Both of them had various wounds and were bleeding at various patches of their body.

"Are you two alright?" Taylor inspected them quickly with her eyes.

Ari shrugged. "Nothing I haven't experienced before. Many were ill-trained to use what powers they had. You look worse than we do." She surveyed Taylor up and down.

Taylor groaned, the aches finally coming in full force. "I feel worse. I'll survive though."

"Good, we need to get topside and leave the city," Liam said firmly. "That behemoth is almost upon us. It was attracted to Zabökar by the fires and explosions caused by the riots."

"No!" Taylor shouted. "We need to get my friend back. She's coming with us. That Bara...baton guy took her! We need to find her."

"That could be anywhere in this city. If he took her, chances are he's not going to kill her or he would have already. You'll see her again." Liam made a motion to leave.

"Why did you come back for me?" Taylor turned to Ari.

"What?"

"You heard me." Taylor crossed her arms, daring Ari to refuse to answer. "Rakkis stopped you from chasing me, and that was the last time I saw you. Either he convinced you to give up following me, or he defeated you and brought you back to your father. So, which was it?"

Ari seemed miffed it was phrased this way. She folded her arms and looked away. "He convinced me to leave you alone."

"Uh-huh, because of your father?"

"He wanted to leave you here to die in the city." She returned her gaze back onto Taylor.

This caused Taylor to pause as she considered the reasons why. "I'm no longer useful to him, am I?"

"You stopped being useful the moment the last experiment ended," she confirmed.

"Was it him? Was it your father who captured me years ago and made me suffer experiments to the point I couldn't remember who or where I even was?" She glared at Ari.

"Yes." Ari stood firm, but Taylor could tell there was some regret in her eyes.

"You never told me this," Liam butted in, getting angry at her. "I was the one that found Taylor running around half naked in the city and took her far away from here! You're telling me you were responsible for that?!"

"No, my father was."

"But you were complicit in it!" He jabbed a finger at her.

"Will you shut it?" She looked bored now. "At that time, I barely even knew or cared about who Taylor was. I wasn't involved. My father had me doing other things."

"Why did you come back then? If he was dumping me off to die and taking you with him, why risk your life coming back?" Liam seemed interested to know the answer as well, standing alongside Taylor now. Ahya was peeking out the other side and "looking" at Ari too.

"Long story short, I wasn't overly happy with how he treated my mother's last wish. I mean, he supposedly made me in her image as a symbol of his love for her. When I saw how casually he just dismissed his promise to her after all these years and using me as bait to get you to act to attract the High Council's attention, it got me thinking back to what you had said to me about my relationship to him." She caught the smirk on Taylor's face. "Think whatever you want. If you want to catch your friend, he's getting further and further away with her."

"How can you tell?" Liam asked.

Ari tapped her red iris. "He's still within range of several security cameras nearby. I can see them flit by as they cross them. He may be able to escape my physical senses, but he can't hide from mechanical eyes."

"Right." Taylor led the charge up the natural ramp formation. She had no clue where to go since she was blinded by the hood on her way here, but if Barateon went this way, it had to be the exit as well. "When I get my hands on that guy, I'm going to rip him from limb to limb for harming Nina!"

"My, my, you sure got bloodthirsty since I last saw you." Ari, jogging beside her, was impressed. "My little Taylor, growing up."

"Shut up." Taylor was frustrated Ari was mocking her. "I'm just…super angry right now. I saw my friend get eaten alive in front of me, then got blood poured all over me while having to have Ahya consume and heal Nina inside my tail, then finally face the real person responsible for my mother's death. It's a bit much to take in right now, ok? I just want it all to be over!"

They rounded a bend and could see the fluorescent lights ahead through the gloom, indicating the subway platform wasn't far off. "I can understand that sentiment. I don't like killing people myself, but I have no qualms ending their life if they seek to harm those I love and care about," Liam remarked, sharing a smile with Taylor.

"You're one of the Arbiter's experiments, aren't you?" She glanced at his odd plates adorning parts of his fur. His powers certainly gave the impression he was like her and Ari.

"We'll go with that," he grunted with a grin.

The exit was only a few meters ahead, but Taylor had a curious thought. "How did you two find me? We're in the middle of nowhere

460

underneath Zabökar in a place I'm positive not many people know about."

Liam gestured to Ari as they continued to jog down the corridor, its rocky interior giving way to more mammal-made material and structure. "I actually saw you two fighting while I was waiting in line for your concert. I broke off and tailed her down to where her father was. It was only after seeing her split and not follow him that I confronted her about her altercation with you."

"That's when I searched the city's network infrastructure to find out where you were, but by the time we got to the apartment, you had already been kitnapped," Ari finished for him.

Liam pointed to his nose, "Good thing I had already picked up your scent. It was quite strong, and led us straight to you."

Taylor turned to smile at them both. "I never thought I'd say this—especially to you, Ari—but thanks for coming back for me."

All three stopped abruptly when they broke through the darkness and into the blinding light of the station. They could hear the wind of a train approaching, still adhering to its automatic schedule beneath the city. Directly across the tracks from them on the other platform was a cloaked figure with antlers, covered with a wolf skull. It was Barateon, but Nina was nowhere to be seen.

"What's he doing? He's just standing there." Liam muscles were tense. He didn't seem to like it one bit.

Ari looked up and down the row of support pillars and benches. There was nobody else around. "It's just him. I don't sense anyone else in the area." Her red iris was scanning through the walls. The sound of the train was getting closer.

"Doesn't matter." Taylor bared her teeth. "We're taking him down."

She was already running forward to the edge of the platform, sparks dancing across her fingertips. Her rage was fueling her power right now, and she let loose a concentrated bolt directly at the robed figure. He merely sidestepped the attack, given how telegraphed she made it. It exploded through the wall behind him, busting several pipes, steam exploding through the wall and causing the immediate area to get foggy.

461

The empty train was already upon them. It was zipping past, not even slowing down for their stop. The figure made an upward motion with his hooves and each car unlatched from the track rails below and went hurtling towards them. They all shouted warnings to each other as they scattered. The first somersaulted over Taylor's head as she dove to the floor. Another went spinning at Ari who reversed direction just as it smashed through a support pillar, destroying it utterly.

As each cabin of the subway was reaching the figure, he kept launching them at high velocities toward them. Liam was already a hulking beast and punched one squarely in the undercarriage on one of its spins, shattering all the glass as it crashed to the floor. He shook out his paw, blood forming at the knuckles.

Ari was doing her best to react to the insanely fast metal objects of death by thrusting both floor and ceiling into each subway section, causing half to stop where it got impaled to be melted by the intense heat, while the rest continued their thrust toward the other end of their platform, creating holes in the tiled wall.

It was pure chaos. The train seemed endlessly long. The three of them were doing their best to avoid, stop, destroy, or redirect each projectile sent their way. The entire platform was looking like a littered graveyard of metal carcasses. Skittering across the floor, Taylor used Ahya as a balancing counterweight whenever she had to change directions quickly. She just needed to get close to Barateon to launch a full-scale explosion near him, to at least knock him on his ass.

He saw through her plan and launched the final three cars directly at her position. Taylor screamed in surprise before slapping the ground with both her fists to stop her forward motion. Unleashing the energy she had been building, the very air around Taylor sucked inward, creating a vacuum of sound. The detonation then expanded violently, causing all objects to soar away from her. The figure had to actually move or be crushed by the incoming metal objects of death. They collided with the opposite wall and brought down two more support pillars, causing the entire ceiling above them to quake.

"Taylor, get across, quick!" Ari jutted forward a boiling mix of rock, masonry, and tile across the rails—cooling it as a path across to the other side.

Liam wasted no time and simply leaped his hulking form across the train gap. Taylor was not that physically capable, instead darting across the proffered bridge. The three were just about to inspect the mangled mess Taylor had created on the other side when glass shattered and metal beams making up each section began to twist and warp, ripping themselves from their frames as they went soaring at them to impale them.

Liam pushed Taylor to the side as he dodged two of the metal rods. Ari erupted a wall of brick and tile as several pierced through, narrowly missing her head just inches past her blockade. The ones that had flown past them immediately reversed and came flying back. Taylor stood up at the wrong time. She cried out as one punctured straight through her shoulder, toppling her to the ground with the impact.

Liam went rampaging into the damaged train cars. He lifted one up with a paw and tossed it aside, revealing Barateon hiding behind it. The stag raised a hoof and multiple beams began to warp and twist themselves around Liam, bringing him to his knees and binding him to the floor. Liam's muscles were bulging, veins popping out, as the steel rods began to bend and bubble out from the strain of trying to snap them apart.

Taylor gritted her teeth and screamed as Ahya gripped the rod tightly and began to pull it out. Ari took the time Taylor was down to send two waves of superheated ground in a semi-circle towards the stag. Keeping up the pressure, the whole floor beneath the remaining metal cars and Barateon turned into a quagmire of hell. He brayed loudly as his hooves sunk into the liquid floor, dissolving into the heat up to his knees.

His hold on the metal restraints now gone, Liam busted them with ease, one spiraling off to knock the figure's skull mask right off his face. Grimacing at the pain of having Ahya's tongue sticking right through her body to heal herself, Taylor squinted at the bleeding snout under the cowl. It was not a stag, but a caribou.

"It's not him." Taylor was simmering with wrath. "It's not him!"

"He didn't exactly teleport, did he?" Liam already had him in a stranglehold.

The caribou, now recovering from the agony of losing half his legs, made a futile attempt at using what metal was left near him to skewer Liam. He just swatted the caribou's arms away and ripped them clean off, one at a time. The caribou bawled in abject misery as blood began to pour onto the swiftly cooling grown beneath. It looked like Liam was going to snap his neck for good measure.

"Stop!" Taylor called out. Ahya had finished her restorative work on her shoulder. She walked right up to him, putting a tiny paw on Liam to stand down. "Where is Barateon? Where has he taken Nina? Tell me now!"

The caribou was delirious with pain, but he just giggled and spat in her face. "All hail, Barateon! All hail our unwritten—"

With a fit of fury, Taylor yelled at the top of her lungs as Ahya descended onto the defenseless caribou, munching him off at the knees. Ahya swung herself back, maw to the ceiling, swallowing his wriggling body deeper into her depths. Taylor didn't bother to look, her eyes fixated on the bloody arms. Within seconds, he was no more. Her stomach was now a bloated mass of bile as the taste of him hit her tongue. Taylor immediately vomited.

Liam was looking at her with sorrow, her body shaking as the last vestiges of her stomach left her mouth. "Be careful that your anger does not consume you, Taylor. You may become something that you wish you were not."

"Liam, shut up." Ari glared at him. "You were about ready to rip his head off before she ate him. Don't be a hypocrite."

"It's the intent I'm worried about, not the act," he clarified.

"I'll be fine." Taylor wiped her mouth and unsteadily got back to standing. She was better than fine now. It felt like a surge of adrenaline and stamina seeped into every cell of her body. She gazed around at the chaos around them. The other two looked exhausted, but she was now raring for more, since consuming the caribou. "We can't stop now. We need to find Nina. Do we have any idea where she is? Ari?" She turned to her.

Ari was already scanning, her cybernetic eye spastic in its socket. "It's at the edges of my range, but they are heading to Caelesti Spire."

464

"That makes sense; he is the High Council elder," Liam mused. "But that's in the dead center of town, and we need to get out of Zabökar soon." As if on cue, they felt the vibrations through the ground of multiple, pounding footsteps reverberating the very structure around them.

"Topside, now!" Ari ordered, pointing at the staircase to street level.

The further they went up the steps, the louder they could hear grinding gears, metal, and steam exhaust. A loud metallic roar diffused through the city. Screams of terror rose up and down the city blocks. It was joined by a reaction cry from another quadrant of the city. Taylor balked at the sight of two behemoths stalking just outside the city, their massive forms visible through the skyscrapers.

"There are two of them now?" Taylor's jaw dropped.

The hum of the chains of light reached a fever pitch. Bright flashes pulsed down each one from the spires to the monoliths below, their visages of protection facing outward. They slowly rose off the ground and began to spin in harmony around the circumference of Zabökar. The chains linking to the top of Caelesti Spire rotated in tune to their movements and it became an unfathomable blur.

"What's happening?" Taylor couldn't believe her eyes.

"Now they finally activate it!" Ari scoffed.

"It's the city's self-defensive mechanism. Something not seen since the elder days." Liam admired it.

A blindingly bright, translucent wall began to form from the statues upwards to the tip of the spire, creating a dome around the entire city. People leaving or escaping by foot or road were now trapped within its confines. The two behemoths rose up on two hind legs and smashed their whole weight onto the thin-looking shield, but it held firm. More howls of steam and metal echoed through the night as they were denied entry.

"We'll need to take the underground roads out of the city if they aren't blocked off already," Liam warned.

"Not before getting Nina first!" Taylor was unwavering.

"Then let's get to it." Ari steeled her jaw.

465

21.

COUNCIL

"Do you think it'll hold?" Samantha was quaking in Jake's arms, looking up through the incandescent shield enclosing Zabökar.

"If what I've read and learned about the old defense mechanism of the city is true, it is said to be indestructible," Natalia explained, watching through the shimmering light both behemoths pound on the barrier above.

"Let's not trust too much in it though!" Trevor called out from the front passenger seat, his window down and elbow resting out.

Trevor and Terrati had secured a large, flatbed hover truck for their transportation out of Zabökar. Nobody asked any questions about where it came from and nobody told. Mikhail shoved Trevor to the passenger seat, demanding he drive since he was a former TALOS member. Terrati was bunched in the back with Natalia, Jake, and Samantha.

They had just gotten through the worst of the traffic attempting to leave Zabökar by road, since the maglevs above had no coverage beyond the bounds of the city. Hovering over sidewalk curbs and taking tightly tense alleyways, they worked their way inward to the center where Mikhail was aware of several maintenance tunnels nearby leading down and outside the perimeter of the newly formed barrier.

Terrati slid the window separating the flatbed from the driver compartment open, poking his head in. "Where did you say this maintenance tunnel was?"

"A few more blocks up on the right," Mikhail answered. "But we're going to find Taylor first."

"Are you insane?" Trevor stared at him in shock. He gestured wildly up at the two behemoths. "This place could go up any moment,

467

and you want to waste our time finding a single wolf? She could be damn well anywhere in this city!"

"I'm with Trevor," Terrati agreed. "She's not worth it. I'm not dying for her."

"Then get out of my truck. Natalia and I are finding Taylor." He shouted back through the window past Terrati. "How's that tracking device we found working, Nat?"

The snow leopard slapped the device with a green-tinted screen against her paw. "Stupid Harutan tech. It's pinging off the wall on various targets. They're all congregating there." She pointed over at the tallest building in Zabökar, the Caelesti Spire.

"Might be the power-eaters. We knew they would be after her. Do you see any stray returns anywhere else in the vicinity?" Mikhail pressed.

"No, I don't…" Natalia grew excited. "Wait, yes, there is one lone signature. No, maybe it's two. It's not that far, one block left and then a right. That'll take us right to the spire."

"*Your* truck?" Trevor finally found the words to retort. "Who the hell found you this truck?" He reached over to snag the wheel, jerking it hard back to the right side of the road.

"Get your paws off the wheel!" Mikhail roared, swatting the smaller wolf's arm off, yanking it back to the left.

"I wasn't asking!" Trevor pulled out a gun and aimed it at Mikhail's head.

"Guys!" Natalia shouted from the back. "Stop the truck. You just knocked Samantha clear from the entire vehicle!" She shook her head, mumbling, "Idiots."

Jake was already up and over the side, landing lightly on the cement. He ran over to where Samantha fell. "You all right?" He lowered a paw to help her off the ground.

"I'm fine. Your 'friends' aren't exactly friendly, are they?" She wiped down her jeans and glared at the arguing males in the front.

Jake regarded them a moment. "They're actually not my friends. More like folks with a vested interest in Taylor. Right now, they're just our best chance to get out of here."

"Are you?" Samantha asked, causing Jake to turn his head back to her. "Are you invested in her too?" There was an ulterior motive to that question, he knew.

"Well, of course." This caused her expression to fall. "She's the last thing worth fighting for right now. My life is a disaster, and all I've got left is a promise. I'm going to see it through."

"So you're with Natalia and Mikhail in finding her?"

"I am." He nodded curtly, his mind made up.

She sighed. "Then I'll be with you too on this." They were already on the way back to the truck. Jake was helping lift her back onto the flatbed when she remarked, "She was a very friendly wolf. She doesn't deserve to be left behind."

"Oh great, another one to the lost cause." Trevor said. Jake glared up to the front, peeved over the sensitivity of the wolf's hearing and his rude attitude.

"Will you two just stop fighting? No wonder Taylor chose Ari over us when we left Cheribaum. We couldn't stop bickering amongst ourselves to form a cohesive team. She saw right through us, and it seems not much has changed! I've half a mind to leave all of you here, save Taylor, and leave with her by myself!" She scowled at Mikhail. "That means you too. I don't care how much history we got."

This cowed Mikhail immediately. "I'm sorry, Natalia. I'm just very anxious to find her and get the hell out of here."

"We all are," she said. Terrati rose a hoof to refute, but she overrode him. "Not the time, Terrati. Look, the signal is just a block down near the tower, and if it's not her, we can head on out. Is that agreed?" She seemed upset with this compromise, but she had to negotiate somehow against the hot-headed "A-type" personalities in the truck.

"Sounds alright," Trevor grumbled as he faced forward, followed by other mumblings of assent.

"Good. Now drive, Mikhail," Natalia ordered, taking charge of their current band of misfits.

"So, do we know where we're going once we get out?" Terrati asked the obvious question.

After a few moments of staring at each other, Samantha peeped up. "I do own a ranch south of Zabökar. We could go there for a bit."

Natalia nodded. "That sounds like a plan. We can figure out the rest once we're safely further away from this mess."

To accentuate her point, the behemoths above had started to clang and shift their metal plates that formed their reptilian faces. Their heads began to contort and elongate, a blinding flash of light blooming around the dual cannons aimed at their city. Several swirls of fire began to encircle each face, the vibrating hum filling the entire city with its pulsing. Glass from all the skyscrapers nearest shattered, falling like shards of deadly rain in the distance.

With dual thunderclaps, beams of pure light slammed into the barrier from each behemoth's cannon maw. Their entire bodies in the truck were shook from the impact. Several buildings beneath where the behemoths were perched began to crumble—layer upon layer of floors cascading down into a torrential waterfall of metal, rock, brick, and glass. Clouds of dust kicked up several dozen stories high, and began to spread out through the streets and avenues. The energy from the blasts appeared to siphon up the length of the swirling chains of light to the spires.

They each could see that the barrier was holding strong, however the twin blasts enveloped the two mechanical monstrosities and continued to expand outward. No doubt dozens of flora and fauna were annihilated as the mushroom cloud of death rose to the darkening heavens above Zabökar. The blast did little to deter the two creatures that caused it.

They did not know how many more blasts of that magnitude the shield could take.

"If we're tracking her, then let's track her! Go, go, go!" Trevor slapped the side of the truck.

Mikhail revved the truck as it soared over the streets, engines squealing as he made a sharp turn towards Caelesti Spire. They had no sooner broken out to the central park surrounding the tower, complete with fountains and resting picnic areas, that they saw a horde of rabbits surging towards the structure with Taylor in the lead.

"Son of a bitch." Terrati's jaw fell. Natalia just smirked at his reaction.

"There's no way you're getting through those rabbits if you want to get to her. They seem pretty savage right now," Jake warned.

"You don't think they'd attack us, would they?" Natalia wasn't sure.

Jake shrugged. "If I know rabbits, this has been a long time in coming. Seeing as they're helping Taylor and not killing her, she's made herself their impromptu figurehead with what she pulled at the concert. As long as she doesn't stop them from what they want to do, they'll support her in what she wants to do."

"Well, can't we just go in there and grab her, leaving them all alone?" Terrati suggested.

Mikhail shook his head. "You ever heard of mob mentality? She's their focal point of their righteous rage. She's directing them where to fire their anger onto. Right now, that's the spire and the High Council. We rip her away from them now and all that will be directed at us." He stopped the vehicle, facing the tower.

"Then we need a plan," Trevor fumed.

"Is that Ari?" Trevor pulled himself further out his window to get a better look.

Sure enough, there were some black-robed figures that were being fought on the very steps leading into the primary entrance. Ari was giving her usual blasts of flame, Taylor backing her up with arcs of electricity. Then there was a strange, gigantic beast that looked almost like a wolf, tossing robed figures left and right.

"Guess she chose Ari yet again." Jake had to chuckle, drawing a look from Natalia.

Ari couldn't believe it. She had half a notion to burn the throng of rabbits rampaging their way to cinders, but several in the front of the herd recognized and pointed Taylor out to the rest. It was an uncanny scene. A bunch of smaller rabbits huddled around them and literally pushed the three of them towards the center of Zabökar. Taylor attempted to halt their destructive tendencies when they went to strike out at other mammals, cars, or buildings, but Liam put a stop to her, warning that it wasn't wise at this time.

Being escorted along by the weirdest entourage Ari had even been a part of, they reached Caelesti Spire. Its beams of light spun at a fever pitch. The cultists guarding the entrance were simply fodder for their powers, having not been trained as long in their usage. The rabbits themselves provided the sacrifices needed to distract the remaining few to where Liam, Taylor, or she could finish them off. Things were looking up.

The moment they stepped through into the foyer, they were all flashed several times by the building's DNA scanners. A couple large panels in the ceiling receded up and to the side as two gargantuan mini-guns descended and took aim. The barrels revved up and unloaded scores of bullets into the mass of rabbits attempting to force entry as the trio dove behind whatever furnishings were available.

The pile of corpses was already seven feet high and stretching the width of the dual length doors when the hail of fire petered off and the guns began to fire empty. Several rabbits cast wary looks into the atrium, noses twitching on whether it was safe to finally enter that sudden graveyard of kin. Seeing as the guns above were no longer a threat, they grew emboldened and surged inward, some giving little kisses or a pause of a paw on a head of their brothers and sisters in memorial as they passed over their bodies.

"I'm surprised they still want to help after all that," Ari sneered, shocked at their fortitude.

Taylor glowered at the reptile. "After all they've suffered and forced to do in their lives? I don't blame them! Why aren't we dead?" She turned her head back up at the swiveling guns, arcing back and forth as if on patrol, now that its armory was spent.

Liam helped Taylor back to her hindpaws and pointed at the scanners above the doors, still flashing them. "None of us have ever been entered into their database. We're invisible because we aren't marked as either hostile or friendly. We're neither."

Ari snorted. "Sounds like a serious flaw in their defense system."

"Well, when you force DNA profiling on everyone in the city, I'd imagine they cut corners for cost in the programming." Liam smiled.

"Forget that!" Taylor huffed. "Nina is upstairs. We need to get to her!"

She was already on her way to the elevators, the rabbit horde alongside them, when the three gold-trimmed elevator cabin doors opened, guards surging out with armor and guns. "Let's take the stairs." Liam pointed to the stairwell door not far left of the gold-trimmed elevators.

"Fantastic! I never did trust elevators," Ari said, recounting a bad experience in one when she was younger and enjoying life in Zabökar. Getting stuck in one for hours was enough. The rabbits needed no more cues before they rolled over the guards, pouring out like an avalanche.

Busting through the door, Taylor gazed up the hundred odd floors from the center of the empty well and despaired. "We'll never make it up in time."

Liam growled and enlarged his body, towering over the two ladies. "I can get us up there faster."

Ari beat on his beefy arm as he gripped them both around the midsection. "I can get up just fine on my own!" Ari did not like getting help. She was used to doing things her way.

"I'm sure you could." He chuckled, his teeth flashing.

Ari squealed when Liam leaped several stories in a single bound. He cleared the railing and pounded onto the concrete steps, causing several cracks within its structure. Turning, he took a foot to the railing and bounded up several more floors. He was making insanely good time, their only breaks being when he had to turn around to prepare for the next jump.

"I sincerely hope this Nina is worth all this trouble." Ari disentangled herself from Liam's grip when they reached the top floor. Looking down the dizzying height they traversed, she scooted away quickly to the safety of the wall. She did not exactly like heights. She could handle a little distance off the ground, but this was way out of her comfort zone. However, she wasn't about to let that show to Taylor, her leaked squeal notwithstanding.

Taylor thanked Liam for the lift, looking more energized than ever. "She is. With everyone else I know gone, dead, or already evacuated Zabökar, Nina is the last person I have left that means anything to me. I don't want her to die here."

"Fair enough." Ari sniffed, looking at the lone door into what looked like exquisitely gaudy corridors through the glass window in the middle. "What made you think the High Council will be here at the top floor?" she asked Liam.

"The High Council isn't known to be humble. They would want the best view in the house."

"You're shooting in the dark," she accused.

"Yup." He gestured to the door. "Ladies first."

They entered into a spacious vestibule with marble pillars adorning the corners of the room. Liam had to shrink down to get through the doorway, lest he demolish part of the frame. The trickling sound of small fountains before each inlaid alcove helped to frame the sculpted High Council visages in each. There was an abandoned receptionist's desk opposite the elevators. It looked pristine and peaceful. A far cry from the hellish environment outside.

Just ahead through boardroom-like doors, they could hear a loud argument between several people. Not caring about any etiquette, Taylor and Ari both busted through the twin doors, having them slam against the stoppers.

Within was a circular table with chairs at intervals, the center hollowed out for when speakers needed to be in the middle. The view of Zabökar was impressive, spanning half the room from ceiling to carpet, starting at the far end of the room to the middle—marred only by what was happening outside. Several recesses along the wooden façade wall not built with glass were decorated with yet even more statues. These, however, were brandishing a variety of sharp-looking weapons within their paws, hooves, and talons.

There were a group of mammals on opposite ends of the table on one side. Barateon had dumped his hood and robe and was wearing a mauve business suit. He was talking with Javier Hawkins, Nina's father, with the frightened girl between them. On either side were a collection of other mammals ranging from big cats, to birds, to a few prey. They all stopped and stared over at the entrance.

Javier spoke first, jabbing a finger in Taylor's direction. "You! I remember you! Dyeing your fur won't hide your heathen face from judgment! I saw that travesty on live television. What have you involved my daughter in? Power-eaters? Cultists? The High Council would never do anything like that!" He looked her up and down, blood and gore covered. "If anything, you are the sick one!"

Taylor had eyes only for Barateon, but he was stepping back, enjoying this. She redirected her focus onto Javier. "Involved her in? She involved herself! She was tricked into thinking she could make a difference in destroying the Script through me. I saved her life when your people, your 'High Council', murdered her in cold blood before my eyes. I brought her back to life."

Javier was flabbergasted. He stammered, "What in blazes are you talking about? Murdered? Brought back to life? There are no such miracles in this world. I have half a mind to believe these injuries on her now were your doing!" He flapped a wing at his colleagues. "And as for these atrocities you claimed they committed at your concert of sin? Easily doctored videos and photos. Falsified. We would know if such criminals infiltrated our ranks. The High Council is a solidified unit and has been for centuries with carefully screened processes for inclusion. One of their ilk would simply not get in to lead this great country. We would know."

"You're pretty deluded if you think that," Ari scoffed, folding her arms.

"And who the hell is this?" Javier shook a wing at her, stepping in front of Nina, who was still trembling and looked unsure of what to do.

Barateon stepped up behind him and whispered, "That's the Arbiter's daughter, Ariana."

Javier narrowed his eyes. "Daughter to a traitor, and no less a criminal if you've come with this lot." He indicated Liam and Taylor. Ahya snapped her teeth in vexation. "If there was any security left in this building, I'd have you bound and chained, but as it is…" He looked out at the city, ash flying through the air and fires generating plumes of smoke that permeated the enclosed airspace above. "There is little I can do except ask you to leave. You've done enough harm to my family already. Let us prepare our exit from the city in peace, and you go off and die in whatever way seems best to you."

With a swing of his head, the conversation was over. He turned to address his daughter, coddling her wounds. "Did they hurt you much at the concert?" Nina stared at Barateon, almost seeking his permission with her eyes to say anything. Taylor noticed the slight nod from the stag.

"N-No. Not much at all, Father." She looked terrified for her life.

Taylor finally saw the problem by virtue of where everyone stood. Every single person was in on their cult except Nina's father. He was standing alone. Of all the High Council members, he was the last of them that had yet to be corrupted. Nina had probably recognized them all from her group meetings.

Nina knew that any false move would spell death for her dad, and quite possibly her. She locked eyes briefly onto Taylor, almost silently willing her to stand down and not make things worse. Taylor's heart ached for Nina. She was in an impossible situation where there was no easy solution out of.

"Why are we even entertaining this? That guy is a sadist." Ari pointed directly at Barateon. "The only reason I'm even bothered to be here is because of her." She shifted her finger to Nina. "We're taking her and leaving. I could care less about the rest of you." She cracked her knuckles, getting ready to fight.

Taylor put a paw out to stay her hand and Liam's. The last thing she wanted was to have Nina get caught in the crossfire and die. "Yes, it's true, we only came for Nina." She saw the affronted look of Javier,

476

his wings now more protective around his daughter. "She has suffered enough under this city, this council, and her father."

Javier clicked his beak in indignation. "I beg your pardon, wolf, but you will do no such thing. She's all I have left now. My daughter means the world to me, and she's escaping with us."

Taylor barked out a laugh. Ahya opened her maw and seemed to join in silently. "That's a joke! I was there, remember? In the church? Your own daughter told you off about how you neglected her all those years. No wonder she rebelled and ran away to be in a 'horrid' band. No wonder she got caught up with the wrong people. She was just looking for someone to accept her and be there for her." She smiled at Nina as she said, "Just like she was there for me when I needed someone most."

Ari studied Taylor curiously as Nina's face beamed. There was a glimmer of hope still left in her eyes. It was dashed as Barateon moved forward to place a hoof on Javier's shoulder. "You two go on ahead. We'll deal with these three. Tend to your daughter first, Javier."

The tension was heavy as Javier thanked Barateon, and with a close wing around his daughter, guided her toward the doors. Nina was constantly glancing back to Taylor, wondering if something was going to happen, or if anything was going to get resolved with the power-eaters standing in their midst. Liam and Ari were eyeing the other well-suited mammals, subtly shifting positions to get some distance. The silence of their leaving was deafening.

Javier was at the door when two rabbits flowed in from the elevator with several of their kits swarming around their ankles. Taylor's eyes bulged at the two of them. "Stepan? Eleanor? What are you doing here?"

Stepan locked eyes with Barateon nervously. "We were, um…leaving Zabökar with our family."

"There's nowhere to go from here," Ari jeered.

Taylor jerked a thumb at the suited mammals. "Don't tell me you're going with them." After a few moments of silence, Taylor couldn't believe the hypocrisy of this rabbit. "After all those rallies and wanting to have more rights and stand up for your fellow rabbit, you throw your lot in with them and betray your own kind?" She waved a paw towards the destruction around them through the windows. "You're leaving your kin to die, Stepan. What excuse do you have for that?"

Eleanor was already shifting away from Stepan, gathering her kits around her. She looked guilty as sin. "Family comes first, Taylor." He waggled a small finger at her. "You should understand that. I recall our conversation about family and how you were eager to reconnect with them once more. Nothing is more important than family."

"So you made a deal with them to incite riots and a full rabbit rebellion for what? I thought rabbits stuck together?" Taylor was incensed now.

Liam spoke up beside her. "I understand family, but what purpose could it possibly serve to launch rallies and tell your kind to do all this, only to just leave with the very mammals you claim to despise and fight against?"

Stepan finally got his courage again. "You and I both know there was no hope for overturning the lot us rabbits got in life. I was just in a lucky position to be able to influence the council to spare my family in return for their safety when Zabökar got destroyed."

Javier had been listening to all of this, looking back and forth between Taylor and Stepan. He turned to Barateon. "What is the meaning of this? What is Stepan talking about?" It was clear he was familiar with the rabbit, but wasn't aware of what he was doing under the table.

Barateon closed his eyes and sighed, rubbing his temple. "Javier, old friend, I really wished you hadn't been around to hear that." He signaled two of his colleagues to sweep past Javier and Nina and shut the doors, standing before them like prison guards. He turned his head to Taylor. "It's true, Stepan was in a unique position for us to influence fate. He had the eyes and ears of the rabbit populace in Zabökar unlike any before him. They would listen to him."

"Why use him to rise up against you?" Taylor seemed confused.

Ari stepped forward. "Because you all wanted it to be destroyed to send a message." She addressed Liam and Taylor. "They were never about saving Zabökar, it was about uniting all of the northern countries under one banner: theirs. By letting it fall to the reptiles of Talkar, the very ones my father had been warning them about and proposing

478

solutions to for decades, they could find a common enemy to bring all mammals together to fight against."

"But how would that attract the attention of the behemoths?" Taylor was fumbling in her mind on how it all connected together. She was there for Palaveve and Howlgrav, but didn't really see a connection between the two.

"They are attracted by powerful light and activity," Ari explained, her eyes ever on Barateon. "But they are unable to strike out on their own. Something is preventing them from attacking cities or waging proper war on us."

Barateon chuckled. "Well done, Ariana. You're only half right. The Script is the other half. This blasted Script is keeping all of us from our true destinies. As long as it exists, we cannot harm the other—not fully. We could have allowed the changes that led to the destruction of Palaveve and Howlgrav unite the north, but with the birds of Dirina hoarding all their advanced technology to themselves, we had little leverage to convince them to join under our banner. Since we require their prowess to win this war, we blocked all news of Palaveve and Howlgrav's destruction so the behemoths could come attack us here, because we have need of their power and might. By keeping the citizens here in ignorance, it made this city a far more lucrative target."

"I don't understand. If the Script is preventing harm between cities, then why did two get destroyed, and why are they attacking Zabökar now?" Taylor glanced back at the behemoths as the entire spire shook when they launched another salvo of city-devastating energy, to much the same effect as previous. It felt like the entire spire around them hummed with crackling energy.

"Nor does the Script stop individual deaths and people killing each other," Liam piled on, his muscles flexing and raring to go. He seemed eager for the fight.

"The Script was never meant for you or me." Barateon schooled her as if she were an unruly child. "The nature of the Script goes far beyond the bounds of our insignificant lives."

Ari shifted her head to Taylor, staring directly at her. "My father said it was because of you."

Her entire body slumped, her tense muscles gone. She blinked at Ari. "What? Me? I don't understand."

"He figured you were upsetting Script, and through your influence, caused Palaveve and Howlgrave to be destroyed well before their time." Ari did not seem to relish telling Taylor this.

"We noticed this as well." Barateon grinned. He began walking slowly along the length of the table, away from Javier, towards the windows to survey the destruction around. "We knew the Arbiter's men were after you in Palaveve. We saw news reports of what they had done in efforts to secure you. Blowing up a town to attract the attention of a behemoth, something that they couldn't normally attack."

He spun on a hoof, his voice raising as he spoke directly to Taylor. "Then with Howlgrav. You were involved there as well. We found out after the fact the city was exploded on Ariana's orders to, again, help secure you. Now you are here in Zabökar. The rabbits would have revolted one way or another without your assistance, but you involved yourself in their cause, and all their work out there right now is of your doing—a day later, I might add. Thus…" He waved his hoof out to the twin goliaths. "They averted Script, and are dead set on destroying this city. We waited to capture you until after you set the pyres of rebellion into motion."

"But why am I so special?" Taylor snarled, baring her teeth. "I don't get why I am so gods damned important to anyone!" Ahya was growing and snapping viciously at the air, causing Javier to keep Nina further behind him. The rest of the mammals were unfazed.

"It's why you were brought to our sanctuary tonight," Barateon intoned, slowly pacing back to be with the other council members. "We knew you were born without a Script. You were the first mammal in history to be born without one. By being exposed to whatever the Arbiter created while in your mother's womb, you came out different. We tried pulling a Script on you at the start, but there was none for you. That's why we were so interested in you. You could be the key to solving the question we've been posed with for ages: how to get rid of the Script."

Barateon frowned. Looking back at a tawny dingo, he ordered, "Cherla, bring the otter in."

480

Cherla waved a paw up in the air, and between them, a portal in the ceiling opened. Finnley dropped from above, straight down through the center hole of the table. He groaned and then squeaked as he was yanked up into the air by another mammal's powers. Held in suspension between them all, Taylor could see he was beaten bloody. His facial features were unrecognizable and there were horrendous lacerations all along his body that weren't remotely healed.

"Finnley!" Taylor cried out. "What did they do to you?" The otter just looked at her with a mixture of sadness and hatred. He simply turned away as best he could in the invisible grip he was in.

"What we didn't account for and what we did not believe at first was the testimony of this runt," Barateon seethed.

"I tried to warn you." He coughed on some blood. "You all didn't listen. Taylor is a danger to us all. You mess with the Script with her, everyone you love will die."

"Like we were going to believe a renounced contract merc like you." Finnley slammed into the table with a gasp. "However, after tonight, I believe we are more inclined to give credence to your theory. What we encountered down there tonight was beyond anything we've known. We will need to know exactly what it is, and how it is triggered. Once that is accomplished, we can use better use those few off the Script to change this world."

"I've heard enough," Javier finally interjected. "I don't even know what the heck is going on here. I thought we were discussing how to properly evacuate the remaining citizens after the shield was raised before these people came in." He pointed to all three of them: Liam, Ari and Taylor. A rumble went through the entire building, causing all of them to lose balance. The last blast concussion wave must have split some key foundational structures in the spire.

Taylor began to approach Javier, her eyes flashing over to Nina. "Sir, the people you work with are power-eaters. Disgusting cultists who have ruined my family from the start. In their search of ending the Script, my family has been fractured and destroyed. I barely made it back to reunite with my two brothers, who I hope are safely outside the city."

481

"Yes, I'm well aware of the proof you showed tonight at your concert." Javier glanced back at the two mammals standing guard at the only exit. "And after hearing what I heard just now, I'm not sure what to believe anymore."

Barateon spoke in his most convincing tone. "Javier, old friend, for the longest time we have tried to get you to side with us. At every turn, you have rebuffed our advances to bring you into the fold."

"If I had known what sort of group you were talking about, I would have tendered my resignation from the council right then and there." He puffed up his chest feathers. "We Hawkins have been an integral part of the High Council since the Hordos War. I've traced my lineage back to those proud warriors who lent air support against the reptile invaders. I would not dare tarnish my family name with the likes of what you are being accused of."

Barateon extended out a hoof to Nina. "Yet your daughter has."

All eyes fixated on the swan. Javier's jowls dropped. "Nina? What is the meaning of this?"

Nina was wringing her wings, twisting her feathers in front of her. She kept her eyes to the floor. "I…I joined them because I wanted to make a difference in this world. Nobody else gave me that chance. Nobody else believed that I could."

"You… You ate other people? Like they did?" Javier was beside himself, the shame of a father evident on his face.

Nina nervously nodded. "Only one. I only ever wanted to change the future…to change my future to something better than all this."

"You see?" Barateon cooed. "Even your daughter listens to reason. She's actually quite blessed. She was resurrected tonight from death by that very wolf over there, and is off the Script. She is free to make her own decisions and change her own life." This information got Finnley to perk up. He weakly raised his head to look at the swan through his swollen eyes.

"It's not entirely her fault!" Taylor growled. "She was lied to and manipulated to get to me. She was eaten before my very eyes to prove that I could remove her Script. If anything, she is innocent of all this." She moved forward to make a grab for Nina.

"I think you've said enough, Taylor." Barateon snapped his fingers. Taylor flew through the air and slammed into the wooden wall façade, denting a gaping hole through to the concrete and metal structure beyond. Barateon continued, facing Javier. "And you, old friend, have seen too much."

"No!" Nina screamed as it appeared Barateon teleported behind Javier. The swan gurgled on fresh blood as an entire antler rack had pierced straight through his ribs and chest. With a heave, Barateon tossed the dying bird to the floor before his daughter.

He pointed at Nina. "Bring the girl. She'll assist us in changing the future."

The boardroom erupted into a cavalcade of light, fire, explosions, and portals. Taylor screamed in fury and split the entire front half of the oval table with her lightning. The debris pummeled the mammals before her while one chunk went flying through a portal and right back into her head from behind, knocking her to the floor. Stepan, Eleanor, and their kits squealed and huddled in the far corner of the room, watching the carnage.

Liam leaped above her and squashed the nearest lion, who proceeded to melt the very floor beneath them like acid. They both fell to the level below with a crash. Ari was already turning the entire carpet around her into flames and firing off balls of heated material at the council members, wreathing herself in fire to avoid the less-damaging powers they wielded. These High Council eaters were of a different caliber than their cultist lackeys; they seemed well-trained.

Taylor attempted to make a dash towards Javier in hopes of swallowing him with Ahya and reversing some of the damage done by Barateon. Hopefully it would be enough. She couldn't quite make it there when the stag appeared before her, knocking her to the floor. Ahya swung back around like a condensed weighted ball to knock him off his hooves. He warped again to avoid the blow. Taylor cursed.

Liam roared and leapt back up through the hole created, the lion's face firmly in his large paw, the rest of the body thrashing. He took aim and threw him at two others near the exit, busting the doors open wide. He rampaged towards Barateon, and they engaged in a game of cat and mouse as the stag zoned all about the enraged wolf.

483

Ari tried to help Liam, hurling a super-heated piece of the oval table in Barateon's direction, narrowly missing him. But she was pinned down by four other skillful, competent mammals. The dingo warped above her and with the combined power of another council member's shield of water, blew right through her fire barrier and slammed her to the floor. Cherla cackled as she shoved Ari's face into the smoldering carpet.

Nina was whimpering on her knees beside her father, their wings intertwined by the time Taylor finally made it over to her. She snapped her fingers to get her friend's attention. "Nina, do you trust me?" She already had Ahya out and maw open, tongue slithering out to ensnare her dad into that spacious darkness.

She nodded vigorously. "I do. Please... Taylor, make him better. He doesn't deserve to die because of my mistakes."

Nina wept uncontrollably as she saw her dying father disappear into that tail, his glassy eyes lingering on hers. She dropped her head to the ground. Taylor put a hand on her friend's back. She could feel Ahya getting straight to work on Javier's body, flushing her saliva through the injuries and into his body. Taylor inwardly grimaced at knowing that this would drain a lot of energy out of her. This was the second time she'd be doing this tonight, and she could already feel the toll it was taking on her body now.

"No rest for me." Taylor sighed, ducking low from a bolt of wood thrust at her from the swiftly deteriorating boardroom table. She fired back a salvo of lightning at her attacker, but missed, shattering out the window panes beyond and letting the ash and heat into the room.

Cherla had now directed her attention to Taylor. Opening portals to each of the statues along the walls, she grabbed various weapons from their paws and hooves and began throwing them in her direction. Taylor did her best to roll and smack each metal instrument of death with concentrated bolts, throwing off their trajectories. The dingo was about to throw a great war axe when Liam smacked her across the room, right into a portal she had to create on the fly.

Cherla plunged from above, the tall stairwell behind her through the portal, with the blade of the axe aimed for Taylor's head. Taylor screamed as she put up her hands and caught it just inches from her paws. It hovered in midair for a brief moment as the body of Cherla kept moving due to her velocity. She fell through the ground before Taylor into another portal and disappeared along with the axe.

"How did you do that?" Nina was amazed. "You stopped that axe like it was nothing."

Taylor looked down at her fingers. "I don't know. I didn't even touch it."

"Maybe you can—" Nina warbled, her neck spurting blood as a knife protruded from her jugular. With a twist of the blade and a jerk, she was tossed to the ground, her life essence poured onto the now-filthy carpet beneath. Behind her was Finnley, wiping the blade on her corpse. He had managed to crawl all the way over here to kill her.

"What the fuck did you do, Finnley?!" Taylor was full of wrath. "If Ahya wasn't occupied, I'd have done what I should have let her do weeks ago and eat your sorry ass!"

"I'm sorry, Taylor, but it had to be done." He showed no remorse. "You pushed her off the Script and brought the Authority down on us all. She needed to die as her Script demanded."

"After what I did for you and Fey? I saved his life!" Spit was flying from her mouth. He remained infuriatingly out of her reach, Ahya weighing her down where she was.

"And for what? For me to witness my lover's flesh and blood melt off his bones? To see him mutilate himself before the Authority took him? That was no fate I would have wished upon Fey." He pointed at her firmly. "Yet you were the one who gave him that fate. A fate he could not escape from. A fate Nina couldn't either."

"You don't know that!"

"Consider it a small mercy I granted you to not have to see that happen to her. Nina for Fey. Consider us even." He slipped the knife in between the band of his belt.

Taylor's vision narrowed. Finnley was all she saw. The bedlam around them was inconsequential to the steaming pile of crap in front of her. With claws bared, she let loose an unearthly howl to the heavens. Her entire body pulsed with a bright light as everything in the room went dark. A suction of air gravitated towards her for a split second before her entire body unleashed a catastrophic explosion, thrusting

485

everyone off the floor. It blew out the entire ceiling and walls to miniscule bits.

With the boardroom now open to the air, Taylor collapsed atop Ahya. Her brain was in overload and she couldn't think clearly. Blinking tiredly, she surveyed the strewn bodies throughout the room. Her mind barely registered that success was imminent within Ahya. People began to groan and recover slowly from the miniature detonation Taylor unleashed. Then a sharp sound intensified her focus—the screeching racket of Eleanor.

Stepan and his half dozen kits were trying in vain to stop Eleanor from scratching and tearing at her ears. She was digging deep cuts into their soft membranes, all the while screaming at the top of her lungs. She continued to pound her head into the floor and wall and pull on her ears until one ripped nearly half off. The kits were crying in unison at what their mother was doing to herself.

Then everyone felt it. A darkness crept over their hearts as a presence of despair brought a pall over the entire room. Taylor could see even Barateon was afraid, his nostrils flaring. The entity above them was horrifyingly visible, yet not. Its gaze tracked the movements of the hysterical rabbit.

"Entity detected. Executing," was all it said.

Eleanor screamed her last as her body began to bubble and blood flooded from her orifices. Stepan and the bunnies squealed and all ran from her as she writhed and jerked on the ground. It was over within a minute, leaving nothing left but her clothes, limply hanging on her bones. Everyone simply stared at the gruesome sight, unable to move or even think.

Finnley coughed and gasped. "You saved her too?" He seemed furious as he tried to move, but the dread in all their hearts was too much.

The Authority was still searching. There was one yet alive off the Script now. Taylor could sense Javier moving about within Ahya. She continued to pat her tail as best she could, willing Ahya to keep her mouth shut. She remembered Nina staying inside of Ahya somehow kept her safe. She didn't need to understand why just yet, just that it was true.

"Please stop moving, please stop moving." Taylor was near to tears. The fear was insufferable. It was like the thing was getting closer and closer to her person, studying her. She wanted to shriek to the sky it was that unbearable.

Then it was gone. With a slight rustling of wind gentling kissing the destroyed boardroom, the Authority had moved on. Javier was still alive inside Ahya. There was still yet someone off the Script. She breathed a sigh of relief as she looked around. Ari and Liam were getting back up to a knee, looking around to see who else they had to fight.

A laughing cry from above presaged Cherla's return. Taylor hadn't the strength or reflexes to react. The dingo descended through her portal, her war axe slicing clear through the base of her tail. Taylor's mind went numb, the nerves at her spine firing off like wildfire. Ahya opened up like a wounded animal, nearly spilling out Javier like spewed meat. The dingo looked her directly in the eye mere inches away and sneered before ripping up the axe from the floor.

Her tail was gone. Her eyes watched as the blood gushed from both ends of the severed connection that was no longer there. She tried to reach out for Ahya, her sister, who was in misery. Her tongue was flopping around like a dead fish, her body jerking in throes of pain. The shock was too much. She waved her hands fruitlessly to maintain a grip on reality, but Taylor couldn't stand no more.

Her head fell to the carpet, and the last thing her eyes focused on before darkness consumed her was the dead body of Nina.

22.

DEVASTATION

The entire world was going in slow motion. Taylor rose up from the floor and turned around in a circle. She could see Barateon lethargically getting up to a knee and shouting something unintelligible to Cherla who was beside her. In fact, everyone was moving at a speed where it seemed endlessly long, yet she was moving normally. There was an air of peaceful tranquility, and Taylor felt like she was just floating.

Portals were opening and the rest of the High Council members were retreating into them. Cherla was ordered to smack Finnley upside the head, throw him over her shoulder, and hop into a portal with Barateon. They were all gone, including Stepan and his kits. Most likely transported far away from where they were now.

Her eyes followed Liam and Ari's shocked eye lines behind her, and she noticed at her feet was her own body. It was lying very still. Her eyes were open and staring straight ahead at Nina, blood still pooling around her head. Ahya was continuing to flop as Javier backed up gradually, his face contorted in some form of horror as he looked at his daughter, who lay dead beside him.

"Hey, Taylor," a small voice peeped next to her.

She whirled around to see two small, familiar faces perched on what was left of the boardroom table. An albino skunk and a brown-blotched-furred raccoon. She rushed to them as they did their best to hop into her arms. "Pine! Mitchell!" She cried with joy.

"It's good to see you again too." Mitchell petted her back.

She pulled back and looked at them. "Where are we? Did I die?"

They all turned to the two disconnected parts of her body. Pine dropped down out of her arms first and walked over. "I don't think so."

489

He pressed his paw into her hair, parting it with his fingers. "Doesn't feel like you are yet."

Mitchell leaped out of her grip and investigated Ahya. "But you are dying though. You both are."

"I miss her already," Pine sighed, gazing fondly at Ahya. "She talked with us sometimes when we were feeling lonely."

Taylor tilted her head. "Wait, talked with you? When was this?"

"Every day, actually," Mitchell clarified, smiling at Taylor. "You just can't see us when we do. She's quite lively."

"I don't understand. What are you then?" Taylor knelt down to be with them. She felt an odd sense of unease being beside her swiftly dying body.

"We're apparently manifestations of your own mind," Mitchell joked.

"We actually don't know ourselves, but we're with you all the time and see what you do." Pine grinned.

Taylor narrowed her eyes. "Wait a minute. All that I do?" If she could have in her current form, she would have blushed furiously.

Mitchell shrugged, doing his best to squat and pet Ahya in an attempt to calm her frayed state of mind. "Don't worry about it, Taylor. We don't judge. We never have. We're just happy to be with you and talking again."

There was loud banging out in the receptionist room. It was coming from within the elevator. "What was that?"

Pine's face grew grim. "Other…people who joined us. You keep adding more, Taylor. It's getting crowded around here, and they're not very nice people."

"Not all of them." Mitchell was sharing Pine's gloom. "We've managed to keep them contained, but Sarah is stuck back with them, and we've not been able to see her for many months."

"Wait, Sarah? I'm so lost! What is going on?" Taylor wanted to walk over to those doors and open it up to see her long-deceased friend.

"I wouldn't do that if I were you." Mitchell stared after her, his tone causing her to stop. "Where we are now, we have no idea what they could do to you, Taylor."

490

"And where is here?" She glanced about the room, now open to the elements because of her display of power moments earlier. "This looks like the top of Zabökar to me."

Mitchell answered. "It has always existed for us. This place was created by your magical connection with Ahya. I think it being severed pushed you in here."

Pine rose back up and sadly smiled at her. "It's a place you can move on from, if you wish. We'll both be with you if that happens."

"Or you could stay and help those that need you," Mitchell offered. His paws were ever on Ahya. "Your sister needs you, Taylor. What did you want to do?"

Taylor moved back between Pine and Mitchell as she went to her knees and looked at her amputated tail. All the expression was in her maw. She was in pain, and it broke her heart. She had tried once before to cut off her own tail, but it was too much. She couldn't go through with it. The idea was an appalling thought to her now. Ahya needed her alive. If she left with Pine and Mitchell now, as much as she would want the peace, it wouldn't make her happy.

"I have to go back." She turned to her two small companions. "Will I see you two again?"

"We're always with you, as we said." Pine hugged her.

"Until next time you summon us." Mitchell joined the hug.

"Bye, you two." Taylor held them close as the scenery around her faded to white.

"Ari! What the hell are you doing?" Liam roared. He pointed at Taylor's bleeding nub of a tailbone. "We need to cauterize both wounds now on either side to stop the bleeding before we can get them healed together! What are you standing around for? You're the only one that can do this!"

Ari had been watching with her cybernetic eye, her focus fixated on something invisible happening right before them. Liam's bellow galvanized her to action. "Right." She rushed forward and with full palms, sealed the wounds on both Taylor's backside and where Ahya would have connected to her. The entire spire shook once more, this time more forcefully. "We can't reconnect them here. This place isn't safe."

"We need you to carry her down," Liam ordered Javier, who was already weeping over his daughter's corpse.

"What's the point? Everything I have is gone. My wife lost to the rabbits. My daughter to gods know what!" He glared at the large, strange-looking wolf. "Why should I care what happens to that girl?" He gazed down upon Taylor's inert form.

"Because that girl just saved your life. She did it without a thought for her own safety. She loved your daughter like a sister and saw her die right in front of her, twice." He gripped Ahya by the middle and flung the tailmaw over his shoulder. "If you do nothing else to honor your daughter's memory, then do this last thing for the only friend she had left at the end. Help me bring her down to the ground from here."

The entire building began to shake. The combined shockwaves of the behemoths' blasts and Taylor's latest explosion had rippled through Caelesti Spire and made it extremely unstable. Ari looked out over the edge of that dizzying height nervously. "And how do you propose we get down ourselves? He can fly with her. We can't. There isn't enough time for us all to wait our turn to get a flight."

"You're going to help me." Liam gestured to her fingers. "You can superheat anything around you and mold it into whatever you want, right?"

Ari looked like she didn't like where this was going. "I could, but if you want stairs down this tower, that's not going to happen. Metal is a bit harder to mold than pure rock for me, and takes far more concentration."

"Then concentrate on a slide a few feet in front of us like your life depended on it, because it does!" He gripped her wrist to drag her over to the edge, nearly prompting a violent response from her. "I'll slow us down with my claws, you just focus on getting us a way down."

492

Javier had already loaded Taylor's body onto his back, adjusting her so her limbs wouldn't get in the way of his wings. He nodded at Liam. "For my daughter," he said without emotion.

Javier already took off and zipped down out of sight below the level of the floor. Liam whooped as he pressed Ari towards the edge. "Time to go, Ari. Give us a slide."

"You're a real asshole, you know that?" She was quivering, but was already doing her best to bend and warp the metal structures, beams, and struts out from beneath the surface of the building, giving them a way down.

"Going to need to be steeper than that. We need a quick way down, not a leisurely stroll." He adjusted Ahya on his other shoulder and with his entire bulk, shoved Ari down the first portion of the slide. He raked his claws into the siding, blood and fur stripping away as he grit his teeth from the pain.

"I hate this!" Ari yelled, doing her best to keep something beneath their rumps as they descended the exterior of the towers in a circular fashion. Liam's legs were around her waist to ensure they weren't going insanely fast so that she could keep up with providing life-saving ground underneath.

"You can do this," he encouraged. "If I can withstand how freaking bad this hurts, you can get us down from this tower. We'll heal."

It wasn't more than a few minutes, but Ari was completely exhausted. Her head dropped and her powers evaporated as she had passed out from the exertion, and probably terror. They were about a dozen or so floors away from ground level. This was going to hurt something fierce—if not kill them—if Liam didn't do something fast.

Gripping tightly onto Ahya with one arm, wrapping the other around Ari, he gauged the distance to tallest tree in the gardens below. Using their momentum, he leapt off at the end of the metal slide, soaring towards the foliage of his intended target. He twirled in the air to protect his two charges, then hit the upper boughs of the tree with his upper shoulder and back. He grunted as several more branches rammed into his body.

Feeling a purchase for his hindpaws to grip onto, he spun again to reorient his center of mass with his two passengers, and was now facing down through the branches of the tree. He hopped down from branch to branch until he hit the pavement sidewalk hard, forcing him into a roll. Ari was held fast as Ahya slumped out of his hold and flopped on the ground lifelessly.

Ari was still unconscious. Liam groaned as he let her roll out of his arms and got up to his paws and knees. He looked up to see several people racing towards him. It was a snow leopard and a rabbit. The rabbit went immediately to Ahya and began inspecting her. Beyond them was a truck filled to the brim of other mammals. Javier was delivering Taylor's body into their care. The rest were fending off groups of rabbits with their guns, mowing them down.

"What happened to her?" The snow leopard was horrified.

Liam propped himself up onto a knee before standing, now his normal height and size. "Some dingo up top sliced clean through Taylor's tail. We need to get them back together again."

"How in the world are we going to do that?" the rabbit asked, glancing up from Ahya. "It seems like it's dead."

Liam nodded. "If not just. We need to get them together fast and apply what little saliva Ahya has left onto their shared wound. Please tell me someone here knows what I'm talking about."

The snow leopard nodded. "I do. Jake, please step back. I'll bring Ahya back there." She turned her head back to Liam, Ahya now over her shoulder. "We have a bit of extra room if you two want a ride out. Things are going to get worse."

"Much obliged." He would have tipped his beanie, but growled when he realized it had gone missing—perhaps with the wind when he was heading down Caelesti Spire. He'd have to buy himself another one. He kicked Ari with the tip of his hind paw, causing her to stir. "Rise and shine, Princess. We have a ride to catch."

"I am never doing that again." She grimaced, still woozy as she allowed Liam to help her up.

"I don't plan to get in that sort of situation again." He chuckled. His face grew serious. "But we do need to haul ass." The ground shook, dust kicking up around the edges of the gardens surrounding. The entire tower began to sag.

"Are you coming or not?!" They could see the tiger in the driver's seat shouting at Javier.

The black swan stood stoically, staring up at Caelesti Spire with reverence. "I will go down with my city. Just let me have this moment." He faced toward the spire and began to pray.

The tiger waved a dismissive paw at him and refocused on the road. Liam and Ari had hopped into back of the truck, its backend drooping at the added weight. Feeling a slight scratch along his back, Liam turned to see a rabbit trying to tear him apart with his very paws. Snorting a laugh, he just punched the critter hard in the face, dropping him like a rock.

"I see you've not had it easy out here," he commented.

"My kin didn't exactly see eye to eye with us." Jake looked miserable as he helped the snow leopard realign the tail as best they could against Taylor's rear. A red panda was sitting transfixed beside a gazelle, fear evident in both their eyes.

"Everybody settled in? We're going!" The tiger in the front squealed the hover engines and was tearing off down the road. Several lingering rabbits got run over by the front end, their mangled bodies littered behind them.

Jake was fumbling, doing his best to follow Natalia's instructions. He was trying to hold Taylor's tail steady as Natalia had to stuff her paws into Ahya's mouth and try to pull out what length was left on the tongue inside. For whatever reason, it had shrunk. It was still sticky with potent saliva, but it wouldn't last forever. She took the fleshy mass and moved the tail-mouth with her hind paw to be closer to the base of Taylor's spine, attempting to wrap it around the severed portion.

"Can you please press the tail hard into her backside, Jake? We need to make sure it's a clean heal." Natalia shouted over the rising rumble that was becoming more prominent over the rest of the din around them.

"I'm trying!" Jake looked over at Taylor's face. Her eyes were fluttering open and closed, and it looked like she was in a state of delirium. "Have you done this before? How do you know it'll work?"

"I don't!" Natalia grit her teeth as she struggled with the tongue in staying on the injured cut. All it wanted to do was flop limply. "But I've seen miracles before with this tailmaw. I'm hoping for another one now."

"I said this was a bad idea!" Trevor shouted from the passenger seat.

"Shut up!" Natalia roared. She got close to Taylor's butt and shoved her hand under the tail, holding Ahya's tongue in place with both a paw above and below where it was covering the entire circumference of the wound. She lightly stroked Ahya with a few clawed toes. "Come on, Ahya. I know you got a bit more life left in you!"

A thundering crack pounded, radiating out from the spire. Natalia was focused on Taylor, but all other eyes turned skyward to see the spires crumble from the top down. The entire grounds around the tower sank into a depression before shifting into four quadrants. A large opening in the ground was revealed, causing the remainder of the tower to plummet into the dark depths below. The entire plot of land it had stood on was a massive bay door that was still opening, the surface elements falling in as the doors shifted.

"What in the world is going on?" Mikhail glanced out his window, narrowly avoiding an abandoned car in front.

Terrati gripped the side of the truck bed with his hooves. "Impossible. I thought they didn't have the funds or manpower to finish that project!"

"What project?" Mikhail shouted back.

"Project Draccos," Terrati explained. "Plans for it go as far back as six centuries ago, possibly more. It was abandoned because it was deemed too astronomical to build."

"Well, what the hell is it?!" Trevor barked from the front.

"A warship." Terrati's ears fell as his jaw went slack.

Mikhail slowed the car just a moment as they admired in both awe and terror at the rising machine being propelled higher by gigantic jet engines on all eight sides. The undercarriage of the spiraling aircraft was loaded with cannons and artillery. Each engine could rotate minimally to alter the trajectory of the ship's movement—its current course heading away from the two behemoths that had just crushed several smaller buildings with their front legs.

"How in the world could they power such a thing?" Mikhail asked, stunned.

"Through the energy gathered from the behemoths through the shield and down into the spires." Terrati seemed in awe at the diabolical genius of it.

That caused Ari to look up. "Guys, the barrier is gone." It had disappeared as the tower fell, the chains of light snapping and falling like chunks of deadly debris on the populace below. The poundings of each behemoth rumbled through the ground. Their protection from annihilation was now gone.

"Enough sightseeing. We got to go!" Trevor slapped the outside of the truck.

"No need to tell me twice." Mikhail was off like a shot, leaving the massive airship above them, a hail of gunfire unloading from it onto the two gargantuan machines.

It didn't take long to find the tunnel leading below the streets; Mikhail appeared to know where he was going. The lights within the tunnel flickered and went out as they could all hear the loud wails of the beasts above and the thumping hum of another volley. They cringed as the sound whapped at their eardrums, reverberating through the tunnel.

They could feel it before they heard it. The entire truck jolted as the tunnel shuddered viciously, like the worst earthquake they had ever experienced. They were deep within the maintenance roads, off the beaten path from most of the traffic that traversed through the underbelly of Zabökar. Mikhail continued to drive in the darkness, his night vision and memory leading the way.

"Can this go a bit faster?" Samantha was wailing.

Behind them was a blinding inferno that was traveling their way. The tunnel ceiling was collapsing meters ahead of it, but the explosion was continuing to blast straight through towards them. Jake was panicking, but he knew he needed to focus. He was holding onto Taylor's tail so tight. Natalia was doing her best to keep the slick tongue wrapped around the base, keeping it from moving through all the jostling.

"We're not going to make it!" Trevor yelled, his eyes on the sideview mirror.

"Just let me drive!" Mikhail snarled.

It was deafening. They could no longer hear each other as the entire world seemed to crumble around them. There was a small glint of the light of night, illuminated by the blast above them, just several hundred meters ahead. Jake glanced up to see Liam growing in size. Following the wolf's line of sight, he could see the collapsing roof just feet away, the explosions having petered off. They weren't going to make it.

With his greater bulk, Liam stepped over Natalia, Jake, and Taylor, and raised his paws up. The first chunks of concrete crushed onto his outstretched paws, buckling his knees at the insane weight. He howled as the combined weight of his body holding the ceiling off their truck slammed the hovering vehicle to the ground. The truck was dead in the water as it whined its engine into a high pitch before the rest of the tunnel caved in around them. They had narrowly escaped the blast zone.

As the last of the rumblings and grinding sounds faded away, all that was left was heavy breathing and small whimpers from the flatbed. "Is everyone okay back there?" Mikhail called back into the darkness.

"Just fucking peachy." Liam laughed, his voice straining. "If you all don't want to be crushed, I suggest figuring out a way to get this roof off my paws and not on us. I'm strong, but I don't know if I'm strong for long endurance competitions." He chortled at his ill-timed joke.

"I can help with that. I think I've recovered enough to finally be able to help," Ari said.

She stood up and reached out towards the nearest wall and pressed her hands onto it. Closing her eyes, she felt through the rock and concrete with her heat. She was liquifying the points above Liam so that he could release his hold on the ceiling.

"Ah, watch it!" Liam had to shift his paws as the brightening red singed his fur.

"Quiet, I'm concentrating." Ari fired back, still feeling out the earthen material.

At last, she split the huge chunk in two so that Liam could toss them aside, crushing either end of the flatbed's rails. She even pushed the molten heat higher to where there was an air pocket, open to the night sky. Unfortunately it looked like a hellish light, and Ari stopped, daring not open the gap further. They could still hear the pounding thuds of each behemoth's feet hitting the earth. Liam sunk down in the trunk, exhausted, his size diminishing.

"Zabökar is gone, isn't it?" Samantha sniffed.

Terrati stared up through the hole. "I'm afraid so."

"So much death…" She mourned.

Mikhail relaxed in the driver's seat, the danger passed. He turned around to look back at them. "Well, the truck is totaled. We'll have to walk when all that above blows over."

"Hopefully somebody has a plan on where we're going?" Liam asked.

Jake was still holding tight to Taylor's tail. "I think Samantha had a place we could go to for now."

The rest aside from Natalia turned to the red panda who shrunk back further into her corner of the flatbed. "Yeah… My family owns a ranch not far south from here."

"We'll go with that for now." Mikhail smiled.

"Hey, I think something is working!" Natalia began to cry at having some success for once. Ahya's tongue seemed to be finally able to move and started to grip its own base tightly, its length pulsing and producing more of the saliva from within the slimy muscle. Letting go of the tongue, Natalia wilted back against the side. "Thanks gods. I honestly didn't think that would work."

Jake finally released the tail in amazement. "How is she able to do this? I've never seen her do anything like this."

"Welcome to the club." Trevor chuckled, eyeing the rabbit. "I think you're literally one of the last people who doesn't know she can do this. She's brought back people from the dead before. I'm honestly not surprised this is even possible." He indicated the injured tail.

Jake continued to regard Taylor with wonderment. "No wonder so many people were after her."

Liam grinned. "You've no idea, rabbit. Just heard the High Council head honcho himself spill the beans on all the reasons why Taylor is special. It really is quite extraordinary what she is."

"So, why are you here with her?" Natalia asked the obvious question. Among the group, he was the only outsider they were not aware of.

"I helped Taylor once before get out of the city the first time her father experimented on Taylor." He pointed a finger in Ari's direction, drawing a look of annoyance. "I watched over her for weeks as I took her out west to Galaria. We got separated and now, as fate would have it, we are back together again here in Zabökar. She asked me to take her away once more, and I fully intend to keep that promise to her. Any other reasons as to why, I prefer to keep to myself."

"That's fair." Mikhail was thoughtful. "As long as you intend no harm to her, I don't see an issue with you tagging along."

Liam nodded, scratching the bridge of his plated nose. "Don't misunderstand me. You all seem like a nice lot, but if Taylor asks me to take her somewhere, then I'll make sure that happens—regardless of what you want."

Natalia frowned. "I really think that should be up to the group protecting her."

Liam leaned forward. "She's not a prisoner, she's her own wolf. I'm just the chauffeur."

"What are you gaining from this? What's it to you?" Trevor seemed curious.

"Oh, my date canceled on me and I had nothing better to do." At a look from the group, he rolled his eyes. "Look, as I stated, any other reasons are my own." He propped back up against the truck siding and

500

looked away, rubbing his head and slight horns protruding between the ears.

"Okay…" Trevor chided the response. He instead turned his eyes to Ari. "About your father then, what happened with him? I bet daddy dearest probably isn't happy you ran off to come help us. Or was it on his orders for some other nefarious scheme?" He smirked at the reptile.

Ari crossed her arms and bared her crooked teeth at him. "I chose to come back on my own. Like Liam here, I got my own reasons, but if you must know something about them, then let's just say I wasn't exactly happy with certain decisions being made without my knowledge or consent."

"So you're a good guy now?" Trevor continued to egg Ari on.

"Lay off of it." Mikhail smacked Trevor's arm, eliciting a growl in response. Trevor pointed a threatening iron finger at the tiger.

"No, I still want to get back to my father and ask him about his plans. Something isn't adding up for me, and I want to know why." She sighed, casting her flesh and blood eye upwards. "He's heading back to our homeland of Talkar now."

"Can you track where he is?" Terrati pointed to her red iris.

Ari shook her head. "There's nothing. No wifi signals. No radio waves. Nothing. It's just dead air all around us. It's…eerie. I've never experienced something like this since getting this eye."

"Something tells me he isn't going to be happy to see you when you catch up to him." Natalia mused.

"Probably not, but I am his daughter. I don't think he would do anything drastic to me."

"I beg to differ." A wheezing cough directed all their attention to Taylor, who was hacking up a storm. She winced in pain as each cough racked her body and Ahya jerked grotesquely with each one.

"Don't hurt yourself. Just rest." Natalia was immediately upon her, paws rubbing her back and arm.

Taylor was on her side facing away, but she did her best to turn her head to look over at Ari. "I wouldn't go to your father alone next time. I remember what you told me about failures." Ari said nothing and instead just looked away.

"What do we do now?" Jake asked, fatigue clear in his voice.

"We rest," Mikhail stated plainly. "With what is still raging above us, there is no way it is safe for us to ascend. We'll wait it out for a day or so and then see where we stand. Between all of us, we should be able to break through to the surface."

The intimidating aspect of that wait pressed upon them all as silence descended on the group. Taylor was still grunting and whimpering, her sounds being the only ones in the darkness. Natalia stayed nearby while Jake continued to watch over her front. Samantha looked sad, her eyes ever on Jake and Taylor, but she stayed in her corner. Everyone else ultimately drifted off in their cramped sleeping spaces with the exception of Ari.

Staring at Taylor for a while, Ari came over and took off her leather jacket, placing it over Taylor like a blanket. She stepped back to sit down opposite the front of the truck. Jake looked curiously at her. "What was that for?"

"What's it look like?" Ari seemed peeved at having to explain. "Just making sure she doesn't catch a cold. I...know what it's like to recover from grave injuries." She turned away without looking back.

"Jake?" Taylor whispered after a time.

His ears jumped up and he leaned down low to her mouth. "What is it, Taylor?"

"Thank you, for everything." Tears were dripping down her snout. "You gave me back one final piece of my mother. I feel like she would be proud of me."

"I've no doubt she would be." Jake put a paw on hers, sharing her smile. His eyes trailed down along her body to Ahya. "How is it feeling down there?"

She stared straight ahead. "Numb. I can feel she's working hard back there, but this is different. It doesn't feel like anything I've healed up in the past. I don't know what's going to happen." Her eyes retrained back onto his. "I'm scared. Stay with me tonight?"

Jake patted her paw. "Of course, Taylor. I'll be right here. A promise made is a promise kept." He smiled.

His heart was at peace at last. Taylor was safe, like Murana wanted. Things could have gone a lot worse, but she was here and she was alive. His eyelids grew heavy and before he knew it, he passed out on Taylor, head on her thigh.

It had been nearly a month since the destruction of Zabökar. Taylor was restless. They had all retreated to the ranch Samantha's family owned. With Taylor's insistence, the Curings family reluctantly gave the existing rabbits in their service the option to leave. To the surprise of all, they chose to stay and work the ranch. Taylor could see the pride brimming in Samantha's eyes as the rabbits chose her and her family to spend their days with.

It was a slow process of healing for Taylor. This injury was quite unlike anything she had experienced. She leaned up against the doorframe leading out to the porch, where she watched Jake and the other two rabbits corral some Cowloos. Ahya rose up beside her for pets. She scratched the top of Ahya's "head" with one paw, lifting a latte to her mouth with the other.

She gazed down behind her at the base of her tail. There was a permanent scar there with a bald patch of skin where the fur didn't seem to want to grow back. It was very tender and sore, and she could not stretch out Ahya for any considerable length before it brought stabbing pains along the scar. She tried feeding food to Ahya when she felt hungry, but it took forever for digestion to occur. They were crippled as a pair, and she didn't know how long it would be before they were back to normal.

Ahya dropped back down and fondled the injury with her tongue. *"This feels so weird. I miss my fur right here."*

"I think we both do," Taylor responded back.

"Think it'll go back to normal?"

Taylor took another sip of coffee. "I hope so."

Ahya rose up and remained at Taylor's side at her elbow, trying to get a feel for what was going on before them. *"I'm actually still super pumped you can finally understand me now. You have no idea how many times I screamed for your attention and you ignored me.*"

"Sometimes I feel it was better that way. My head was a lot less busy." Taylor smirked into the cup.

"*Now we can talk deep into the nights about girl stuff like sisters are supposed to do!*" She could hear Ahya cackling in her head. "*I mean, that Liam hunk looks very charming if I do say so myself.*"

"You can't even see him, Ahya. How would you know?"

Ahya licked her "lips". "*I can see him on his voice alone. He sounds delicious. I want him.*"

"You need to cool your jets. We're not like that. He's just a friend who helped us out...twice now."

Ahya gave her a most mischievous grin. "*Fine, be that way. But you were delicious too!*"

Taylor gave a cry of disgust and turned away from her tail. "Ahya would you stop bringing that up? It was a mistake to even have tried it. I was alone, horny, and curious, ok? We're sisters, and that shouldn't be happening!"

Ahya looked offended, swinging around to face Taylor dead-on. "*Excuse me? So it's okay for you to get your rocks off, but deny me when I'm in heat? You're not being fair! I didn't ask to be like this and be stuck to your butt! Give me some sympathy here!*"

"I don't even know how I'm going to survive a relationship with you now. I think I liked it better when you were silent." Taylor edged away from her demanding tail.

"Talking to your tail again, I see," Liam spoke from behind her.

"Ah, Liam!" Taylor nearly lost her cup and had to hold it tight to keep it from spilling. "How long have you been there?"

"Long enough to see you two are fighting again." He snickered. "Has she always been able to talk to you? To some, they might see you as being a bit loopy in the head, talking to yourself like that. Who knows, you might be and just creating an excuse that she can talk to cover for it."

She scowled up at him. "If her voice is a figment of my imagination, please put me out of my misery now."

"*Rude.*"

504

Taylor turned back to the fields beyond the rabbits. Seeing as he was waiting there waiting for her to talk first, she exhaled. "It started happening shortly after I woke up a few weeks ago. I felt like I had heard her a few times before, but only when I was in great pain. I don't know, maybe what happened to my tail caused something to happen in my brain, and now I can hear her."

"And nobody else can," Liam confirmed. She nodded. "Such an interesting case you two are. I would not have guessed you were sisters until you told me."

"I'm the prettier one."

Taylor ignored Ahya. "Regardless if that's the case or not, I want to believe it. After the pain and anguish my mother went through having thought she lost a daughter, I want to believe she is alive and well in Ahya. It makes me feel better about the whole situation."

Liam bowed his head. "I can understand that. Anything to help see you through this difficult time. I'm just glad to see you are recovering."

"Oh, his voice sounds divine! Can I lick his butt?" Ahya was already slinking back around to do just that.

Taylor shifted herself around to face Liam, willing Ahya to push back behind her. "So, what's the news out there? What's going on?"

"Sourpuss!" Ahya clacked her teeth.

Liam scratched his chin, leaning on the other side of the doorframe. "You did quite a number on the High Council's plans. As expected, they have been trying to rally up support for Zabökar's destruction and made entreaties to the other nations. Your message about their true nature went viral before Zabökar was destroyed. Nobody wants to join under their banner at all now, even with their grand warship. Dirina wants nothing to do with them. Their credibility is shot because of you."

"Where will that leave the fate of the northern countries when Talkar attacks?" Taylor had a sinking feeling in her gut.

Liam grunted. "Nobody is joining forces. Each country is holing up within itself and forming their own individual plan for defense. You may have thwarted whatever the High Council was planning, but it'll probably make the northern countries weaker as a result."

505

"Crap." Taylor took another sip. "And the behemoths that destroyed Zabökar? What happened to them?"

"Headed west to Dirina. Gods know what they'll get into over there."

"The Arbiter was right. If those things are just a taste of the might of Talkar, then us mammals are not ready to defend against that. I might have just screwed it all up." She nursed the last of her coffee in the cup. She knew in her heart it would do her no good to stay on the ranch much longer. "Any word about my brothers?"

Liam shook his head. "Mikhail left northward alone to the far edges of the peninsula. We're not sure where your brothers went, nor do we have any contact numbers to call them."

Taylor's face soured. "And the only phone I had with their numbers in was destroyed back in Zabökar."

She had to fight back the tears when she recalled Nina. As much as she hated some of the things Nina did, she couldn't stay completely mad at her for the position she was in. Losing her felt almost as bad as losing Sarah. She lost two of her greatest friends in that city, as well as her mother. She didn't even have a clue where Uncle Sebastian was, or if he was even alive. And now her two brothers were currently missing somewhere out there. She fidgeted with her pine tree necklace. It felt hopeless.

Liam was studying her. "You going to be alright?"

She nodded quickly, letting the necklace drop. "Yeah, I'll be fine."

"She's not all right."

Taylor frowned at her tail before turning to Liam. "I saw Ari leave this morning. Did she say where she was going?"

"Yep. She was going south to track her father down, and see if she could stop him from marching right on into the capital of Talkar."

"And she's going on alone? Even after what I said?" Taylor scrunched her snout in frustration.

"Not alone. Natalia offered to help." This caught Taylor's attention. "I was just as surprised as you. The two of them are going to be headed westward towards Balkar."

Taylor gave a slight nod. That accounted for everybody. Trevor had left weeks ago to retire off in the far-flung country of Livarnu, wanting nothing more to do with any of this. Terrati followed him. Quite the unlikely duo. "Looks like everyone is leaving us." She looked down at the porch sadly.

"Good, less distractions. We can have Liam all to ourselves." Ahya rolled her tongue out with glee.

Taylor pushed Ahya further away from Liam, snubbing her silent laughter. "Then I'd like to leave too."

Liam turned to face her. He seemed nonchalant about most of the news happening in the world, but grew serious at this request of Taylor's. "Why would you say that?"

She shrugged. "I feel like disappearing. I came back to Zabökar hoping I could make a difference. I had no plan. No grand design from the start. I was just fumbling, thinking I was doing the right thing. In the end, I just made it worse. I discovered there was so much corruption wherever I looked. Everyone was backstabbing each other, and even those I thought were friends were enemies in disguise. I don't know who to trust. You've been strangely one of the few constants who hasn't betrayed me."

"Are you sure about leaving?" A sly grin came back to his features. He gestured with his chin out to the fields. "I've heard Jake has become quite smitten with you. He won't leave your side, going on and on about some promise he made to your mother. It's pretty endearing, if not a tad pathetic."

"Ah, Jake! He sounds juicy too. Can we have both? I just want to munch on him a bit, just a bit!" Ahya faced the direction where the rabbit voices were coming from.

Taylor shook her head. It was certainly weird having a tail that was in heat when you weren't. Would certainly explain a few things about her past experiences with her. Flouting that train of thought, she addressed Liam's question. "He's not pathetic. He's sweet. However, I don't really want to involve him in my affairs anymore. He's finally got his freedom out here with rabbits who share his passions."

"Then shouldn't he have the freedom to choose what he wants?"

"Well, yeah, but I feel like our current friendship is still tainted by the law that is still widespread in the northern countries. Wherever he goes with me, he'll always be judged, and then so will I. I couldn't put that burden on him, forever questioning if what he's chosen was his freedom or his compliance." She set the cup down on a small circular table next to the bench on the porch. "Besides, he's off the Script now, and if what happened up in that tower is true, the Authority will find him the more he is with me. He's safer here where he has less chance of changing anyone's Script."

"Yeah, that's probably for the best then." He was watching Jake laughing with his own kind.

"I would rather just leave quietly before he notices. He's done more than enough for my mother…for my family. He deserves some happiness here. So it's probably best if I just disappear. Less chance of me affecting anyone's Script, let alone destroying it so this war can begin. The further I'm away from everyone after me, the better."

"Well, if you say so." He resituated his black beanie atop his head. "You may be right, though. With Zabökar gone, there are literally no major targets of note to strike in this region. Jake could be safer near the site of where it once was than anywhere else…at least for a while. No saving lives unnecessarily for him!"

Taylor caught him adjusting the beanie. "Oh, you got yourself a new one."

He snorted. "Of course! These rugged good looks just wouldn't be complete without my beanie!" He tapped his pants cargo pocket. "I even bought spares just in case this time!"

"You look good in them." She giggled.

"Why thank you, little lady." He dipped his head in mock greeting.

"*What the heck is a beanie?*" Ahya's maw looked confused.

"So, you never did tell the others why you came back to save me, or why you bothered to save me the first time," Taylor pointed out.

"Well, if you must know, you'll probably need to get yourself another cup of coffee. It'll probably be a long story." He turned to head on into the large farmhouse.

Trailing in after him, they headed into the kitchen. The rest of the Curings family were out harvesting the grain for the fall. They were alone at the dining table with new, fresh steaming mugs in their paws. Liam adjusted himself in the small chairs meant for mammals half his size. Taylor took the one adjacent to him. She noticed a leather jack slung over the back of it.

"Ari left her jacket." She pet a paw on it and felt its texture before sitting down.

"Guess it's yours now if you want it."

"Isn't it a bit big?"

"Nothing I can't tailor down to your size." He snorted at his own pun, drawing a vexed look from Taylor. After taking a sip and relishing it, he looked at her gesturing to himself. "Jake was not the only person your mother made a deal with to watch over you."

"*Wow, our mother was popular!*" Ahya seemed impressed.

Taylor had to bark a laugh at the insanity of it. "First Jake, then Trevor, now you. Who hasn't she hired to watch over me?" She shook her head before taking a drink. "It seems like everywhere I turn, there is someone out there she has been in contact with."

"Your mom was a very extraordinary wolf. What we saw on the surface with those videos and documents you released to the public at the concert was just a small snippet of who she was as a person. She was also the Dark Flame Wolf."

Taylor's smile faded. "Yeah, I know. Something she adopted to cope with the pain of having to lose her brother to those vile people who are right now roaming free in that damned warship. They destroyed my family." Her nails dug into the mug.

"I'm sure we'll get to them in time," he assured her. "But I bet you've got some happy memories of your mother."

"I do."

"If you wouldn't mind, while we are still enjoying our time here, would you care to tell me a bit about her?" Liam relaxed back into his chair, waving a paw for her to continue. "What's the last thing you remember?"

APPENDIX A:
CHARACTER GLOSSARY

Major Characters (in order of appearance)

Murana Delante Wolford
Age: 52 (at death;35 at Taylor's birth) – Birthday: Jase 20 – Species: Wolf

Taylor's mother who was a reformed criminal and vigilante that terrorized the criminal underworld of Zabökar for years before being caught and coerced into working for the city to lawfully work off her crimes and pay her debt to society. After being tasked to go undercover one last time to infiltrate and blow the whistle on the Arbiter's operations, she was caught and pulsed by his DNA ray project. Taylor and Ahya were the result of this mishap. Her family life began to unravel where she first lost her first husband and then her daughter as she ran away after eating her first victim. Having nothing else left but to expose those who ruined her life, she longs for the day her daughter returns home.

Jake Thumpings
Age: 25 (22 in flashbacks) – Birthday: Nevmelpah 30 – Species: Rabbit

A rabbit with high aspirations for his future. He trained most his life to be a cop and protect others of his kind when a friend of his got snuffed in a sexual film enabled by the law that governs their sexuality. He was once a bouncer for the band '*Bad Luck*' which Taylor was a part of. Murana tasked him to deliver one final message to her daughter via a necklace. His reunion with Taylor back in Zabökar was less than ideal, but he still remembered his promise to her mother and intends to fulfill it.

Taylor Renee Wolford
Age: 19 (varying in flashbacks) – Birthday: Jasu 8 – Species: Wolf

Protagonist of the story. Was born with a unique tail with a mouth in it that can swallow most sized mammals whole. She returns to the city of her birth in search of her family and to make amends for running away from home. She reunites with an old bandmate and friend and uses her limited time to recapture her lost youth and hopefully have some fun along the way while trying to stay out of trouble with the law. She grows to understand there are bigger things out there to fight for after meeting Jake again.

Ahya Wolford
Age: 19 (varying in flashbacks) – Birthday: Jasu 8 – Species: Taylor's tail (Wolf?)

The mute tail of Taylor's with a fanged mouth at the end of it. With a tip of crimson, Ahya is not one to be easily missed or forgotten. Has unusual powers within her saliva to heal almost any wound and literally bring people back from the dead under certain circumstances. Is discovered late that she might be related to Taylor more closely than anyone could have guessed.

Nina Hawkins
Age: 18 – Birthday: Mala 24 – Species: Swan

Former bandmate to Taylor in their death metal band, '*Bad Luck.*' A rebellious teen with influential ties to the High Council through her family. She was one of the few people who were nice to Taylor and looked up to her. Upon reuniting, she takes it upon herself to watch over and rekindle the past friendship between them. However, there seems to be a dark secret she is keeping that she is afraid to tell born from the insecurities with her family.

Ariana "Ari"
Age: 19 – Birthday: Dulhanpah 28 – Species: Crocodile/Tortoise hybrid

The daughter of the Arbiter and a force of nature. She is both hot-headed and calculating. With powers to liquefy solid material around her and manipulate it in various ways, she is more than capable of watching over Taylor in Zabökar on her father's behest. Although more jaded and acting older than she appears, she is still a teenager and is prone to making errant decisions and mistakes. Has been found to be very sore about the topic of her relationship to her father and her singular drive to please him.

Trevor Novak
Age: 46 – Birthday: Sempah 29 – Species: Wolf

A former cop turned military turned bounty hunter. Once hired by the Arbiter to track Taylor down, he was set lose into Zabökar with a retirement that he can no longer enjoy with anyone else. Sporting numerous injuries from his time as both cop and service member, he has learned a bitter sense of dark humor to go along with his missing limb. Once served alongside Taylor's dad, Anthony Wolford, back on the force, but now wants little to do with her or her family now that Gregor is dead.

Finnley Lillibard
Age: 27 – Birthday: Agroa 17 – Species: River Otter

Joined the mercenary lifestyle on Fey Darner's insistence and has proven himself to be a valuable asset. Short-tempered and impatient, he has been known to get in fights with others. Is in love with Fey and greatly respects his opinions and wants. Was injured by Taylor in the previous altercation with the Arbiter's paid enforcers and now wants nothing else to do with the mercenary life now that they've been disavowed. Is frustrated that Fey refuses to leave alone the fact he's off the Script.

Fey Darner
Age: 25 – Birthday: Sempah 12 – Species: Elk

The former appointed leader of the band of mercenaries sent by the High Council to bring Taylor back for them. Now disavowed, he is obsessed with his new lot in life now that Taylor removed him from the Script by saving his life from certain death. Is in love with Finnley Lillibard and enjoys crazy colored tropical shirts.

Mikhail Joan
Age: 40 – Birthday: Oblepah 31 – Species: Tiger

Showing scars from missions past across his face and body, Mikhail was part of an elite force working from within a secret subdivision of Zabökar's police force: TALOS (Tactical Aviation and Land Operations Service). Now disavowed, his only goal is to secure Taylor from the Arbiter and High Council's grasp and whisk her away to safety. Considers Taylor almost like a surrogate daughter. Served in the military with Natalia previously and considers her like family. Has lost his sense of smell due to previous torture.

Natalia Ruyemov
Age: 31 – Birthday: Mele 2 – Species: Snow Leopard

Coming from the far western country of Livarnu, she was prior military for her country and served alongside Mikhail, whom she considers like family. She had a little sister, Sarah, who was sent to Zabökar on an exchange student program, but was eaten by Ahya as Taylor's first victim—has since forgiven Taylor for the loss. She now seeks, alongside Mikhail, to take Taylor away from the dangers of Zabökar.

Terrati Cavier
Age: 29 – Birthday: Juhous 15 – Species: Gazelle

Although skittish at first impression, Terrati is a trained spy and knowledgeable about many places and underground agencies. He is also an expert sharpshooter and proclaimed master negotiator. Now disavowed like the rest of his team, he is uncertain of where his future lies and tarries around Zabökar looking for the right opportunity and person to leave with. Is fascinated by Taylor and Ahya, but would rather not get involved with them.

Liam McHowl
Age: 29 – Birthday: Jase 6 – Species: Wolf (hybrid ?)

A stranger of origins unknown. He met Taylor once before when she first escaped the Arbiter's experiment lab. He agreed to watch over her and escort Taylor far away from Zabökar. They lost track of each other on the way to Palaveve. Now crossing paths once again by fate, he is again willing to protect her and ensure she get to safety. He has unusual powers and seems to know more than he lets on yet refuses to divulge his reasons for what he does or shares much of his past.

Secondary Characters (in order of appearance)

Manchas Wendell
Age: 54 (34 in flashbacks) – Birthday: Agroa 29 – Species: Kudu

An officer in the Zabökar police department who tasks Murana Wolford on her final undercover mission to infiltrate the Arbiter's operations. Keeping in contact with her discretely, he is her point of contact on all things official. He mysteriously disappears when the sting happens and nobody knows who he was or where he went to.

The Arbiter
Age: 150+ (???) – Birthday: (???) – Species: Tortoise

An aged denizen from the far southern country of Talkar. Traveled north to Zabökar due to a promise he made to his late wife to save the mammals from their impending doom at the hands of his reptile brethren. Genetically created his own daughter from both his own DNA and that of his wife, who was a crocodile. Appeared in Zabökar thirty years before Taylor's birth and was once appointed member of the High Council before being shot down by his colleagues and forced to go underground with his operations. His initial protect was busted by Murana's successful undercover operation, but he has slowly built up from this loss over the years. He needs Taylor for reasons unknown.

Anthony Wolford
Age: 38 (at death) – Birthday: Alahon 22 – Species: Wolf

Former husband to Murana Wolford. He died when Taylor was still young due to a punk kid at a routine traffic stop. Once worked with Trevor Novak on the police force. Loves his wife and family unconditionally and would do anything for them.

516

Kowolski Summers
Age: 31 (in flashbacks) – Birthday: Oblepah 21 – Species: Tiger

Colleague of both Murana and Anthony Wolford on the force. He was a part of the sting that disbanded the Arbiter's operations. Cheated on his wife, with three other wives. Unknown legal situation, but outlook isn't good.

Samantha Curings
Age: 23 – Birthday: Frehous 16 – Species: Red Panda

A lustful girl who has an addiction to rabbits. She wants to sponsor Jake Thumpings like she has sponsored two other rabbits previously. Her family owns a ranch south of Zabökar where she sends those she sponsors. Meets Taylor at a rabbit rally in hopes to feel better about her own anxieties at how she treats those she lusts after.

Tony Clahoon
Age: 24 – Birthday: Jasu 4 – Species: Rabbit

One of the few rabbit friends Jake Thumping's has. Is more content to work within the system that governs their species and is excited to be sponsored by a cheetah that Taylor knows very well by this point, Sabrina Fahpar. Ahya unfortunately puts an abrupt end to his limited dreams.

Stepan Longare
Age: 31 – Birthday: Alahon 15 – Species: Rabbit

The appointed leader of the rising rebellion of rabbits in Zabökar. He sponsors and runs the rallies that rile up the rabbit population to do great harm and chaos to the streets and people above. Is married with children and puts family above all else, even at the cost of others.

517

Pine

Age: 12 (???) – Birthday: (???) – Species: Skunk

An albino skunk Taylor had lived with back in Palaveve. Was proven to be a figment of her imagination by Ari. However, there might be more to him than meets the eye.

Mitchell

Age: 13 (???) – Birthday: (???) – Species: Raccoon

A mangy raccoon Taylor had lived with back in Palaveve. Was proven to be a figment of her imagination by Ari. However, there might be more to him than meets the eye.

Rakkis Guerradde

Age: 26 – Birthday: Juhous 1 – Species: Chameleon

A peculiar reptile who only seems to respect and follow the Arbiter due to some life debt he owes the tortoise. Willingly agreed to undergo experimentation to develop his own tailmaw and unique powers that make him a lethal threat—even Ari does not like entangling herself with him. Has an odd way of speech and doesn't exactly seem to be all there. Lacks empathy. Finds the oddest things amusing.

Marle

Age: 14(???) – Birthday (???) – Species: Giraffe

A young calf found by Anthony Wolford and his team when they initiated a sting on the Arbiter's operations. Her whereabouts and fate is unknown.

Vergin Tannenbaum

Age: 46 (26 in flashbacks) – Birthday: Nevmelpah 22 – Species: Wolf

Colleague of both Murana and Anthony Wolford on the force. He was a part of the sting that disbanded the Arbiter's operations. He has had great relations with Trevor Novak when on the force and lets certain protocol violations slide for his friends.

Henley Houser

Age: 27 (in flashbacks) – Birthday: Frehous 11 – Species: Wolf

Colleague of both Murana and Anthony Wolford on the force. He was a part of the sting that disbanded the Arbiter's operations. Had an unfortunate encounter with one of the powered mammals during the sting and suffered grave injury. Final status is unknown.

Steven Stinkman

Age: 35 (19 in his flashback) – Birthday: Sempah 1 – Species: Skunk

Oldest brother to Taylor and Ahya and was adopted by Murana Wolford. He is hard-working and is very proud of what he has accomplished. Is knowledgeable about many topics and strives to broaden his wealth of information. Worked his way up to pursue his passions as a journalistic reporter for ZCN (Zabökar Community Network). Known to be a momma's boy and is embarrassed about his species' ability to spray pungent musk.

Max Thrash

Age: 32 (13 in his flashback) – Birthday: Mele 23 – Species: Raccoon

Older brother to Taylor and Ahya and was adopted by Murana Wolford. Nocturnal by nature, he gravitated to music and was the inspiration for Taylor's love of it. Performed on stage as drummer to '*Bad Luck*' before moving on to start his own jazz club. Has a blunt and impersonal way of speaking to people, but loves his family deeply and will do what he can for them. Has been diagnosed on the autism spectrum. Might also have moonlighted as a vigilante sidekick to his adoptive mother, Murana.

Barateon Therator
Age: 57 – Birthday: Mala 30 – Species: Deer

The chief elder of the High Council alongside Javier Hawkins. Is a well-respected member of the council and guides the decisions and future of Zabökar. He was responsible for shooting down the Arbiter's plan and getting him removed from the council. May have ties to a shadowy organization.

Hank Eultide
Age: 29 (start of his flashbacks) – Birthday: Jahous 17 – Species: Muntjac

He was the initial point of contact for Murana and Anthony Wolford for the High Council after the events of the sting which caused Murana to be pulsed by the Arbiter's DNA ray. His job was to record and document all things pertinent to Murana's pregnancy and the child that was born in case anything unusual surfaced of note. In return, the Wolford family was supplied a lot of money on contract.

Ramon Herrara
Age: 21 – Birthday: Nevmelpah 29 – Species: Spotted Hyena

The former band leader of '*Bad Luck*' and the leader of the newly formed '*Horny Toads*.' Has a strong dislike for all things Taylor and encouraged the rest of the band to actively avoid her during her stay in the band. Has influential ties through his father in Zabökar, who is a famous banking CEO. He is very addicted to mind-altering drugs.

Loray Irroni
Age: 20 – Birthday: Mele 12 – Species: Porcupine

A well-educated porcupine that preferred the calling of music over educational pursuits. A former bandmate to Taylor from *'Bad Luck.'* Speaks eloquently and is very mild-mannered. Is very keen on the social networks and what is trending. Has little backbone when it comes to those in authority over him.

Bailey Cooper
Age: 17 – Birthday: Oblepah 9 – Species: Opossum

Former bandmate to Taylor from *'Bad Luck.'* He has extreme narcolepsy and tends to fall asleep during concerts, but has the unique ability to wake up and figure out exactly where they are in a song to keep going. He was the replacement hire when Max Thrash left the drums position. He is very interested in hacking and is a skilled IT (Information Technology) technician.

Sebastian Hrunting
Age: 30 (start of his flashbacks) – Birthday: Jase 3 – Species: Wolf

Emergency room nurse in Zabökar and surrogate father to Taylor when Anthony Wolford died. He was tasked to take care of Murana in her older years when the cancer began to settle in and she couldn't take care of herself, let alone Taylor. Becomes Murana's second husband by common law and stays with her until the end. Adores Taylor and Ahya unconditionally.

Javier Hawkins
Age: 60 – Birthday: Dulhanpah 17 – Species: Swan

The father to Nina Hawkins and one of the two chief elders of the High Council. He is a proud avian who prides his species' contribution to Zabökar. His daughter believes he's lost his way being in his lofty position for so long that he looks down upon the common populace of the very city he is supposed to serve.

Harold Bremingham
Age: 39 (in last flashback) – Birthday: Agroa 28 – Species: Black Bear

The stalwart chief of the Zabökar police force, very loyal to those in his employ and would do anything for his colleagues if they've earned his respect. He was a major proponent for the capture and arrest of the Dark Flame Wolf, aka. Murana Wolford—proclaiming himself the expert on all things about her. Reluctantly allowing her a chance to turn her life around in exchange for service to the city, he has grown fond of Murana and her family over the years. That still did not mean he trusted her further than he could spit.

Kiera Santonni
Age: 27 (in flashback) – Birthday: Sempah 12 – Species: Gazelle

The police department provided psychiatrist that helped Murana get over her past and insecurities after the death of her husband, Anthony Wolford. She was considered almost like family with how much intimate knowledge she knew about Murana and her family.

Gulia Hawkins
Age: 58 – Birthday: Jahous 24 – Species: Swan

The wife to Javier Hawkins and mother to Nina Hawkins. She is an elitist socialite that preferred to stay on the cutting edge of gossip. She is proud of what her husband has accomplished and favored her now dead sons over her daughter.

Eleanor Longare
Age: 28 – Birthday: Jasu 2 – Species: Rabbit

Wife to Stepan Longare. Has an unfortunate encounter with Taylor, but is pulled off the Script by Ahya shortly afterwards. The Authority finds her because of this.

Cherla Lafleur
Age: 36 – Birthday: Jase 16 – Species: Dingo

A younger High Council member with the ability to create portals in space to transport people and objects through. She is a member of the power eater cult. Has a wicked streak a mile wide.

Unseen Characters (in order of reference)

Buchanan Tillus
Age: 26 – Birthday: Mala 8 – Species: Elephant

Colleague to both Murana and Anthony Wolford on the force. He is shot and killed by a botched rescue mission headed up by Murana herself.

Lawrence Kurren
Age: 29 – Birthday: Alahon 19 – Species: Waterbuck

Colleague to both Murana and Anthony Wolford on the force. He is shot and killed by a botched rescue mission headed up by Murana herself.

Sally Nopps
Age: 21 – Birthday: Jase 26 – Species: Rabbit

A rabbit declared a whore by Tony Clahoon since she ignores the rabbit breeding laws and tries to get pregnant illegally.

Sabrina Fahpar
Age: 32 (at death) – Birthday: Frehous 25 – Species: Cheetah

She was a recent appointee of the High Council. Went rogue to seek Taylor on her own to eat her and consume her powers all by herself. Was discovered to be a power eater and was promptly devoured by Ahya during Taylor's rescue. Was going to be Tony Clahoon's sponsor.

Gregor Trepani
Age: 43 (at death) – Birthday: Frehous 12 – Species: Wolf

Co-bounty hunter with Trevor. He served military service with Trevor and even saved his life during this period which earned him a life debt. However, he was killed by Finnley Lillibard during a dispute over who would take Taylor back to Zabökar.

Mrs. Hircus
Age: 73 (at death) – Birthday: Jase 1 – Species: Kamori

An elderly goat living in Palaveve that was an honorary grandmother to many orphanged kits and cubs in town to include Taylor. She believed in the Script and the old magic that governed it. Gave Taylor a kitsune plush as a gift. She died in the explosion that destroyed Palaveve.

Sarah Ruymenov
Age: 11 (at death) – Birthday: Mala 28 – Species: Snow Leopard

Natalia's younger sister who died at an unfortunate age. Was Ahya's first kill.

Klera Faliden
Age: 62 – Birthday: Juhous 19 – Species: Tiger

Mikhail's mother-in-law who offered asylum during Taylor's stay in Cheribaum. Is an excellent cook and motherly to all.

Francis
Age: 21 – Birthday: Dulhanpah 5 – Species: Rabbit

A waiter at the Java Rabbit café located in Cheribaum. Had an extremely intimate misunderstanding with Taylor.

Terry Fitzgerald
Age: 26 – Birthday: Mala 17 – Species: Deer

A buck Fey saved from certain death, pulling him off the Script in the process. He went on to stop a bank robbery and saved many lives. The Authority finds him because of this.

Mereliah
Age: UNK – Birthday: UNK – Species: Heavenly

The goddess said to be responsible for gracing the world with the Script. People pray to her daily for good fortune in their Scripts. It is unclear if she really exists.

Alacoth
Age: UNK – Birthday: UNK – Species: Heavenly

The demonic lord that the power eaters follow. He is the purveyor of strife and chaos—hellbent on freedom for all peoples from the Script at any cost; a sentiment shared by his followers. It is unclear if he really exists.

APPENDIX B:
LOCATION HISTORY

Zabökar History and Trivia

The largest, most technological city of mammals for miles around. Named after the very country it resides in. No city has ever been so great or as well known. The exact founding of Zabökar is unclear, but many historians place its birth around thirteen centuries ago. It was the first experimental attempt at joining mammals and birds together, both prey and predator, under one banner to live in harmony. It continues to remain a success to this day, with multiple, smaller cities copying their example.

The birds shared their technological prowess with the mammals to create technologies that would ultimately become the levitating traffic system in Zabökar among other marvels. They even joined forces with the reptiles from the southern country of Talkar to share in their knowledge and partnership. It is quite unclear as to what went wrong, but the reptiles revealed themselves to be a threat and both mammal and bird joined forces against the reptile nation in what became known to be as the Hordos War—two centuries after the founding of Zabökar.

The war devastated most of Balkar, once said to be a verdant grassland filled with beautiful forests. The avian nation of Dirina crossed the Grune Mountains with their floating cities and laid waste to the reptile armies, pushing back their numbers south through the isthmus back into Talkar. Mammal sympathizers within the reptile nation defected to the north and assisted in the victory against Talkar. There was an undocumented division between mammal and bird at this time and they retreated north into Dirina, taking their technology with them, leaving the mammals to build the great wall that would separate north and south.

Some believe the acceptance of mammal sympathizers into their ranks may be the cause of this division, which caused bitterness among the mammals now that their greatest allies had abandoned them. As a result, although the mammals were grateful for their assistance, all friendly reptiles were isolated to a reservation on the Hordos peninsula south of Zabökar, named after the very war they helped win. That fact combined with their overall treatment throughout the north has generated resentment in their secluded community.

The few birds who remained behind to assist the mammals in building the great city of Zabökar also helped establish the esteemed High Council, which has jurisdiction over several counties around it. It was clear a more equal, yet centralized system of government was needed to combat future threats and calamities. The town's rising spires can be seen for miles and its impressive defense system is known the world over. Consisting of eight monolith statues resembling each of the original members of the High Council at the foundation of the city. Connected together by magical beams of light, the city has never been assaulted or won over since construction.

Zabökar went through many reconstructions as the central Caelesti Spires rose higher and higher to continue to cover the ever-expanding city. Buildings and structures were built higher to match the growing skyline. However, corruption began to seep down through the city and multiple aspiring entrepreneurs left Zabökar nearly two centuries ago to form Howlgrav in the neighboring country of Galaria to the southwest—a miniature version of Zabökar. As Howlgrav expanded and grew, it invited multiple scientists and brainchilds into its borders. Much of the current technology in use in Zabökar today not invented by the birds were first invented in Howlgrav.

The High Council fearing Galaria was getting to be too powerful and seeking to maintain their centralized government in the north, launched an attack on Howlgrav within its third decade of existence. They wiped out the city and killed all of the brilliant engineers that had provided so many great technological boons to both cities. The mass howling of mourning over the graves of their loved ones from this disaster gave Howlgrav the name it still carries to this very day. Nobody sought to make a city as grand as Zabökar since this disaster.

Zabökar today continues to enjoy its prosperity and showcases its wealth and success to everyone who visits. In efforts to maintain any remaining birds' cooperation to their fair city, the High Council has promised cushy payment and jobs to any and all birds willing to preserve the peace between prey and predator with their exclusive commodity of eggs. This single act has stratified the entire social structure of the city to specific classes of citizenship—something felt most strongly by those on the bottom.

As checkered as the history of Zabökar has been, it still remains a testament to the combined cooperation between species to create something revolutionary. It is also the birthplace of Taylor Renee Wolford.

Named districts in Zabökar

Milk District

So named for its original population of cows, goats and other milk-producing mammals that were paid handsomely for their biological product. The original location of this subsection was within what is now considered as downtown Zabökar with its high rises and penthouse suites. Sandwiched squarely between the Furon River as it arcs through the city on its south side, it is a bustle of activity and nightlife for many a rebellious teenager—filled with shopping malls, rave clubs, theaters and ritzy coffee shops, it is the epitome of capitalistic Zabökar. Its original population of milk givers have since moved to the outskirts of town in recent centuries due to the heavy urbanization of the downtown area—preferring instead to be near the green pastures surrounding the city.

Meerkat Town

Built on the west side of the eastern half of the Furon River, this district thrived on fish and seaborne imports—with boats traveling from the northern delta down the river to the wharf. A thriving community of fishmongers, restaurant entrepreneurs and entertainment venues took shape here. There is even a yearly fair held on the boardwalk every fall complete with rides, food stands and outdoor musical acts. Further in from the river and south is where the majority of the smaller residents reside just shy from the inner downtown skyscrapers—the reason why it gets its name. It is one of the oldest districts in the city and supposedly has been built upon multiple times throughout the centuries to its current form seen today.

The Bits

Sandwiched between Meerkat Town to the east and Outer Hedges to the west across the Furon River, The Bits lies south of the Milk District at the bottom of the river bend. Neglected by the city planners since its construction, it has fallen into disrepair and its structures do not reach the grand heights of everything around it. Filled with homeless and rampant crime, most people tend to avoid this area if they can. The southern reaches are slowly sinking into the Furon River due to lack of maintenance. The Marsh House is also here on the northeast side near Meerkat Town.

Outer Hedges

A newer development built on the west side of the Furon River at the bottom of the bend. It is filled with higher class residences and seeks to be an inviting alternative living location for the avian citizens of Zabökar. Not many common folk can afford the expensive living offered here.

The Leans

A newer development built opposite The Bits across the Furon River. It gets its name based on how it looks when viewed from above or from a map app, its gridded quadrants looking like they're leaning one direction or another. It comprises mostly of industrial warehouses and business storage alongside a smattering of office buildings.

APPENDIX C:
"BAD LUCK" SONG LYRICS

OUTCAST

(Long growl)

Lost in the urban haze
Alone and unloved by all
Shunned from above to loss
Recognition since denied

From under your feet crushed
Stifled by your belief
Suffocating on disappointment
I've got nowhere else to run to

I'm an outcast
Killing your expectations
Watch me pour my blood
To be what you hate me for
I'm your darling outcast *(Long growl)*

Sinning the fathers for their crimes
Be the embarrassment that I crave
Rising up through your petty lies
Let me cut your vision of me
Watching it bleed all over your heart

I'm an outcast
Killing your expectations
Watch me pour my blood
To be what you hate me for
I'm your darling outcast *(Long growl)*

BRING THE FALL

Kings on high judge not their designs
Stamped souls to be traded for lies
Suckling up the rot
Feasting on the remains of yore

Coerced to comply, you bend
Tempted by the lie, you turn
Relishing the peak, you sigh
Facing your demise, you cry

Bring the fall *(Long growl)*
Fuck your tatters
It no longer matters
On judgment day
Your feet turn to clay
Nothing to stand on
All that you gained now gone
Bring the fall *(Long growl)*

Pittance spared for naught your descendants
Ivory towers all soaked in blood
Kingdom's treasures locked away in vaults
Busted wide by those you have deceived.

Rising up from hell, you run
Nowhere to seek help, you break
Chased down by your tell, you scream
Choking on the dream, you die

Bring the fall *(Long growl)*
Fuck your tatters
It no longer matters
On judgment day
Your feet turn to clay

Nothing to stand on
All that you gained now gone
Bring the fall *(Long growl)*

Looking on legacy
Nobody to remember
Buried under our feet
You brought your fall *(Scream)*

SCRIPT HATER

How I've hated what I've become
Joyful paths all undone
No ending future bright
The Script sees all
Choices that I cannot make abound
Quells not my inner rage

Cut my skin with a jagged knife
Watch my blood pour out my sin
Scream on high that I cannot die
Script destroys all reason and soul

Rebel against the fates of your gods
Place trust in what you cannot see
Your spot in life has since been decreed
Not left but to rip it at the seams

Script of my life, I despise
Burning hatred in disguise
Script Hater
Script Hater

(Screams and growls)

You suck my joy from out my day
Written unseen by gods now dead
Matters little what choices I make
When the heavens laugh at your fate

Rebel against the fates of your gods
Place trust in what you cannot see
Your spot in life has since been decreed
Not left but to rip it at the seams

Script of my life, I despise
Burning hatred in disguise
Script Hater
Script Hater
All my life I've hated you
All my life I'll kill you
Script Hater

(Screams)

BETRAYAL

The ones who claim to protect you
Gave no warnings that they'd harm you
When you look up to their heavens
You'll see through their deceptions

Forgotten children you have become now
Passed on in favor of their passions
Rotting our own city from within it
Feasting on our corpses like a fattened cow

Liars rampant
Nothing to trust
Eating our children
Leaving their taint

Betrayal cuts so deep
Stirring our minds to weep
On and on it sinks lower
Wretched lives offered up to their tower

Betrayal cuts so deep
Stirring our minds to weep
Over and over it kills us slowly
When those on high think themselves holy

Stab, stab, stab them all
Burn, burn, burn them all
Kill, kill, kill them all

Nothing left to avenge but betrayal

(Long scream)

APPENDIX D:
AUTHOR THOUGHTS AND NOTES

This second book in Taylor's series was a difficult one to write, but not terribly difficult to plan out. Let me explain. The book in its current form was because of the initial plan to have Taylor's books as a trilogy. The bloated nature of this second book was a direct result of having it originally requiring to set up so many events that would lead us into the conclusion that was supposed to be book 3. This all changed while I was writing book 1 and realized I needed a bigger canvas to tell this story and expanded it out to six books. However, we were left with all the events that still needed to happen within the confines of book 2, and so here we are with one of the most complex plots I've ever had to devise since I first started writing.

There were so many loose ends that needed to be either resolved or continued from the first book: Fey and his team of mercenaries, Taylor and her group, Arbiter and this new villain, a potential threat from High Council and more. It was hard starting off the second book. I had much of the middle and almost all of the ending sequences planned, but the first third of the second book was a mystery to me. Trying to figure out how all parties got from point A to where they needed to be in Zabökar at point B was a nightmare.

That was when I came up with the disjointed time skip option that concludes around chapter 6. I reasoned the most striking way to start off Taylor's second book was not starting with Taylor at all, but going straight with someone we barely knew anything about but have heard mention in the previous book: Murana, her mother. In fact, all of Murana's scenes were written in order from start to finish in a single go over the course of several weeks—months before any other scenes were written for book 2. This was done specifically to keep my head in Murana's mindset the whole time and not get distracted by other characters while I focused on her story arc.

Filtering in Murana's scenes throughout the book, carefully skipping two chapters purposefully, I arranged the flow of information to feed into each other. Past informs present and present informs past. My inspiration for this sort of storytelling was inspired by The Godfather Part II. I wanted the reader to be informed about revelations at specific moments right as the characters were learning about them. The flow of Taylor's arc and scenes seemed to naturally match what I had already created months earlier when I wrote Murana's sequence with the exception of two chapters, which as stated, I skipped inserting a scene for her.

Finally settling on the disjointed storytelling to begin the novel, I wanted to introduce Taylor back into it in an unorthodox way. What better way than to start with her planned ultimate love interest, Jake Thumpings, and work his introduction into the story first and then bring the two together in the most violent, shocking and conflicting way possible! I did not want an easy romance to blossom. I wanted something that would be a slow burn and would be rife with issues from start to culmination, making the end result all the sweeter and worthwhile.

Book 2 is a far more sexualized story than previous because of several things: the most obvious is that we were now formally dealing with the rabbit issue introduced oddly in the first book and so Taylor's involvement there demanded more interaction with such sexual topics regarding them. The less obvious reason is her budding sexuality that was denied as a teenager growing up and the freedoms she gets to enjoy while in Zabökar. This is her story of attempting to rekindle her youth and eventually realizing that what was lost can never truly be recovered and she must take what can be salvaged and move on and not dwell in the past. A lesson she will continue to struggle with even past this book. Nina was born from this purpose and I adored every moment writing for her.

The hardest part about arranging and writing this particular book was the myriad of new and old characters I had to juggle. Many character groups had their own agendas, motivations and arcs to complete in Zabökar and it was difficult to manage enough page time for all of them. The most important story arc was, of course, Taylor and Nina's, but Jake was a close second with his story weaving in and out of the High Council mercenaries'. Ari had her own journey to complete involving a nice heelturn towards the end that I was extremely happy how it resolved. Finally, Fey and Finnley had their small arc that was necessary for the endgame events and helped explain the supernatural events occurring behind the scenes in the rest of the character sequences.

Other new characters were introduced like Steven and Max. They were always planned to be the older brothers to Taylor and I was finally happy to reveal them. Although they had less impact on the overall story than I would have liked, I was still satisfied with their small "cameos" in the story which helped establish their characters and by the end, I feel I've pushed them off on their path for a more "meatier" storyline in book 3.

Rakkis was an interesting addition and one I teased at the end of book 1. He, like Steven and Max, did not have too much to do in this story, mainly because this story was Taylor's story. It was about her past, her mother, her origins. It was her arc to complete. Rakkis was just a side character to propel her to where she needed to be. His role will be more developed in the coming books, but I felt it necessary to introduce him early here for future use. His dialogue quirk of referring to himself in third person plural was something that came to me on the spot and really gave him some extra creepiness that I liked.

Now one of the biggest changes in the book was the inclusion of Liam and the exclusion of Sebastian (Uncle Seb Seb!) outside of Murana's segments. Sebastian was originally going to meet Taylor at the graveyard in chapter 15 and they have a nice reunion there. However, upon outlining how I was going to finish off the remainder of the book, there was not much for Sebastian to do and he would have been just another "puzzle piece" that I needed to figure out how the hell

I was going to get him out of Zabökar before it all went down. So to make it easier on myself, I just simply said he was no longer in the city and to compliment his disappearance, I also shooed out Steven and Max towards the end to simplify my juggling of characters. Sebastian may yet appear in the future.

The original idea to suddenly introduce Liam at the start of book 3, but it was an awkward transition and one I wasn't overly happy with. So, I instead pushed him forward to where Sebastian was going to be in chapter 15 and made him more integral to the endgame plot. I needed to have him form a sort of bond with Taylor early so their relationship in the next book starting off would make far more sense. In the end, it was one of the best decisions I made since his planned skillset was instrumental in getting our protagonists out of some really hairy situations that could have easily written me into a corner!

The biggest takeaway from this entire experience was to not bloat my novel with so many plot lines where I had to juggle characters to such an extreme degree. I'm amazed I got something coherent out, but extremely satisfied at how it all came together at the end. There always could have been a few characters who could have received a bit more love and attention on the page, but I feel I did my best in giving everyone their due time and purpose in the story—if nothing else, I set up some of the new characters to have arcs of their own for future books.

This second book was always about finally answering the big questions about Taylor and her origins. The history of her family played a big factor into that. I figured it would do no good to keep pushing off the secrets to Taylor's story to later books. Book 3 onwards would deal with bigger issues and crises and Taylor's core history would have no place there. We needed to hook readers into her more as a character and thus make them more willing to follow her throughout the remainder of her series when things start getting far more fantastical.

The secret of Ahya was always planned from the start, before word one on page one of book one. I'm so overjoyed to finally reveal this secret to you all. May there be many more happy revelations to come!

Thank you all for reading this second book and hope you are looking forward to the rest!

AUTHOR BIOGRAPHY

Matthew Colvath was born in California, USA, where he grew up in the 'golden age' of gaming when Nintendo and Sony were having their 1980s feud and movies had a more simple and light-hearted fantastical flair to them. Movies and games captured his attention and drove him to pursue game design to tell stories and express his creativity. His interest in game design petered off, but his passion for storytelling did not.

Graduating in 2005 with a bachelor's degree in Communications from CSUS in Sacramento, Matthew faltered in direction in his life and after a year of aimless ambition decided to join the US Air Force. He was with the USAF for nearly 11 years and went through two deployments with the B-52 bombers up in Minot, North Dakota.

Through these years, he was honing his writing craft through fanfic. Being a self-taught author, he cut his teeth first on these low risk writing projects before tackling his first professional work with Legend of Ahya: Target of Interest. Now having separated from the military and picking up a career in IT (Information Technology), he currently resides in Germany with his wife and two boys where he continues to write the rest of Taylor's saga.

Made in the USA
Thornton, CO
05/08/22 16:07:37

759ab112-354a-4be8-93f2-3ec902afe150R01